I0586587

Copyright © 2025 by Sherilee Gray

All rights reserved.

No part of this book may be reproduced in any form or by any electronic or mechanical means, including information storage and retrieval systems, without written permission from the author, except for the use of brief quotations in a book review.

Cover Designed by Jay Aheer at www.simplydefinedart.com

Print ISBN: 978-1-0670738-1-7 (Paperback)

Print ISBN: 978-1-0670738-2-4 (Hardcover)

THE THORNHEART TRIALS

BOOKS 4 - 6

SHERILEE GRAY

An Oath at Midnight

THE THORNHEART TRIALS

BOOK #4

PROLOGUE

Magnolia

M<small>Y HEART RACED SO FAST</small>, I felt dizzy.

He was back.

It was *really* freaking hard, but I sat as still as I could and stopped myself from turning to look at him again. The sly glances I'd managed his way; there was no missing how utterly magnificent he was. Goddess, he was living, breathing midnight. Every part of him, from his pointed beak to his vicious-looking talons was black. His feathers, so shiny, I was desperate to feel how silky they'd be against my fingertips.

He was beautiful.

I'd spotted him for the first time a month ago. He'd been perched in the huge oak tree that bordered our cemetery, and every day since he'd come closer. I wanted to talk to him, badly, but I had to wait. He needed to approach me, that's what Willow and Iris said.

He needed to come to the realization that he was my familiar on his own. If I tried to force the connection, I could freak him out and he might leave. But it was *so hard* to wait. So hard not to run over to tell him that he was mine. That we'd be best friends forever, and that no matter what happened to either of us, we'd always have each other. Butterflies went wild in my belly, and I forced myself to breathe through them.

I couldn't take it. I had to peek at him one more time, and I glanced over my shoulder.

Coal-black eyes locked with mine, and something invisible, but *huge*, hit me so hard that I rocked back, sucking in a startled breath. Happiness, the kind I never knew existed, filled me, and it was so vast there was no stopping the smile from spreading across my face.

The big black crow's wings extended, and with a *caw*, he dove from the tree branch and flew away.

I jumped off my seat. "Don't go! Come back! Please, come back!"

What had I done? What if he never came back? What if I'd ruined everything? I wanted to run after him, but I'd never be able to catch up to him... and if he didn't want to be found, I'd never see him again.

I couldn't remember the last time I cried, but tears welled in my eyes now.

My head jerked back, a cry bursting from me. I touched my forehead, and my fingers came away coated in blood. A rock lay at my feet.

I looked up at the sound of laughter. Amelia and her best friends Leah and Claire watched me. Each holding rocks in their hands. Amelia smirked, and her familiar, Scott, a feline shifter at her side, puffed out his chest with a smirk.

I straightened. They hated me, all of them. I wasn't sure why, but it'd been that way since we met on my first day of elementary school. Amelia had taken one look at me and decided I was a threat to her, that's what Wills said, anyway. She said that jealousy made people act like assholes.

Scott tilted his head to the side, his green, feline eyes moving over me. "You get uglier every time I see you."

Amelia threw her head back laughing as Scott took the stone from her hand.

"Start running." He grinned. "We're just trying to help you. Look at yourself, you could use the exercise."

I stood there in shock, blood still dripping down the side of my face. "Aren't you a little old for this playground bully bullshit?" I said, pleased when my voice came out strong and not as shaken as I felt.

"Run," he said again with more force, throwing the rock in the air and catching it. "Or I'll open up the other side of your face."

"Run, you stupid bitch," Amelia said, then snatched the rock back from her familiar and threw it.

I covered my head with my hands, ducking.

The rock was snatched out of the air, followed by a thud as black boots hit the ground in front of me.

It was him—my crow.

But there were no feathers this time. No, this time, he was in his human

4

form. I straightened, taking in the boy in front of me. He was tall, towering over me, and thin. He wore black jeans and no shirt, and through his dirt-streaked skin I could see several tattoos on his back and arms.

The witches across from us stared at him in shock. Scott flexed his biceps, hands fisted at his sides, and took a step forward. I couldn't see my crow's face, and he said nothing, just shook his head, making his glossy black hair move in a way I knew it'd feel as silky as his wings would.

Scott stopped in his tracks. He was still scowling, trying to look tough, but there was real fear in his eyes. "I'm finished with these fucking losers," he announced, then spat on the ground and strode away, Amelia and her friends rushing after him.

I stood still and silent behind my crow, waiting for him to turn around, and prayed to the mother that he wouldn't shift and fly away again. The muscles in his back flexed, and I held my breath, but he didn't change forms and fly away, he turned.

When his black eyes met mine, he jolted, and his lids slammed down. The fan of his thick, black lashes quivered against his cheeks for several seconds, before they slowly opened and he looked at me again.

I had no idea what he was thinking, so I swiped my tears away and smiled tentatively. "Thank you for stopping them." His head was dipped, his glossy black hair hanging forward, obscuring some of his face, but there was no missing how beautiful he was in this form as well. His brow was broad, his jaw square but a little pointed. His nose was prominent but refined, and his cheeks were sharp. I wanted to brush his hair out of the way and get a better look at him.

He said nothing, just studied me with those obsidian eyes.

"You've been watching me," I said.

He nodded.

My hands trembled with excitement, with fear that he'd leave again. "Why didn't you say hello?"

Still, he said nothing, but his chest rose and fell faster, his eyes searching mine.

"You don't need to be afraid of me or hide." I smiled gently and took a small step closer. "I'd never hurt you. Not ever."

His feet shifted, his head still dipped.

"My name's Magnolia, what's yours?"

His chest expanded and a shaky breath rushed past his perfectly formed lips. "Bram."

Goose bumps lifted all over me at the sound of his voice. It was impossibly deep, deeper than I expected, yet soft as well somehow.

He didn't move, didn't look as if he were going to try to leave again, and

5

I couldn't hold it in any longer. "I've been waiting for you," I said. "For so long...my whole life."

His head jerked back, his hair falling away from his face, and his gaze grew impossibly intense.

"You know, don't you? What we are to each other? That we belong together?"

His fingers curled and uncurled at his side, and his nostrils flared. "Yes," he said, and something changed in the way he stood, in the look in his eyes. It was understanding. Relief. And the wall he held between us dropped and crumbled to dust.

I needed to get closer to him. I let the feeling fill me, guide me, and closed the space between us. He didn't step away as I wrapped my arms around his waist and pressed my cheek to his chest. "You're finally here. I finally have my familiar." His arms tentatively wrapped around me as well. "We'll be together forever, and nothing will ever tear us apart."

CHAPTER I

Magnolia

Six years later

I LAUGHED as Bram dipped low, spinning as we flew above the forest canopy.

His low chuckle rumbled through his chest, and I couldn't wipe the smile off my face. He'd partially shifted, so instead of going full crow, he was wings only. He looked like a dark angel in this form, a deadly, tattooed, obsidian-eyed, goth angel.

He tightened his arms around me and did another wide loop. I cackled again, and he flashed me a grin.

How long had it been since we'd done this? Hung out, laughed, just... had fun. Too long. Things had been strained between us for so long, but today we'd both called an unspoken truce, and I refused to be the one to break it and dredge back up all the hurt that had been simmering between us—or let my anger get the better of me. Today he was here, we were together, and I *would* bank the inferno constantly blazing in my gut and enjoy every damn moment.

Bram pointed to the forest floor through the trees. A group of demons looked up at us, pointed teeth bared, running to try and keep up, as if they had a hope in hell at getting anywhere near us. This part of the forest was infested with demons and other creatures. The hounds had killed and driven most of them from their territory, and a lot had settled here. This area had always been infested with monsters, though, and they all wanted to take a bite out of you.

We were on the outskirts of the Roxburgh State Forest and far from civilization. The area had been left to run wild a long time ago, and Bram's people, who also lived out here, and the bat shifter colony not far from it, used it to their advantage.

If you didn't have wings, getting anywhere near them was impossible.

They used the deadly forest as a first line of defense, and it had worked for them both for a very long time.

A cluster of tree houses appeared in the distance, and Bram changed direction. My hair whipped around my face, and I shoved it back so I could take it all in. The tree houses in Bram's village were all different shapes and sizes, eclectic and beautiful in their own way, and were joined by intricate swing bridge-like walkways high in the trees. The village was fairly spread out, and their warriors set up their places on the outer edges, protecting those more vulnerable from attack—if anyone managed to make it through the first line of defense, that is. Bones, demon mainly, hung from the branches and swing bridges like macabre wind chimes, skulls mounted on every post and above every tree house door, a final warning to any enemies that might come too close.

The demons heeded that warning and avoided the crows' territory. They'd learned long ago that getting too close would cost them their heads. Crow shifters were a rare breed, dark and deadly and preferring their own company. Most of the people here barely left the area or ventured to the city.

We landed on the deck of one of the larger tree houses. It belonged to Payne, Bram's older brother, and he had not one but three demon skulls nailed above his door. It flew open now, and Maeve, Bram's niece, ran out, her long, glossy black hair streaming out behind her.

Bram lowered me to my feet and lifted her into his arms, pressing his face against her little throat. "Happy birthday, Maeve," he said low.

She hugged him tightly back. Maeve was sweet and shy, watchful of strangers, and she'd warmed up to me a little the last couple years.

Maeve was Payne's only child. I had no idea what happened to her mother. I did know she was a witch named Farah, but she'd been gone when I met Bram and Payne refused to talk about it with anyone, even his family.

Uma, Bram's aunt, walked out, wiping her hands on her apron and grinned. "You're here, finally."

Uma was a small female, her black hair streaked with gray, and she had sharp eyes. Like most shifters, crows were long-lived. I had no idea how old she was, but she looked as if she were only in her late forties.

"Glad you're home," she said to Bram, giving him a tight hug.

She released him, then held her arms out to me. I let her pull me in for a hug as well and somehow managed to stop myself from pulling away or flinching. I was having a good day, but my scars often made it hard to forget they were there. Sometimes, it was as if they were alive, crawling all over my body—making me feel as if the people who put them there were right there as well.

I fought my shudder as she released me, and I stepped back. I was short, but even I had to look down at Uma. The older female had only recently come home from England. She'd lived with her mate, at one of the crow villages there, for seventy years. After Uma's mate died, she came home. Bram said she couldn't be there anymore, the reminders of her female were too painful.

Maeve only had eyes for the gift in my hand and looked ready to burst out of her skin. Laughing, I handed the little crow the gift Bram and I had for her.

She sat on the ground, tore away the paper, and gasped. Her eyes flew to Bram. "I love it!" The art set we'd gotten her was in a cool wooden case with all the paints, brushes, and markers a kid could need.

Bram pulled the other gift he had for her from his pocket and placed it on her lap.

"Another one?" She tore that paper off as well, and gasped. "Wings! Did you make them, Uncle Bram?"

He nodded, looking uncomfortable. Bram didn't like a lot of attention, even from his own family.

"He spent hours carving it," I said, admiring the wings Bram had labored over for his niece. Each feather was incredibly detailed and utterly beautiful.

She turned it over and saw the little space Bram had carved out. It had a small cork in it. Her gaze shot up to us.

"I added some herbs, a spell for protection and good health," I said. I didn't know if Maeve would develop magic abilities from her mother's side, but I wanted her to know what was possible, and to feel comfortable asking me anything if she ever had questions.

"Thank you, Magnolia." She smiled wide.

It'd taken us a while to get to this point. Bram's family had struggled to understand our relationship. Like why he'd moved away from his people, or why he had trouble leaving my side. Crows didn't trust easily, and it didn't help that I was a witch. For years, his brothers thought I'd cast a spell over him, that I was controlling him somehow.

They seemed to have accepted me a little more now, but I knew they still resented me for keeping him from them. It didn't matter that neither of us had any control over our connection. And honestly, I didn't blame them. I hated being parted from Bram as well.

Talon dropped out of the sky, landing in a crouch in front of Bram. "You're needed."

Bram raised a brow.

"Secret birthday shit," Talon said. "Let's go."

They both shifted and exploded into the air. Bram was the youngest, then Talon, Rook next, and the oldest was Payne. Payne was the exception to the whole acceptance thing, he didn't just resent me, he didn't trust me, and sometimes I thought he might actually hate me. I watched Bram disappear over the treetops above us, until I couldn't see him anymore. Uma covered my hand with hers, startling me, and drawing my attention back to her.

"How have you been, honey?" she asked, and there was concern in her eyes.

"I'm good," I said, lying. She continued to stare, seeing right through my lie. "Bram's talked to you?"

Uma shook her head. "No, my nephew keeps his own counsel, but I know things must be difficult for you at the moment."

"So you know what he's doing? What this new job is that takes him away all the time?" He'd started a new job eighteen months ago, leaving at all times of the day and night, a job he said he'd had to sign an NDA for and couldn't share with me. His "job" had been taking him away more and more frequently, and I had no idea where he was going, what he was doing while he was gone, or why, when he came home, he was often injured.

She didn't answer, which was answer itself. Cool, everyone knew but me. Flames licked my insides, my anger trying to rear its head. I forced it back down.

"You don't need to know," a deep voice said behind me.

I turned to see Payne materializing from a dark corner, shifting into his human form. Crow shifters had several forms: human, shadow, bird, and wings only, and Payne took full advantage of the shadows, looming in dark corners, silently watching...judging. His dark eyes locked on me, his lashes so thick and dark, it looked like he had coal around his eyes.

All four brothers had those lashes. They were all similar in appearance. Black hair and eyes, tall, tattooed, but Bram and Payne were the most alike. Bram wore his hair differently than his brothers, though. They wore theirs tied back and had one or both sides shaved, and all three had a series of lines inked there. I'd asked Bram what it meant, and he'd just shrugged and said it was what their warriors did, that it was tradition.

"Be nice," Uma said to him.

Payne's wide chest expanded. "Of course."

Uma's eyes narrowed. "I need to check on the meal. If you upset Magnolia while I'm gone, we'll be having words."

He inclined his head, and his aunt bustled off. His dark gaze slid from his aunt, and he smiled down at his daughter. "Go help your aunt, little feather."

Maeve jumped up, doing as he asked, and Payne scooped up the wings Bram had carved, turned it over, pulled out the cork, and dumped the tiny leather pouch filled with herbs and other ingredients for the spell I'd put in it for his daughter over the side of the deck, then put it back. "She doesn't need your spells. She doesn't need anything from you."

Yeah, that hurt, but I wasn't surprised by it, and I refused to let him see how shitty he'd just made me feel. My anger rose again, and I blew out a breath as I jammed it back down, though I knew from experience, that would only work so long. "You said I don't need to know about Bram? Why?" I said instead of telling him what a giant asshole he was. I knew Payne wasn't my biggest fan, he'd never bothered hiding it. I'd never really cared, but for some reason, right then, I kind of hated the resentment I saw in his eyes when he looked at me.

"Because it's none of your business."

"Bram's my best friend, my familiar. We share everything," I said, and this time there was no controlling the bite of anger in my voice.

"Obviously not," he said and eyed me for several long, uncomfortable seconds. I'd always had a kind of sixth sense. It had never developed into anything more than that, but I'd always just known things—not like a psychic, but at a gut level. I'd lost touch with that side of myself the last couple of years, but I was slowly getting it back—and there was something wrong about Payne, something off. No, he wasn't a danger to me, not physically, but looking into his eyes sent a shiver down my spine, always. "You've seen the picture of our mother?" he asked cryptically.

"Yes." I'd seen it many times. Bram had a framed photo of his parents in his room at home.

"Do you know how she got the jagged scars down the side of her face?"

"Fighting with a demon." Bram didn't like to talk about his parents. They'd died when he was young, and eighteen-year-old Payne had taken responsibility of his brothers. Things had been tough for all of them. "But I'm not sure what that's got to do with anything. I want to know what's going on with Bram..."

The coldness in his black eyes intensified, shutting me up.

He angled his head to the side of the house, telling me without words to follow. He led me around to the other side of the deck and stopped at the railing, his rough, scarred, and inked hands gripping it as he stared out at the large clearing in front of us.

I'd seen it many times, of course, and right now it was covered with wildflowers, a riot of color and sweet perfume. It was beautiful, but I didn't know why he'd brought me around here.

"She was younger than you are now when it happened." He pointed to a spot in the distance, on the other side of the clearing. "My father told me that was where she burst from the trees, a hoard of demons behind her. One tackled her, taking her down. She fought and killed it, then kept on running."

I stared at him stunned. "Why didn't she fly away? Why didn't anyone help her?"

He turned to me, and I forced myself to stand my ground and not retreat when his black eyes locked on mine. "Because she was determined to pass the test, to win our father. She'd known he was hers since she was fifteen. My father knew it as well, but he had to wait until she was old enough, and because of who he was, he waited for her to make the first move. She needed to decide what she was willing to risk to be with him. But she'd decided as soon as she realized he was fated to be hers. My mother trained hard, and when she turned eighteen, she was finally ready to claim my father, to become his mate. She went to him and told him she was leaving, and that she'd be back in two days."

I frowned. "I don't understand. What test? Ready for what?"

"She told him to wait for her right there," he said, ignoring my questions, and motioned to the edge of the clearing below us, to the chain-link fence across it. "He knew what she was about to do, what she had to do if they were going to be together. He also knew there was a chance she wouldn't make it, but there was no stopping her. He told me he'd never been more terrified in his life or more proud. When she broke through the trees that day, he was waiting, like she'd asked him to." Payne's Adam's apple slid up and down. "It killed him to stand by while she fought, but if he'd helped her, she would've failed. Our people would've seen her as weak, someone in need of rescuing, and not a fitting mate for their future leader."

I stared out toward the forest filled with demons and other creatures. *Holy shit.* "I had no idea."

He gripped the railing tighter. "It's called the demon run."

"Jesus," I muttered. "Why would anyone do that?"

His nostrils flared, his knuckles turning white. "Our people are strong. Fierce. There's a reason others avoid us and why we keep to ourselves. We

12

are predators, without mercy or remorse. It's in our blood, it's the way we're made." He looked down at me. "We don't have kings and queens, but my father led and protected his people until the day he died. They look to me and my brothers to lead them now. And whoever my brothers mate, will need to be just as strong as our mother was. They'll need to be resilient, courageous...merciless. They need to be willing to risk everything to be with us."

The way he was looking at me—an uneasy feeling settled in my belly. I quickly looked away. "Does every mated couple do the demon run?"

"Only those who want to mate a warrior. Not many can handle a male with that kind of strength. We may try to fight our true natures..." I felt his gaze burning into me now. "But it always comes to the fore. Being with a male like that is not for the faint of heart. Our mates need to be as strong as us, and the demon run is how they prove it."

Bram called my name from the other side of the tree house, and there was an edge to his voice. He hated when he didn't know where I was, and no matter how irrational it was, there was no missing his concern. Pretty ironic, since he did the same to me all the time.

I turned to go, but Payne stopped me, I turned back and he stared at me for several uncomfortable seconds. Whatever he was going to say, I wasn't going to like it.

"Do you understand what I'm telling you?"

"Not in the least, so instead of scowling, how about you enlighten me?"

He crossed his inked arms. "Bram will meet a female one day, a female the fates have chosen for him, one worthy of him, one who is willing to prove to him and his people that she's strong enough for him."

Pain shot through me like a barbed dagger, followed by pure undiluted rage. "Why are you telling me this?"

His hand shot out and he gripped my shoulder, his hold firm, unforgiving. Pain speared through the scar beneath his palm. I gritted my teeth.

"I don't give a fuck that he's your familiar. When that day comes, you *will* step aside. You'll let him go," he said, no, demanded, his voice sending shards of ice through me.

I stared at him in shock.

Bram called again.

"I need to get back." I pulled away, dislodging his hold on me and rushed off.

As soon as I rounded the corner, Bram closed the distance between us, reassuring himself the same way I did after he'd been gone, and pulled me close, his face pressed to my throat. Bram liked to touch me, to be close, it'd always been that way since we found each other. He was the only person I could tolerate touching me most of the time, but sometimes, even that was too much, and now, under the weight of his brother's stare and after the conversation we'd just had, I eased away in the guise of checking out the cake Talon and Rook were placing on the table.

"Is this what you were doing?" I asked Bram.

His lips twitched. "I'm the best with frosting."

He was.

Payne joined us. I felt his gaze on me, and I did my best to ignore him.

Rook lit the seven purple candles, the flames glinting off his necklace made of fangs, demon mostly, but others as well, then Talon nudged Bram and we all sang happy birthday to a beaming Maeve.

I tried to relax after that, to enjoy the rest of the evening, but after what Payne said, it was impossible, and the anger stayed, no matter how hard I tried to shove it down again.

No matter how hard I tried not to think about why I felt this way.

))) ● (((

"Land here," I said to Bram when we flew over my family's two-story, Victorian house.

He frowned but did as I asked. "You need something from your room?"

"I need some time on my own," I said, shoving my hands in my pockets and balling them into fists.

Bram rocked back like I'd backhanded him. It fucking stung, knowing that I'd hurt him, but I was hurting as well, and with all this anger inside me, I didn't want to take it out on him—and I would if I didn't get away from him right now. His family knew what he was doing, where he was going, but not me. *We* were family, closer than family, yet he refused to tell me anything. The cut of that, after talking to his aunt, was deeper tonight, and I couldn't hide it from him or hold it in any longer. If I didn't get some distance between us, we'd fight. I'd say shit I'd regret, we'd hurt each other, and I didn't want tonight to end that way.

He knew it as well, which was why he didn't say anything, why he stood there with pain in his eyes, with a look that said he didn't recognize me anymore. Well, he wasn't the only one. His Adam's apple slid up and down his throat, and he took a step back. "Whatever you need."

"Night, B," I said and rushed inside, shutting the door behind me.

"Drink?" Else asked from the kitchen counter, startling me. She was in her favorite fluffy pink robe and her soft, silver hair was still damp from her shower. She looked tiny tonight, and fragile. I wanted to wrap my arms around her and hold her tight, to let her comfort me and to beg her to never ever leave me, but my scars were alive, the pain more than I could stand. I didn't know why, but I could barely stand my own arms against my sides, let alone someone else touching me.

I did my best to hide the way I was feeling when I turned to her, but I couldn't hide shit from Elswyth Thornheart. No one could. I shook my head. "I'm fine."

My great-aunt was seventy-four years old, and looked like a sweet, little old lady, but she was smart, sarcastic, and a powerful healer. She and I were alike in a lot of ways. We both had an aptitude for potion making, and though I was nowhere near the healer she was, my talent for it had finally shown up several months ago and was steadily growing.

"You look like you could use some cocoa," she said, her brown eyes softening.

I forced a smile. "I just need a good night's sleep."

"Okay, pumpkin." She shuffled past with her steaming mug. "See you in the morning."

"Night."

A good night's sleep was what I desperately needed, but I didn't have a whole lot of them anymore, especially when Bram was away, or we slept apart.

I waited for Else's door to close and slipped back outside. I quickly glanced up at the tree house. The lights were on. Bram was inside.

Spinning around, I raced down the road to our cemetery, opened the iron gates and ran through, then I yanked off my jacket, shoved it against my face, and screamed into it, releasing all the pent-up rage inside me. Rage that wouldn't leave me alone, that had only grown with every passing month. That anger had lived inside me for two and a half years. I knew when it started, but I had no fucking clue how to control it. Or stop it.

Lying on the ground beside Gran's grave, I stuffed my jacket under my head and stared up at the stars, trying to fucking breathe. Sometimes I felt as if I were truly losing my mind.

I kicked off my shoes and pressed my bare feet and palms to the earth, relishing the texture of soft grass beneath me. I couldn't be with Bram right then, so this place was the next best thing.

The power from our cemetery danced over me, reaching through my hands and feet, and I felt it filter through me. Even after death, witches exuded magic; it poured from our bones into the earth. Everything in this place was useful and held power. The dirt, plants, the grass. Mom and Art tended gardens here, so Else and I always had a supply of ingredients for the tonics and potions we made for the store, and it was strongly warded, for the same reason.

Breathing deep, I bathed in the light of the moon and worked at calming myself.

It was a long time before my eyes finally grew heavy. I tried to fight it, knowing what would come, but the way I felt tonight, it was inevitable. Then I couldn't fight it anymore.

I shivered, wrapping my arms around myself, naked in every way a person could be. Clayton's cold blue eyes slid over my bare skin, and I whimpered, wanting to recoil, but I couldn't move. He gripped my throat, pumping more of his magic into me, causing me to tumble more and more out of control. I was lost, here, but also in the world he was spinning in my mind. His hand slid over my breast, squeezing roughly, a look of disgust on his face.

"You are utterly repulsive. You make me sick, Magnolia." He closed the space between us, his hand going lower, shoving between my thighs, the other taking my forearm in a bruising grip. "Your family is in agony. They're bleeding because of you. Do you see them? Can you hear their screams?"

More of his magic pulsed through me and I screamed, I screamed with them.

He smashed his cold lips against mine in a hateful kiss, biting me before he lifted his head, a twisted smile on his face.

"Kill me," I choked out. "Please, kill me."

My eyes flew open, and I sat up with a gasp.

The images were still there, in my mind, and I gripped both sides of my head. *It's over. He's dead.* The images he fed me, the sounds, they weren't real. Bram, my sisters, Mom, Else, Arthur, they're okay. Everyone's okay.

Snatching up my shoes and jacket, I ran from the cemetery, sprinting along the dirt road back to the yard and across the damp grass. I raced up the ladder to the tree house and through the door. Only then could I breathe, only then did the racing of my heart and the terror in my gut begin to calm.

I walked into Bram's room. He was on his side, the sheet at his hips, revealing an expanse of smooth, golden skin. I craved the warmth of it, of him. I tiptoed to the side of the bed, eased the covers back, and tried to get in without waking him.

"Come here," he said in his sleep-roughened voice.

My scars had calmed for now, the pain was gone, so I let him pull me into his strong, warm arms, let him hold me in that comforting, familiar embrace, soothing me the way only Bram could.

CHAPTER 2

Bram

I WOKE to the rustle of leaves, and the creak of the tree house. That sound always soothed something inside me.

The clouds were thick, the room washed in muted gray. I looked down at Magnolia again, curled against my side. We'd gotten home late after visiting my family. I studied the familiar curve of her cheek, the bow of her upper lip. She'd seemed distracted most of the night, then she'd gone straight up to her room when we'd gotten home. She'd been angry and trying to hide it from me, but I didn't miss it. I knew exactly why she was angry, and I deserved it.

I'd come to my tree house in the backyard and tossed and turned until I finally went to sleep. I'd woken again around three a.m. to Magnolia crawling into my bed.

I brushed the hair away from her face. Even in sleep she looked tired. My beautiful, wild, tortured, brave, maddening-as-fuck, little witch.

I swiped my thumb over the scar on her forehead, the one she'd gotten the day we first met.

One of many scars Magnolia had on her body now.

Scars she'd gotten when a sick, twisted monster had used magic to carve slices into her skin. I'd held her thrashing, bleeding body in my arms while she screamed in agony and fear. I'd been utterly helpless, unable to fight an invisible enemy attacking my reason to live.

That was two and a half years ago. The monsters were gone. One locked up, the others dead—one at my hand. That day still fucked with me, though. It felt like yesterday. I dreamed about it most nights. Sometimes about a different outcome, one that I couldn't bear to contemplate in the waking hours, one that took Magnolia from me. And other times, I dreamed of their screams, of their blood on my hands, of making the ones who hurt her pay again and again.

The anger she carried now, it started then, the kind of anger born from hopelessness, but it had grown into something more. Something she struggled to contain every single day, and I didn't know how to help her.

What the fuck would have become of me if we'd never found each other? My entire life, something had been missing, there'd been this feeling, this gaping nothingness inside me. It'd gotten worse after my parents' deaths—then I found my Magnolia, and I was whole for the first time. She'd been my world since.

You know, don't you? What we are to each other? That we belong together?

Her words filled my head, the ones a fifteen-year-old Mags had said to me that day. Yes, I'd known. After I found her, it was all I knew. I'd been sixteen, nearly seventeen, and maybe, if I'd been younger when we met, the truth of what we were to each other would have grown more gradually. But I hadn't been, and along with a deep knowing that Magnolia was my witch and I was her familiar, came the undeniable truth—that she was also my mate.

Something I never imagined would happen for me, and definitely not when I was so young. It wasn't something I'd ever wanted. I'd seen what loss and pain looked like when my father died, when my mother died soon after of a broken heart. I'd wanted none of it.

Then I'd seen Mags. She'd been at her family's cemetery. I'd been drawn there, pulled to that spot by a force deep inside me, unable to resist. I'd seen her hair first, black and thick and wavy—then she'd tilted her face up to the moonlight.

I'd stopped breathing.

She'd been perfect to me in every way. Everything my secret teenage heart had dreamed up had been sitting right there. She'd been too young for me then, and I'd been prepared to wait, for as long as she needed. To wait for her to come to the same realization as me.

It never happened, though.

My best friend, my mate, didn't want me the way I wanted her. She didn't recognize that part of the bond between us and thought of me only as family—maybe even a brother.

She was my everything, and being by her side the last six years had been a privilege and an honor, it was what I'd been born to do, but the last couple of years, after someone tried to take her from me during her sister Willow's trial, everything had changed.

I'd changed.

And so had Mags.

My gaze slid lower. While she slept, her shirt had slipped off one of her shoulders, revealing more silvery scars. She hated them. I hated how they got there, and how that day, and the ones leading up to it, irrevocably altered everything between us.

I looked at her face again. Her lips were full and deep crimson. Her dark lashes rested on her pink cheeks, her beautiful amber eyes locked behind closed lids. My crow's song built in my chest, like it often did at times like this, but I swallowed it back down and willed her eyes to open. I craved the way she looked at me, the same way I craved the wind on my feathers. Those eyes, they'd never hidden anything from me. The day we met, there'd been no lies when she'd looked at me, only truth.

We'll be together forever and nothing will ever tear us apart.

She'd said it and meant it. I'd believed it with everything in me.

I wasn't so sure anymore.

When she looked at me now, there were secrets.

She blinked, waking, and immediately gave me a sleepy smile, cracking my heart right down the fucking middle—because I had secrets of my own. Secrets I was forbidden to share. Secrets, that even if she did want me the way I did her, made it impossible for us to ever be anything more than we were.

"Hey," she said.

"Hey."

Rolling into me automatically, she curled her arm around my middle. I lay back and she rested her head against my chest.

She yawned. "So what're we doing today."

I opened my mouth to answer, but the thud of boots hitting the deck outside reached us.

A throaty *caw* followed. Rook. He liked talking even less than me.

Mags pulled away from me, sitting up, her gaze instantly growing distant. "I guess that answers that."

The peace between us shattered. "Mags..."

She climbed out of bed, shoved on her boots, and walked out of the room.

I tugged on my jeans and followed her out as Rook walked in.

He greeted Mags with a chin lift, and she forced a smile in response as she strode past.

I went after her, jumping off the deck and landing on the ground before she could get down the ladder. I stood in front of her before she could storm off. "Wait."

I expected fire, her anger, because that's what we did now, snapped and snarled at each other out of fear and desperation. Instead, when she looked up at me, that tiredness was back in her eyes. "It's fine. Go."

That look, the defeat in her voice, it fucking terrified me. "Mags—"

"Whatever it is you're doing, just be safe, okay?"

I studied her expression, hating what I saw. Distance yawning wider between us. Every time I left her, every time I kept another secret from her, the canyon between us grew deeper, wider. "I want to tell you," I said, but giving her that small amount was all I could.

"But you can't, right?" Her gaze slid from me to the house on the other side of the yard, already checking out, already gone.

I'd taken the kind of oath that was binding for a lifetime. Only family, mates, could be told more. And though Mags meant more to me than anyone on this earth, she wasn't family, not in the blood sense, and we weren't mated. There was one other way—if she found out on her own. But the idea of her finding out that way? No, I couldn't fucking stomach it. That'd be the worst thing that could happen.

What would she think if you did tell her? Would she still look at you the same if she knew the things you'd done? If she knew what you truly were? How deep your darkness truly went?

She pressed her hands to my chest, and at the innocent contact, my heart smacked hard against the back of my ribs. I wanted to pull her close, my instincts screaming for me to press my face to her throat, nuzzle her smooth skin, to breathe her into my lungs.

"Be safe," she said and smiled up at me. It was forced, false. "I'll see you when you get back."

Then she dropped her hands and strode away, back to the house.

Rook dropped to the ground beside me. "Tell her how you feel or move the fuck on."

My brothers had picked up I had feelings for her, but they didn't know she was my mate, and I wasn't in a hurry to tell them.

I ignored him, watching until Mags disappeared inside. If I told her how I felt, I'd destroy what we had now. Yes, it was volatile and shaky, but she still cared, she still wanted me around.

After what Clayton did to her, she'd closed off completely when it came to any kind of romantic relationships. They made her uncomfortable, even in movies. She'd turn off the TV if anything even remotely sexual happened.

Telling her the truth was the worst thing I could do.

I used to hope that one day she'd see it, feel it for herself. That I'd wait forever if I had to.

I didn't wish for that anymore. I hoped like fuck she never felt it. I never wanted her to see the dark corners inside me, the twisted things in my mind, the things I needed to do just to stay sane. No, she could never see what I truly was, and if we were mated, there'd be no hiding it.

"Let's get the fuck out of here," I said.

Rook shifted, and took flight.

I did the same, following my brother.

What was another black mark on my soul?

›)〉〉●《《

Magnolia

The road to the keep was bumpy as hell. I gripped the steering wheel and tried to breathe through all the anger and pain. It wasn't working. Only one thing would help me.

I parked, and as I walked up the steep track to the keep, a wolf howled in the distance, alerting everyone of my arrival. Since Iris moved here with her mate, Draven, she'd become familiar with the different howls the wolves made, different pitches and lengths, and she was walking out of the keep to greet me as I strode across the clearing.

Iris was the second oldest out of the four of us, she could talk to animals, take on their traits and also did this weird thing that wasn't exactly shifting into an animal, but also kind of was.

She grinned. "I wasn't expecting you. This is a nice surprise."

I let her hug me, the coolness of her cheek brushing mine. The damage from her ex-boyfriend, Brody's, attempt to kill my sister had left a permanent black mark on her face. I squeezed her in return, though it was hard today. When I was like this, full of banked rage, I didn't want to be touched. I felt every scar as if it were a fresh slice, heard every twisted word that'd been muttered in my ear on repeat. The monsters were only in my head, but they were as real to me now as they were back then—when I'd made the biggest mistake of my life, breaking a blood oath and almost causing the death of my entire family.

My soul had been damaged that day, a fissure of darkness creeping through. It grew wider by the day, settling deeper, and there was no stopping it.

"Maybe we could visit later?" I said to Iris. "I'm actually here to train. Is Ash around?"

She gave me a look, one I didn't like, one that said she saw way too much of what I was trying to hide. "She's getting ready to leave on patrol, so you may as well hang out with me—"

"Thanks." I rushed off before she could finish, dashing around the side of the keep. I spotted Asher with several other wolves, including Draven.

Asher and I had gotten off to a pretty rocky start, and when she offered to train me six months ago, to help me deal with my anger, I'd turned her down flat. But my anger had continued to grow, had become so overpowering, the darkness inside me digging so deep, I'd scared myself, but worse, I was scaring everyone around me.

So much so that I shoved down my pride and asked her to train me.

Asher was cool, I could admit that now, and it turned out fighting the wolf, focusing my anger outward, helped me a lot. She wasn't family. She didn't give me a pass or go easy on me. She pushed me to my limits, forcing me to get a handle on my anger, and to work through what I was feeling. I learned quickly that using anger to fuel you, at least my brand of wild and uncontrollable anger, was the fastest way of getting your ass kicked.

She spotted me and strode over. "Can't train today, feisty. I'm rostered on patrol."

"Let me come with you."

She snorted, her golden eyes sparkling. "You think you're ready to take on a real live demon, little witch?"

I gritted my teeth. "Yeah, I do. We've been training for nearly six months. I can hold my own. You know I can."

Her expression grew serious. "This isn't playtime, Mags. One of those fuckers gets hold of you, it'll tear you to pieces."

Draven strode over. "What's going on?"

"She wants to come with us."

He didn't spare me a glance. "No."

I planted my hands on my hips. "You didn't even think about it."

"Don't need to," he said in his deep, growly voice.

"I'm ready, you know I am," I said, working really hard at not letting my anger get the better of me and firing attitude at him. Draven was not the kind of male to be talked into anything. He'd tell me to fuck off if he thought I wasn't in the right headspace. We'd talked about the possibility of this, when I was ready, and I was. More than ready.

He crossed his arms, looking down at me, his vibrant green eyes deadly serious. "My mate would fuck me up if you got hurt, you know that, right? And I won't be very fucking happy either if I have to carry you back in pieces."

"You've seen me train. And I'm going to need to know how to fight on my own, the mother will call me soon…"

"You still have time," he said.

I bit back a curse. So far, she'd called my sisters, one year apart. Going by that timeline, I had another six months. "The more practice I get, though, the better my chances. I want to do this, Draven."

"What you want and what you're ready for are two different things," he said.

"I am ready."

He turned to Asher. "You've been training her. You think she's ready to go out in the field? Keep in mind, it's your head on the chopping block if anything happens to her."

I bit back another curse.

"Physically, she's up to it. But what about in here, feisty." She tapped the side of my head, and I shoved her hand away. "You let your anger get the better of you out there, you'll wake up to the horrific sound of demons singing 'Kumbaya,' an apple jammed in your mouth, while they roast you over an open fire."

Draven's lips twitched. I ignored him, curled my fingers tight to control my temper, and nodded. "I've got it under control."

She flicked my forehead. "You sure?"

"Ash—"

She did it again. "Yeah?"

"Yes, I'm sure."

She gave me a shove. "Positive?"

I gritted my teeth. "Asher—"

She grabbed my forearm, a trigger spot for me, which she well knew, and tugged me forward. I snapped and swung at her instantly. Ash grabbed my fist midair and shoved me back. "You're not ready for shit. Get your ass inside before you get hurt."

Fuck. "Ash, come on."

She shook her head. "You came to the keep 'cause you're pissed off. That's more than fine when we're training. But that won't fly when we're on patrol."

"Asher, please—"

"You heard her," Draven said. "Get inside."

Then they turned their backs on me and ran into the surrounding forest, leaving me behind. I stood there breathing hard, fury exploding through me as I spun away and strode back across the clearing.

Iris called my name.

"I need to leave," I said, not looking back, and jogged to my car.

A minute later, I sped away. Not sure where I was going, or what I was going to do. The tree house was empty. Bram was gone.

Nothing made sense anymore.

My life fucking sucked, and I didn't know what the hell I was going to do about it.

CHAPTER 3

Magnolia

I GRABBED a sprig of rosemary and plucked several yarrow flowers from the dried herbs hanging above me, then added them to the bubbling pot of healing elixir I was currently standing over. If I stopped stirring before it was done, the batch would spoil, and I'd have to start over again. Stock for several of our elixirs was low at The Cauldron, the shop owned by my oldest sister, Willow, and Else and I were busy trying to replenish them.

Else limped in. Her prosthesis gave her trouble in the morning and her limp was always more pronounced.

"Almost done, pumpkin?" she asked as she dumped a bunch of lavender on the worn wooden counter.

"Yeah." I lifted it off the burner, finally able to stop stirring, and put the brew aside to cool.

She came over and eyeballed it. "Should fill about forty bottles, I reckon." She ran a gnarled finger down the list in our order book. "That'll do for now. We'll start on the rest of these in the morning." She patted my shoulder, and I forced myself not to flinch. "Go do what young people do. I'll clean up."

I snorted. "Oh no, you don't. Connor will be here any minute. You're not getting out of your CEA meeting by using me and a messy workshop as an excuse." Else had recently been roped into joining the Coven Elders Assembly. They'd been trying to get her to join for years. I was pretty sure Connor had been the reason she'd finally caved.

She scowled. "I wasn't doing that."

"Yes, you were. Now, go pretty yourself up for your gentleman caller. I'll clean up here."

"You're a smart-ass, you know that?" she muttered as she headed across the room.

"I take after you."

She flipped me the bird, and I laughed as she walked out. Connor was her *very* good friend, though she hadn't confirmed or denied that they were dating. The male was a saint, though, always calm and steady. It also helped that he thought Else's grumbling was totally adorable.

I pulled my phone from my pocket and checked it again, and my smile slipped away. Still no word from Bram. It'd been thirty-six hours. I was worried. Goddess, I felt sick all the time when he was gone. When he was away, everything was just...worse.

I forced myself to focus on cleaning, putting things away, but my inner demons were in full swing without Bram here to distract me, and they were pushing in from all sides. I rubbed my forearm. Phantom pain throbbing below my skin, where the bruise had been, a perfect outline of Clayton's hand. It'd been visible for two weeks after.

He was dead, but when Bram was gone, my fucked-up mind brought him back to life. The darkness let him creep back in, reminding me of how stupid I'd been, how naive, how I'd let him use me to get to the people I loved most in this world, and no matter how hard I tried to force him back out, I failed every damn time.

Voices traveled in from the hall. Else and Connor, and there was no missing the alarm in their voices. I strode out, and as soon as I spotted Else, I knew something was wrong.

"What's going on?"

She turned to me and all color had drained from her face. "There's been another one," she whispered, her hands shaking. "I knew there would be, I goddamn knew the council was trying to downplay it. Idiots."

"Another murder?" A rock settled in the pit of my stomach.

"Another execution." Else sat heavily in the seat behind her, a look on her face I'd never seen before.

I gripped the doorframe. "Who?"

Pain filled her eyes. "Margot Huxley."

Margot was my age. We'd gone to school together. She and I and another guy named Jamie had been kind of friends. We'd all been loners, preferring our own company, but we'd hung out sometimes, occasionally ate lunch together if we were in the cafeteria at the same time. If we were forced to do an assignment with someone else, or some other group activity, they were my first choice and I was theirs. I hadn't seen her in a while, but whenever we ran across each other, we made time to catch up. "Is there a chance it could be unrelated?" I asked, my heart a lump in my chest.

She shook her head. "They carved judgment into her skin, Mags..." Her shrewd brown eyes locked on mine. "You need to be careful. Don't go anywhere on your own, not until this animal is found. Promise me."

I nodded and walked woodenly back into the workroom, still in shock. The first victim, Clara Hope, had been older than Margot, and the same word had been carved into her when they found her. I hadn't known Clara. She was Willow's age, but their deaths had to be by the same psycho.

Roxburgh already had its fair share of monsters. We didn't need another one.

Images flashed through my mind—of my own monster.

The way he'd touched me, making my skin crawl from the utter wrongness of it, of the images he'd projected into my mind. Images so horrific and real—

Gasping, I grabbed on to the edge of the counter as more of them filled my head, one after the other.

Blood, gore, flaying skin, dismembered limbs—the screams. Oh goddess, the screams of my family, of Bram.

I squeezed my eyes closed and tried to fight it.

For hours Clayton had filled my head with horror, until something had broken inside me, until I believed what I saw and heard. Until my screams were just as loud as the ones in my head.

And now I heard Margot as well—I heard her screams of terror and pain. As though the darkness in me was on the same frequency, broadcasting that horror right into my mind.

Opening the small box on my workbench, I slid the false bottom aside, took out the key, and rushed to the old dresser across the room. I quickly opened the heavy wooden doors and crouched, moving the stack of old recipe books out of the way. I'd found the key over a year ago and had no idea what it was for. Then several months ago, I'd discovered the drawer. I unlocked it now, taking out the small, black leather book I found there, and ran my hand over it. It had belonged to my grandmother and was half full of spells she'd created, spells I knew without doubt she'd kept hidden. Because Gran had been like me—more than I'd ever known.

A sense of calm washed over me immediately.

I'd put hours of work into the contents of this book. Hours alone in this workshop while Else was out and about, while Bram was gone, hours deep in my fear, in my rage, in my terror that history would one day repeat itself —of Clayton gripping my arm, pumping me full of dark magic while he whispered in my ear, reminding me of the horrors he'd made me see, of what could happen if I wasn't vigilant, if I wasn't strong enough—turning words into a twisted reality in my head.

This little book full of spells and recipes, of potions and elixirs, was my safety net. This was how I slept at night. When I channeled my anger into the spells I wrote in it, the same book Gran had used, it calmed me, it banked the inferno in my gut like nothing else could.

If anyone came for my family again, I could destroy them with what was written in this book, with my words, my magic.

Flipping to the back, I lifted out the small business cards there. One from Rose, the name of a counselor she wanted me to speak with. I don't know why I'd kept it, probably because it'd seemed so important to her. The last thing I wanted was to dredge up my pain to a complete stranger.

I put it back and studied the second—Umbra Sanitarium. It was an institution, a place for witches who skimmed too close to the dark side, those who dabbled in dark magic and got burned or needed help back to the light.

It was touted as a place of healing. But Umbra was also a prison. We recently found out that was where Cora had been sent. The evil bitch was Else and Gran's cousin. She was being held in a separate area, a place for those who couldn't be saved, who didn't want to be. I clenched my teeth. Two and a half years ago, Cora and her grandson Brody had plotted against our family, and with the help of Clayton Whitlock, they'd made their move. Cora had murdered the previous Keeper of our coven in the hopes the position would pass to her grandson, but instead of her branch of the family, it went to ours—and she'd almost succeeded in killing us all to get what she wanted.

Willow was Keeper of our coven now, but after she passed her tasks and trial, the mother had thrown us a curveball. Because the position of Keeper had moved to a new branch of the family, each of us—me, Rose, and Iris— had to pass a task and trial of our own to prove our line was worthy of keeping the magical gifts she'd bestowed on our coven over the centuries. To lose those gifts would be devastating. A coven that couldn't hold on to its power became a target for those who could.

My sisters had all gone through their trials and passed. It was now down to me.

The ritual was nonnegotiable and included a demon-infested forest and some up-close-and-personal time with a giant serpent possessed by Mother Nature. I wasn't looking forward to her inevitable bite, which would pump me full of her magical venom, leaving behind a permanent tattoo-like mark. The black tattoo would eventually become colorful, if I passed the ultimate task she gave me. But that wasn't all. A magical combat trial was the final piece of her twisted puzzle. If I didn't win that? Bye-bye magical gifts.

I stared at the nondescript card again before sliding it back into the book. My darkness nudged me, pushing again. I didn't know if I could hold it back indefinitely, but if I ever got really bad, I'd do what I had to so no one got hurt.

The moment I broke a blood oath, one I'd made to my family, by going to Clayton for help—the trajectory of my life had changed. I didn't know how exactly, I just knew it had.

After that day, after we battled Cora, Brody, and Clayton at our cemetery, everything had fallen apart.

Bram had started going away, leaving me, and I'd felt the darkness crawling closer.

I became someone else, someone full of anger, who lacked any kind of control—someone I didn't like very much at all.

It'd been two and a half years and I still hadn't worked out how to live in my own skin again. I was lost, and I wasn't sure I'd ever find my way back.

I slid the book into the drawer and closed it. But maybe that was a good thing. The old Magnolia had messed everything up, had almost gotten herself and her family killed.

That wasn't who I was anymore, but I did know, if this new monster came for any of us, I'd destroy it.

>>>●<<<

"Come by the clubhouse Friday night. We're having a party," Willow said as she grabbed her bag and strode toward me.

I often helped Willow out at The Cauldron, and today I was working the afternoon for her since she had some appointment she needed to get to. Wills was an earth witch, she could manipulate wind and the plants and trees, move boulders, and could cause a fairly decent earthquake if she wanted to. She also had a magical blade that warned her of danger.

"Whose birthday is it?"

She chuckled. "Lothar."

The hounds had taken to celebrating birthdays recently. It started when Willow threw a party for Warrick, and now they all wanted one. It was getting out of hand, but the hounds loved to party hard and were taking full advantage. "What kind of party are we talking about?"

"Nothing too wild," she said, reading my mind and giving me a nudge. "You know you want to. Everyone will be there."

Everyone except Bram. When he vanished like this, he could be gone days. My belly gripped. I really hated how we'd left things before he left. I hadn't even said goodbye. I rubbed my chest, the ache there wouldn't subside. "Maybe."

"I want us to hang out. I feel like we haven't talked in ages. Come, okay? It's important."

I opened the door for her. "I'll try."

As she passed, she gave me a look that said I'd better be there, and then she strode out. I pulled my phone from my pocket, checking it again. Still no word from Bram.

I'd dreamed about Margot all night, and I was exhausted today. To keep my mind off everything, off Bram, and Margot, I needed a menial task, something that forced me to concentrate. Grabbing a notepad and pen, I got to work taking stock of our inventory in the storeroom. Willow didn't do it nearly often enough. Then she'd run out of something, and Else and I would be left scrambling to make more.

My and Else's tonics and potions were stored in the back for safety, only the harmless stuff was displayed out front. I was working my way along the shelves by the register when the door opened and three witches walked in. My spine straightened, but I didn't let what I was feeling show on my face. I wouldn't give them the satisfaction.

Amelia, as always, was in front, with Leah and Claire following. Always following. It was seriously pathetic.

"Oh, look who it is, ladies!" Amelia said. "I haven't seen you in so long, Magnolia. What have you been doing with yourself?"

No, we hadn't seen each other in a while, we'd barely had any interaction since we finished high school, which was the way I liked it. "Working," I said. "Is there something you need?"

She grabbed a basket. "Just a few bits and pieces for my new place, you can't be too careful. I plan on strengthening my wards." She leaned in. "We heard about Margot." She screwed up her face, eyes wide. "Sounds like she was *tortured*...they carved into her before they finally...you know..."

My fingers curled into fists, and I turned away before I swung at her.

There was silence behind me, my disgust in her gossiping over Margot's horrific death was received loud and clear. I ignored them and got on with what I was doing while they made their way around the store, talking under their breath but loud enough for me to hear, like we were still in fucking high school.

What I wanted to do was kick their asses out, but again, I wouldn't give those bitches the satisfaction.

Leah finally walked over and peered at me through the shelf I was standing behind, her familiar, a small dog named Biscuit, tucked under her arm. "Sorry, we didn't realize you and Margot were friends," she said, a ridiculous, overly innocent look on her face that said she did in fact know.

"Do you have everything you need?" I said, ignoring what she'd said completely.

"Oh, um...almost." She smiled in a way that had my hair standing on end. "So...how's Bram?"

Amelia laughed, giving her friend a little shove. "I knew you couldn't help yourself."

Leah blushed.

Just hearing Bram's name from her mouth had fire shooting through my veins. "What are you talking about?" I moved out from behind the shelf.

"Oh nothing," Leah said. "I just saw him out last night. He was at The Bank with another guy I assume was his brother. The hair color, and those eyes. The two of them together..." She bit her lip and grinned. "They were a whole lot of eye candy, and I wasn't the only one who thought so. They were surrounded by females."

Bram was at The Bank? What the fuck was going on? Why was he at a club? I locked down my emotions, which was hard, but I refused to let her see me react.

"Bram can do what he wants," I said, even as the pain in my chest became almost unbearable.

Leah leaned on the shelf beside me. "I'm really glad to hear that because I got his number from a friend of a friend and was thinking of asking him out."

It took every ounce of willpower not to slam my fist into her smug face. Over my rotting corpse would I let this grasping bitch anywhere near Bram.

"You guys definitely aren't, you know, together?" she asked, watching me like a hawk ready to tear its prey's eyes out, while she stroked her familiar like a comic book supervillain.

I shook my head, finding it impossible to speak without firing a whole lot of verbal poison at her. The urge to pull my knife and make her bleed was there as well, and that was even harder to resist—which should worry me, but I wasn't thinking rationally right then.

"Did you hear me and Scott bought a new place?" Amelia said, hating that the attention was off her for even a moment. "That's why I'm here. I want to make sure the apartment has a strong ward. I like to be ready for anything."

"Awesome," I said. "You truly are perfect for each other." Her familiar, Scott, was a narcissistic creep.

Her gaze sliced to me, and I could tell she wasn't sure how to read my tone. I didn't give a shit. She could read it however she liked. We may be adults now, but I had a long memory, and I was petty as shit. I had no plans on letting go of the way they'd treated me.

"Yes, we are," she said, her eyes locking on mine as she handed me her basket. "Maybe you'll find out for yourself what that's like, Magnolia. I'm sure your mate will turn up...someday." She smiled, and it was full of spiteful glee.

I refused to engage. If I opened my mouth now, I'd tell her what an asshole I truly thought she was. And honestly, I didn't trust myself to stop there. My fingers curled into a fist at my side as I finished ringing her up. Shoving everything into a paper bag, I slid it to her.

She opened her mouth to say something else—

"Bye," I said before she could.

She shut her trap and, with a snotty look, turned and headed for the door.

"Tell Bram to expect my call," Leah said before she walked out after her friends.

I gripped the edge of the counter to keep from launching over it. I wasn't okay. Not at all. Bram had apparently been out partying with one of his brothers yet wasn't able to call or text me?

Cool. That didn't feel like being kicked in the gut multiple times *at all*.

So many thoughts, dark ones, flew through my mind. I shoved them down. This was Bram, *my* Bram. He didn't like partying, he barely spoke to anyone but me and his brothers. I needed to calm the fuck down. Until I spoke to him, I wasn't going to jump to any wild assumptions.

Somehow, I managed to keep a lid on everything I was feeling the rest of the afternoon. Just after I closed up the shop and was heading to my car, my phone chimed.

When I checked it, my relief was so strong, my legs actually went weak.

Bram. Finally.

Be home tonight.

⟩⟩⟩●⟨⟨⟨

Mom and Arthur were setting themselves up in front of the TV to watch their favorite gardening show when I got home.

"Another cushion, my sweet Daisy?" Art said.

I smiled. I loved the way he always called her *his*.

"You're back," Mom said when she saw me. "I was getting worried. Grab some dinner and come watch TV with us."

I plonked down in the chair by Art. "Bram's coming home tonight. I'm going to wait at the tree house. I'll eat when he gets here."

"I made apple sponge pudding," Art said.

It was Bram's favorite and one of Arthur's specialties. "I hope you used the big dish?"

He flashed me a smile. "Sure did."

Arthur was middle-aged with dark brown skin and kind eyes. He was an owl shifter, but preferred his human form, and Mom's familiar. He'd been in love with her from the moment they found each other. It took Mom a little longer to work it out, but they were now deeply in love, and we were all thrilled about it.

Art was loving and protective and the closest thing any of us had to a father, since our own sperm donors were either absent, wastes of space, or in Rose's case, a psychotic, power-hungry piece of shit. We all adored Art.

Both Mom and Art had also welcomed Bram into the fold when he showed up and promptly built himself a tree house in our backyard. They were the best, and I'd do anything to protect them...and to make up for what I'd done. If I could only give them back half of what they'd given me...

I stood. "Enjoy your show. I'm gonna take some food to the tree house."

"Okay, baby," Mom said, squeezing my hand as I walked past, then stopped me by holding fast. "Promise me you'll be safe. After what happened to Margot... I can't think why anyone would want to hurt her." Her hand trembled around mine. "Promise me, Magnolia."

"I promise." I kissed the top of her head. "Besides, Bram will be here." Though as I said it, I wasn't sure it was the truth. It used to be, but not anymore.

I shut those thoughts down and loaded a basket with food, getting double helpings of dessert, and headed out the back door. It was dark, but it was still hot. I hated summer. The last thing I wanted was my skin and all my scars on display. People mostly just stared, but there were always others who didn't think there was anything wrong with asking how I got them.

I reached the tree house, attached the basket to the pulley, winching it up to the deck, then locked it in place. I climbed up after it, and grabbed the basket. Bram had built this place when he was seventeen, and he'd lived here since.

I walked into the tree house and switched on the light.

It was beautiful, a work of art, and even better than his tree house back at the village. The living space was fairly big, with enough room for a kitchenette and a short breakfast bar on one side, a decent-sized couch and flat-screen TV on the other. The windows in this room were all different shapes and sizes. He had designed and made each one with different colored glass that bathed the room in a rainbow of colors during the day. His bedroom was off the living room, and only a bit smaller, and there was an ensuite as well. The entire tree house was bigger than a lot of apartments in the city.

It was my favorite place in the entire world.

I put the food in the fridge and tidied up the living room, then stripped the sheets from the bed and put on fresh ones for him. I always liked fresh sheets after I'd been away, even if it was only after a night or two.

Then I opened the reading app on my phone, so my mind didn't wander back to Margot, and lay down to wait.

CHAPTER 4

Magnolia

My eyes snapped open, and I sat up, blinking into the dark room. "Bram?"

"Yeah." The bathroom door opened. "Go back to sleep." He shut himself in and the water turned on.

I stared through the darkness. It'd been too dark to see him, but something wasn't right.

The door finally opened again, and I flicked on the light and gasped.

Bram stilled, his jaw tightening, his gaze dropping to the floor. "I'm okay."

I flew out of bed. "What the hell happened to you?"

His wet hair had fallen forward, covering his face. My hand shook as I lifted it to his bruised stomach and chest, to the bloody slices scattered across his smooth, inked skin. He'd pulled on shorts, but the rest of him was bare, and I took inventory of every mark on his lean, muscled body.

"Please," I whispered. "I can't take this anymore. I can't bear it. You're hurt, you keep getting hurt, and I'm terrified that one of these times you'll leave me...and you won't come back." I finally said it, the thing that terrified me the most. I couldn't survive without him. I just...I couldn't. I wouldn't want to.

He reached for me, and I pushed his hands away, scared and angry as hell. I couldn't be hugged by him then; I couldn't hear how much he cared

35

about me when he wasn't being honest with me. I knew he loved me, I was his best friend, but that didn't make the secrets any less painful.

I wouldn't let him touch me, but the need to touch him, to heal him, was overwhelming. Brushing his hair back, I took his chin and tilted his head to the side. There was a bruise on his jaw, a cut by his eye.

"It's nothing serious." His voice was full of grit and lifted goose bumps all over my body.

"Lie on the bed so I can tend your wounds."

"Maggie—"

"Please," I said, my heart squeezing at the use of his nickname for me, one he used rarely and only when we were alone. I had trouble meeting his eyes all of a sudden, something else that was new. More distance, more pain.

He did as I asked. We'd done this several times now, but he'd never been this badly hurt before.

I grabbed my basket of healing supplies from the bathroom. I'd taken to leaving one here since he'd needed them more often. "Can you at least tell me what kind of creature did this so I know the best treatment to use?"

He didn't answer, just shook his head.

I muttered a curse and pulled out a generic poultice and the herbs and balm I'd need, then started cleaning the cuts...or scratches. I wasn't completely sure what they were.

"I'm okay," he said into the quiet room.

"Bullshit."

He didn't contradict me, lying still as I slowly and methodically cleaned out his wounds and smeared them with Else's healing balm to get the regeneration of tissue started. Then, laying the poultice over the top, I closed my eyes, held my hand over it, and muttered the spell that would go one step further. "Blood and bone. Flesh torn, skin bruised. Return what was broken...again to what was." Warmth radiated from my palm as I said the rest of the spell, a spell that was unique to me. Like all healing witches, the spells needed to be of our own making, since no two witches had the exact same healing power. Mine had come to me in a dream, at least part of it, and I'd developed the rest from there.

I checked under the poultice and the bruise beneath hadn't healed completely, but it'd lost some of the angry purple and the slice in his skin had thinned, the deeper tissue beginning to heal already. I moved to the next. A slice across the rigid muscle of his abs, and repeated my spell, doing it over and over again, until I was shaking and exhausted from all the magic I'd drained working on him.

I moved to the next—

Bram grabbed my hand, stopping me. I looked up.

36

"No more. Bed, Magnolia. Now."

I'd gotten the worst of them, but I couldn't bear to think he was in pain. "I'm fine, let me finish—"

"I don't need it. Bed," he said in that incredibly deep, velvety voice of his. It'd surprised me the first time I'd heard it. I loved his voice. I could listen to him talk all day, if he was the kind of male to talk nonstop, which he was not. His voice had only grown deeper, grittier as he'd gotten older. But that wasn't the only thing that'd changed. The way he spoke, the things he said.

The last couple of years another side of Bram had come out, a more demanding, blunt, forceful side. Gone was the shy boy I'd met that first day. He still didn't like to talk much, not to anyone besides me and his brothers, but a dominance radiated from him now that he hadn't had when he was sixteen, but it'd sure as hell grown over the years. He'd always been protective, but he could also be seriously possessive.

I'd tell him to stop being so goddamn bossy now, if I wasn't so exhausted. I stood on shaky legs. I'd expended a lot more of my power than I'd realized—

My legs gave out, and Bram cursed, jackknifing up. He hooked me around the waist and planted me in the bed beside him.

"I should be the one cursing right now," I muttered, giving his shoulder a pathetically weak shove.

He pulled me close, ignoring my pitiful struggles, and pressed a kiss to the top of my head. "Rest."

I should resist, ask him about The Bank and what he'd been doing there. I could say a lot of things, but I didn't want to fight. He wasn't going to tell me no matter how angry I got anyway.

And honestly, I didn't have a fight in me. So I let him manhandle me to where he wanted me, wrapped in his arms, his face to my throat, because I was just glad he was home.

Then I closed my heavy eyes and let the heat of his body soak through me.

·))◉((·

When I woke again, Bram was dressed and in the middle of lacing up his boots.

"What's going on?" I sat up.

His jaw clenched.

"You're leaving again." My stomach tightened into a painful knot.

"One night. I'll be back sooner, if I can."

"Right." I jerked back the covers and shoved my feet in my boots.

"Cool." Deja vu hit. I was living my own personal *Groundhog Day*. I said my lines, then he said his. Nothing changed.

He grabbed my hand when I tried to walk past. "Mags…"

I looked up at him. "What? What could you possibly say that will make this okay?"

His hand around mine tightened, and he tugged me closer before his other arm hooked around my waist and held me tight, so tight I struggled to breathe. "I'm sorry," he said roughly.

Tears sprang to my eyes, but I fought them back and pushed away from him. "Yep, you've said that already, I don't know, like three thousand times." I stared up at him, waiting, hoping he'd say something more. He didn't. I shook my head and walked past him. "See you later, I guess."

Then I strode out of the tree house.

)) ⟩ ● (((

"Come on, maybe it'll be fun." I grabbed Jasmine's hand and pulled her along after me.

"I don't feel like going to a party," she grumbled, while several butterflies fluttered around her head. Like Rose, who didn't have just one familiar but instead countless—in Rose's case, bats, she could call and control—Jazzy had butterflies.

I wasn't sure how it worked, and she hadn't elaborated yet. We didn't like to push because Jasmine wasn't one to share unless she needed to. She liked to sort through things on her own first. She'd had a lot to sort through lately, not only with her sister gone so often but with learning to deal with her gift. She was a medium, like Zinnia, and could communicate with the dead, something that had once terrified her. Else and Mom were trying to help her, but it was tough.

"Willow said we all have to be here. It'll take your mind off everything." Jasmine was nineteen and our cousin. She was living with us while Zinnia, her older sister, was living in Limbo—with Death, as his consort. It was all pretty complicated and fucked up, but Zinnia had no other choice. She had, however, negotiated the terms of her time there. She stayed with Death every other month until Jasmine turned twenty-one, after that she would have to stay there permanently.

Well, that wasn't fucking happening. We had two years to figure something out, and we wouldn't rest until we'd found a way to get her out of the bargain. Zinnia wasn't as hopeful as us, and she didn't talk about her time there when she came home. This was her month to be away, and Jasmine desperately needed a distraction, and I did as well.

We got out of the car and strode toward the clubhouse. There was a huge garage to the right of it, and both had the Devil Dogs logo painted on the side of the building.

The clubhouse was in Linville, a thirty-minute drive from Roxburgh, and the hellhounds who lived there looked and acted like a human motorcycle club, for the sake of the humans in this town. They lived all together in the den they'd dug out below the main building, and Willow lived here with Warrick, her mate and alpha of the hounds.

Jazzy and I walked in and were hit by a wall of sound and pure undiluted testosterone. The latter so thick you almost needed a shovel to get through it. Leather, motor oil, bulging muscle, and lots of hair. The hounds were huge, all close to seven feet, and had lived the majority of their extremely long lives in Hell.

Tonight, they were partying. Mom and Arthur had just walked in ahead of us, and everyone else was already here.

I turned to Jazzy. She looked cute in shorts and a baggy, black T-shirt. She was no stranger to the hounds and hung here with Willow a lot. She also liked to draw, and Roman, the hounds' tattoo artist, had gotten her to work with him a few times. Jazzy had asked for payment in ink, and now her arms and hands were decorated with a bunch of small tattoos. Flora and fauna, animals and insects. They were pretty and delicate and suited her. "Let's go get a drink."

Jasmine nodded, but she was still taking in the room with wide eyes, and I knew the moment she spotted Ren because she froze. Ren was a fox shifter, and Willow's familiar. He was the same age as Bram, twenty-two and model handsome. Add in the scars he'd collected over the last couple of years living in the wild, demon-infested woods...well, he was a lot rougher around the edges than he used to be. He had females throwing themselves at him left and right.

Ren had embraced partying and lots of sex as his coping mechanism, after all he'd been through. It was concerning, but at least he was back with us.

"Jazzy?" My cousin had a mega crush on him, and right now there was a female, a wolf shifter from Draven's pack, running her fingers through Ren's auburn hair with one hand, while the other slid across his stomach.

"I'm not really in the mood for this," Jazz said, though I had to read her lips over the loud music.

Willow strode over with a huge smile on her face, but her eyes gentled as they slid to Jasmine and who she was watching. "Come and hang with me and Warrick."

Jazzy sucked in a breath and dragged her gaze from Ren, who was now making out with the wolf, and she smiled, though it was more a baring of teeth. "Yeah, I'm just...I need a Coke." She strode off across the room, toward the bar.

Willow looked over at Ren and worry shifted across her features before she turned back to me. "Try to have fun, okay?" Then she followed Jasmine.

The hounds could get wild, but this was a bit more relaxed than some of their parties, despite the making-out sessions here and there. I spotted the birthday hound and strode over.

"Hey, Lothar. Happy birthday."

He glanced down at me and gave me a chin lift.

"So how old are you?" I asked.

"Stopped counting a few hundred years ago."

I smirked. "Damn, that old?" He didn't look old. He looked like a male in his early thirties. He was hot and broody and at times scary as hell. But you could say that about all of the hounds, honestly.

He shifted, his whole body turning to face me. "You ever come so hard you lose consciousness, Magnolia?" His deep voice resonated right through me.

I blinked up at him. "Uh..."

He flashed his teeth, white and sharp, and it was sexy and terrifying all at once. "You ever want to, you know where to find me."

I laughed. The brazenness of these hounds was unmatched. Not surprising, considering they were created by Lucifer and were emotionally deficient. They understood loyalty, they knew anger and lust well, but that was about as far as their emotional range went—the rest was beyond their grasp. Warrick and the other mated males were the exception—after they mated, their emotions developed, to different degrees. "Warrick might have a problem with that, don't you think?" I said. My bother-in-law was extremely protective.

Lothar shrugged. "I was at your twenty-first birthday party, sweetheart. You're a female, old enough to decide who she fucks." Then he waited, watching me for a response, I assumed.

I didn't have one. "That I am. So, I'm just gonna...go over there."

"I'll be here all night, you change your mind."

"Noted," I said and hustled across the room to the table Ren and his wolf were leaning against, along with several other hounds and their females, well, the ones they'd chosen for that night, at least. One of the males handed me a beer, and I settled in. Ren was too busy to talk, so I chatted with one of the wolves.

But slowly, over the next hour, they all drifted off in pairs to find a room and some privacy, no doubt.

I ended up at the table alone, watching everyone around me.

Draven had his arm hooked around Iris's neck, and they were sucking face every few minutes. Rose and Ronan were here as well. She was on her mate's lap, and every now and then, he'd tug her down for a kiss. Six months ago, Rose discovered who her biological father was, and the reason she'd been sick most of her life—now she had these awesome white wings and could fly. She was also a seer and, through scrying, received messages and visions.

I glanced across the room. Willow and Warrick were just as bad with the PDA. She stood leaning against the bar, Warrick behind her, one hand resting on her belly, the other resting on the bar in front of her. And yep, every so often he'd lean in to kiss the side of her neck, telling her without words what he wanted, and she'd turn to him and give him the kiss he was silently asking for.

What would that be like? To have that? To be wanted like that?

An image of Bram filled my mind, of how he'd looked last night. Bruised and cut. After I'd healed him, I'd drifted off, but I'd woken again a couple of hours later. He'd been asleep, lying on his back, his muscled body defined by the moonlight filtering through the room. His face had been relaxed, his thick, black lashes resting on his cheeks, and his lips, full and deep burgundy, had looked so incredibly soft.

For a split second, goddess, for just a moment, I'd actually had the insane urge to lean in, and—

I swallowed hard.

Then Clayton's hateful face had filled my head, like it did now, and had turned the soft feeling that had filled me into something jagged and awful. As if he were standing in front of me, blocking what lay ahead, stopping me from seeing anything good, or real. He was here with me now. I saw his cold blue eyes staring back, mocking me, making me feel sick to my stomach.

But worse, I felt his lips on me, cold and hard. He'd been my first kiss, my only kiss. My hand lifted to my mouth, and I rubbed at my lips, trying to take away that cold, awful feeling.

Suddenly, I couldn't breathe. I was suffocating. I rushed across the room, plugged the code into the keypad by the door, and ran down the stairs to the den, and the coolness and silence it offered. The stone walls made it soundproof, and the wall sconces offered a soothing, warm glow. I strode along the wide cavern, not knowing where I was going, only that I needed a moment alone. The hounds slept down here. They each had their own quarters, and there was also a common area, a gym, a fighting pit, and cells for locking up and torturing their enemies—and I'm sure a lot more I didn't know about.

A deep thumping sound echoed down the cavern, rapid and repetitive. It was coming from the gym. I made my way there on autopilot and opened the door. It was Relic. He was in a pair of shorts and nothing else, his long hair tied back in a knot, his body straining as he smashed his bare fists into the stone wall over and over again. I guess when you were immortal and impossibly strong, a normal leather punching bag didn't quite cut it.

He stopped and turned, sensing me as soon as I walked in. He was panting, but not as much as he should be, not after trying to punch through a cave wall in the name of fitness. Relic planted his hands on his hips. "Mags, hey, what's up?"

I'm freaked out and lonely as hell. How about you?

"Why are you down here and not up there with the others?" I said instead.

He shrugged a massive shoulder. "Felt like punching shit."

The male was a bit of a mystery. Relic was one of the next generation of hounds, only hundreds of years old instead of thousands. I assumed he was as emotionless as the others, though he definitely hid it better. After leaving Hell, the hounds taught themselves to imitate emotion to fit in, and Relic had mastered the skill. He was also Lothar's son, which was extremely weird since Relic looked only slightly younger, like a guy in his mid-to-late twenties.

"Your dad seems to be enjoying himself," I said.

He shook his head. "It's fucking weird when you say shit like that."

"You don't call him dad?"

"Never." Relic flexed his scarred fingers. "We're brothers, all of us, doesn't matter how we were created or by who."

I skirted a pile of free weights. "Why?"

"Because we're fucking old. Shit gets blurred when you've lived as long as us." He ran a hand over his hair. "So why are you here and not upstairs?" he said, asking me the same question.

"It was getting a bit much." My gaze slid to his mouth. He had nice lips. He was also extremely hot and loved to flirt shamelessly with my sisters and me whenever he came by the house. I should be attracted to him, I should welcome his attention, right? That would be normal. A normal response to a male like him.

Clayton flashed through my mind again and nausea gripped my belly. I rubbed my forearm when that phantom ache below my skin throbbed harder. "Kiss me," I blurted, surprising myself. Whether or not Relic was surprised, I couldn't tell. I should take it back, but I didn't.

He tilted his head to the side. "Why?"

I huffed out a laugh. "I ask you to kiss me, and you ask why?"

"Yeah, I'm asking why. You're sure as fuck not into me. And Willow would slit my throat if I laid a finger on her baby sister."

When Clayton kissed me, it'd been hard, punishing. His teeth had scraped against mine, his taste had turned my stomach, his fingers had dug into my flesh so hard he'd left bruises.

I needed him gone. I needed Clayton gone.

A weird desperation filled me, and I had to curl my fingers into fists so Relic didn't see them shaking. "What does it matter? Just fucking kiss me. What's the big deal?"

He crossed his arms. "Talk to me."

"I don't want to talk." I crossed my arms as well, feeling so incredibly vulnerable. I hated it. "You literally suck face with anyone who throws themselves at you, but I'm the exception?"

"Mags—"

"Forget it." Humiliation burned my cheeks. What the hell was wrong with me? I spun to leave, but he moved fast, stopping me.

"Wait," he rumbled in his impossibly deep, barely human voice.

"It's fine. I just want to go."

He growled a little and held me fast. "You're definitely not into me?"

"I'm definitely not," I said, giving him the truth. He didn't look offended in the slightest.

"But you want me to kiss you and you won't tell me why?"

"That's right."

He ran his hand over his hair again. "The females in your family have been sent to fuck with me, I'm sure of it." Then he cursed under his breath, took my face in his hands, dipped low, and planted one on me.

His lips were warm and soft, but also firm. They brushed over mine softly once, twice, then he took my chin in his hand and opened my mouth, swiping his tongue inside. I touched his in return. He tasted nice, mint and a hint of bourbon. He made a growly sound and sucked my lower lip gently, then lifted his head.

His otherworldly golden eyes were glowing brighter. "Well?" he said roughly.

I stared back.

I felt—

Nothing.

His face seemed to morph, change. It was all in my mind, but there was no stopping it, his gold eyes flashing to frigid blue. The nausea rocketed back, twisting my gut, and I threw a hand over my mouth, gagging.

"The fuck?" Relic said, jerking back. "Are you gonna hurl?"

I lifted a hand and shook my head. "It's...it's not you," I said through my fingers. I was definitely close to hurling, though, and my scars burned, pain radiating through me. I wanted to fucking scream.

"You just gagged, right after my mouth was on yours. I'd say that sure as fuck has something to do with me." I took a step back, and he grabbed my arm, stopping me. "Talk to me. What the fuck is going on here?"

The pain heightened under his grip, and my fingers curled into a fist all on their own. Instead of lashing out, though, I yanked my arm free, and he let me. Still the look in his eyes said he wasn't going to let me leave without some kind of explanation, not after that little display. He knew about Willow's trial, because the hounds had been a part of it. He also knew what had happened to me, some of it, anyway.

So I gave him what he needed and hoped he didn't ask more questions, because I sure as hell wasn't in the frame of mind to answer them. I tugged down the collar of my shirt, flashing him some of my scars. "Just dealing with some old demons," I said and held his bright gaze, silently asking him to drop it.

His gaze moved over the scars, then came back to mine. "Babe," he said gruffly, somehow conveying a whole lot of feeling in that one word, and again making me think he felt a lot more than a lot of his brothers.

"It's fine. I'm fine. I need to go." I took a step back, and he let me walk away this time.

I strode out into the cavern and guilt hit me, along with a sense of wrongness over that kiss that made me feel sick all over again. I wasn't sure why.

Bram's face filled my mind, and I forced it back out.

Shoving down the feeling inside me, I rushed back upstairs.

CHAPTER 5

Magnolia

I PUSHED OPEN THE DOOR, back into the noise, laughter, and chatter of the clubhouse. I was heading toward the door and freedom when Warrick whistled loudly, silencing the entire room.

I forced myself to stop and turn to him and Willow, who was now pressed into his side. His arm was around her, tucking her in close under his arm—and my big sister was, goddess, she was beaming, glowing with joy. Willow was gorgeous, but I don't think she'd ever looked as beautiful as she did in that moment.

"Ready, dove?" Warrick said to her.

She smiled up at him and nodded.

Warrick looked out to the room full of family and friends and flashed his vicious-looking white teeth. I'd never seen him smile like that, and I stilled along with everyone else in the room.

"It's not just Lothar's birthday. There's another reason we brought you all here tonight 'cause we've been through a lot of shit the last few years and for once we've got something good..." He shook his head. "Something... fucking awesome to share with you." His arm tightened around Wills.

"I'm pregnant!" Willow cried.

Mom shot to her feet with a cry and ran to Willow—Iris, Jasmine, and

Rose following—the hounds howled their approval. There was no stopping my own smile. I shoved down my own crap and walked toward them—

The door to the clubhouse flew open, and several members of the witches council along with their enforcers walked in, magic swirling around them. The hounds closed ranks immediately, blocking their way. Calvin Adler stood in front, eyes wild. He'd taken Cesare Sartori's place on the council when Sartori resigned a few months ago. I didn't know much about him, except he'd quickly grown a reputation as a hothead.

There'd been two other resignations. Sapphire Eldridge and Sara Hayashi, and of course they'd both endorsed their own children as their successors. Which was why Sapphire's asshole son, Isaac, was standing with Calvin, and Asuka Hayashi was at his side.

"You better have a fucking good reason for walking in here," Warrick said, voice cold. "She told you already she's not fucking selling," he said, pointing at Isaac. "Bringing your council buddies here won't change her mind."

A couple months ago, a company approached Willow, offering to buy her store for some development project. Willow rejected their offer. A few weeks later, someone tried to torch the store next to hers. She did some digging and found out the company was headed by Isaac, and he didn't just want her store but the whole block.

Willow pulled away from Mom and pushed her way to the front, stepping out beside Warrick, who was staring them down. "Is that what this is about? What's going on, Nathan? Why are you here? This place is warded, how did you get through?"

Nathan Trotman had always been someone we could trust, for a lot of years the only one we could trust on the witches council, and right now he looked seriously rattled. "We broke it under the dangerous witch clause in the council's code of conduct."

The room went silent. There were three ways to break a ward: the first, a spell that literally judged your intentions and only worked if they were good; the second was known only to council members and they were forbidden to use it unless it was a matter of life and death; the third, the worst kind of dark magic.

Willow jerked back, as shocked as the rest of us. "What?"

"Willow Thornheart, you are required to come with us for questioning in relation to the murder of three witches—"

"What the hell are you talking about?" she said, her confusion obvious.

"You're not taking my mate anywhere," Warrick snarled.

Willow put her hand on his arm to calm him because her male was about to start tearing the council members to shreds. "There's been another murder?"

46

Calvin stepped forward. "Yes, there's been another murder."

"Who?" Willow asked, paling.

His jaw tightened, fury in his eyes. "As if you don't know! You fucking murdered Katana!" His hand shot out, magic buzzing from him.

Warrick stepped in front of him, grabbing his fist, and got in his face. "She did nothing. You aim your magic at her again, and I'll turn you inside out."

"Katana's dead?" Willow asked, moving around Warrick again. He locked his arm around her, pulling her back. "Why the hell would you think I did it?"

Isaac Eldridge placed his hand on Calvin's shoulder, and there was a smug-as-fuck look on his face. "Justice will be done, Cal, I promise you that." His gaze slid to Willow. "This was inevitable, wasn't it? You wanted everyone to know how powerful you were during your trial, and you took pleasure in defeating my family, in watching your mate kill my brother, but you let that power go to your head, you let it corrupt you." His eyes darkened, filling with hatred. "You let it turn you into a monster."

Willow's gaze sliced to Asuka. They were friends, had been since school. No, they weren't as close anymore, but Asuka had to know Willow wasn't capable of this. "I didn't do it. You know me. You know I'm not capable of what they're accusing me of."

Asuka looked pained. "They found Katana in your shop, Willow, in your bedroom in the back. She was tortured and killed, like the others."

Willow said, her spine stiff, "My shop is warded. Did the council break that one as well?"

"It was already down."

"And that's not a fucking red flag to you?" Willow bit out. "We keep the store warded at all times. Somehow, someone broke it. They're trying to set me up."

"Or that's what you want us to think," Asuka said, without heat.

Willow stared at her friend, stunned. "This is insane, you have to see that?"

"Time to go, Willow," Isaac said, fucking glee dancing in his eyes as he motioned their enforcers forward.

They weren't listening to her, to reason.

Warrick roared, the sound rattling the windows, his canines extended. Willow grabbed his arm and shook her head. Warrick and the hounds slaughtering the council would only make this worse.

Warrick's furious stare slid to me, then toward the door to the den. I knew what he wanted, and I eased my way back through the crowd of people. They truly thought Willow had murdered those females and bringing enforcers here, onto the hound's territory rather than waiting to get her on her own, said how desperate they were to bring her in, and just how guilty they believed she was. I quickly plugged in the code right as the room erupted into chaos. The hounds ran forward, getting between Warrick and Willow and the council as magic snapped through the room.

Warrick snatched Willow off the ground and ran toward me, I opened the door and slammed it shut, the locks clicking into place behind them.

Calvin strode over, grabbed me, and shoved me back. "Open the fucking door."

"Can't, sorry, I don't know the code," I said.

He gripped my wrist tight, so tight I knew he'd leave a bruise. "Yes, you can, you lying, little bitch." He forced my hand over to the keypad. "Enter the fucking code. Now."

Warrick and Willow needed more time. I assumed there was a secret exit, but I needed to buy them as much time as I could.

Draven closed in, baring his teeth. "Let go of her or I'll take off your fucking head."

Calvin spun around. "She needs to open the door, or we'll be taking her in as well for her interference."

I yanked my hand from his. "It's fine, I'll do it."

I pushed a bunch of numbers, then tried the door. A red light flashed, and it remained locked. "Hang on. Let me try again."

Calvin hissed behind me.

I did it again, punching in some random numbers. Again, it flashed red. He was an asshole, but his cousin was dead, had been murdered brutally, so I understood his anger, but he was directing all that rage at the wrong people.

He spun me around and slammed me into the door, the handle digging into my spine, making me wince. "My cousin is dead, and your sister murdered her. I'm not in the mood for your bullshit. Open the fucking door. Now!"

Draven threw him back and stepped in front of me. "She doesn't know the code. Maybe you should ask one of the hounds."

The door opened behind me, and Relic stepped through, stopping me from falling through with his body, and closed the door behind him, tight.

Calvin's nostrils flared. "Let me through, hound."

"Your council holds no authority here. You're trespassing. Leave, or you'll be slaughtered where you stand," he said, his barely human voice resonating through the room.

Calvin roared, then turned back to me.

"Touch her again, and see what happens," Relic said and flashed his wicked-looking canines.

Isaac strode forward and grabbed Calvin's arm. "They can't hide forever, we'll get her," he said, his sharp gaze slicing to Relic, then to me. I felt his hatred down to my bones.

Calvin stormed off, and Iris and Rose rushed over to me.

Relic, Ronan, and the rest of the hounds strode after the councilors, seeing them off the property.

"Good work, Mags," Iris said.

"They got away. Willow's safe," Mom said, but there was fear in her eyes.

"Warrick won't let anything happen to her or the baby," Rose said, wrapping her arm around Mom's shoulders.

Ronan strode back inside and over to us. "The hounds are leaving tonight, they're following Warrick."

"Where are they going? Where would War have taken Willow?" Draven asked.

"Home," Ronan said before anyone else could.

Warrick was taking Willow to Hell, where no one could reach her, not even us.

)>)>·◉·(((

Bram

Magnolia wasn't in the tree house.

I shoved down the panic, jumped from the deck to the yard below, and strode toward the house.

Coming home and finding Mags in my bed was the fucking highlight of my day. She slept in my bed more often than her own, and always after I'd been away. The fact she wasn't there, waiting for me now, stung.

She didn't owe me anything. She'd given to me, constantly, and without expectation of anything in return. She'd been there for me since the day we found each other, even with all the shit I was putting her through, still she gave. She was pissed off, yes, but she put that aside to care for me. She made sure I had food in the fridge, that my wounds were tended, my place was clean, and I always came home to fresh sheets.

She constantly fucking worried about me.

All I'd done lately was take and cause her pain.

Acid churned in my gut.

Had she finally given up on me? Was this the day she finally told me to fuck off and never come back?

The house was dark. I used my key and quickly let myself in, taking the stairs two at a time to her room. Mags had moved to Willow's bedroom when she'd left. It was on the top floor, the tower, and far enough from

49

everyone else in the house that she could make noise, play her music, and not bother anyone else.

Light glowed from under her door. She was here and awake, which meant she was avoiding me. I gripped the handle, tapped on the door, and eased it open.

She stood by her dresser, and when her gaze met mine, there was something in her eyes that had me gripping the door handle tighter. "Why are you still up?" It was two in the morning.

"Couldn't sleep. It's been an...eventful night."

She didn't run to me and throw her arms around me like she usually did. No, she stayed back, and I felt the distance acutely between us. I took her in. She was wearing her favorite jeans and the boots she'd bought last week. Her red shirt had a neckline that dipped way too fucking low and hugged her little, curvy frame far too fucking close. "Did you go out?"

"A party, at the clubhouse." She stood and grabbed her robe. "We need to talk, but not now. Tomorrow," she said and started toward the bathroom.

I shoved my fingers through my hair. "Will you come to the tree house when you're done?" I tried to keep the desperation from my voice.

She crossed her arms. "Not tonight."

"Why?" Jesus, it felt like a dagger in the chest.

"I just...my head's all over the place. I just wanna sleep in my own bed."

She was pulling away. She'd needed to be alone after Maeve's party as well. We didn't do alone. We were better together, always. "Bullshit."

She released a wary breath. "I'm tired. I don't want to argue. You have no idea how messed up tonight was." The "because you weren't there" went unsaid. Her hands went to her hips, and her amber eyes locked on mine. "So, if you're around tomorrow, and you still want to talk, or argue, we can do it then."

"Don't be like that." The adrenaline pumping through my veins hadn't calmed from earlier that night, and every muscle in my body tightened. I had to stop myself from grabbing her and tugging her closer.

Her eyes never left mine. "Like what?"

Fuck. I felt as if my world was falling apart, slipping away beneath my feet, and I didn't know how to stop myself from falling with it. "You're pissed off. So let me have it." I deserved her anger. I needed it. This indifference she was giving me, I fucking hated it.

"Go to the tree house, Bram. I can't do this with you right now." She walked past and reached for the door handle. A scent hit me like a wet fucking rag to the face and possessive fury exploded through me.

My hand shot out, grabbing her arm, stopping her. "You smell like hound." The words were out, hard and accusatory, before I could stop them.

"Like I said, I was at the clubhouse," she said, not looking at me.

My other hand snaked out and caught the side of her throat. I tugged her closer, struggling to contain the possessiveness, the rage at what I was positive I could smell on her. I dipped my head, dragging my nose along her throat to the corner of her mouth, and a series of hoarse, rhythmic *clicks* rumbled from deep in my chest. My crow right there.

"Bram?"

"Relic," I snarled. "His mouth was on yours."

She was mine, my mate, whether she knew it or not, whether she ever acknowledged it or not, and another male had put his fucking mouth on her.

I lifted my head and stared down at her. "He kissed you."

Her eyes were wide. "I asked him to...but none of that matters—"

"You want him?" I barely stopped myself from rocking back. The effect of her words, a physical blow.

"No." She trembled slightly. "I wanted Clayton gone, and Relic was there."

My eyes slid shut, and my vision filled with blood, with death, with agonizing screams. Clayton's. Warrick had torn him to pieces that day at the cemetery, but as far as I was concerned, he'd died too easy. When I opened them again, Mags was staring up at me, her breathing erratic. I wanted to claim her mouth. I wanted to be the one to wash Clayton from her lips. That wasn't Relic's to take. It was mine, it should have been mine.

"Bram—"

"Don't," I said harshly, unable to control all I was feeling. "Don't ever kiss him again, understand? You kiss him again and I'll kill him, Magnolia. I'll fucking end him."

Our eyes locked, and we stared at each other as seconds ticked by. I waited for her to tell me I was out of line. To ask me why I'd said what I just had. She didn't, like every time I veered too close to possessive or all but declared her mine, she broke eye contact first and pulled away. I wanted to grab her and shake her, to roar at her to see me—*to fucking see me.*

Somehow, I had to contain what was flaring up inside me—a male staring down at his female and wanting, needing, so badly to wash away the stain of another male's kiss from her lips.

But if I did that, I risked fucking up everything. I risked losing her completely. So no, I wouldn't kiss her, but I also couldn't pretend I didn't need her. Especially after being away from her. "You're sleeping with me in the tree house," I said, a demand leaving no room for argument. "You can shower there."

For once, Magnolia didn't argue. Deep down was she afraid of what I'd say if she resisted?

Fucked if I knew, but something was seriously wrong, and the sooner I had her in my bed, in my arms, the better. She let me take her hand and lead her back down the stairs, out of the house and across the yard. When she reached for the ladder, I stopped her, yanked off my shirt, and partially shifted. My wings exploded from my back, and I scooped her up and flew to the deck and carried her inside. As soon as I put her down, she walked into the bedroom, grabbed one of my shirts, then strode into the bathroom, shutting herself in—or maybe me out?

Fuck.

I stood there, staring at the door for long seconds, then finally sat heavily on the bed. Every time I left, every time I did what I had to, I felt myself slipping deeper into the shadows, into the role of monster. I became something, someone else without Mags to hold me steady, and it was leaking into my life here, it was ruining what she and I had.

But the truth was—I'd never felt more myself.

Because I was a monster.

Because that was exactly what I was meant to be.

CHAPTER 6

Magnolia

I LOOKED OVER MY SHOULDER, checking out my back in the mirror. There was a dark bruise low on my spine and another around my wrist. I grabbed the balm from the cabinet and smeared it across my skin before tugging on Bram's oversized shirt.

Bram was in bed when I walked out, his arm propped up behind his pillow, dark eyes on me.

My belly churned, my heart and mind rioting. Usually just being in the same room as Bram calmed me, not tonight. My belly hadn't stopped churning over what happened at the party. When would I see Willow again? How the hell were we going to prove she was innocent? And my heart was still beating hard after what happened in my room. I studied Bram now. There was something in his dark eyes I didn't recognize. I'd tried to pretend I never saw it, but I did, more and more often lately. The realization that he'd kept pieces of himself from me, that there were parts of him that I didn't know, unsettled me. Wounded me.

I tugged back the covers and got in, and he immediately pulled me in close.

Neither of us said anything.

Bram was protective to the extreme, but tonight he'd threatened to kill

Relic if I ever kissed him again. And the look in his eyes, so cold, so devoid of all emotion except rage when he said it—he'd been deadly serious.

It was a giant step over the line, but I didn't call him out. Something in me said not to. No, it screamed it.

His arms tightened around me, and I willed the tension from my body, relaxing into him. If anyone walked in here now, they'd think we were a couple—that we were lovers. Was it weird to other people, how close we were? I'd never really thought about it too hard. I'd just done what felt right, and being with Bram as often as possible was what felt right. That's the way it'd always been. I guess that's why his unexplained absences were so painful.

I was the most important person in his life, and he was mine. And once upon a time, we'd told each other everything.

I rested my head on his chest and slid my arm across his stomach.

He dipped his head and breathed deep, scenting me. It was subtle, but I felt it, heard it. Thankfully, I'd washed all traces of Relic away. Whenever he'd gotten possessive in the past, this was the part where he'd apologize for overreacting. He'd say he was just worried about me, or only wanted the best for me. As the silence dragged out, I realized that wasn't going to happen. Not this time.

A weird feeling slid through me.

His hand traveled over my back, and I jerked.

He froze. "You're injured."

I needed to tell him what happened, but I'd been prepared to completely avoid it until morning because saying it out loud meant it was true. That my pregnant sister was in hiding, that she was most likely in Hell, and I had no idea when I'd see her again.

"Magnolia?"

"A lot's happened the last few days." My hand was on his chest, and his slid to my wrist, lifting it. Every one of his muscles beneath me tightened.

"Who the fuck did this?" he snarled and rolled me off him so I was on my back. "What the fuck is going on?"

Pain stabbed at me, as everything that had happened while he was away hit me again. I ignored it. I'd gotten good at that. "There was another murder, a couple days ago...Margot. She was tortured, carved up and killed," I said woodenly. He didn't move, his black eyes locked on mine. "Then there was another one tonight. The witches council came for Willow, they think she did it." Art had talked to councilor Trotman and he'd shared, probably more than he should. "The evidence against her is overwhelming. The witch killed tonight was found at The Cauldron. There was no break-in, no sign of forced entry. The body was found in Willow's old bedroom in the back."

54

Wills had lived in the shop for years before she moved home during her trial. There was a small apartment behind the store, but we didn't use it anymore. The door between the back room and the storeroom had been closed and locked. No one could remember the last time we'd actually been in there.

"There were traces of blood and hair, but not just the latest murder, the other two as well."

Bram cursed viciously. "Where's Willow now?"

"They got away. The rest of the hounds are with them. Willow's pregnant...we were there to celebrate, then..." My voice cracked.

Bram pressed a kiss to my forehead. "War will keep her safe until we can figure this out."

"I know," I said, fighting back angry tears.

He ran his thumb over my bruised wrist. "Who did this to you?"

"One of the new councilmen. I got in his way so he couldn't go after Willow and Warrick. His anger got the better of him. If I hadn't, he'd be dead. Warrick would have torn him to shreds. He should've thanked me, not shoved me against a door."

Bram's jaw clenched, and his eyes turned frigidly cold. "He'll pay for that."

"It was his cousin who was murdered tonight. He's an asshole, but I think he deserves a pass on this one." Bram didn't look as if he agreed. I blew out a breath. "Isaac Eldridge was there as well, the smug bastard."

"That prick's overdue for an ass kicking."

Bram wasn't wrong.

"You know where War took Willow?"

"We don't know for sure, but we're guessing they're in Hell. It's the safest place for them right now." Saying that out loud seemed insane, but besides Lucifer himself, the hounds were one of the most feared creatures down there. No one and nothing would get near Willow.

"It's going to be okay," he said. "We'll get through this."

I nodded and hoped he was right.

His arm tightened around me. "You think you'll be able to sleep?"

"I don't know." I glanced up at him. "If I do, will you be here when I wake up?" There was bitterness in my voice. I hadn't meant for it to come out like that, but the hurt was impossible to hold in anymore. I shouldn't have said anything. The storm was over, and those words had the power to open the floodgates again.

His eyes slid to mine. He'd heard it as well. "I'd never leave without telling you. You fucking know that."

I studied him. Bram had changed so much. For a long time, when we were around others, he'd preferred his bird form, to hide and go unnoticed.

He didn't do that anymore. There'd always been a darkness to him, but it had deepened in ways I couldn't describe. There was also a hardness to him that had never been there before. It'd happened slowly, but there was no missing it now. "I thought I knew a lot of things. Turns out I was wrong."

Don't say it. Do not say it.

I didn't want another confrontation, I'd had enough emotional turmoil for one night, but I couldn't not say something. Not when it was eating at me. "Amelia was in the shop yesterday; Leah and Claire were with her. They saw you at The Bank with one of your brothers."

He stilled against me.

I slipped my arms from his waist and hugged myself. "It's true, then."

"Mags—"

"Leah said you and your brother were surrounded my fawning females... Oh, and she also said she had your number and planned to ask you out."

"That's not what happened—"

"How about you explain it to me, then? So I can understand." I'm the one who said I didn't want to fight, and here I was, starting one. "So you're, what? Going out with your brothers to pick up females, then lying to me about it for some fucked-up reason?" As I said the words, my anger grew. "Or maybe you're fucking demons? That would at least explain why you're coming home so messed up?" I shifted farther away from him. "I'm not one to judge. If fucking monsters is your thing, then just tell me—"

"I'm not fucking demons," he said, his obsidian gaze unwavering. "I'm not fucking anyone."

He reached for me, and I swiped his hand away and sat up. "You could. You could go out with Leah, fuck her, let her scratch up your chest. I'm sure she'd be into it. You can do whatever the fuck you like, you already are, right? Just don't come to me and expect me to heal you afterward."

"Mags—"

"Christ, I'm not even an afterthought, anymore, am I?"

"Magnolia," he all but snarled.

I shoved off the covers, fully worked up now. "No, you go off and do whatever it is you do, go out and party with your brothers, or whatever. I honestly don't give a fuck anymore." I stood, heart pounding, feeling sick to my stomach.

He shoved back the covers and stood as well, taking a step toward me.

I lifted a hand, warning him to stay back. "I can't do this." The words escaped before I knew they were coming, but I didn't try to take them back, because I meant it. "I can't wait around at home for you, scared out of my mind, not knowing if you'll ever come back. You've checked out. You're my best friend, and I'm losing you." I was shaking, my emotions rioting through me. "You were mine. I was yours. We were inseparable, now we're—"

One moment I was standing there, the next he was in front of me, lifting me off my feet and planting me back in bed.

"Stop," he bit out and loomed over me. "You haven't lost me. You will never lose me." His nostrils flared, his big body shaking. "I need you to trust me, Magnolia. I need...I need you to tell me you know I would never do anything to hurt you. Ever. I'd fucking die before I purposely caused you even a moment of pain." One of his big, rough-skinned hands took hold of my jaw, his coal-black eyes on mine. "I would tell you everything, fuck... everything, if I were able to, but I can't. I want to tell you what I'm doing, where I'm—"

He made a choking sound.

"Bram."

He gasped for breath. "I would...I'd—" He choked again, then again tried to speak, and it was like some invisible force had him in a choke hold and was squeezing.

I slammed my hand over his mouth. "Stop. Stop trying to talk."

Oh goddess. He couldn't tell me, not because he didn't want to but because he was physically unable to. "You're being gagged by a silencing oath, aren't you?"

He said nothing. But he didn't deny it. He just continued to stare deep into my eyes, silently asking me to see the truth as his breathing slowly evened out. He was bound so tightly that he'd choke, most likely to death, if he even tried to tell me. Which meant whoever he was answering to was extremely powerful. Silencing oaths were rarely used. They were forbidden by everyone—except those in the highest of high-level positions.

"You really can't tell me, can you?"

He continued to hold my gaze, saying nothing.

No. He couldn't.

·)))·◉·(((·

"Magnolia," Bram's voice was low, insistent.

My hair was brushed back from my face, and I struggled to open my eyes.

"Mags. Wake up."

My mind was fuzzy, then everything snapped back into focus—the murders, what happened with Willow, what I'd learned about Bram—and my eyes flew open. I groggily tried to sit up. "What's wrong?"

I expected it to be morning, or that I'd slept in. But it was still dark outside, the moon high in the sky.

"I have to go," Bram said, tucking my hair behind my ear. "Something's come up."

Disappointment washed through me. It still hurt, but at least now I knew he'd tell me where he was going if he could. "When will you be back?"

"Tomorrow. This shouldn't take long," he said.

I nodded and covered his hand still lingering at the side of my face. "Be safe. I'll be here when you get back."

He was watching me, his body incredibly still.

His gaze dipped to my lips.

I found it hard to breathe all of a sudden, and tension stretched out between us. The kind that I tried to pretend didn't exist, the kind that had panic firing through me. I quickly looked down, breaking eye contact, while my heart hammered behind my ribs, so hard and fast, I felt dizzy.

He slid his hand from under mine and stood. "Go back to sleep," he said as if nothing had just happened, as if he hadn't felt that tension as well.

I nodded, but there was no chance of me going back to sleep now.

He planted a kiss on the top of my head and walked out, and I lay there for a while, listening to the leaves rustling. But it was hot, and my mind was all over the place. Places I didn't want it to go. So I got up, wandered into the living room, and turned on the TV.

Not that I paid much attention to what was on. Goddess, where was Wills now? Was she already in Hell? Or had Warrick taken her somewhere else? Who and what had called Bram away in the middle of the night? Honestly, if it wasn't for the fact he could fly and I couldn't, I would've followed him by now.

My mind was so busy, it took me a moment to realize my voice wasn't the only one in my head.

Come to me, daughter of Coven Thornheart, echoed through my mind.

I stilled. That's what I thought I heard. I shot to my feet.

Oh fuck.

The mother—she was calling me.

This wasn't supposed to happen yet. I had another six months. And this sure as hell wasn't supposed to happen without Bram.

I couldn't wait for him to come home, though. When the mother called, you went, no matter what. I couldn't even ask Relic to go with me because he'd left with the other hounds. There was Asher, but her loyalty was with Draven and Iris, and I didn't want my family knowing about this, not yet, and she'd definitely tell them. My family couldn't help me, or come with me, it wasn't permitted, and they'd want to. Badly. Telling them would only cause them worry, when there was absolutely nothing they could do to help me, and I was convinced if they knew, they'd try to find a way even though it was forbidden.

I couldn't risk it, not after everything my sisters had been through to get us this far.

I called Bram as I shoved on my shoes. When he didn't answer, I left a message asking him to call me back. I didn't want to tell him over the phone. I didn't want him distracted if he was doing something dangerous. He'd call back as soon as he could. I took the ladder to the yard below and ran for the house. I didn't believe in coincidences. And being called on the night my sister was accused of murder—yeah, that sure as hell wasn't one. I quickly let myself in, changed into something more suitable for running—and fighting—grabbed my knife, loaded a backpack with a few things I'd been working on, grabbed my car keys and slipped out of the house.

Oldwood Forest was twenty minutes away, and I gripped the wheel for dear life the whole drive, running through everything I knew about the meeting place, about what would happen when the mother came, what could happen afterward, over and over again. I still had to make it to the meeting spot in one piece, but the most dangerous part was afterward.

All three of my sisters could have lost their lives if they hadn't had help after the mother was done with them. I needed a plan, one that would mean me getting out of the forest alive. I didn't love the idea of becoming the main dish at some demon dinner party.

The clearing loomed up ahead, the forest opening so dark I couldn't see anything beyond it. It was creepy as hell, but I had no choice, this was happening and I had to be ready for anything.

Pulling over, I checked my knife again, pulled on the dark hoodie I'd swiped from Bram's room to help me blend into the shadows, tugged on my backpack, and walked into the forest.

CHAPTER 7

Magnolia

SOMETHING WAS FOLLOWING ME.

I hadn't seen it yet, but it'd clocked me fifteen minutes ago and had been on my tail since. Its smell gave it away first. It was disgusting, like rot and manure, but also perfect for my needs.

Other than my new friend tailing me, I'd managed to go unnoticed. I'd heard demons in the distance—voices, calls and whoops and growls, and what sounded like some kind of party in full swing in the opposite direction —but the darkness had provided excellent cover.

And Asher had trained me well. She'd taught me how to move sound-lessly through the forest, where to walk, what to avoid. And what I was about to do? She herself had done once, and it'd gotten her out of a tough spot when she'd been a young wolf and found herself alone in a forest full of hungry demons. I was close to the meeting spot, so close, I could feel the humming of it, calling me.

The demon tracking me darted to the other side of the path, getting closer. I'd only seen him in my peripheral vision, but the demon looked smaller in size, a similar height to me, which made sense or it would've attacked already, possibly one of the smaller scavenger breeds.

Just a little farther. I was only a few feet from the clearing now. Gripping my knife, I pretended to trip and stumble, dropping to the ground—and waited.

As expected, as soon as it thought I was wounded, it struck.

I spun just as it reached me and buried my knife in its throat, then jerked the blade to the side. Spinning, I swept its feet out from under it, flipped it over, and sliced through the tendons on each leg, then across its wrists so it couldn't run or fight.

It roared and thrashed while I covered its mouth with my hand, pulled a piece of string and a large needle from my pocket, and curled it tightly in my fist. "Thread the needle with this twine, seal your mouth shut for all of time." It was a variation of a spell Willow used once, and it had left an impression. Hers used invisible magical thread, mine on the other hand did not. I'd need to be conscious to maintain a spell like that, but I wasn't sure I would be after this, so real thread was best this time.

Gripping the demon's ankle, I dragged him after me. He was small but heavy, and he struggled as I towed him into the middle of the clearing. He stared up at me with wide, furious eyes, a stare that said he wanted to tear me into tiny pieces.

"You were about to eat me, asshole, you deserve what you got. So keep your mouth shut, or you'll tear your lips off along with your stitches." I pulled my top over my head and tossed it aside.

Getting naked in front of this creep wasn't my idea of a good time, but I had no choice and quickly removed the rest of my clothes. Stripped down to nothing, I strode to the squirming demon and made a couple more holes in him, then covered myself in his blood, disguising my scent with its seriously nasty one. The demon was finally too low on blood to fight, and thankfully passed out.

There was a circle of stones in the middle of the clearing, and I whispered a simple spell, igniting a blazing fire inside it. All that was left was to let the mother know I was here. Pulling from my pocket the small jewel-handled knife Mom had given me when I was thirteen, I made a slice in the side of my thigh. Blood slipped from the slice instantly.

Dropping my knife, I closed my eyes and recited the words. "Guide me, old ones. I am your servant, the Keeper's sister chosen to fulfill the rite of Coven Thornheart." A gust of wind hit me, whipping around me out of nowhere, it swirled faster and faster, blasting against my naked body. "I'm here to accept my task. Whatever you ask, I will undertake."

The wind grew stronger, so fierce it was hard to draw breath.

Then finally, a rattling sound reached me, followed by a hiss.

She was coming.

The mother wasn't all goodness and light. She wasn't all evil and darkness either. She was both, she was everything, and I felt that now. It danced through me, over my skin, lifting goose bumps all over me.

I had to fight my fear to hold my ground. She had no corporal form, so when the mother did need to make an appearance, she inhabited the body of her massive pet serpent.

My heart thundered in my ears as the rattling grew louder, closer. There was a hiss by my ear, then hot breath brushing my skin before I felt a raspy, tickling sensation against my thigh. She was tasting my blood, making sure I was exactly who she'd called to her.

Open your eyes, daughter of Coven Thornheart.

Her voice echoed through my mind, and I made myself do as she bid—then bit back my gasp at the sight of her. She was massive, her huge head swaying, black eyes looking through me, as if she could peer right into my soul.

You've come alone. Brave or stupid?

"Probably a little of both," I said.

She hissed, her head jerking forward, and I slammed my mouth shut.

There is greatness in you, child, if you choose to take hold of it, but it's volatile. Your sisters, they were full of light. Not you. You have shadows, so many of them, and you are blind to so very much.

I stayed silent, her words sending a chill down my spine and terror through my heart.

You must complete the task I give you by the time the vines meet. If you fail, you will be unworthy of trial, and gifts past will be returned to the mother. If you complete your task yet fail to win your trial, again, your coven's gifts will be returned to the mother.

"I understand," I said.

Her massive head swung my way, her black eyes meeting mine. *Your inner rage is a gag, a blindfold, it's the heavy cloak you hide behind. If you can't find a way to best it, child, you will fail this test. You will lose everything.*

"I'll do whatever it takes to pass this task," I said, a knot in my stomach.

We shall see.

Her head jerked back suddenly. I didn't have time to suck in a breath or brace before she struck. Her massive jaw wrapped around my torso, and she sunk her fangs into my body, my stomach and lower back. I knew it was coming, but still I stood there in shock as fire blazed through me, suspending me there for what felt like forever when it must have only been seconds.

Finally, she released me. I swayed, stumbling to the side, fighting desperately to stay on my feet as she spun and slithered back into the forest. Her venom pumped through me now, hard and fast, and my legs gave out from under me. I fell to the ground, naked and alone in the middle of the woods.

Darkness creeped in at the edges of my eyes...I grabbed for my bag.

But it was too late.

I passed out.

〉〉〉●〈〈〈

Groaning, I forced my eyes open. It wasn't easy.

It was still dark.

And somehow, I was still alive. The demon blood had worked.

The fire had gone out, and thankfully, the demon I'd captured was still unconscious. I couldn't see much of anything as I felt around for my clothes. The weakness was so strong, I ignored everything but Bram's over-sized hoodie and my boots. It was a struggle, but I finally pulled them on. Then grabbing my knife and pack, I fought to stand. It wasn't easy, and it took almost all my energy, but I did it.

I stumbled back toward the trees, muttering a protection spell as I went, calling on my ancestors to protect and guide me, since I had no one else.

I tried as hard as I could, but with how unsteady I was, there was no way I could be quiet. I sounded like a goddamn elephant stomping through the forest. I stumbled over my own feet again and hit the ground hard. Darkness tried to creep into the edges of my sight—a rustling came from the trees to the right of me.

More demons. And I was about to pass out again. *Fuck.*

With the last of my strength, I jerked off my pack and pulled out several of the glass vials I'd put in there, crushing them in my hands. The glass cut through my skin, but that was the least of my worries.

The potions in these vials would disorient anyone they came in contact with, causing hallucinations, delirium, blindness, and a constant ringing in their ears. It seriously fucked you up. It was only temporary, the effects usually lasting about thirty minutes. I'd just surrounded myself with it, which meant I'd unfortunately be getting a dose as well. The darkness around me grew heavier. I didn't know if it was the potion or from my meeting with the mother at this point.

I just hoped it kept me safe until I woke up.

Then everything went dark again.

〉〉〉●〈〈〈

I didn't know how many hours had passed, but I woke with a gasp, the horrors of my hallucinations dissipating like smoke.

That was the third time I'd used the potion.

There were several demons wandering around, their hands over their ears, staring blindly into the distance—I looked down at myself—still in one piece.

I left the clearing...it had to be hours ago, but I'd been falling in and out of consciousness and lost track of time completely.

The walk in had only taken me twenty minutes, walking out had taken me a hell of a lot longer. I stumbled to my feet as a disoriented demon crashed through the trees toward me. It was foaming at the mouth, eyes dilated, staring blindly ahead, following the sounds I was making.

With a cry of desperation and exhaustion, I stumbled to the side, spun, and slashed its throat. It didn't stop, too lost in its own hallucination to even feel it. It swiped at me, and I spun again. Approaching from behind it, I wrenched back its head and hacked it off. The last thing I needed was it wandering out onto the road and terrifying some human driving by.

It turned to ash, and I pushed on, one shaky step at a time, toward my car.

My vision was blurring again by the time I reached it. I yanked the door open quickly and locked myself in before I passed out again.

›)〉●《‹‹

I woke just before dawn. Orange streaked the still-dark sky, the first rays of sunlight struggling to break through the darkness. With trembling hands, I shoved the key into the ignition and started the car, then pulled out onto the road.

I'd done it, on my own.

And I'd survived.

›)〉●《‹‹

Bram

Pulling off my shirt, I tossed it aside and sat.

I'd put this off as long as I could, but it was time. The markers were building up, I couldn't delay it anymore.

I was a warrior of our people. This was the way our father, our grandfather, his before that, had worn their hair. This was a rite of passage, letting everyone know what I was.

A warrior and provider for my people.

Resting my elbows on my knees, I dipped my head, while Talon sectioned off a thick strip of hair down the middle and tied it back. Payne got down on his knees beside me, pulled his knife from its sheath, and began slicing away the hair at the sides. It fell to the wooden deck as Payne muttered the ancient words of our people, the vow of our warriors.

Talon stood back, leaning against the railing, watching, while Rook prepared the ink he'd be adding to my skin.

The blade was scraped against my scalp, taking it back to skin.

What would Mags think when she saw me? How would I explain it? I couldn't. It was one more thing I couldn't share with her. Something important that I had to keep from her.

I'd brought her here, she'd met my brothers, my people, but she didn't know what we were at our core. I'd made sure of it.

Crows were true predators.

She knew we were deadly hunters, but she didn't know the extent of it, because I'd never shared it with her—no, I'd actively kept it from her, afraid of what she'd think if she knew my true nature. I'd also spent a lot of years trying to suppress my desire to hunt. But after what happened in the cemetery that day, stopping that fucker from hurting Magnolia, there was no suppressing it. Not anymore.

And letting that side of myself, my dark urges, free, had felt so right.

Just as a wolf was compelled to howl at the moon, a crow was compelled to hunt—and kill.

This was who I was, what I was born to be.

I was a crow.

A warrior.

A killer.

Which meant my job was perfect for me and my brothers. We fulfilled a necessary service, and we fed the dark need inside us.

Rook came forward, taking Payne's place. He gripped the top of my head, tilting it to the side and pressed his tattoo gun to my skin. "Say their name," Rook growled low.

The ink loaded in Rook's gun was laced with blood. Every soul I sent to the afterlife, a piece of them would stay with me in the markers I'd carry on my skin, that was my burden.

It was the price we paid for embracing what we were, but this one, I wanted it. He deserved that disgrace, and I hoped his soul burned for eternity.

My lips peeled back from the hatred filling me before his name could pass my lips. "Brody," I snarled.

No, tonight wasn't my first kill, that was in the Thornheart cemetery two and a half years ago—when I killed the male holding a knife to Magnolia's throat.

When the fighting ended that day, before his body had been taken, I'd collected Brody's blood because deep down I knew this day would come. I wished I could add a marker for Clayton Whitlock as well, and hated that Warrick had killed him before I could.

The buzz of the gun, the bite against my skull, had me breathing hard. Not from the pain—no, I welcomed the pain—it was from the fucking rightness of it. Payne's hand came down on my shoulder and squeezed.

Again, I wondered what Mags would think if she knew the truth. I wasn't afraid she'd hate me or fear me because I killed, I was more worried about her looking into my eyes—and seeing how much I liked it.

Rook finished and quickly cleaned the gun and loaded the new ink laced with the blood of another of my kills.

I said the next name, and the next, and I kept on saying names until I had eight markers on the side of my head.

Maeve had come out to watch and was sitting on Talon's shoulders.

"What do you think?" he asked her.

She pressed her hand against the shaved side of Talon's head, something she often did to Payne as well, since she was a baby. "I like it. I'm gonna be a warrior too when I'm a grownup, like Daddy," she said and wrapped her arms around Talon's neck, resting her chin on top of his head and grinning. "I'll have more markers than all of you."

Payne muttered a curse.

Talon gave her leg a squeeze. "Yeah, you will, little feather."

Rook chuckled low as he wiped the side of my head with a damp cloth.

Payne strode over and held out his hand. "How do you feel?"

I took it, and he pulled me to my feet. "Good. Right."

He nodded. "Stay and have a drink with us to celebrate."

"Yeah, maybe." I checked my phone, I'd forgotten to turn the sound back on after we'd been hunting. There was a message from Mags. I listened to it, then called her back. No answer. She was probably asleep. "Another time," I said to Payne. "I need to get back." Mags had no idea what just happened here, what it all meant, but I needed to be close to her, now more than ever.

I needed to be close to my mate.

The only female I wanted—that I would ever want.

I ran my fingers over my hair, nerves firing inside my gut.

The need to be close to Magnolia pumped hotly through my veins.

After last night, finding out all she'd been through—Margot's death, the shit at the clubhouse, seeing the bruises that fucking prick Adler had given her, the way she blew up at me—I needed to smooth things over with her, and that wasn't going to happen if I was never here. I needed to be here for her more. I just didn't know how I was going to make it all work.

All I knew was I couldn't lose her.

I knew loss.

And Magnolia was a loss that would fucking end me.

Darkness swirled around me, through me. There wasn't one thing I wouldn't do to make sure that never happened. To make sure I never lost her. I'd tear it all down before I let that happen. I'd snatch her from her world, and I'd make a new one, just her and me.

I'd fly away with her and never come back.

She wasn't expecting me home so soon, and my need to see her was a deep, relentless ache inside me now. I quickly headed across the yard toward the house.

The sound of a car pulling up out front reached me. Magnolia's car, I detoured and jogged around the side of the house.

The driver's door was open. Mags was struggling to get out—and she was covered in blood.

I sprinted to her, scooped her into my arms, and frantically searched her, trying to find where the blood was coming from. "Where're you hurt? Where's the blood coming from?"

That's when I smelled it, not just Magnolia's blood—demon as well.

"Take me...t-to the tree house. I don't want anyone else to s-see me like this," she said.

My wings exploded from my back, tearing my shirt to ribbons. Clutching her to me, I flew over the house and landed on the deck of the tree house. Shoving the door open, I strode to the bathroom.

"Where're you hurt?" I asked again as I lowered her to her feet and, still supporting her, helped her out of her boots.

"I'm not s-sure," she said and swayed to the side, her eyes rolling into the back of her head, almost blacking out.

Fuck. I pulled her against me and carefully pulled up my hoodie that she was wearing. She was completely fucking naked underneath, her small curvy frame covered in dried blood and mud. I needed to wash all this off to see the damage. I turned on the shower and carefully lifted the hoodie over her head, tossing it aside.

"I'm n-naked," she slurred.

"I don't give a fuck. I need to see what we're dealing with."

I kicked off my boots and scooped her up, stepping into the shower still in my jeans, and held her under the water. I let it wash away the worst of it, not wanting to rub at her skin in case I made something worse.

"What happened? Why are you naked? Did someone force you...did they..."

She groggily shook her head. "N-no one...t-touched me." She went limp then, blacking out for a moment before jolting back to consciousness.

I grabbed a washcloth and carefully cleaned the rest of the mud and blood away. The more of her skin I revealed, the more relieved I became. There were some superficial scrapes and grazes, her hands were all cut up, but nothing life threatening.

What the fuck was going on? "Why are you having trouble talking? Who did this? Did you run into Adler–"

"I was...at Oldwood," she rasped.

"What? Why?" I swiped the washcloth over her stomach, taking away the last of the dried blood.

And froze.

Fuck.

Markings, ones that I'd seen before, on each of her sisters. My gaze shot to hers. "No," the word burst from me.

Her lids were heavy as she struggled to stay conscious. "Y-yes. After you left. I called you, but..." Then her eyes drifted shut, and she went limp in my arms again.

"Maggie? Magnolia?" Her breathing was slow and even. She'd passed out again.

Fuck, I'd called her back a couple more times on the way home, but when she hadn't answered, I was positive she was asleep, tucked up safe in bed.

I made sure I got all of the blood off her and quickly shut off the water. Wrapping her in a towel, I carried her into the bedroom and laid her on my bed to carefully dry her off. I rolled her to her side to make sure I hadn't missed any injuries. A few more scrapes, but nothing deep, nothing that needed stitches or for me to get Else.

The black thorny vine markings on her skin swirled low on her stomach, around her belly button, and there was a mirror image in the middle of her lower back. They looked like tattoos, only these, I knew, would move and grow. The vine from her stomach and one on her back would reach out until both vines touched. If she hadn't passed the task the mother had given to her by the time that happened, she'd fail.

I stared at those markings and tried to fucking breathe. We knew this was coming, that the mother would call on her, but we thought we had another six months. I thought *I* had six months.

When Mags's turn came, I was supposed to be there with her, to protect her from the demons that infested the forest. I planned to be there with her every step of the way. Instead, she'd gone alone. She'd been alone and vulnerable.

The only explanation I could come up with for all the demon blood on her skin was that Mags had covered herself in it to disguise her scent. She'd killed a demon.

Magnolia had met with the mother. She'd fought at least one fucking demon, then she'd walked back, all by herself.

She could've been killed.

I could have lost her.

Breathing heavily, I tore my eyes from her, then rushed to grab the basket filled with her healing supplies, the one she kept here for me, and pulled out Else's balm. I carefully applied it to every scratch, scrape, and bruise on her smooth, pale skin. When I was done, I grabbed one of my shirts and carefully pulled it over her head, working her arms through the sleeves.

I wanted to keep her as she was, I wanted to hold her close to me, her bare skin against mine, so I could feel her alive and breathing and warm. But she wouldn't be cool with that. Mags wasn't shy about her body, at least not in front of her sisters, some spells required the witch to be naked. I made myself scarce during those times. Yes, I'd accidentally walked in on her during a spell once or twice, but best friends didn't sleep together naked.

It didn't matter that she was so much more than that to me.

I quickly yanked off my wet jeans, pulled on some dry shorts, and got under the covers with her, carefully pulling her into my arms.

"Bram?" she said suddenly, startling awake.

There was no missing the fear in her voice. "I'm here." She was so used to me being gone, so used to doing it all on her own now, when that was never how it was meant to be.

She sighed, relaxing against me, and fell back to sleep—or losing consciousness, I wasn't sure which.

After the mother bit a witch, her potent venom pumping through their veins, it took them out for at least a day, and staying conscious was damn near impossible. "How the fuck did you get out of that forest?" I said against her damp hair, talking to myself, not expecting her to respond.

"My potion," she muttered. "Th-the one I've been working on."

I dragged in a ragged breath, every muscle in my body locking tight. "The one that causes hallucinations?"

She nodded against me. "I c-covered myself in it."

So anything that came close to her while she was unconscious got a dose, which meant, she would have as well. Fuck. *Fuck.* "What if one of them had attacked you while they were still out of it?"

"They didn't," she said.

What else could either of us say? She'd done all she could to protect herself, because her familiar hadn't been there to do it for her.

This wasn't how it was fucking supposed to be.

I pressed my nose to her hair and breathed deep, the monster in me needing reassurance, needing her in my fucking lungs. I was born to walk beside her, to protect her, to make sure she was always safe. And I'd failed.

I'd failed her.

I'd been failing her for the last couple of years.

I pressed my mouth to the top of her head again. No more. "I'm not going anywhere, Mags. I promise, I'm staying right here."

She didn't answer, not this time.

I didn't know if she'd passed out again—or if she didn't answer because she didn't believe me.

CHAPTER 8

Magnolia

MY EYES SNAPPED open when something cool touched my stomach.

It was morning, light filling the room, and Bram was sitting on the mattress beside me. His hair had fallen forward, covering most of his face, and he was so focused on what he was doing he hadn't noticed I'd woken up. I looked down as he smeared healing balm across a scrape low on my belly.

I was wearing one of his T-shirts and a pair of his boxers. They were low on my hips, and there was more balm on a scrape on my ribs, and another beside my belly button, right over the new markings the mother had given me.

"Hey," I said, my voice croaky as hell.

His gaze shot to mine. "Fuck, finally."

"Why am I dressed as your female alter ego?"

His gaze darted down my body and back, and the tendons in his muscled forearms popped. "You don't remember?"

I remembered a lot of last night, and the rest was slowly coming back. "The drive home's still a bit fuzzy. I got here, then you...appeared, and you..." He'd lifted me into his arms, flown to the tree house, stripped me naked and cleaned the blood and mud off me before he'd tended my wounds. I looked up at him again and wanted to squirm as the memories flooded me. But this was Bram, my best friend. So I was naked, so what, right? "Yeah, I remember. Thanks for taking care of me."

He sucked in a sharp breath and shook his head. "You're thanking me now?" His jaw clenched. "I know I've been doing a shitty fucking job of taking care of you, of being there for you, I know that, and I promise, I'll be here from now on. When you need me, I'll be here."

He meant it, but he was lying to me, and to himself. It wasn't intentional. He was deep in denial. Seeing me messed up last night had scared him, and he wasn't thinking logically. "You can't promise that, Bram, and I don't expect you to. I know you can't tell me where you go and what you do, but you're bound by a silencing oath, which means you're working for the kind of people who don't like to be ignored."

The muscle in his jaw jumped. "Let me worry about that."

"You want to protect me? I feel the same way about you. If something happened to you because you ignored an oath? I'd never forgive myself. I've done that, remember? Trust me, you don't want that."

His expression didn't change, and he didn't agree with me or argue his point, because he was going to do whatever the hell he liked.

"Bram—"

"How are you feeling? You were out of it last night."

Okay, he wasn't going to talk about it now. Fine. But if he thought I'd just drop it completely, he was mistaken. "I'm fine." I slid my legs out of bed and stood. Not as shaky as I thought, and my hands that had been cut up were already healing. I walked to the bathroom and lifted the shirt to take a closer look at the markings on my stomach. "Shit." Thorny vines swirled around my belly button and spread a little out to the sides.

"Check your back," Bram said, leaning against the doorframe.

"Seriously?" I turned and looked over my shoulder. Okay, that was excessive. "The mother obviously decided less wasn't more where I was concerned. The belly design wasn't enough, noooo, she thought I needed a tramp stamp as well?"

"They suit you," Bram said.

I glanced his way, and his gaze was moving over my exposed skin, lingering on my belly. Warmth curled right under the design, stealing my breath, and I dropped the shirt. "You're just saying that so I don't freak out." The shirt was way too big and had slipped down over one of my shoulders, uncovering more of my scarred skin. "I guess I should thank her. At least they cover a few of my ugly scars." He made a strange sound, and I glanced up at him again.

He shook his head, making his glossy black hair shift in a way that, if I was close, I'd reach up and touch it. I loved his hair. I'd told him a million times over the years how jealous I was of it.

"There's not one fucking part of you that's ugly," he said.

I stilled. The way he'd said it lifted goose bumps all over me. We stared at each other for several tense seconds, and my heart slammed into the back of my ribs, so hard I lost my breath for a moment.

I tore my gaze from his and busied myself by washing my hands, even though I didn't actually need to wash my hands, but the weird tension between us was too much. "I haven't felt the call to my task, but I don't need it, I already know what it is," I said drying them off.

"You do?"

"Willow gets accused of murder, then the same night the mother calls me, six months ahead of schedule." I strode toward him, and for a moment I didn't think he was going to move, he kind of paused, staring down at me with a look I couldn't decipher, but then he tucked his hair behind his ear and stepped back.

My breath was knocked from me and I blinked up at him. "What have you done?"

He tensed.

"Your hair." I reached up, and he held still as I brushed it back on one side, then the other. "You shaved it."

"It's how our warriors wear it," he said roughly.

Like his bothers. "And you're a warrior now?"

"Yes."

There was new ink on the side of his head, eight lines, something else the warriors in his village had. "And these?" I said as I ran my fingers over them. "Can you tell me what they are?"

"A warrior's markers," he said but didn't elaborate.

It was all he could or would tell me, which was nothing at all.

I dropped my hand. "It suits you."

His gaze searched mine. "Yeah?"

I nodded, then turned away and strode out to the living room, my heart in my throat. It was only hair, but something inside told me that it was a lot more than that, not just one more secret between us.

"So you're looking for a murderer," he said, following and picking up the conversation about my task where we'd left off.

"Looks that way." Now I just had to figure out where the hell to start.

·)·)·)·●·(·(·(·

I'd showered and changed, and Bram and I were making a late breakfast. He was wearing his usual black jeans, boots, and worn tee, the fabric straining around his biceps in a way it never used to. He'd tied the wide strip of his black hair back, and I kept sneaking glances his way. He looked so different.

73

He was still my Bram, but also...not—though then that went deeper than just his appearance.

The front door opened and closed, and I couldn't see them, but I heard Iris and Rose talking as they walked in. We were having a family meeting this morning to discuss what we were going to do about Willow, and though it was terrible timing, I needed to tell them I'd visited the mother last night, and my suspicions about my task before they started looking into it. The mother would see it as interference. A witch couldn't get help from her coven when her task had been set, and knowing my sisters, they'd already formed a plan.

"I can't believe she's calling her favor in now," Rose was saying. "The timing couldn't be worse."

Iris made a sound of agreement. "Have you heard from her at all since you and Ronan went to her cottage?"

"No, and I'd kind of hoped she'd forgotten about our bargain."

"What will you do?" Iris asked.

Rose let out a frustrated breath. "What I won't be doing is asking her. It's too dangerous."

"Our baby sister is twenty-one years old. She doesn't need us to protect her from everything, not anymore. Is she still struggling with some things? Yes, but don't write her off. When Bram started vanishing, it crushed her, but she's been getting better, controlling her anger, she's grown so much stronger, become a lot more independent. And she's been training her ass off with Ash."

Well, fuck. Thanks a lot, Iris. I felt Bram's eyes on me, and I couldn't bring myself to look at him.

"I thought you were just hanging out with Ash, learning a few moves?" he said softly, so he didn't blow our cover.

I don't know why I hadn't told him the extent of my training. Maybe it was me being petty. He was keeping something from me, so I was from him.

"What do you think Agatheena will do if you break your bargain?" Iris asked Rose before I could answer him.

I lowered my butter knife, and Bram tensed beside me at the mention of that witch's name.

"It's fine. I'll just take her what she wants," Rose said.

"But she asked for Magnolia, not you."

Rose cursed. "She asked me for the favor, no one else was mentioned."

"What exactly did she say? What words did she use?" Iris asked.

Rose was silent for several seconds. "A favor, at a date and time of her choosing."

"There was no mention of who," Iris said. "She's a powerful witch who dabbles in dark magic. You think pissing her off is a good idea?"

Okay, that was enough skulking in the kitchen.

"This is my mess. I'm not asking Mags to clean it up for me," Rose said, her startled gaze slicing to me when I walked out into the hall, Bram right behind me. "You're here," my sister said, guilt written all over her face.

"Yep, and I heard every word."

Rose paled. "Mags—"

"What does Agatheena want me to do?" I said and felt Bram close in behind me, volatile energy radiating from him.

"I don't want you involved with this." Rose crossed her arms. "Just forget you heard anything."

I snorted. "Well, that's not going to happen."

"Tell her," Iris said.

I could have hugged her but was having one of those days when touch wasn't something I could tolerate.

Rose sighed and pulled something from her pocket. "She wants you to take this to her." She held up a small vial.

"Why me? And what is it?"

"It's blood from a very powerful vampire. Another debt apparently. Ronan collected it." Rose chewed her lip. "I have no idea why she asked for you. It makes no sense. She and I made the bargain. If I'd known she'd do this, I would have told her to shove it." Rose cursed, looking worried. "I don't like this. She's half demon and extremely powerful."

"She wants me to deliver it, I'll deliver it. Everything'll be fine." I shoved my hands in my pockets as a tremor moved through them for some unknown reason. "And I'll even keep my attitude in check so she doesn't eat me."

"Don't even joke about it. I'm not actually a hundred percent sure that she doesn't eat people."

"Awesome." Shit was just getting better and better. Yesterday, I woke up and it was like any other day. Within forty-eight hours, I learned Bram was bound by a silencing oath, my sister was accused of murder and was in hiding, the mother called me, and now I had to visit a witch who may or may not be a cannibal. I'd obviously pissed the fates off somehow. "There has to be a reason she's asking for me." I took a steadying breath. "Maybe it has something to do with my task?"

Iris sucked in a sharp breath, and Rose's eyes went huge.

"Your task?" Iris said. "What do you mean, your task?"

"Magnolia?" Rose whispered.

"How did I not see it," Iris bit out, not letting me answer either of them.

"Look at her," she said to Rose, "She's barely recovered. Show me," my sister said.

I knew what she was asking and lifted my shirt, showing her the vine markings on my stomach and back.

"Holy shit," Rose said.

I dropped my shirt. "My words exactly."

"It's too soon." Iris planted her hands on her hips. "What the hell is going on?"

"My guess? My trial has something to do with this mess with Willow."

Rose blinked rapidly, then yanked me into her arms, hugging me tight. I had to fight my wince and the urge to pull away. She needed it, and I had to let her. When she pulled back, she looked up at Bram. "Thank the goddess you have wings, at least you didn't have to fight your way there and back."

Bram's entire body went rock solid beside me.

Rose frowned, not missing his reaction. "You were...there, weren't you?"

"He didn't know," I said quickly. "It's fine, I'm fine."

"You went alone?" Iris yelled.

"Keep your damn voice down. I don't want Mom knowing, not yet. She'll only worry, and there's nothing she can do to help me."

Iris bared her teeth like one of the wolves she lived with. "How the fuck did you survive it?"

"It doesn't matter, I did. It's over and done with. Let's move on," I said, the tension around us so thick I couldn't bear it. It wasn't Bram's fault, and I hated the way they were looking at him.

"Do you have someone to go with you to Agatheena's?" Iris asked, not looking at Bram.

Rose appeared even more pissed, her eyes flashing to her bat's, turning black for a second before returning to blue. "Relic would. Maybe we can get a message to him somehow? What about—"

"I'm standing right here," Bram said, and that volatile energy grew, swirling around us both.

Bram never usually said boo, but that had changed, especially the last year.

Iris stared up at him, and her head tilted to the side. "You can't blame us for asking, Bram. You've not exactly been around lately. Magnolia literally fought her way in and out of Oldwood Forest *alone*, something I can't even fucking bear to think about."

"You have been *extremely* busy," Rose said, and the look in her eyes as she stared up at him gave me pause.

"Magnolia comes first," he said, and there was a whole lot of grit in his voice.

"Does she?" Rose's stare was utterly frigid. "She didn't last night."

Whoa. What the hell? I knew they were pissed off on my behalf and hated seeing me upset when he left, but my sweet sister looked ready to go into battle. "Rose, there are things you don't know—"

"Did you tell her you visited The Vault a couple nights ago?" Rose asked, not looking away from him. "Is that where you were last night instead of protecting Magnolia?"

"No," he ground out.

I spun to face him. "The Vault?" I thought he was at The Bank, the club above it. Apparently, that was only half of the story. The Vault was below the popular nightclub and a place where blood drinkers went to feed and fuck willing donors. Bram wasn't a blood drinker, which meant the only reason he would be down there was to—

His eyes clashed with mine, but he said nothing. Not one fucking thing. I spun away and snatched the vial from Rose's hand. "I've got this. I'll let you know when I'm back."

"Mags, hang on. You can't go alone—"

Bram growled behind us, like a wolf or a freaking hellhound. "She won't fucking be going alone."

At his tone, both my sisters jolted in surprise. He'd never spoken to them like that, and they'd been too caught up in their own stuff, with living their own lives, to notice how much he'd changed. They noticed now.

"No," I said. "I won't. I'll ask Asher."

"Like fuck you will," Bram said, grabbing my hand and gripping it tight. "You're pissed at me. I deserve it, but I can't do anything about that. I will be going with you, though. So it's your choice. Either be pissed off all day, or get the fuck over it, because I'm your familiar and no one protects you but me. Understand?"

The room went utterly silent. Rose was blinking up at him stunned. Iris was wide-eyed, and going by her expression, she couldn't decide if she was angry or impressed.

I knew what I was. Yanking my hand from his, I spun away and stormed from the room, Bram hot on my heels.

"Call when you get back, or we're coming after you," Rose called after us.

I strode out the door, and Bram grabbed my arm before I could get in the car.

"Stop it," he said. "We're not doing this. Do you hear me? We're not fighting about this. Whatever you're thinking, it's wrong. So completely fucking wrong."

"I'm thinking you went to The Vault to feed and fuck a vamp," I said.

He did that thing where he locked eyes with me and said fucking nothing, like he wanted me to read his damn mind. The oath. He was there because he had to be. But he couldn't tell me why, or what happened. I pulled my arm free of his hold and dragged in a steadying breath.

I was acting like a jealous girlfriend. I needed to rein it the hell in. Whatever the details were, he couldn't tell me, and getting pissed at him for something he had no control over wasn't very constructive.

"I'm sorry," I said, and it wasn't easy to gather control of my anger, but I managed to bring it down from inferno to simmer. "Let's just focus on what we need to do, okay?"

He nodded, but his jaw was tight as hell. "We'll drive to the edge of the forest, then fly. It's dangerous. There're creatures there that make the demons we're used to look like kittens."

"Fantastic."

Bram bared his teeth. "They come anywhere near you, I'll tear them to fucking shreds."

A weird swirly sensation spiraled through my lower belly. "Noted."

CHAPTER 9

Magnolia

I TRIED REALLY hard to clear my head and focus on what I needed to do as we headed for the forest—and not on what Bram might or might not have done while he was at The Vault. I was failing.

The forest ahead thinned, and I pulled over on the side of the dirt road. The track that would lead us to Agatheena's cottage was just ahead. I slid my smaller knife in my pocket, the one I used for spelling, then reached under the seat and pulled out my bigger one.

Bram watched me. "Where'd you get that?"

"It was a gift." I got out of the car.

He did the same and rounded the hood. Slipping the knife from my fingers, he tested its balance and weight. His fingers curled around the hilt, gripping it tight, so tight his knuckles turned white. "From who? Relic?"

"What? No."

I frowned and took it back, strapping it to my thigh. "Asher. She gave it to me two months ago." I glanced up at him. "The first time I managed to take her down to the mat."

His brows shot up. "You took Asher down?"

"I've taken her down several times now," I said and grabbed my pack, pulling it on.

His dark eyes searched mine. "So, what Iris said, about you training?"

"It's true. And I'm good. Really good. I can take care of myself now. So you don't need to worry about me." It wasn't the reason I'd gone to Asher in the first place, ignoring my pride and with my tail between my legs, it had been about an outlet for my anger. But the more Bram was away, the more I realized I'd need to take care of myself, that Bram wouldn't always be there to look out for me like he used to be.

His nostrils flared, the muscle in his jaw twitching before he looked away.

"Bram?"

"We better get going." He tugged off his shirt, tucking it into the back of his jeans, then scooped me into his arms.

His wings unfurled, beating hard, and we lifted off. A moment later we were above the forest, looking down at the treetops.

"You don't like that I can fight?" I asked when the silence stretched out.

He shook his head. "I don't like that you had to learn because of me."

"I didn't do it because of you, I learned for me." I tightened my arms around his neck and pressed my forehead to his cheek. Goddess, my heart couldn't take much more of this, all this animosity and hurt, and just plan weirdness, between us.

"And the other thing Iris said about when I started leaving all the time?" I felt his throat working and his voice had grown incredibly deep. "I crushed you?"

"Don't," I said instead of answering, because we both knew the truth and there was nothing either of us could do about it now.

My world was in a spin, and he'd always been my steadying force, I needed that from him again now. I needed that more than anything right then. "Can we just be us. For today, can we just be Mags and Bram again, the way we used to be?"

His chest expanded, and he turned his head, pressing his lips to my forehead. "Yeah," he said against my skin before he turned back and focused on where we were going.

The farther we flew, the darker and denser the forest became. Strange sounds, cries and calls and growls, echoed up from below. Bram said there were creatures here that I'd never seen before, that the demons who lived out here had no choice because there was no way they could pass for human like the ones who lived in the city. And when Bram pointed to one below us, I understood what he meant. It was tall and skinny, gray in color with a greenish tinge at its joints. It also had pointed ears and holes where its nose should be.

The roof of a cottage appeared in the distance, peeking through the trees. "There."

I felt Agatheena's power then, like a dense fog wrapping around us.

Bram circled the area a few times, making sure there weren't any demons or other creatures right below us, then landed. His wings folded in and disappeared, but he didn't release me as he scanned the trees surrounding us.

With how dense the forest was here, the sun could barely break through. It made the air damp and heavy.

I pulled the knife from the sheath strapped to my thigh as Bram and I listened for anything approaching. "I can't believe she lives out here on her own."

"Not entirely on her own," Bram said when a demon roared in the distance.

I turned to the cottage. Rose was right, it looked like something from a Grimm's fairy tale, where a child-eating witch lived, or one working on evil spells and plotting revenge.

Smoke drifted lazily out of the chimney, even though it was the middle of summer, and the cottage itself looked almost part of the forest—its moss-covered stone walls butting up against thick tree trunks, a couple growing right through the thatched roof.

Her wards would be impenetrable, they'd have to be out here.

"What now?" Bram asked, his gaze sliding to the thick pines that stood on either side of the worn dirt path, and what hung from them.

Bones, some clean, some still covered in blood and gore dangled from thick twine. Skulls from different breeds of demon, and other creatures I had no chance of identifying. There were jars filled with bits of fabric, floating eyeballs, fingernails, and several others with organs of some kind stuffed into them. Another was half filled with a multitude of different colored hair all matted together.

The path led to the cottage's front door and branches arched over the top, forming a leafy canopy, also covered in Agatheena's macabre decoration.

"Now we let her know we're here." Rose had shared what happened when she came here, so I was prepared.

I reached out, and her ward sent fire coursing through my veins. Cursing, I yanked my hand back, clenching my fingers and shaking them out.

"Didn't tickle, then?" Bram asked.

"No, smart-ass. And I'd say that was just the warning." I walked to one of the pines. "Rose said Agatheena needed her blood, for confirmation of who she was. She said to look for a smooth patch on the side of the tree. It'll be darker in color."

Bram nodded and searched with me.

"Got it," he said a minute later.

I took a closer look. In the middle of a knot was a smooth, indented patch. The tree was lighter wood, but this spot was a deep mahogany color.

"Yeah, that's it." I slipped my big knife back in its sheath and pulled out my small one, the one Mom had given me on my thirteenth birthday. Every witch in our coven had one, since we often used blood magic, and unlike my other knife, this one wasn't big enough to take my hand off.

Bram scanned the trees again as I made a slice in the tip of my finger. Blood bubbled to the surface, and I pressed it to the center of the darker patch in the tree.

Bram took my hand as soon as I was done, some of Else's balm already on his finger. "Now what?" he said distractedly as he smeared it over the cut, something he'd been doing since I first cut myself in front of him six years ago.

A low creak echoed from the cottage, the door swinging open slowly a moment before a very old and tiny, hunched-over female walked out with a raven perched on her shoulder.

"Now I go visit with Agatheena, and you wait here for me," I said, not taking my eyes off the old witch shuffling toward us.

"Like fuck," he snapped. "Where you go, I go."

"Magnolia Thornheart," Agatheena said as she drew closer. "I wasn't sure your sister would let you come." She smiled, briefly flashing red demonic eyes and yellow, pointed teeth, reminding me of her demon blood. As if I could forget.

"She wasn't either," I said. "But I convinced her."

Agatheena chuckled.

I took a step forward, and Bram hooked an arm around my waist, not letting me go any farther. "Rose said you asked for me specifically, why?"

"I like you," she said, stopping in front of us. "I knew I would."

Her skin was wrinkled, and her gray hair was wild and wiry. I had no idea how old she was, but I'd say *very*. The only thing between us was her ward, and my heart banged a little harder when her now piercing green eyes locked with mine. The raven on her shoulder looked up at Bram and bobbed, making a high-pitched *caw*.

Bram replied, a gritty sound coming from low in his chest.

"Why am I here, Agatheena?" I asked again.

"You'll find out, but first." She waved toward one of the jars hanging on the tree. "It needs a lock of your hair before it'll let you past," she said.

I wasn't sure what *it* referred to, the ward or the tree. Either way, I needed to add some hair to her collection. I guess I should be grateful she didn't demand an organ.

"I'll be waiting, so get a move on," Agatheena said, then headed back up the path and into her cottage.

"I'm coming with you," Bram said as I pulled a piece of hair forward from underneath and sliced off a small section.

I glanced up at the cottage and back at him. "Ronan wasn't allowed past her wards, but she didn't say you couldn't. Maybe it'll be okay?"

"I don't give a fuck if it's not. I'm coming." He unscrewed the lid of the jar and held it out.

I shoved my hair in, and he did it back up, letting the jar hang.

"Let's get this over with," he said and curled his fingers around mine.

I lifted my hand, and the buzz of power that had zapped through me was gone. "The ward's dropped. Let's go." I stepped through, turning back when Bram pulled on my hand—

He snarled as his fingers were ripped from mine and he was tossed backward, landing hard on the forest floor. He shot to his feet and bolted toward me but was thrown back a second time. He jumped to his feet again and stormed forward, his black eyes filled with rage. "This isn't happening. You are not going in there without me."

He was afraid for me, but I had no choice. "I have to do this. I'll be okay."

"Don't you dare walk in there," he said through gritted teeth.

I was already stepping away. "I have to. Rose owes her, and she called me here for a reason. Maybe she can tell me something about Willow, or my task."

"No," he bit out and stepped forward, reaching for me without thinking —and was tossed back a third time.

Agatheena obviously got sick of waiting, because her magic suddenly coiled around me and dragged me right up the path and to the front door before Bram could storm back to the path entrance.

The door opened, and I was thrust inside before it slammed shut again.

I looked around. There were more...*things* hanging all over the cottage, from the walls and ceiling. Things that would turn anyone's stomach.

Agatheena walked out of a room to the side, the kitchen. She was sucking on a pipe, blowing out blue smoke.

She held it up. "You gonna throw a hissy fit? Or are we all good?"

"I'm good."

She grinned, showing me those pointed teeth of hers again. "You tell me if you change your mind. I'll give you a dose of my blue smoke and all your stresses will melt away."

Bram yelled my name.

"Your male might need it, though. If he's anything like your sister's mate, he'll caterwaul until you're back."

"He's not my mate. He's my familiar."

The kettle whistled, and she lifted it off the stove, put some basil, chamomile, lemon balm, and lavender in a couple of mugs, then poured water over them—a mix used to help with relaxation. I didn't see her add anything else, but there could've been something already in the mug. Her familiar flew from the living room, cawing, and landed on her shoulder. She chuckled. "You see it, too, Dolores?"

The bird bobbed its head.

"The eyes are useless when the mind is blind," she said, and pulled something from her pocket and held it up, seed. The bird ate it from her hand.

Bram roared my name again, his panic coming through loud and clear.

Agatheena ignored him and carried the mugs over to the table, putting one in front of me. "Sit."

I did as she said.

"First things first." She held out her hand.

I stared at it, wrinkled, fingernails more like claws.

"The blood," she added.

"Oh, right, shit." I fished it out of my pack and handed it to her. "One vial of powerful vampire blood, as requested."

She took it from me and slid it into her pocket.

This female was terrifying, no doubt, Rose was right about that. There was a darkness that flowed from her that sent a shiver through me, but I didn't feel in any immediate danger.

She dabbled in dark magic, I was sure of it. This little, old female did what she wanted, and that piqued my curiosity. "Can I ask what it's for?"

"No," she said, then studied me, closely.

I struggled not to squirm in my seat.

"You feel it, don't you, child? The line I walk?" she finally asked, like she could read my mind.

"Yes." There was no reason to lie. "How do you do it? How do you stop from falling into total darkness, from letting it overtake you?"

"Some of us are born with a little darkness in us already. Only those witches can do what we do," she said, her piercing gaze not leaving me.

"We?" I straightened in my seat, preparing to stand. Now I was afraid, but not of her.

"If you stand, I will make you sit, understand?"

I nodded and forced myself to stay put.

Bram had lost it completely outside. Roaring my name, cursing, and trying to break through the ward over and over again, going by the thud of his body hitting the ground repeatedly as he tried to get in, when he knew better, when he knew it was impossible.

"Can I tell him I'm okay?" I asked, lifting out of my seat again.

"No."

An invisible force shoved me back down.

"You'll be back to him soon enough. And you saying it won't appease him. I doubt he'd believe you. He knows too much about magic."

The raven on her shoulder *cawed* again and shook out its feathers.

There was no point arguing, her mind was made up. "You still haven't told me why I'm here," I said, an uneasy feeling flowing through me.

"A message, obviously." She gave me an exasperated look. "Why the hell else?" She motioned to my drink. "Drink your tea, and I'll give it to you."

I looked down at it. "Are you going to read the leaves?"

"No, I just don't want good herbs going to waste. And I don't get much company, so we're going to drink tea together first, then I'll give you your message."

I sniffed the drink, then took a sip. "It's good."

"Of course, it is." She chuckled. "You're not nearly as jumpy as your sister."

"You met her after being sheltered and sick for most of her life. You wouldn't recognize her now," I said, giving more information than I should to this witch, but I truly didn't think she was as bad as everyone thought, the possible cannibalism aside.

Bram roared my name again, and goose bumps lifted all over me.

"You know why the fates chose a crow as your familiar, don't you?" she asked.

"No, but I'm glad they did." Her gaze remained steady on me. "Is this the part where you tell me?"

"You already know, Magnolia, but whatever, I'll humor you." Her gaze sharpened. "They chose a crow because they have an innate darkness in them. They're born with it, and so were you. Your own darkness grew, though, and changed, after whatever it was that caused those scars all over your body. And your male?" She chuckled. "Well, there's a reason a group of crows is called a murder."

I stilled. "What do you mean?"

She motioned to my tea, and I quickly took another sip.

"The mother called you," Agatheena said, ignoring my question and changing the subject.

I forced myself to meet her shrewd gaze. "How do you know that?"

Her lips curled up, and those sharp teeth had me biting back my next words.

"I know a lot of things," she said. "You're very impertinent for someone so much weaker than me. You're lucky I like you, Magnolia Thornheart."

There was a tone to her voice that said she was humoring me, that if I pissed her off, she'd cut out my tongue, or some other part, going by her choice of home decor. "According to my sisters, I have a death wish and anger issues," I said, gripping my mug tighter.

"Are they right?" she asked.

"Probably."

She laughed again, and I guessed as long as she found me amusing, I'd be okay. Bram roared, so loud my scalp prickled. I needed to get out of here. I took another sip of my tea, and she nodded her approval. This whole thing was so freaking weird.

"Your task, it'll be a test of strength—magical, physical, but mostly..." She tapped the side of her head. "But mostly a test of what's in here. Are you mentally strong, Magnolia? Because you'll need to be." She shot out of her seat and pressed a finger against the center of my chest. "And in here. Your heart will need to be sure, true."

What did that even mean? I blinked up at her when she stayed where she was, standing over me. This close she was even more terrifying, especially when one of her pointed claw-like nails was digging into my chest. I assumed she was waiting for a response. So I nodded.

She pulled her hand back and sat. "If you're not, and you fail, you'll not only hurt your coven but you'll lose everything and everyone you care about." Her green eyes burned into me. "Including the crow."

Fear filled me, so frigid it chilled me to the bone. "What do I need to do?"

"That darkness inside you, Magnolia, you can't deny it, not anymore. You couldn't even if you wanted to. It's too late." She didn't look away. "If you accept it, if you loosen the binding you have around it, it can help you control that rage burning inside you that's been burning for so long. But you need to be very careful. The spells you've created, they're potent, but you already know that. Do you know why?"

I shook my head.

"Because they were created with hate in your heart, with rage and thoughts of vengeance burned into your soul. That's the quickest way into darkness."

She was right. That's exactly how I'd created my spells and potions, every one of them in my book, I'd written in a frenzy of emotion, usually anger, and always pain.

She covered my hand with hers. "The darkness can be your friend...or it can be your enemy. But like any new acquaintance, you must be on your guard. Don't trust it easily. It'll lie to you, flatter you, try to bring you closer, to tip the scales. Only the strongest can walk the path between dark and

86

light. Only the strongest can dip their toe into a pool of terrors and walk away only missing that one toe."

"And the others, those not strong enough?" I held my breath.

"They become one of the terrors."

CHAPTER 10

Magnolia

I WALKED out of the cottage, my mind racing as Agatheena's words, her warnings, flew through my head.

I glanced up and saw Bram, and my breath caught.

He stood at the end of the path, waiting just beyond the ward. He looked...wild. His shirt was in tatters on the ground, his tattooed chest and arms glistened with sweat, his wings extended, his face contorted with fear and rage.

I rushed down the steps, breaking into a run.

His black gaze was locked on me as he gripped one of the tree trunks bordering the path, holding himself back. He bared his teeth, his chest heaving, struggling for control, no doubt afraid Agatheena would suddenly snatch me back.

"I'm okay," I called when I was almost to him. Then finally, I was there, and I closed the space between us, running through the ward to reach him.

Bram snatched me off my feet with a feral snarl, clutching me to him, and shot into the sky.

"Bram?"

He tucked me closer and shook his head.

"I'm okay," I said again.

His arm was banded around me, holding me tightly to his front and his long, thick fingers dug into my waist, not giving me an inch of space. I didn't fight it. I needed him close as much as he did me. It'd always been this way between us. Physical closeness was something we both seemed to need from each other. Even on my worst days, when I couldn't stand to be touched, Bram was usually the exception. Being close to him calmed the storm inside me.

I rested my head on his shoulder. "I'm okay," I whispered once more, because he needed to hear it. I'd say it a hundred times if I had to.

We flew over the treetops, past the demons and other creatures below us, back to the edge of the forest. Bram kept his arms locked around me the entire time, every muscle in his lean body rock solid.

His arms flexed around me as we landed by the car, then his hold loosened, but he didn't let me go. His chest was pumping when he looked down at me, his midnight eyes moving over my face.

"Bram—"

"I thought I'd lost you. I thought she was hurting you and I couldn't get to you..."

I took his face in my hands, silencing him, with my fingers brushing over the newly shaved sides of his hair. He trembled, and a shiver moved through me as well at the look on his face. I knew there was more to the fear in his eyes, the desperation. It wasn't just about today, it was about the past few months, the last couple of years, of us growing more and more distant.

Losing me was his biggest fear, just like the thought of losing him was mine. What happened at the cottage had just brought that into sharper focus.

"You didn't lose me." I brushed my thumb over his jaw, feeling the stubble there.

He was no longer the boy who'd rescued me from a group of bullies; he was a full-grown male. We were both so different, had gone through so much, and if that wasn't enough for us to navigate, it felt as if there were a whole lot of outside forces trying to tear us apart.

This energy between us had always been there but had steadily grown more intense, more volatile over time and swirled around us now. I didn't know what it meant, but sometimes it scared me. I did my best to ignore it now. "No matter what happens in the future, you will never lose me. I promise I won't let anything tear us apart."

His dark gaze was intense, and I dipped mine, finding it hard to look into his eyes all of a sudden, and landed on his beautifully sculpted mouth. It was darker than usual—

His fingers slid into my hair, and he fisted it in a way he never had before, sending electricity zapping across my scalp and shooting through my belly. My gaze flew to his, and he tugged me forward as he dipped his head, and for a moment I thought he was going to...that he was—

He pressed his lips to my forehead, then released a shuddering breath before finally letting me go.

My heart was thundering in my chest for some stupid reason. "L-let's go home," I said and stepped back.

He nodded, and I walked around the car, opened the door and tossed my pack in the back. Bram got in on the passenger side.

I opened the driver's door and, as I did, a snarl came from behind me.

I spun as a demon burst from the tree line. Bram exploded out of the car, but I'd already delivered a flying kick to its face. Its head jerked back, and it lost its balance, falling to the ground. I advanced, bringing my boot down hard in its ribs, then dropping to my knee, I slammed my knife into its throat, thrusting the blade to the side and semi decapitating it. I jerked the blade the other way, then dropped the knife, spun around, gripped the sides of its head, planted my feet against its shoulders, and, grunting, yanked its head off the rest of the way.

I fell back as the demon turned to ash. *Gross*. I was covered in it. Panting, I dusted my hands off on my jeans and jumped to my feet.

"What the fuck, Mags?" Bram stood watching me, his shock obvious.

"Told you I could take care of myself," I said and got in the car, and yeah, I was secretly pleased he'd seen that. That Bram had seen with his own two eyes what I could do.

He got in as well and stared over at me. "But that...that was..."

"Impressive?"

He thrust his fingers through his hair. "Yeah, that...and fucking terrifying."

I grinned, and he blew out a shaky breath. I gave his hand a squeeze and started the car. "You'll get used to it."

He didn't look convinced.

››᠈●᠂᠂

Later that afternoon, we headed to the city. I needed specialty supplies, and even if The Cauldron hadn't been off-limits while the witches council investigated, they were things we didn't stock and never had.

It was getting dark, and Bram was silent beside me, so deep in thought that a heavy energy rolled off him. I'd shared some of what Agatheena had said to me, and his fists had been clenched ever since. Seeing me take down that demon wasn't helping the situation.

Nerves curled in my gut, but I refused to let the fear take hold. The things Agatheena had said about me, yes, they'd scared the shit out of me, but they were also true.

That darkness inside you, Magnolia, you can't deny it, not anymore. You couldn't even if you wanted to. It's too late.

I'd known what I was doing when I made those potions and came up with those spells. I'd felt the darkness while I did it, and instead of retreating from it, I'd embraced it. I'd been too filled with anger to do anything else. Knowing that it had always been part of me was actually kind of reassuring, and finding Gran's book, knowing that she'd been the same as me and kept control of it, helped me as well.

If I was going to survive my task, and the trial that followed, I needed to embrace who I was. I needed to walk the path between darkness and light, like Agatheena said, like Gran obviously had.

I just had to make sure I didn't slip too far into the shadows.

"It's too dangerous," Bram said into the silence.

I glanced over at him. "What is?"

"Everything, all of it," he said roughly.

"You know there's nothing I can do to stop this, that I have to pass this task."

He ran his fingers through his hair. "Yeah, I know."

His hair was down and fell to one side. It suited him, but it was still taking some getting used to.

I made a turn and the energy around us immediately grew thick, lifting the hair on the back of my neck.

Bram stiffened beside me. "You're sure about this?"

"Yes." And I was, but I still had to get my head around the shift. All my life I'd been told dark magic was wrong, that witches who practiced it were evil. I'd never considered there was a space in between. I'd been fighting it so long, embracing it—the shadows swirling inside me—was frightening but also a relief.

I scanned the street ahead. This part of Roxburgh was known to humans as "the wrong side of the tracks" where the "bad guys" hung out, and they actively avoided it. Good thing, too, because this was a demon neighborhood. Those still living here had once been ruled by a powerful female named Vorena. Willow had bartered with her in the past, and by all accounts, she'd been utterly terrifying, but she had kept her demons in line. Then she'd been killed, and the demons who wanted to hurt humans had run free. The knights of Hell had done their job, had taken them out, and the demons who were allowed to remain here were the ones who had controlled themselves and continued to follow the knights' rules. They were watched closely, and as long as they kept to their end of the bargain, they kept their heads.

The new demon in charge was named Rune and, word had it, he was placed here by Lucifer himself to keep those still here in line. I'd never met him, didn't know what kind of demon he was, and after the things I'd heard about him, I wasn't in a hurry to get acquainted. He lived in what had once been known as the Sunnydale Insane Asylum back in the 1800s. The building had long ago been abandoned and decommissioned, and before he moved in, teenagers used to dare one another to spend the night in the creepy, haunted building.

Coming here was a risk, but with Bram able to get us out quickly, if need be, I wasn't overly worried.

We got out of the car and headed up the street. Bram tied his hair back as we strode along the pavement. It definitely made him appear more intimidating, though I wasn't sure if that was his intention or not.

The street was lined with shops, demon-run cafes and clothing stores, bars and supermarkets. This was their world, where the demons who were humanoid in appearance, and didn't have a driving desire to kill or torture or eat humans, were allowed to reside.

As we walked by, heads turned, some openly staring at us with other-worldly eyes, some sniffing the air to find out what we were, others scowling with open hostility. Two male demons walked out of a bar in front of us and turned our way. They stilled, one tilting his head back as he stared directly at me and scented the air.

It was—unnerving.

Bram's hand was suddenly gripping the back of my neck, pulling me closer, in a hold that was utterly possessive. It was for the demon's benefit, of course, they'd be less likely to try anything if they thought I was claimed —it didn't matter that I could kick both of their asses on my own.

Bram touched me all the time. I had no idea why my heart was suddenly racing again, or why I couldn't stop myself from sucking in a sharp breath.

What the hell was wrong with me?

We carried on, passing them, and both demons eyed Bram, their gazes sliding up to his face, his head. Their eyes widened, and they quickly looked away.

I shot a glance at Bram and did a double take. He was baring his teeth in their direction, his smile so sinister, so full of promise, of the most horrific kind, it sent cold chills shooting up my spine.

His fingers squeezed the back of my neck a little more firmly, and he pulled me in closer. I let him. I wanted to walk back out of here in one piece, and if Bram somehow made the demons here uneasy, I wasn't going to complain. I also wasn't going to think about it too hard or ask him all the questions now firing through my head, because I got the feeling he wouldn't be able to give me the answers I wanted.

I spotted the shop up ahead. *Malicious Brew* was scrawled on a sign swinging in the summer breeze.

Bram strode up to it and opened the door. We walked in, and a whole lot of different smells assaulted us, potent, not entirely unpleasant, but different than what I was used to. A mix of herbs and roots, of plants and elixirs and other things we didn't stock at The Cauldron or use at home.

The demons here catered to those with darker desires and tastes, and I guess that included me now.

The sound of door hinges creaking in the back of the shop echoed through the room, and I turned as a demon walked out. A stunning female with peridot eyes, wide and tilted up in the corners. Her small nose was slightly upturned, and her mouth was full and lush. Her hair hung to her waist in blood-red waves, and she had several tiny plaits hanging down each side of her face.

She strode forward, her gaze moving over me before sliding the length of Bram, then her spine stiffened. Her gaze darted to me, then back to him.

Bram shook his head for some unknown reason, and the female in front of us seemed to understand because her posture lost some of its rigidness.

"What do you want?" she said, her pale, yellow-green eyes still on him.

"It's me you'll be dealing with," I said, stepping forward.

She tore her eyes from Bram, and they narrowed. "You're not one of my regular witches."

"Will that be a problem?"

She shrugged. "No, as long as you and your...shadow..." Her gaze darted to Bram and back. "Don't try anything that we'll both regret."

"I just want my supplies, then we'll go."

She nodded, but her gaze kept darting to Bram, like she expected him to pounce at any moment. "Well?" she said impatiently. "What do you want?"

I slid the list from my pocket and handed it to her. In the past, I'd made a lot of my potions by foraging, in safer parts of the forest, usually around the keep after I'd trained with Asher, and by mixing a few things together that witches were strongly advised not to.

She looked down at the list. "You got money? 'Cause you'll need plenty of it."

Well, shit, that tone said I'd probably need a lot more than I had.

Bram pulled a roll of cash from his pocket. "Get her what she wants."

I'd seen more rolls of cash like it in his tree house. His "employer" paid well.

She laughed huskily, her gaze coming back to me. "Ahhh, now I get it. I guess the cash is worth the risk, huh?"

I frowned. "What?"

"The risk of lying down next to him at night and not waking up?"

"What the hell are you talking about?" I asked, looking between her and Bram.

"Your boyfriend, he's a crow." She gave me a look that said she thought I was missing several brain cells.

"Just get what she asked for," Bram bit out, cutting her off.

Her eyes flashed at his demand, but she didn't bite back. She spun and strode off, presumably to do what he said.

I turned to him. "What the hell was that? What was she talking about?"

"No idea," he said, crossing his arms. "She's a demon."

He said it as if that explained everything. "What does she mean, risk not waking up?"

His gaze hit mine. "How the fuck would I know?"

The bite to his voice, his obvious overreaction to my question, told me he was lying, and I hated the feeling.

The demon strode back, stepping in behind the counter, and dumped my supplies on top. I walked over as she rang everything up.

"I'm out of belladonna, but I have rosary pea. It's more potent, you'll need less. It's heavy-duty shit, and I'd advise you to leave it here if you don't know what you're doing with it."

"I'll take it." Abrus precatorius, or rosary pea as it was more commonly known, was deadly. No, I'd never used it before. Like belladonna, it was forbidden by the council to grow ourselves, but I knew how to handle plants and herbs, deadly or not.

She smirked. "If you say so. As for the vamp blood, leave a number and I'll call if I get some in."

"You have any idea when?"

"Could be days, could be weeks. Harvesting that shit isn't like plucking a bunch of herbs from your back garden, sweetie."

I ignored her attempt to get a rise out of me, and it wasn't easy. "So you have a lot of regular witches coming here?"

"Yep," she said as she wrapped the rosary pea and slid it in the bag with my other supplies.

"From here or out of town?"

"Both." She grinned, and I realized she had sharp, elongated fangs, not vampire or shifter, these were all demon.

Were these other witches like me, like Agatheena? Did they carry darkness inside them along with light? Or were they pure darkness? Did I know them?

The other female slid the bag toward me, and Bram handed her a wad of cash.

She grinned. "I'll call if we get some blood in."

I nodded, and we walked out. The street was fairly busy, and I could hardly believe everyone around us were demons. The knights always said not all demons were created equally, and I finally understood what that meant. Those around us were nothing like the monsters we encountered in the forests.

Not everyone here was harmless, of course, but if they wanted a life outside Hell, they had to obey the rules, and, apparently, most of them had been.

As we headed back the way we came, several questions were on the tip of my tongue, like, what the hell was the demon in that store talking about when we walked in?

I dropped my keys and stopped to scoop them up. Bram kept walking, not realizing I'd stopped. I straightened, about to jog to catch up, when someone hooked me around the neck and jerked me in close to their side.

"Hey, gorgeous," a roughened voice said against my ear. "Wanna party?"

"Not even a little bit." I clenched my fist, about to dislodge him the way Asher had taught me, when a dark shadow materialized behind him.

One moment Bram was a shadow, the next he stood behind the demon, one hand gripping his chin, the other pressed to the side of his head, and that vicious, sinister look was back on his face, his features distorted by rage.

"Release her, or die," he said in a voice I barely recognized, a voice that projected pure hatred and violence.

The demon released me instantly, but Bram didn't let go. No, his arms tensed, his muscles flexing. He was going to break the demon's neck anyway.

"B," I said, gripping his forearm, "he let me go. Let's walk away."

The demon nodded. "Listen to your female. I was just messing. Didn't mean any disrespect. Saw a pretty girl on her own, thought I'd take a shot. My bad."

"Bram," I said again.

His nostrils flared and his bicep bulged.

"Bram," I said more forcefully.

His black eyes shot to me and locked on.

"Let go. I'm okay. No harm done," I said, keeping my voice as calm as I could.

Finally, he released a slow breath, dropped his hands and stepped back. The demon instantly took off.

Bram and I stared at each other for long seconds, that weird tension growing between us again, and I suddenly found it hard to breathe normally.

Then I felt it—so strong, I jolted.

"What is it?" Bram said, closing the space between us.

"I'm being called somewhere." A terrible feeling filled me, gripping me behind the ribs. "Something awful's happened."

CHAPTER 11

Bram

Mags sat in the passenger seat, staring blindly ahead. "Turn left," she said as a great shudder moved through her small frame.

I'd seen a lot of things since we found each other. I'd been with her while she spelled, performed rituals, and used potions. I'd seen her cut herself more times than I could count. I'd also been around during her sisters' own tasks and trials. I thought I'd seen it all, was prepared for what was coming—I sure as hell never expected this feeling growing inside me right now, now that it was finally Mags's turn. I felt fucking helpless, powerless, and I didn't know how to deal with the feeling.

I wanted to take this from her, all of it, but I couldn't. When she'd walked out of that fucking cottage, after what felt like forever, I was so close to saying something—to *doing* something I could never take back.

I'd never wanted to kiss her more than in that moment, and I'd barely resisted the urge.

Then that female demon had almost told Mags what I was. That wasn't fucking done. You talk about us, about what we are, you die. She'd need to be dealt with. Then the fucker on the street had put his filthy hands on Mags. I'd almost snapped his neck. I still wanted to go back, find him, and end him.

Throughout the day, the ever-present darkness inside me had gone from a low hum to a silent roar. I thought I could keep my shit tight, but that was easier said than done. And the closer I got to that darkness, the deeper it pulled me in, the more the crow, the predator, the male who craved his mate, roared along with it.

"Take the next right," she said, her voice lost, distant.

I dragged in a steadying breath, forcing myself to focus. We had no idea where we were going and what we were about to walk into. Fuck, the thought of her doing this without me turned my insides to stone. As much as I craved the hunt, needed it, being by her side, making sure she was safe, surpassed it all.

I'd called Rook, and he was going to try to cover for me, but that wouldn't work forever. Ignoring an assignment wouldn't be tolerated, and sooner rather than later, I'd need to go for my own sanity.

"We're close," she said, gripping the door so tight it had to hurt. "There."

She pointed to an old garage. The faded sign above it hung on an angle. Sɪᴅ's Gᴀʀᴀɢᴇ. The building was covered in graffiti, and weeds had burst through the cracked concrete in front of a rusted roller door.

Magnolia continued to stare out the window, her big amber eyes wide. She bit her lower lip.

"Mags?"

"I don't want to go in there," she said, her voice barely more than a whisper.

Neither did I. What I wanted to do was drive away and never come back. To take Mags away from the danger that she was about to face, away from the mother and her fucking sadistic test of strength, away from everyone—to a place where no one or nothing could come between us. Where she'd be mine alone. Just her and me.

But I couldn't, because nothing was that easy, and the shit swirling around us was way more complicated than that—and I couldn't see a way through it.

"Let's go," she said and shoved her door open.

I grabbed a flashlight from the glove box and rounded the car as she strapped that massive fucking knife to her thigh. A knife she more than knew how to use, thanks to Asher.

Taking her hand, we did a quick scan of our surroundings, then moved through the shadows, walking down the narrow alley between the garage's concrete wall and the decrepit building beside it.

It was quiet back here. Silent.

"Can you scent anyone nearby?" she asked.

"No." But I tilted my head back and scented the air again just to be sure. *Fuck.*

"What is it?"

"Blood. A lot of it."

Magnolia stared up at me, her gorgeous eyes wide. "It's another murder, isn't it?"

She wasn't actually asking, she already knew. We didn't need to go in there to know what we were about to find, but we had to anyway. The door was locked, so I quickly picked it. As soon as it opened, the scent of death hit us, sweet and sickly.

I turned on the flashlight and shone it around the room. It was the old workshop and mainly empty besides a few tires and a car completely stripped of anything worth anything.

The scent grew stronger as we walked deeper into the wide space.

The door to what I assumed was the office, was ajar. Mags motioned to it before I could.

I walked ahead and pushed the door open, Mags right behind me. *Fuck.*

The room smelled like fear and decay, and the scene before us was something I'd never seen before. I tried to stop Magnolia from walking in, but she wasn't having it. This was her task, and no matter how gruesome this was, she had to see it for herself. I kept my arm around her middle, holding her close to me, and good thing because her knees gave out when she saw it for herself.

People killed for different reasons: a sense of justice, or a need for revenge, or to feel powerful. Some killed because it turned them on, giving them some kind of sadistic pleasure. Some just couldn't deny their predator's nature, no matter how hard they tried.

And some killed out of raw anger, or hatred. That's what we were looking at here.

Mags's hand flew to her mouth and she retched. "Who would do something like this?"

I didn't move any closer, not wanting to disturb the scene, and shone the flashlight at the dead witch. Their eyelids were swollen mostly shut, but I could tell there weren't any eyeballs behind them. Their mouth had been sewn shut, and I was pretty sure their teeth had been pulled out first. "Someone who wanted to make a point." I trailed the light lower. The face would be impossible to ID, since it was barely more than pulp. "Someone filled with rage." The witch wore blood-soaked trousers, and his shirt was in tatters on the floor. There was bloody wire dangling from the ceiling, where I could only assume their hands had been strung up above their head on an iron hook, before both arms had been cut off, and taken. "The witch is male." They'd been sliced open, their organs spilling out.

"A wallet," Mags said, motioning to the floor.

Leaving that behind was no mistake. "They want to make it easy for the body to be identified."

Mags grabbed an old rag from the desk and crouched to pick it up. She flicked it open. "Fuck." She looked back up at the body again. "That's Calvin Adler."

Well, fuck. "And with Willow missing—"

"They'll pin this on her as well," Mags said.

"He's from a prominent family. They have money, influence, power," I said, eyeing the scene, searching for any clues as to who would have done this. I stepped closer, carefully so I could check his back. "They carved Judgment into his flesh."

"Like the others," Mags said.

"He's missing his heart as well," I said and took a closer look. "Maybe some other organs too. And those slices around his shoulder, they're clean. His arms weren't just hacked off, care was taken there." It was the only part of him that showed any control.

"Why? What the hell does that mean?"

I did another quick search of the room. "We need information on the other killings, what was done, if any limbs or organs were taken."

Mags put the wallet back on the floor where she found it. "We need to get out of here. There might be cameras?"

"There aren't."

She looked up at me. "How do you know?"

Because I knew all the places around this city where you could go undetected. "This part of the city, people don't like to be watched. Most of the cameras have been destroyed."

She nodded, believing me, trusting me. I kept my arm around her middle, keeping her close as we backed out of the office. She was trembling hard against me. Mags was tough as hell and incredibly brave, but this horror show was too much for anyone.

She'd been trying so hard to keep it together, so when her legs gave out again and I held her up, I pressed my face in the crook of her neck, so she felt me right there, skin on skin. "I've got you. We're nearly out, just a little bit more."

She nodded again. "W-who would do this? W-what kind of a monster would torture someone like this?" Her breath hitched. "No one deserves to die this way. No one."

"I know," I said as I got her through the next door and finally back outside.

She sucked in fresh air and, getting her legs back under her, pulled out of my arms. Pacing away on shaky legs, she bent at the waist, her hands on her knees, and breathed deep. I stayed quiet, letting her get it together.

Finally, she looked up at me. "What he must have suffered. What they all must have suffered. Margot..." Tears sprung to her eyes, and she squeezed them shut, shaking her head as if she was trying to shake the images out of it. "Goddess, she must have been so scared."

I took a step toward her, but she straightened and took a step back. At times of high emotion especially, Mags couldn't tolerate touch, but I was usually the exception. "Mags..." I wanted to pull her back into my arms so fucking badly.

"What kind of a person can just...take someone's life like that, goddess, *enjoy* it, without remorse? How can they live with themselves? Who the hell do they think they are playing God? They don't get to choose. They don't have the fucking right."

My gut tightened, twisted. Would she see me the same way? A monster playing God? If she knew the things I'd done, that I wanted to do? What I needed to do to stay sane?

I'd lose her forever.

Yes, the circumstances were different. Very. But it still amounted to the same thing. Me taking lives and feeling zero remorse afterward. Feeling nothing but relief.

"We need to go," I said.

She let me take her hand, and I released a relieved breath. Touching her, feeling her warmth, the silky texture of her skin against mine, calmed me. She often sought out my touch as well, because it was the same for her. The reason for that was the same for both of us, even if she didn't know what that reason was.

But I did.

No, I couldn't make her mine, but as long as I had this, as long as I could hold her close, breathe in her scent, have her near, I'd be okay. It was ironic that it was her calming touch, her presence, that kept the violent need I constantly had for her swirling inside me, under control. Her touch made not being able to make her mine in truth bearable.

As long as I still had her, I'd be okay.

I just had to make sure she never gave up on me—that she never let go.

CHAPTER 12

Magnolia

Foxglove Funeral Home was owned by Ren's parents, and the only mortician the witches in Roxburgh used. If there was a magic-related death, they took care of it. The last thing we needed was to draw the attention of the human police.

Ren lived in a small apartment in the basement, and his parents had a house just down the street. Taking the steps, I opened the main door and we walked inside. Low classical music drifted out from hidden speakers, and it smelled of orchids, and the vanilla perfume Ren's mom, Sally, always wore.

She walked out of her office then and smiled brightly when she saw us. "It's so nice to see you both."

"Hi, Sally." Bram and I used to pop over often and hang with Ren if he wasn't at our place already, but not so much the last couple years. "Is Ren around?"

"He's in the basement." The phone started ringing. "Head on down," she said and rushed back to her office.

I hadn't seen Ren since the party at the clubhouse. He'd walked in with the female he'd left with earlier, after the mess with the council was over. We'd had to tell him Willow and the hounds had gone, that they'd had to leave him behind. The look on his face, before he'd shut all emotion down, had hurt to look at.

Bram opened the door for me and we took the stairs. Music drifted up, telling us exactly where Ren was. The mortuary door was open, and Ren was sliding one of the cold cabinets closed. I knocked.

He turned and his brows lifted. "Hey."

"You got a minute?"

"Sure." He was in jeans and a T-shirt and wore a black rubber apron over the top. "What's up?" He undid the apron, lifted it over his head and hung it up.

"I was hoping you could tell us about the murdered witches, they were brought here, right?"

He crossed his arms. "So it's true? You're hunting their murderer?"

"Yeah, and so far, we're hitting a bunch of dead ends."

Ren strode to the small desk in the corner, opened up the laptop, and tapped a few keys. "Dad was called to a house in Cicada Drive. He said the place was empty. No one had been living there."

"This was Clara Hope?"

"Yeah. The witches council had taken her down, but she'd been strung up with wire around her wrists, but only one arm." He turned to me, and the shutters came down, like something had switched off inside him. "I looked after her when she came in. The other arm had been removed, the cut clean, done with precision. It was odd. Some of the cuts were like that, done with purpose, with control. Like the one down her midsection, when they'd removed her internal organs. Her other injuries...yeah, not so much. Her mouth had been sewn shut as well."

I took a steadying breath, my stomach churning. "And Margot?"

Ren's eyes gentled. "The same. She was missing an arm, mouth sewn shut. Her eyes had been taken as well."

I forced myself to focus on why we were here and not let images of my friend like that overtake me. "Where was she found?"

"Like Clara, Margot was in a vacant house, but this one was a new build in some up-and-coming neighborhood."

"Anything else you can think of?"

He shook his head. "Sorry. That's all I've got."

"No, that's really helpful. Thanks, Ren." He slid his hands in his pockets, suddenly looking uncomfortable. I hated it, that he still had walls up between us and him.

"How you doing?" Bram asked him.

Ren met his gaze and something passed between them, a knowing. And I felt like crap for not thinking about how much Ren would be suffering with Willow gone, how she would be as well, being parted from him like this, especially after how hard Ren had to fight to find his way back to her.

Ren's gaze slid away. "Yeah, all good. Wills is safe, that's all I care about."

He was in pain, but there was a wall around him so thick and sure, I knew better than to try and comfort him. He didn't want it. I got the feeling Ren was more at home in his pain now, that the old Ren was buried so deep after what he went through two years ago, there was no pulling him back—that he was gone for good.

›)➤●《‹

Several hours later, Bram lay on my bed, feet crossed, one hand behind his head, scrolling through Nightscape for any information he could find on the victims. The social media app used mainly by witches and shifters was a good place to start. The victims' own pages could have information that might be useful.

I'd been searching on my laptop for the last two hours and hadn't found one fucking thing. No, I wasn't expecting to find a big red glowing arrow pointing to the killer, but I wasn't expecting a giant brick wall in front of me either. People were dying, horrifically, and I didn't know why, or where to even start.

Calvin's tortured body flashed through my mind, and I gripped the edge of the desk as a shudder moved through me. I'd barely slept last night. I'd been on Nightscape almost constantly since we got home, waiting for Calvin's death to be mentioned, but there still hadn't been a report that he'd been found. The comment section of posts about the other three victims, however, was full of speculation and gossip about who did it and the condition of the bodies.

I'd seriously considered sending in an anonymous tip about Calvin, several times, because I couldn't stand the thought of him there like that, all alone. He was dead, the pain was over, but I didn't care. If it were someone I loved in that room? I shuddered again.

His family had to be worried.

In the end, I hadn't, because all fingers would point to Willow and Isaac would leak it to the press making everything worse for her, because that's the kind of asshole he was. It'd be splashed all over Nightscape within hours.

I forced the images from my mind and looked at Bram again, and the inferno died down to embers. Calm instantly moving through me.

I'd had him home with me almost another full day, and I was too scared to mention it in case I jinxed it. I let my gaze slide over his long, lean body.

Though lately he'd filled out. His biceps and thighs were thicker, the skin on his hands rougher. My gaze slid up to the side of his head, to the markings inked there. "Did Rook do the new ink?" Rook was a talented tattoo artist and usually did all the work for their people.

"Yeah," he said without looking up, but I didn't miss how his entire body kind of paused at my question.

"Do you ever think you'll be able to tell me what those lines mean?" I shouldn't push, but this was my best friend. We shared basically everything, or at least we used to.

He lowered his phone, his obsidian gaze moving over me. "I don't know."

Not a definite no. "Are there any circumstances at all, where you would be able to tell me?"

He stared at me for long seconds, a look in his eyes that made my belly feel weird, warm. "Yeah," he finally said.

My mind raced. I really wasn't expecting him to say yes. "About the new ink, or everything?"

His gaze dipped to my mouth, then back, and he licked his lips. It was unconscious, I was sure, but something about it, about the look in his eyes made the warmth in my belly swirl. "Everything."

My pulse sped up as I stared down at him. Goddess, that tension was back, and it was growing thicker by the second. My gaze went to his perfect lips all on their own, and the swirls intensified. This was Bram, my best friend, my belly shouldn't be swirling. But it was, and it wasn't the first time. It also wasn't the first time I'd thought about his lips, or how they'd feel against mine—what he'd taste like.

Other things...

I shoved those thoughts back down as deep as I could. I'd never risk ruining what we had by going there. I'd never risk losing my best friend because I wanted to appease my curiosity. And even if in some alternate reality he'd want me that way as well, it was pointless because I was broken. The idea of being intimate with anyone, even Bram, sent actual terror through me.

I cleared my throat. "But you can't tell me what those circumstances are?"

His gaze didn't leave mine. "No."

The finality of it wasn't just in the word itself, but his tone. And right then he was impossible to read. "How do you feel about that?" I asked.

"How I feel is irrelevant. The situation is what it is," he said, purposely keeping his expression blank.

Frustration filled me. Fine, anger. "That's a fucking cop-out. I'm starting to get the feeling you're glad you can't tell me your secrets, and that even if you could, you wouldn't want to."

He said nothing.

"How do you feel about it, Bram?" I asked again.

His gaze slid from mine to the window, out to the late-afternoon sky. He was quiet so long I didn't think he was going to answer my question. But then he looked at me again, and the weight in his gaze had me freezing in place.

"It's not an easy question to answer for a lot reasons," he said. "But you're right, there are things...things I'm glad you don't know." He licked his lips again and released a ragged breath. "But if it were possible, if things were...different. If there were certain guarantees, I would want you to know. I'd want you to know all of it."

Certain guarantees? What did that even mean? But there was no point asking because he couldn't tell me, and now I felt even more frustrated than before. I tore my gaze from his and turned back to my laptop. His gaze stayed on me. I felt it. He was waiting for me to say more, but there was nothing else to be said.

Not sure what else to do, I typed all four of the victims' names into the search bar and hit enter. Links to social media popped up, a website for one of Calvin's businesses. An article here and there. I clicked to the next page of results and saw a hit for Roxburgh High School. I clicked on it and scanned an article from the school paper. It was from twelve years ago, naming the prom committee, and three of the victims were named in the article. Calvin Adler and his cousin Katana and the first victim, Clara Hope. "I might've found something." The other members were Chase Golden, Jenna Barlow, and Robert Hazark. Robert was now married to Jenna—and he was also Margot's stepbrother.

Bram got up and read the article over my shoulder. "Can you find anything else?"

I tried, but nothing more came up. "Do you think we'd have better luck at the school?"

"Only one way to find out. We'll go when it gets dark."

"Nothing like a little breaking and entering to top off the day," I said and yawned.

Bram took my hand. "First, you need sleep."

I protested but then gave up and let him tug me from my chair and lead me to the bed. "I have too much to do."

"You won't be any use if you're exhausted," he said, then pulled me down onto the bed with him.

He tucked me in close. "Sleep. I'll wake you when it's time to go."

He was right. I needed sleep or I'd be a liability if something went wrong tonight. "Promise you'll wake me?"

His hand slid up and down my back. "Promise."

›)❯❯◑⟨⟨‹

Bram

Mags threw her leg over my hip, her hand sliding low on my stomach.

I squeezed my eyes closed.

Fuck. This was agony. The kind that hurt but you craved it anyway.

I looked down at her. She was still asleep, and I couldn't bring myself to wake her. Thankfully, there was still plenty of time before we'd have to leave. I brushed her hair back from her face. Better to go in the middle of the night, anyway.

I'd always preferred the night—not a crow thing, a me thing. I liked the quiet and calm during those hours. I never used to talk much, still didn't, unless it was with Magnolia. I didn't like people looking at me, didn't like being the center of attention.

The only person I wanted noticing me was her.

Mags made a breathy little sound, and my cock grew harder. This wasn't new. When Mags slept beside me, I wanted her. I always wanted her. Usually, though, I could control my shit. I could will my dick down. The last thing I wanted was to make things even weirder between us. And Mags waking up and accidentally brushing up against my hard cock would definitely make things weirder. The way she'd looked at me earlier, yeah, she definitely felt the growing tension between us. I just didn't know what she thought it meant or what would happen when it grew more intense, because it would, it had to. There would be a breaking point.

And I was terrified that when that day came, the truth would come out, and we'd never be the same again—or worse, Mags would withdraw, that she'd pull away from me. My fucking chest hurt even thinking about it.

She curled into me more firmly, and the warmth of her little body, the press of her full curves plastered to my front, had me gasping for fucking air. There was no willing my erection away, not this time.

Fuck. I needed a minute.

Carefully, I slid a pillow between us, so she was resting on it and not me, then eased from the bed. My gaze moved over her. So fucking gorgeous. Every inch of her, inside and out. The grip in my lower gut tightened and my hands fucking shook from how much I wanted to get back in that bed, how much I wanted to touch her.

How much I wanted her to touch me in return.

"Fuck," I muttered and forced myself to leave the room. I needed to get out of there, just for a minute, just to get myself under control.

The house was silent, everyone asleep, so I took the stairs, walked out the back door and across to my tree house, then flew up to the deck. I kept walking, through the living room, past the bed, and into the bathroom. I needed to cool the fuck off before I went back into her bedroom.

Stripping off, I turned on the shower and stepped in. It was hot tonight, and the cool water felt good on my overheated skin, but it did nothing to ease the ache burning through me. I tried to stop myself from going there, from letting thoughts of Mags and me, of us, doing things that we never could, from filling my mind. It was dangerous, those thoughts, but tonight I was weak, my control for shit. Especially when her warm curves were still imprinted on my flesh, as if she were right there with me.

I slapped my hands against the tiled wall and let the water run down my back as images flooded my mind. When I was younger, I'd been shy, quiet. I'd always been that way. I met Mags when I was sixteen, the freaky, skinny kid with the scary, black eyes. She hadn't been scared, though, she hadn't shied away or flinched when she met my gaze like everyone else, like other girls who weren't from our village. Not that I'd been interested in chasing females back then. I'd never touched a girl, never kissed one, never fucked one, and I still hadn't because Magnolia was it for me, whether she was mine in truth or not. And she always would be. No matter what happened between us, that was a truth that would never change.

Images of Mags and me in her bed filled my head, of her waking beside me, her big amber eyes sleepy and soft like they always were in the morning. And instead of smiling up at me, then resting her head on my chest like she usually did, I cupped the side of her beautiful face with one hand and fisted her hair with the other, then tilting her head back, I took her mouth, owning it. Because it was mine, she was mine. Kissing her deep and hard, washing away Clayton's hateful kiss and Relic's fucking kiss as well, making her taste all the hunger inside me, all the longing and pain and heat that blazed hot inside me, the fire for her that had never gone out since the day I met her.

Squeezing my eyes tight, I ran a hand down my chest, imagining it was hers, over my abs, then curled my fingers around my cock, gripping it tight.

)))·◎·(((

Magnolia

108

. . .

I blinked into the dark room. The only sound was rain hitting the roof. My hand shot out, searching for Bram, but the bed was empty.

Panic filled me instantly, and I threw back the covers, shoved on my shoes, snatched up my phone, and rushed down the stairs to the kitchen.

It was 1:00 a.m. He wouldn't leave without saying goodbye. He wouldn't. Still, the panicky feeling grew as I grabbed one of the raincoats by the door, then slipped out to the backyard.

I jogged across the soggy grass to the tree house and quickly scaled the ladder.

"Bram?" I called as I shoved open the door.

The rain was coming down harder now, loud against the tin roof, and if he'd replied, I hadn't heard him. I strode through the living room and into the dark bedroom. The bed was empty, but the bathroom door was open and light spilled out. I didn't hear the shower running until it was too late.

A low moan echoed off the tiles, and I spun around.

And froze.

Get out of there, now, my mind screamed, but I couldn't move. My feet were cemented in place, and I couldn't look away. My mouth went dry, and my heart hammered in my chest.

Bram stood behind the glass, one forearm braced against the tiles, his head pressed against it, his eyes screwed shut. Muted light danced over his naked body, highlighting the intricate tattoos that covered his back and arms, and showcased every muscle, every ridge, every vein and tendon— his other big, rough-skinned hand was wrapped around the impossibly hard length of his cock.

He bit his lip, as though he was trying to hold back, but another groan escaped as he stroked himself hard and fast.

My breasts felt tight all of a sudden, my nipples hardening. *Walk away. Get the hell out of here!*

"Baby," he said hungrily yet tenderly, voice full of grit. "Fuck me."

A throb started between my thighs, the muscles deep inside contracting with a violent pulse of need at the rawness of his words. My response was so strong and unexpected, I had to bite back a moan of my own.

I retreated several steps, deeper into the shadowed room, because I still couldn't make myself leave.

His breathing was choppy, broken, and as he continued to stroke, each breath turned into a desperate, gasping sound, low and pained, almost like a sob.

The sound had my heart clenching behind my ribs. Who was he imagining behind those tightly closed eyes? Who was he calling baby in that hungry voice? Did he wish she were here? Did he wish he was fucking her in that shower right now? This was so wrong, but jealously wrapped its boney fingers around my throat, the choke hold so tight I barely stopped myself from storming into the bathroom and demanding answers.

Bram hissed through gritted teeth, then with a growl, he came. And, oh god, the sounds he made lifted goose bumps all over my skin.

He slumped against the tiles, panting hard.

I backed up before he opened his eyes, running silently across the living room and out the door, closing it as quietly as I could, then rushed down the ladder so fast I almost slipped and fell but somehow managed to not land on my ass, and sprinted back to the house. I quickly hung up the jacket inside the door and raced back to my room, kicked off my shoes, and dove into bed, slamming my eyes closed.

I lay there, heart racing, mind spinning, waiting for him to come back, and I'd barely calmed myself down when I heard the door open and close, followed by his light tread on the stairs.

He tapped on the door. "Mags?"

I yawned, stretching as the door opened, giving my best impression of someone still sleepy when I was so freaking wide awake it wasn't funny. "Hey." I looked around, trying to appear confused. "Did you go some-where?" I was not a good actor, but this was the performance of my life and I had to deliver, because he could never know I saw him. Never.

His hair was damp, and he'd tied it back again. His gaze moved over me, an odd look on his face. "We still had time, and you needed the sleep, so I took a shower."

Images of what he'd done in that shower slammed into my mind. Christ, it was burned into the back of my eyes for all eternity. "Oh, right." My mouth was dry, and I had to swallow several times. "I guess we should get going, then."

"Yeah." He frowned a little, still with that odd look on his face.

I shoved back the covers and grabbed my shoes. They were muddy and wet. I quickly shoved them on before he could see.

"You'll need a jacket, it's raining out," he said, his voice going deeper, rougher.

I tucked my hair behind my ear, my very damp hair, then inwardly cringed. I couldn't meet his stare that I felt burning into the top of my head as I did up my laces, then grabbed a jacket from my closet. "Ready."

He didn't say anything about the hair or the shoes, but he had to have noticed. How could he not? Why did I go looking for him? Why couldn't I have just stayed in my damn bed?

And how the hell would I get through the rest of the night after what I saw?

I wasn't sure I'd ever be the same again.

CHAPTER 13

Magnolia

THE SCHOOL LOOMED AHEAD. The main building and the dilapidated chapel behind it were *old*. Both were made from large slabs of gray stone and had this whole gothic vibe going on, and at night, shrouded in shadow, the campus looked seriously foreboding.

"I never thought I'd come back here," I said as we got out of the car. There was a big sign on the side of the building announcing the upcoming prom, the theme was Starry Night. I snorted.

Bram walked around and stood beside me, slinging an arm around my shoulders. "Do you wish you'd gone to yours?"

"Not even a little bit."

He scowled at the huge building. "This place is a fucking shithole."

"That it is." I gave him a nudge. "I know you, Talon, and Rook went to the village school, what about Payne?"

"Yeah, him too."

"Why? I know your people like to keep to themselves, but that can't be the only reason?"

He glanced down at me. "Crows can be volatile when they're young. There are few things more dangerous than an adolescent crow pumped up on hormones and ruled by their hunting instincts. Safer to keep us home where we can be kept in line." He took my hand and started toward the building.

"Hunting?"

He didn't answer.

The lightbulb went on. "Oh...like that, was it?" I said and chuckled, even as that unwanted jealousy rushed back.

"Like what?"

"Hormonal and on the hunt? You're kept home so you don't break hearts and knock up half the city," I said and was glad it was dark when my face heated for some stupid reason. *You just saw him jerk off, that's the freaking reason.* "I can see your brothers doing that as teenagers...you, not so much."

I smiled, joking around, trying to keep things light, but he didn't laugh or even smile.

"I was never really interested in any of that, and once I found my best friend, nothing and no one else mattered," he said.

I swallowed hard. He had to be joking. "And before we found each other? Did you go out with anyone at your village?" What the hell was I doing? We had an unspoken rule that we didn't ask each other about this stuff. Everything else, yes. Sex and romantic relationships, never. I didn't know why or when we both decided that was how it would be, but we'd been avoiding this conversation for six years, and *now* I decide to bring it up and break all the rules?

But then so much between us had already changed. Maybe that rule didn't apply anymore. Maybe it shouldn't. Neither of us were kids anymore.

His expression told me he was thinking the same thing, and he waited, I assumed for me to take it back or change the subject. I didn't.

"No one at the village," he finally said, surprising me as he led me around the side of the main building.

An image of him in the shower flashed unbidden through my mind. *Baby.* His throaty voice igniting invisible sparks across my skin.

That swirly sensation curled low in my belly again. "Are you dating anyone?" I blurted, unable to hold it in. We spent enough time apart, it was definitely possible.

His step faltered, then he glanced over at me. "No." He didn't elaborate, and we both went quiet. I thought that was the end of the conversation, then he said, "Are you?"

I shook my head, trying to subtly rub my clammy hands on the front of my jeans. "No. Have you...ever dated anyone?" My heart was racing. Yes, we'd always been in each other's pockets, but we'd had hours apart while I was at school. The idea of sharing him with someone else, anyone else— honestly, I hated it. It was selfish, but I wanted him all to myself.

I couldn't expect him to be alone forever, though, and like Payne had so bluntly said, eventually, Bram would meet someone.

"No," he said, startling me.

"No?" He couldn't mean it. "No one at all?"

He shook his head as he walked to one of the side doors. It was darker around here, but we both had the hoods of our jackets up in case anyone saw us, or if there were security cameras around.

"You?" he asked as he quickly picked the lock.

I swallowed several times. "No."

We walked into the dark building, and Bram pulled a small flashlight from his pocket, shining it up at the alarm system. We only had a few minutes. I quickly sliced an X into my palm and held it up in front of the control panel. I'd learned the spell from Iris, who'd learned it from a witch who frequented a bar she used to work in. It was a simple but seriously effective bit of blood magic.

The alarm instantly shut down, along with any cameras inside the building.

Bram produced a small jar of Else's balm and grabbed my hand. He swiped some over it, then covered it with a large Band-Aid. He carried them with him, always. "Thanks."

He took my other hand and led the way down the wide hall. "Where are we going? Office?"

"Library. This way." I took the next right.

"Where was your locker?" Bram asked.

"A couple corridors over. Why?"

He shrugged. "Trying to imagine you here, walking these halls." We passed a group of pictures. Sports teams. Pride of place, of course. His jaw tightened. "Being ogled by all these asshole jocks, no doubt."

I laughed. "Ah, nope. No one was looking at me."

His nostrils flared, and he shook his head. "The little goth girl, so fucking untouchable, putting out all those come-closer-and-die vibes? All they wanted to do was get closer." He scowled harder. "They were looking at you, all right."

His words stunned me. "You're wrong. They hated me. Pretty much everyone hated me when I went here."

"You scared them because you never have and never will play by the rules. And you never conformed or tried to fit in. They wanted you, they just didn't have the balls to take their shot."

Where was this coming from? "You're wrong," I said again. "I was invisible." And that's the way I liked it.

"I'm not, and you weren't. I guarantee, every boy here was one hundred percent aware of your presence in this school."

My heart did a little flip. "How can you be so sure?"

Bram glanced at me as we approached the library door. "Because you are fucking gorgeous, Magnolia."

He pushed the library door open, leading the way, while I tried to freaking breathe again. He'd never said that to me before. Not ever. "Are you actually trying to say that every male in existence wants me?"

"Yes."

Our eyes locked for a moment, and we both went still...and utterly silent. He was a male who existed, right? Was he including himself in that bold statement? He didn't look away, didn't say a damn thing.

My heart kicked in my chest, and I forced a laugh. "Well, you're my best friend, so you're biased." I pointed to the other side of the room. "The yearbooks are over here." I tried to get my racing heart back under control as we strode over.

Bram didn't respond but kept his fingers firmly wrapped around mine. There was no reason for us to be holding hands, but we always did. If we were together, we were touching or sitting or standing close. I'd never thought too hard about it. I'd assumed all witches and familiars were like that, were as close as us, but over the years, I learned that wasn't the case. It was an *us* thing. Why was I thinking about this now? And why was I so aware of the way the rough skin of his palm felt against mine.

"Where did you sit when you came in here?" he asked.

I'd loved the library. I liked books, and it was always peaceful in here. No one bothered you. "Over there," I said, pointing to a table on the other side of the room, an area that no one liked but me because the lighting wasn't as good and you couldn't see who came and went from my little dark corner. I hadn't cared who came and went.

"Yeah, this scent is familiar. You used to smell like this place when I'd meet you after school."

I laughed. "What can I say...I spent a lot of time here."

He flashed me a grin. "While I waited outside, counting down the seconds for you to finish."

"That was the worst part, being away from you." We'd texted constantly, but I'd felt like a part of me was missing for six hours a day.

"It was fucking torture," he said as I led him between the shelves.

The tone of his voice lifted goose bumps all over me. "You were always right outside the gates waiting, and I was always desperate to get out of here to see you." I chuckled. "Like we'd been away from each other for weeks not hours." I glanced at him. "All the girls thought you were my boyfriend." Why the hell had I told him that?

His throat worked as he stared up at the row of yearbooks in front of us. "The boys as well," he said with certainty.

I lifted our linked hands. "Not surprising. No wonder no one asked me to prom," I said, laughing again, but it sounded strained.

His lips curled, but it wasn't a smile—there was no humor, the look on his face was menacing as fuck, the same grin I'd seen when we were in the demon neighborhood. "Probably a good thing," he said, obsidian eyes somehow darkening.

"Oh?" Again, I was trying to inject lightness into the conversation, because something dark and heavy had fallen around us, and it was definitely coming from Bram. "I'm guessing, if any of them had hurt me, you would've kicked their asses?"

He shook his head. "If anyone hurts you, or even thinks about it, I'll kill them."

Like he had two and a half years ago, when Brody held a knife to my throat. Bram had shifted into his shadow form, materialized behind Brody, and viciously broken his neck. I shoved the memory of that awful fucking day from my mind. "Well, lucky for you, you don't have to anymore. Thanks to Asher's excellent tutelage, I can do it myself."

He turned back to the shelf. He didn't like that.

"I'll always need you, B, you know that, right?"

He nodded, but it wasn't very convincing, and slid a couple books from the shelf. "You check these." He passed them to me and grabbed more for himself.

We sat on the floor and started flipping through the books.

I got through the first one, shoved it aside and grabbed the next. I stopped at a picture of the kids who'd written for the school newspaper. Willow stood in the back. I'd forgotten she'd done that. She'd worked on the paper for a few years. Her story ideas were regularly shot down because, more often than not, they were way too controversial. It used to piss her off.

Bram slid his book my way and pointed at a picture. "Prom committee."

I looked over the picture. "All the victims are either in that picture or related to one of them." I pointed to Robert Hazark standing to the side, his arm around Jenna's shoulders. They'd married seven years ago. "Margot's stepbrother. Clara Hope is the one holding Chase Golden's hand." All of them were the rich kids, the ones with influential families. "Calvin and Katana Adler." They stood beside each other in the back. I looked at Bram. "Could this really be what links them? There has to be something else."

"What's your gut telling you?" he asked, surprising me. "Close your eyes."

I didn't do this as much anymore. I'd stopped listening to my inner voice, to my instincts. But I did as he said and quieted my mind, letting my instincts guide me. Encouraging them to rise from below all the other noise, all the crap floating around in my head. I opened my eyes and stared down at the picture again. "My gut is telling me this is definitely a lead." I studied their faces. "Do you think one of them is the killer?"

Bram looked down as well. "Possibly."

I felt nauseous.

"But then why would they try to pin the murders on Willow?" he said.

I had no clue, and I didn't know how much time I had left to find out. There was only one person I could think of who'd want to frame Willow. Who hated her beyond reason.

"What is it?" Bram asked.

"What about Isaac?"

His expression darkened. "You think he could have something to do with this?"

"At this stage, it's just a wild hunch." I pulled my phone out. "But the way he hates Wills... He'd love to destroy her. And they've had recent issues with him trying to buy the stores along her block." I did a quick search. "The real estate company he heads is called Dark Star Investments." The website popped up, and I clicked the "our team" section. There was a picture of Isaac, the founder and CEO, and at the bottom of the page was a list of the company's directors/shareholders. Robert Hazark, Chase Golden, Clara Hope, Calvin Adler, and Maria Watson were listed. All but Isaac and Maria had been on the prom committee. "Look at this." Isaac was a very busy boy. The council wasn't a full-time position and most of the councilors had other employment, businesses or whatever, but it did take up a lot of their time and energy—looked like Isaac had some friends to help him out.

Bram looked down at it. "What are you thinking?"

"Something insane," I said.

"Like Isaac killing off his own shareholders to make it look like Willow? Like she's going after them for coming for her?" he said.

That's exactly what I was thinking. "Come on." I put away all the books except the two with the pictures we'd found. Those I shoved in my bag. Then I strode to the librarian's desk and jiggled the mouse, waking up the computer.

Bram moved to stand behind me. "What're you looking for?"

"Copies of the school newspaper during the time Wills was working on it. They must have it all on file." A space to enter a password popped up on the screen. "Dammit." I turned to Bram. "You think Talon could hack into the school system?"

"Yeah, easily."

"Do you think he would if I asked?" Talon wasn't outwardly hostile to me, but I wasn't sure he'd be willing to do me any favors.

"He'll do it," Bram said, the "I'll make sure of it" went unsaid.

We left the way we came, taking the long halls back to the exit. I reactivated the security system, Bram locked the door after us, and I tugged up my hood before we jogged across the grounds and back to the car.

When we got home, I was too wired to sleep, and the nap I'd had earlier wasn't helping. We strode across the yard to the tree house, and Bram dragged off his shirt, scooped me into his arms, then flew us up to the deck. I plonked down on the couch when we got inside, pulling a yearbook out of my bag to flick through it.

Bram turned on music. It was low and moody, the way he liked it, then he grabbed a couple drinks from the kitchenette and put one down in front of me. "How much time do you think we have to solve this thing?" he asked.

Nerves darted through me. "I don't know." I lifted my shirt, angling my body so he could see the vines created by the mother. "Any change?" I'd looked at them several times a day since she'd impaled my torso with her monster-sized serpent fangs, and so far, so good.

He reached out, brushing my skin with his fingertips, and I barely suppressed my shiver.

"I don't think so," he said, studying them intently.

I dropped my shirt. "At least that's something."

Bram sat and quietly sipped his drink while I got back to flipping through the yearbook. The same people had been on the prom committee for two years in a row, going by the pictures in both books, and there were other pictures of them together as well. "They were friends outside the committee," I said and flipped the page. There were pictures from the prom itself, and several members of the group were together, laughing, dancing, and a few other candid pics around the school as well.

I sat forward. "Check this out." Isaac and Maria Watson had gone to prom at Roxburgh High. Isaac was beside Clara, and Maria had her head on Chase's shoulder. I studied their faces. "They've all been friends since they were teenagers."

Bram slid his arm along the back of the couch behind me and took a look. "And somewhere along the line they pissed off the wrong person?"

"Yeah, or they already had a complete psycho in their midst." I studied their faces. They looked close, really close. Isaac was a prick, but would he murder people who were so obviously his good friends to get back at my sister? I wasn't so sure—but then people were capable of a lot of horrible things with the right motivation.

Willow defeating his brother, Elmer, and causing their coven to lose the mothers gifts was enough to send someone like Isaac over the edge, but then Warrick killing Elmer defending Willow—that was some seriously strong motivation right there.

Bram studied the prom pictures. "You sure you weren't disappointed you didn't go?" he asked, surprising me. I'd asked Bram if he'd go with me my last year of school, and the look on his face had been answer enough.

"I honestly don't think about it, like at all." We hadn't talked like this for so long, and these last couple of days, having him here, had been awesome, but different—definitely not how things had been before. It was like we were trying to establish our new normal, because there was no going back to the way we used to be. We'd both been through some things, had been forced to grow up a lot, and had too many secrets.

"I should have taken you," he said, glancing over at me.

"Neither of us like people. We would've hated it." I took his hand, linking our fingers. "I don't feel like I missed out. If I remember correctly, we had our own prom. We hung out up here, eating pizza and listening to music."

The song changed, and he stood suddenly, tugging me to my feet.

"What are you doing?" I said, laughing as he pulled me into his arms.

"What I should've done that night. If we were having our own prom, we should've danced," he said, holding me close.

I chuckled and wrapped my arms around him as well, resting my head against his chest. "I much prefer this prom."

"Me too," he said low, his voice rumbling through his chest.

Suddenly I became highly aware of the way he felt pressed up against me. We stood close, slept close, but we'd never done this. "Have you ever danced like this before?" Today was the day I asked *all* the questions apparently. He said he hadn't dated, but it didn't mean he'd never danced with anyone. He went to The Bank...and The Vault, it was highly probable he had.

"No," he said.

I lifted my head, looking up at him, and grinned. "Is it everything you hoped it would be?"

His lips curled up. "And so much more."

We were just being Bram and Mags, but there was something else between us, something new—that tension was back. I forced myself to ignore it and hung on tight.

Goddess, he was everything to me. *Everything.* What would I ever do without him? "What happens when you meet someone?" I said, the words, Payne's words, yanked from me by an invisible force. They were pulled from a place of fear, so much fear that one day I would eventually lose him, that what we had couldn't last forever. Over time things changed for everyone, and that included the relationship between a witch and their familiar. We were proof of that.

His expression was utterly unreadable. "Meet someone?"

"Your mate," I choked out, each word a spike in my throat.

Something that looked a lot like pain filled his eyes. "I'm not leaving you, Mags. Not ever."

"You deserve to be happy." My throat grew tight. "When I went to Clayton...when I fucked everything up...I didn't just hurt my family, I hurt you. I kept what I was doing a secret, and when you found out, you stuck by me, you never tried to make me feel shame or guilt, you were there, like you always have been."

"You did nothing to be ashamed of. Fuck, Mags, you were trying to help your sister. We all fuck up. We all make mistakes." His expression hardened. "You've more than paid the price for it."

"I just... I want you to know when I was with him..." Bile churned in my gut, and my forearm burned, the phantom ache there flaring up. "While I was being held by him—"

"You don't need to talk about it," he said, his eyes dancing with undiluted fury.

If Warrick hadn't killed Clayton that day at the cemetery, Bram would have hunted him down and torn him to pieces. I knew that with complete certainty.

I'd tried to talk to him about it several times, what happened while I was with that monster, but it'd always been too hard, the memories too painful. He knew about the emotional torture, the images Clayton had projected into my mind that had almost driven me insane, but not the rest. My sisters did, I'd recently shared it with them one night when we were all together, but talking to Bram about this stuff had been way too hard.

I swallowed several times. The conversation was well overdue. "I knew I'd made a mistake the moment I got to his place." My mind took me back there now. "I'd tried to make the same deal as Willow, a marriage of convenience, one where he'd gain access to our cemetery, and in return, he'd help find a cure for Rose." I shook my head, remembering the moment I realized I was in trouble. "I'd been so fucking naïve. I'd thought he was handsome. I'd followed him on Nightscape like all the other starry-eyed little idiots. I knew it was Willow he truly wanted, and I was okay with that. I just wanted to help Rose, to be the hero, and sacrificing myself to some handsome rich guy didn't seem such a hardship. It wasn't real, it'd be for show. I could marry Clayton and go back to my life. But he insisted on a proper marriage, and when I refused, everything went...wrong."

"Mags..." Bram growled out, his expression stark.

I pushed on. "He grabbed me, he put his mouth on me. I tried to fight him off, but he...he was too strong."

Bram flinched.

"He didn't rape me," I said quickly. "But he...he touched me. He stripped me naked and made me stand in front of him, then he told me how ugly I was. How my scars were hideous and no male would ever want me. He used his magic to make me, to make me feel every word, every insult like it was a physical touch, a physical blow, until it was so bad I...I begged him to kill me—"

Bram snarled in rage. "If I'd had the chance, what you saw in that garage last night would be fucking child's play to what I would've done to that piece of shit. I would have made him scream until his vocal cords gave out, until they bled."

I stared up at him, but not in shock. I knew Bram was capable of it, I'd always known it. Yes, a darkness surrounded my crow, I'd felt it the day we met. I hadn't needed Agatheena to tell me.

His black eyes burned down at me. "Does that scare you?"

"No." Nothing Bram could do or say could ever scare me.

"Because I'd do it, I'd fucking destroy anyone who hurt you. I know you can fight. I know how fucking strong you are, but I still would, because I was born to protect you, because I need that. I'd need to do that for both of us."

His words were a vow, and I believed every one of them. If I'd known what I did now, if I'd had my spell book and my potions, Clayton wouldn't have gotten the chance to lay a hand on me. "I didn't tell you that to hurt you or upset you. I told you that because, as time goes by, you might want to move on. You might find a female, and I don't want you to miss your chance for happiness. I don't want you to stay here with me out of duty or pity."

He searched my gaze, his eyes filled with so much rage and pain. "What if it's you who finds someone else?"

"That's the thing, that's what I'm trying to tell you...that will never happen. Clayton, he...broke something inside me that day. The magic he used, the things he did and said, he shattered something inside me. I don't want to be touched that way, not ever again. I don't want to be claimed. I don't want to have to explain my ugly scars to someone else, or have them look at me with disgust. I don't want a mate." I gave him a shaky smile, because this night had taken a turn I hadn't expected it to. I rubbed at my forearm again, trying to wipe Clayton's touch away, then forced a grin. "I'm going to die a virgin, and I'm okay with that."

Bram covered my hand still rubbing at the phantom pain under my skin and gently lifted it away, not missing it. Never missing anything. "He's not here, Mags," he said fiercely. "He can't fucking hurt you anymore."

My lips trembled. "Bram..."

He took my face in his hands, and they were trembling. "You need to listen to me, and you need to hear what I'm saying. You, Magnolia Thorn-heart, are so fucking beautiful, inside and out. There is not one part of you that's ugly. Any male would be lucky to have you, even if none will ever deserve you." He swiped his thumb over my cheek, and I realized I was crying. "I don't know what will happen in the future, but I do know nothing and no one will ever be more important, will ever mean more to me than you. And if you want to stay right here, you and me hanging out in this tree house for the rest of our lives, and that's all you want, I'm here. We can sit in this room, listening to music until we're old as fuck." He pressed his lips to my forehead. "Maggie, if that's what you want, I'll happily die a virgin right alongside you."

CHAPTER 14

Bram

MAGNOLIA HAD FINALLY PASSED out exhausted, and I'd sat beside her, so full of rage—rage with nowhere to go, and no one to work it out on—that I was close to losing my fucking mind.

I knew that piece-of-shit Clayton had touched her. I'd known more had happened than what she'd told me, and now that she'd shared the truth? I didn't know what to do with it because that motherfucker was already a corpse.

I don't want to be touched that way, not ever again. I don't want to be claimed.

I don't want a mate.

Her words sliced me down the middle a second time. She meant what she'd said, but she'd also said them standing in my arms, pressed so tight against me, nothing separated us.

How could she not see it? How could she not feel this thing between us? Every day our connection grew stronger, more volatile. I shoved my fingers through my hair and tried to calm the hell down. How could she think I'd ever leave? That anything on this earth could tempt me away from her? I could handle a lifetime of wanting her, of never having her the way I desperately needed her—as long as she was right here, with me.

But something had to give, and it would, whether I fought the truth of what we were to each other or not, and I was terrified of what would happen when that day came.

The living room door opened, and Payne walked in without knocking.

I scowled at him.

His gaze slid to Mags tucked against me, her head on my chest, and his jaw tightened.

"You ever knock?" I said low.

"Not like there's anything to walk in on, baby bro," he said, eyes hard. "So what? You just sit there awake and play mattress while the princess sleeps?"

"What do you want?" I asked, trying to keep my voice down.

Payne crossed his arms. "Fun time's over. You're needed."

"I'm needed here."

"That's not a choice you get to make, and you know it."

My fingers curled into a fist. Not now. I couldn't go now. "She needs me."

"I don't give one single fuck. You'll be no good to her if you don't take care of yourself. You need this. I can tell just looking at you."

I hated that he was right, especially after what Magnolia told me, but I couldn't leave her. "I'm not going anywhere."

Mags stirred and groggily opened her eyes. "What's going on?" She lifted her head, then she spotted Payne.

"Bram's needed elsewhere," my brother said to her.

"And I said I'm not going," I fired back.

Her fingers curled around my bicep, drawing my attention back to her. "You need to go."

"Mags—"

"It's okay. I'll be okay." She looked back at Payne. "He'll get in trouble if he doesn't go, right?"

Payne's gaze slid from her to me and back, and he nodded. I would, but not the kind of trouble she thought.

She gave my arm another squeeze. "You have to go."

I stared down at her, and the look in her eyes was a gut punch. She wanted me here, needed me, but she was letting me go anyway, putting me first. The darkness swirled inside me, a wild storm that needed release. I wanted to stay, but Payne was right, I needed this as well, badly. I tucked her hair behind her ear. "I'm sorry."

"It's okay, B. Go do what you have to, then come home," she said, her voice still husky from sleep.

I couldn't bring myself to let her go. "I'll be back as fast as I can."

She nodded and eased off my chest, sitting back, doing the hard part for me. "I'll see you when you get back."

I stood and followed Payne to the door, then turned before I walked through. My stomach was in knots, but I couldn't work out what I was feeling. All I knew was something about this moment felt...final. I couldn't explain it. There was a voice in my head saying that once I walked out this door, for better or worse, everything would change, that nothing would ever be the same again.

I took her in, the way she looked in that moment, locking it away in my mind. "Promise me you'll stay safe while I'm gone."

She pulled her knees up, wrapping her arms around herself. "I promise. Now I want the same from you."

"Promise," I rasped.

I shut the door and shifted, then flew into the night sky.

And even though I wanted to go back to her as soon as I'd left—there was also no stopping the dark excitement that filled me.

Time to hunt.

›)〉●((‹

Magnolia

I tapped the steering wheel and checked out the massive house in front of me.

It'd been thirty-six hours since Bram left. Thirty-six long freaking hours. He'd texted once this morning to check on me, but nothing since.

I couldn't just wait around and do nothing, so I'd spent the day doing more research on the prom committee. They still had a tight connection socially and in business, and not just Dark Star Investments. I looked down at the open yearbook on my passenger seat, at their smiling faces in their prom picture, and back up at the massive house in front of me.

It belonged to Robert and Jenna Hazark.

I didn't know if one of the witches in that picture, the ones still breathing at least, had anything to do with the killings, but if I were one of them, and I was innocent, you better believe I'd be on high alert after several people I knew had shown up savagely murdered. My wards would be rock solid, and my place would be locked the hell down tight.

The Hazarks obviously didn't think the way I did. The gates to the house were thrown open and several cars were parked out front. Were they having some kind of party? Fucking odd thing to do after what happened.

125

Calvin still hadn't been found, but if they were as tight as I thought, they had to know he was missing.

Another car rolled in. I couldn't see who was driving, but I recognized the female in the passenger seat. Maria Watson, shareholder in Dark Star and Chase's date for prom back in the day. Like the others, she was a witch from a prominent family. Maria also owned a bunch of high-end clothing stores. Emmaline and Marcel was the name of her boutique chain. The stores stocked designer labels and were named after her sister and brother who both died when they were just teenagers. In the article I found, it said they'd died in a tragic accident of some kind.

Shoving my door open, I jogged across the street to get a better look at what was going on. She parked beside a Lamborghini Miura. Its license plate was GLDNBOY. Not hard to guess who that belonged to. Chase Golden was a manwhore who'd inherited his wealth and never worked a day in his life. He had several businesses that he had nothing to do with, and according to gossip on Nightscape, was the biggest player around. He'd been nicknamed golden boy in high school because he had the looks to match. Perfect chiseled features, golden-brown eyes and thick, blond hair that had a slight wave that all his followers were "desperate to run their fingers through."

I'd only ever had a couple of encounters with him, both times at The Cauldron, when he'd come in for supplies, and both times he'd been a slimy douche canoe.

Maria got out and headed for the house as a Holden's Catering van pulled up on the other side of the Lamborghini. The door opened, and Jamie Graves got out. Jamie was my age, a fellow loner from Roxburgh High and my occasional science partner and study buddy. He'd gotten a job at Holden's straight out of high school.

Looked like I'd just found my way into this shindig.

I waved when he spotted me, and there was no missing his surprise.

"It's been a long time," he said, giving me a wary smile when I strode over, his confusion at seeing me there, obvious.

"Too long. You heard about Margot?"

He nodded. "I was gonna call..."

"I was too." It was bullshit, and we both knew it. We might have thought about it, but the actual calling, that wasn't something either of us actively did unless we totally had to. "I thought I'd see you at the funeral, but then they made it family only..."

"Yeah." He shut the van door, and his gaze darted from mine. "Though, I'm not sure you would've been welcome there."

The rumor mill had been busy. "Willow didn't do it, Jamie. She's innocent."

His head tilted to the side. "I hear they have evidence."

"They're wrong. Someone's setting her up."

He was quiet a couple beats. "So why are you here?"

"I'm trying to clear my sister's name."

"And you think they know something?" He motioned to the Hazarks' mansion.

"I'm sure of it."

Genuine concern filled Jamie's eyes. "If you're right, and Willow was framed, then there's a psycho out there who won't like anyone poking around in their business."

I scanned the parking lot, making sure no one was watching us. "Maybe not, but I don't really have much choice."

"Christ, Mags. It's too dangerous."

"It's not exactly voluntary." I shoved my hands in my pockets. "The mother called, and I had no choice but to answer."

"Fuck...yeah, of course. I heard about your sisters." Disbelief filled his eyes. "So this is your task? Finding a fucking psychotic murderer?"

"Yep. I'm not sure the mother likes me all that much."

"No shit," he said, looking furious on my behalf. "And that's really why you're here?"

"It is, but I need you to keep all of this to yourself, no one can know." I trusted him. No, we'd never been besties, but he, Margot, and I, we'd been there for each other when we'd needed to be. We'd only had each other in that shitty school, and the loyalty between us had always been rock solid. I glanced at the house and back. "So how big is this party?"

"It's not really a party. Jenna Hazark called and wanted catering for an intimate dinner. I'm not sure on the number of people. I'm just setting up, then getting lost."

So not a party, which meant I couldn't just blend in with the other guests. "I need to get inside. You think you can help?"

He blew out a breath. "I mean, yeah, I can get you in...but I can't lose this job, Mags. I just got a promotion—"

"If I get caught, your name won't be mentioned."

He contemplated for only a second. "I've been instructed to set up, then lock the door on my way out. There's a separate door into the kitchen that locks when it's closed. The best I can do is text you when I'm finished. I'll make sure you can slip in when I leave."

"Perfect," I said, ignoring the nerves in my belly.

"They've lowered their wards for me to get in, but they'll put them back up once I'm gone. If they catch you, if you do something crazy, I'm not sure I can help you—"

"They won't and I won't." I squeezed his hand. "This is amazing, Jamie.

I owe you." The ward could definitely be an issue, but I'd worry about one thing at a time.

"I'll text when the coast's clear." He started toward the house, then turned back. "And I hope you catch the asshole who hurt Margot. I really do. Call me if you need anything else."

I nodded my thanks. I'd catch the monster who tortured and murdered our friend, who was trying to frame Willow, no matter what. I would find out who this sick fuck was, and I'd expose them. I'd make them pay.

Jamie's text came through thirty minutes later. A thumbs-up.

I watched him drive out, then pulling up the hood on my sweatshirt and making sure to avoid the security cameras, I rushed around the side of the house. He'd wedged something in the door, so it hadn't closed properly, and I slipped inside.

The kitchen was quiet, empty when I walked in. I assumed the Hazarks had staff, they'd have to for a house this size, but it didn't look like anyone was here right now. They'd opted for a caterer instead of their own chef, and with a kitchen like this, I'd be surprised if they didn't have one. Odd. You'd think they'd want all hands on deck tonight since they had guests.

I eased the swinging door open and slipped into the hall. The clink of glasses and the low murmur of voices came from deeper in the house.

The halls of the grand house were still, silent. I followed the voices, rounding a few more corners. Definitely no staff wandering around.

Stopping at the end of the hall, I peeked around the edge. There was a room on the other side of the main foyer. The door was open, and I could see Jenna playing hostess and Robert, her husband, beside her. They were talking to someone, but I couldn't see who.

"I'm starving," someone said.

"Once Ryan gets here, we'll move through to the living room." They had to be talking about Ryan Alway. He was a witch, younger than the Hazarks and the other prom committee members, and he was all over their social media profiles. From what I could ascertain, he worked for several of them, a "guy Friday" if you will, for the group. "I had the caterer set up in there."

The living room? Okay, also weird.

Jenna sipped at the amber liquid in her glass. She looked pale, her eyes red and puffy. She was in pain, they all were, and I felt like a total jerk for eavesdropping on their grief, but I had no choice if I was going to find the killer.

Somehow, I needed to listen in, and I didn't have much time to get situated. I didn't know my way around this place, so I followed my nose, which wasn't hard, their meal smelled amazing. I rushed back the way I came, turning left instead of right this time, and found the living room a few doors down. There was a table set up. The food was laid out buffet-style, a stack of plates and silverware at one end. This was most definitely a casual get-together, but then these guys were besties, so there'd be no need for airs and graces.

The room was decorated in dark tones. There was dark wood furniture, and two large cozy couches, one by the door, the other opposite it. Across from me was a wide window covered by long, navy-blue curtains, and by the looks my only option for a hiding place. I rushed over and peered behind them. There was a low window seat covered in throw pillows. Perfect.

The sound of chatter reached me.

They were coming. I dove in behind the curtains and quickly made myself comfortable. I could be in for a long night, and there was no escape, not until the room cleared out.

My heart raced. This was probably a terrible idea, but my spidey senses weren't wailing at me to get the hell out of there, so that was something.

They walked in, their conversation subdued. I felt the dark cloud of their grief instantly, and wrapped my arms around myself. I really wished Bram was here. I always felt more in control when he was with me. Always.

Promise me you'll be safe while I'm gone.

This might be breaking that promise, in his eyes at least, but it was too late to back out now. I wasn't leaving until I found out what the prom committee knew, and I'd never get the chance again.

There was a small gap in the curtain, and I leaned forward to watch.

Robert grabbed a plate and immediately started loading it with food. Jenna picked up a cherry tomato and popped it in her mouth, then sat on the couch furthest away.

"Any word from Calvin yet?" Maria asked, hugging herself.

"No, and I've been by his house. His housekeeper was there. He hasn't been home for several days."

Isaac.

Both he and Maria weren't part of the original prom committee, but if the pictures in the yearbook were anything to go by, they'd been friends for years. Maria leaned into him, burying her face against his chest, and Isaac curled his arm around her.

"He's dead, isn't he?" Jenna said.

Ryan sat on the couch beside her. "We don't know that."

"He'd never do this, just vanish and not tell us where he was," Chase said, sitting on the floor at Jenna's feet. He looked a mess—his hair was all over the place and his eyes were bloodshot. Jenna threaded her fingers through his hair, and he leaned into her touch. "First Clara, then Margot and Katana...now Calvin—"

"Don't even say it," Robert bit out.

"Why not? It's fucking obvious someone's targeting us!" Chase cried.

"Not someone. Willow fucking Thornheart," Isaac growled.

"I don't understand," Maria said, visibly shaking. "Why would she do that?"

"The Thornhearts are power-hungry bitches. Having that cemetery isn't enough for them," Isaac all but snarled. "She used her connections to stop our development. We made a move against her, and she didn't like it. So she's doing to us what she did by setting her dog of a mate onto my brother, she's eliminating us."

The guy truly hated us, more than hated, but he was insane if he thought Willow would go on a killing spree over that.

"She'll pay for this. I'll make sure of it," Isaac said, actually shaking.

Robert threw his plate suddenly, with a roar. It smashed against the wall, mashed potatoes and beans sliding to the floor. "How? No one knows where she is and she's picking us off one by one. The twisted bitch is too powerful for us to stop. Willow Thornheart's turned into a monster like the hellhound she's fucking," Robert said viciously.

I had to bite my lip hard, my fingernails digging into my palms as fury filled me.

Maria rushed to Robert, wrapping her arms around him, tears rolling down her face. "I'm so scared."

Isaac clenched and unclenched his fists. "I have every enforcer on the council's payroll searching for her. I promise, we will get her."

They truly believed it was Willow. This was utter madness.

"You're doing everything you can, Isaac," Jenna said, still playing with Chase's hair like he was a puppy at her feet. "As long as we look out for each other, like we always have, we'll be okay. We know she's coming, and we can prepare for it." She smiled at Isaac and held out her hand. He went to her instantly and took it. "I'm so glad you found your way back to us. You're one of us and always have been."

"You know what a fucking monster my mother is. I hate that I let her control me for so long, and stayed away because of her. And now Elmer's gone...that bitch got her mate to kill him..." He shook his head and took an angry breath. "You, all of you, you're the only family I have left." He leaned in and kissed Jenna...*on the lips*. "I used to hate going back to school after the summer." He pressed his forehead to hers. "It fucking killed me."

"I hated it as well," Maria said, lips quivering. "Being sent away felt like a punishment after I met all of you."

Jenna smiled sadly, a tear sliding down her cheek. "Those summers, we had so much fun. All of us together."

Ryan ran his hand down her leg, and she reached over and grabbed his dick through the front of his pants. Then Isaac pressed his lips to hers, kissing her again. Only this time, he didn't pull back.

What the actual fuck was going on here?

Robert took Maria's hand, and they sat down as well. Maria climbed onto his lap, then they were kissing as well. Chase crawled closer, and Maria pulled away from Robert, then kissed him, while something similar was happening between Jenna, Isaac, and Ryan.

Holy fuck.

Okay, I wanted to get the hell out, right the fuck now, but I was stuck.

"Shall we go to the playroom?" Chase asked.

Playroom? Jesus.

Jenna shook her head. "Not tonight. I just want to be close to you all. I just want this."

Things progressed from there. People switched partners, and somewhere along the line, most of them ended up on the floor. Maria yanked up her dress, climbing on top of Isaac. "Oh fuck," she groaned.

Isaac arched beneath her, his moans making me feel nauseous. Robert climbed off the couch and moved in behind her, undoing his pants, and joined the fray. All three groaned. Then they were moving, fucking.

Chase sat on the couch, and Jenna slid down between his spread thighs, unzipped his pants, and sucked his cock into her mouth. Ryan moved in behind her, eyes wild, excited, and shoved her dress up, then jerked open his pants. Jenna made a muffled cry when he slammed into her, then started fucking her almost brutally.

I was trapped in a room while a bunch of witches had an orgy—and one, or more of them, could be a serial killer. This sure as hell hadn't been what I thought I'd find when I came here tonight.

This was bad, really bad. My skin crawled as their moans and cries grew louder, the sloppy sounds, the scent turning my stomach.

Maria moved faster, both Robert and Isaac fucking her at the same time. Chase had Jenna's hair fisted, and Ryan looked almost angry as he savagely fucked her from behind. Jenna seemed to love it, though, and her screams for more made my stomach rebel.

A panicky feeling filled me, and I squeezed my eyes closed, doing my best not to hyperventilate.

I had to get the hell out of there before I had a panic attack. I had no idea how long this would go on for, but I couldn't be in this room a moment longer. The door was close. So damn close. No one was looking my way. They were all fully occupied.

Easing out from behind the curtain, I dropped to my hands and knees and quickly crawled behind the couch closest to me.

There was no way they heard my panicked breathing over Jenna's screams and Ryan's obscene grunts and groans, but I held my breath as I rushed for the door.

As soon as I made it out, I clambered to my feet, then ran like hell back the way I'd come. Slipping out the kitchen door, I pulled it quietly closed behind me, dragged fresh night air into my lungs, and rushed for the gate.

I felt for a ward, but there wasn't one. They'd forgotten to put it back up. Thank fuck.

CHAPTER 15

Magnolia

GRIPPING THE STEERING WHEEL, I headed for home, my mind in a whirl. There was so much to unpack from all I saw and heard at the Hazarks', and I wasn't sure where to begin. The witches who started off on the prom committee had stayed tight. No, they weren't just close, they were *close*, and I had to assume that'd been going on for a while now.

There was more, though, there had to be. I growled in frustration, and again wished Bram was with me. We were like two halves of the same person, mind, body and soul, and I was lost without him.

A weird pain swirled in my gut, spreading to my chest, and I rubbed at it. I took the next turn, but the sensation kept growing, twisting into a feeling of...intense wrongness the farther away from the city I got—it was like the call to my task, like last time, when we found Calvin, but also... different, and it was screaming at me to turn around and go the other way.

I had to follow it, right? To let the intense feeling guide me.

Last time, when I was led to that garage, the feeling had come from within. This time it was an outside force. Someone was guiding me, and they were insistent. It didn't feel malevolent exactly, but there was a sense of darkness.

I felt...I felt the way I had when I was in Agatheena's cottage.

It was Agatheena, she was guiding me, I was sure of it. She wanted to show me something. I wasn't sure why, but I didn't think she meant to hurt me. Maybe she was actually trying to help me? I could also be wrong and she was sending me straight into a trap. But the sense of urgency inside me, the dread when I tried to ignore it, was so fierce and all-consuming that all I could do was let her lead me where she will.

I drove along dark streets in a part of the city I'd only ventured to a handful of times. It was near the demon neighborhood, but I felt the urge to stop before I got that far. Strapping my knife to my thigh, I pushed the car door open, got out, and scanned the streets. There were a couple dive bars nearby. Across the street was a diner, closed for the night, and between it and the thrift store next door was a dark alleyway.

And, of course, *that* was where I was being urged to go.

Awesome.

Muttering a protection spell, I pulled my knife free, letting it hang loose at my side, and strode across the street. I treaded as light as possible into the shadows, searching the dingy, narrow space. It carried on ahead to another older building behind the diner. The place was crumbling, and at some point most of the windows had been smashed.

The door hung on its hinges, black nothingness yawning behind it. I really didn't want to go in there, but my senses screamed louder for me to do just that.

Fuck.

My senses on high alert, I gripped my knife tighter and stepped over the threshold. Broken glass crunched under my boots as I moved deeper into the building. The hair on the back of my neck stood on end the deeper I went. Something was in here, something evil.

Why the hell would Agatheena send me to this place? I was starting to think that perhaps her motives hadn't been so wonderful after all.

A roar echoed through the building somewhere in the distance. It was unhinged and full of rage—and still the force driving me forward persisted. The sense of rightness, that this was where I needed to be, was so strong, my flight instincts were completely overridden. This was the part in a horror movie where everyone screamed at their TVs while some moron left their nice safe house to go "check out" the scary noise outside. I was the moron in this situation, I knew this, yet I kept walking because I *had* to.

My breath shook as I stepped through another doorway, my pulse thundering in my ears. A murmured voice came from nearby. I couldn't hear what they said, but I had no trouble hearing the harsh, loud reply. "You think you can stop me?" a male voice said. "Others have tried and failed."

Some of the wall had crumbled away, and a florescent sign close by cast the room in a wash of blue. Taking a deep breath, I eased closer to the door and peered around the edge, because something else was pulling me closer now, something—familiar.

It took me a moment to register what I was seeing. Stunned, I watched the scene playing out in front of me.

A male stood there, panting, fists clenched, legs braced apart. He had a busted nose and a split lip. Fury lined his face, and his twisted, hate-filled eyes were laser focused on his opponent.

I turned to the second male, my gaze sliding over him, tall and muscled, a look etched on his face I'd never seen. Familiar, all of him—but also a complete stranger.

Bram's eyes danced as he beckoned the other male forward, a low rough sound falling from his lips that had goose bumps lifting across my arms.

The male roared and ran at Bram. He laughed darkly when the other male swung at him, the menacing sound setting off a flurry of swirls in my lower belly. Bram dodged the incoming blow and returned one of his own, so hard his opponent dropped to his knees.

The deranged grin stayed on the other male's face, though, even as he staggered to his feet. "Have you ever heard a female beg for her life?"

Bram said nothing.

"It's beautiful," the other male said. "Do you have a female? A mate?"

Bram still said nothing.

"I'll take that as a yes." The creep laughed. "When I'm done with you, I'll find her, and while I kill her, slowly, I'll tell her you were too weak to save her."

One moment Bram stood across from the creep, the next he was in his shadow form. I tracked his movement as he shot across the room, wrapped an arm around the male and threw him back against the wall. Bram solidified in front of him, his long fingers wrapped around the shorter male's neck, his talon's punching through, sharp and deadly. He made a grating, rattling sound that came straight from his chest, his crow right there in his eyes. He dragged a knife from the sheath at his hip, then pressed it against the other male's throat.

"You're not gonna do it," the other male rasped, that grin still on his smug face.

"No?" Bram leaned in.

"If you kill me, then you'll be no better than me."

That menacing smile tilted up Bram's lips. "That's right," he said. "Only my victims deserve it."

The other male's eyes widened. "Please, don't. Please, I beg you."

Without hesitation, Bram slashed through the begging male's throat. Blood sprayed his shirt and neck as he sliced deeper, his eyes locked on the gasping male staring up at him with obvious shock in his eyes. Then not done, Bram pulled back the knife, and slid it deep into his chest.

My heart was hammering so hard I felt dizzy from it, my stomach churning.

Bram sneered back, not looking away until the guy slumped, until his last breath gurgled from his sliced throat.

My feet finally unfroze, and I stepped into the room.

Bram's head jerked up, and our eyes clashed. Neither of us moved or said a word for several heart-stopping seconds. Bram's nostrils were flared, his breathing heavy. The blood painting his shirt and skin looked black under the glowing blue sign shining from outside.

Finally, and without looking away from me, he yanked his blade free and straightened, letting the dead male crumple to the floor. He wiped the blood off on his thigh, then slid the knife back in its leather sheath, a look in his eyes I had no hope of reading. I didn't know this Bram. In this moment, he was someone else. Someone he'd never introduced me to.

"How did you find me?" he asked, his voice low and rougher than I'd ever heard it.

Electricity zapped between us like a current firing from both of us and clashing in the middle, drawing us closer and pushing us apart at the same time. "Agatheena. I think she led me here."

He nodded, his gaze sliding the length of me and back. "Are you afraid?" His head dipped for a split second, giving me a glimpse of the Bram I knew and loved, then his dark gaze slid back to mine and my lower belly trembled. "Of me?" he finished.

I shook my head, though honestly, I wasn't sure what I was feeling. "You just killed a man while he begged you not to," I said. "Why?"

"Because he deserved it."

"And you get to decide that?"

Bram took a step closer, and I took one back, not because I was afraid, but because I was overwhelmed, by this, by him. Goddess, every part of me felt oversensitized, raw.

He watched me do it. "You are afraid."

I shook my head again. "How do you know him? Why did you do it? Does this have anything to do with my task?"

"I don't know him, and because he enjoys killing females. Does unspeakable things, then he kills them. And no, this has nothing to do with your task."

Agatheena had wanted me to see this. To see Bram like this. To see the truth. I looked down at the male slumped on the floor. He was the evil I felt when I walked in here. I didn't feel it anymore, the feeling left the moment he'd died.

"Is this your job, the thing that takes you away?"

The muscle in Bram's jaw jumped. "Yes," he finally said.

I could tell he was testing it out, testing to see if he could talk. He'd made an oath, but I'd just walked in and seen his secret for myself. Maybe that voided it? "You kill people?"

"Yes," he said.

"So you're some kind of...assassin?"

He nodded. "I hunt bad people and I kill them."

"Why you?"

"Because I'm a crow, it's what we're born to do."

My head was in a whirl. "And your brothers?"

He held his body unnaturally still, watching me closely, and he nodded again.

"And you...you enjoy it, don't you? You enjoy the kill," I rasped.

He didn't look away, didn't flinch or try to hide. "Yes," he said.

I felt as if I were spinning out of control. "Is that why you didn't want me to know?"

"Yes."

I swallowed hard. "And this part of you—"

"It's always there. I'm a shifter, Magnolia. I'm not human. My animal side has always been dominant. I think you know that."

I did. I knew it. It was one of the many things I'd loved about him.

"Crows enjoy the hunt, the kill," he said. "Not to do it is ignoring the very core of our nature." He took several more steps toward me, and this time I didn't retreat, I stayed where I was. Because no matter what I'd just witnessed, this was Bram. My Bram. "And I do it because if I don't, I could become one of the monsters I put down." He took another step toward me, his chest heaving. "We are as dark as our feathers, as the shadows we shift into. I kill because I have to, but also because it's what I am. Because I need it, and yes, because I enjoy it."

He took the last two steps, closing the space between us.

"The oath... Why can you talk to me about it now? Because I saw you?"

"Yes."

"And that's how it is with everyone?"

"Yes."

"Because they don't usually live long enough to tell anyone what they saw?"

His chest heaved, and he tucked a loose strand of my hair behind my ear. "Yes."

I stared up at him. He was splattered with blood and had a strange look in his eyes. I was the exception to that rule. He'd never hurt me, not for any reason. I stared back, looking at a stranger. Goddess, I hated so much that he'd kept this from me, that he'd held a part of himself back from me. "Now I know all your secrets," I said, my voice husky, my heart racing, belly swirling.

He took another of those heaved breaths, gripped my chin in his blood-stained fingers and shook his head. "There's one more."

His eyes were fathomless, intense, and my heart thundered harder. I'd seen this expression before, but only when he thought I wasn't looking. Like the times I woke and found him watching me, or the times we watched a movie and I'd turn to him, only to find his eyes locked on me. Every time, the urge to retreat had slammed through me, and it did now. "Bram—"

"Why do you think I'm the only one who can touch you, Magnolia? Why we need to touch? Why do you think the moment we met, we were so intensely drawn together? It wasn't just because I was your familiar—"

I pressed my fingers to his lips, stopping him. My pulse was racing so hard I felt close to passing out. What was he doing? What the hell was he doing?

His fingers curled around my wrist, and he gently pulled my hand away, shaking his head. "You know, Mags. You know."

"No." I shook my head. "You're not thinking...this situation, it's..."

His fingers slid around the back of my head, into my hair, his gaze dipping to my mouth.

"Bram," I choked out.

He pressed his forehead to mine. "Maggie," he whispered on a shuddering breath and leaned in, his lips a breath from mine.

I jerked back, but he held me fast, not giving me an inch. "Please," he rasped.

My heart exploded in my chest, cold sweat breaking out all over me and I reacted, as if my hands were being controlled my someone else. I shoved at him, pulling from his hold. "No."

We stayed locked like that for long seconds, his gaze searching mine.

Neither of us moved, then finally, pain sliced through his obsidian eyes, and his hand dropped away, releasing me.

As soon as he did, my world cracked down the middle. Terror like never before filled me from the top of my head to the tips of my toes. He couldn't do this. I couldn't do this. He was ruining everything. "Bram..."

He turned away, striding for the door. I rushed after him, but I didn't know what to do, what to say. So many thoughts and feelings stormed inside me. We walked out of the building and down the alley, back to the street.

"Where's your car?" he asked, voice devoid of emotion.

"Bram."

He spotted it and strode over. I expected him to get in with me.

He didn't.

Bram wouldn't meet my gaze. "I need to...go away for a while."

"Hang on. No, you can't do that. You can't leave me—"

"I promised I wouldn't do that, remember?" He was trembling, his entire body vibrating. "And I won't."

"When will you be back?"

His fingers curled and uncurled at his sides. "I don't know. I won't be gone long. I just...I need some time."

He needed time...away from me.

My best friend just tried to kiss me, and I'd pulled away. I said no. I wanted to scream. This wasn't happening. It couldn't be happening. "My task...I need you," I said in desperation, trying to keep him with me.

His hand lifted as though he was going to touch my face, but then he dropped it. Fuck, that hurt so damn badly. "Asher's more than capable of having your back while I'm gone."

"I don't want Asher...I want..." I let the rest fall away.

His lips curled in a broken smile before he leaned in, pressing a kiss to my forehead. Then he shifted into his crow, retreating completely, the way he used to, and exploded into the night sky.

My shattered heart splintered into so many pieces there was no chance of ever putting it back together.

"I don't want Asher... I want you," I choked out.

CHAPTER 16

Bram

TALON WAS FUCKING BOUNCING with anticipation. Rook looked the way he always did, sinister as fuck, but tonight excitement made his onyx eyes glitter. I'd always been more like Payne, able to keep a tight hold on my control. Not now, though, and definitely not tonight.

Tonight, the blood would flow, and there was no hiding how much I craved it or the thrill of the hunt pumping through my veins.

I wanted to take all the pain and anger and helplessness I was feeling, then listen as it echoed into the night, in the screams of fuckers we'd been sent to kill.

We watched our prey laugh and drink and fuck. The smell of death surrounded their camp, so much of it that it coated the back of my throat. The hyenas were rogue and had been on another killing spree, snatching humans from the city and bringing them back here to torment and eat. Their clan had lost control of them, and other shifters in the area were getting nervous. The last thing any of us needed was the attention of the human authorities.

One of the hyenas laughed, the sound high and deranged, before he tore a piece of thigh meat from a dead male and shoved it into his wide mouth, while another two, covered in human blood, fucked on the ground beside the body.

The human part of me retreated and the predator came to the fore, taking over, dominating. I let it, relished it. It was less painful that way.

I studied my prey. I'd kill the laughing one first, the sound was grating my last nerve. His smile was pissing me off as well.

I'll tear his tongue out before I slit his throat. Yeah, that's what I'll do.

On the other side of the campfire, it was much the same, but my brothers could take care of them. I had dibs on the fucker stuffing his face.

"What are you thinking?" Payne asked beside me.

"Chuckles is mine." We didn't often hunt all together, only when there was a group like this one.

Payne nodded. "He's yours, but that's not what I meant."

I didn't look at him, my big brother was way too perceptive. "Not sure what you're asking."

"Something's bothering you."

Yeah, I wasn't hiding shit. But then the love of my life had just shoved me away when I'd finally worked up the courage to kiss her, after six years of wanting her and fighting it. And my favorite part? When she'd looked at me like I'd lost my fucking mind for even thinking we could go there.

Mags had seen the real me. She'd seen what I truly was, and she'd pulled away so fast my fucking head spun. Her resounding "no" still rang through my mind, hammering me in the skull over and over again. I didn't know if the outcome would have been the same if I'd tried to kiss her at a different time or place, like not right after murdering someone in front of her. I guess I'd never know. But the realization that swiftly followed had been brutal and undeniable—the female I lived and breathed for, my witch, my mate, my Magnolia, didn't want me the way I did her.

So yeah, it was kind of hard to keep that shit locked down. Honestly? I felt like I was dying. Or maybe I wished I were dead? It was a toss-up.

"Magnolia," Payne said. "She's the only one capable of fucking you up like this."

I dragged in a harsh breath. "I tried to kiss her," I said, because they'd find out eventually. Why hide it?

He was quiet a beat. "What happened?"

"She didn't want to be kissed...by me."

I still didn't turn his way, but I saw his surprise in my peripheral vision. "She turned you down?"

"Yes." There went another one of those daggers thrusting into my chest.

After another pause, his hand came down on my shoulder. "At least now you know and can finally let her go."

My brothers didn't like Mags and couldn't fathom the connection between us. "I'm her familiar, she's my mate, whether or not she wants me is irrelevant. I can never let her go." I'd tried to explain how it was between a witch and their familiar, and they'd struggled to grasp it, mainly because the idea of having no control over a situation freaked them the fuck out.

Payne's gaze burned into me for several seconds as the enormity of what I just said and what it meant for me sunk in. "Mate?"

"Yes, mate." And my mate had rejected me. I would live beside the only female I wanted for the rest of my life, but she would never be mine. Anger filled me, no, fucking rage. Maybe things would've been different if Clayton hadn't hurt her, if she hadn't withdrawn so deeply into herself, maybe...

I scrubbed my hands over my face. No. That was all bullshit. I didn't know why she didn't feel the mating bond between us, but she obviously didn't because if she did, she would have welcomed my kiss, she would've wrapped her arms around me and fucking held on, she would have...

Stop.

I gripped the sides of my head. My mind needed to shut the fuck up.

It was done. Over.

The hope I'd been clinging to for six years needed to fucking die.

"I'm sorry," Payne said. "I know you don't want to hear this, but mate or not, she wasn't right for you. Others at the village have taken lovers after the loss of a mate and so could you. She was selfish, like all witches. They can't be fucking trusted. You don't have to stay tethered to her—you're a warrior, the son of a chieftain, you deserve a female who would do anything to prove her worth to you."

"Don't," I bit out. "Magnolia isn't Farah. You don't fucking talk shit about her. Not ever. You say one more thing against her and you and I will have a problem we won't ever come back from. There will be no other female, not for me, not ever. Understand?"

Payne's lips peeled back and a throaty *caw* rose from his chest. We didn't mention his ex, Maeve's mom, ever. Payne refused to talk about her, but I didn't give a fuck. Instead of losing his shit like usual, though, that steely control kicked in and he bit back whatever he wanted to say and turned to our brothers. "Ready?"

Talon grinned evilly and Rook dipped his chin, his eyes sliding to his prey.

Payne's wings burst from his back. "Let's go."

We took flight, dropping from the sky, right in the middle of the hyena camp. They shot to their feet, and the moment they got a good look at us, fear filled their eyes. They knew exactly who we were and what it meant when my brothers and I dropped in.

We were the boogeymen. Monsters whispered about but never out loud, afraid if they did, we'd come for them as well—and we would.

I strode toward my target as Talon laughed. Payne moved with purpose, killing with precision, and Rook, like me, was playing with his prey. These twisted fucks deserved to suffer for what they'd done, and they would.

But when I shadowed out, surprising the fucker who had human blood smeared on his face and soaked into his clothes, there was no excitement, not for me, not anymore, not even as I watched the life bleed from his eyes —only a moment of relief.

When we left a while later, the ground was soaked with their blood. I was bitten and clawed, and I relished in the pain. This was the part where I'd go home to Mags, and I could admit that sometimes I let myself get hurt just so she could tend my wounds. A kind of twisted foreplay in anticipation of having her hands on my bare skin.

The urge to go to her, to go to my tree house in her backyard and pretend nothing was wrong, that nothing had happened between us just so she could touch me now was so damn tempting. But I couldn't do it. If I went back now, I'd fucking beg her to want me. I'd crawl on my knees in front of her. I'd fall at her feet and fucking beg for her to take this pain away.

Because without hope, I was lost. Magnolia was my sky and earth, my moon and stars. She was my reason. My everything. She was my fucking oxygen.

And without her, I wasn't sure how to breathe anymore.

CHAPTER 17

Magnolia

My world had been ripped out from under my feet. I didn't know anything anymore, not even my own feelings. I was confused and felt sick to my stomach. I missed Bram so badly it hurt, and I'd spent the night in his bed alone, crying so fucking hard my throat was raw this morning.

I'd tried calling him multiple times—he hadn't answered.

He hadn't come home. I knew he wouldn't but still I'd hoped he'd change his mind, that I'd wake up in his arms and everything would go back to the way it was.

I shoved my mug away, the coffee only making my stomach worse.

"We got a corpse," Asher said across from me.

I'd called her early this morning, filled her in on everything that was happening, well, everything except what happened with Bram, and she'd agreed to come with me today. Ash also had a way of forcing me out of my own head, and I needed that more than ever.

I took her phone, scanning the post on Nightscape. Calvin's body had been found last night by some teenagers. They'd broken in to hang out and get drunk and found a decomposing, mutilated body instead. I quickly read the rest of the article and scanned the comment section, then wished I hadn't. There were a lot of familiar names taking potshots at Willow, accusing her of all kinds of fucked-up shit.

I slid the phone back to Ash. "Now they'll be even more convinced it was Willow. I'm not even sure the council's looking elsewhere. They're staying quiet right now, and it's not fucking helping." I tapped the table. "Isaac is involved in this somehow, beyond being fuck buddies with the prom committee."

"You think he's our killer?"

"After what I saw at the Hazarks', your guess is as good as mine. Do I think he's capable of doing some seriously fucked-up shit? Definitely. But torture and murder his friends to get his revenge on Willow? I don't know. But I don't trust him. He's up to something."

"Jenna said she was glad he came back to them, right? They haven't been tight this whole time. He weaseled his way back in. Are you sure the closeness you saw between him and the others, and I'm not talking about the orgy, was real?"

I slumped back in my seat. "I don't know."

Asher eyed me over her mug. "Okay, feisty, what's up with you? I mean, besides the whole hunting-a-psycho thing?" Her brow arched. "You're acting all...I don't know, emo."

"I'm not."

"Does it have anything to do with the fact that I'm here instead of your shadow man?" She made a show of looking over my shoulder to the vacant space behind me. "When Bram's here, he's hovering behind you like Lurch, only a hot, goth version. What did you do?"

"I don't want to talk about it."

She shrugged. "Honestly, neither do I. Just thought I should check, since that's the kind of shit Iris makes me do now." She stood, the chair scraping on the wooden floor, then winked. "But you're all good, right? So let's get the fuck on the road before you change your mind."

I swiped my keys and phone from the table, and we headed out of the house. Asher strode right past my car, where I was opening the driver's door, and over to her truck. "I don't do passenger princess, princess."

I snorted. "Maybe not, but you do an excellent impression of an asshole, asshole," I said and walked to her truck instead of arguing. I didn't have the energy after crying for hours and zero sleep.

"Aww, look at you, throwing attitude." She grinned, flashing her sharp canines. "It's cute the way you try so hard to be like me. Maybe someday, but you've still got a long way to go, pup."

I opened the door. "We're nothing alike."

"Loves to fight, has an attitude, angry most of the time, will cut a bitch." She ticked off each description on her fingers. "Sound familiar? We could've come from the same litter...except you'd be the runt."

"And you'd be the cun—"

"Cunning one?" She smirked. "Why, yes, how insightful of you, Magnolia. Now get in and stop bitching."

I flipped her off and got in.

She started the truck and turned to me. "So where to?"

"Council chambers." I needed to talk to Councilor Trotman. He was a good male. He'd also taken our side and treated us fairly in the past. I needed to know if they were looking at anyone else for these murders, or if they were content to pin it on my sister.

Ash nodded as she scrolled through the music app on her phone. A moment later metal filled her truck. She cranked it up and roared along with the lyrics in a deep, demonic voice like the guy blasting through the speakers. Then she planted her foot on the gas, and we sped off.

I let the music crash through me, welcoming the chaotic beat because it made it impossible to think. I'd done enough of that last night, replaying what happened in that run-down building over and over again.

Several songs later, Asher sped into the council's parking lot. We got out and strode up to the main doors.

I pulled my ID from my wallet, showing the guard. All witches had one. It allowed us access to the building, identifying us and the coven we were from. I signed Asher in as my guest, then we were scanned, the magical kind. It checked us for spells or incantations that a witch could use on themselves or others to cause harm. The guard gave us the all-clear and let us in.

Heads turned as we walked in. On my own, I wasn't overly intimidating, though I often got second looks and wide berths. I guess when you exuded a whole lot of anger, people felt it. Add Asher into the mix, both of us dressed in black and more than likely wearing matching resting bitch faces, and we weren't the most approachable-looking people in the building.

And yes, though I tried to deny it, she was right, we did have similarities, and right now, we were both putting out some serious stay-the-fuck-back vibes. Mine weren't intentional, it was just how I was these days, and I assumed it was the same for Asher. She was an alpha female and a warrior, and no one could mistake her for anything else. Most people felt it and steered clear of her path.

A male strode around the corner almost crashing into us. He actually cried out in alarm as he threw himself back so fast that he almost fell on his ass, proving my point.

"Sorry," I muttered, and we carried on down the hall.

"I think his balls just retreated back inside his abdomen," Asher said.

They totally had.

She nudged me. "So, when are you coming out to train? You haven't been to the keep in a while."

"Are you going to let me go on patrol with you?"

"Maybe," she muttered.

"I met the mother in Oldwood Forest on my own. You think I managed that without spilling some demon blood?" I said, feeling frustrated all over again.

"Well, that was a fucking foolish thing to do, feisty," she said, her tawny eyes slicing my way.

"I didn't exactly have much choice. Bram was gone and..." A wave of pain rolled through me.

"I assumed he'd been with you. You didn't think to call me?"

I glanced at her. "I didn't want anyone knowing. You and Iris are besties. I couldn't trust you'd keep it to yourself. My family would've freaked out if I told them. You know how protective my sisters are, and if they knew, they would've tried to get around the rules to help me. I couldn't let that happen. And even if they didn't, what was the point of them sitting around all night worried out of their minds?"

She scowled. "You couldn't trust me? Are you fucking serious?"

Asher was pissed, for real, and I kind of felt like an asshole. "Would you have told Iris?"

Her jaw tightened. "Maybe."

"Exactly. Can we just drop it now?"

"Fine, but if you need to do something else like that, something on your own, at least let me know where you are."

I glanced her way again. "You are literally here with me now. And are you seriously telling me you let Draven know where you are at all times?"

"If I'm doing something that could get me killed, you fucking bet I do." Her eyes narrowed. "And FYI, you do anything else that dumb, I'll kick your ass."

I bumped her with my elbow, trying to lighten the mood. "You could try."

Asher scoffed. "You took me down once. I was having a bad day."

I'd taken her down more than once, but keeping her down was another story. I wasn't even close to her level. I wasn't sure it was possible. "Nice rewriting of history you did there."

She bumped me back. "Shut up."

We stopped in front of Nathan Trotman's office.

"So what's this guy like? Does he have a stick up his ass, or what?" Ash asked.

I knocked. "Nah, he's actually a good male."

"Come in," Trotman called.

I opened the door, and we strode in. Trotman was about Mom's age. He had dark brown skin and kind eyes, and always wore nice suits. He took us in, and sat back. "Magnolia." He looked around. "I'm not sure you should be here."

"Why? Am I a suspect as well?"

He straightened his glasses. "Of course not, but if people see you here with me, it'll make it harder to help your sister."

"And you want to help her?"

He held my gaze. "I'm a friend of your family." He pointed to the door, to the offices beyond it. "And they know it. I'm already being left out of important discussions where this case is concerned."

Shit. "Look, I just want to know who else the council's looking at. Who are your other suspects?"

He looked pained. "There are no other suspects, Magnolia, and things aren't looking good for Willow. She had a public altercation with Calvin Adler, and now he's been found brutally murdered, and that's on top of all the other evidence we found at The Caldron when we found Katana's body." He glanced at the door behind us, then back again. "There's also the way the victims' mouths were all sewn shut...they're saying it's her calling card."

Fuck.

"No one's forgotten how Willow used that spell during her trial," he added.

These were all things I'd considered but hoped had slipped by everyone else. "Do you think she did it?" We needed Trotman on our side because the rest of the council seemed to have already made up their minds.

"I can't talk about this with you—"

"Do you?" I asked again more forcefully.

He sat back. "She told me she was working for us during Rose's trial, helping us when the demonology department was robbed and that guard went missing. She lied to me, putting her own interests, and that of Coven Thornheart above everything else. She's changed—"

"You think she did it, don't you?"

"I think she's lost her way. I think being mated to a hellhound hasn't helped the situation," Trotman said.

I couldn't believe what I was hearing. I nodded, fury firing through me. "You actually think she did it." I folded my arms so I didn't flip his damn desk. "I will find whoever's responsible for these murders and clear my sister's name. You're wrong about her. So fucking wrong."

He stood. "I want to help her. If you know where she is—"

"I wouldn't tell you. And I promise you, the council's enforcers don't have a chance in hell of getting anywhere near her. No one can, not even me." I ground my teeth. "There's someone else you should be looking at, someone who hates Willow and would love to see her ruined."

Trotman frowned. "Who?"

Was he serious? "Isaac. You know their history. He'd love nothing more than to take Willow down. I honestly think he's involved in this somehow and using his position at the council to his own advantage."

"That's a serious accusation."

He didn't look convinced, like at all. "And I don't make it lightly."

He said nothing for several seconds, his gaze devoid of all its usual warmth. "If that's all, Magnolia, I need to get back to work."

I wasn't getting through to him, and I wasn't going to.

We walked out and I struggled to control the fire burning in my gut.

"Not so sure he's such a good guy anymore," Asher said. "Seems to me he's sold his soul to this place and the rest of the power-hungry assholes here."

I didn't want to believe it, but Asher might be right.

A door opened ahead of us and Asuka walked out. Her gaze darted our way, and as soon as she saw me, her already pale skin, grew even more so, and she reversed so fast I was surprised she didn't leave skid marks as she shut her office door. The sounds of the lock clicking into place was loud in the quiet hall.

"I guess we know where she stands as well," Ash said.

I guess we did. "Nothing's making sense. Trotman, Asuka, they *know* Willow. That they both think she's capable of this...I feel like I'm in the fucking twilight zone."

›)›●(‹‹

We spent the rest of the day chasing our tails. Nothing new, nothing that could help me or Willow. We drove by the Hazarks' place, then the Golden mansion after that, then Maria's. They were all locked down, not surprising after the discovery of Calvin's body.

My phone chimed and I snatched it from my pocket so fast I almost dropped it.

Brutal disappointment quickly followed.

Not Bram.

Tears instantly sprang to my eyes. You'd think I'd be all cried out, but apparently not. I swallowed them down, and Asher arched a brow at me when I glanced her way. "Mom wants to know if we'll be there for dinner."

Goddess, this was killing me. What was I going to do? How could I make this right?

Ash gave me a hopeful look.

"I'll tell her to save us a plate."

"Nice." She grinned, then her gaze slid over my face and her grin vanished. "What the fuck is up with you?"

"Nothing. I'm fine."

"Don't give me that shit, you're on the verge of tears. You didn't even cry when I dislocated your shoulder that time. Something's fucking with you, and despite what I said back at your place, I am a good sounding board, so fucking talk, feisty. Or I'll pull this car over and we won't move until you do."

I stared out the windshield, my fingers curling and twining together. The look in Bram's eyes, the way he held my chin with his blood-stained fingers, the way he'd leaned in... "Bram almost...he almost kissed me." My breath hitched just saying it out loud.

Ash was quiet several beats, her gaze going from me to the road, then back. "Okay...so what's the problem?"

I curled my fingers into tight fists because my hands were shaking. "Bram's my best friend. He's my familiar."

"Right."

"I knew you wouldn't understand," I said, wishing I hadn't said anything. Talking about this was too damn painful.

"What did you do when he tried to kiss you?" she asked.

Squeezing my eyes closed, I tried to flush the memory from my mind. "I pushed him away. I said...I said, no."

She nodded. "And you said no because?"

"Because he's my best friend."

"You said that already. Tell me what you were feeling in that moment?"

I rubbed my now sweaty palms on my thighs. "I don't know."

"Yes, you do. Was your heart racing?"

My mouth went dry. "Well, yes—"

"Belly all flippy?"

Yes, it had been. There were serious flips. I didn't reply, but the look on her face said I didn't need to.

She glanced at me again. "You ever thought about kissing him? Looked at him and thought, damn, he's fine? You ever imagined what it would be like to get naked and let loose on each other?"

Yes, yes, and yes. Suddenly, I was struggling to breathe. "Don't...I can't...I can't do this—"

Ash pulled the truck off the road suddenly, stopping in the middle of nowhere. "Look at me."

"Ash—"

"Look at me, feisty."

I turned in my seat and forced myself to look at her, because I knew that tone. We were staying right here until I did what she wanted.

"You're scared. I get that," she said. "Fear is a powerful thing. It makes us think we can't have the things we desperately fucking want. It lies to us, it makes us think we *can't*, when we sure as fuck *can*." She took my hand in a tight grip, forcing me to keep looking at her when I tried to look away. "He's in love with you, Mags. We all see it. He's so in love with you that being close to you is Heaven and Hell for him, all rolled into one."

My mouth opened, closed. I tried to pull my hand from hers, to retreat, to not freak the fuck out at her words.

She held tight, but her gaze softened, something I'd never seen before. "You had to know that."

Yeah, I was definitely struggling to breathe normally now. Because, goddess, I did. Didn't I? I'd tried to tell myself that wasn't what I saw in his eyes. I tried to pretend that wasn't what I felt from him when we were together, that the tension between us wasn't so thick sometimes, I found it hard to draw breath. A couple of years ago, things between us had started to change. I'd started seeing him...differently. There'd been several times when I thought he was going to kiss me.

Then Clayton happened, and I'd shoved it down. I'd pretended I'd never felt the thing inside me slowly unfurling, desperate to bloom.

"I'm scared," I choked out. "I'm so fucking scared, Ash."

"You won't lose him, you have to know that. Whatever happens from this moment on, he'll still be there for you. And you know why, don't you?"

I licked my dry lips, my pulse racing all over again. "How did I miss it, how—"

"You weren't ready to see it, and maybe you aren't totally ready now, but you have to decide if you want to be. Don't let this slip through your fingers." Her voice changed, becoming more forceful. "Don't you fucking dare do that. Nothing will ever compare to what you could have with him... with your mate." Shockingly, her throat worked, emotion filling her eyes. "The years I had with Boone were the best of my life. You're scared, I get that. But you know what's scarier? A lifetime never knowing a love like that, happiness like that. Never sharing a connection with someone, a connection that even if I tried, I couldn't explain the enormity of it. I could never describe the way it feels." She shook her head.

"Ash...I had no idea." She'd been mated.

She shrugged. "I don't talk about it, because it's mine, and because he still lives with me in here." She pressed a hand to her chest. "I try to make the best of the time I have left on this earth, because Boone would want me to. But I'm just killing time until I'm with him again. He was it for me. There will never be anyone else who could take his place. You need to think about that when you make your decision. There is no one either of you will ever want the way you want each other."

My lips trembled and I growled, shutting it down, refusing to cry again. "But I'm...I'm fucking broken. I don't know if I can give him all of me, I don't know if I can...if we could ever..."

Her hand tightened on mine, the other gripping my shoulder, and she jolted me, roughly. "Snap the fuck out of it."

I blinked up at her.

"You're not fucking getting it, feisty. Bram is your mate. *Your mate.* There isn't one thing you can't figure out together. Not one. He knows you like no one else, he knows what you can and can't handle. *He knows.*"

He did.

He'd always known what I was feeling, thinking at least—until recently, when we'd both closed ourselves off to it. Ignored it.

"I can guarantee no matter how long it takes, he'll wait," Ash said. "He'll wait, because making you happy, pleasing you, caring for you, is all he'll ever want and need." She gave me a sad smile. "Mags, he's already been waiting, and he'll keep on doing it. He'll wait an eternity for you."

CHAPTER 18

Magnolia

ASHER WAS FULLY FOCUSED on eating the plate of food Mom had put down in front of her, but I couldn't even choke down a bite.

"Eat, then rest. You look exhausted," Mom said and kissed the top of my head before walking out of the room.

There was no way I could rest, not when everything Asher had said to me earlier was on repeat in my head.

I scrubbed my hands over my face, feeling utterly lost. I missed Bram so fucking much.

I couldn't do this, not without him. Not any of it.

I couldn't sleep.

I couldn't think.

I couldn't fucking breathe.

I missed him so much, I ached. I ached for him. Goddess, it hurt.

Asher cleared her throat, and I looked up.

"What are you thinking?" she asked, looking at me as if she could see everything.

"That I need Bram, and that I'm going to get him."

She smiled.

"Will you help me?"

She lowered her fork. "What do you need?"

"A ride. But first I need to get a few things together."

She slid my plate her way. "I'll be right here when you're ready."

))》●《((

I double-checked the spell book, making sure I'd added everything. Satisfied, I started filling the glass vials with the potion.

What I was about to do, it'd be even more difficult than my trip into Oldwood and my visit with the mother, so I'd taken what Agatheena said to heart. The only way to succeed was by embracing who I was, by walking the path between dark and light, and thanks to the ingredients I'd gotten from the demon store, I was more than ready to do it.

"What are you making there, pumpkin?" Else said from the door, startling me.

I slammed the spell book closed and dragged a rag over the vials.

Else limped closer and sat on the wooden rocking chair she used by the fire when she needed to take a load off. "You know there's nothing you can't tell me, don't you, Mags?"

Guilt filled me. "I know."

She nodded. "There's nothing that you could do or say that would change how much I love you, how much we all love you."

I nodded.

She nodded as well. "Iris let slip the mother called you, and about your trial. I wish you'd trusted me enough to tell me yourself. I know I can't help you, but anything you need, anything at all, in here or in the library, anything, you help yourself, okay?"

"I do trust you. I should've told you. I'm sorry." I let out a shaky breath. "Does Mom know?" I was closer to Else than almost anyone, and she was right, I should have been the one to tell her.

"Nope."

Mom was a different story. Else would know the right things to say, the best way to break it to her. Mom worried about me so much, and she'd already had to watch my sisters go through this, feeling terrified and helpless. I wasn't sure how she'd handle it this time. "I know I should do it myself, but would you tell her for me? I can't bear to see the worry in her eyes."

"I'll tell Daisy." She studied me for several seconds. "I don't know what you're about to do, or what you've got under that rag, pumpkin, but whatever it is, whatever you have to do during this trial—it's the right thing. Trust your gut, what's in your heart, and it will lead you right, understand?"

I nodded.

154

Then she stood, but before she left, she turned back. "I'd feel a lot better if you had Bram with you, though." Her lips quivered. "You're the toughest witch I know, Magnolia Thornheart, strong and unstoppable, like your grandmother. Goddess, so much like her. I don't know how the hell you got to the mother and back on your own that night, sheer stubbornness no doubt." She smiled shakily, then sniffed. "But we need our familiars at times like these, and if you're lucky enough to still have one, you hold them close. Promise me no more going it alone, that you'll take Bram with you."

"I will," I said and gave her a shaky smile of my own. "As a matter of fact, I'm on my way to get him right now."

))➤●((

An hour later, Ash and I were deep in Oldwood Forest. It was a different part than where I'd met the mother, and Ash had driven me in as far as she could go. I took in the dense forest that lay ahead. I had to go it alone from here if I was going to do this right, and I was determined to do just that.

"You sure about this?" Ash asked.

I grabbed my pack and checked my knife. "Yes, I've never been more sure of anything in my life." I looked at her across the cab of her truck. "I need to do this."

She nodded, her gaze growing intense. "I respect that, and I won't get in your way, but you need to keep your head on straight. Focus at all times, control your emotions, don't let your anger take hold."

I thought she'd stop me. I thought she'd go to Draven and rat me out. She hadn't. "I'm focused. I'm in control." For the first time in a very long time, I wasn't confused. I had a better handle on my anger now than I had for a long time. I knew exactly what I wanted. The other stuff was there— the fear, the memories, the pain—but I wasn't going to let them stop me, not this time.

We got out of the truck, and I pulled on my pack and strapped my knife to my thigh.

"You want me to keep an eye on the prom committee while you're gone?" Ash asked.

I shouldn't be going. It was reckless, time I didn't have to spare, but I couldn't not. Without Bram, I would fail this task—because I was only half alive, half a soul, without him. "Thanks, but I'll be quick. There and back in a flash."

She nodded and leaned into the truck, taking something from under the seat, and tossed it to me.

I grabbed it. "What's this?" I unrolled the canvas. A dozen small throwing knives shone up at me from their harness.

155

"Strap them to your chest," she said.

I did as she said as she walked around the truck and undid the massive hunting knife strapped to her thigh. She held it out to me. "Take this as well."

"Ash—"

"Take it. A couple good whacks and you'll just about take a head clean off, even those thick-necked fucks."

She wasn't going to take no for an answer, and I wanted to hug her for it. I resisted. Asher wasn't the hugging type. "Thanks." I strapped it on as well.

"I know I've given you shit in the past about going on patrol, but you've been ready for a while. Draven was nervous, being protective. I should have forced the issue. I didn't and I'm sorry." She gripped my shoulders. "But you're a fucking warrior, Mags. I'd trust you to have my back any day of the week."

I swallowed thickly.

"And don't forget, if you even think you're about to be outnumbered, run like fuck. Demon blood's your best camouflage. Go high when you need to rest, but only if you really have to. Staying in one spot for any length of time's the worst thing you can do. If you don't have time to remove their heads, incapacitate and keep moving. It's a better option for conserving your energy anyway, and a wounded demon's easy eating and will distract the others in the vicinity while you get the fuck out of there."

I nodded as she went over all the things she'd taught me the last six months.

She tapped the side of my head. "You control what's going on in here, and you can do anything, Mags, yeah?" She released me and stood back.

"Thanks, for everything, Ash."

Her jaw tightened, then she held out her fist. I pounded it, and she strode around the truck and opened the door. "Don't die, or I'll never hear the end of it from Iris."

"Not planning on it," I said, refusing to let her see the nerves rioting inside me. "See you in a couple days."

"See you in a couple days." Her gaze grew intense. "Now go get your male."

Then she got in her truck, turned around, and drove away.

I pulled my phone from my pocket and scrolled down to the number I needed.

It rang twice. "Yeah?"

"Payne, it's Magnolia. Is Bram with you?"

"If he's not answering your calls, then take the fucking hint. Don't call again."

"Wait!" I said before he hung up. "This is important. And it's you I want to talk to."

"We have nothing to say to each other."

He was the most arrogant asshole I'd ever met. "I'm going to tell you something, and I want you to keep it to yourself, for now, anyway."

A beat of silence. "And why would I do that?"

"Because if you give Bram my message now, he'll come for me, and he can't do that."

A low growl. "Cut to the chase, witch."

"In thirty-six hours, I need you to tell Bram to stand behind your family's tree house and face the clearing."

More silence, and this time it was heavy as hell.

"Payne?"

He laughed darkly.

"Will you do that?" I asked, refusing to let his reaction piss me off.

"You're not fooling me. First, if you think you're strong enough to do the demon run in thirty-six hours, you're even more fucking clueless than I thought. Witch, you aren't capable of making it in the forty-eight allowed. I see through you, though. You think I'll tell him and he'll come running to stop you. But I won't let you use him anymore. Bram's a warrior, not your fucking lapdog. You are selfish and self-centered, and I won't let you twist him up in knots only to cast him aside again. It won't fucking work."

Each of his words left a bruise. It fucking killed me to think about the pain I'd caused Bram. "I will be there in thirty-six hours. I love Bram, and I'm going to prove it to him."

"It's your funeral," he said, then he disconnected.

I didn't know if he'd pass on my message, but either way, I was doing it, and I hoped like hell Bram was waiting for me at the other end.

Agatheena's words filtered through my mind. *Your task, it'll be a test of strength—magical, physical, but mostly...*" She'd tapped the side of her head. *"But mostly a test of what's in here. Are you mentally strong, Magnolia? Because you'll need to be."* Her finger had pressed against the center of my chest. *"And in here. Your heart will need to be sure, true."*

I hadn't known what she meant at the time, but I did now. My heart was sure, and it was true. I knew what my heart wanted now, what it needed. I needed Bram in my life, not just for this task but for all my days and all my nights. For forever.

I'd always needed him, and not just as my familiar—I needed my mate.

Shoving my phone in my pocket, I started running.

CHAPTER 19

Magnolia

PLANTING my foot on the demon's chest, I yanked Asher's knife from its throat. Blood sprayed me, and I dragged my forearm over my eyes so I could see, then scooped up more of its blood and smeared it over any exposed skin to cover my scent. I'd been doing it regularly, but still some of the creatures in these woods scented me.

I hadn't slept in thirty-five hours. I was cut and clawed, there were several bites on my arm and one on my side that I was pretty sure was getting infected, and I had one hour to reach Bram, and a lot of ground still to cover.

Shoving the knife back in its sheath, I spun from the flailing, bleeding demon and ran like hell. Roars and hisses echoed behind me, from breeds of demons, from creatures I'd never encountered before I'd walked into this forest. I shuddered, but now knew more about than I'd ever wanted to.

Hopefully, the demon thrashing about back there would keep them busy for a short time and give me the chance to put some distance between me and them.

A snarl came from my right several seconds before a demon ran at me. They tended to do that, gave themselves away before they attacked. It was all the time I needed. Spinning, I kicked it in the head. It stumbled back, then came at me again. I tumbled into a roll as it lunged, jumping up and kicking it in the back. It face-planted, and I quickly slashed the tendons above each knee and ankle. The demon screamed, and I jumped to my feet and kept running.

I was fueled by adrenaline and desperation at this point. I'd finished the last of my water a few hours ago. I was hungry as hell, but without water I wasn't sure I'd be able to choke down my last energy bar.

A group of four...not demons, but *creatures*, appeared out of nowhere. Their hideous faces were wide, noses pointed and bony, bloodshot eyes protruding. I cringed. If my belly wasn't so empty, I'd be dry heaving from their smell alone. I yanked a glass vile from my pocket and threw it with force at the rock by one of the fugly fuckers' hairy feet. It smashed, and my potion did its thing, the vapor exploding around them and sending them deep into a hallucination haze, blinding them to me.

I only had two vials left. One like the potion I'd just used, inducing confusion and causing hallucinations, and the other, well, that one caused a little more damage.

I yanked my knife free, using it on the next demon who ran at me, somehow taking him out of commission with my frenzied hacking. Yeah, I was running out of steam, and fast. Digging deep, I thought of Bram, of how much pain I'd caused him, of how much I missed him, needed him, of how much I wanted to show him what he meant to me, and gritted my teeth, pushing harder.

I only had twenty minutes left.

Light broke through the trees ahead. I was almost at the edge of the forest. So close. Almost at the clearing between this forest and the crows' village. I just had to get there. I just had to find the strength to run that clearing.

The excited calls and whoops, the growls, grew in volume behind me. I focused ahead, about to pick up the pace, but was forced to slam on the brakes instead.

Demons.

They hadn't seen me yet, but ahead of me were more demons than I had a single hope of getting by.

Fuck.

The hungry sounds grew louder behind me, more of them closing in from all directions.

I needed to make a move. Now. I looked up at the massive tree beside me, its thick branches reaching out to the one beside it. With no time to waste, I gathered every bit of strength I could muster and scrambled up the wide trunk, somehow finding foothold after foothold, like I was being guided by someone else.

The demons crashed through the forest beneath, searching for me. I'd never seen so many demons or hideous creatures in my life. If I fell now, I'd be torn to shreds in seconds.

Taking a deep breath to steady my nerves, I stepped out onto one of the thick branches, using the one above to steady me, then onto another that touched the tree beside it. I focused on my balance, making my way to the next tree, then the next, slowly working my way to the edge of the forest.

What I planned to do when I got there? I had no fucking clue, but I had to think of something fast, because time was almost up.

If I was going to prove to Bram that I was worthy of being his mate, I had to finish this.

Failure wasn't an option.

>)>●(((

Bram

I gripped the railing, refusing to rub at the ache in my chest. No, I let it sink deeper. I'd done this to myself. I'd known she wasn't ready, and I'd pushed for more anyway. I'd ruined everything.

Gritting my teeth, I dragged in a breath, then another, trying to calm the fuck down. It didn't work. Nothing worked.

I didn't know what to do with this feeling inside me. This violent twisting behind my ribs, the knives in my gut, the hammering in my skull —it was unbearable.

Magnolia was my everything, but right now, being with her was as painful as being parted from her.

The thud of boots on the deck came a moment before Payne grunted, then growled something under his breath. I turned to find him pacing, lips peeled back, fists clenched.

He'd been acting weird since yesterday. He glanced at his watch, again, something he'd been doing all day.

"What the hell is up with you?"

"Fuck." He growled and planted his hands on his hips. "Fuck," he said again. "Let's go."

"Where?"

"Just fucking follow me." He looked at Talon and Rook. "You two as well."

The three of us looked at each other, then at Payne's retreating back.

Talon rolled his eyes. "Guess we're following."

I pushed away from the railing, strode the edge of the deck, and jumped to the ground after my brothers. Payne walked to the chain-link fence between us and the wide clearing that bordered the forest beyond it.

"Okay, we're here," I said to Payne, then stilled and tilted my head. Roars and howls, a fucking lot of them, echoed from the forest beyond the clearing.

"Something's riled them up," Talon said, walking up to the fence as well. He shaded his eyes and searched the tree line.

Payne's jaw tightened, and he looked antsy as fuck. "You." He pointed at me. "Stand here."

"You having some kind of episode?" Talon asked our older brother.

Payne ignored him. "Here, Bram, now."

I frowned and walked up to the spot my control-freak brother was pointing out, confused as hell.

The demons and other creatures in the forest grew louder, their howls and snarls filled with excitement, with hunger and rage. "What the hell's making them lose their shit like that?"

Rook shifted, a look suddenly crossing his face like a lightbulb just switched on before his gaze sliced to Payne, then back at me.

"Why the fuck are we standing here?" Talon asked, sounding pissed and just as confused as I was.

The roars from the forest grew in volume. I'd never heard anything like it. I felt it in my chest, in my gut. Why the fuck was my heart racing?

Payne looked down at his watch.

"Payne?" Rook growled out.

Payne looked up and grabbed my shoulder in a bruising grip, then pointed to the edge of the forest. "Watch."

There was a strange note to his voice that had every muscle in my body locking tight, that lifted goose bumps all over me. I turned, searching in the direction he pointed, when the creatures in the forest lost their shit to a whole new fucking level.

Something small dropped from one of the tree branches along the edge. I squinted, trying to see what it was—

A dark figure shot up from the ground and started running—fucking sprinting.

Demons, creatures of all shapes and sizes, burst from the forest edge, making chase.

I gripped the fence, my heart hammering harder.

The small figure was dressed in black.

Short.

Curvy.

They turned to look behind them, and a long, black ponytail whipped out.

My entire body jolted.

Magnolia.

Oh fuck.

I gripped the fence about to jump it, to get to her—

Three pairs of strong hands grabbed me, yanking me back down, stopping me from getting to her, from helping her. I fought harder.

"Let me fucking go!" I snarled, losing my shit completely.

Payne gripped me harder. "You know what this is," he growled into my ear. "Fucking look. Look at her."

My heart was beating so hard that black spots were dancing in front of my eyes, not hearing him, not really. "Get the fuck off me."

My brothers held me tighter, not giving me an inch.

"Your little witch has spent the last thirty-six hours fighting her way through a forest full of monsters to get to you," Payne said. "To show you how much you matter to her. Don't take that from her. Let her finish this."

I gripped the fence so tight the wire cut into my fingers. No, that's not what this was. It couldn't be.

"She knows what you are, Bram," Rook said, his voice low. "And still she's running to you. She's not scared, she doesn't want you to rescue her, she's on a fucking mission," my usually quiet brother growled out. "Fucking look at her."

He didn't need to say it, she was all I could see. My wings exploded from my back, every part of me wanting to jump this fence, to snatch her from danger, to protect her.

A demon charged her from the left. Mags pulled something from her pocket and tossed it hard at the fucker. It screamed, grabbing at his now *melting* face. Several more came from the right. Her hands moved so fucking fast, grabbing and tossing throwing knives that were strapped to her chest, taking them down one after the other. Another one came from the left. Her hand shot out, and she slammed a knife into its throat, wrenched it out, then head down, arms pumping, she kept sprinting toward me.

"Holy fuck," Talon muttered.

She was covered in mud and so much blood, I could smell it all the way from here—demon blood and her own—and my crow shrieked, its talons clawing at my subconscious to get to her. To get to my female.

She was close now, and when her eyes came to me, locking on, my fucking knees went weak.

There was a roar and a huge fucking creature broke from the pack, barreling after her on all fours. Fuck, it was gaining on her. My wings started beating.

"Wait," Payne growled beside me. "She got this far without you. Trust her."

The creature pounced, and Mags flipped into a seamless tumble, rolling to her back. The fucker was taken by surprise and couldn't stop. Mags thrust her knife into its chest as the creature ran right over her, its own forward momentum dragging her blade down its belly, gutting it as it ran over the top of her.

Without missing a beat, she rolled, jumped to her feet, and kept sprinting.

Thirty yards.

Twenty.

Ten.

My heart smashed into my ribs. "Come on, baby."

She was almost to me.

My brothers released me, and I took several steps back as she closed the last few yards between us, as she threw herself at the fence, scrambling up it. The demons making chase slammed on the brakes as soon as they saw us, quickly falling back, not dumb enough to come any closer to our territory.

Blood pumped through my veins so hard and fast, I felt fucking dizzy as I watched her.

Mags jumped down, her boots thudding against the hard-packed earth. Then she straightened, demon blood dripping down her face and coating her clothes, her hands.

I tried to speak, but nothing would come. I was in shock. In fucking awe.

"You forgot something when you left," she said, chest heaving.

"What's that?" I choked out.

"Me," she said and ran at me.

I caught her up, lifting her into my arms. She wrapped herself around me, and I buried my face against the side of her throat, my skin to hers, breathing her in.

Uma and Maeve, the rest of the village had come to see what was going on, congregating behind us, and they hooted and cheered now.

Several seconds ticked by, both of us clinging to the other, then she cupped my jaw. "Look at me," she whispered against my ear.

Trembling, I lifted my head, afraid to believe what this meant, what was happening here, but hoping like fuck this was what I thought it was.

Her fingers slid over the shaved sides of my head, her amber eyes searching mine. "I made a mistake," she said.

I swallowed. "What was that?" My voice was so fucking deep and broken, I didn't recognize it.

The pulse in her throat fluttered wildly. "When you tried to kiss me... Instead of listening to the fear, I should have listened to my heart."

I brushed my thumb over her jaw. "And what was your heart telling you?"

She licked her lips. "This." Then her gorgeous mouth came down on mine.

My fucking pulse went haywire, my knees nearly buckled, and my body went up in flames. Wrapping my arms around her tighter, I groaned, fucking positive this had to be a fever dream, or maybe I'd died and this was Heaven.

"I love you," she said against my lips, then parted hers, sliding her tongue over mine.

I fucking short-circuited, gripping her tighter, taking everything she was giving me, afraid she'd change her mind and take it back, that she'd stop—that I'd fucking wake up in bed alone.

Then she whimpered into my mouth, her scent, the heat of her body, the tang of blood coating her skin and clothes...hit me, lit me up, and I knew it was real. This was no dream.

I wrapped my arms around her tighter, and beating my wings, I lifted off the ground.

I finally had my Magnolia in my arms.

Where she belonged.

CHAPTER 20

Magnolia

BRAM SHOT INTO THE SKY, and I hung on tight, lifting my head to look down as we flew over tree houses. Bram's hand gripped the back of my head and he pulled me down again, to take my mouth. He kissed me deep, hard, his body shaking as soft rattles and growls resonated through his chest, vibrating against mine, his crow coming through loud and clear.

I couldn't believe this was happening.

This was Bram. My Bram. And we were *kissing*. I fisted his shirt, holding him close, kissing him back, and it felt so incredibly fucking right.

But it had always felt right when I was in his arms. My body, my heart, had known this was where I belonged, but after what happened with Clayton, my mind had shut it down, it had denied and resisted what was right there all along.

Bram dropped from the sky, landing with a thud on the wooden deck outside his tree house, the one he'd built with his brothers when he was a kid, the one he used when he came to the village.

I clung to him as he strode through the door and kicked it shut behind us. I couldn't take my eyes off his as he lowered me to my feet. His hands were low on my sides as he walked me backward through the living room and into the bedroom.

165

His glossy obsidian eyes smoldered down at me. "You're so fucking beautiful," he said in that deep yet quiet voice of his.

The rough velvet of it had goose bumps pebbling across my skin. "So are you," I said, eating up the sight of him. I knew his face better than my own, but I'd never seen the expression he currently wore, or the look in his eyes. It was desire, only now he wasn't trying to conceal it. He wasn't hiding anything, any part of him. I knew it all, had seen it all. First in that run-down building with blood on his hands, and now standing in his arms, the full force of his need etched into his handsome face.

His hands slid up to my waist, his grip tightening as he tugged me closer...squeezing a whimper of pain from me.

Bram hissed, pulling back instantly. "Your injuries." He scanned my body. "They need tending."

"I'm okay," I said and lifted to my tiptoes, going after his mouth.

Bram gave me what I wanted, pressing another kiss to my lips before he ended it too damn quickly.

I whimpered again, not in pain this time. "Don't stop."

He pressed his forehead to mine, the tremor still moving through his big body. "I don't ever want to stop, but I need to check your injuries. The scent of your blood is making me want to storm the forest and kill everything in it. So let's do that first, yeah?"

I didn't want to. I wanted to stay where I was, I wanted him to keep kissing me, but I knew he was right. So I let him lead me into the bathroom. He crouched down, helping me out of my boots, then tugged my blood-soaked pants carefully down my legs. His hair was loose and falling to one side, and I slid my fingers through the thick, black strands, needing to touch him, to never stop touching him.

He tilted his head back, looking up at me. "Okay?"

I nodded. "Are you in any doubt now about how much I love you?"

His eyes flared and hands slid up the outside of my thighs to my waist. His fingers gripped me there, lightly this time. His throat worked, then he wrapped his arms around my waist, shaking harder as he pressed his face against my belly and breathed deep. I kept my hands in the soft warmth of his hair, my own emotions rushing through me.

When he looked up at me again, his eyes glistened. "I thought I'd lost you. I never thought you'd... Fuck, seeing you running across that clearing..." His throat worked.

I shook my head. "You will never lose me." I brushed my fingers over the shaved sides of his head. "I lost my way for a little while, but I've found my way back...back to you."

He rose to his feet and took my chin in his hand, tilting my head back before he kissed me again, wild and deep, stealing my breath once more.

"You know what we are, don't you, Mags?" he said against my lips, then lifted his head and took my chin again, holding it, demanding without words that I look into his eyes, that I don't shy away or retreat. "What we are to each other?"

I did, and the dominance in his gaze, his voice, the way he held me, sent a delicious shiver through me. "Yes." I thought he'd shown me all of him, but this was another part of Bram I'd never seen, not really, not like this.

"You are my mate, Magnolia. I felt it from the moment I met you. I've waited so fucking long for you to feel it, too, to see it. So make no mistake, you are mine." He pressed another kiss to my lips. "And I want to devour every fucking part of you, own every inch of you, I need you to know that, but we're not going to rush this. I can wait. I'll make you mine in truth, but not until you're ready for it, okay?"

My heart thundered wildly in my chest, and I nodded.

I wanted him, I did, in every way, but I was also scarred, inside and out, in more ways than a person should be, and Bram knew that better than anyone.

He stared down at me, a look of...of wonder on his face as he tucked my hair behind my ear, then leaned in and kissed me gently, as though he couldn't bear not to touch his lips to mine just one more time. "Now, we're going to clean all that demon blood off you before I lose my shit. Your wounds badly need tending, and you need to eat and rest."

I fisted the front of his shirt and tugged him closer. "You think we can fit some more kissing in there somewhere as well?"

He grinned, his abs tightening against my fist. "We fucking better."

Goddess, he was handsome.

He stepped back and tugged off his shirt, then shoved down his jeans. Stripping so he was just in boxer briefs, he reached in and turned on the shower.

"We need to get these clothes off," he said as he gently peeled my shirt up and off, flinging it aside. When he turned back and took in the state of my upper body, he hissed again, his hand trembling as it skimmed carefully over the cuts and bites, the bruises marring my skin, adding to the scars already covering my body.

He shook harder, but with rage this time, as he took in the rest of me. I stood in front of him in only my underwear. He'd seen me like this before—he'd seen me completely naked, more than once—but for the first time, I knew he was looking at me as his female, his mate, and one day soon, his lover.

What did he see when he looked at me? All I saw when I looked in the mirror were imperfections. All the ugliness of my past, immortalized on my skin. I shoved that down, locking it away, refusing to let it ruin this moment.

Bram helped me into the shower, and lathering soap in his hands, he slowly, methodically, ran them over my body, washing the blood and dirt from my skin. As his hand drifted over my chest, he paused, looking down at me, checking I was okay with it. I nodded and bit my lips when his palm grazed my nipples.

His nostrils flared as I ate up the sight of him, tall and lean and muscled. His stomach muscles were tight as hell, and my gaze trailed over the warrior tattoos decorating his body, then down to the V at his hips that led my gaze even lower...

My belly heated, clenching tight. He was hard, straining behind the soaked fabric of his underwear, but Bram seemed content to ignore it, laser focused on getting the smell of demon off me.

His hand slid over my stomach, and he leaned in and kissed me again. My body fired to life in a way that it hadn't for so very long. My nipples tightened, heat flooding me. I squeezed my thighs together, moaning against his lips. "Touch me."

I was weak, hungry, my mind spinning, fuzzy for once, not letting anything else in except for my desperation for Bram's touch.

His hand didn't stop moving over my skin. "You sure?"

"Yes, please. I need you to touch me."

"Tell me where."

I took his wrist, leading him where I needed him, pushing the tips of his fingers under the elastic of my underwear. "Please," I said.

His gaze was locked on mine, searching for any sign that I didn't want this as he slid his fingers down the front of my underwear.

"Fuck," he growled, the sound bouncing off the tiles.

He hooked one strong arm around me, holding me up, and pressed his lips to my forehead. "I need you to tell me if you don't like it, if you want me to stop, okay?"

I nodded as he curled his fingers around my pussy, the middle one pressing deeper. I shoved my forehead against his chest, digging my fingernails into his biceps.

"You're so hot. So fucking slick." Bram groaned as he slid his fingers up and back. "Good?"

"Yes, don't...don't stop."

He fisted my wet hair with his other hand and tilted my head back. "Eyes on me, Magnolia."

The rough, possessiveness in his voice sent a shiver through me. I blinked up at him through the spray and steam, licking the water from my lips.

His gaze dropped to my mouth, then back, and his eyes darkened. "I want to make you come, Maggie, so fucking badly. I want to make you feel good."

The use of that nickname—the one he used so sparingly, the one that I loved so much—and the vulnerability I saw in his eyes had me moving closer, holding him tighter. "It d-does. It feels so good."

His fingers slid higher, circling my clit, and my legs tried to buckle under me again.

"Yeah, right there," he muttered. "Faster?"

I nodded, digging my nails deeper. "P-please."

His chest heaved with his panted breaths as he focused solely on getting me off. His fingers didn't let up, demanding my surrender. I cried out and bit my lip harder when the pleasure started to grow.

He pressed on my lower lip with his thumb, pulling it free, and shook his head. "No hiding from me. We've hidden enough from each other. Not this, never this." He dipped his head, sliding his tongue over my abused lip. "I want to hear it, how good I make you feel, I need to hear it. Give it to me, Mags."

At his words, the feeling growing inside me intensified, its grip on me tightening even more. I panted, sharp sobs bursting from me the closer I got to my breaking point. I squeezed my eyes closed.

"Eyes on me," he said again. "Now."

I forced my eyes open, and when they met his, a sound vibrated through his chest, soft yet deep, rumbling through him. It was almost melodic, a mix of growls and rattles, along with something that could only be described as cooing. I'd never heard it from him before. He nuzzled the side of my face, my neck, sucking the skin there.

At the next swipe of his fingers, I gasped, a cry bursting from me, then I shattered, calling out his name as I came for him, gasping for breath.

Black dots filled my vision, and this time when my knees buckled, there was no stopping it.

Bram scooped me up. "I've got you," he said.

Then everything went dark.

)))●(((

Bram

I worked my way across Magnolia's body, liberally using Else's healing balm and some of the other concoctions Mags had made and used on me many times. There was a bite on her side that was starting to look puffy and pink around the edges. Infection would have set in if it'd been left any longer.

It was a good thing she was out cold, it meant she wouldn't feel it when I cleaned it out. I rinsed it a second time with herb-infused warm water. There was a clear outline of a vicious set of teeth deep in her skin.

My hand shook as I dabbed the area clean. Only now that things had quieted down was the shock setting in.

I would never forget the image of Magnolia running across that field, a forest full of monsters right behind her. She'd been powerful, god, magnificent. My Mags was a fucking warrior, but I'd never been as terrified as I was in that moment.

There'd been so many other emotions there as well. Fuck. Pride, possessiveness, hope, love—lust.

My gaze trailed up to her face. Her eyes were closed, her chest rising and falling slow and even. Her lips were puffy and darker from our kisses, and I wanted to taste her again so badly. I wanted to taste every part of her. My need was so great and my gut was in constant knots, but I meant what I said, I'd wait. Yes, I wanted Magnolia in a way that, if she could feel it, see it, would probably scare the hell out of her, but I'd wait another lifetime for her if I had to.

She needed to be ready for me, which meant the ball was in her court. I'd lived with the aftermath of what Clayton fucking Whitlock did to her. I knew how much she'd struggled to live with it, to get past it. It'd been the hardest thing she'd ever done, and I wouldn't undo all that work by pushing for something she wasn't ready for.

The way she'd asked me to touch her, pleaded for it, the way she'd called out my name in the shower, the sounds of her coming for me, kept running through my mind now, and I sucked in a sharp breath when my cock grew heavier.

It's not like I wasn't used to it when I was around her, but it was different than before. Before I had no hope of ever making her mine. Before, I hadn't touched her pussy or felt how slick and hot she was *for me*. I'd resigned myself to never having her, to never knowing these things. Now it wasn't a matter of if, but when.

I dragged in another fortifying breath and willed my dick down as I smeared more balm on her side, rubbing it into the wound as best as I could, then adding another layer before I dressed it with a thick bandage. I'd stripped Mags out of her wet bra and panties while she was out cold and tugged the shirt I'd put on her down to cover her nakedness.

It was late, had grown dark outside, and I climbed into bed beside her, getting as close as I could so her body was plastered against mine. Wrapping my arms around her curvy, little body, I closed my eyes and breathed her in.

A sense of peace I hadn't felt in a long time, not since the day I found her, filled me. Mags made a breathy little noise, wriggling against me, finally regaining consciousness. I didn't move behind her, still afraid she'd wake up and change her mind, that she'd pull away, that she'd say this was all a huge mistake.

She didn't, instead, her hand covered mine, threading our fingers together. "Night, B," she whispered.

"Night, Mags," I said, and kissed her jaw.

How the fuck was I supposed to sleep now? It felt like Christmas, all my birthdays, every good fucking thing all rolled into one.

Mags was here with me. She was finally mine.

And I was never letting her go.

CHAPTER 21

Magnolia

SUN FILTERED INTO THE ROOM.

I blinked several times, letting my sleepy brain clear, then remembered where I was. With Bram, at his village.

In his bed.

I'd shared a bed with him more times than I could count, pressed against him, draped over him, but this...this was different. We'd kissed, he'd touched me. He'd made me come.

We'd admitted to feelings we'd both hidden from each other, and in my case, from myself, for far too long.

He was plastered against my back, his hand up under the shirt he must have put on me while I was out cold. His palm was flat against my stomach, hot against my skin. I could tell without looking, he'd tended my wounds while I'd been out. I could smell the balm. There was half a glass of water by the bed. He'd given me water, but I had no recollection of it. I shifted, reaching for it now, my wounds smarting as I carefully moved while trying not to wake him.

He muttered something as I lay back, the hand on my belly pressing me into him more firmly and one of his knees lifting, sliding between mine. Heat spiraled through me, and I tried to keep my breathing even, but it was impossible, because all I could think about was the way he'd touched me in the shower. The sounds he'd made when he'd looked into my eyes, the dominant way he'd quietly asked—no, demanded—submission from me. How desperately I'd wanted to give it to him. I'd asked him to touch me, but he'd run with it. He'd taken control, and he'd made it so I didn't have to think, so I could just let go.

I'd never experienced anything like it, but I wasn't surprised it was Bram who'd given it to me.

His fingers flexed against my stomach, and he growled as his arm curled around me more tightly, his thigh lifting higher, until it was pressed firmly against the bare flesh between my legs.

His mouth went to my ear. "Morning."

Somehow, I managed to suppress the shiver that danced up my spine at those roughly spoken words. I really wanted to squeeze my thighs together, but it was impossible. "Morning."

Bram's thigh applied more pressure while the hand on my stomach started to slide up and back, getting a little higher each time.

"You sleep okay?" he asked in that same gritty-as-hell morning voice.

It did things to me, it always had, I'd just been in denial about it. But there was no hiding what it did to me now, not this time. He had to feel it. "Yeah...you?"

He nuzzled my throat. "No." His lips trailed along my skin. "I lay awake all night, too scared to close my eyes in case I woke up this morning and it turned out yesterday was all a dream."

His hand slipped higher, and I sucked in a breath, a sensation moving through me that was full of contradiction. My scars were so incredibly sensitive. I wanted more, but at the same time, it was almost too much. I wanted to arch against his touch and shove his hand away at the same time. I was in sensory overload, and my subconscious was pulling up images of the only other person who had ever touched my bare skin...

I quickly rolled to my back so I could see Bram, so every part of me knew this was him, because he was safe. He was my safe place.

He looked down at me, eyes sleepy, hair mussed, and I hated that my body was still in flight mode; that even now I had to fight against the need to flee when I was touched. My scars burned under his hand and, as he slid it higher, I sucked in another breath and covered it with my own, halting him.

Worry filled his eyes, and I quickly reached up, hooked him around the back of the neck and pulled him down for a kiss before he could speak, before he could apologize or freak out that he'd done something wrong. Because it wasn't Bram, it was me.

He came to me instantly, his kiss soft, gentle, exploring, knowing I needed him to slow down and giving that to me. I hated that I needed time.

Bram would never hurt me. Never. I knew that to my very soul. He'd give up everything for me in a heartbeat. He'd give me the world if he could.

My scars burned hotter, and I moaned against his lips, the mix of pleasure and pain saturating my body, making me gasp against his lips. I pulled him closer, fighting it, willing the pain overwhelming me away. But it didn't leave, it heightened.

Then it was too much. Oh, goddess, it was as if every scar had been torn open again. I shoved at Bram's shoulder with a scream of pain. He lifted off me immediately, and I looked down at myself, expecting to see blood, to see knife wounds appearing all over my body like they had that day.

"What is it?" he barked, his gaze slicing over me, fear stark in his eyes as if he expected to see the same. As if he were reliving that awful day as well.

Panting, I shook my head, sweating, body trembling. "I—I don't know. It felt like...like it was happening again."

His chest rose and fell with his labored breaths, and his jaw tightened. "I pushed too hard, too fast."

"No, that's not it. You touch me all the time—"

"This is different. I'm touching you differently, Mags. The only other person to touch you that way..." A look of pure hatred filled his eyes. He was imagining what he'd do to Clayton if he had the chance, I could see it on his face. He shook it off, his eyes softening when they came back to me. "I promised I'd take it slow, then I rushed you. It won't happen again."

I wanted to scream in frustration. I didn't want that monster getting between us. I wanted him wiped from my mind, from my skin. "What if..." I sat up and pushed on his shoulder.

Bram let me, dropping to his back. "You don't need to—"

"I know I don't, but I want to. I want to be close to you. If we have to go slow because I'm so fucking messed up, fine, but I want to keep trying..." I moved over him slowly, ignoring the way the bite at my side throbbed, along with all the other aches and pains all over my body, and rested my hands on the mattress on either side of his head. "We can't stop, okay? We can't stop trying. We need to push, because I want you...I do. I just...I just..." I didn't know what to say, how to make him understand.

He brushed my hair away from my face, and held it against the back of my neck. "You're not messed up, you're perfect—in every conceivable fucking way. You think I'm going to get frustrated with you? That I'll change my mind because we can't have sex? That I'll lose interest?" His thumb swiped over my cheek. "Just knowing you want to be with me is enough. Being with you, just near you, is *enough*. I need you to let that sink in. I need you to believe it, because it's the truth. If it takes a week or a month, or a year, before you're cool with me touching you, I'm fucking cool with that. If it takes a year before you're ready to have sex, more, fucking never, I am cool with that. I'm crazy, insanely, obsessively in love with you, Magnolia, and that will never ever change no matter what we do, or don't do. Not fucking ever, understand?"

I swallowed and nodded. Goddess, everything he'd just said hit hard, so hard I had to fight back tears. I had no idea what to say to that, so I leaned in and kissed him. When our lips met, he lay still, letting me lead, his hands at his sides. I explored his mouth loving the way his chest rose and fell faster as I did. He was right, I was scared he'd give up on me if I couldn't be everything he needed, even though I knew better than that. I knew Bram better than that. "You're obsessively in love with me?" I said against his mouth.

"Are you really in any doubt?" he said. "I have been since you hugged me outside your family's cemetery." He blinked up at me. "You became my entire world that day, Maggie."

"You became mine as well," I said and pressed my face against the side of his throat before I lost the fight and started crying. He rubbed my back, his touch light, cautious, as I breathed heavily.

We stayed like that for a long time, and soaked it in, breathed him in. Reminding my stupid brain every now and then that I was with Bram, and that Bram was crazy, insanely, obsessively in love with me.

For a minute, I thought he'd gone to sleep, then his hand slid up my back and into my hair, fisting it gently. "Baby?"

Baby. "Yeah?"

"Look at me."

I lifted my head.

"Do you have any questions about what you saw the other night," he asked, his gaze searching mine.

I did. Several.

I slid my hand up his chest and lightly wrapped my fingers around his throat, like I'd be able to feel it, stop it if his oath kicked in and tried to choke him again. "How do you decide who to kill?"

"We don't, we're given targets," he said, thankfully without any trouble.

"By who?"

"Pack heads, the witches council, others of all kinds. They call us when one of their own goes rogue and humans are involved. Maybe they can't deal with it themselves, for some reason, or it's too risky or dangerous. That's when they hire us to do the job."

"If the council didn't know about our connection, do you think they would've called you and your brothers in to hunt for Willow?" I asked. "In their eyes, she's a murderous witch out of control."

"I don't know. If humans were involved, then probably. But we don't just kill because someone wants us to. We make sure they deserve to die before we end a life."

"Do the people that hire you take the silencing oath as well?"

"Yes."

"And you...you wanted to do it? Go after your targets?"

"Not at first, I tried to resist, but like I said, we're more animal than human. Payne made sure I had no choice but to join the family business, because hunting is something we need and ignoring our animal instincts can be detrimental, it could turn us rogue or worse."

"You could lose your mind if you don't kill?"

"Yes."

"And all crows are like that?"

"To an extent. Most are satisfied to hunt in the woods every now and then—animals, occasionally demons. Those of us who grow into the warriors of our race, the protectors of our people, are closer to our crows, to that base part of ourselves and we need the...outlet. This work gives us what we need to stay sane and healthy, provides our people with the money we need to thrive, and the humans stay safe."

"But you could get hurt, worse."

A dangerous-as-fuck look transformed his face. "Hunting and killing, we're made for it, Mags. You don't have to worry about me."

What he'd said should probably worry or frighten me. It didn't. Maybe it made me twisted, but instead heat bloomed low in my belly, a throb humming to life between my thighs.

Bram's nostrils flared, and he made a low grunting growl sound, one that was totally animalistic.

"That sound, it's your crow, yes?"

He nodded and licked his lips.

"What does it mean?" All the sounds they made had their own meaning. He'd explained that to me a long time ago. I thought I'd heard all his sounds until now.

"It means I can smell how wet you are right now, and my crow is pleased," he rasped.

I wasn't embarrassed. I wanted him to know how much I wanted him. I couldn't give him all of me, not yet, but I at least wanted him to know my body did even if my mind was fucking with me. I pressed my mouth to his. "And the sound you made in the shower?"

"When I made you come?" he asked, voice gritty as hell.

"Yes," I lifted my head, looking down at him.

"It's the sound...the song, we sing to our mates. It comes from within us, pure instinct. Wild crows obviously can't kiss, so they nuzzle each other, and our people, being closer to our crow, do both, we sing and

176

nuzzle our females to show affection and to let them know how much they're loved." Bram had always done it, pressed his face to my neck, nuzzled me. I hadn't known the significance. He tucked my hair behind my ear. "Our songs, they're incredibly intimate and something we don't do in front of others. No two songs are the same. It's something just for the two of us."

My heart clenched. "Was last night the first time you've done it?"

"It's the first time I've allowed myself to do it. I've wanted to, more times than I can count, when I was alone with you, but I wanted you feeling what I was when I finally allowed it to happen."

My eyes drifted shut as I fought back more goddamn tears. Just thinking about the last six years, the pain he must have suffered thinking I'd never want him the way he did me, it hurt to think about it. The guilt was unbearable. He was my familiar, my best friend, my everything, and I'd hurt him.

His warm palm pressed against the side of my throat, his rough-skinned fingers curling around the back before he drew me down. His forehead touched mine. "Mags, look at me."

I did as he asked, blinking down at him.

"Don't," he said roughly.

"But I—"

"You have nothing to feel guilty about."

Like he always had, he was able to see what was in my heart. "I hurt you."

He shook his head. "We hurt each other."

He gave my throat a light squeeze, and the heat between my thighs intensified.

"How can we have a moment's regret when it all led to now? To this moment."

He was right, regrets were pointless. "We may have taken the long route, and yeah, there are a few more hurdles to jump, but the happily ever after is right there on the horizon," I said and gave him a wobbly smile.

"It's right fucking here, right now."

The door banged open in the living room. "Rook's inking, get your ass up," Payne called through the door. There was a pause. "Morning, Magnolia."

For once there wasn't even a hint of resentment in his tone. Even when he'd tried to hide it for Bram's sake, I'd heard it, or seen it in his eyes.

"You've got five minutes," he added, then the door closed behind him.

It took some serious convincing, but I eventually managed to drag Bram out of bed. Yes, I wanted to stay right there, but I also didn't want to piss off his brothers. They'd pretty much despised me since Bram found me. I thought I might finally have their respect, and I didn't want to mess that up again.

Bram grumbled as he pulled on jeans. He didn't bother with a shirt. I'd seen him bare chested more often than not over the years, but now, it was hard for me to keep my hands off him. I guess that wasn't new either. But now it was heightened, like to the millionth degree.

My jeans were ruined, so I had on a pair of Bram's track pants. I was swimming in them, they looked ridiculous, but the sexy, smoldering smile Bram gave me when I tugged them on, yeah, I'd wear them every day to get that smile.

We walked out, and Rook was bent over Payne, who sat with his elbows resting on his knees while his brother inked another marker on the side of his head.

I glanced up at Bram. "Why do you do that?"

"To count our kills. It's always been done among our warrior ranks. Originally, it was to show our enemies we were not to be fucked with. Now it's mainly to uphold traditions."

My gaze automatically went to Bram's head. He'd collected more than a few. "And I guess it still warns off your enemies?"

He bared his teeth in a wicked smile. "We don't have any, Mags, we killed them all."

Talon laughed, the sound lifting the hair on the back of my neck. "The ink's also laced with their blood. We carry in our skin a part of every soul we send to the afterlife. It's the price we pay for embracing what we are."

Okay, that was intense. I turned to Bram, and he was watching me closely. Did he think I'd judge him for it, judge his people for something they'd been doing for probably thousands of years? I felt the opposite. Taking a life meant something to them, and they carried it with them the rest of their lives. I gave his hand a squeeze.

Payne stood, drawing my attention back to the scene in front of me. Bram's oldest brother gave me a chin lift. "You're looking better this morning, and you don't stink of demon."

"Why, thank you. I feel a lot better." That was as much of the touchy-feely stuff as I was gonna get from that particular male. Talon was grinning at us, and Rook said nothing, which was standard for him.

Maeve came running out of Payne's tree house. "Let me see," she said, tugging on her father's hand.

He immediately crouched so his daughter could see his new ink. She traced it with her little finger. "Are you winning?"

"It's not about winning. You know that." Then he grinned wide, surprising the hell out of me. "But yes, baby, your daddy is winning."

Rook chuckled low, and I was stunned a second time. I'd never heard anything other than the odd word and the occasional grunt from him.

"Now that you and Bram have stopped pining and started boning, you gonna be a good wifey and follow our traditions?" Talon asked, motioning to the chair Payne had just been sitting in.

Bram growled. "For once, how about you keep your mouth shut."

He took a step toward his brother, and I planted my hand on his stomach, stopping him. We weren't "boning" as Talon so charmingly put it, but just because we hadn't been able to mate in truth yet didn't mean I didn't want to do other things a mate would do for her male. "What traditions?"

"Dinner on the table at six on the dot and always ready and willing to submit to your male and fulfill all his needs—"

"What does submit mean?" Maeve asked her father.

Payne's gaze sliced to Talon, and if looks could kill, he'd be shredded on the floor.

"It means to do as you're told," he said to her.

She screwed up her face. "Why would Uncle Bram want that—"

"We'll talk about it later," Payne said, and I got the feeling later would never come.

"There's only one way our females submit," Rook said, low and gritty. "And it's not in the fucking kitchen."

Talon laughed, and Payne's lips twitched.

My belly did that heat-and-swirl combo again, and I looked up at Bram.

His jaw was tight. "Ignore my fuckwit brothers. Considering Rook and Talon have never had females of their own, I wouldn't consider them experts on the subject."

Talon flipped Bram off. "Not sure why you're acting all coy," he said to Bram, then looked at me. "Okay, I was messing with you. Our females do what the fuck they like. We only have one tradition. If a warrior has a female, she usually hangs with him when he gets a new marker, you know, to show everyone she's proud of him, that she's proud to be his—"

"Talon," Bram bit out.

"What? It's one of my top fucking fantasies. Only when I do it, we'll both be naked," he said.

"You're naked, you can ink your fucking self," Rook muttered.

"What do I do?" I asked, warily.

Talon grinned. "Don't worry, it's nothing kinky. All you gotta do is sit on his lap and distract him from the pain."

Bram cursed under his breath, shoved Talon out of the way, and sat on the chair.

"Is that what usually happens?" I asked Rook, who seemed the least likely to make shit up.

Rook's cold, black eyes slid to me, like he was surprised I'd asked him, but then he nodded.

Okay, then that's what I'd do.

"Hair outta the way," Rook said to Bram.

Bram searched his pockets for a hair tie.

"Let me." I took the one from my own hair, and Bram faced forward again, sitting back while I threaded my fingers through his hair, gathering it up. His brothers went silent, and I felt their eyes on me while I tied his hair in a knot the way I knew he liked it, getting it out of the way so Rook could do what he needed to.

Then I walked around him to get on his lap. If my job was to distract him, I'd need to be able to look into his eyes, so I straddled his spread thighs, and he looked at me in a way that sent a tremor of pleasure down my spine. His brothers were still silent and not even trying to pretend they weren't watching us.

I took his strong jaw in my hands. "Ready?"

His hands slid lightly up my thighs and rested on my hips, careful of my scars. "Yeah."

Payne grunted, the sound one of approval, but I didn't look his way or at Rook when he stepped up with the tattoo gun. I kept my eyes on Bram. He'd trusted me with the truth, with all of him, and I didn't want him to regret it. I wanted him to see that I loved all of him, even the part of him that was a predator who needed to hunt and kill.

"Say his name," Payne said.

Bram said the name of the male he killed, then the buzz of the gun started. Bram held my eyes as Rook pressed it to the side of his head. The only sign that he felt it was his lashes fluttering a couple times. I ran my fingers over his stubbled jaw, then leaned in and pressed a kiss to his lips. His hands squeezed my hips, and he kissed me back, slow and easy, and I kept on kissing him as Rook inked his new marker.

Someone cleared their throat a little while later, and I realized the buzzing had stopped and Rook had stepped back. I smiled against his lips. "I'm proud of you," I said. "Proud to be yours. I love every bloodthirsty inch of you."

He grinned.

"Never seen anyone covered in more blood than you, little witch," Payne said.

"Truth," Talon said and laughed, and Rook actually smiled, well, kind of. His lips twitched.

"I'm no crow, but if I was, I'd probably have more markers than you," I said to Payne.

He smirked. "Sure you would, short ass."

Was Bram's surly brother actually teasing me?

I took Bram's jaw and angled his head to the side so I could see the new marker. "Do you remember them all?"

"Yes," he said.

I traced one above his ear. "Was this the first?"

He nodded.

"Who was it?"

He took my hand away and cupped my jaw. "Brody."

I stared into the dark depths of his eyes.

"I collected some of his blood before his body was taken away, because I knew I wanted to carry him on me. I wanted to look at it and remember the way it felt to snap his fucking neck. The way his body looked crumpled and lifeless on the ground. He was the first marker I got Rook to do. He's the kill I'm most proud of. I'm only sorry that Clayton isn't beside him."

I was breathing heavy, my heart pounding. Everything he said, I felt it, deeply. It didn't scare me, it turned me on. I squirmed on his lap. "Bram..."

"Hang on tight," he said and stood. His wings unfurled and I quickly locked my arms around his neck before he shot upward, higher, right up to the crows' lookout, high in the trees.

We landed and I released him, looking out at the view. I turned back, and Bram advanced. He backed me up against the railing, grabbed it each side of me, so he wasn't touching me, but caging me in. I looked up at him, and my breath caught.

"Don't want to push, Mags, and I'm not asking for more than this, but I need to own that mouth," he growled. "I need it. Right the fuck now."

I needed it too. I rested my hands on his chest and lifted to my toes. "Take it."

With a snarl, he kissed me hard, his tongue delving deep. Still, he didn't touch me, even lost in his hunger. What he'd just done, getting the new marker, my acceptance, my pride in the male he was, had affected him, deeply. But he wasn't the only one. His body trembled and he was hard, straining against the front of his jeans, I felt it when he brushed against my stomach.

He'd made me feel good last night, he'd made me come, and I wanted to do that for him as well. I wanted to show him how much he mattered, how much I wanted him. I tugged open the button of his jeans, then slid down the zipper.

His hand covered mine, and panting, he lifted his head. "You don't need to—"

"I want to. I want to touch you," I said and shoved his jeans lower. I pushed my hand down the front of his underwear, and a shuddering breath burst from him when I lightly gripped his cock.

Hunger filled his gaze, his chest pumping hard as I explored. He was like hot iron in my hand, his skin silky smooth.

"Tell me what to do," I said, unsure and desperate to make him feel good. "Tell me how you like to be touched?"

His Adam's apple slid up and down his throat. "Just having your hands on me is enough. Anything you do feels fucking amazing."

I curled my fingers around him more firmly and stroked from root to tip. Hips rocked forward instantly, and his head dropped forward on a groan. "Like that?"

He nodded, breathing hard. His hair had fallen forward, hiding his face from me, and when I did it again, his biceps bulged, the veins in his forearms standing out as he gripped the railing tighter.

Fluid leaked from the slit at the head of his cock and I spread it with my thumb, using it to ease my way. I dragged my hand down and back once more and Bram hissed through clenched teeth.

His head lifted, and dominance rolled off him. His dark eyes were intense, utterly gorgeous. The transformation sent a delicious shiver through me. "Hold me tighter, baby," he said. "Both hands."

I did, stroking him again.

He held my eyes and started thrusting his hips, rolling them. He stood over me, still gripping the railing either side of me and I couldn't look away. He was so beautiful. His tattooed arms and bare chest glistened with sweat, his muscles straining as he worked himself in my grip.

"Dreamed about this, Mags, kissing you, your hands on me." He took my mouth in another hard kiss, wet and deep, hungry. He sucked my tongue and nipped my lips, making me dizzy from how good it was. "Fuck, I can't get enough of you," he said against my lips. "Tighter, faster," he groaned.

His thrusts grew wild, brutal and I imagined how it would feel if he was inside me. Heat pooled between my thighs. I was panting as well, watching him like this was so incredibly hot.

Then he jerked, his cock pulsing in my hands as he came for me, his entire body jolting with each thrust.

Finally, he dropped his head to my shoulder, shaking, breathing hard.

I kissed his neck, working my way to his ear. "Goddess, Bram, you are so fucking hot," I said, throat tight, body electric.

He lifted his head, fisted my hair and kissed me hard and deep and wild. I never wanted him to stop.

But then his fingers grazed my back, right over the vines stretching out from the center, reminding me that I had somewhere I needed to be, that this little pause from my task was over.

I didn't want to go back, I wanted to stay right here forever, but I couldn't do that.

I needed to get back to the city.

CHAPTER 22

Magnolia

I JOGGED down the stairs after a quick change of clothes, and there was an unmistakable tingling along the markings on my back and stomach. It'd started a few minutes ago.

Bram stood at the bottom.

"We have somewhere to be," I said.

He frowned. "Yeah?"

Mom walked out of the kitchen. "Mags?"

The fear in her eyes said it all. Else had told her about my task.

She didn't ask me about it, she just closed the space between us and pulled me into her arms, trembling. I let her hold me. My scars ached, but I grit my teeth and gave her what she needed, because there was nothing I could do to ease her fears.

Her smile was strained. "You must be hungry. I made you sandwiches. Let me get them." She rushed off, and I let her do that as well, forcing myself to ignore the sense of urgency filling me, because feeding the people she loved was what she did, especially when she was feeling helpless and it was all she could do.

She handed us both wrapped sandwiches.

"Thanks, Mom."

"Promise me you'll be careful," she said, eyes glistening.

"Promise."

We strode out to the car a few minutes later. "We need to head to the city," I said.

Bram took the car keys I held out for him. "Your task?"

I nodded.

The sense of urgency grew as we drove. It definitely wasn't Agatheena meddling this time, and the feeling was so strong that I had to grab for the door handle, sucking in a startled breath.

Bram shot me a look. "Okay?"

I nodded and gripped the door tighter. "Turn right, then take the next left," I said, when we hit the city, letting my instincts guide me.

I directed him down street after street until we reached one of the oldest parts of the city. The buildings were ornate, solid. Most of this street had been developed a few years back, new bars, clubs, and restaurants. A couple of the hotels had been refurbished. This was where the wealthy locals or visitors came to play.

"There," I said, pointing to a parking spot ahead of us.

Bram parked, and I shoved the door open and followed the persistent feeling pulsing through my veins. Bram jogged to catch up as we strode past shops and clubs. It was late enough that most of the shops were closed, and early enough that the bars were still pretty quiet and the clubs hadn't opened yet.

I stopped in front of a cobbled walkway between two buildings. The stones were black, but every so often there was a red one, like a trail leading you somewhere. There were vintage lanterns on either side that provided dim lighting and a small bronze plaque set into the brick wall to the right with "Red" etched into it. "Down here," I said.

Bram grabbed my arm, stopping me. "Careful, we don't know where that leads." He slid his knife free.

I nodded, and pulled mine as well as we walked up to a massive, glossy red door. I tried the handle. Locked. "Keep watch."

I picked the lock, opening the door, then quickly sliced an X in my palm before the alarm went off, about to use the same spell I had at the school, then paused, when I didn't feel the usual vibrations. "The alarm, the cameras, they're already off."

I bunched my shirt in my hand, applying pressure to stop the bleeding. Bram's nostrils flared, gaze darting to my hand. But we didn't have time for him to treat it, not when we didn't know what was behind the set of double red doors ahead of us.

We walked into a foyer and each of us took a side, knives gripped in our hands, and grabbed a door handle.

Bram nodded, and we opened them together—

185

Then froze.

Bram scented the air. His eyes flared, and he cursed before he grabbed my hand, yanking me closer.

I'd filled Bram in on everything that had happened while he was away on our way back from the village, including what I'd witnessed hiding behind the curtains in the Hazarks' living room. A week ago, I would've been surprised that this was where I'd been called, but not now, not after what I saw. It was a BDSM club. Thankfully, it was currently closed.

The walls were painted black, and there were racks and benches and all kinds of contraptions I'd never seen before dotted around the room. There were also couches, a couple beds, and a small stage.

"You think this is one of the prom committee's hangouts?" Bram asked, taking in the room.

"I don't know, but it would make sense, right? Chase mentioned a play-room. So I guess, this is what they're into." I tried to imagine this place full of people, and my belly swirled. Was I intrigued? Yes. Was it my scene? Oh, hell no. "I guess we should look around."

We checked out the rest of the large main room, then headed down a hall in the back, where there were smaller ones. All different themes, with different devices. I assumed they were for people who wanted to play in private.

The last door was ajar. My instincts skyrocketed. I motioned to it and Bram pushed it open. He stopped abruptly and I bumped into him.

"Fuck," he bit out.

I stepped around him.

Chase Golden.

He was all fucked up, but I recognized that hair instantly. His wrists were bound with wire, secured above his head, mouth sewn shut, face swollen and bloody. His shirt was open and "judgment" was carved into his chest—

His body jerked.

"He's still alive," Bram bit out, yanked out his phone, and quickly called for an ambulance. "We need to leave, now," he said when he disconnected. "It's only a couple minutes away."

A door slammed somewhere in the building. I took off, sprinting in the direction of that sound, Bram right behind me.

We'd interrupted the killer.

I ran down the hall, bursting into the main room and sprinting for the exit. The door flew open before I could reach it, and I slammed on the brakes as a tall male in a dark suit filled the doorway, blocking my way.

Demon, or at least half. I sensed it instantly.

He scowled down at us. "What the fuck are you doing in my club?"

That's when I recognized him. "Brent? I mean...Mr. Silva."

His scowl deepened, and I had to stop myself from shrinking under his hard stare. Brent Silva was a powerful sex demon. I'd only met him a couple of times, when I was with Willow, but it was a long time ago. I knew he owned several clubs, I just didn't realize what type of clubs they were.

"Did you see anyone when you came in, did you pass anyone?"

"Answer me," he demanded.

Bram stiffened and took a step forward, and I grabbed his hand, doing my best to hold him back. "I don't know if you remember me? We've met a couple of times. My name's Magnolia. I'm Willow Thornheart's sister," I rushed out. "Did you see anyone?"

Recognition filled his gaze and some of the fury dissipated. "No, I didn't see anyone. Now how about you explain why you broke into my club?"

"It's a long story..." Sirens wailed, they were close. Too damn close. "Look, I don't have time to explain. Someone tried to kill a guy in one of your private rooms. His pulse is weak, but he's still breathing. The ambulance is almost here and it'd be a lot better for us, and for Willow, if no one knew we'd been here."

His dark eyes burned into me. "Did you do it?"

"No."

"I'm gonna need an explanation."

"And I'll give you one, but the witches council can't know I was here."

Someone banged on the main door. We were trapped.

Brent's gaze slid to Bram and back to me, his jaw like granite. He pulled something from his pocket, keys, and tossed them to me. "Behind the bar, up the stairs. Wait up there."

I nodded, and Bram and I ran across the room, in behind the bar and out the back. There was a door on the left. We rushed through, and up a set of stars. I unlocked the door at the top and we shut ourselves in.

It was a small apartment. It didn't look like anyone used it, just the bare minimum of furniture. I strode to the window and peered around the edge of the curtain.

Witches, shifters, others, we had our own ambulance and hospital, and when the medics down there realized Golden was a witch, they'd contact the council. If they knew I was connected with the crime scene in any way, well, it wouldn't be good for me or Willow.

I turned back to Bram. "If we hadn't gotten there when we did, Chase would be dead now." My hands balled into fists. "They were here. Whoever's behind all of this, they were right fucking there, and I let them get away."

"We had no idea what we were walking into. Chase is alive. He might know something. I fucking hope so, because whoever did that, they need to be put the fuck down."

He wasn't wrong. Whoever hurt Chase and tortured and killed the others was a twisted monster.

The kind only death could stop.

>>>●<<<

The council descended on the club like I knew they would. Hours passed and somehow, while we waited, I fell asleep.

The phone in the apartment rang, startling me awake. I lifted my head from Bram's chest. The room was dark. I had no idea how long we'd been up here, but it was late, the moon high in the sky.

Bram grabbed the phone, because there was only one person it could be. "Yeah?" he listened. "On our way." He hung up, then turned to me, tucking my hair behind my ear. "He wants to see us."

Shit.

We took the stairs back down, and slipped out from behind the bar. A low, throbbing beat filled the room. The club was in full swing, business as usual, like nothing had happened.

Bram's jaw worked as he looked around.

Some people were dressed seductively, some barely dressed at all, and some were straight-up naked. There was a couple on the low stage, a mostly naked male was strapped down, his back and ass streaked red, while a female in leather walked around him. Others in the room watched or were engaged in their own...scenes.

Bram's chest expanded. "Can I touch you? I need...I need everyone to know you're mine."

He needed it, and right then, I could thankfully tolerate it. "Yeah."

"He let go of my hand and gripped the back of my neck possessively, pulling me into his side. "Stay beside me, and don't talk to anyone."

"No one's going to hurt me or touch me. Places like this have rules. Brent wouldn't let his members harass one another." Bram looked ready to tear someone to pieces. "It's going to be fine," I said, and hoped I was right.

He didn't look reassured.

We walked around a big male sitting at one of the tables, a female wearing a collar, kneeling at his side. Her head was dipped, and his big hand was threaded in her hair, stroking her like she was his pet.

Bram's grip on my neck tightened, and he snarled when several people looked our way. They weren't just looking at me, but Bram didn't seem to notice that. No, he only saw the eyes that came my way, and he seemed to puff up like a cobra ready to strike.

I leaned into his side, wrapping my arm around his waist, trying to reassure him. Brent was already pissed at us for breaking into his place, the last thing I needed was Bram going full predator and killing a bunch of people for looking at me the wrong way.

"Down here," he said and led me toward the hall where we'd found Chase.

Most of the doors along it were closed, but I could hear the moans and cries of pleasure and pain coming through them. We turned left at the end of the hall and walked up to another set of glossy red doors. Bram tensed beside me.

"What do you know about this guy?" Bram asked.

"Brent's half sex demon and owns several clubs, I assume, like this one."

Bram bared his teeth.

"B, you gotta calm down," I said, looking up at him. "What's gotten into you?"

He took my chin between his thumb and finger. "You ran for almost two days through a demon-infested forest to show me you want me. I watched you run from a bloodthirsty hoard, fight and kill to get to me. Baby, my crow didn't miss it, the male who knows he has his mate at his side, didn't miss it. I was already protective of you, possessive as fuck, and overnight that shit has reached an entirely new level. Anyone even looks at you, at *my* female, the wrong way, and I will fucking end them...that's what's gotten into me."

I blinked up at him several times, my heart in my throat. What the hell did you say to that? I touched his arm, trying to calm him down, when I was far from calm myself. "I've been around my sisters and their mates enough to understand this is something you have to work through, just please, no matter how strong the compulsion is, do not kill Brent. He's a good guy, by all accounts, and a friend of Willow."

"He won't die if he shows the proper respect. If he's a good guy, like you say, then we shouldn't have a problem." He turned back to the door.

Shit. I knocked.

"Come in," a deep voice called.

I opened the door and walked in. Brent stood from behind his desk. He wore dark trousers, his jacket was off and draped over the back of his chair, his shirt unbuttoned at the throat and his sleeves were rolled up. His hair looked like he'd been thrusting his fingers through it, and there was a heavy sliver chain around his neck, glinting against his lightly tanned skin, a metal ring hanging at the base—a collar.

"Hey, we're really sorry about earlier. That was kind of...fucked up.

Thanks for giving us somewhere to wait it out." I motioned to Bram. "I uh... didn't get to properly introduce you before. This is my—"

"Mate," Bram finished and pulled me a little closer.

Brent studied us a moment, his lips twitching. "Take a seat."

We both sat, then Bram's hand shot out and grabbed the arm of my chair, dragging it right up against his, and gripped the back of my neck again.

"Bram," I bit out. "Take a freaking breath."

Brent grinned. "Newly mated?"

"Um...not yet."

He nodded. "It's hard to control at the beginning. Wait until you actually mate," he said and gave me a pitying look.

Surely Bram couldn't get worse than this?

Brent sat back. "Brother, you can relax. I'm mated. I'm not looking to take your female or hurt her."

Bram did seem to relax a little then, at least the death grip he had on my neck loosened.

"Did you have any trouble from the witches council?" I asked.

Brent shook his head, a tight smile curling his lips. "No. They came in, cleaned up and left."

I assumed the council would move in. But for them not to be able to see who did this or the previous murders, with their access to a whole lot of powerful witches, made it obvious there was dark magic involved, or they would have brought a seer in and Willow would be off the hook already. Whoever was behind this was wiping their tracks clean with the kinds of spells that had been forbidden for centuries. "Any camera footage? The cameras were already off inside when we got here, but what about the ones outside the club?"

"Disabled as well." Brent's chair creaked as he sat forward, his dark eyes on me. "Tell me, Magnolia. How easy was it for you to break into this place?"

My face heated. "Honestly? Even if someone hadn't already disabled your alarm and cameras, it would've been a piece of cake."

Brent's jaw tightened. "Fuck."

The door opened and a curvy brunette about my height and wearing a black leather corset and short pleated red skirt, walked in. "What's got you cursing?" she said.

She rounded the desk and sat on the arm of her husband's chair. Brent wrapped his arm around her waist, and when he looked up at her, his face softened. "Our security's for shit."

"Hey, Chaya," I said.

Chaya ran her fingers through Brent's disheveled hair, then turned to me. "Hey, Mags, it's been a while."

Thankfully, right now neither Brent nor Chaya seemed overly upset with me, but still, I'd broken into their place. "I really am sorry for breaking in like I did. If I'd known it was your club, or there'd been another way—"

"I'm not pissed about it anymore," Brent said. "But I am pissed that you, and whoever got in before you, were able to do it so easily in the first place, and I'd like you to help me stop it from happening again."

"You want me to ward the club?"

"Yes."

Maybe I could use this to my advantage.

"And what does Magnolia get out of it?" Bram said before I could open my mouth. "She was able to break in, yeah. But like you say, someone did that before her, or they'd been able to hide out until everyone left. She found that guy before the attack turned into a murder. Honestly, you should be thanking her."

Chaya's lips twitched.

"Don't push it," Brent said to him.

"My wards are exceptional. No one will get past it," I said before Bram and Brent started a pissing contest.

Brent's eyes narrowed. "Fine, what do you want?"

"I need access to your client list and who was here last night. I wouldn't ask if it wasn't important."

He shook his head. "My clients come here expecting privacy. It gets out that my security is that weak and I share private information, I lose my business."

I leaned forward, resting my forearms on my knees. "I would never repeat or share any of the names on your list, but I need it. Willow's in trouble. She's been forced into hiding. The council wants to convict her for a bunch of murders she didn't commit. My entire coven could lose everything, including our magic, if I don't catch this fucker. And odds are good, you have a sadistic murderer on that list."

They both stared at me for several long seconds, then Chaya pressed her mouth to Brent's ear and said something I had no hope of hearing.

Brent nodded, then opened his laptop. "I signed a confidentiality agreement, along with my clients." He tapped a few keys. "I'm sorry, I can't tell you anything, Magnolia."

Chaya stood, taking Brent's hand. "We need to step out of the office for a few minutes to check on something," she said. "Will you excuse us?"

They walked out and shut the door firmly behind them. I frowned. "What the hell was that?"

Bram was already up and around the desk.

"What are you doing?"

Bram looked up and grinned. "He couldn't tell us, but what if it's on the screen and we happen to see it?"

I rushed around the desk, and the members list was right there, along with another list, members who'd signed in the night before Chance's attack. Brent had left it open for us. I quickly did a search for the obvious names.

They were all members, and they were all here last night.

"We'll need a copy of that and the full list of members as well," Bram said and tapped a few keys.

The printer started up a second later, spitting them out. I snatched everything up, folded it and stuffed it in my pocket.

The door to the office opened a minute after we sat back down. They were probably watching us on their security cameras.

I stood again, and placed the keys to the apartment on his desk. "We need to head off, but I'll be in touch, and we'll make a time for me to come and ward the club."

"Make sure you do," Brent said, holding my gaze before he stepped aside.

Bram and I strode out, through the club, out the door and down the alleyway.

"Where do we start with these? There has to be a couple hundred names on the members list," I said as we walked toward the car.

"We start with anyone who's remotely connected to the prom committee. Business associates, friends, family, anyone who went to Roxburgh High, especially if they were at Red the night of Chase's attack."

CHAPTER 23

Magnolia

WE GOT out of the car and looked up at Maria Watson's apartment building. She lived in the penthouse, thanks to her family and their money.

"She hung up on me," I said, shoving my phone in my pocket. As soon as I gave Maria my name, the line went dead.

"Surprised?" Bram asked as he shut the car door.

"Not at all." I shielded my eyes and looked up at the wide balcony jutting out from the top floor. "We just won't give her a choice."

Robert and Jenna had locked down their home and weren't answering calls, at least from numbers they didn't recognize. Ryan had snarled down the line for me to fuck off, and there was no way Isaac would talk to me.

Another person had almost died, and I had nothing, no leads. They hadn't released his name to the public, but I'd seen on Nightscape that the latest victim was alive and had been put into an induced coma.

They'd also thrown in that Willow was still "at large."

There was no way to question Chase, no way to find out if he knew who tried to kill him. Isaac's smug face kept popping into my head, his gleeful expression when they came for Willow at the clubhouse, the way he was with Calvin that night, oily, manipulative. He'd treated Calvin like his attack dog. Calvin had lost it, then one command from Isaac, and he'd backed away snarling.

Then Calvin had turned up dead as well.

Isaac had to be involved in this somehow, and the more I thought about him and his actions in the past, the last couple of weeks, the more convinced I became that he was capable of almost anything.

With no other leads, we'd spent most of the night looking up names on Brent's list. There'd been a few surprises, one of them being Rook's name. I'd shown Bram, and he'd raised a brow but hadn't seemed overly shocked that his brother would frequent a place like that.

Besides the prom committee members, and Maria and Isaac, there were three other people who were linked to at least one of them, all via business of some kind, and who had been at the club the night of Chase's attempted murder. Chloe Chan, a wolf shifter, was the first. She was the Hazarks' realtor and had been a member of Red for several years. Ryan Alway had only been a member of the club for the last four months. I shuddered, and I knew firsthand he was deep in the inner circle. And the last was a shifter named Luke Donaghy. The male was rich and powerful and, since moving back to Roxburgh, had made a name for himself as someone not to mess with, but he'd also formed strong alliances with not only several powerful witches but shifters and demons as well.

He seemed to have gained their trust, not an easy thing to do in this city. People tended to shoot first and ask questions later. He'd been a member of Red for five months.

The connections were tenuous at best, but it wasn't like I had much else to go on. Whoever hurt Chase, they'd chosen Red for a reason. The only one I could come up with was to expose the prom committee. They wanted everyone to know what they were into, to ruin them, and to humiliate them, and a member of their tight inner circle murdered in a BDSM club would most definitely cause a stir. Bram and me showing up had ruined that plan. And not only had Chase lived, but he'd been taken away by the witches council before any Nightscape reporters could descend.

"Ready?" Bram asked.

I nodded.

"Will you be okay? I'm gonna have to hold you close," he said.

"I'm okay right now." And I hoped like fuck I stayed that way, for a little while at least, for both our sakes. Bram needed to be able to touch me, and I needed to be touched. This increase in my scar sensitivity, especially when it came to him, was honestly starting to scare me.

"You'll tell me if it gets too much?" he said as he tugged off his shirt. He tucked it in the waistband of his jeans, and his wings sprouted from his back.

"I will."

He scooped me up, and I wrapped my arms around his neck. There was a low vibration fluttering across my skin, and I wasn't sure if my scars were waking up and taking notice or it was just my body's reaction to being so close to Bram. His hold was firm but not tight, his muscles rock solid. Then he pressed his nose against my throat and breathed deep. A quiver rolled through him and he groaned in a way I knew was involuntary.

"Jesus," he muttered.

I bit my lip. Just being this close had my pulse fluttering like mad. "You okay?"

He cleared his throat. "Yeah, you just...you smell really fucking good."

I fought my own shiver. "You smell pretty good yourself." And he did, so good. I thought about the way he'd looked while we were up in the lookout, the sounds he'd made, the way he'd watched me. I moistened my lips, my belly flipping about.

His gaze slid to my mouth and back, and his nostrils flared. "Fuck," he muttered, then his jaw tightened and we shot up, his wings beating hard. We soared higher, looping around the side of the building, up to the top floor. He hovered above.

Maria sat below us, relaxing on the balcony, reading.

This was probably a terrible idea, but I was running out of time and options.

Bram tucked in his wings and dropped, landing on the penthouse balcony with a thud.

Maria screamed and jumped off her banana lounger, tossing her book at us. Bram caught it.

I lifted my hands. "We're not here to hurt you, Maria. We just want to talk."

Her eyes were wide as she stumbled back. "I told you I don't want to talk to you."

"I just have a couple of questions, then we'll leave, okay?"

She started shrieking, uncontrollably.

Bram shadowed out and popped up behind her. He clamped his hand over her mouth, and she started struggling, completely freaking out.

"We're not going to hurt you," I said again. "We just want to talk. Calm down." I looked up at Bram. "If you promise not to scream, he'll take his hand away."

Her wild eyes were locked on me.

"Okay?"

She jerkily nodded, and Bram eased his hand from her mouth.

"W-what do you want?" she said.

"We just want to ask you a few questions. That's all."

She nodded again.

"I promise, we're not here to hurt you," I said a third time, because she still looked terrified. "I'm trying to clear my sister's name. She didn't do the things people are saying. Someone's hurting your friends, and I know it's not her. The real killer is out there, and I want to find them and stop them." I kept my hands out at my sides. "Will you answer my questions?"

She took several shaky steps away from Bram, and her expression changed from fear to disbelief. "This is so weird, and intrusive...you know that, right?"

I did. "I'm sorry we scared you, but this is important."

Maria crossed her arms. "You really are just like her, aren't you? Just as self-righteous and self-important as your sister. You think you can just come here like this? That even if it isn't your sister butchering my friends, which it is, that *you* have the skills to find the killer when the witches council hasn't been able to? The arrogance of your family is astounding."

She seemed to have gotten over her fear quickly. I bit back what I wanted to say because that wouldn't help right then. "Has Chase's condition improved?"

"That's none of your business," she bit out.

"Do you have any enemies? Can you think of anyone who'd want to hurt you or your friends?"

The outrage left her eyes and was replaced with a look that sent a shiver down my spine. "Yes, your psycho sister."

My fingers curled into a fist, and I had to work really hard at controlling my anger. "Why would Willow want to hurt you, Maria? You've had literally nothing to do with each other."

"There's no one else. And your sister has had it in for us since high school. She's hell-bent on sabotaging all of us."

I was starting to think this was a complete waste of time. "You went away to school. She doesn't know you. And why on earth would she risk everything to go on a killing spree targeting your friends?"

Maria planted her hands on her thin hips. "She wrote that awful piece for the high school newspaper her senior year, showing everyone how spiteful and jealous of us she was, and no, I wasn't at the same high school as her, but her attack on my friends was spiteful and cruel. She's held on to that grudge all these years, going out of her way to mess with them. I mean, she set her attack mutt on Isaac's brother! She got her mate to kill for her. How can you be so blind?"

"That was self-defense. *Elmer* tried to kill her. I was there, Warrick did what he had to."

Maria shrugged. "That's what she wanted you to see. What she wanted everyone to see. Maybe she made him attack her? Did you ever think of that? Maybe she hexed him somehow so her mate would kill him? All I know is your sister hates us, and she's made it her life's mission to hurt us at every turn."

She was delusional. "She never talks about any of you, Maria. She doesn't waste time thinking about you, any of you. You said she was holding on to a grudge? Are you saying the article she wrote was some kind of retaliation?"

She colored. "There was this...harmless prank, and she got all bent out of shape."

"What prank?"

She jerked her chin up. "Just kids' stuff. Peroxide in her shampoo."

I remembered that. Willow's hair had ended up with green streaks through it. She'd been allergic to peroxide as well, and she'd been covered in an awful rash. She'd never said what happened, and I assumed she'd tried to dye it herself. I was still pretty young, so no one filled me in on the facts. No wonder Wills wanted revenge back then.

"What your friends did was shitty, but I know my sister and she wouldn't go on a killing spree over something like that, something that happened so long ago. And why now? Why all of a sudden would she come after you and your friends? You have to see how insane that is."

"If she doesn't care about us or what we do, then why did she stop us from buying the property we wanted? She could move her store anywhere, but no. Instead, she rejected our generous offer, then made sure everyone else on the street rejected our offers as well."

"She was protecting her store and the others around her." Wills knew everyone on that street. We all did. The other stores were mainly owned by witches or shifters, and they knew what happened during Willow's trial. One look at Isaac's name and they would have shut him down even without her saying a thing. "She has friends there. Loyal ones. They wouldn't want Isaac there any more than Willow would."

"You think you know your sister, the Keeper, the big deal, but you don't. Isaac was kicked out of an...an exclusive club because of your sister, without explanation, I might add." Her hands shook, her eyes filling with fury. "That was Willow's doing as well."

She was talking about Red, it had to be. "I'd say that probably had more to do with Isaac being a dick than Willow stepping in." I was seriously starting to lose my patience with this nonsense.

"Wrong, Isaac did some digging. Your sister is a friend of the owner—"

"That doesn't mean she had anything to do with him being kicked out."

Her face colored again, with anger this time. "Isaac just wants your awful family to leave him alone, but Willow won't stop. And then there was all the stuff during Iris's task as well. We just want her to leave us alone." A tear streaked down her face. "No, she killed our friends, and she won't stop until we're all dead."

I ground my molars. Maybe I was just a horrible person, but I was struggling to find sympathy for her. "You're wrong."

Her eyes flashed. "She has all this power, and she lords it over everyone. She's selfish and conceited."

What the actual hell was she talking about? "You don't even know her."

Her eyes narrowed. "I know all I need to. She's let power go to her head, then she mated a monster and turned into one. She's as vicious and deranged as the dog she lies down with. Now get the hell out of here before I call the witches council and report you."

Isaac had poisoned her. He'd poisoned all of them against my sister. The guy was a master manipulator, that much was obvious, and Maria had fallen for his bullshit.

There was no talking her around—she clearly couldn't think for herself, and the last thing I needed was the council breathing down my neck. Though, I wouldn't be surprised if she called them, anyway.

Bram scooped me up and dove off the balcony.

"Well, that was a waste of time," I said when he landed.

He gave the back of my neck a gentle squeeze, then released me. "Where to now?" he asked when we got back to the car.

"Let's go to the Golden mansion." I'd tried calling the hospital, but they weren't giving out information on Chase's condition, not unless you were family. I'd lied and said I was Leah, his bitch of a cousin, but then they'd asked for a password. Not surprising since reporters from several Nightscape news and gossip pages had apparently been hounding the hospital staff for details.

So far, Chase was the only one to survive one of these attacks, and people wanted to know all the gory details.

We rolled up to the mansion a short time later, and the gates opened immediately.

I glanced at Bram. "Maria had to have warned everyone about us."

"Without doubt." I'd expected the gates to stay firmly closed and locked, honestly. I'd planned to try to pay off one of their staff members to get the intel. This was definitely a surprise.

Bram parked the car, and we got out as the main door to the house opened and Leah Golden walked out. *Great. Just freaking wonderful.*

Chase and his cousin weren't all that close from what I'd understood. She certainly didn't look upset as she skipped down the stairs in her short, floaty sundress. She also didn't look my way once. Her eyes were firmly on Bram.

That explains why we were let in so easily.

"Hey," she said as she strode toward us. "Maria called." She glanced at me and screwed up her face. "You scared the hell out of her, and if anyone else was here, they wouldn't have let you in. You're lucky it's just me." She turned to Bram. "I volunteered to house-sit. Chase has a couple dogs that need feeding and..." She motioned to the huge house and grinned. "Staying here is no great hardship." She honest to god batted her lashes at him. "It does get kind of lonely, though, all on my own—"

"How is Chase?" I said, cutting off whatever was about to come out of her mouth next. It didn't take a genius to work out what she was hinting at.

Her gaze sliced back to me. "Why do you want to know? How is it any of your business, Magnolia?"

"I'm sure Maria filled you in. I'm trying to clear my sister's name."

"Good luck with that." She rolled her eyes and dismissed me, turning back to Bram, and the hungry look she gave him lifted my hackles. "How've you been, Bram? I haven't seen you around in a while."

Heat rose from my gut, filling me with instant fire. I didn't like her looking at Bram, let alone talking to him.

His eyes narrowed. "Is Chase still in a coma?" he asked, voice low, clipped, and ignoring her question.

She clasped her hands in front of her, squeezing her boobs together so they bulged out of her dress, and licked her lips. "If you say please, I'll tell you."

Bram's eyes darkened dangerously.

Her eyes went wide, but not from fear, from excitement. She giggled nervously and lightly hit his arm. "I'm just kidding around." She looked at me. "And not that it's any of your business, but yes, he is. The doctors say he'll be like that for a while. He was pretty fucked up when they brought him in, even the best healers said it could take weeks before he's ready to be woken up."

Shit.

She turned back to Bram. "So, um...did Magnolia tell you I was going to call? I tried a few times, but you didn't pick up. I assumed you didn't know it was me." She held out her hand. "Give me your phone and I'll add my number to your contacts, so you know who's calling next time."

"No," Bram said.

She blinked up at him, a confounded look on her face. "No?"

He curled his arm around me, and I leaned into him.

Fury filled her eyes. "You said you weren't together!"

I shrugged. "We weren't, now we are."

"You did that on purpose!" she fired at me.

I laughed, I couldn't help it. "Are you serious?"

"I told you I was interested in him, and you moved in. You couldn't stand that Bram might want me—"

"He doesn't and never did, and I can assure you, Leah, neither of us spared you a thought when we finally got together." I shook my head. "He's my mate. You never stood a chance."

A low laugh rumbled from Bram, dark and sexy, and my belly quivered.

Her mouth pinched up. "Get in your car and get lost, and if you come back, I'll set the dogs on you."

"Thanks for your help," I said, and we got back in and drove away.

Chase had been my best bet.

What the hell was I going to do now?

CHAPTER 24

Magnolia

I SCROLLED through the articles from the school newspaper. Talon had worked his computer-hacking magic and gotten us access to the high school server.

Most Likely To... by Willow Thornheart.

I clicked the file open and quickly scanned it, and bit back a laugh. "Well, this would've definitely pissed off the prom committee."

Bram read it over my shoulder and grinned. "Yeah, that'd do it."

Robert Hazark: Most likely to get turned on by his own reflection.

Jenna Barlow: Most likely to marry a complete and utter loser.

Chase Golden: Most likely to catch something and have his dick rot and fall off.

Clara Hope: Most likely to live off Daddy's ill-gotten gains.

Calvin Adler: Most likely to marry his cousin.

Katana Adler: See above.

I had no idea how she'd managed to sneak that one into the school paper, but I knew without a doubt that's what happened. No editor would have let that run. "Willow isn't cruel, but she was obviously pissed off. I'd bet anything the peroxide prank wasn't the first either." I turned in my seat to face Bram and sighed. "What does any of this mean? We're not getting anywhere with this. So they hated each other in high school, big freaking deal. Everyone hated me, but you don't see me running around torturing and murdering a bunch of people. They can't seriously believe Willow is doing this because of what happened back then?"

"We know she's innocent, but the evidence is there. The murder at The Cauldron and all the DNA planted there. Her lip-sewing spell being replicated, at least something like it, and Calvin's murder after their altercation at the clubhouse," Bram said from my bed.

He was right, of course, but still. "None of this is making any sense." I rubbed my temples, then covered my face with my hands, trying to keep the out-of-control feeling inside me at bay.

"Hey," he said and came to me, kneeling down beside me. "It's gonna be okay. We'll figure this out."

"What if we can't?" I thought about my sisters and how scared they must've felt, how heavily the burden their own trials must have weighed on them. Rose's was only six months ago, and we were still reeling from the aftermath of it, especially with the sacrifice Zinnia had made for her and the coven.

And before that, Death had come to Rose in her dreams repeatedly, tormenting her, blackmailing her. We'd almost lost her—

An idea struck. "What if...what if I could get inside Chase's head while he's still in a coma?"

"And what? Dig through his memories?"

"I don't know. Maybe I can talk to him, or see what he saw? It has to be there, right? All of it. Including who hurt him."

Bram straightened. "Okay, but how?"

I chewed my lip. It was risky, but it was all I had. "I've heard of a spell, it's...it's forbidden, but—"

"No," Bram said.

"We don't have any real leads, B, we're coming up against brick wall after brick wall. I'm just saying we get our hands on the spell. I don't have to use it, right? It can be a last resort, an insurance policy, if all else fails."

He gripped the side of my chair. "And what happens if you get caught?"

"I won't, and I'm pretty sure I can use it like a blueprint, use the bare bones but change the spell to suit me. I can make it my own, then I wouldn't be breaking any rules, right?" It was a technicality and we both knew it. But I wouldn't let my coven suffer because I failed to do my task, not after all my sisters had been through to get us this far. I'd do whatever it took, they'd done the same, and I wouldn't let all the risks and sacrifices they made be for nothing.

Bram's fingers brushed my arm. "Where's the spell?"

He wasn't going to like this. "It's in an ancient book. It's dark, so dark it can't be kept at the library or the council chambers..." I took a steadying breath. "It's at Shadow Falls."

Bram cursed viciously. "You meddle with that kind of darkness, and the council will come after you."

He was right, of course, but it was a risk I was willing to take. "I'll cover my tracks. I can do it, you know I can. I need you to trust me."

"I fucking do, and you know it. But this?" He shook his head. "It's too dangerous. If they come for you, you'll either end up in Umbra Sanitarium... or worse."

"Agatheena said I can straddle darkness and light, and if I can do that—"

"I don't give a fuck what Agatheena said. It's not her head on the chopping block." He stood and moved to the bed.

I followed and pressed my hands to his chest and pushed. He sat, and I moved in between his thighs, threading my fingers in his hair. "What can I do to ease your worries?" Because I needed to do this, and I needed Bram with me.

He pushed his fingers through the belt loops of my jeans and pulled me closer. "Nothing, and I won't get in your way, as long as you make me a promise."

"What promise?"

His obsidian eyes held mine. "You only use that spell as a last resort, like you said."

"I promise."

He shook his head. "That's not all of it." He tugged me closer. "If you're forced to use it, and for some reason it doesn't go our way...if the council comes for you? You have to let me keep you safe, even if that means I get you the hell out of Roxburgh and we never come back."

I dragged in a breath, but he was right, if the council came for me, we'd have to run. If we didn't, I'd be locked up, or worse. I'd be put to death and my body placed at Shadow Falls with all the other dark witches.

I wouldn't use the spell lightly, and I'd use every precaution. I wouldn't tip the scales into darkness, I was sure of it, but if Bram needed my promise, he had it. "I promise."

Bram

We flew over the barren forest, the trees brown and sick or dead. The evil from the falls was so potent it poisoned everything around it. This place had been used as a burial ground by witches for centuries. It was where they put the witches who'd gone dark. Their covens didn't want them in their cemeteries, tainting the earth and their magic. So they brought them here.

Both Willow and Iris came here during their trials, and both nearly didn't make it back out. I wanted to tell Magnolia no. I wanted to fly away from here and not let her walk into that cave. But that wasn't how we did things, or at least it hadn't been before I'd fucked everything up. Mags and I had always been either all in or all out, together, and I was more than familiar with the determined look in her eyes—she'd do anything to save her coven, which meant, like it or not, we were here at this fucking twisted place, because she would come here, with or without me.

We landed on the stone path, and the roar of the falls left no room for anything else, not that there was anything. No wildlife, not even demons came here.

"This way," Mags said and straightened the bag she'd slung over her shoulder. She walked ahead, her lips moving rapidly, chanting a protection spell over and over again. We both knew it wasn't going to do much, but she was hoping it bought us at least a few extra minutes when we walked in there.

The crones who haunted this place couldn't be stopped, not easily. We'd need to be on our guard, and we'd need to move fast.

The path led us behind the falls itself, a furious wall of water on one side and stone on the other. The spray of water hit my overheated skin and the stone beneath our feet was slippery as hell. I grabbed the back of Magnolia's shirt, terrified she'd fall as we carefully made our way to the cave opening.

The temperature inside was frigid, the air musty. Mags rubbed her arms and looked around the open cavern. The cave went deep into the rock, and I stared into the darkness. I couldn't see a damn thing, but still the hair lifted on the back of my neck.

There was a dais to one side with dried, rusty-colored blood staining its rough stone surface. Mags froze in place as she looked at it, her eyes wide. Willow had almost died right there, and I could see the horror of that in Magnolia's eyes.

"Where's the book?" I said low, trying to pull her from whatever living nightmare was filling her mind.

Mags jolted and turned to me. Her teeth were chattering. "I—I can feel them, the crones. They were at rest here, for so long, but not anymore, and they're...they're so angry," she whispered.

I went for my knife on instinct, even though I knew it was utterly useless. "What do we need to do? We need to move, baby."

Mags turned to the cave wall, where linen-wrapped corpses were tucked into gruesome stone bunk beds. "The book is with a crone named Frances. She was one of the first brought here a really long time ago." She strode to the wall. "Which means she should be at this end somewhere." She slid her hands under one of the bodies, wincing as she felt around, then pulled her arms free before lifting back the linen covering the witch's skull. Shaking her head, she re-covered the bones, then moved to the next.

I tried the one beside her. Nothing. Then lifted back the linen. "What am I looking for?"

"This book is powerful, dangerous. They would've concealed it. Look for unusual markings on the skull." She moved to the next and cursed. "Where the hell is it?" She tilted her head to the side and all color drained from her face.

"What is it?"

Her gaze sliced to me. "They're coming."

Fuck. I moved to the next corpse, jostling it to check underneath. The linen draped across its face fell away. Hollow skeletal eye sockets stared blindly ahead, its jaw hanging open—and there was a symbol carved into the bone. "Here."

Mags rushed over. "This has to be Frances. That's a concealment rune, not one I've ever seen before, but I'm sure that's what it is."

It was the darkest kind of magic, and witches who adhered to their rules and laws wouldn't ever have occasion to see anything like that. Magnolia was walking a dangerous road right now, and I had no idea how to help her. How to keep her safe from what might come of this.

"It's here, it has to be," she said.

Whispers echoed from the shadows, rising from the dark caves beyond the cavern. I couldn't hear what was being said, but the voices were clearly angry. I heard it, felt it. "What do we do?"

She pulled something from her bag and handed it to me. "Surround us with this."

It was a mix of salt, herbs, and cemetery dirt. I quickly did as she instructed as Mags pulled her blade from her pocket and sliced her finger, then traced the rune carved into the skull with her blood.

The scent of my female's blood had the predator in me screeching, clawing to be released. There was nothing my crow could do, though, no physical form to attack, no body to claw. Nothing to kill. I was used to the feeling, the drive to protect when Mags cut herself, but that roar inside me was at a whole new level now. It was so fierce that it was almost impossible to control.

She started chanting.

"Reveal your secrets to me, I command you, show me what I cannot see." Her eyes were wild as she again traced the rune etched into the skull. "Reveal your secrets to me, I command you, show me what I cannot see," she said again, her voice rising, her body shaking harder. "Show me what I cannot see. Show me what I cannot see," she cried as wind whipped around us. The whispers turned to screeches as the spirits of the crones exploded into the cavern. They flew at us, screaming louder when they reached the salt line protecting us, battering it over and over again.

The rune smoldered, then short flames ran along the lines etched into the bone, scorching it.

Magnolia thrust her hands under the body, and this time when she pulled her hands back, she held the book.

"How did you know to do that?"

She glanced at me. "I didn't."

Shit. "How the fuck are we gonna get out of here?" I roared over the crones' furious screaming.

"Overlapping salt circles," she said, quickly and carefully turning the pages of the ancient book.

"Take the book and let's go."

She shook her head. "We can't take it. It's too dangerous." She turned another page, then another.

The salt beside me was slowly being eaten away by the crones' constant attacks.

"Got it," Mags said and pulled out her phone and snapped a picture, shoved the book back where it came from, and covered Frances's skull with linen. Then she held out her hand for the bag of salt.

I handed it to her, and she poured another circle, overlapping the edge of the one we were in. But the crones were working together and the wind they'd created had become a wild storm in the cavern, whipping around us, not letting the salt settle in a thick line. The one surrounding us was thinning with every passing second.

"Fuck," Mags said and reached for something in her bag.

The circle broke—

Cold, grasping hands grabbed me, wrenching me away and tossing me across the cave. My body slammed against the hard stone wall, jarring every bone in my body.

"Bram!" Mags screamed a moment before she was tossed across the cavern as well and pinned to the opposite wall.

I roared, fighting, but the crones were too strong.

A force slammed my head back, and light danced across my vision.

She is ours, a distorted voice whispered in my ear.

CHAPTER 25

Magnolia

THE CRONES' laughter echoed through the room as they attacked Bram. His shirt was torn off and scratches were appearing across his skin, then bruises, slices.

"Let him go!" I screamed, fighting. "Please, let him go!"

The crones hissed with fury, ignoring my pleas, holding me fast.

You're staying with us, little witch.

You are ours.

We're going to make you bleed.

Tear you limb from limb.

Their whispers filled my head, their cold breath brushing my skin and chilling me to the bone. Bram roared, fighting, blood dripping from his body and down his face.

This wasn't happening. I wouldn't let it. No one I loved was getting hurt, not again, not because of me.

I screamed in fear, in rage, and words filled my head. A spell swirled, coming from deep inside me. Again, somehow, I just knew what I needed to do.

My hands were being forced against the wall. I fought, managing to get my knife from my pocket, and carved a hexagon into my palm, one inside the other, then sliced across them from point to point until the lines criss-crossed my palm, and I repeated the words filling my head. "Hear me, darkness, crawl from your slumber deep in the shadows and leash these restless souls, bind the evil in their bones, and thrust them back from where they came." Hissing through my teeth, I lifted my hand. "Eyes blinded with blood. Hands, feet, mouths bound with skin," I yelled, then slammed my palm against the stone wall with a cry.

Fire burned through my hand, blasting, exploding inside me. I screamed as a force flowed from me, a wall of magic pouring from my body, so heavy and wild that it threw the souls back, dragging them screaming back down into the caves they'd come from. I dropped to the floor, and silence filled the cavern again.

Bram hit the ground, and I scrambled to my feet, running for him. "Bram? Oh, goddess, what did they do to you?"

He coughed, then staggered to his feet. "I'm okay. Let's just get the fuck out of here."

I wrapped my arm around his waist, and we stumbled across the cavern and out through the wide entrance, then ran along the path under the falls. I stopped as soon as we were far enough away. "Let me see you?"

He leaned against the trunk of a dead tree, and I cupped his face, taking in the scratches just below his eyes, letting my hands hover an inch above his chest, using my magic to search for any serious injuries. There was nothing life threatening, but he was cut up badly. "You're okay, you're going to be okay."

He fisted my shirt at my belly, pulling me closer. "What the fuck happened back there?"

"I don't know, they were...so much stronger than I thought they'd be. I'm sorry. I almost got us killed." I rested my hands against his chest, then I pulled the one I'd cut back with a hiss.

Bram grabbed my wrist.

"What the fuck did you do to yourself?" He uncurled my fingers.

"I don't know." The design I'd carved into my hand had welted, now puffy like badly healed scar tissue. "They were attacking you, and a spell...it just...it came to me. It flowed through me and forced them back."

"It just came to you?"

"Yes." I didn't want to think about what that meant. Not yet.

I quickly checked the photo I'd taken on my phone, worried that somehow the crones had wiped it clean or somehow messed with it, but thankfully, it was still there.

"That ever happen before?" he asked as he pulled a small jar of healing balm from his pocket and smeared it across my palm.

"Kind of." I quickly scanned the spell.

"Should we be worried about that?"

I didn't look up. I didn't want him to see the worry in my own eyes.

"Magnolia? Should we be worried about it?"

I forced myself to look at him. "Honestly? I don't know. There's no one I can ask." I looked back down at the spell, not wanting to talk about it anymore. I'd worry about that later, after I'd found the killer. "So this isn't just a spell...there's a potion as well. These ingredients, some of them I've never used before."

"You don't need to worry about it yet, though, right?" Bram said, letting me change the subject.

"Right." But something told me it was only a matter of when, not if I was going to need it. That was why I'd come here today, that feeling was too strong to ignore. Yes, I'd try to pass this task without it, but this spell, it might be the only way to save my coven.

Bram tugged on my shirt again. "Ready?"

I nodded, and he lifted me into his arms. His blood instantly soaked through my shirt, and I felt enraged all over again. "I need to look after your wounds."

"They're superficial," he said as we lifted off.

Bram flew fast, and I could hear his heart pounding hard against me. I held on to him, even though I felt impossibly raw right then.

As the minutes ticked by, my scars began to tingle, itch, they started to burn hot, painful.

Not now. I wanted to fucking scream in frustration.

The urge to pull away, to escape Bram's touch, hit me hard, but that was impossible while we were in the air. My anger rose because I fucking hated that right then, being in Bram's arms was close to actual torture.

Goddess, it hurt. So bad.

When we finally landed, I was breathing heavily, ready to scratch my own skin off.

"Mags?" Bram asked when I pulled away, stumbling back.

"My scars," I said, fighting back all I was feeling. I didn't want him to see the truth of just how bad it'd gotten. I didn't want him to see that his touch had hurt me because that would hurt him, and I couldn't bear it.

He stepped forward, reaching for me, and I stepped back, cringing away from him.

Bram froze, his dark eyes missing none of it. "You're in pain."

"I'll be okay."

He lifted his hands. "I'm not gonna touch you, I promise."

"I'll be okay in a minute. Just give me a minute." I motioned to the bedroom door. "Let me look after you, please. That's what I need right now. Let me take care of your wounds."

He watched me closely, then nodded and did as I asked, walking into the room and sitting on the edge of the bed for me, like we'd done so many times before. I rushed to the bathroom on shaky legs and grabbed my basket.

Bram's gaze didn't leave me as I took out my mortar and pestle and several bags of herbs, dropping a small spoon of each into the stone bowl. "We need to cleanse as well as heal. I don't know what those twisted bitches did to you, but they were able to cut you, and I don't want their evil anywhere on you." I added some lavender oil and worked it and the herbs into a paste, followed by a scoop of healing balm. I mixed it all together, then, holding my hand over the potion, I let my magic pulse through me and into it, whispering a spell to increase its power.

"Put that on your hand first," he said, watching me.

"I will, I just need to—"

"No. You first," he said. "Now. I would, but..."

But right then, I'd pull away if he even tried. I quickly did as he asked, smearing some over the angry new scar on my hand, then grabbed a cotton pad and started on Bram, smearing it over all the cuts and scratches, the bruises they'd given him. "Bitches," I muttered.

Bram was quiet for several seconds. "One of them spoke to me."

"What did they say?"

"That you were theirs."

A shiver moved through me. "Well, they were wrong. And I won't ever be going back to that place, so they're shit out of luck." At least while I was alive. If this mark on my hand meant what I thought it did, my family might have no choice but to put me there one day, anyway. The darkness in me might be too great.

"No," Bram growled out. "You won't ever go back, and if you even think about it, I'll fucking tie you down and never let you out of my sight."

Instead of being irritated at his order, my body heated, my belly doing that swirling thing it did around him. "Is that so?"

"Yes."

"Did I tell you how bossy you've gotten lately?" I said and swiped some of the healing oil over another scratch on his chest. Bram was silent again, and I looked up.

His gaze locked with mine, then he shook his head. "No, but I'm not too worried."

My heart raced faster. "Oh? And why is that?"

His nostrils flared and he breathed deep. "Because you love it."

My face heated, but I didn't look away. "Caught that, did you?"

210

"Yeah, I fucking did," he said, his voice gravelly as hell.

I carried on, cleaning and treating the wounds on his chest, while his gaze burned into me. I felt the hunger rolling off him, but he didn't move, didn't attempt to touch me or kiss me or pull me closer. I loved him for it and wanted to cry at the same time.

"It's okay," he said.

I kept my head down. "No...it's not."

"We talked about this, Mags. I want you, of course I do, but this is enough. You think I lied about that?"

I shook my head.

"Good."

"But Wills and Warrick and Iris and Daven, Rose and Ronan—"

"Aren't us. We'll work out our own thing, yeah? And who says we have to touch each other to give pleasure. There are other things we can do," he said roughly.

"There is?"

He nodded. "But right now, we're going to talk through what we know about this task," he said, changing the subject, trying to distract me. "Okay? So tell me what you know so far."

I wanted him to elaborate on the "things we can do," but I felt too raw to go there right then, and Bram knew it, hence the change of subject. "We know a group of friends and the people close to them are being targeted, tortured, and killed. Body parts, skin, and other organs have been taken from each scene for reasons unknown, and all have had judgment carved into their skin."

Bram nodded. "What else?"

"We know the prom committee's relationships aren't platonic. They partake in group sex, they frequent Brent Silva's club, Red. And after what I saw at the Hazarks', we know they sometimes bring others into their circle. Like Isaac, Maria, and Ryan. All of whom are also members of Red, well, except for Isaac who was kicked out. They're in each other's pockets, and they've been that way since they were teenagers."

"They're convinced Willow is the one hunting them," Bram said. "Someone planted evidence at The Cauldron, and they're using some old high school resentment, and Isaac's investment company, trying to buy Willow's store, as well as the death of his brother and Willow's supposed grudge against his family as a motive. And they pranked Willow, right? I doubt she's the only one they did that shit to. They're entitled assholes, all of them. We've seen them in action. I have no doubt they were the bullies in high school. We've been searching for someone they fucked with recently, but maybe we need to go back farther than that."

"Like another high school prank gone wrong?"

Bram shrugged. "They were dicks to Wills; it's easy to assume they were dicks to a lot of other people as well."

"You think someone could hold a grudge that long?"

"If the damage they'd caused was bad enough? Yeah, I do."

CHAPTER 26

Magnolia

"Do you think Chloe knows anything?" I asked Bram as we walked out of her office.

Chloe Chan was all about money, and the prom committee had that in spades. The wolf shifter made a killing off them, no pun intended, as their sole realtor.

"It doesn't make sense to kill them off," Bram said.

This was true. I couldn't see her cooking the geese that laid all the golden eggs.

We'd started with the two members of Red who were in business with or worked for the group, then narrowed it down to those who were also Roxburgh High School alumni. If that didn't bear fruit, we'd have to cast a wider net.

Thankfully, Chloe was several years older than me and had left school before I started, so didn't recognize me when we showed up. She bought my fake name and our ruse as organizers of the next RHS reunion and that we were after stories to include in a reunion yearbook. High school was hard for a lot of people, and those people tended to remember the assholes, the kids they'd been forced to avoid in the halls or the cafeteria.

But Chloe hadn't fallen for my attempt to draw her into any "off the record" gossip. No, she wasn't going to say a bad word about any of them, not when the prom committee funded her very nice lifestyle.

We got in the car as another pulled up across the street. "Is that Ryan Alway?" He got out of his car, and Chloe strutted out of her office.

"Yep."

She smiled wide and strode over to him. They kissed, deeply, then she got in his car and they drove away.

"Ryan sure likes mixing business with pleasure."

"I guess they work closely. Ryan and Chloe most likely scout out potential investment properties before they take it to Isaac and the other shareholders."

I locked this new bit of info away with everything else, and we headed for Luke Donaghy's office next. Going by the yearbook we'd taken from the library, Luke hadn't been one of the cool kids. He'd been awkward, kind of nerdy, the skinny mathlete with glasses and braces.

And a far cry from the male who'd rolled back into Roxburgh six months ago, quickly making a name for himself as the kind of guy you did not want to fuck with—and not just in business—and he'd most definitely grown out of his awkward phase.

"Do you think the rumors about Luke are true?" I asked Bram. Luke had been the same year as Willow. They hadn't been friends, as far as I knew, but they'd shared several classes together.

Bram stared ahead, but his fingers tightened on the wheel. "I know they are."

"You think he's capable of murder?"

"Yes."

I turned in my seat. "So you know him?"

He shook his head. "I know of him, because that's the world I'm part of and because he likes people to know. He also introduced himself to Payne not long after he moved back."

"What did Payne think of him?"

"He said he'd prefer to work with him than against him," Bram said. "Payne couldn't work out what he was, though. Shifter, most likely, at least that's what he puts out there. Luke wasn't forthcoming, but he's powerful."

"So he could totally be our killer?" I said, beginning to feel a little edgy meeting this guy.

"It's possible."

"Oh goody." We'd called and made an appointment to see him, using the same school reunion bullshit and, surprisingly, he'd agreed to see us.

Bram parked the car, and I looked out the window and up at the building where Luke had his offices. It was architecturally designed by an award-winning architect, twenty stories high and made of black iron with tinted windows. It looked like some dark lair, or the fortress of some evil, maniacal supervillain. "What's his line of business?"

"He calls himself an entrepreneur and has his fingers in all sorts of pies," Bram said.

"Sounds messy."

"Oh yeah, from what I hear, he's more than happy to get his hands dirty." Bram glanced my way. "I'm not sure going to see this guy is a good idea."

It was probably a terrible idea, but we needed to do this. Not only was I feeling the call from my task but my inner spidey senses were definitely telling me I needed to speak to this guy. "I feel drawn to this place, Bram. We need to do this."

The muscle in his jaw jumped. "Fine, but if I decide we need to leave, we're getting the fuck out of there, yeah?"

I nodded my agreement and reached for the door handle. Bram tugged the sleeve of my shirt, stopping me.

I turned back and he leaned forward, his eyes dark and hot as they held mine before they dipped to my mouth and back up. "But first, I want you to kiss me."

The gravel in his voice had tingles dancing all over me. He was being careful, not touching me, not even brushing his fingers over my skin, but still letting me know that he wanted me. A kiss I could handle, and I instantly gave him what he asked for, resting my hand on his chest, I leaned forward and pressed my mouth against his. Heat spiraled through me, and I cupped his jaw, my thumb brushing across the corner of his mouth. Bram groaned and licked the seam of my lips, and I opened for him immediately.

"Can I touch your hair?" he said roughly against my lips.

"Yes."

He instantly gripped a handful in his fist and tilted my head to the side so he could kiss me harder, deeper, his hunger for me unmistakable. I didn't want to stop, there was no way I could pull away, but eventually, he slowed things down and lifted his head.

"That was...nice," I said and grinned up at him.

"Nice?"

"Okay, stupidly hot."

He licked his lips. "Definitely a more accurate description."

I hadn't been able to stop thinking about what he said last night, and that kiss had his words flying around my head again.

"What is it?" he said, seeing right through me.

My cheeks warmed. "It's nothing."

He grabbed my shirt at my belly, fisting it, stopping my retreat, but again being careful not to touch me. "It's not nothing. Talk to me."

"Bram...honestly, it's nothing."

He studied me for several seconds, and I thought he'd drop it. Instead, he leaned closer. "I'm your male, Magnolia. We may not have mated yet, but we should be able to talk about anything, no matter how hard, or"—he swiped his fingers over my hot cheek, allowing himself that brief contact— "embarrassed we are."

"I'm not embarrassed," I said, and I wasn't totally lying.

"Good, so tell me what you're thinking."

I blew out a breath, attempting to steady the butterflies in my belly. "I've been thinking about what you said...last night."

"What did I say?" he said, but judging by the way his gaze had heated, he knew exactly what I was talking about.

"Don't play with me, B. You know exactly what I'm talking about," I said.

"I haven't even begun to play with you, Mags," he said, his voice so impossibly deep I barely suppressed a shiver. "I've had a long time to think about it, what I want to do to you. I tried not to, I did, but there was no stopping my mind conjuring up all kinds of dirty shit. All the things I'd do if you were mine."

Guilt and frustration filled me. "But my scars, I'm not sure I can—"

"You saw me, didn't you?" he said, tugging on my shirt again. "That night I left your room while you slept. When I came back, you were in bed, but you were faking it, weren't you, baby?"

Oh goddess. I swallowed, audibly. "Yes."

"I woke up beside you, and I was so fucking hard, wanting you, I had to go to the tree house and get in the shower. I told myself I just needed the cold water to cool me down, that I had to stop thinking about you like that, but there was no stopping it, and I closed my eyes and let the fantasies play out. After that, I had no choice but to stroke my cock while thinking of you, and it wasn't the first time, Mags." He tucked my hair behind my ear. "You saw me, didn't you?" he asked again.

I nodded, struggling to breathe. "Yes." I gripped the side of his neck. "And you were...goddess, so beautiful."

His nostrils flared. "You liked it. You liked watching me?"

I nodded again.

"Have you ever thought about me like that? Have you ever touched yourself while you did?" he rasped.

I blew out a shaky breath. "Yes."

Bram's chest was rising and falling rapidly, and a husky *caw* rose in his throat. "You have?"

"Yes."

"Fuck," he snarled.

"That's what you were talking about? When you said there were other things we could do? You were talking about us doing that...together?" I said.

His mouth was so close now, his breath brushing my lips when he spoke. "Would you? Would you do that? Touch yourself and let me watch?"

His black eyes were locked on mine, the heat of him, his scent filling my head, making me freaking dizzy. "Yes. Will you?"

"Yes," he said without hesitation.

I wanted him, really, really badly.

A shudder moved through him, and his nostrils flared. "How the fuck am I going to think about anything else now?"

A car horn blasted somewhere nearby, jolting us from the intimacy of the moment. I cleared my throat. "I ah...I guess we better go in."

"I guess so," he said and tugged on my shirt one more time before releasing it.

"You think you can manage to hold my hand?" he asked.

I took his. "Yeah." My hands had the least amount of damage, and holding hands was usually fine, but with the way my scars had been lately, I wasn't sure how much longer that would last. There was no pain now, though, no burning when his skin touched mine. I'd been trying not to think about it, why the pain was getting worse, but something was very wrong, and we both knew it. It wasn't just because of what Clayton did to me. There was something else, something inside me, and it was growing in strength.

We walked into the building, got in the elevator, and I hit the button for the fifth floor.

"You should probably take your hair down. If he's a shifter and he sees your markers, he'll know what you are," I said.

Bram gripped my hand tighter. "I don't think putting my hair down will hide it, not with this guy." He pulled the hair tie out anyway, letting his hair fall around his face. "But no reason to broadcast it."

The doors slid open, and we strode up to the reception desk.

"We have an appointment with Luke Donaghy," I said to the receptionist. He asked for our names. "Brad and Magda. We're here about the Roxburgh High School reunion."

The guy smiled. "Ah, yes. He's expecting you. Go through."

"Thanks."

"Brad and Magda?" Bram said, lips twitching as we headed for the office door.

"I thought they were the closest to our own names, less chance to mess up." I grinned up at him.

"After today, if you ever call me Brad again, we'll have a serious problem," he said, an expression on his face that had me biting back a grin.

"Hey, you could totally be a Brad. You've got those big shoulders now. You could be the quarterback of the football team, Brad." If quarterbacks were dark goths with murderous tendencies. Bram was so far from a Brad it wasn't funny.

"Would a Brad sit you in a chair, strap your legs wide, and make you play with yourself until you come so many times you passed the fuck out?" he said.

I sucked in a sharp breath, my gaze flying to him. Bram laughed, and it was dark and dirty. A throb started between my thighs. "That wasn't fair."

"Oh, I'm definitely not planning on playing fair," he said, then knocked on the door before I could reply.

A deep, masculine voice called for us to come in.

Bram opened the door and walked in, and I followed, trying to focus on why we were here and not the images now filling my head.

Luke sat behind a massive desk. The wall behind him was all glass and the view utterly breathtaking. "Brad and Magda?" he said and stood.

Bram stepped forward and shook his hand. Luke looked at me, and I waved instead. I could hold Bram's hand, but the idea of touching anyone else sent more dread through me.

He frowned, but then motioned to the chairs opposite him. "Please, take a seat."

I pulled a notepad and a pen from my bag and we both sat. "Thanks so much for agreeing to speak with us, Mr. Donaghy."

"Call me Luke." His sharp gaze moved over me before sliding to Bram.

"We're gathering stories from past students of Roxburgh High School, for a reunion yearbook. And as a successful Roxburgh High alum we thought you might have some fun stories to share? We'll include a brief bio as well, just a few details about you alongside it. What you're doing now, that sort of thing," I said, spouting the bullshit I'd come up with.

He sat back. "I don't really have many fond memories from my time at RHS, if you want the truth. I was a bit of a loner."

I grinned. "You and me both. I spent most of my time in the library."

"So did I." His gaze darkened. "I'm positive I'd remember you, Magda. How old are you, sweetheart?"

Bram froze beside me a moment before his hand came down on my knee, in a tight possessive grip. Pain instantly fired through me, my scars burning under my skin. I jolted, and he immediately pulled his hand back with a hiss.

"You okay?" he asked, alarm in his voice.

He'd felt territorial and his instincts had taken over completely. "Of course." I smiled at Luke and forced a chuckle. "I fell over this morning and grazed my knee. Don't mind us."

218

Luke tilted his head back...then breathed deep. His lids fluttered. "*Mmm*, you smell good. Very good, but I don't smell blood, Magda." His gaze was hot when he refocused on me. "I wonder why you're lying to me?"

Bram shot to his feet. "You smell my female again and I'll tear your fucking face off."

Luke slowly rose from his chair, buttoning his suit jacket as he did. "Finally, a little honesty. And you can try it, boy."

Bram took a step forward, and I jumped to my feet, getting between them. "Let's all just calm down, okay?"

"Why are you here?" Luke demanded. "Because you're sure as fuck not working on some nonexistent high school reunion." His gaze slid to Bram over my head. "And I can smell the death all over you, crow. You can hide your markers, but I see right through you."

"He's not here for you," I said to Luke. "He's helping me."

"Oh, I know he's not here for me," the other male said. "If I thought he was, he'd already be dead."

Bram laughed; it was cold and nasty. "I'm sure my other kills thought the same thing, unfortunately I can't ask them, since they're all rotting in the ground."

Luke snarled and leaned forward, planting his hands on his desk.

"We're sorry we lied about our reason for being here," I said quickly, before he bounded over that wide desk and all hell broke loose. "Bram definitely isn't here to...kill you." I couldn't believe those words just came out of my mouth, like it was a reasonable clarification. "But I do need to ask you some questions."

"I'm not sure why you think I'd answer," he said, his expression now stoic, even though fury still burned in his eyes.

"I know we went about this the wrong way, but I would really appreciate it." He was about to tell us to get lost, I could see it all over his face. "You might remember my sister Willow? Willow Thornheart. She was the same year as you. I think you shared a few classes?"

He stilled, then straightened. "You're Willow's sister?"

I didn't know if he and Willow knew each other well, but I knew my sister was a good person. She sure as hell hadn't been cruel or a bully in high school. "Yes, and I'm sure you've heard the accusations being made against her."

"I have. They're utter bullshit, of course," he said, surprising me.

"You don't think she's guilty?"

His glaze flicked to Bram, then he slowly sat back in his chair, so I did the same. Then I grabbed Bram's hand and tugged him down as well when he continued to loom.

"No," Luke said. "I don't."

Was that because he knew my sister wasn't the murdering kind or because he was the one doing the murdering? "So you remember her from school?"

"She was one of the few people who were kind to me back then." He smiled and it was...terrifying. "She spoke up more than once when I was outnumbered and getting the shit kicked out of me."

"Why did they pick on you?" I asked, genuinely interested but also trying to get him to open up.

He tapped a finger on his desk. "Because they didn't know what I was. They sensed something...something wasn't right. I scared them, I guess, so they attacked first."

I wanted to ask what he was, but I didn't think he'd like that, especially since he seemed to have gone to a lot of trouble to hide it. "Did you ever have any trouble with Robert and Jenna Hazark, or Chase Golden, Clara Hope or Calvin Adler and his cousin Katana? I know you do business with them now, and move in the same...um, circles, but they were a tight group even back then, and I get the feeling they weren't the nicest in high school."

He studied me for several seconds. "They were bullies then and now. Narcissists, all of them. I've enjoyed coming back and...repaying them for their treatment of me and a few others from back then."

"Does repayment include torture and disembowelment?" Bram asked.

Luke smiled, but it didn't reach his eyes.

Bram stared back. "How about removing and collecting limbs?"

"You think I'm killing them off?" Luke asked.

"Are you?" Bram asked without looking away.

"Do I look like a vicious killer, sweetheart?" Luke asked, turning back to me.

Well, yeah, he kind of did.

"I mean, you'd know," he said and tilted his head toward Bram.

Bram bared his teeth.

Okay, testosterone was flying all over the damn place. We needed to move this along. "Can you remember anyone else they bullied back then?"

"You're grasping at straws, you know that, don't you?" Luke said.

"Maybe. Humor me."

A small smile curled his lips, and this time it did reach his cool blue eyes. They actually sparkled. It was unsettling as hell. "I like you, sweetheart, you're tenacious."

"She's not your sweetheart. Say it again and I'll slit your fucking throat," Bram said.

Luke didn't spare him a glance, but the muscle in his jaw pulsed. "The only reason you're still sitting in my office and not out on your asses is because I liked Willow. She was a good person, and I haven't encountered many of them over the years. Yes, they fucked with other kids. Mainly those younger than them. There was a group of kids that hung out at the library, a poetry group. They were their number one targets."

"Can you give us names?"

"No. As I said, I was a loner."

"Is there anything else you can tell us?" I said.

"No." Luke stood. "Now get the fuck out of my office."

"Thank you for your time." I grabbed Bram's hand, tugging him from his seat and dragged him from the room and into the elevator.

I blew out a frustrated breath and turned to him as the doors slid shut in front of us. "Well, you were in fine form back there."

"He was looking at you like he wanted to fuck you," Bram said by way of explanation.

I thought he looked at me like he wanted to take a bite out of me, and not the good kind. "Do you think he's our killer?"

"He's capable of it," Bram said, then shook his head. "But I don't think so."

Shit.

I didn't think so either. "The yearbook, the one with Willow's piece in it, there were several poems scattered through it as well, I'm sure of it."

Maybe one of them was our killer? Or maybe it was time to cast that wider net? I wasn't sure. I wasn't sure of any fucking thing.

CHAPTER 27

Magnolia

I FLICKED THROUGH THE YEARBOOK. I'd showered while Bram had heated us up the dinner Mom left for us, and now we were back to scouring for clues.

"You find any?" Bram asked, sitting on the couch opposite me.

"Two. The first was by Maria's brother, Marcel, the one who passed away in some accident with his younger sister, and it's seriously dark." It was called "In the Dead of the Night." "If the guy hadn't been dead for years, this would put him at the top of my serial killer suspect list."

I leaned forward on my wooden kitchen chair, and turned the book so Bram could read it. He scanned the poem, and I knew when he screwed up his face that he'd gotten to the bit about stabbing his broken heart and letting it bleed into the mouth of the person who broke it, so they could taste his pain. "Fucking hell," he muttered.

"My thoughts exactly. There's another one." I flipped the page. "By a guy named Thomas Alway."

Bram looked over at me. "A relative of Ryan's?"

"That'd be my guess." I crossed my legs, and his dark gaze slid over my bare skin. My belly swirled.

"Any good?"

"It's about a flower."

"Sounds riveting." Bram flipped a few more pages. "There any pictures of the poetry group in here?"

"None." I was guessing they were lucky to get their poems in the yearbook, let alone a photo as well.

He nodded, then looked back up at me. His stare was intense. "Love it when you wear my shirts," he said.

"Yeah?" There was another swirl, this one dipping lower. I'd put one on after my shower.

He nodded and moistened his lips. "Nearly every one I own, you've worn. I used to think about how they'd been against your bare skin." His gaze grew darker still. "You ever notice that I always wore whatever shirt you'd slept in the night before?"

I hadn't thought too much about it. I usually tossed the one I'd worn on his bed after I dressed, I'd assumed he'd just grabbed the first one he saw. "You did it on purpose?"

"Fuck yeah. Your scent was all over it, and knowing your bare skin had been right up against it and was now right up against mine, it helped satisfy the possessive male in me."

I'd had no idea. None. "And how does it make you feel now?" I asked, my heart racing faster, an ache building between my thighs.

"Like a fucking caveman." His gaze dipped to my legs again. "I can smell how wet you're getting, Mags, and every time you cross and uncross your legs, I'm tipping closer and closer to the edge."

"What do you want to do?" I asked, the pounding of my heart making my voice quiver.

His nostrils flared. "I want you to spread your legs wide for me and let me taste you." He shook his head. "The last fucking thing I want is to hurt you, baby. I know your scars are causing you pain, but knowing you need me, that you're aching for me, my crow is growing restless. No pressure, okay? You don't want it, we wait until you do. But know the only part of me that would touch you, is my mouth against your hot, little pussy."

His chest was rising and falling fast, watching, waiting for what I'd say. I was breathing hard as well now, my skin burning up, but for once it was in a good way. I placed the yearbook on the floor, and slowly uncrossed my legs. "I want it."

"You sure? I don't want to make you—"

"You're not making me do anything. I want it. Please," I whispered.

He bared his teeth and it was wicked and sexy as hell. "Panties off, baby."

I stood and slid them down my legs, kicking them aside.

"Sit back in the chair, ass on the edge."

I did as he asked, excited, wanting what he said so bad.

He got off the couch and sat on the floor, then positioned his legs between the wooden legs of the chair I was on, before gripping them and dragging, it and me, right up to him. My legs had nowhere to go and I automatically spread them wide.

Bram's face was level with my bare pussy.

"Legs on the couch either side of me, and lean back," he rasped.

I did, bending my knees, and bracing my legs either side of him, before leaning back. I was already wet, the ache inside growing unbearable. "Bram," I whimpered.

"Lift the shirt and show me how wet you are."

My hand trembled as I did as he asked. I was hot and flushed, and needy as hell.

Bram groaned. "Fuck. Look at you." He looked up at me. "Fucking dreamed of this. You have no idea how long I've thought about how you'd taste, Magnolia. I thought it was a craving that I'd never get to satisfy, a secret you'd never share with me." His biceps bunched and he tugged the chair closer and breathed deep, and his eyes drifted shut on a full-body shudder. "Fist my hair, move me how you want me, take what you want, rub, grind, do whatever the fuck feels good."

I slid my fingers into his hair and whimpered again at the picture he painted, at the feel of his hot breath against my bare, damp flesh.

Then he leaned in, closing the small space between us and covered my pussy with his mouth, then dragging his tongue through my slick flesh with a deep groan. I pushed back against the chair, fisted his hair tighter, and spread wider for him.

Bram's eyes were closed, lashes fluttering as he feasted on me. Sucking and licking me, exploring every inch. He opened his eyes as he swirled his tongue around my clit, then sucked on it gently. I cried out, my stomach quivering, my legs shaking. He worked me until I couldn't stop myself from grinding against his mouth.

"Can you take one of my fingers?" he growled.

"D-do it."

Bram flicked his tongue over my clit as he slid a long, thick finger inside me. I arched against the seat with a groan and rocked against his hand. He started fucking me with his finger then, and working my clit, sucking and licking it so good.

My orgasm roared up on me, slamming through me and I cried out, coming hard, my inner muscles clutching and gripping around his finger.

Finally, I collapsed back and Bram lapped at me gently setting off delicious aftershocks, before sliding out his finger. I looked down at him, watching as he slid it into his mouth and sucked it clean.

"Good?" I asked.

"What do you think?" he said, his voice little more than a snarl. "Fuck, Mags, I want to live right fucking there, between your thighs."

I stood on shaky legs and shoved the chair out of the way, then dropped to my knees, reaching for the front of his pants, and yanked them open.

"Mags?"

"Now it's my turn," I said, tugging down his jeans and underwear. His hard cock sprang free.

"I don't expect you—"

I sucked his long, thick cock deep into my mouth as deep as I could. I wasn't ready for everything, not yet, but I wanted to give him this. I could do this for him. I wanted to, badly.

Bram barked out a curse, his hips lifting.

I had no idea what I was doing, I just knew I wanted to make him feel as good as he'd made me feel. I wanted to know his taste. I wanted to know everything. He was too long to take all of him, so I stroked the base the way I had at the lookout, while I sucked and licked the rest.

His fingers thrust into my hair and the sounds that came from him made me hot and bothered all over again.

I sucked him harder, faster, over and over again.

He hissed through clenched teeth. "I can't...I can't hold back, baby. I can't..." His cock pulsed in my hand a moment before his come flooded my mouth. He called out my name, fisting my hair, his hips thrusting and twisting beneath me.

I swallowed him down, and kept sucking him until he was done. When I released his cock, he loosened his grip on my hair and brushed it away from my face, before tilting my head back. His gaze was full of a dark possessiveness I'd never seen before. I loved it.

He swiped his thumb over my swollen lips. "Maggie," he rasped.

That's all he said, all he needed to say. It was all there in my name. I was his, and he was mine, no matter what.

He pulled me in for a gentle kiss and I wanted to curl up in his lap and stay there forever, but I couldn't, the scars on my body wouldn't let me have that.

A thump came from outside the tree house, followed by a bang on the door. I lifted my head, my stomach sinking because I instantly knew who it was and what it meant.

Bram cursed as he stood, and helped me up. He tugged down my shirt and wrapped the blanket on the back of the couch around my shoulders.

Tucking himself back in his jeans and doing them up, Bram strode to the door, that he'd thankfully started locking, and opened it.

Rook stood there, his expression almost violent, but then that was how he always looked. "You're needed," he said and didn't elaborate, he didn't need to.

"No one else can handle it?" Bram asked.

Rook shook his head.

"Payne and Talon?"

"Another hunt," he said and ducked back out.

Bram's jaw tightened.

"Go." I hadn't missed how aggressive Bram had become the last few days. He needed this.

The muscles and tendons in his forearms bunched. "You sure?" he asked, and I could see the conflict in his eyes.

I curled my fingers around his. "You'll be back as soon as you can, and I'll be careful."

"You'll call Ash?"

"I will."

Bram closed the space between us. "I'll be as quick as I can."

"I know." I dropped the blanket when Bram gripped either side of my shirt at my waist. Holding the fabric tight, he pulled me close without actually touching my skin, then leaned in and kissed me. I could taste myself on his lips.

"I don't wanna leave you," he said against my mouth, a growl in his voice.

"You'll be back before we know it."

He held my shirt more firmly, the fabric tightening around my waist, almost having the same effect as a hug, before he released me and stepped back. The lack of contact was killing me, and I could see Bram was struggling as badly as I was without it. We'd gotten each other off, and it was amazing, but what would have made it even better? Lying in his arms afterwards. We both still needed more.

"Be safe," he said, then with one last quick press of his lips to mine, he walked out and closed the door behind him.

I stood there and stared at that door for far longer than was sane. Shaking myself out of it, I finally sat and jotted down everything I knew. Isaac's name glared up at me. On a whim, I pulled out my phone and hit Brent's number.

He answered on the third ring. "Yeah?"

"Hey, it's Magnolia. I know you have a whole confidentiality thing, but I wanted to ask you something."

There was a beat of silence. "You can ask."

"Why did you end Isaac Eldridge's membership?"

Another beat. "Usually, I wouldn't tell you shit, but I think we've already crossed that bridge. I kicked his ass out because he was getting too rough with females who weren't into pain. He crossed the line. And I would have kicked him out sooner, but the females in question only came forward after I saw it myself."

I recoiled. "So you're saying he has an aggressive streak?"

"Yes. And there's something else, something I hadn't really thought too much about until now. They were all redheads. I just assumed that was his type, but the level of violence he was dishing out, it was more than that."

Fuck. "Thanks, Brent."

We ended the call, and I instantly hit Asher's number.

She answered on the second ring. "What's doing, feisty?"

"You free?"

"Yep. Where are we going?"

-)⟩⟩-◑-⟨⟨⟨-

It was dark by the time I pulled up outside Ryan Alway's apartment. Clouds had gathered, rain was brewing, and it was muggy as hell. But this was where I was supposed to be. I had planned to go to Isaac's place, but the moment I got in the car, the vines had started tingling in the middle of my back and I'd been led here. What part Ryan played in all this, I had no idea, but going by the alarm bells wailing through my head, there was definitely a link between him and my task.

It was hot, and I yanked up my sleeves as I looked up at the second floor. The lights were on at Ryan's place, and I could see a shadow moving behind the curtains. He was home, thank fuck. As soon as Asher got here, we'd head up.

Ryan knew something, that much was obvious, and I wasn't leaving until I'd extracted every bit of information I could from the little creep. That night at the Hazarks', the way he'd been with Jenna, the look in his eyes—I shuddered—Isaac wasn't the only one with a violent streak. The guy had given me the major icks.

The door to the building opened and Ryan strode out, heading down the street, hands in pockets, whistling while he walked. *Shit.* My internal alarm wailed again, screaming at me to follow.

I had no choice. I followed my instincts. I quickly texted Ash, letting her know the direction I was headed. Ryan walked faster, carrying on for a couple blocks, and I was forced to pick up the pace to keep up with him. He turned down the next street, and I jogged after him, rounding the corner—

Fuck.

I slammed on the brakes.

He was leaning against the building, arms crossed, waiting for me with a smirk on his face. "You're not very good at the whole stealth thing, are you, Magnolia?" he said, gaze burning into me.

My heart kicked to life in my chest, and I forced a chuckle. "Obviously not. When did you make me?"

"I saw you sitting in your piece-of-shit car outside my very nice apartment. What the fuck do you want?" he said, the amused expression falling away.

"To talk to you, that's all."

He tilted his head to the side. "Aren't you persistent. And what would we have to talk about?"

I got the feeling this guy wouldn't believe anything less than the truth. Besides, I knew without a doubt that Maria and Leah Golden would have filled the whole prom committee in after we'd stopped by to talk to them. "I'm trying to clear my sister's name, and I was hoping you'd help me."

"You really believe she's innocent?" he asked with what appeared to be genuine surprise on his face.

"I know she is."

He studied me for several seconds. "Fine. Honestly, I'm curious how you think I can help." He motioned ahead. "I was on my way to a wine bar. You have a drink with me, we'll talk."

I pulled my phone from my pocket. "Sounds good. What's the name of the bar? I was meeting my friend, and I need to tell her where we're going."

"What friend? Your familiar?" he asked.

"Nope, Bram's busy tonight."

He smirked. "Oh dear, trouble in paradise already, huh?"

Dick. "Not at all. The name?"

He chuckled, amused with himself for some reason. "Angelo's."

We walked the block to the bar in silence. He glanced my way at regular intervals, his lips curled in what I'm sure he thought looked like a congenial smile, but I couldn't work out what was behind it. I was usually a pretty good judge of character, but I wasn't getting a read from him right then. Nothing but dead air.

He opened the door to the wine bar and led me to a table in the back. We sat, and he smiled again. It was...friendly. "How far away is your friend? Are we ordering for them as well?"

"She prefers to order for herself," I said.

"Just us, then." He stood, then strode to the bar, even though I hadn't actually told him what I wanted.

I shifted in my seat, taking in my surroundings. The place was quiet. The people that were here mainly sat at the front near the large windows. Bram wouldn't like this, not one bit, but we were in a public place and Ash was on her way.

Ryan was laughing and chatting with the barman like they were old friends. Finally, he walked back with two glasses of red wine. He put one down in front of me. "This is one of my favorites." Then he rounded the table and took his seat again. "Try it." He lifted his glass, swirling it, then breathed it in deeply, then grinned, about to take a sip.

I leaned across the table, wrapped my fingers around his glass and took it, then slid mine across the table toward him. "A girl can never be too careful."

His eyes narrowed. "You think I'm going to drug you? Do I look like the kind of guy who needs to drug his dates?"

"I wouldn't know. And this isn't a date," I said.

"We're two young, attractive people enjoying a nice glass of wine, seems like a date to me. Try your wine."

Such a fucking creep. I forced myself to take a sip while he watched me intently. It was nice, I guess. I wasn't much of a drinker, wine or otherwise. It was hard, but I managed not to screw up my face.

"Well?" he said. "Do you like it? It's stunning, isn't it?"

Stunning? What a dick. I pitied Chloe or any other female he dated. I'm sure he thought he was impressing them with his apparent knowledge of fine wines, but he just sounded like a douche bag. "It's okay, I guess. I don't know much about wine."

He sat back, his frustration clear. "But you must know if something tastes good or not?"

"Of course."

"Take another sip."

He was offended, and that sounded more like an order than a request, but you caught more bees with honey, right? I wanted him to talk, and a few drinks might actually loosen his tongue. I forced myself to take another sip.

"Well?" he demanded, watching me closely.

"It's good." Still tasted like vinegar to me.

He smiled. "Don't feel bad, not everyone has the kind of refined palate to really appreciate a truly superior wine."

"Oh, I don't feel bad," I said.

His smile widened, giving me an indulgent look, like he thought I was an adorable little moron. "You're one of those tough girls, aren't you, Magnolia?" he said, the smile turning into a smirk. "All bluster. You talk a big game but can't actually deliver. Under all the black clothes and eyeliner, you're scared out of your mind."

"What do I have to be scared of, Ryan?" I asked, doing my best to keep my temper in check. It wasn't easy. I wanted to throat punch this asshole, badly.

"You tell me?"

That smirk was still front and center, and my fingers curled into a fist at my side. I shook my head. "I have no idea what you're talking about. I just want to ask you a couple questions."

"Then ask," he said, taking another sip of his drink.

The tips of my fingers felt a little tingly. "How long have you worked for the Hazarks, Chase Golden and Maria Watson?" I shook my hand out, trying to get the blood flowing again.

"Seven months, and I work for Dark Star."

"So you work for Isaac as well?"

"Yes," he said.

A dull thump started behind my temples. "What do you do for them?"

He sat forward. "Anything they ask of me. I'm their assistant. I'm there to assist in any way they see fit."

A cold sweat coated my skin, and my hands felt kind of numb. "Do you know Thomas Alway?"

"Yes."

"How?" My head spun.

He took his wallet from his pocket, pulled out his license, and slid it to me. "Thomas Ryan Alway" was printed on it. "I dropped Thomas years ago. It's kind of old and stodgy sounding."

He was Thomas Alway. One of the kids the prom committee relentlessly bullied.

My head did another loop. Something was seriously wrong. I tried to stand, but my legs gave out. *Fuck.*

Ryan leaned in and slid his fingers under my chin, tilting my head back. "I also use Ryan because I didn't want anyone to know who I was, not right away. I'm a lot hotter now than I was in high school, you know. I've lost a lot of weight. No one guessed I was the sad boy from the poetry group that no one would look twice at...unless they were about to spit on me, that is— or kick the shit out of me."

My eyes grew heavy, and Ryan stood, laughing like I'd told some amazing joke. He pulled me out of my chair and tucked me under his arm. "I think you've had enough to drink, honey."

I tried to open my mouth, to call for help, to tell him to back the fuck off, but he was already leading me through the bar and out the back, and no matter how hard I fought, my limbs were utterly useless. His hand delved into my pocket, and he took out my phone, switched it off and tossed it in the dumpster, then looked down at me. "You're wondering how I knew you'd switch drinks? I didn't, but I added a little insurance just in case you did," he said and smiled. "I'm immune to it. I'm sure you're wondering that as well. I ingested small quantities, slowly over time, increasing the amount until I built a tolerance to it."

He was completely insane.

He all but carried me out the back and through an alleyway, then back out onto the street behind the bar and lifted his hand. A cab pulled up beside us, and Ryan stuffed me in, got in beside me, and rattled off an address I didn't recognize.

"The wife and I...celebrated our anniversary a little too hard," he said, slurring his words, pretending to be drunk. I guess so that the driver didn't think he was taking advantage of some poor drunk girl. So he didn't try to help me or ask if I was okay.

"Ready to have a little fun, Magnolia? I know I am," he said low against my ear.

Inside I was screaming, but the words wouldn't come. My entire body was paralyzed. I could hear everything, feel everything, but my body wouldn't work. I was in serious trouble. Asher wouldn't know where I was, and with my phone back there, she had no way of tracking me.

We didn't drive for very long, and when the car pulled over, I willed my limbs to move and my mouth to work, but nothing. Ryan lifted me from the car, laughing and pretending we were having a grand old time as he dragged me away.

There was a big for sale sign at the front of the house, with a picture of Chloe Chan's face on it. He pulled a key from his pocket and opened the door to the house. A new build, like he'd taken Margot.

He unlocked the door. "Chloe's a decent fuck, but she really is as dumb as a post," he said and slid the key in his pocket.

It was big and empty. There was plastic sheeting still on the floor, cans of paint, tools scattered here and there. He was using Chloe's real estate business to help find places he could take his kills. I tried to talk again, and all I managed was a moan.

Ryan set me on the floor, but I couldn't hold my head up. He crouched in front of me, taking my chin in his hand, and shoved my head back roughly before swiping the drool from my chin. "Messy girl. Look at the state of you." He tutted. "Not so tough now, are you, Magnolia?" He laughed. "Are you cursing me out in your head? Attempting some gruesome spell? I like to think so, better than pleading for your life, that'd just be pathetic. Now, I'm going to set up, so you wait right here, okay?"

He released me and stood, and I fell to my side, hitting the ground hard.

Unfortunately, it didn't take long before he was back, yanking me off the floor and dragging my limp body to the wall in someone's freshly painted living room. He'd drilled a hole through the wall, into one of the studs, and attached a piece of thick wire, then using his body, he pressed me against the wall, gripped my wrists tight in one hand, and twisted the wire around both of them, so tightly it cut in. Agony shot through my forearms when he released me, the wire the only thing supporting the dead weight of my body. The wire cut deeper, and warm blood trickled down my arms.

I tried to speak again, to use the power of my blood to spell, but still no words would come out.

Ryan walked to a bag in the corner, took something out, and strode back. He held up a needle and thread. "We need to make sure you can't talk when the drug starts to wear off. And, of course, use your sister's calling card, right? Since she likes to sew people's mouths closed."

Then he pressed my lips together and started sewing.

I screamed, the sound exploded through my mind, but again nothing passed my lips. The pain was unbearable, but I couldn't fight, couldn't move. I thought about all the people he'd killed before me. How they must have suffered. Still conscious while he tortured them, while he removed organs and hacked off limbs.

Ryan was a monster, and the way he was breathing heavily, the excitement in his eyes—he got off on this. He was enjoying every moment.

Ryan wanted people to think it was Willow, but he couldn't even replicate the spell she'd used during her trial with Elmer Eldridge when she sewed his mouth closed and the one the witches council was using as evidence of her guilt. It wasn't a spell; it was a psycho with a needle and thread and no magic at all. The council was either somehow blinded to the truth or more interested in hurting Willow, hurting our coven, than finding the real killer.

I knew who was framing her, finally, but I didn't know why, and unless I thought of a way to get the hell down from here, I'd never get the chance to tell anyone.

CHAPTER 28

Bram

My HEART POUNDED, excitement filling me as I watched the life drain from the vampire's bloodshot eyes. It wasn't often we were hired to take out a vamp, but there were things going on among their leaders, things that put chasing a rogue deep in bloodlust low on their list of priorities.

This one had been snacking on humans in the basement of an abandoned theater for days. I tossed his limp body to the floor, then removed his head with my axe. I straightened and screwed up my nose. The stench of rotting corpses was strong as hell in the confined space. He'd been too lost to his thirst to be careful, and if anyone found these bodies full of fang marks, well, it might lead to questions. Questions we didn't want the humans asking.

Removing a vamp's head, then burning them was the best way to ensure they stayed dead, which meant there was only one thing to be done.

Rook poured gasoline over the bodies, dropped the can, and I flicked open my lighter and tossed it. Rook climbed out the window and I followed, the room going up in flames behind us.

"I'll text Nero and tell him it's done," I said.

Rook dipped his chin, shifted and flew away.

I strode across the parking lot, smoke billowing from the building

233

behind me, and pulled out my phone. I'd had it on silent while we'd hunted and froze when I got a look at the screen. I'd had multiple calls from Asher.

My gut fucking knotted, followed by an adrenaline spike as I hit her number.

Something was wrong.

Something had happened to Magnolia.

I fucking felt it, the dread in every part of my body.

"Where the hell have you been?" Ash hissed down the line.

"Where is she?"

"No fucking clue. I was supposed to meet her at a wine bar. Found her car but no sign of her."

I swallowed down my roar. "Where are you?"

"Downtown, on Grant Street, outside The Crest apartments."

I disconnected, yanked off my shirt, my wings bursting from my back, and exploded into the sky. That was Alway's apartment building. She'd gone to talk to him on her own. *Fuck.*

An image of Calvin's body after we'd found it in that garage slammed into my head, and fear like nothing I'd ever experienced gripped me by the throat. Ryan. He had her. It had to be him.

He'd just marked himself for death.

Ryan was going to die today, screaming.

›·›·●·‹·‹‹

Magnolia

Ryan was toying with me.

And no one was going to stop him.

No one was coming to save me. No one knew where I was.

He had all the time in the world, and he was making the most of it.

He sliced down the front of my shirt, yanking it open, then stood back and stared at my mostly naked body. He tutted. "Not much I can use here. You're scarred almost everywhere, not a fan of the ink either. Not very appealing, are you, Magnolia?" He rubbed his chin. "Your organs will be useful, maybe your legs?" He shook his head, his gaze lifting to mine. "Don't get me wrong, I mean, I'd fuck you...I just wouldn't tell anyone about it. You know, because you look like...that."

He stepped closer. My body was still utterly useless, but I refused to let him see my fear and hoped he saw all the hatred I felt burning through my eyes.

234

I let that hatred swell and curl inside me, let the anger build higher. That anger, it felt safe. I'd used it to protect myself for so long, and it was wild and dangerous. Recently I'd been able to control it, contain it, but right then, I needed it. I needed that wild rage inside me more than ever.

Agatheena's words filtered through my mind. I was light, but I was also darkness. Like Gran, like so many other witches who were forced to hide the power their darkness gave them.

Ryan pressed the tip of his knife to the underside of one breast and slid it around the curve, not hard enough to cause real damage but enough to cause pain, to slice skin, to create a new scar. He carried on up to a point in the center of my chest, then back down and around the other breast. Warm blood slid down my ribs.

All I could do was take it—but instead of drowning in the pain and horror, I embraced it, all of it, and let the darkness grow inside me, let it feed on the surge of power that spilling more of my blood gave me.

Then the words came like they had at Shadow Falls, a spell derived purely from darkness, one that was all my own. It was dangerous, but it was either go dark or do nothing and let this evil little fuck cut me up and kill me. Let him walk free to do the same to others.

"Your lungs could be of use. Your ribs as well," he was saying.

I shut out his voice and focused inward. I'd never spelled this way before. I wasn't even sure it could be done. Ryan obviously didn't think so. I'd only ever spoken the words of my spells out loud, but this time it wasn't my corporeal body that was casting the spell, no, this time it was my spirit. I repeated words over and over in my head, words that would sever the tether between my physical form and my soul. I needed to release it from my body.

I'd read about astral projection, but I'd never attempted it. I wasn't even sure it was possible while you were still conscious, but I continued to repeat the spell filtering through my mind.

Something wrenched inside me.

I looked down at my hand, and when I tried to lift it this time, it moved. My soul lifting from my physical body.

The tether snapped and I stepped away, away from Ryan and his knife slicing my body.

I wasn't dead or alive, I was in the in-between.

The darkness inside me grew.

Aiming my hands at Ryan's back, I yelled one of the spells I'd created, a spell I'd written in my book when I'd been filled with hatred and vengeance after Clayton hurt me. Ryan froze in place, a horrified look on his face, as I used my powers to control the knife in his hand. He cried out in terror, watching his own hand lift. Screaming when I forced him to angle the blade downward, then bring it down hard, sinking it into his own thigh.

The scar on my palm tingled and burned as I forced him to bend to my will, to pull the knife back out, to raise it high again, ignoring his screams and begging me to stop.

But before I could bring it back down, I staggered back. My head spun wildly.

What was happening?

My soul was ripped away from the room, the house. I was dragged at an unnatural speed through the city, the forest, deep among the trees—and right up to Limbo's gates.

I threw up my hands. *No.* But the boulders rolled, reforming into an arch, the door opening, and I was pulled through, dragged along a path made of skulls, past souls wandering aimlessly through a dark forest, and through the door of a stone fortress.

My mind spun again. I fought for consciousness but blacked out. I don't know how much time passed, but consciousness came and went.

"She entered my world. She chose this," a monstrous voice said, so horrifying it sent terror through every part of me.

"Send her back."

Zinnia.

It was Zinnia. She was here as well, and she was angry.

I tried to open my eyes, but I couldn't. I felt a hand take mine. Zinny was right there, right beside me. "I've asked for nothing," she said, fury in her voice. "I've lived by your rules. You owe me this."

Silence, and it was deafening. "I owe you nothing, wife. We made a deal. By being here you are merely holding up your end of our bargain. If you want me to send her back, there will be a price, for her...and for you."

"What kind of price? What will happen to her?"

I tried to speak, but I was fighting not to be pulled back under.

"You ask only of her price. Do you have no concern for you own?" he said.

"You already know I'd do anything for my family, and the worst has already happened. I'm here, living this nightmare with you," Zinnia fired at him, then squeezed my hand. "Tell me what her goddamn price is?"

"That is not your concern," he snarled. "She either lives or she dies. Choose."

"You're a fucking monster," Zinnia snarled back.

"Are you only coming to that realization now?" He chuckled, and the sound lifted painful goose bumps all over me.

"I hate you."

"Choose," he said.

Zinnia growled under her breath. "For once, can you just do something because it's the right thing to do? Just send her back, no deals, no payment...please."

There was a heavy pause, the tension growing impossibly thick, so thick I could feel it even in my semiconscious state.

"Mors...please," Zinnia said, using Death's true name.

There was a snarl. "I told you what would happen if you spoke my name again, wife."

"I remember," she said.

Another pause. "And you will come willingly?" Death asked.

I had no idea what they were talking about, but it didn't sound good.

Zinnia didn't reply, not quickly enough, anyway.

The tension snapped, and a jarring crash came next, followed by stone hitting the floor. "She lives or she dies. Choose," he growled, his rage rolling over me.

"Hang on a minute—"

"Choose," he said again, the word deadly calm this time. "Or I will choose for you."

"She lives." Zinnia squeezed my hand again. "Now send Magnolia back."

Her hand was torn from mine, and I was dragged back the way I came, past the lost souls wandering the dark forest, along the path made of skulls, and through the stone archway.

Then I was flying through the forest, the city, through the door of the house—and slammed back into my body, the force knocking the wind from me.

I searched the darkness. Something moved, a shadow. It filled my vision standing in front of me, looming. No, not a shadow, Death, draped in his hooded cloak. I was still unconscious, that was the only way he could be here, away from his realm.

His frigid blue eyes glowed from under his hood. "Magnolia Thornheart, you live because I allow it. You entered my realm without my permission, now you must pay a price."

"What price?"

"You are now my reaper. When I request it, you will collect souls and escort them to me."

The darkness around us was heavy. In here, in my mind, it was just him and me. "Do I get a choice?"

"No," he said, and the world around me shook from the violence in his voice.

"What will happen to me?"

"You will become an extension of me. My reapers are my right hand. I am Death, you deliver it."

"I won't kill for you. I won't do it."

He slammed the twisted wooden staff in his hand on the floor. "You will do whatever I say, or I will rip your soul from your body and take you back." Then he held a large, scarred hand in front of his hood, palm up, and blew across it.

Black smoke flowed from under his hood and into my face. I coughed, choking as it crawled inside me, taking hold, gripping on to my own darkness with unrelenting claws.

"Until you learn to control it, your touch is death," he said.

What? "I can't touch anyone?"

He shook his head.

"How do I control it?"

"No two reapers are the same."

And if I didn't learn to control it, I'd never be able to touch Bram again. I'd never be able to hug my mom, or Else or my sisters, or hold Willow's baby.

"You think this is a punishment, witch," he said, his soul-shaking voice slicing through me. "But I feel the darkness inside you, so vast it would have eventually taken over. I've given you a way of channeling it."

He made it sound like a good thing. It didn't feel that way to me.

Death took a step back. "You will hear from me, reaper."

He lifted his staff, about to pound it on the floor, to make his exit.

"Please, don't hurt Zinnia," I said quickly. "Don't hurt my cousin." I didn't know if a being such as him was capable of kindness or mercy, but I knew without a doubt he was capable of cruelty.

He froze, his glowing eyes boring into me, and I wanted to shrivel up and die under that frigid stare, to vanish from the face of the earth. Looking into them was like staring into a nightmare come to life.

He said nothing, then finally, he slammed his staff on the ground.

Then he was gone.

Consciousness returned with a harsh jolt.

I was back in that room with Ryan, and it was as if time had stopped. He was still screeching, blood pouring from his leg. I tried to move, and this time I was able to. I wasn't paralyzed anymore, the numbness completely gone.

Ryan looked up at me, murder in his eyes as he stumbled toward me. I kicked out, slamming my foot into his chest, hard. He stumbled back, falling on his ass.

I didn't have time to waste. With a scream, I forced my mouth open, tearing the stitches, ripping through flesh so I could speak, and yelled my spell. This one most definitely came from a place of hatred, and now that I was Death's reaper, I didn't need to hold back. My voice was strong, cold, pure venom as the words fell from my torn lips.

Ryan was thrown back, and his body slammed into the wall. He yelled and thrashed, but the hold I had on him was strong. It was his turn to feel powerless. Goddess, it was easy, so easy for me when I allowed my anger to fuel me.

The next spell I called, the words came to me without even thinking, in a language so old I didn't understand it. The wire around my wrist moved, untwisting, loosening as I spoke.

The door crashed open, and I turned to see Bram and Asher run in.

Bram took one look at me and roared.

He ran for Ryan as Asher rushed for me.

The wire released, and I fell to the floor. "Stay back," I yelled at Ash.

Then my power collapsed, my magic drained. Ryan fell to the floor as well, then instantly jumped to his feet and ran at me. Pain overwhelmed me, every bit of strength I had, I'd used up. Ryan got to me first, dragging me off the floor, holding me in front of him, a knife to my throat.

"Stay back or I'll slice her throat," Ryan screamed.

"You're already dead," Bram snarled, about to shift, to turn into a shadow.

My mouth and the tips of my fingers were burning, I assumed from my injuries, but then the dark thing that Death had given me reared up, coming to life, and snapped its teeth, taking a bite. Ryan made a choking sound, then his hands loosened and released me. We both fell, hitting the ground hard.

He was dead, I could tell without looking. His soul...I *felt* it leave his body. Time stilled. Then Ryan's soul stood, looking down at his body in horror, then at me, and I could see it all. His face twisted, and he took a step toward me—

A male...no, a monster, appeared out of nowhere. He grabbed Ryan. Ryan screamed and fought, but the hellish male subdued him easily. The monster paused then, looking at me. I couldn't make out his face—I knew he had one, but no matter how hard I tried, I couldn't see it. His head tilted to the side. A demon.

Then he gave me a nod and vanished, taking Ryan with him.

Lucifer's own reaper, and he'd dragged Ryan to Hell. Somehow, I just knew that as well.

Then the room exploded back into action and Bram and Asher rushed for me.

I lifted my hands, scrambling back. "No, you have to stay back. You can't touch me. No one can touch me."

CHAPTER 29

Bram

MAGNOLIA SCRAMBLED BACKWARD. "I mean it, stay away."

Blood dripped from her torn mouth, her clothes had been cut off her body, more blood dripped from under her breasts, covering her ribs and stomach. She was huddled against the fucking wall, and she wanted me to stay back? She had to be confused? Or seeing things that weren't there.

"It's okay, Mags," I said, my voice cracking. I took another step closer. "It's me. You're safe now."

She shook her head. "Y-you need to listen to me." She lifted her hands as if to ward me off. "Don't come any closer."

I froze in place. "What's wrong with your hands, baby?" The tips of her fingers were black. "What the fuck did he do?"

She shook her head again. "N-not him. Not Ryan. Death. He...he made me a reaper." More blood ran from her ruined lips. "Oh goddess, I'm a reaper."

"You're hallucinating or confused—"

"No." She struggled to her feet, swaying in place and grabbing for the wall to hold herself up. "If you t-touch me, you will d-die, just like Ryan did." Her entire body was trembling from pain, from shock. "I'm Death's servant."

240

Getting her out of that place and back to the tree house was fucking torture. Mags kept passing out, and I was forced to stand there and do fucking nothing. I was jumping out of my skin, my entire body aching to pick her up and hold her to me.

She'd wake, struggle a little farther across the room, then black out and fall again. She managed to pull my shirt on to cover herself, and Ash and I laid out a drop cloth. Mags finally crawled into it, and we carried her outside and got her in the car—then she passed the fuck out again.

When we got to the house, she insisted on climbing the fucking ladder to the tree house, terrified her mom or Else or one of her sisters would accidentally touch her.

Now she was in my bed, still out cold.

She'd been asleep for two days, and the longer she took to wake, the more out of control I felt. I didn't exist without her. I was fucking nothing. I needed her to open her eyes and look at me.

Thank fuck Talon was able to hack into Ryan's phone and track it.

My gaze traveled over her, down to her pale hand and black-tipped fingers. I wanted to take it in mine, to feel the warmth of her skin so fucking badly. But I couldn't do that. Before she'd passed out again, she'd managed to fill me in on everything that had happened. Ryan had nearly killed her; he'd nearly taken her from me.

Then fucking Death had made her one of his reapers.

Whenever I left her, something bad happened. I should never have left her alone. No matter what, we were always stronger when we were together. Always.

My mind filled with images of Magnolia in that fucking house, bleeding. It was the second time someone had used their knife on her, had cut her. If Mags hadn't killed him, I would have torn Ryan to pieces. I wished I had.

Magnolia's family was freaking out and Daisy had literally collapsed when she'd seen Mags lying here. The reality of how close we'd all come to losing her to that piece of shit had hit her hard. Rose and Jazzy had clung to each other, and Iris had called the council and told them where to find Ryan's body and what he'd done to Magnolia. They couldn't doubt Willow's innocence now, the evidence of Ryan's guilt was right fucking there, sliced into Magnolia's flesh for fuck's sake.

I lifted the small jar of balm from the bedside table as I took in Magnolia's face. My fucking chest ached just looking at her. Her mouth was looking a lot better, thanks to some new and improved heavy-duty balm

Else had come up with, but the thought of what almost happened to her...I couldn't bear it.

I opened the lid and swiped a cotton ball through it, making sure my skin didn't touch hers, and carefully dabbed it on her lips.

Her lips had changed as well, and not from her wounds. The color was brighter, candy-apple red. Like all poisonous things, they were colorful and enticing. One touch and I'd be dead. God, I felt the poison flowing through her.

I'd searched for information on reapers while I waited for her to wake, and the red lips and the black-tipped fingers came with the job.

The fates had made her for me, and me for her, yet they seemed to be throwing every fucking thing they could think of at us to keep us apart. I wanted to tear down the fucking walls.

"Wake up, Maggie," I choked out. "I need you. Come on, baby. Please, come back to me." She didn't move. Her eyes firmly closed.

Someone knocked on the door, and I dragged myself away to see who it was.

Rose held up two plates of food. "I brought dinner. She awake yet?"

"Not yet." I took the food from her and put it on the counter.

Her eyes softened. "She will wake, Bram. Her body just needs time to heal."

"Then what happens? When she wakes, will Death call her away?" I paced across the room and back. "I've been reading everything I can on reapers, but there isn't much."

"We've been looking as well. Reapers have always been elusive; their job is kept secret for obvious reasons. If we knew how they worked, we'd try to avoid them or kill them. It's not for us to know." All pretense of calm evaporated, and Rose cursed viciously, shaking with fury. "Why would Death do this? Hasn't he taken enough from us? He got what he wanted, he forced Zinny to be with him in Limbo, he can't have Magnolia as well."

My fingers curled into tight fists, and it was only because Rose was there that I didn't tear everything in my small living room to pieces. "Mags said if she can figure out how to control it—"

"But how long will that take?" Rose said. "What if she never learns? Me and Iris are hitting the books again today. There has to be something. If there's a loophole or a way out of this, we'll find it."

I nodded my thanks.

"I'm just glad her task is over. Ryan's dead. She found the killer, at least that's something."

Yeah, thank fuck for that. I didn't want her leaving my side. I wanted her safe in my tree house, with me. She'd been through so fucking much. Magnolia needed time to heal.

"Let me know when she wakes, okay?" Rose said, then headed back to the house.

My phone dinged. Payne. My brothers had been calling, texting, checking on Mags regularly, but Payne was especially feeling it. The way he'd treated her in the past, the fact he'd insisted on me going on that vampire hunt—yeah, he was struggling with the guilt. But not as much as me. The fact that once again, I hadn't been here for her when she needed me most was fucking killing me.

I strode back to the bedroom.

Magnolia was awake, and staring back at me.

I rushed for her, and she jerked away, her hands flying up.

Fuck. I stopped in my tracks. "It's okay, I'm not gonna touch you, baby."

She blinked up at me, once, twice, and a tear streaked down her cheek. Then another. I wanted to pull her into my arms so fucking badly, but all I could do was stand there and watch her cry.

Right then, I was willing to die just to hold her one more fucking time.

"I was hoping it was all just some fucked-up dream," she said and lifted her hands, looking at her fingers. "But it's true. It actually happened. How long was I out?"

"Two days. And we'll work it out," I said, because there was no other option.

She touched her healing lips. "How?" She fisted the covers. "We can't do this. It's impossible, Bram."

I took another step closer, unable to stay so far away. "Nothing's impossible."

"I'm a reaper. I'm literally poisonous. One touch and you die." She shook her head. "I can't stay here. I can't be around you or my family. I'd never forgive myself if I... I could kill one of you. It would be so easy, one accidental touch, just one."

"You're not going anywhere, you hear me?" I growled out.

She looked up at me, her eyes filled with despair. "I can never be your true mate, we can never touch, or even kiss anymore, we can't...sleep together. This is it. Looking at each other from across the room. I won't do that to you, I won't—"

A roar exploded from me. "Stop!" I snarled. "Stop trying to fucking leave me or send me away. I'm not going anywhere, and neither are you, do you hear me? Death said you can learn to control it, so you'll fucking learn. This is not the end for you and me. It can't be because there is nothing else. There is only this. There is only us." I strode from the room, grabbed her plate of food, brought it back and set it beside her. "Now eat your fucking dinner, because you need your strength for whatever is thrown at us next."

She looked a little shocked, not something I saw on Magnolia very often. "B—"

"You need anything else?" I said, gentling my voice, but I was not having this fucking conversation.

"No," she said and licked her still-healing lips. "I'm sorry I freaked out."

"I hope you're sorry, because I don't want you saying that shit to me ever again." I blew out a frustrated breath and planted my hands on my hips. "Female, you are mine, no matter what. I've told you, more than once. I thought you understood. I see now I was wrong."

A small smile curved her lips. "I think I'm starting to get it now."

"Fucking finally," I said, then I sat on the end of the bed. "Now eat."

"Yes, sir," she said.

"Still managing to be a smart-ass I see? You must be feeling better."

Her lips twitched, and she picked up the fork and ate a piece of potato, then another. She looked up at me. "Are you just going to sit there and watch me eat?"

"Yes." She wasn't leaving my damn sight, not until I was positive she wasn't going to try a disappearing act.

"You get more and more like your brothers every day," she said. "So bossy and surly."

I growled under my breath. "You're fucking lucky I can't touch you right now."

Her gaze flicked up. "And why's that?"

"Because I'd take you over my knee and spank your round ass until it glowed." It wasn't the first time I'd wanted to do it, and it wouldn't be the last. But then I wanted to do a lot of things to Magnolia.

Her cheeks colored, then she snorted and rolled her eyes, trying to lighten the moment, to deflect. "So Rook was right, then, huh? What he said about your males being dominant? I mean, he is a member of Red."

She wanted me to joke around with her, to make me forget she'd just tried to leave me. But I couldn't, not then and not about this. "Yes, we are. We're dominant, we crave control, and that spills over into all aspects of our lives."

She lowered her fork. "Jesus, Bram." She blew out a breath. "You're being serious?"

"Yes."

"So you do...want to spank me?"

"For what you said about leaving me? Yes, badly." I stood because I needed to cool off. I was scared and I wanted to kiss her so fucking much I ached. "I need a shower. Finish your dinner, then we can watch a movie, okay?"

"Okay," she said.

I turned back before I closed the bathroom door. "And if you're gone when I come out, I'll come after you and drag your ass back, so do us both a favor and keep your ass in my bed." Then I shut myself in the bathroom, turned on the shower and prayed the cold water would help calm me the fuck down.

>)) ●《((

Magnolia

I stepped out of the shower and wrapped a towel around myself. Bram had walked out of the bathroom half an hour ago in only a pair of track pants, his hair wet and hanging over his face. His dark gaze had slid to me in the bed instantly, and I'd seen his relief.

He'd expected me to run.

I won't lie, I had thought about it. I didn't know if I'd ever get a handle on this thing Death had forced on me, and keeping everyone I loved safe was more important than anything else, but I couldn't do it to Bram—or to me. So I stayed.

I dried off, my body still a bit sore and bruised, but with the help of Else's balm and tonics, I felt better than I should. I turned to the mirror, my gaze trailing over my bare skin again, my new scars.

Then froze.

The vine markings the mother had given me were still reaching for each other, still a few inches between them, and they were black. Ryan was the killer, and he was dead. If my trial was over, the vines should have changed color, right?

Which meant, it wasn't fucking over.

I pulled on my underwear and tugged on a clean shirt I'd taken from Bram's dresser and walked out. Bram was sitting on the couch in the living room.

He turned when I walked in, and his gaze darkened as it moved over me. "How do you feel?"

"Physically? Pretty good, actually." I gripped the bottom of my shirt and lifted the side, showing him the vine markings from the mother. "But we have a serious problem."

His gaze instantly dipped to what I was showing him, and he stood, stalking closer. I took a step back, and he pulled up short. "Fuck." He looked from the vine markings and back up, then shoved his fingers through his hair, his biceps bulging, abs tightening. "How can that be?"

"I don't know. Someone else has to be in on it with him. Isaac. It has to be him." Bram's chest was pumping, the veins in his forearms bulging. He was furious on my behalf. I wasn't that freaking happy, either, to put it mildly, but for once anger didn't come, because I didn't want to think about it, any of it. I was struggling to do anything but watch Bram. Goddess, I couldn't take my eyes off him. He was beautiful like that.

I took in every raw, furious, wild inch of him, and my body heated.

Bram stilled and his nostrils flared before his eyes locked with mine. "You sure you're not in any pain."

"I'm not in any pain," I said.

He straightened. "But you've got an ache you need to ease, haven't you, Magnolia?"

"Yes." The word slipped from my damaged lips all on its own.

He watched me for several long seconds, his abs tightening with every one of his labored breaths. "Take the shirt off, baby," he finally said.

At his rough command, a throb started deep inside me. I did what he said, lifting his shirt over my head and tossing it aside. Clayton and Ryan had both tried to make me feel ugly, unworthy, but what those monsters thought of me didn't matter. I only needed to look into Bram's eyes to see he thought the complete opposite.

"So fucking beautiful," he said, making sure I knew it. "Cup your tits for me, Mags, give them a squeeze."

I did, and a shuddering breath escaped when my palms pressed against my hard nipples and I squeezed lightly. I did it again.

"Good?" he asked, watching me closely.

"Yeah."

"Play with your nipples. Gently squeeze them."

I did as he said, imagining it was his hands on me, that the warmth of my skin was his.

"I'd lick them and suck them deep into my mouth," he said, raw need on his face. "Lick your fingers for me, Mags, and do it again. Make them slippery for me, show me."

I was so turned on now that I struggled to catch my breath. My fingers slipped over my hard nipples, and Bram reached down and squeezed the obvious hardness behind the front of his track pants. He groaned, then shoved the pants down, kicking them off.

He was only in his boxer briefs now, and the outline of his erection made my heart pound. I could see how thick and long he was, the ridge below the fat swollen head, all perfectly outlined, and remembered how he felt in my hands, in my mouth.

"Slide your fingers down your stomach, nice and slow," he said roughly. "That's it, now down the front of your panties."

246

As he watched me do it, he shoved his hand down the front of his underwear, and I could see him grip his length and squeeze. Liquid heat trickled over my fingers.

"Tell me how wet you are," he demanded, the dominance rolling from him now.

"So wet," I said. "My panties are soaked."

"Show me your fingers."

I slid my hand free and showed him.

"Fuck," he growled. "Put them in your mouth, lick them clean for me. Tell me how good you taste, Mags."

Again, I did as he said, slipping my fingers into my mouth, tasting my own arousal for him. A moan slipped free, because having him watching me, wanting me, was so goddamn hot.

"You're making me fucking jealous, Magnolia, tasting your pussy for me. Panties off, baby," he bit out. "Toss them to me."

Sliding my fingers down the sides of my underwear, I pushed them down and stepped out. He held out his hand, and I threw them to him. He snatched them and pressed them to his face, breathing deep with a rough growl. "Fuck."

His hand was stroking faster inside his boxer briefs, and I couldn't take my eyes off him.

"Spread your legs for me," he rasped. "That's it. Now show me. Show me how you get yourself off thinking about me, imagining me fucking you. Show me exactly what you do."

My knees quivered and my face heated, but I did what he asked, needing to please him, desperate to get off, to show him what he did to me. I ran a finger over my slick clit, then circled it.

"Spread your pussy for me, so I can see," he said, every muscle in his body tight and straining.

I did, then repeated the move, circling my clit, and a whimper broke free. Having Bram's hot gaze on me was exciting as hell. I'd never been this turned on. "I—I want you naked," I said. "I want to see you."

He shoved his underwear down instantly, kicking them aside, and his heavy cock jutted from his strong, lean body, thick and so impossibly hard. He gripped it immediately and started stroking again. The head glistened, leaking with every stroke.

I wanted to squeeze my legs together, the ache was so bad.

"You hurting, baby?"

"Yes."

"Do you push your fingers inside when you get yourself off?" he asked through gritted teeth, his black eyes utterly wild now.

I nodded, another moan escaping.

"Do it," he ordered.

I'd been waiting, needing him to tell me what to do, craving it, and as soon as he did, I felt a deep pulse inside me, another rush of arousal. I slid my fingers lower, pushing one inside me, just the tip, in and out, teasing Bram and myself.

"More," he demanded. "Push it in, Magnolia. Fuck yourself for me."

I did it, helpless to do anything else. I slid in and out, and his gaze was locked on what I was doing.

"You're so fucking wet, baby. It's all over your hand. Fuck. Add another finger, that's it, can you feel the stretch?"

"Yes, I feel it." I worked myself with two fingers, pushing deep, seeking out that spot inside me that made me come hard every time.

"Faster, deeper, Mags," he said.

The wet sounds of me finger-fucking myself and Bram stroking his cock, along with our labored breaths, filled the room.

"Now rub your clit with the other hand," he said, panting.

As soon as my fingers grazed my clit, the pleasure shot higher. I rubbed once, twice—and tipped over the edge, coming hard and calling Bram's name. My inner muscles pulsed around my fingers, and I couldn't stay on my feet. I dropped to my knees while I carried on working my clit, wringing out every last bit of pleasure I could while Bram watched.

Panting, I looked up at him. "Please," I rasped, not sure what I was asking for but needing something more.

But Bram did, he knew what I needed. He walked toward me, his hard cock still in his hand. He was stroking hard and fast, his face a mask of wild hunger. "Sit on your heels, hands on your knees," he said.

I did as he asked, and he moved closer, too close, but I was so lost to this moment, all I wanted was to see Bram come for me. Then he looked into my eyes and groaned, stroking himself hard and fast.

With a shout, he came, pumping furiously and angling his cock so he spurted across my breasts, emptying himself on me as he called my name.

It was beautiful. He was beautiful.

"Rub it in," he said, still breathing hard, trying to catch his breath. "Do it." He stared down at me with bright eyes.

I did. I lifted my hands to my chest and rubbed his come over my skin.

He watched me, a fierce expression on his face. "I don't need to touch you to make you mine, Mags. Do you doubt it now?"

I shook my head. I was his, no matter what happened next.

I would always and forever belong to him.

CHAPTER 30

Magnolia

WE KEPT our heads down as we strode through the foyer of the council building. They'd let Bram and me through without issue, which meant Maria hadn't called to rat me out after we dropped in on her.

Though it wasn't like they had a leg to stand on, not after the prom committee's assistant-slash-sex toy attempted to mutilate and murder me.

It was lunchtime, and after we'd watched Isaac drive away from the building, Bram and I had made our way inside.

We strode down the hall to where the councilors' offices were located and stopped at the end, in front of the door with Isaac's name on it. Bram quickly picked the lock and we let ourselves in.

"You search the shelves, I'll get his desk," I said and started riffling through his drawers. Nothing of importance jumped out at me. I yanked open the next drawer and was hit with the scent of vervain, a common herb among witches and one that held great importance. It was used during our wedding ceremonies and was the first herb a witch planted in her own garden when she left to live with her mate. On its own it was harmless. I picked up a lone juniper berry that had rolled to the back of the drawer beside a small square of brown leather—mixed with a few different things, however...

"This anything?" Bram said.

I looked up, and he was holding a vial.

"Where was it?" I stood.

"In the box."

There was a small decorative wooden box on the shelf. He handed it to me, and I popped the cork and took a sniff. "It's lavender oil." I sniffed again, and there was a bitter undertone that was easily recognizable. "And snake venom." It was rare and expensive, so not often used, unless you were wealthy.

"What do you use if for?"

"On its own, nothing too nefarious. Add vervain, juniper berries, and a few other things, like the skull of a rodent, and a few drops of blood, put it in a leather pouch, and you have a fairly powerful enchantment charm. You can bend people to your way of thinking." The spell was most definitely forbidden.

"You think that's what he's done here?"

"You can't spell at the council chambers, but I think at some point this is where he'd stored his ingredients. I'd guarantee he's used it on the other council members. Trotman and Asuka haven't been themselves through this whole thing. They'd never believe Willow was capable of the things they've been accusing her of. Maybe even the prom committee as well."

We quickly left, making sure everything was where we'd found it, and got the hell out of there. Trotman and Asuka weren't in their offices, so I called and left them messages to call me back. I had to be careful how I approached this. Right now they were under Isaac's thrall, and the longer a person was under a spell like that, the stronger it became. They might not believe me even if I told them what we found.

We walked out and got in the car. "Let's try Trotman's house. Maybe he's at home."

Bram started the car and we headed out.

That's when it hit me, that tight grip in my gut, the feeling of wrongness.

"What is it?" Bram said, glancing at me, instantly sensing something was wrong.

"I'm being called somewhere. It's strong, Bram. Something's happened."

I let the feeling inside guide me.

It led us to the edge of the city, then into an affluent part of Roxburgh. "Turn right," I said, and we drove for a little bit more. "Take the next left." As soon as Bram turned, I knew exactly where we were going. "Pull over here."

"Fuck," Bram said beside me when he looked through the window at Chase Golden's mansion looming ahead of us.

A sick feeling filled me. "I have to go in."

When we reached the security gate, the ward sent tiny shocks over my skin. It was a strong one, which was not surprising. I wasn't on the council, so there was only one way I was getting through this ward—I had to prove good intent. If your motives were honest and you had no intention of causing harm, the spell would let me through. It could literally see into your heart and was the impartial judge that would grant you entrance or not. Which was why blood was required. You gave the spell life, and for a short time, its own beating heart.

I pulled my knife from my pocket, and Bram made a growly sound. I looked up at him, surprised.

"You've bled enough."

"I don't have any other choice," I said as I sliced an X into my palm.

Bram actually flinched, something he'd never done before, but he said nothing more. I quickly held my palm against the gate. Time was ticking. I felt it. I recited the spell, repeating it over and over, faster and faster.

Pins and needles flowed across my chest and down my arm, then through my hand still pressed against the gate. A surge of power pulsed through me, and I had to plant my feet when it tried to shoved me back. The force of it was so incredibly strong that I wasn't sure I'd be able to hold my ground. Usually, someone needed to stand behind you, to hold you in place, but Bram couldn't help me, and I cried out as I gripped on to the iron bars of the gate with everything I had, fighting not to let it throw me back.

Bram stepped closer. "Magnolia?"

"I've got it," I ground out.

Then finally, the ward dropped and the gate unlocked.

I stumbled back as the power receded and the gate swung open. Quickly righting myself, I ran through, and we rushed up the stairs. I pounded on the door. "Leah? Open up!"

Nothing. Not a sound came from inside.

I banged on the door again, still nothing.

Bram quickly picked the lock, and we burst inside. Biscuit ran around in circles barking, then tore off down a hall. We followed, down a flight of stairs and through the kitchen. The feeling inside me was unbearable now. "Whatever it is, it's through there," I said, pointing to the door in front of us.

But I already knew, didn't I? There was a body behind that door. Ryan was dead, but my task wasn't over. Someone else was working with him or helping him. Isaac, it had to be.

Leah's familiar was losing his mind, shaking and barking. I scooped him up and shut him in the kitchen, then watched as Bram turned the handle and pushed the door open.

It was oppressively dark, and he felt around for the light.

It was a garage. I could tell by the smell.

He flicked on the lights.

Oh, goddess.

Leah.

She was naked, propped up against one of the pillars, blood soaking the concrete floor around her. Bram and I rushed over. She was dead. There was no need to check for a pulse. Goddess, both of her legs had been taken.

I touched her cheek. "She's already cool."

I tried to remain emotionless as I studied the scene.

It was different than the others, like someone had tried to make it the same but hadn't quite pulled it off. Her wrists were bound with wire, the wire wrapped around the pillar to hold them up. The stitches through her lips were wider apart than the others, than the ones Ryan had given me, and they'd used different string. This was thicker.

The word "judgment" was carved into her forearm, but again, it looked different than the others.

"It's messier, done in haste," I said.

Bram walked around her. "They didn't take quite as much pleasure as Ryan did."

"No, they wanted to get it over with quickly." Her chest had been opened up and her ribs were missing, her insides spilling out.

I crouched down. "They didn't take as much time to torture her." I checked the pockets of her discarded clothes for her phone, but it wasn't there. The ward had been active when we arrived, which meant whoever did this either used dark magic to get in or Leah knew them. "Check if her phone's somewhere in the house. There might be something important on it."

Bram nodded and strode back into the house.

Leah hadn't been my friend. We hadn't liked each other, but she sure as hell didn't deserve this. I stared down at her. "I'm so sorry, Leah."

"Don't move." A voice echoed through the garage behind me. "Keep your hands at your sides so I can see them. If you even attempt to spell, I'll take you down. Now turn around...slowly."

I recognized the voice. Asuka. I turned, and she stood with her hands held out in front of her, magic swirling, ready to spell. Peter Lewis, another council member, stood beside her. Two more witches watched me on either side of them. Both were extremely powerful and worked as enforcers for the witches council.

"I didn't do this," I said.

The enforcers fired up their magic as well. It snapped out and wrapped around me, tight, binding me and my magic.

"Magnolia Thornheart, we're taking you into custody for the murders of Katana Adler, Calvin Adler, Margot Huxley, Ryan Alway, Leah Golden, and the attempted murder of Chase Golden," Asuka said.

"What? You can't be serious? You're making a mistake. I'm telling you I didn't do this. I didn't do any of it."

"We just heard you apologize to that girl for killing her," Peter said. "Her blood is still on your hands."

I looked down and realized I'd gotten blood on my hands when I'd touched her. This wasn't looking good, not at all, not with all of them under Isaac's enchantment spell. "I found her like that. I touched her to see if she was still warm, to work out how long she's been like this."

Peter Lewis strode forward. "Look at her palm and her fingers. She's been practicing dark magic." He turned back to me. "We're taking you in, you twisted little bitch."

He reached for me.

"No! Don't touch me!" I tried to move back, but I was bound too tight.

He grabbed my arm in a tight grip, then he froze for a split second, his eyes widening before they rolled back in his head. He dropped like a stone, falling to the floor. Instantly and unmistakably dead. I watched his soul rise from his body, and a beam of light shot down, surrounding him, then he was gone.

The room snapped back into focus, time returning to normal, and everyone exploded into action. Asuka cried out in shock. The witches fired more of their magic at me, binding me so tight I could barely breathe. Bram banged on the door, roaring my name. They knew what Bram was, and they were using magic to lock him out, the kind that even his shadow form couldn't get past.

"How the fuck did she do that? She's bound?" one of the enforcers said.

Asuka shook her head. "The foulest of dark magic. Nobody touch her."

"What about her familiar?" one of them said.

"Leave him."

Because they knew if they tried to take him, if they let him through that door, they'd all be dead.

Using magic, they dragged me from the room and out to a waiting van. They forced me in, the enforcers keeping plenty of space between us, and we sped off. As we drove away, I spotted several other witches standing in the yard, their hands aimed at the house. They were keeping Bram locked inside so he couldn't follow me.

"This was a setup," I said, trying to fight the bindings, but it was too strong and I couldn't reach my knife. "Someone told you to come here, yes?"

"Someone saw you breaking into the Golden mansion and called it in,"

Asuka said. "Are you really going to sit there and profess your innocence when I just watched you kill Peter right in front of me?" She shook with fury. "You killed and tortured all those witches. You tried to pin it on Ryan Alway, killing him and hurting yourself. It's even starting to look like you tried to frame your own sister, unless she's in on it with you." Hatred burned in her eyes. "You disgust me."

"You know Willow. You know she's not capable of this, and neither am I."

"I thought I knew her, but after seeing this? I'm not sure about anything anymore. Only that death and pain follows your family everywhere you go," she said.

There was no getting through to her. She wasn't going to listen. "Where are you taking me?"

"Where monsters belong. Umbra Sanitarium, to await judgment," she said, then slid up the soundproof glass barrier between us, shutting me out.

My blood ran cold. There was no getting out of that place. If a witch went where I was going, she never came back out.

Twenty minutes later, we pulled up outside Umbra. The enforcers opened the door, then used magic to force me out onto a gurney, like I was their own personal marionette puppet. Thick leather straps snapped around me, securing me tight.

The wards were heavy, and I tried to flex my magic, but it was useless. I was being fully suppressed. All the witches here, with the exception of those working at this place, were as powerless as humans.

They wheeled me down a hall to an elevator, and one of the enforcers hit the button for the basement after I was wheeled inside. I tried to stay calm, but it was impossible. My family, Bram, they'd sort this out. I wasn't guilty, the truth would come to the surface. It had to. Innocent until proven guilty, right? That was how it was supposed to work.

Except, they'd just caught me with Leah's body, her blood on my hands —and then watched me kill a male in cold blood right in front of them, and with Isaac's enchantment spell holding them hostage, there was no way they'd listen to reason.

I wasn't getting out of this, was I? How could I? Isaac had turned everyone against our family.

The elevator doors slid open, and they wheeled me out.

There were cells on either side, and as they pushed me along, witches screamed and called for help from behind thick glass walls. They hissed and laughed and called out spells that couldn't work. If they hadn't been mad when they were brought in down here, they would be now. Having your magic suppressed like this was mental and physical torture. I'd only been in the building for a matter of minutes and already I felt as if I was being scraped raw from the inside out, from my magic trying to fight against it.

We reached the end of the hallway, and they opened a cell door. The straps released and invisible hands shoved me off it.

Magic tugged at my clothes next, tearing the fabric from my body, yanking the shoes from my feet, leaving me naked on the ground. One of the witches tossed a gown at me, then they shut the door, locking me in.

Their footsteps echoed off the walls as they walked away.

Then the lights went out.

›)》●·《‹‹

Bram

I couldn't find her, couldn't feel her. The council had dragged Magnolia away, and I didn't know where they'd taken her. I paced the kitchen. When all else had failed, I'd come home to Magnolia's family, my family.

Daisy walked in, pale, her phone in her hand.

"You know where they took her?" I asked.

"Oh, goddess, they took her to Umbra. Trotman said they're keeping her there until judgment is passed, but after what happened when they found her? He said there's no way they'll let her back out."

"She's a reaper, for fuck's sake," Iris said, gripping the back of a chair. "That position has to trump any of those fuckwits at the council."

Else limped in, carrying a thick book. "We have no way of proving it. She has the markings, but at this point they're going to believe it's dark magic over her being one of Death's little helpers."

"They said there's a symbol on her hand, and not a good one," Daisy said shaking. "They say she used dark magic, that it's the only way she could've gotten it." She shook her head. "But Mags wouldn't do that, would she, Else? She'd never do that."

Else sighed and sat at the table. "She would and she did, just like your mother before her."

Rose rocked back. "What?"

Else shrugged. "You don't have to be either or, despite what the witches council will have you believe. Mags is like her grandmother, the darkness comes natural. She hasn't gone bad, Daisy, she's just using what she was born with. Your mom thought she might end up at Shadow Falls one day, but that never happened, because she wasn't a dark witch, she just occasionally used dark magic. There's a difference. Pure evil goes to those falls.

My sister wasn't evil, and Mags isn't either. Neither of them have an evil bone between them, *that's* the difference."

"She's the same person she always was," I bit out. "Agatheena said she could balance darkness and light, and she has been. Yes, she was struggling with it, but Death told her she won't struggle anymore, now that she's a reaper."

Daisy closed the space between us and rested her hand on my arm. "We know she's still our Mags. Things have just...taken a turn I wasn't expecting." She turned to Else. "I've seen my baby struggling. I wish I'd known." Her lip quivered. "Why didn't you tell me about Mom?"

"She saw what happened to other witches when they even veered toward darkness. She knew the rules and our laws like the rest of us, and she'd never do anything to put this coven at risk. But for Mags, I see now it was stronger, far more powerful. That girl, she must have been fighting so hard for so long."

"We need to get her out of that place," Iris said through gritted teeth. "I won't leave her there. I won't do it."

Else sat back in her seat. "Mags being held there is wrong, we all know it, but if we go charging in there or try to break her out, not only will the mother see it as interference but the council will see it as a declaration of war. We want her out, but we need to be careful how we approach this."

"I think we need to trust Mags."

Everyone turned at the new voice in the room.

Willow stood in the doorway, Warrick behind her. Ren, Relic, and Jagger hovered at the door as well.

Daisy ran to her oldest daughter, pulling her into her arms, Iris, Rose, and Jasmine following.

"I missed you so much," Daisy said, brushing her hair back. "But it's not safe, the council still thinks you could be involved."

Warrick growled. "I tried, but she wouldn't stay the fuck put."

"No one has to know I'm here, and if they do, well, there's a bunch of hellhounds and my familiar to get through first," Wills said. "Lucifer told me what was going on. I couldn't stay away. I won't let Mags rot in that place, but she's not powerless. Give her a chance to figure this out, and if all else fails, we declare war."

Figure it out? "No, we get Mags now," I growled. "She's been in there too fucking long already."

Several heads turned my way at my barked words, surprise on more than one face.

"Didn't know you could speak, crow," Warrick said and snorted, then dismissed me, turning back to Daisy. "Not cool with us making a move if it puts my mate in danger—"

"Then your mate stays out of it," I bit out. I wasn't in the mood for the hounds and their bullshit, not tonight. "Because nothing is getting in the way of me getting to mine, especially not you or your brothers, understand?"

The room went silent.

Warrick straightened and turned my way, his gaze slid over me, then up to the side of my shaved head before his eyes met mine again. "Nice markers. They new?"

Relic chuckled behind him.

"No." My gaze slid to Relic. "And I'm looking to add to them. Just give me a reason."

Relic smiled wide, flashing his long canines.

Warrick moved around Willow to stand in front of me. "You telling me you'd take on the whole pack to get to our Mags, crow?" Warrick said.

"She's my Mags. And I wouldn't need to. You're not the only one with brothers who like tearing shit apart," I said.

Warrick barked out a laugh and thumped me on the arm. The male had more power than one being should have, but I managed to stand my ground and not rock back. "Good to hear, brother," he said and gave me another bone-jarring thump. "But we're not going off half-cocked and risking anyone in this family, not until we know there isn't another way."

"I don't give a fuck what you do. I'm going to bring my female home," I bit out, then strode out of the house.

CHAPTER 31

Magnolia

My scars felt as if they were being torn open.

I lay on the floor, my arms locked around my knees, and tried to breathe through the pain. The floor was cold through the thin cotton gown, somehow making it worse. It'd never been this bad. No one was touching me, but I was on fire. I bit my lip harder, drawing blood, then cried out, unable to hold it in another moment.

"Hurts, does it?" a voice called.

A familiar voice.

I ground my teeth, of course those assholes would put me in a cell opposite Cora—the evil bitch who'd tried to kill us all during Willow's trial. I wouldn't be surprised if they were watching our reunion for their own entertainment. It took everything I had, but I managed to crawl to the glass wall and pull myself up.

Cora watched me, several feet back from the glass of her own cell, her expression filled with glee. She'd changed, a lot. The sweet old-lady facade was long gone. In front of me stood a stooped crone with yellowed teeth and bloodshot eyes. Her once soft, gray hair was a tangled mess on her head.

"Still a twisted bitch, then?" I said, staring back at her.

"Apparently, it takes one to know one, Magnolia. I hear you've been a very bad girl." She made a tutting sound. "Torturing and killing all those people like you did. Feels good, though, doesn't it? Making people bleed?"

I gripped the glass wall, hissing as another wave of pain washed through me. "I'm nothing like you," I said through gritted teeth. "You're a monster, and you're exactly where you belong."

She tilted her head to the side. "You really do feel it. You don't know how much that pleases me." She smiled wide. "But it's obvious you do."

The pain shot higher, and I sucked in a breath. "W-what are you talking about?"

"The spell I used to stab you...over and over and over and over again." She threw her head back and laughed like the deranged lunatic she was. "Your screams were so loud, I could hear them from next door. I wanted to watch so badly."

Her words made the blood in my veins turn cold. "My scars? That's what you're talking about?"

"Of course," she said between cackles.

My legs almost collapsed from under me as another wave of pain hit me. "Why do they still hurt, Cora?" I growled out.

"In general, or right now?"

"Both."

Her laughter stopped abruptly. "You haven't worked it out?"

"Tell me!" I screamed, all semblance of self-control shattering under the constant agonizing onslaught of my scars.

She rushed up to the glass wall of her cell, her gaze locking with mine. "It wasn't just a spell to hurt you, Magnolia, it was a hex to corrupt you, to destroy anything good in your life. Your grandmother was dark, did you know that? She tried to hide it, but it was there. I felt it. Dark senses dark, you know. I sensed it in you as well. I just had to give you a little push to bring it out. The rotten apple, that's what you are. The rot in your coven that would spoil the rest. It was my backup plan, in case you lived. Turns out it worked very well. The pain is your body trying to fight it, to get it out, and it gets worse whenever you try to be happy, like one of those science experiments with rats, shocking them to make them avoid something they want again and again until they give up entirely." Her eyes flashed. "And it's even worse now because I'm near. Magic binding this place or not, it senses me, it's part of me and it's working harder for me."

I gasped in agony and horror.

"You really did go above and beyond my wildest expectations, though. I hoped, but I never imagined anything like this. You're a monster." She laughed again as she stared at me, unmoving, just watching and enjoying her triumph.

The fucking bitch had hexed me. I wanted to claw at my skin and tear her out of me. She was the reason the pain grew worse when Bram touched me. I was finally reaching for happiness and her hex had tried to put a stop to it.

The pain hit me again, and I retreated into the corner of my cell, where Cora couldn't see me, where she couldn't take pleasure in the damage she'd done, and dropped to the ground, crawling into a ball and gritting my teeth as pain sliced into me over and over again.

I bit down on my lip. I wouldn't let that bitch hear me cry.

This wasn't how this was supposed to end. I had to get out of here.

Anger filled me, and the darkness inside was a furious storm.

I used it to fight the pain, to fight Cora's poison inside me—then I felt it, a shadow memory of Death's claws, the way they'd felt taking hold on me. It sent dread through me. Everything in me wanted to retreat from it, but something told me to do the opposite and I did, I gripped on to it in return.

Something wrenched inside me, like a dislocated limb being forced to the side and snapping back into place. Finally, the relief came. The sense of wrongness disappeared, replaced by a power that surged through me, not like my magic but something new and exhilarating and terrifying all at once.

There was a knowing that came with it, now that I'd quieted my mind and allowed it in.

I was a reaper.

No doors or bars, no magic, could hold me. I struggled to my feet.

I was Death's servant.

Nothing could stop me.

›)➢·◐·⋘⟨⟨

Bram

Umbra Sanitarium loomed in the darkness.

It was warded. I felt the vibration of magic the closer I got to it.

Still, I felt her.

I felt my Magnolia.

She was in that fucking place, and I was going to get her out. I wasn't sure I could do it alone, though. "What do you think?" I asked my brothers.

Payne studied the building. "I think your plan's sound."

"It could bring heat our way. If you're having second thoughts, I'll understand," I said to them.

Payne smiled. It was vicious as hell. "There won't be any heat, baby brother, I promise you that."

Rook grunted. "There is? Easy fix." He dragged his thumb across his throat.

Talon laughed. "Bring on the fucking heat." Then he bounced on his feet and cracked his neck.

"Magnolia's one of ours now," Payne said. "We look after our own."

"I'll take first shift?" Talon said and exploded into the sky.

The only way to get in was using someone who already had access, someone who worked at Umbra. The cleaning crew, a doctor, a cook, it didn't matter. Talon would see them coming, and we'd stop them and take their place before they were let in.

I paced away and back, near fucking vibrating with the need to get to her.

"Breathe," Payne said. "We've got this."

I opened my mouth to reply when a crack of sound rolled from the building, making the ground shake. "What the fuck?" A shimmering light wavered around the asylum, then the fucking ward dropped. I felt the invisible shield crashing down with a ground-shaking rumble.

"Magnolia." Somehow, she'd done it.

My brothers and I shadowed out and shot across the field behind the building. The world swam around me, spinning and moving as we flew around the side and to the main doors, Talon swooping down to follow.

The massive iron doors wouldn't stop us. Not much could, which was why we were so deadly. With the ward down, I easily slid through the tiniest gap and into the building.

I let my instincts guide me down the hall to the stairs beside the elevator, my brothers following close behind.

I was about to dive down the stairwell when the numbers above the elevator flashed, shooting up from the basement. I stopped, because I felt her so fucking strongly now. Shifting into my human form, my heart hammered in my chest, and I stepped back.

The elevator dinged, reaching our floor.

Then the doors slid open.

Mags stood there, head down, looking so fucking small. Her black, wavy hair was wild covering her face. Her little curvy frame was swamped in a plain cotton gown, her feet bare. Then she lifted her head, and I fucking froze. She stared straight ahead—her eyes white, fingers black tipped—and her fucking bones were glowing, I could see them through her skin, making her face a skeletal mask.

She stumbled forward.

"Mags," I choked out.

She walked out, hugging herself. Then she doubled over with a groan of pain and fell to the floor.

I ground my teeth, wanting to scoop her up in my arms so fucking badly I had to curl my fingers into fists at my side. Because I couldn't. I couldn't touch her. I crouched beside her. "Maggie? Look at me, baby."

She blinked up at me, her skin, her eyes returning to normal. "B-Bram?"

"I'm here." This was fucking torture. "I need you to stand, can you stand?"

She nodded, then spotted my brothers and, gasping in pain, dragged herself to her feet.

"What the fuck did they do to you?" There was no mistaking the pain etched into her beautiful face.

"My scars, they're...bad," she said and grabbed for the wall. "That evil bitch, she's down there. She did this." She gritted her teeth, looking around. "How did you get in here?"

Seeing her in pain again and not being able to touch her was fucking torture. "You took down the ward."

"I thought...I hoped. We need to go." With a hiss, she gave my brothers a wide berth, then headed for the door.

"What evil bitch, Mags?"

"Cora."

I snarled. "Payne, get her out of here. I'll catch up."

"Leave her," Magnolia said. "She doesn't matter."

I shook my head. "She needs to die."

Magnolia stared up at me. "Don't. Don't let her get off that easily. Let her rot in there," she said, eyes locked on mine.

I'd imagined killing that female ever since she used her magic to attack Magnolia. I wanted to break the bitch's neck. I wanted nothing left of her but a marker on the side of my head.

"We need to go," Payne growled.

He was right, of course. Getting Magnolia out of here was more important than my thirst for revenge. It was fucking hard, but I nodded.

Three witches exploded from the stairwell, braced for a fight. Asuka was one of them. My brothers and I closed ranks, standing in front of Magnolia.

"Get out of the way," Asuka said. "You walk away now, we'll forget you were aiding a prisoner."

Like the rest of the council, Asuka knew our value. Losing us and our services would be bad for all of them. Very bad. Making us an enemy? Even worse. "You know what we can do," I growled. "You don't step aside, all three of you will be dead before you open your mouths to spell."

"Magnolia Thornheart is a killer—"

"Are you fucking stupid?" I snarled. "She's been trying to clear her sister's name, who is also fucking innocent. Ryan Alway killed those witches, but he wasn't doing it alone. Someone else is still out there. You didn't see the differences between the previous murders and what was done to Leah Golden?"

Asuka shook with rage. "Magnolia had blood on her hands!"

"She checked if Leah was cold, which she was. If you'd checked yourself, you would've known that. If Magnolia had killed her, she would've still been warm. The witches council has failed, repeatedly, so focused on Coven Thornheart, you blinded yourselves to any other possibilities. Which was why we are now hunting the killer ourselves."

"The mark on her hand!" Asuka cried. "The tips of her fingers. Darkness. She's been corrupted. She killed Peter."

"She's a reaper, appointed by Death. She told Peter not to touch her, and he did, anyway, which makes his death his own damn fault. If you'd stopped to listen to her, we could have explained all of this, and we wouldn't be standing here now."

She looked at the witches on either side of her. They were faltering.

"I don't know why the council is so blind with this," I said. "But something isn't right. We all see it, but for some reason, you and the other council members don't."

Asuka blustered.

"It's Isaac," Magnolia said, stepping out from behind us. "I know you won't believe me right now," she said to the councilor, "but he's enchanted you, and others, I'm sure of it, to make you see what he wants you to. Check his office. Please. I think he killed Leah."

Asuka gave Mags a look as if she thought she was insane.

I was done with this. I wanted Mags out of here. "We're leaving, and you're not going to stop us. If you're stupid enough to try, you will die," I snarled. "Now step the fuck aside."

The others moved and Asuka, seeing she had no other choice, finally wised up and did the same.

"I didn't hurt anyone, Asuka," Magnolia said. "And neither did Willow. Deep down you know it's true. I'll bring you your killer. I'm close. I just need a little more time."

Asuka said nothing, just stared at Magnolia, looking angry and afraid. She didn't believe us. She truly thought Magnolia and Willow had done all those twisted things.

We rushed out of the building, and a car sped up beside us.

I braced for attack, until I saw who was in the driver's seat.

"Get in," Ren barked.

My brothers shifted and exploded into the sky, and Mags and I jumped in the back seat.

Fucking Relic sat in the passenger side, and he glanced back, looking over Mags as Ren planted his foot on the gas, speeding from the parking lot. "You solid?" the hound asked Magnolia.

"Yeah...yeah, I'm okay."

The farther we got from Umbra and Cora, the more the tension in her body and pain on her face eased.

"Thanks," I said to Ren.

"You know I've got you," he said.

I did. Ren was my friend. He was family, though I hadn't been there for him either for a long fucking time, so wrapped up in my own stuff.

Relic tilted his head back, scenting the air, and his jaw tightened before his gaze slid to me in the rearview mirror. "I get you've claimed Magnolia, brother," he said roughly to me, "but if you wanna actually protect her, you need to stop fucking around and figure out a way to mate her."

"Relic," Magnolia bit out. "Mind your own damn business."

Every muscle in my body tightened. I didn't like him talking to her, or fucking looking at her. "Magnolia can look after herself, but I guarantee, no one will be getting anywhere fucking near her from this day on. As for when we mate? Like she said, it's none of your fucking business."

The hound scowled. "Immortality is the only real way to protect her."

"What the fuck are you talking about?"

"Like your sisters?" he said to Mags. "The deal with Lucifer."

Magnolia made a choking sound. "What deal? You're telling me all my sisters are immortal?"

I stared at him in fucking shock.

Relic's chin jerked back. "You didn't know?"

Magnolia sat forward. "No, I sure as fuck didn't."

"My bad," Relic muttered.

She turned to Ren. "Is that true?"

Ren shot Relic a look. "Warrick made the deal for Willow, and included her sisters. Lucifer countered, only if they mated. They each found out when they did."

Well, shit. "You okay?" I asked her.

"Scratch that," Relic said. "Forgot reapers are already immortal. So you're good. No harm no foul."

Her eyes widened in alarm. "Are Ronan and Draven immortal as well?"

"That's how the deal works."

Mags spun to me.

I was a shifter, I was long lived, but I would die. "Mags, it's okay."

She shook her head. "I don't want to be immortal. Not without you."

Fuck. "You don't need to think about this. Not right now."

Ren turned into the driveway of Magnolia's house and shut off the car.

She shoved the door open, then turned back to me. "I need to talk to my sisters. I won't be long. Will you wait for me in the tree house?"

I nodded, and she took off into the house.

CHAPTER 32

Magnolia

EVERYONE TURNED to look at me when I walked into the kitchen, jumping to their feet, Mom and Else barely stopping themselves from running at me and hugging me like they were desperate too.

"How?" Mom said.

"I'm a reaper, nothing can hold me. Somehow, I tapped into it," I said to the room, then turned to Willow. "Glad you're back."

Her gaze moved over me, making sure I was in one piece. "Back at ya."

"How's the peanut?"

She grinned. "The peanut's perfect."

"I'm going to make you something to eat, you must be starving," Mom said, trying to feed me since she couldn't show affection the way she usually did, by pulling me in for a tight hug.

"I'll help," Else said. "Then we can sit down and figure this thing out."

I turned to my sisters. "Can I have a word?" They followed me into the living room.

Iris looked worried. "Are you okay, truly?"

Her worry wasn't a surprise since we were all worried. There were so many fucking things to be worried about, but I couldn't let this go. "I am. Now that I'm out of that place." I wanted answers, and I wanted them now. "Are you immortal? All of you?" I said.

266

They were momentarily stunned by my sudden change of topic, then they looked at each other, something passing between them before they looked back at me. "Yes," they all said together.

"Were you ever going to tell me?"

"Of course, when you mated," Willow said.

"Well, therein lies the problem. I can't touch Bram without killing him, and even before Death made me a reaper, my scars..." I looked up at my sisters. "They hurt... And they've grown more painful the last few months. A hug, a simple goddamn touch causes excruciating pain."

Sadness filled Rose's eyes. "You never said."

"I was handling it, until...I wasn't." I gripped the back of the couch. "They put me in a cell across from Cora—"

"They did what?" Iris said, furious.

"Yeah, and she had a few things to say." I told them about the hex she'd put on me, that it was inside me still, infecting me with her darkness to draw out my own, to stop me from finding happiness. "I want it out," I said to my sisters. "Now."

Willow nodded. "We've got you, Mags. I think if we work together, we can do it."

"What's going on?" Jasmine asked, walking into the room.

"We're going to the cemetery," Willow said. "And we could use your help. Will you come?"

"Of course," she said, taking in all the serious faces in front of her.

"Let's go while Mom and Else are busy," Rose said.

We slipped out the front door and headed down the path to the cemetery. I thought about Bram as we walked, about how much I wanted to be his mate and of how that might never be. An eternity of never being touched by him was not a welcome prospect, but an eternity without him at all wasn't a life I wanted. I didn't want to live forever if I didn't have him with me.

The moon was high when we pushed open the iron gates. "I got out of Umbra, but I still don't have control over this whole reaper thing. I can feel the poison inside me, on my skin. What if I never can? What if I can never touch Bram, never mate with him, and I lose him. He'll eventually grow old, and I'll be stuck here without him," I said, voicing my deepest fear as we weaved through the headstones.

Jasmine frowned. "But if you mate, you're both immortal, right? The reaper thing won't matter if Bram can't die."

"But we can't mate if we can't touch," I said.

Jazzy's cheeks darkened. "Oh, right."

Rose cleared her throat. "I mean, to mate you've just got to, you know, both finish while he's..."

"Inside you," Iris said. "Seems easy enough to me."

Willow nodded. "All you have to do is get yourselves *close* to the finish line, and just before you both, you know...Bram thrusts inside—"

"You think that will work?" I said cutting her off before Jazzy died of mortification. "I won't risk Bram, not on a maybe."

"Give me sec," Rose said, and she sliced her finger and stared into the blade's shiny surface. Her eyes rolled back in her head.

"She's getting good at that," Iris said.

Rose couldn't see into the future, not really. But images came to her, visions. Sometimes she asked for them, sometimes they came on their own.

Her eyes rolled down and she smiled at me. "It'll work."

"You're positive?"

"I mean, I didn't see you *doing it*, thank the goddess, but I did see you and Bram a week from now, and you were cuddled up on the couch together."

That was good enough for me, Rose's visions hadn't been wrong yet.

"We have a plan," Wills said and clapped her hands. "Mate tonight... catch a killer tomorrow."

"As much as we want to, we can't help her," Rose warned, sounding frustrated as hell.

"I know, but I have complete faith in Mags." Willow strode deeper into the cemetery. "And she needs to wrap this up fast. The council won't let what happened tonight go. We have to assume they're rallying the troops as we speak. If we don't come up with the real killer ASAP, they'll come after us, all of us."

"So no pressure," Iris said, giving Willow an exasperated look.

"We can always move to Hell, right?" Rose said with a strained laugh.

"Or Ronan could hide us," Iris said.

Ronan could make us all disappear if we needed him to. Rose and Ronan's place looked like a vacant lot to everyone else, but vanishing into thin air was no way to live, not long term. It was a good thing I knew exactly what I needed to do next. "I have a plan. We're not going to Hell or living in an invisible little world of Ronan's making, not just yet."

"I'm glad to hear it," Willow said. "Now let's break this curse so you can go jump Bram's bones."

Jasmine laughed, her cheeks flaming. It was good to hear. She'd been closed off and quiet for so long.

"So how do we do this?" Rose asked.

Willow smirked. "Well, first, we get naked."

Jasmine groaned at the same time as me.

Of course, we did.

꒰꒱◐꒰꒱

I was naked, lying on the ground under the cemetery's ancient oak tree. A wooden bowl containing a little of my blood sat beside me.

The bowl had always fascinated me. It was stained with the blood of our coven from centuries past, from spells and incantations that witches in our family had performed, like the one we were doing now. One of our ancestors made it long ago from a branch that fell from the oak after it was struck by lightning, and it was incredibly powerful.

My sisters and Jazzy stood around me, and one by one they called for the tree and our ancestors to cleanse me of Cora's darkness, to shatter her hex, and each time they called, they dipped a finger in my blood and traced one of my scars.

My entire body felt alive, buzzing. My scars were warm but not burning —instead of stabbing pain, they tingled.

They all called to the tree again as Willow painted the last scar with blood, then she straightened and sliced an X into her palm and began the chant.

Iris joined in, slicing the same mark into her own palm. Rose next, then Jazzy followed, all cutting the same X into their palms before they clasped hands surrounding me.

Their feet bare, toes pushed into the dirt and heads dipped, they repeated the spell one step behind the other, creating an unbreakable wall of words, of sound and magic that echoed around us.

The chanting grew in volume and speed. Magic snapped through the air, lifting the hair on my arms and the back of my neck. They were crying out now, shaking from the force of the magic they were using, giving everything they had to break the hex.

Cora's darkness gathered inside me, steadily building in intensity. The hex was like a serpent in my gut, twisting and writhing, fighting against the magic, fighting to stay where it was. I gritted my teeth, biting back my scream.

They dropped to their knees and placed their hands on my stomach and cried out the final words of the spell. My spine bowed as Cora's darkness, her hex, was dragged from my belly, pulled down through my back and forced into the ground beneath me.

I cried out as it left my body, as her evil was drawn away by the roots of the mighty oak and pushed down into the earth where it couldn't do anymore harm.

I collapsed back, shaking from relief and exhaustion.

It was gone and the change was instant.

It'd been so long since I felt like this, it took me a moment to recognize it—to recognize myself. All this time we hadn't known why I'd changed so much, not entirely. Clayton and what he did to me was a big part of it, but Cora's evil had made it so much harder. She'd been locked away, but her hex had been slowly poisoning me. Now it was gone. It was finally gone.

Willow grinned down at me. "How do you feel?"

I climbed to my feet. "Like me."

Rose, Iris, and Jazzy grinned as well.

"I think we should tell Mom about this later, yeah? She's already freaking out," Iris said.

"Agreed," Rose said, throwing her arm around Willow's shoulders. "We better get back. She'll be wondering where we are."

Everyone got dressed, and I tugged back on the plain cotton Umbra gown, and headed across the cemetery toward the gates.

"We'll pass on your apologies, then, Mags?" Willow called after me, her chuckle reaching me as I broke into a run.

I wouldn't go another night without him.

Not one more.

)>》●《((

Bram

I paced from one end of the tree house and back, wearing out a fucking track. I'd been waiting for Magnolia for over two hours. I got her and her sisters had a lot to talk about, but I was climbing the fucking walls.

Shoving the door open, I walked out onto the deck again, searching the backyard.

If the witches council made a move tonight, I needed to be with her so I could stop them, even if that meant killing every single fucking one of them.

The moon was high, lighting up some areas of the yard and casting others in deep shadow. The sensor light at the side of the house flicked on, and a moment later Mags rounded the corner.

My heart smashed against the back of my ribs at the sight of her, like I'd been plugged into an electrical socket. The white cotton gown she wore clung to her as she ran, her black, wavy hair streaming out behind her.

I strode to the ladder as she reached it, and my heart did another of those heavy thumps when she tilted her head back and smiled up at me. It knocked the wind right out of me and made me fucking weak at the knees.

She climbed the ladder, and when she reached the top, I took a step back and kept going, backing into the tree house, unable to take my eyes off her. The scent of her blood hit me, and I snarled. "Why are you bleeding?"

Magnolia shook her head. "I'm okay. We did a ritual, one that needed my blood." Then she gripped the bottom of her gown and lifted it off, tossing it aside.

She stood in front of me completely naked. Streaks of blood had been painted over every one of her scars. "What is this? What did you do?" I was fucking panting, because my female was naked and not only could I smell her blood, but I could smell how much she needed me. Wanted me.

"While I was in Umbra, I found out the pain I was feeling was because of Cora. Every stab of her knife forced some of her evil inside me. She hexed me, but it's gone now."

"It's gone? No more pain?" I choked out.

"No more pain."

"Thank fuck. Knowing you were in pain... It was killing me." My skin felt tight over my bones, and my palms itched to reach for her. Being this close to the female I loved, knowing that if Death hadn't done what he had to her, I'd be pulling her into my arms right now, carrying her to my bed and finally making her mine—I won't lie, it fucking cut me to the core. But I shoved it down. Mags didn't need to feel that from me. It would hurt her, and I'd rather die than do that.

"I found out something else tonight," she said, her voice barely more than a whisper.

I searched her amber eyes but wasn't able to read what I saw. I don't think I'd ever seen that look on her face before. "What did you find out?"

"Do you trust me?" she asked.

"You know I do."

"With your life?"

"I'd fucking die for you," I said, and she knew that as well.

"I want to be your mate, Bram, in truth."

I hauled in a ragged breath. "I want that, too, baby, more than anything. You'll get control over this thing, I know you will, then we can—"

"No, I want to be your mate now. I want you to make me your mate tonight," she said, her voice shaky.

I stared at her, at the way her eyes sparkled, the excitement on her face. "There's a way?" I didn't want to hope, but I couldn't stop it.

"Yeah, there's a way," she said, the pulse at her throat fluttering wildly. "You game?"

"Fuck, yes, I'm game." There was no need to think it over, I'd do anything to make her mine.

I gripped the couch to hold myself back as she explained what we had to do.

"Rose used her powers. She said you'd be okay, and she hasn't been wrong yet." She chewed her lip. "But I guess there could always be a first time, right? Maybe we shouldn't—"

"We're doing it." Magnolia trusted her sister and her gift. If she didn't, she wouldn't be proposing this to me now.

Silence stretched out between us.

Her hands were fisted at her sides, her feet pressed together, her naked body streaked with blood. Her hair was wild around her face, and her eyes were wide and bright. She was the most stunning thing I'd ever laid eyes on.

And she was waiting for me to tell her what to do, like I had the last time we were standing here like this.

"Bedroom, Magnolia," I said, the strength of my need for her deepening my voice. "Get on the bed."

She licked her nearly healed lips and did as I asked.

I followed, watching as Magnolia crawled onto the bed and sat in the middle. Her long hair fell over her shoulder, and she stared up at me. Her deep cherry lips were glossy and full, and I was desperate to taste them again.

Fuck, she was beautiful. I couldn't believe this was finally happening, that I was finally going to claim my Magnolia in truth. I'd waited for this day for so long. I swallowed hard, my mouth dry as hell. There was something I needed to ask first. "Can I mark you? I know you hate your scars, and I'll understand if you don't want more, but crows, when they mate—"

"Do it, whatever it is, I want you to do it," she said, no hesitation, trusting me with her body, trusting me to take care of her, like she always had.

I swallowed again, the sound audible in the small room. "You sure?"

"Positive. I want your mark on me, Bram."

The predator in me spread its wings and flexed its claws. "Lie on your back and spread your legs for me. Show me what I've been missing. Show me what you're gonna give me." Her breasts shook with her labored breaths, nipples taut. She did as I asked, lying back and letting her legs fall wide.

My skin was burning and tight. Reaching back, I gripped my shirt, dragged it over my head and tossed it aside. "More, Magnolia, spread yourself for me. Are you wet, baby?"

Her hand drifted down her belly and, panting, she did as I asked, and slid a finger over her pretty, slick flesh. "I'm...I'm so wet," she said.

"I need you dripping for me, Mags. I don't want you feeling a moment of pain, just pleasure when I push inside you for the first time." I squeezed my hard cock through my jeans.

"Take the jeans off," she said. "I want to see you."

"Not yet. If I start stroking now, watching you like that, I won't last." I dropped to my knees at the end of the bed, my gaze reaching hers between her spread thighs. "Play with your clit, Mags. Make yourself come fast for me, can you do that?"

She nodded and slid her fingers over her clit while her gaze held mine. Her scent filled the room, and it was driving me closer and closer to the edge of sanity. I wanted to taste her again, tease her, make her scream my name over and over.

Magnolia whimpered, the muscles in her thighs tensing and releasing, her belly quivering. Her lids lowered, eyes heavy with lust. She was breathtaking. "You close, baby?"

"Yes."

I growled when she rubbed her slick little clit faster, and I had to press my hard dick against the mattress to ease the ache, barely stopping myself from thrusting against it. She cried out, and I fisted the covers to hold myself back when she arched against the bed. Her pussy clenched and released as she came for me, so wet she glistened from it, soaking the covers beneath her ass.

Standing, I undid my jeans, shoved them down and kicked them off, squeezing my cock again through my underwear, then shoved them down as well because I couldn't hold back now. "Show me your hand, two fingers out." She instantly did what I asked and I bent down and spit on them, needing part of me inside her right the fuck now. "Push them inside for me, Mags, but not all the way in, not yet."

She trembled, breathing hard, still not fully recovered from her first orgasm. Her second would be with me buried deep inside her. She nodded and pushed her slick fingers inside, and her hips lifted instantly. She drew them out, then back in with a whimper.

The color on her cheeks deepened, and she was breathing heavily. "You're already close, aren't you, baby?"

"Yes."

I stroked my cock faster. "Your reaper power kicks in fast, so I need to try not to make any contact with your skin before I slide inside you. I'm gonna need you to roll over for me, baby. Ass in the air, those fingers still in your pussy."

She did as I said, and I had to squeeze my cock hard not to come when her perfect round ass was aimed right at me, pussy spread and ready to be filled.

"Nice and wide, that's it, chest to the bed. I'm gonna get up behind you now, so don't move, the only thing moving are your fingers, okay?"

"Okay," she groaned.

She was so wet, her juices dripped down her fingers.

I moved as close as I dared. "I don't want to hurt you, Mags, but I'm gonna need to shove my cock inside you hard and fast. I can't ease into you, and you're gonna have to push back to take me deep."

"I k-know. It's okay." She moaned into the covers, her fingers still thrusting in and out.

I stroked my cock again and groaned. I was gonna go off as soon as I was inside her. Holding back was the hardest thing I'd ever done. "Deeper now, baby, faster. Get yourself to the edge. Do it. Quickly now."

The sound of Mags fucking herself for me was more than I could take.

"Bram," she moaned. "Oh, I'm...do it. Do it now."

"Brace," I growled, lined my cock up with her wet-as-fuck entrance, and slammed my hips forward. The head of my cock punched inside her. "Take me," I snarled as she shoved back, taking me all the way to the root.

She screamed, and her pussy clamped down on me, clutching and gripping over and over. I roared as I pulsed inside her, coming hard, filling her. My talons exploded from the ends of my fingers, and I grabbed her shoulder, holding her in place as I pulled out and slammed back in.

Then my eyes rolled into the back of my fucking head, pleasure, euphoria, joy filling me. My crow's song bubbled up from my gut, my chest, bursting from my throat—

Then everything went black.

CHAPTER 33

Magnolia

"Bram!" I spun around.

He lay slumped on his side, face gray, chest deathly still. With a cry, I shoved him to his back, pounding my fists against his chest, once, twice. "Bram," I screamed.

He gasped, his eyes flying open, and sat up. He was shaking hard.

I quickly tried to back away, terrified if I touched him he'd stop breathing again, but his hand shot out, locked on to my arm and he hauled me against him.

"No...wait..."

He rolled me to my back and took my face in his hand.

I blinked up at him, afraid to move, to freaking breathe.

A grin curled his lips. "I'm touching you. You're touching me. I'm still breathing." He pressed his forehead to mine, then he kissed me hard, gripping me tight to him. "You're mine, Maggie. For eternity, you're mine."

A tear streaked down my face, relief and happiness overwhelming me.

He pressed his face against my neck and breathed me in as he ran his hands over my body. "Finally," he said against my shoulder, then lifted his head. He swiped the tear from my cheek. "I've missed you, Mags. Fuck, I've missed touching you so much."

"I've missed you too." We held each other for a long time, just running our hands over each other, reveling in it while we breathed in the other's scent.

Finally, Bram lifted his head and tucked my hair behind my ear. "You okay? Did I hurt you? Your scars? Any pain?"

"No, no pain." I shook my head. "Not anywhere."

He released a relieved breath. "Don't move." He got off the bed and strode into the bathroom. When he came back out, he was holding a washcloth. He carefully spread my thighs, wiping me clean, and when he looked up at me again, his expression was impossibly hot. "I know we don't have much time, but if I don't taste you again, Mags, right the fuck now, I think I'll lose whatever grip I have on my sanity."

"Well, we don't want that," I said, as desperate for him to touch me again, to be with me any way he wanted to.

He tossed the cloth aside and came down on top of me, brushing my hair back from my face. "It's gonna be you and me forever, Mags." His body trembled against mine. "An eternity of loving each other, because fuck, I love you, Magnolia, so much," he said, staring into my eyes.

"I love you too." My heart raced wildly.

His eyes grew heavy, and he took my mouth in a deep, hard kiss that literally made my toes curl. Then he was kissing his way down my neck, not caring about the dried blood streaking my skin, and sucked a nipple into his mouth with a moan. I shoved my fingers into his thick hair and squirmed beneath him.

He looked up at me. "I can't take my time like I want to. But fuck, I want to worship every inch of this beautiful body."

He sucked and kissed his way across my breasts, toying with my nipples, then down, over my ribs, my belly. His strong hands slid between my thighs, and he spread them wide as he shifted farther down. Then, holding my gaze, he dragged his tongue through my pussy, wringing a cry from me. His lids fluttered and a deep, rough groan rolled from him.

Wrapping his arms around my thighs, he gripped me tight to him, and I arched against the mattress when he used his tongue and lips, tasting me, pleasuring me while he snarled and groaned. His fingers flexed against my thighs, digging in when he slid his tongue deep inside me, his growl vibrating through my body, and I was so sensitive already, I couldn't hold back.

I fisted his hair harder. "Bram, oh shit, I—I'm going to—"

One moment he was between my thighs, the next he was looming over me. "I want to feel you come while I'm inside you again."

I nodded, rolling my hips against him. "Please."

He kissed me once more, then lifted to his elbows. "Fuck," he said as he looked down between us. We both watched as he gripped his cock and rubbed the head through my slickness before notching himself at my opening. "Ready?" he said, his obsidian gaze smoldering.

"So ready."

He rocked his hips forward, pushing inside me, and we both groaned. He stayed there for long seconds, panting hard. "Fuck, you're so hot and tight." With another moan, he eased out, then thrust back in, all the way this time. His hiss as he ground against me set off tingles all over my body.

He came down on top of me then, and I wrapped my arms and legs around him, nothing between us now, and I held on tight as we rocked and strained against each other.

"You feel so good," I said against his shoulder.

"Fuck, Mags, so do you." He thrust deep inside me, grinding again, as if he couldn't get deep enough. "I want to stay here for eternity, inside my mate," he rasped, then kissed me.

We moved together, harder, faster, until our harsh breathing and the sounds of our bodies colliding filled my head. Bram's gasping grunts mingled with his crow's song. A husky, growly melody that was just for me. Waves of pleasure built inside me, higher and higher, and there was no holding it back, not anymore.

I arched in his arms, crying out as I came again, shaking and clutching him to me.

Bram groaned before he pulsed hard inside me, filling me again.

We clung tight to each other, sweat, and blood from the ritual, all over us as we slid together, as we finally collapsed in each other's arms.

I lay there listening to his heart pounding.

"Was it how you imagined it'd be?" I asked when I could finally catch my breath.

He lifted his head and smiled down. "My imagination couldn't have come up with anything as fucking beautiful as this."

))) ● (((

The night air was warm, moving through my hair as we flew through the sky. I tightened my arms around Bram's neck and could feel the tension rolling through him. He wasn't happy about my plan, but there was no other choice. Not only had the vines on my skin grown even closer, but I'd just broken myself out of Umbra. In the eyes of the council, I was a serial killer on the run, and they would assume my family had aided in my escape or were hiding me. Time had well and truly run out.

Asuka and the rest of the council weren't going to back off, and she hadn't believed what I'd said about Isaac. As soon as they had enough witches to stand behind them, they were coming after us—all of us.

Which was why my house was currently surrounded by wolf shifters and hellhounds and my sisters, Jazzy, Mom, and Else were taking turns to walk the perimeter of our property, spelling to keep our wards strong. No one was getting in and no one except Bram and I were getting out, not until this was over.

I had no choice but to end this thing tonight, and there was only one way that was going to happen. I needed proof. There was no room for a misstep. When I took Isaac down, I wanted to hand the council indisputable evidence.

We landed, and Bram immediately took my hand as we strode down the demon-filled street. I hadn't been back to this place since the last time Bram and I ventured here, but there were things I needed. Ingredients the demon-run store had that I couldn't get anywhere else.

Bram pushed the door open, and the same female as last time stood behind the counter. When she looked up and saw us, she sighed heavily. "You're still alive, then."

"You seem disappointed." I strode up to the counter.

She shrugged. "Just surprised." Her gaze moved over me. "But you're different." Her eyes narrowed. "What's changed?"

I pulled my hands from my pockets and wiggled my black-tipped fingers. "I'm a reaper."

She took an abrupt step back. "You're not—"

"Here to collect your soul?" I shook my head. "Nope. But I'm hoping you have some oleander and that vial of vampire blood." I had the spell I'd gotten from Shadow Falls, and if this was going to work, I needed that blood.

Her shoulders relaxed a little. "The oleander I can help you with. Still a no for the vamp blood. You're going to have to source it yourself."

"What about Ronan?" Bram asked.

If only. "It needs to be one hundred percent vampire."

"We'll take the oleander," Bram said, then he turned to me. "I think I know someone who can help us with the blood. He owes me."

We left the demon neighborhood a short time later, and Bram flew us to the other side of the city.

The Bank was packed when we walked in. The vampire-owned club always was on the weekends. I'd been here several times, and it could get wild. I had no idea about The Vault, the separate club in the basement. I'd never been able to get down there since it was only for blood drinkers and those willing to offer themselves up as donors.

Bram kept a tight grip on my hand as we strode through the crowd on the dance floor, then stopped in front of the door on the other side of the room.

The big vampire standing in front of it greeted us. "We got business with you tonight, crow?"

Bram shook his head. "Ender here?"

He jerked his chin up and opened the door, stepping aside.

Bram strode through, pulling me after him, and we made our way down the stairs. "Why were you here that time? The time Leah and the others saw you?"

He stopped in front of a massive, round iron door, made from an old safe.

"We had business with Nero. They lost a couple of their elders and were in the middle of a reshuffle. There's been fighting over who takes their place. They didn't have time to deal with a couple rogues, so we were called in to do if for them."

"Why does Ender owe you?" Pretender or "Ender" to most, worked for Nero. I knew this because Iris had met him during her own trial.

"He fucked up, made a mess he didn't want Nero to know about. We cleaned it for him."

By all accounts, Nero was an utterly terrifying and very old male who would kill you without blinking an eye. "Is there anything else I need to know before we walk in there?"

He curled his fingers around mine. "Just stay close to me, okay? Don't leave my side." Then he turned The Vault's big handles and pushed the door open.

We walked into a large room. Music played, and the scent of blood and sex filled the air. Blood drinkers of every kind were hanging out, some feeding from donors, some fucking for all to see while they did it.

Bram headed across the room, his hand tightly around mine. Unlike the others here, the male we were walking toward wasn't in a suit—or completely naked. He was wearing black jeans and a hooded sweatshirt. The hood was up, and the shadows from it concealed most of his face. He was leaning against a tall table, looking at his phone and ignoring everyone around him, including several people overtly trying to get his attention.

He turned then and watched us from under his hood as we approached.

"Bram," he said when we finally reached him.

"Ender," Bram returned, then smiled, and it wasn't friendly.

Vibrant lilac eyes glowed from under Ender's hood. "You're here to collect."

Bram nodded. "You have somewhere private we can talk?"

Ender jerked his chin up, and we followed him deeper into the club, down a hall, and through a door at the end. We walked into a bedroom— and *wow*. It was a freaking horror show.

"Someone has a major fairy-tale fetish," I said, looking around stunned. "What the hell is this place?"

"A place we don't talk about if we want to live, so keep that in mind," Ender said.

I turned away from the four-poster bed draped in pink and finally got a good look at the male. He was...well, there was no other word for it, beautiful. Like he could give Ren a run for his money in the male model stakes, and that was no easy feat. I blinked up at him, momentarily mesmerized. The guy was so gorgeous, he didn't seem real.

"I know your sister Iris," he said. "And I've seen you upstairs." His gaze slid over me, and there was no mistaking the hunger in his eyes for anything else. Though, I wasn't sure which kind, lust or he was contemplating taking a bite out of me.

Bram stepped closer. "Don't look at my mate, and don't talk to her."

"Let me guess? Touch her and die?" Ender said with a rough laugh.

I pulled my hands from my pockets and flashed my black-tipped fingers. "Literally."

Ender's violet eyes slid to Bram. "You brought a fucking reaper in here?"

"She's not here for your soul, but we would like some of your blood," Bram said.

Ender's eyes narrowed. "I don't have a soul, and I'll take a pass on the blood donation."

Bram and the vampire locked eyes. "You owe me, big. Don't fucking test me on this."

Ender's nostrils flared, and though he was wearing a baggy sweatshirt, I could see him tense for a fight. I quickly stepped forward. "You have my word it won't be used against you or anyone else you know. I need it for a spell, nothing more. And if there's any left, I'll destroy it," I said.

His gaze slid to me. "I want a blood oath."

Bram grabbed the front of his shirt, and they snarled in each other's faces. "Not happening—"

I rested my hand on his forearm. "B, it's okay." Then I looked at Ender. "I'd do it, but I'm not sure how? My blood gets anywhere near you, I'm pretty sure it'll kill you."

Ender flashed his fangs. "We're already dead, sweetheart. You can touch me all you like."

I hadn't thought of that.

I'd broken my last blood vow, and everything had gone to shit afterward. Nerves filled me, but what choice did I have? And there wasn't a chance in hell I'd break this one. I didn't know if vampires had souls or not, but they were the undead. "Fine, let's do it." I pulled my blade from my pocket and made a slice in my palm before I changed my mind.

Bram closed in behind me, his front pressed to my back, and his arm came around me, locking around my middle. I didn't have to turn around to know he was staring Ender down. But I guess if it kept my new, seriously protective mate under control, I wasn't going to argue.

Ender cut his own palm, then held out his hand. "Take it and repeat what you said."

I pressed my palm to his, and he curled his fingers around mine firmly. "You have my word that your blood won't be used against you in any way, and I'll destroy whatever's left."

He nodded his approval and released my hand. "You got something for me to put it in?"

I pulled a vial from my bag. He took it, sliced his wrist and filled it, corked it and handed it back. He covered the cut with his mouth, and when he pulled his hand away, the slice had already sealed. "Use it wisely, little witch."

I carefully put it in my pack, and when I looked up, Ender was swiping his tongue over his palm.

His eyes flashed. "Fuck, you taste good. You ever wanna return the favor, I'll accept a donation from you anytime."

Bram growled, viciously, and slammed his fist into Ender's face. The vampire's head jerked back and blood sprayed from his nose. He laughed, flashing blood-coated teeth and fangs.

Bram grabbed my hand and towed me toward the door.

"We're square now, crow," Ender called after us. "Don't forget that."

CHAPTER 34

Magnolia

THE HOSPITAL WAS easy enough to get into, but Chase's room, not so much. He had a guard stationed in front of the door.

Bram eyed me, then the guard, from our current spot down the hall. The nurse's uniform I'd acquired was a little on the tight side.

"Did it work? Do I look different?" I said, holding my bag containing the potion I'd carefully mixed.

He frowned. "Yes. I don't like it."

I had enough of Ender's blood to work another spell. One where I could take on someone else's likeness. I just had to keep a personal item of theirs with me at all times. I'd broken into a few lockers and found a necklace that belonged to one of the nurses and, presto-chango, I was now Nurse McGill.

This was another spell the council didn't approve of. It was outlawed when they first came to be. It was definitely on the dark side of the magic spectrum, and if Death hadn't used his mojo on me and made me one of his minions, this spell alone probably would have tipped my internal scale into the pool of terrors Agatheena spoke of. Using my magic to infiltrate Chase's comatose brain and ferret around in his memories? Yeah, that would've definitely done it.

"Time to go," Bram said.

A nurse had left Chase's room a short time ago, so I'd have some time before another one showed up. I lifted to my tiptoes to give Bram a kiss, and he jerked his head back.

I grinned up at him. "Sorry, forgot."

"I'm sure Nurse McGill's a nice lady, but no kissing until you have your face back, yeah?"

"Roger that." I patted him on the butt, and he jumped. I grinned. "Right, see you in a couple minutes."

Bram shook his head at me, and I strode toward the guard. "Hey," I said when I reached him.

He smiled and instantly stepped aside. I walked into Chase's room and shut the door behind me. Piece of cake.

Chase lay still in his bed. The bruises on his face were gone, but I had no idea what condition the rest of him was in. His other wounds were dressed or under the covers. I hovered my hand over his forehead, using my healing ability to feel out the damage to his mind. What I got was a whole lot of nothing. Well, mostly nothing. He was there, I could feel him, but he'd withdrawn completely. It was like he'd shut down his mind to hide from the horror of what he went through.

I got it, and I didn't blame him, and my evening with Ryan hadn't been half as bad as what Chase had endured. I still understood, though. I'd wanted to check out multiple times a couple of years ago, but I hadn't because of Bram, and I'd used anger to get through it instead. That anger hadn't all been mine, though. Cora's hex had made everything worse.

A tap came from the window. Bram hovered in front of it, his wings steadily beating behind him. I rushed over and opened it for him.

He quickly climbed in and jumped down. "Let's do this." He strode to the door and carefully and quietly turned the lock.

I pulled a vial from my bag and stood beside the bed. "Hey, Chase, I wish I didn't have to do this, but it's our only hope of catching the person who did this to you, okay?"

Bram raised a brow.

"I'm taking invading his privacy to a whole new level. If he can hear me, I'd like to give the guy a little warning." I popped the lid off my potion. I'd used Frances's spell and her ingredients, but I'd also tweaked it a little and made it my own. Her way caused the recipient a lot of pain, intentionally as far as I could see, mine did not.

I held the vial out to Bram, since I couldn't touch Chase, and he dipped his finger into it as I recited my spell and drew the symbol I'd shown him on Chase's forehead. On the second recitation, I dipped my finger in the potion and drew the same symbol on the center of my own hand, then the third time, I hovered my palm above Chase's forehead.

"If my hand gets too close to him, you'll need to hold it up," I said to Bram.

He nodded, and I closed my eyes, uttering the spell a final time.

Oppressive darkness filled my mind's eye immediately, the hospital room, Bram, no longer there.

There was just...nothing.

"Hello?" I called into the darkness, my voice echoing through what had to be Chase's mind.

Something fundamental had fractured the day he was attacked, and instead of just locking away the awful memories of what happened to him, he'd slammed everything behind a door and thrown away the key.

He'd been trying to protect himself, but he'd taken it too far, and now he was lost, stuck in the dark, unable to find his way out.

"Chase? Are you here?" There was a shuffling sound to my right. A figure huddled in the corner, curled in a ball. "Chase?"

His head lifted, and he stared up at me wide-eyed. "What are you...why are you here?" He slowly rose to his feet. "Am I dreaming?"

"It's not a dream. I'm in your room at the hospital, and I don't have much time." I took another step closer to him. "I need you to help me. I need you to show me who hurt you."

He scrambled back into the shadows. "No. I can't. I can't do that."

"I know you're afraid, but they can't hurt you here. In here, they're not real," I said, holding out my hand to him. "If you don't want to wake up yet, that's okay. But I need to see who did this, Chase, so I can stop them."

"I—I don't know," he said. "I can't remember. I don't want to."

"I know, and you don't have to. I can do it for you. I just need you to show me where it is. Where the memory is," I said.

"You won't make me go?"

"You can stay right here."

He sat down on the floor again and wrapped his arms around his knees. "Chase?"

"You can stop them?" he asked, his voice so childlike now it was unnerving.

"I promise, I'll stop them. They won't hurt you ever again," I said and hoped that was true, for everyone's sake.

He buried his face against one arm and pointed to a door that hadn't been there before on the other side of the room.

The door was tall and wide, and as I got closer I saw that blood dripped from the cracks around it. I gripped the handle, took a deep breath, and turned it.

It flew open, and Chase screamed behind me. I quickly threw myself through and slammed the door behind me—and almost dropped to the floor when everything Chase had been feeling, physical and mental, slammed into me.

The images spun around my head, blood, so much blood. Chase trying to scream but unable to with his lips sewn closed and from the drug he'd been given. The pain was unimaginable, the kind that had you begging for death rather than endure a moment more.

I fell to the floor, shaking, and covered my head with my hands. It was too much. Oh, goddess, it was too awful.

"Magnolia?"

My name echoed around me, coming from a distance.

"Mags...baby?"

Bram.

His voice calling me back snapped me out of the despair, the horror. Time was running out. I needed to get the fuck up. Now.

"Maggie!" Bram's voice was louder, more urgent.

I pushed off the floor and struggled to my feet, then forced myself to open my eyes, looking through Chase's eyes, looking out at that room we'd found him in at Red.

I struggled to breathe through the agony and fear as the door opened across the room, forcing myself to keep watching as someone walked in and shut themselves in with Chase.

Ryan.

If it was only Ryan, if he was there on his own, this was all for nothing. I had nowhere else to go from here, there wasn't enough time.

The door behind Ryan opened again.

I felt myself being pulled back through the one in Chase's mind, the memory fading. I just needed another minute.

The second person closed the door and walked in. They were talking to Ryan. I could hear them, I could hear everything, but I couldn't see them. My eyes wanted to close again when the newcomer stepped closer, but I forced them to stay open, to look into their eyes—

Then I was sucked back through the door and it slammed shut. A moment later I was yanked back to consciousness.

"Magnolia?" Bram said, shaking me.

I blinked, and the hospital room came back into focus.

"I didn't think you were going to wake up," he said hoarsely. "You scared the fuck out of me."

I straightened, feeling sick to my stomach. "I know who it is. Who was working with Ryan."

)))·◉·(((

I held the phone tighter. "Where is she?"

Isaac hissed down the line. "I'm a bit busy right now, Magnolia. We're outside your mother's house. If you don't want anyone to get hurt, you better come home."

"Or better yet, you could break the enchantment spells you have over the other council members and your business partners and call them off."

There was a beat of silence. "I don't know what the fuck you're talking about."

"Yes, you do. Did you do it because you truly believed Willow was the killer, or are you in on it with Ryan and Maria?"

"In on what?" I could hear the hesitation in his voice.

"Ryan and Maria are the ones killing your friends. Did you agree to help them so you could get your hands on my sister's store and the other properties, so your development could go through, or just because you hate my family, you sack of shit?"

"You've lost your fucking mind," he snarled.

Chanting started in the background, the council had their army, and they were about to start a fucking war. "I've seen it. I saw Maria hack up Chase. I fucking saw it. Call the council off, now! You start a war with my family, and you will lose. You're not just taking on my coven, you're taking on the hounds, the wolf pack, the bats, the crows, and the knights of Hell as well."

He released a shaky breath. "How did you see it?"

"I looked into Chase's mind. He showed me."

"And you're sure it was Maria?" he asked.

Anger hit me. "Let me guess. She convinced you to enchant everyone?"

A shaky breath rattled down the line. "I was sure it was Willow. Positive. Maria said...she said I should do it so Willow didn't get away with killing our friends like she did Elmer. I thought I was doing the right thing... I thought—"

"You thought it was a fast way to get Willow locked away so you could buy the property you wanted and take down the witch you blame for your brother's death all in one go."

"I didn't know," he said. "I didn't know what Maria and Ryan were doing."

"Then call the council off before you start a war you can't finish, and tell them what happened."

"Stop," he yelled. "Stop the spell!" The chanting in the background stopped.

"Where is she, Isaac? Where's Maria?"

"I don't know." He cursed. "She hasn't been answering my calls."

I cursed and disconnected. "How the hell are we going to find her?"

"You're a reaper," Bram said beside me.

I paced the roof of the hospital. "I don't even know what I can do?" I said to him, feeling fucking helpless.

"Reapers can find their targets anywhere. They have access to any place they want. Nothing can stop them," he said.

He was right. I rubbed my hands over my face. "I'm not even sure how I did it in that cell."

"Those powers are there. They're part of you. You just have to pull them forward again."

He was right, of course. Everything had been so crazy, I hadn't had time to really think about what I could do, apart from the whole touch-me-and-die thing. I needed to slow things down, panicking wasn't going to help me.

Bram strode over and took my hands. "Sit."

I sat and Bram did the same.

"Close your eyes."

I did.

"Breathe deeply. In and out. I want you to focus inward. I want you to remember how you felt, what you did in that cell."

I did, and that same darkness swirled inside me. Cora's darkness was gone, but my own, Death's, they were there, and they were powerful, fierce. I gripped on to it, like I had the day before.

And this time it clicked into place with ease, the power pulsing through me, so strong and wild, violent.

"I haven't been called to collect Maria's soul, so I can't just find her. But I know how I can," I said and opened my eyes.

Bram was watching me intently, a fierce expression on his face. "You're fucking amazing."

"Not without you." I leaned in and kissed him. I wanted to keep on kissing him, but that would have to wait.

"How do we find her?" Bram asked when I lifted my head.

"I need to hold something of hers."

"Easy," Bram said, tugged off his shirt, tucked it in the back of his jeans and scooped me into his arms.

CHAPTER 35

Magnolia

THE WIND SWIRLED AROUND US. Maria's apartment was dark, empty, not that I expected her to be here. Would have made things a hell of a lot easier, though. Resting my hand on the banana lounger I'd seen Maria sitting on last time I was here, I closed my eyes.

Shadows rushed in at the edges of my mind, a vision flashing in front of me. It felt kind of the same as when Death dragged me to Limbo, but this time my soul was still with me, and I was being shown where to go, rather than actually being taken there. My fingers and lips burned and I knew I'd transformed. I was the reaper.

A massive building filled my mind's eye. "I've got it." Bram's palm was warm against the side of my face, and I blinked up at him.

His expression was fierce, his gaze unfaltering. My bones were literally glowing through my skin and he was looking at me as if I were the most beautiful thing he'd ever seen. "Whatever happens tonight, remember, you're not in this alone. I'm with you every step of the way."

"I know."

He dipped his head and kissed me, not caring that I looked like a monster right then. I released my reaper powers, letting them flow out of me, feeling myself transform back to normal, and kissed him back harder. I never wanted to stop. I wanted this task over with. I wanted my trial in the rearview mirror and for something to be easy for us.

"When this is over, you want to go away on a vacation?" I said.

"Where are we going?"

"I don't care. As long as it's just you and me and no one else, it'll be the best place on earth." He flashed me a grin and my heart went a little crazy in my chest.

"Let's get this the fuck over with, then, baby. We got somewhere to be." His wings unfurled, large and shiny black.

My dark angel.

He scooped me in his arms.

"Where to?"

"Roxburgh High School."

Bram cursed but held me tighter and dove off the side of the building.

He flew fast, and I tucked my face into the side of his neck when my hair whipped around me. I had no idea what we were going to walk in on when we found her. Maria's motives were still a complete mystery. Why would she kill all those people? People that she pretended to be friends with, more than friends. The level of evil for someone to do that, to lock emotion away like that? I mean, I'd watched her in the living room comforting her *friends*, seeking comfort in return while crocodile tears had rolled down her face, grieving for people who she and Ryan had mercilessly and brutally murdered.

Yeah, there was something terribly wrong with her.

We reached the school, and the parking lot lights lit up the area. A couple of cars were parked there—and Isaac's was one of them. Jenna and Robert's was the other.

"Isaac must have gone straight to her after our call." Either he was in on it or he'd stupidly decided to confront her himself.

Bram flew behind the main building, landing in the shadows. I had my knife strapped to my thigh, though, I'd only needed to touch Maria and she'd go down. Killing her wasn't the goal, however. "I need to take her alive. The council needs proof, and I'm going to deliver it to them."

Bram nodded.

Maria hadn't attended this school, yet she seemed fixated with it. We strode to the back entrance, but my instincts told me that wasn't where I needed to go, so I let them guide me. "Around here."

The grounds had numerous smaller buildings, but when we rounded the corner, I knew exactly where I was being led.

The old chapel was one of the original buildings, but it'd been left to crumble after an earthquake a year after I started here. The cost to fix it had been more than the school could afford, but it was also a historical building, and the school and community were trying to raise funds to eventually have it restored.

"The chapel." Sticking to the shadows, we sprinted around the back of the old building. A light flickered through one of the windows.

The building was warded, one that bound magic, similar to the one at Umbra. This one allowed you entry, but strangled your magic. I didn't need it though, not now that I'd tapped in to my reaper powers.

I slid my knife free as Bram gripped the handle, easing the door open.

The chapel itself was quiet, the candlelight dancing over the remaining stained-glass windows that had survived the quake. The pews were jostled from their perfect formation and covered in dust.

"I'll check back here," Bram said quietly.

I nodded, then froze when a muffled cry came from the back of the church. We rushed toward it. Jenna was trussed up on the ground. She looked up at us with huge, terrified eyes. I pressed my finger to my lips, telling her to be quiet, and yanked the gag from her mouth.

"Where is she?"

"Basement. She's got Robert and Isaac," Jenna said. "I d-don't understand what's going on."

Bram quickly untied her. "Go," he said.

She shook her head, lips trembling. "Not without Robert."

I held her terrified gaze. "We'll do our best to get him out of here alive, but you need to go get help. Get the council and tell them what happened."

A tear streaked down her cheek, but she nodded.

"Stay low, stick to the shadows," I said.

She slipped out, and we moved on silent feet down the center aisle and in behind the ornate pulpit. There were heavy, dark wooden doors against the walls on either side of the room. Bram checked the first. "Pastor's office," he whispered.

I nodded and gripped the door handle of the opposite door, opening it as quietly as I could. A terrible but familiar smell hit me almost immediately—rot. Death.

Candlelight flickered at the bottom of the stairs, and we started down. My mind kept throwing scenarios at me, of what this could be, of why Maria and Ryan had done this, but the truth was, I had absolutely no idea.

Someone's voice carried up to us.

Isaac.

We paused on the stairs.

Isaac was trying to reason with Maria, but there was no missing the tremble of fear in his voice. "Tell me Ryan forced you into it," he was saying. "This isn't you. It can't be."

"You don't know anything about me, Isaac. And you never really bothered to ask, did you? If you weren't fucking me, you were using me for my money. Don't pretend you ever cared about me, when we all know the only person you care about is yourself. You're all the same, every one of you."

Bram took the next step, and switched forms, shadowing out so he could check around the corner. He rematerialized again a moment later and waved me forward. Maria had Robert and Isaac on the far side of the basement, where numerous old bookcases filled with junk created several walled-off sections.

"I don't know what you're talking about," Robert said. "We love you."

"No, Rob, you love yourself, and you and your friends are *fucking monsters*." Maria screamed the last, then laughed, the switch unnerving, the sound deranged. "Well, it's my turn to be the monster, and it's your turn to feel pain. I want you to feel the kind of loss that breaks you, mind and soul, the kind of pain that drives you to do anything to make it stop."

I eased closer. What the hell was she talking about? How had they hurt her?

"What are you going to do?" Isaac asked.

"I've already done it. I just need a couple things from you, and I'll have everything I want." The sound of another door opening echoed through the room.

"Oh goddess," Isaac rasped. "What the fuck have you done, Maria?"

"Come meet your new friends, my dears," she said, I assumed to whoever had just revealed themselves.

And going by Robert's scream of pure terror, Maria wasn't the only monster in the room.

There was a scrape and a groan, then shuffling sounds. I stepped closer to the shelves in front of me and peered through. Maria stood in front of Robert. Isaac was beside him, and they were both tied up. Isaac had a pretty bad gash on his head, and blood dripped down the side of his face steadily.

"We still need an arm, Rob, and I thought you'd be the perfect candidate."

Bram looked at me, and he didn't need to say a word. I nodded. We couldn't just stand here while she started chopping limbs, we needed to do something.

Bram and I stepped out from behind the shelf, and Maria's head swung our way. Fury filled her eyes. "Emmaline, Marcel come to me."

They were the names of her brother and sister, the ones who'd died while Maria had been away at boarding school.

Another scrape came from the corner, and what walked out turned my blood cold. Bodies, but not human, not anymore, stitched together like Frankenstein's monster.

"How?" I gasped.

"Dark magic, Magnolia, the kind you're all too familiar with." She ran the backs of her fingers down the side of "Emmaline's" patchwork cheek. "Their spirits were lost, so full of rage they refused to cross over, so I worked out a way for them to be with me all the time." Emmaline seemed to have all her body parts. Marcel, on the other hand, was still missing an arm.

"You cut up your friends and the people they loved to use their organs, their body parts, to turn your brother and sister into zombies?" Because that's what I was looking at. The undead. This wasn't reanimation, this was shoving a couple of lost and angry spirits into vessels and hoping for the best.

But to create them, she would've needed more...*parts* than the ones we knew about. She'd killed others to create these monsters.

"That's not what they are," she spat. "It's Emma and Marcel. I have them back."

"No, you don't. They stopped being your brother and sister a long time ago. Spirits that refuse to pass over become angry." I held her wild stare. "And you know what the undead need to stop their bodies from decomposing." Blood, flesh. Human flesh. And if they hadn't developed a hunger for it yet, they would very soon. "You killed others, you had to have. Where are they?"

She waved a hand. "They're not important."

No, she made sure only the prom committee and their loved ones were found, so they knew they were being targeted.

Emmaline turned to me and I jerked back when I realized whose eyes Maria had used when she'd created Emmaline. They were Margot's. They were dull and lifeless, but they were my friend's eyes. "Why did you do this?" I choked out.

She strode over to Robert, crouching down in front of him, and fisted his hair. "You know, don't you, Rob?"

He shook his head, eyes wide.

"Rob here doesn't understand the word no, do you, Robert? And when you cornered my baby sister in the library one day when no one else was around, and she said no, you didn't listen then either. No, you took what you wanted."

Robert's mouth opened and closed, true horror filling his eyes. "I thought...I didn't know..."

Maria turned to me. "We were going through some of Emmaline's things a few months ago, and I found her old diary. You can imagine my horror, my utter disgust to learn the people I loved and trusted were the reason I no longer had my brother and sister. I'd let them touch me, fuck me. I scrubbed my skin raw that night."

"What happened?" I asked, feeling sick to my stomach.

"It started off with bullying, a lot of it. My brother and sister, the rest of the poetry group as well. First Clara pretended she was interested in Marcel. Her acting skills really paid off, didn't they, Rob? She made him fall in love with her. She said she wanted everyone to know, that they should go on a date, and when he got there, Clara and her friends laughed at him, mocked him, humiliated him."

That explained the poem Marcel wrote. "That's why you chose Red when you attempted to murder Chase, to expose them, to humiliate him, all of them, the way they had Emmaline and Marcel."

Her eyes narrowed on me. She wanted me dead as well, it was written all over her face. I'd gotten in her way, I'd killed Ryan.

"Ryan was Marcel's best friend," Maria said. "And he'd been dating Emmaline for six months. He loved her." She shoved Robert's head back and stood. "Marcel and Emma were close, only a year apart, more like best friends as well, and after Robert forced himself on my sister, she withdrew, stayed in her room. I never knew why, not until I found her diary, but it was all there. Everything they did to both of them."

It was all clicking into place. "What did they do?"

"They made a suicide pact. They came here to this chapel, where no one would find them, and hung themselves from those beams, right there," she said, pointing to a spot above her. "Robert and Jemma, Chase and Clara, and Calvin and his bitch cousin Katana, they tortured my sister, bullied and tormented my brother, until they couldn't take it anymore."

"You showed Ryan the diary, didn't you? And he agreed to help?" I guessed.

Ryan had been in the poetry group as well, another of the prom committee's targets, no doubt.

"He was more than happy to help me, and he relished taking his pound of flesh." I bet it was Ryan's idea to carve judgment into each victim as well. "He wanted Emma back like I did. We wanted them both back, and with Isaac's help, and his little enchantment spell, of course, it wasn't hard convincing everyone it was Willow running around killing everyone."

Which was why Leah's murder had been different. Maria had been forced to kill Leah herself with Ryan dead. "Why Willow? Why me?"

"I never meant for you to become the prime suspect, that just kind of happened." She strode to Isaac and gripped his jaw. "Isaac wanted to believe it was Willow so badly that he didn't think twice when I suggested he tip the scale and help her get convicted faster." She shoved his head aside. "As for why? Because it was easy, because I had Isaac in my pocket and he hated your sister, and because your family is powerful and hoard that power, keeping it for themselves. Willow was strong, even back then, and she did *nothing*. She let those monsters roam the halls and terrorize people weaker than them, than her, and she did *nothing* to stop them. She's Keeper of her coven—she strolls around this city like she fucking owns it—but she's just the same as the rest of them."

"If Willow had known, she would have stopped it, Maria. She stood up for others at this school. If she'd seen them hurt Emma, she would have stopped it, I know she would."

"Lies!" Maria screamed. "Get them," she said to her brother and sister.

I expected them to move slow, but they were *fast*. Emma came at me, grabbing for me. I tried to shove her back, but she was strong as hell. I touched her, but because she was already dead, nothing happened. I didn't think even hacking off body parts would do much.

Marcel had other ideas completely, and instead of coming for me and Bram, he pounced on Robert, tearing into him and taking a bite out of the side of his throat. Robert screamed as blood pumped out of him.

Maria watched on, stunned.

"Untie Isaac and get Maria out of here," I called to Bram, as Emmaline came at me again, mouth open, lips peeled back, trying to take a bite out of me.

Bram did as I said, slashing the ropes around Isaac's feet and hands, while Marcel chowed down on Robert, who was now unmoving and obviously dead. Isaac sprinted for the exit, while Bram grabbed Maria. She kicked and screamed, hitting and scratching him, trying to get him to let her go.

"Run, Mags," he roared.

I spun with force, kicking Emmaline's legs out from under her. She hit the ground, and I sprinted for the stairs, Bram and a spitting, screaming Maria right behind me. We bolted to the top and I slammed the door shut after Bram, turning the old iron key in the lock, then dragged a heavy wooden seat over and jammed it under the handle.

Bram threw Maria down, and Isaac stepped forward, offering his belt. Bram quickly and efficiently tied her hands together with it, then used his own belt for her ankles.

"That door's not going to hold them long," I said when everything went quiet. "Once they're done with Robert, they'll come looking for more."

"What do you want to do?" Bram asked.

"We need to hand Maria off to the council, then deal with those monsters."

"I'll take her in," Isaac said, still visibly shaken.

"You'll have to excuse me for not trusting you," I said. "You know, since you tried to frame my sister for murder and all."

He shoved his shaking fingers through his hair. "After finding all that evidence at The Cauldron, I truly believed she was doing it. I had no idea... I never would have—"

"Save it."

The door opened and Asuka strode in, Jenna and several other council members behind her.

Bram immediately hauled Maria off the floor and dumped her at Asuka's feet. "You need to get her out of here."

Asuka looked at me, her expression stricken. "I'm so sorry, Magnolia. The council's withdrawn all charges. Willow's included in that, of course." Her gaze slid to Isaac, and she all but bared her teeth. "We found the enchantment charms you hid in our houses. You'll be held at Umbra Sanitarium while you await trial."

The council enforcers moved in, grabbing him and hauled him and Maria away.

A crash came from the basement.

"It's not over yet," I said. "Maria and Ryan weren't just killing for the hell of it. They were collecting body parts to build new bodies for her dead sister and brother." I motioned to the door. "That's them, behind door number one."

Asuka paled. "The undead?"

"Yes." Tingles danced across my back and around my side, swirling around my belly button, the markings the mother had given me heating until they were burning under my skin. I yanked up my shirt. "Bram?"

He rushed over, crouching to check them. His hand covered my side before he looked up at me. "They're touching, but they're colorful."

I'd passed. I'd passed my task.

I didn't get a chance to reply because pain arrowed down my spine, and I staggered back.

Bram grabbed hold of me. "Mags?"

I dropped to the floor like a dead weight, and a silent scream tried to burst from me as power exploded through my body. It built higher and higher, surging in waves; the gifts the mother had given our coven strengthening and solidifying inside me.

Bram cupped my face. "Mags?" he snarled. "What the fuck's going on?"

I tried, but I still couldn't speak, my back arching against the stone floor when another wave crashed over me, through me. The pain increased, until I couldn't take any more—

Another surge of power caused my body to jerk under the strength of it —then it seemed to wash away, taking the pain with it.

"Magnolia," Bram called, shaking me.

"I passed," I choked out. "I passed my task. I-it's okay. I'm okay."

He pressed his lips to my forehead, then scooped me up in his arms. "What the fuck was that?"

"Our coven's powers taking hold. It's done."

"Thank fuck," Bram said, fisting my hair and holding me tight against him.

A crash came from below the church, then another one.

Bram cursed and helped me to my feet as a council enforcer ran into the church, his face white, visibly shaken. "Whatever was in the basement, it got out. Looked like two of them. They ran into the forest."

"They're strong and fast," I said to Asuka. "We don't know how old they are, but they're only going to get stronger with every hour that passes."

Shouts, screams, came from outside.

"Maybe they doubled back?" I pulled my knife free and ran outside. The witches who came with Asuka had backed up, awe and horror on their faces.

Then a rattle echoed through the night—a sound I recognized all too well.

The mother, in her serpent's vessel, was sliding across the school field, heading straight for me. I dropped my knife and braced, not sure what was about to happen.

She stopped in front of me, so close, her hiss blew my hair back. Her massive head swayed as her black eyes locked on me.

You passed your task, young witch, but you are no longer the mother's child alone. You are Death's servant, and you have an unfair advantage.

She stared down at me, and I wasn't sure what she wanted me to say. "I didn't seek Death out, mother."

Did I ask you to speak?

I shut my mouth.

A combat trial is now pointless. You would win, easily. But your touch cannot kill the undead.

She paused, and I didn't know if it was for dramatic pause, but I was close to jumping out of my skin.

One final test for you...and your sisters. Her head shot forward, her tail rattling with the sudden movement. *No mates, no familiars. The four of you, alone, must destroy the undead, and you, reaper, will deliver their souls to Death.*

CHAPTER 36

Magnolia

My SISTERS WERE GATHERED around me, dressed for battle and ready for anything.

"I'm sorry you have to do this," I said.

"Don't." Willow planted her hands on her hips. "This isn't on you, and who's to say this wouldn't have happened anyway? You're the last, this might've always been the mother's endgame."

"Wills is right," Iris said. "It makes sense this is how it ends, all of us fighting together."

Rose took Iris's hand. "We're stronger together." She looked over her shoulder. "I just hope Ronan stayed at the house with the others."

Willow blew out a frustrated breath. "War's being a stubborn ass. I have a feeling they won't do what they're told."

"Oh, I know they won't," Iris said. "But Ash is going to do her best to talk sense into them, or at least stall them. She's an alpha; she knows their language."

I searched the sky and the surrounding trees for Bram. If he was here, he was staying out of sight. "They're worried, and in Bram's case, hopped up on newly-mated-male possessiveness. He won't be stopped. Tell me he'll eventually calm the hell down?"

Iris laughed. "That's a myth they tell us to make sure we mate them. The truth is, it gets worse the longer you're with them, not better."

"Just wait 'til you're pregnant," Willow said. "Relic promised to try and stop Warrick if he loses it and comes after me. Or get a bunch of his brothers to hold him down, whatever works."

It was going to be hard on all of them. Our mates were going to have to fight every one of their instincts to come after us, to protect us, but they also knew what we'd been through to get to this point, and they wouldn't mess that up for us, not unless they absolutely had to.

"How fast do you think Marcel and Emma are moving?" I asked Rose.

She'd gotten back from a reconnaissance flight a few minutes ago.

"They're moving fairly quickly, but we won't have any trouble catching up."

"Probably because they're not hungry yet," Iris said.

No, they'd only eaten Robert a couple of hours ago. "We need to be quick. They won't be satisfied long." I strapped my knife to my thigh. "I think if we send Rose back up, she can keep us updated on their position and can use her powers to knock them back if she absolutely has to, though we don't want you draining too much of your magic." I checked my pack, making sure my vials were easily accessible. It wasn't just Emmaline and Marcel we had to worry about in that forest. "Iris, if you go wolf and run ahead, it'll drive most of the demons back." Since Draven's pack had been culling the demons around their keep ruthlessly for a few years now, they tended to avoid a wolf when they sensed one. "And, Wills, do not engage. Do not get close, not to the demons or the fucking zombies. Peanut comes first. She's more important than this trial, more important than anything, understand?" I pulled on my pack and adjusted the straps. "None of you get close enough for Emmaline or Marcel to touch you. If they get hold of you, they're not letting go and then they're taking a bite out of you. We corner them, then I finish them the way we planned, agreed?"

Silence greeted me, and I looked up from strapping on a set of throwing knives. All three of my sisters were watching me—surprise, but mostly pride on each of their faces.

"You got it," Rose said and bit her lip. I knew it was to stop it from quivering.

"Good plan," Iris said.

Willow grinned. "Well, aren't you the little badass."

"Why yes, yes, I am." I grinned. "Though, obviously, I defer to you. You are the oldest."

Willow shook her head. "You don't need to defer shit to me, Mags. Your plan's perfect."

That felt good, really fucking good. After two years of fucking up, of worrying my sisters, worrying my entire coven—feeling in control, feeling like me, and making my sisters proud, felt amazing. "Okay, let's go catch us a couple bloodthirsty zombies."

Rose's white bat wings unfurled, and her eyes flicked to black. "I'll stay back, but I'll try to slow their progress," she said, then lifted off.

Iris called on her wolf, and her eyes changed from brown to blue. Physically, she stayed the same, no matter what animal she chose to surround her. But you could still see the animal, and a translucent wolf enveloped Iris now. "I'll call the animals when I get close. They'll help drive them back this way."

Then she jogged into the forest, and Wills and I followed. It wasn't like we'd be able to keep up, not when she went wolf.

Fifteen minutes later, we were deep in the forest and our plan was working. The scent of Iris's wolf had the demons scattering, and until now, we hadn't seen any. The one that had just stepped out onto the path ahead of us was tall, gray, and its mouth was wide and full of razor-sharp teeth.

Willow moved fast, firing her blade at it. The magic knife never missed and sunk deep into the demon's throat. It charged at us, and I rolled, sweeping its feet out from under it. It hit the ground hard as Willow's knife dislodged itself and flew back to her hand. I quickly pulled mine from its sheath and finished what Willow started, removing its head. I didn't want her getting anywhere near this demon.

"Nice decapitation, little sister," she said when we kept running.

"Thanks."

We met three more demons a few minutes later. Willow fired her magic at the forest floor and tree roots burst from the ground, wrapping around them, stopping them from running at us. I pulled a vial from my pack and tossed it at them, and we kept running, their screams echoing behind us.

Wills smirked. "Vicious little thing, aren't you?"

"Something we have in common."

She chuckled. "These undead fuckers better not be too much farther. Another couple of hours and my morning sickness will kick in."

"Trust you to get your morning sickness at night." My phone buzzed. Rose. "Your wish has been granted. Rose says they're less than a mile away from here."

"Good, let's get this over with."

We jogged for a little while longer, then spotted Iris just ahead. She was crouched behind a boulder near a cluster of trees, and she pressed her finger to her lips when she saw us. We slowed down and bent low, moving as quietly as we could to join her.

"Rose blocked their way, threw a few obstacles in front of them, sending them off course. The animals helped, but I told them not to get too close," Iris said.

Something heavy hit the ground, and I peered around the boulder. Rose was in the air, and she was using her power to throw dead trees and rocks at Emmaline and Marcel, driving them back in our direction.

"They're moving quicker," Iris said as Marcel picked up one of the boulders and tossed it aside like it was nothing. "Fuck, and stronger."

She was right. "We need to act now, before they're impossible to stop." We had a plan, we just had to execute it perfectly. So, no pressure at all.

"Promise me you'll stay back," I said to Willow. "No matter what, okay?"

"I don't make promises I can't keep, but I promise to try."

"Stubborn witch," I said.

"Takes one to know one."

I looked up at Rose and gave her a thumbs-up, then turned back to Iris and Wills. "Right, you stay the fuck here," I said to Willow, because it needed to be said again to our headstrong sister. Then I turned to Iris. "Call them."

Iris silently called on her magic, and in minutes the forest went from birdsong and the occasional growl from a distant demon to a low-building thunder as every animal within hearing distance headed our way. Sounds of thousands of small feet, flapping wings, chirping and squawking, squeaks and growls and hisses filled the air.

Rose's little bat familiars joined them. They burst through the trees and, swarming, flew around Emmaline and Marcel, animals, birds, bats dive-bombing them.

They both roared and shrieked, making inhuman sounds that lifted the hair on the back of my neck. Iris and I rushed out from behind the boulder, and despite the animals attacking, both sets of milky but lifeless eyes slid to us. Goddess, Calvin's and Margot's eyes, and the hunger aimed our way sent ice through my veins.

"Fuck," Iris said beside me.

They sprinted for us, moving so fucking fast there was no way we could outrun them. Wills called out a spell from behind us, sending her magic into the ground. Tree roots shot up, trying to latch on to their legs as they ran, but they were moving too fast.

Rose flew in front of them and, gritting her teeth, fired her power at them full force. It slowed them down enough for the tree roots to coil around their legs and arms, stopping their forward momentum. They tore at the roots, snapping them as if they were toothpicks. Rose lowered to the ground and, planting her feet, cried out as her power battered against them, as she fought to hold them back. Iris called out orders to her little animal army, and they dove at them, scratching and biting, disorientating Emmaline and Marcel.

I ran for them.

Marcel suddenly wrenched his only arm free and grabbed Rose. Emmaline snapped her teeth, and before I could get to them, Marcel bit down on Rose's bicep.

She screamed in horror and pain.

I slammed my blade into his skull, and it was as if I'd done nothing. He shook his head, as though my blade was nothing more than an annoying bug, and tore at Rose's flesh. A zombie died when you destroyed the brain, but Emmaline and Marcel weren't actual zombies, they were stitched-together meatsuits controlled by angry and vengeful spirits.

Wrenching my blade free, I sliced through his cheek and twisted the blade downward, into the hinge of his jaw. It dislocated and fell limp, releasing Rose. She stumbled back, and Iris grabbed her, pulling her away and wrapping her belt around Rose's upper arm to stop the blood pouring from her.

Marcel made a throaty gurgling sound as he tore the roots from his limbs, and broke free—then ran straight at me. Emmaline right behind him.

Marcel tackled me to the ground, dragging his upper teeth over me, unable to bite down hard without his jaw. Iris kicked Emmaline's legs out from under her, as I hacked at Marcel's arm, through ligaments as he thrashed on top of me. I dug the tip of my blade into his shoulder joint and smacked the end of the pommel, once, twice, popping the bone out. Rendering it useless.

Shoving him off, I sliced the tendons in his legs and ran for Iris. Rose was shrieking, her claws extended from the ends of her fingers, scratching, trying to get Emmaline off Iris.

I screamed a spell as I ran, one that would render Emmaline blind, but it didn't work. Marcel and Emmaline shouldn't exist, and though we could spell *around* them—Willow's earth magic, Rose's burst of power, and Iris's animals—the magic wasn't working on them, which meant we were in serious trouble.

Iris's struggles suddenly stopped. She went limp, blood everywhere. Willow ran forward, unable to stand back any longer.

"Emmaline!" I yelled to get her attention off Iris.

Her head came up, her eyes slicing to me a moment before she bounded to her feet and sprinted for me. Willow ran for us, her hands outstretched, screaming now, calling on her earth magic. Emmaline collided with me, teeth rabidly biting, tearing at my flesh. I shoved my forearm against her throat, trying to hold her snapping mouth away from my throat, and stabbed and sliced at her patchwork flesh.

Willow tried to drag her off, and Emmaline shoved her back with so much force, she flew across the forest floor and into a tree trunk. Willow crawled back to her feet, blood dripping down her face and her arm, not stopping, still calling on her magic, until the earth shook from it.

Roots again flew at Emmaline, dragging her back, whipping around Marcel as well. Willow kept coming, wrapping vines and roots and branches around and around them both. I dragged myself up, blood pouring from the scratches and bites all over me.

I pulled a handful of vials from my bag. "Get back," I yelled at my sisters and closed in on the struggling, snapping undead monsters Maria had created.

Willow stumbled back and Rose grabbed her, pulling her down beside her. With a cry of rage, I threw the vials with force, and they smashed against the trunk Emmaline and Marcel were bound to.

Their skin instantly started smoking, sizzling and bubbling, their flesh melting from their bones, the bones corroding and disintegrating, their bodies quickly turning to nothing but pulp at the base of the tree.

I turned back to my sisters. Iris was still unmoving, Rose and Willow clinging to her as they watched Emmaline and Marcel dissolve before their eyes. Until all that remained were two souls, confused and angry and afraid.

Power surged through me, not magic but the power Death gave me. A staff appeared in my hand, a smaller version of Death's. Somehow, I knew what I needed to do. "Come with me now," I said to them. "It's time to go."

"We don't want to," Emmaline said. "We're scared."

They'd resisted and missed their chance to go to Heaven. They didn't belong in Hell. But they couldn't stay here, which meant the only place left for them was Limbo. "It's going to be okay," I said.

"Will we be together?"

I held out my hand. "Yes. You'll be together forever."

Emmaline took it, and Marcel took hers. I lifted my staff and banged it on the forest floor, then I was flying through the trees, not just my soul this time but my physical self, all of me, and taking them both with me.

We flew up to the pile of rocks, and I banged my staff again. The rocks reformed into Limbo's gates. We flew through the gateway, along the path of skulls, but instead of traveling to Death's fortress, I took a worn path to a cottage that appeared in the distance.

Emmaline smiled.

"You know this place?" I asked.

"My grandmother's cottage," she said. "It's our favorite place."

I led them to the door, and my skeletal face was reflected back at me in the glass panes. I don't think I'd ever get used to that. Emmaline let go of my hand, then she and Marcel walked in, shutting the door behind them.

Then I was flying back the way I'd come, back through the gates and the forest, back to my sisters. They hadn't moved. What felt like fifteen minutes to me had been no time for them. I looked down at the staff and willed it away. It vanished.

"It's done. They're in Limbo," I said, rushing over to them.

"Thank fuck," Willow said.

I helped her up. "We need to move. Our wounds need treating."

We were immortal, yes. But I wasn't willing to risk it. I had no idea what would happen to one of us if we were close to death. What if we ended up like Chase Golden, stuck in a coma for eternity? Anything was possible.

Rose stayed in her shifted form, she was stronger that way, and half carried, half dragged Iris back the way we had come. I wrapped my arm around Willow and took her weight as she limped along.

The way back took a hell of a lot longer, and it didn't help that we were weak from blood loss. Several demons came at us, and I took them down, killing each and every one before they could attack. Adrenaline pumped through me, and that was the only thing keeping me standing.

"We're almost there," I said when I spotted the forest opening ahead.

That's when I saw our mates. They were headed toward us, and they were moving fast. With snarls and glowing eyes, they crashed through the forest like the monsters they were to get to us.

Then they were there, snatching us off our feet—and getting us the fuck out of there.

EPILOGUE

Bram

Three months later

THE ENTIRE COVEN WAS HERE, my brothers, Maeve and Uma as well. Daisy had insisted on a proper mating ceremony, and I wasn't going to argue. Not that I wanted to. I'd take any excuse to show everyone that Magnolia was mine.

My mate laughed at something Rose said while she danced with her sisters. Then they were all laughing, happy, carefree for the first time in a fucking long time. Daisy joined them, twirling around and throwing her arms around her girls, now that Magnolia had learned to control her powers.

It had taken some practice, but her control over it became easier and easier with each passing day. Now she could lock them away until she needed them. She'd also ushered several souls to Limbo for Death. She was handling it a lot better than me. I hated that there was somewhere she could go that I couldn't follow.

She'd also been talking to a counselor, someone that Rose knew. It was helping and I was fucking proud of her.

"When's the bedding?" Talon said beside me.

I shook my head at my brother. "We're not doing that. We're not at the village. They do things differently here. Besides, we are already mated."

"You marked her already?" Rook asked, dark eyes sliding to Mags.

After a crow mated, he had his female display his mark on her skin, to show every male with eyes in their heads that she was taken and to touch her was to sign their own death warrant. "I marked her the first time we mated."

"Uma will be disappointed," Payne said.

"Some of the warriors at the village might think she's still fair game," Talon said and shook his head. "You start slitting throats, we lose good warriors. Best she wear something that shows it off next time you bring her home."

"Fine," I said, and possessiveness filled me because deep down I needed them to see it as well.

Magnolia ran to me then, and I pulled her into my arms, sliding my fingers into her thick hair. "You're fucking beautiful."

She grinned up at me. "Dance with me?"

"I only slow dance," I said.

"Sounds good to me."

She took my hand, dragging me out to where the rest of her family was. War, Draven, and Ronan had all claimed their mates as well. Daisy and Art, and Else and Connor were all dancing.

I pulled Mags close. "Happy?"

"Are you really in any doubt?"

"No." I tilted her back and kissed her candy-apple lips. I wanted to kiss her all the time. I had to restrain myself often, or I'd be permanently attached to her gorgeous fucking mouth.

Payne lifted Maeve in his arms, and they came out to dance as well, swaying beside us.

"I wish my parents were here. I wish they got to meet you, that they saw how fucking happy you make me."

"I think they know," she said.

I smiled down at her, holding her tight to me. "So you think you can handle an eternity with me?"

"I think I'll manage," she said and smiled back. "I can handle anything when I'm with you."

I felt the same way.

I kissed her again then, because I couldn't stop myself, and I didn't have to, not anymore.

Then we danced. We danced the rest of the night.

›)›●(((

Jasmine

. . .

Ren was looking at me again. I felt his amber eyes burning across my skin.

I glanced up and he looked away. Coward.

"What do you think?" I asked Rome who was checking out the picture I'd drawn for my next tattoo.

"Yeah, Jaz, no problem," Rome said and sipped his beer.

Roman did all the tattoos for the hounds—and me. His skill was second to none, but I guess that's what happened when you'd had a thousand years of practice—and I'd taken full advantage of it the last six months. I'd traded a few of my designs for his services, and it was working out well for both of us.

The party was in full swing around us. Mags and Bram's mating was a good excuse to blow off some steam after a stressful few years, and everyone was here—except Zinnia. Her absence was a constant ache. She'd gone back to Death two weeks ago, and her month at home hadn't been long enough. It was never long enough.

I glanced Ren's way again. *Busted.* Again, the fox shifter was staring at me. He gave me a chin lift this time, then turned back to the wolf shifter he was talking to. She was gorgeous and confident, all the things I wasn't. I focused back on Rome. "Cool. I'm helping Wills with the nursery next week, if you're free?"

"I'm free," he said, then winked at Esmeralda, a third cousin of ours.

She blushed while simultaneously undressing him with her eyes. That was my cue to get the hell out of there. It was getting late, and I'd reached my social integration limit. Time to sneak back to my room.

I spotted Ren walking down the side of the house, and I knew I shouldn't. I really shouldn't. But I couldn't stop myself from following him —and wished I hadn't when I rounded the corner.

The wolf was with him, and he was leading her through the front door.

"Bathroom's through there," he was saying to her. She kissed him, giving his ass a squeeze before she dragged herself away.

I should be used to it, but seeing him with her—I felt sick to my stomach. I was about to retreat and get the hell out of there when Ren turned, spotting me, and I had no choice but to keep walking. He smiled instantly, flashing me his flirty grin, the same grin he'd just given his wolf, the same grin he gave all the females who happened to venture into his orbit.

A smile that meant absolutely nothing.

"Hey, Jazzy." His gaze trailed over me, hot, lingering. "You look pretty."

That smile, that look from him in that moment while I felt so lonely for Zinny and guilty over my jealousy of Mags and Bram's happiness was more than I could take. I snapped.

I usually shied away from him when he did that shit, because it meant nothing. I wanted a genuine interaction, instead I got the player. I wasn't a fan of this iteration of Ren, not at all. Anger shot through me, and ignoring the way my heart pounded, I gave him back what he had me. I let my gaze trail over him slowly, before my eyes met his again.

He looked surprised, momentarily stunned, but then he smirked, turning it back on.

Idiot. "You know, I used to think you were a good guy."

His head tilted to the side, his gaze flat, giving me nothing. "And now?"

"Now I think you're a slimy fucking creep, and you kinda make my skin crawl," I said, angry at myself and taking it out on him. His head jerked back, his eyes widening in surprise, not flat anymore, and I won't lie, it was seriously satisfying. "I mean, you were literally kissing a female five seconds ago, then you have the stones to look at me like that?"

"Hang on a minute, I was just—"

"You were just what? Do you even know?" I was so done with pining after this guy. Why did I care? Why? I had to be missing some fucking brain cells. "Behaving like a slime ball comes so naturally to you now, I don't even think you're aware of it."

Ren's lips curled, and he leaned against the wall, not taking his eyes off me. "You kind of sound like a judgmental bitch, Jasmine."

My heart felt as if he'd gone psycho killer on it, rendering it nothing more than a bloody pulp behind my ribs. "I don't really give a fuck how you think I sound." *Yeah, good cover, Jasmine, your voice is hardly shaking at all.*

"Really? You look like you're about to cry." He straightened from the wall and stepped close, too close.

I could smell the wolf's perfume on his clothes and bourbon on his breath. He was drunk. He dipped his head, his face an inch from mine.

"Or maybe you wish it was you I was kissing, that it was you I was taking home to fuck?" he said low, rough.

Ren was a lot of things, but he wasn't cruel. Apparently only I could bring out that side of him. That invisible dagger stabbed me in the heart one more time, then it was jiggled from side to side, over and over, turning the already damaged organ into mincemeat, making sure it was well and truly dead. He was right, I was close to crying, but I sure as hell wouldn't let him see it.

I shoved him. "I'd sooner fuck a cactus, asshole. Smile at me like that again, look at me the way you did...look at me at all, and I'll knee you in the nuts so hard you'll black the fuck out." Then I stormed off, up the stairs, his laughter following me.

I didn't know him anymore. I wasn't sure he knew himself.

He wasn't the fun-loving male I'd met when I was a little girl, or the wounded creature I'd delivered a message to a few years ago after receiving my very first message from the spirit world. He was someone else, someone I didn't like all that much.

It was a pity my head and my heart weren't in cahoots—instead they were bitter rivals.

One was telling me to forget about him.

The other was telling me to never let go.

Which sucked for me since there was literally nothing to grab hold of.

A PROMISE OF ASHES

THE THORNHEART TRIALS

BOOK #5

PROLOGUE

Jasmine

Three years ago

GRUMBLING, I yanked up the sheet. It did nothing to stop the chill across the back of my neck. I'd shoved my lower leg out of the covers before I went to sleep, and now, with it still hanging out, goose bumps prickled over my skin. I slid my foot back under and reached for my quilt, then remembered it was mid-July and my quilt was folded on the chest at the foot of the bed —because I didn't need it.

Adrenaline spiked through my body, my heart thumping hard in my chest.

I squeezed my eyes shut tighter. Everything was fine.

Just go back to sleep because this isn't happening. It can't be.

We were traveling to Roxburgh early in the morning to help my cousins with something involving our family cemetery. I needed a good night's sleep.

Perhaps I was asleep? Maybe this was a nightmare?

A whisper. Close to my ear. I froze, terror seizing me by the throat, and I choked down my scream. *Not a nightmare.* I'd prayed to the mother every single day, ever since Zinnia received her gift. I prayed that if she gave me one, it would be different, and then I received my empathic powers—and I thought I was in the clear...

Another whisper. Closer. More urgent. Desperate. My eyes snapped open, and I cried out, recoiling until I was pressed against the wall.

My room was crowded. There were at least ten of them. Souls. All trying to tell me something. Some whispering, some shouting, others unable to do anything but show me, like a grizzly game of charades. Battered and bruised. Insides on the outside. Missing limbs. Mouths open in soundless, tortured screams.

I closed my eyes, covered my ears, but they were relentless. Wishing them away wasn't going to work. They weren't going to stop. Logically, I knew that.

Zinnia knew how to control it. She'd mastered her gift, using magic and sigils to quiet the noise, but when a soul was persistent, there was only one thing she could do—listen. Make them feel heard. But I didn't want to. I didn't want any part of this. This wasn't a gift; it was a curse. A living hell. Yet I knew, deep down to my soul, there was no escape from it. The only way to make them go away was to hear them out.

I was breathing so hard, I was on the verge of hyperventilating, and the tight band of fear around my chest wasn't going anywhere. Slowly, I lowered my hands from my ears and opened my eyes. The ghostly figures swarmed forward, crowding me. I wrapped my arms around myself, sucking down desperate breaths, trying to hear what they were saying.

They were talking over one another, but their fear and horror came through loud and clear.

"P-please, one at a time," I said, but they weren't listening. It was as if they'd been waiting for this very moment, waiting for me to acknowledge them, and they were afraid if they didn't get it out now, they'd never get the chance again.

Ren.

The name filled my mind until it became almost a chant.

Tell Ren. Tell Ren. Tell Ren.

Over and over again, amid their whispers and cries, Ren's name was said. These souls, they had a message for Ren—my cousin Willow's familiar.

Their words, the images, rolled into one, and the message became clear.

"I u-understand," I said, trying to get them to stop.

They didn't. They came at me over and over again, battering my subconscious with everything they were feeling, that they'd felt during the most horrific moment of their lives. Sharing with me on repeat their grizzly deaths.

I was right there with them. I gasped for breath. "Stop, please. You can stop now. I'll tell him."

Their screams grew louder, more urgent, more panicked. Darkness crawled in from the corners of my vision. My heart that had been racing so fast seemed to suddenly stop. I gasped and grabbed for my chest. *Thump.* My heart took a sluggish beat, followed by a long pause. *Thump.* Another pause, longer this time. *Thump.*

The blackness swam forward, my sight fading.

Darkness. Quiet pressed in.

Then there was nothing.

"Jazzy?"

I blinked at the sound of Zinnia's voice. She was on the bed, lying beside me.

She brushed my hair back from my face. "You're back."

My gaze shot around the room, but it was just the two of us here now, and it was light outside. "There were souls, Zinny." I sat up and my head spun. "So many."

"Take it easy. Don't stand yet. Passing out happens sometimes. It's the whole straddling-life-and-death thing the first time, it's a real kick in the head. It shouldn't happen again."

"It never happened to you."

"No, but you're sweet and caring and feel everything deeply."

Her gaze was steady, sympathetic, and even though I knew what this was, what it meant for me, my stomach sank. "I don't want this."

"The mother gave you this gift for a reason, Jazzy. Trust her."

I shook my head. "I already have a gift. I don't want this one."

"She sees the goodness in you, baby sister, just like I do, like everyone who meets you does, and she knows what good you can do with your gifts and how many people's lives you can touch." She brushed my hair back from my face. "I promise, Jazzy, it'll be okay. And you won't be doing this alone, you'll have me."

I wrapped my arms around my sister and clung to her because I couldn't do this without her. "There's something else I need to do when we're in Roxburgh," I said against her sweater.

She ran her hand over my hair. "What's that?"

"They gave me a message...for Ren."

><>●<<

We finally finished the ritual, the reason we'd made the trip here, and I could feel it, the difference. Our family's cemetery had been tainted by evil, poisoned by darkness, and it'd taken almost two hours, and the combined magic of Zinnia and me, my cousins Willow, Iris, and Magnolia, as well as my aunts Daisy and Else to remove every last drop from the soil. I stomped my numb feet to get the blood flowing again.

"All right?" Zinnia rasped, then cleared her throat.

Our voices were hoarse from chanting for so long. I nodded, though it was a lie. I was far from all right, but it wasn't like I could do anything about it. I quickly finished dressing, pulling on my shirt, and shoved on my sneakers.

"Okay, let's head back..." Iris trailed off as she looked across the cemetery.

I knew who she was looking at without having to turn around.

Ren.

Zinny had given me her sigil necklace to wear so I couldn't see them, but I still felt them. The souls, they surrounded me now because he was here. The closer we'd gotten to Roxburgh, the more I'd felt their presence. They were eager for me to pass on their message.

Zinnia turned and waved at him. I took a steadying breath and turned as well. A large red fox moved out of the shadows.

"Ren?" Willow choked out when she saw her familiar. He'd been staying away from even her, and it was causing her so much pain. She missed him terribly.

She took a step in his direction, but Zinnia stopped her before she could go to him. "He's here because I asked him to come," she said gently.

Willow stared at my sister in shock. "What? Why? How?"

"I got his number from Else. I wasn't sure he'd come." Zinnia rubbed my back, trying to keep me calm. "Jazzy has a message for him." She gave me a nod.

Willow's gaze sliced to me. I could tell she wanted to say more, to ask me what it was, but she didn't.

My mouth was dry, and I swallowed repeatedly, trying to control my breathing when I felt the souls surrounding me press closer. Gathering my courage, I started across the cemetery, heading to Ren.

I hadn't seen him in at least a year. In his human form he was, well... beautiful, like model gorgeous. He'd never been conceited about it, though. He'd always been kind to me, to everyone, and funny. I hated that he was suffering, and despite how much I didn't want this "gift," I was glad that my first message was for Ren. I only hoped it helped.

He stood utterly still as I approached him. He didn't shift from his animal form, but I knew he was in there, that he'd hear me.

Not sure what else to do, I crouched in front of the large fox. Touch came naturally to me, was part of the first gift the mother gave me. Providing comfort was something that went hand in hand with my empathic power—that and the ability to soothe and heal others' emotional damage. So I ran a trembling hand across his neck. I could feel his anguish, his self-loathing, his helplessness. It rolled off him in agonizing waves. Still, he didn't move, his amber eyes remained fixed on me.

I gave him a shaky smile, hoping to put him at ease when my own heart was pounding like mad in my chest. "Hey, Ren."

He blinked at me.

I swallowed several times, sorting through the noise, narrowing everything down to what I needed to tell him. "They want me to tell you, they don't blame you."

He jerked back, but I couldn't let him retreat, not until he heard it all. I took his furry face in my hands, not letting him pull away. "Your guilt is keeping them here, Ren. They can't move on. They can't be at peace until you try to find it as well," I choked out, emotion welling inside me.

Ren shifted suddenly into his human form, stumbling several steps away from me. He looked around startled, as if he hadn't meant to shift. Tears trekked through the dirt on his cheeks.

"Ren!" Willow called.

"Ren," I whispered, "Don't go."

He backed up, then spun and ran into the woods.

Willow cursed behind me, her pain sharp, jagged.

The souls surrounding me retreated, satisfied that I'd delivered their message, but I barely noticed because all I could see was the horrified expression on Ren's face, the agony in his amber eyes. These souls were all people Ren had killed while possessed by an evil spirit, his body used, forced to commit all kinds of evil while he was taken along for the ride, witnessing every disgusting, twisted act. His guilt, that he hadn't been able to stop it from happening, was drowning him.

I forced myself to stand and walk back to Zinnia and my cousins, though it was the last thing I wanted to do.

Something new and powerful filled me, like a tether in the center of my chest was trying to tug me back, telling me to go after Ren, that he needed me.

It was hard, but I ignored it...because I didn't understand it.

Why would Ren need me?

CHAPTER 1

Jasmine

"THIS PLACE IS the creepiest we've been to by far," I said and peered into the shadows.

"Agreed." Zinnia's fingers unconsciously slid over the hilt of the knife strapped to her hip.

The private cemetery was seriously old, the final resting place for the people who'd owned this land through the generations. Human teenagers dared one another to come here at night, trespass on the grounds, and walk through the crumbling headstones.

"I can feel them," I said. There were several spirits lingering here.

Zinnia nodded. "Me too. They're calm."

I hitched my bag higher on my shoulder. "Definitely not feeling anyone pissed off enough to try to burn a house down."

Zinny looked toward the old groundskeeper's place. "We should probably check out the cottage."

"I was afraid you'd say that." I reluctantly followed her. The old building was nestled among weeping willows, their branches swaying, making them look like bony monsters and shrouding the place in darkness. The cottage was mainly made of stone, except for what was left of the shutters on the windows and the wooden door that was currently creaking and banging against the half-rotting frame in the wind. You could guarantee if a place looked like something from a grizzly horror movie, that was the place we needed to "check out."

"Don't worry, baby sister, I'll protect you." Zinny chuckled.

I snorted and rolled my eyes, but I was glad as hell she was here.

As we got closer, a chill breeze brushed past me, lifting goose bumps across my arms. "You feel that?"

"I felt it."

Zinny had spent the last month at home, and we'd tried to cram in as much time together as we could. I'd rescheduled most of my clients needing clairvoyant help, but not those in need of emotional healing therapy. That wasn't something I could or would put off. Thankfully, I hadn't had many in need of healing this month, so I could devote every remaining hour helping Zinnia. Her time with me was almost over, though, and in a few days, she'd have to return to Limbo—to Death. We'd really been hoping she'd have found what he wanted by the time she had to return, something she could use to bargain with, since that was Death's preferred currency.

He'd asked her to find some missing souls, promising to grant her a boon if she succeeded. She'd planned to ask for more time with me. Unfortunately, so far we hadn't been successful. And it wasn't just Limbo, Hell was missing souls as well. When the reapers had shown up to collect them, they'd been gone without a trace.

We'd spent most of her month home investigating volatile spiritual activity in the city. So far, they'd been your average spooks. Souls who were stuck here for different reasons, tied to a person or place, who weren't scheduled to be reaped until whatever had them tied here was resolved. Not everyone died, then instantly headed where they were supposed to go. We were yet to find out what we were dealing with here—if it was one of the missing souls destined for Limbo or Hell or your average ghost with unfinished business.

This particular soul had been going up to the main house and scaring the fuck out of the family. The place had been empty for years, and when the aunt of the current owner died after a long stay in a nursing home, her niece, who had inherited the place, moved her family in.

There'd been the usual stuff—footsteps in the hall at night, lights going on and off, doors opening and slamming shut—but more alarming were the fires. There'd been one in the family room, when the fireplace door had opened and a burning log was tossed out, and another in the kitchen, where a wooden spoon slid across the counter and over the gas flame when the owner left the room. She was adamant none of her family were responsible. Her aunt had never said anything about any paranormal activity at the house, so either the soul was new—hopefully one of our missing friends—or it was old and having new people in the house had disrupted it.

An icy blast rushed from the cottage when I opened the door. "I think we're at the right place."

"Best we work quickly, then," Zinny said, taking the black candles from her pack and setting them out in a square around us. She grinned over at me. "Wooden floor."

"Oh, I noticed. Thank the goddess for that small win." I pulled out a can of spray paint and quickly sprayed the protection sigils on the worn planks under us. If the floor had been made of anything else, we'd be getting naked right now and covering our skin in a special oil for extra protection. Witches and nature, trees especially, were intrinsically connected, which meant they were like a conduit of power.

Zinnia lit the candles. The wax was mixed with a potion she and Else, our great-aunt, came up with a few years ago, and it was highly effective protection against your average soul. For ones like the one we were about to tangle with, not as much, but it did provide an extra layer of protection, and layering up in these instances was always the best bet, which was why we laid out a line of salt mixed with cemetery dirt as well. Always have backup.

I turned so Zinny and I stood back-to-back.

"Ready to meet our friend?" she asked.

"As I'll ever be."

I took off the sigil charm I wore around my neck and placed it outside the square, followed by my leather cuffs inlaid with the same silver sigil. Zinny did the same, then her hands clasped mine and she started the chant, with me joining in a couple beats behind her.

It didn't take long. A rumble echoed in the distance, and the ground trembled beneath our feet. Not thunder or an earthquake, a highly pissed-off soul who didn't like us forcing them to come to us.

The wind inside the small shack whirled angrily, the door opening and crashing shut with more force. My hair whipped around my face, and my eyes watered. A high-pitched sound began, steadily growing in volume, until it was a shriek that made my ears ring.

"They're almost here!" Zinnia yelled over the noise.

I braced as the ground shook harder. The soul was old and filled with rage. "Not one of the souls we're looking for."

"No," Zinny yelled. "Way too old and powerful."

Souls were at their weakest right after a person died. If they were one of the ones we were looking for, there wouldn't have been anywhere near this much resistance. The door flew open with force, crashing against the wall, then flung back, slamming shut. A female shrieked and rushed at us, then screamed louder when she hit our protection barrier. She flew back, then rushed at us again, around and around the barrier we'd made, looking for a way in.

"We're here to help you," Zinnia said.

I watched over my shoulder as the spirit came to an abrupt halt in front of her. "You can not help me!" she shrieked.

"We can. We're not mere humans. We're more. We've helped souls just like you. Let us try."

Her hazy form flickered, her mouth opening in a soundless scream, her neck stretching in an odd way before her face snapped back into place. She flew around us again, floating to a stop in front of me. "I don't like it here," she said, her voice changing, becoming almost childlike.

"We can help you leave. I promise," I said. "What's your name?"

"Elizabeth." Her gaze darted around the room. "I don't like it here," she said again. "He'll come back. I have to leave. Let me leave."

"Who's coming back?"

"Mr. Stetson." Her form flickered again. "He'll hurt me! I don't want him to hurt me anymore. Let me leave. I want to go home!"

"Colin Stetson? He lived in the main house." We'd done some research on this place. The groundskeeper had shot Stetson, then paid for the murder with his own life. He'd been hung right here on the property.

She nodded, her gaze darting around in terror. A doll appeared in her hands. "He comes here when Papa's working. He hurts me." An image appeared in the corner—Elizabeth sitting by the fire, the way she looked now, probably seventeen or eighteen. The vision continued as the door opened and a well-dressed male walked in. She turned with a smile, but it dropped as soon as she saw who it was. She shook her head and backed up as he strode toward her, grabbed her by the throat, and shoved her against the wall.

The image dissolved and nausea hit me hard. The male who employed her father had been abusing her for years, if the doll was anything to go by. "He killed you, didn't he, Elizabeth?"

"That's why you want to burn the house? He's still here as well and you want him gone?"

She nodded again.

Her head whipped around. "He's coming!"

Zinnia's hands tightened on mine as the door flew open again and a second soul rushed in. It was Stetson. There was a gaping hole in his chest where Elizabeth's father had shot him.

He ignored us, a smile curling his lips. "There you are, Lizzy. You can't hide from me, girl."

She was trapped here by our spell and now so was Stetson. Elizabeth crumpled into a ball in the corner, shaking in terror. He'd been hurting her even now. The power of his emotion had trapped her here with him, even in death.

"Stetson!" I yelled, trying to get his attention off Elizabeth, but he was focused on his target.

"Blood," Zinnia yelled to me. "We'll call up Hadeon."

I nodded and sliced my palm. Hadeon didn't like being called, but this was an emergency. We could destroy Stetson's soul, but this monster deserved to suffer.

We joined hands again, and Zinny began the chant. "Hell, take this soul so dark, remove it from the mortal realm, never to return." I followed, oldest to youngest, always, so there was a chorus of voices, repeating the spell one over the other, an unbreakable loop of words and magic flowing from us.

We spelled faster, louder. The floor beneath Stetson shook.

The ground shuddered, and he stopped in his tracks, a look of confusion on his face. The floor glowed bright, heat and an orange-red light filled the small space. A loud rumble echoed beneath us, then the ground opened.

A second later, Hadeon, a demon and one of Hell's reapers, appeared. Seeing a reaper "on the job" was impossible unless the reaper chose it, and most didn't. Hadeon always showed himself, at least to us, although he did keep his face concealed. He looked to us, and although I couldn't see his features, I felt his displeasure. "He's one of yours," Zinnia said. "Take him."

His head tilted to the side. "Not your lapdog, witch. Being Death's consort means nothing to me," he said in a low rumbling voice.

"My association to him has nothing to do with this. I've called on you many times over the years."

He growled. "Didn't like it then, like it even fucking less now." Still, he turned to the souls, both of which stood frozen in place. Hadeon moved to Stetson and lifted a hand, power radiating from him, ascertaining if Hell was where the soul was destined to go. He growled again and both souls unfroze, then he grabbed Stetson, who screamed as soon as the demon's hand curled around his wrist in an unyielding grip, and dragged him to the glowing hole in the ground. Then, without looking at us again, they were gone.

Elizabeth stood to the side, her eyes wide as a white light, warm and welcoming, shone down beside her.

"No one can hurt you ever again," Zinnia said.

"Your father's waiting, Elizabeth."

She dropped her doll and stepped into the light.

Then she was gone.

I released the breath I was holding. "Fine. I don't mind creepy-as-hell cottages when that's the outcome."

"Truth," Zinny said. "I hope they make that asshole scream for an eternity."

I blew out the candles. "Unfortunately, Death's still missing his souls."

"We still have a couple days," Zinny said, but there was a note of defeat in her voice, and I hated it.

"Let's get out of here," I said, trying not to think how little time we had left.

CHAPTER 2

Jasmine

ZINNIA CURLED her arm around my neck and bumped her hip into mine. "This is probably your best idea yet." We walked down the stairs to the main tunnel below the hellhound's clubhouse and into their underground den.

I bumped her back. "Do you really love the design?"

"It's stunning, Jazzy." Hemlock, her familiar, poked her head out of the hood of Zinny's sweatshirt to take a look around, then pressed her little face against Zinnia's.

"Hey, Hemy." She gave her head a scratch.

Hemlock was a sweet black rat and extremely shy. Most mediums had gentle familiars, and usually animal, not shifter, since they were less intimidating to the souls we communed with.

The first time Zinny went to Limbo, she'd left Hemy with me, not sure it was safe for her there. Now Hemy went with her, and I was glad she at least had the comfort of her familiar when she was away from us.

I inwardly shook myself. I couldn't even think about her leaving, not yet. Zinny didn't talk about what she did while she was away. I'd tried to ask her, and she always shut me down. Now it was an unspoken rule for me, and my cousins as well, not to bring it up unless she did.

She never did.

It'd always really just been the two of us. We'd grown up in Philadelphia with our mom, not that she'd been around all that much. Our dad left when I was a baby. Like Mom, he was a free spirit. Being in one place for any period of time wasn't something either of them handled well. We never saw Dad after that and had spent school holidays here in Roxburgh with my aunts and cousins. When Zinnia was old enough to look after me on her own, Mom had taken off to see the world. I didn't blame her for it, I knew she loved us, she just had a restless soul. But at times like this, I wished she'd put her daughters first and come home. But that just wasn't her.

She texted occasionally to let us know where she was, that she was okay, and we'd learned a long time ago not to expect more. Or anything at all.

"Do we have time to check out the nursery first?" Zinny asked, stopping outside Willow and Warrick's place. Willow's mate had dug through the wall, connecting three of the original rooms and turning it into one underground apartment. He'd also put in several skylights to let in more natural light.

"Yeah." I knocked, and my current tiny familiar, a mourning cloak butterfly who had been with me a while now, and had been resting on my shoulder, fluttered up to rest on my hair just above my ear. Wills asked me to paint a mural in Violet's nursery when she was pregnant, and now I hung out there a lot when I wasn't working. If I wasn't with her or one of my other cousins, I was usually with Relic or Roman.

Relic was my gym buddy, he'd also taught me a few self-defense moves. After what my cousins had been through the last few years, he said Thornheart females needed to be ready for anything. And Roman had become a friend—well, as much as you could be friends with a thousand-year-old hellhound with limited emotions. But being an empath, spending time with hellhounds was kind of a nice break from all the noise. The emotions they were capable of were far from complicated.

I'd asked Rome to teach me to tattoo after Zinnia left. Basic tattooing was sometimes needed in witchcraft, especially when you were dealing with souls, and I'd used my new skills several times already. That led to designing tattoos for Rome and his brothers when they asked, which they did more and more lately. In exchange, Roman gave me the ink I wanted. Both of my arms were now covered in pretty, delicate tattoos, mainly flora and fauna, animals and insects. I loved them; it was kind of an addiction.

The door swung open, and Warrick stood there, Violet nestled against his chest, holding her close with one massive arm. "Yo," he said and opened the door wider for us to come in.

Zinnia swiped Violet from her daddy as we walked in.

"I've come to show Zinny the nursery," I said to War as we headed into

324

the new living room he'd created—and had to force my expression not to change, or to instinctively retreat, like I usually did.

Ren was on the couch beside Willow.

Our cousin jumped up, a wide smile on her face. She pulled Zinny in for a quick hug. "Hey, I didn't know Jazzy was bringing you over for a visit."

Ren stood as well. "Hey," he said, his voice deep, a raw quality to it he hadn't had before the evil spirit had possessed his body. What hadn't changed, though, was how devastatingly handsome he was. He was rougher around the edges, of course—the scars and that hardness he wore like a shield—but Ren was still utterly beautiful. Tall and muscled, that angled jaw and the sharp cheekbones—and that mouth. I'd dreamed of pressing mine against it so many times, against lips that had been sculpted by the goddess herself and designed to tempt us mere mortals with all kinds of wicked thoughts.

Zinnia smiled at Ren. "Haven't seen much of you the last few weeks. Glad I am catching you now, before I leave."

"Yeah, you two haven't been around much," he said with an easy grin, a grin that didn't reach his eyes. They never did anymore. There was a hollowness there, and I knew I couldn't be the only one who saw it.

His gaze slid to me, and he ran his fingers through his deep russet hair, making his scarred bicep bulge, not that I was looking. I didn't give a shit about his biceps, or any other...parts of him.

Yeah, right.

Fine. I was in love with the asshole. That didn't mean I liked him very much right now. We'd barely said two words since Magnolia's mating ceremony four months ago. Since I blew up at him after I saw him with one of the females he regularly fucked. He'd had the nerve to look at me the same way he'd just looked at her, like someone he wanted to go a round with between the sheets. Like I was no different than all the others, just some Band-Aid to numb his pain for a few hours. If he'd been sober, he'd never even consider taking it there with me...which had kind of made it worse.

I would've been just another distraction from the things he needed to deal with but wasn't. He'd been drunk, I should have let it go. Instead, I'd let my hurt take over, and I'd reacted. I'd called him a bunch of not very nice names. Ren's surprised expression was branded on my frontal lobe for eternity.

"Hang on a minute, I was just—"

"You were just what? Do you even know? Behaving like a slime ball comes so naturally to you now, I don't even think you're aware of it," I bit out.

The surprise vanished and his lips curled. He leaned against the wall, not taking his eyes off me. "You kind of sound like a judgmental bitch, Jasmine."

I inwardly winced, studiously not looking at the male now standing only a few feet away from me, because that hadn't been the worst of it. He'd dealt a final blow that day, and it had hit way too close to the bone.

"I don't really give a fuck how you think I sound." My voice shook. *Goddess, my heart was eviscerated in my chest.*

"Really? You look like you're about to cry." He straightened from the wall and stepped close, too close.

I could smell the wolf's perfume on his clothes and bourbon on his breath. He dipped his head, his face an inch from mine.

"Or maybe you wish it was you I was kissing, that it was you I was taking home to fuck?"

The rough way he'd said it sent tingles down my spine even now.

"How you been, Jaz?" he asked.

Embarrassingly, I jumped, not expecting him to actually speak to me directly. I tucked my hair behind my ear, then hovered my fingers above the mourning cloak butterfly in my hair, feeling her wings flutter, trying to cover my reaction and calm myself down. "Um...yeah, fine." I turned back to Wills. "Zinny wants to see Violet's mural before we get our tattoos. Rome said he could do them today."

Ren straightened. I wasn't looking his way, but still I noticed the movement. I ignored that as well.

Violet let out a cry in Zinnia's arms, and before Willow could reach for her, Ren was easing her out of Zinny's arms and laying her carefully over his shoulder. "I got you, Vi," he said in a low, rumbling voice that made my heart do all kinds of flips and flops in my chest.

Wills watched them, her heart in her eyes, then turned back to us. "I love that idea." We followed her through the living room and along the short hall to the bedrooms. "So what tattoos are you getting?"

The tension in my spine eased the farther away from Ren we got, even though the feeling of longing that hit me when he was in the same vicinity had increased to painful levels.

"Our flowers together. Jaz designed it. Wait until you see it," Zinnia said when I didn't respond. My sister raised a brow, not missing how distracted I suddenly was. I grabbed her hand, ignoring the look, and led her to Violet's room. I hadn't told her how I felt about Ren. I didn't want her worrying about me when she had her own stuff to deal with. I had a bruised ego and a broken heart, both of which I'd given myself. There wasn't anything anyone could do about that but me.

"Holy shit, Jaz, this is amazing," Zinnia said when we reached Violet's room.

She stood at the door, and I watched as she stepped inside, taking it all in. Pride filled me. I'd put my heart and soul into every inch of wall I'd painted. I wanted Violet to look around and find something new every day.

An insect or an animal, a flower or herb she hadn't noticed before. There were animals sitting, sunning themselves with their families, others hidden behind trees and flowers and shrubs, a tail, an ear, a paw peeking out if you studied the walls hard enough. A tiny family of mice you really had to search for.

"It's so beautiful," Willow said. "The amount of time Jazzy spent making this room magical for our baby girl...I'll never be able to repay her."

"I told you I don't want anything. I loved every minute of it." I glanced to a spot in the corner and wondered if Willow had noticed the golden amber eyes glowing gently among the leaves and the tip of one pointed, orange ear. I hadn't meant to do it, it just...happened. It was kind of humiliating, but I couldn't bring myself to paint over it.

Had Ren seen it? There was no missing how much he adored Violet. He was Willow's familiar, he was here all the time. He could have seen it.

I fought against the heat that traveled up my neck.

When we walked back into the living room, Vi still over Ren's shoulder, with one of his scarred, rough-skinned hands supporting her little booty, the other on her back. He was swaying side to side as he talked to Warrick. My belly swooshed as he pressed his nose to her head, kissed her softly, and breathed in her scent.

He turned when we walked in, his gaze coming straight to me and lingering before it slid to Wills. During our argument, I told him to never look at me again. He hadn't taken the note. Was he messing with me? I wasn't sure what else to think because I still felt his eyes on me all the damn time.

I studiously ignored him as we walked back through the living room.

"Don't forget movie night tonight," Warrick said when I opened the door.

"We'll be there," Zinny said as we walked out.

))⟩⟩·◉·⟨⟨⟨

"Catch," Relic called and tossed me a bag of Peanut M&M's.

I snatched them up. "Sweet, thanks."

Once a week, the common room down in the den was made into a makeshift theater. Every Monday night the hounds rearranged the couches and chairs and set up the projector Willow got for them. She was trying to teach them about emotion and the right and wrong way to behave in different situations. The hounds felt loyalty, anger, lust, but tender emotions were a mystery to them, at least until they mated. I came most Mondays. The hounds' commentary was worth it, even if some of the movie picks weren't my fav. It had been Relic's turn to choose last week, and he picked a gory '70s flick, *The Texas Chainsaw Massacre*. I was hoping for less blood this time.

"Don't say I don't do anything for you," he said and plonked down on one of the recliners.

"I would never." I grinned at him as I opened the bag and shoved a handful in my mouth.

Zinny scooted down and opened her bag of Skittles. Hemlock was curled around her neck, getting comfy. "What are we watching?"

I bumped Roman with my elbow. "Do you know what movie we're watching?"

He rested his beer on his massive thigh. "*Romance is a Stone* or some such bullshit."

"*Romancing the Stone?*"

He shrugged.

"Yeah, that's the one," Relic said and tossed a pretzel in his mouth. "It's Wills's pick this week. She said we'll like it."

Zinny snickered beside me.

I glanced around the room. Warrick, Wills, and Violet were snuggled up on a couch. All of the hounds were here except those on security detail, and there were a few others here as well, wolves, mainly females.

My wee mourning cloak settled in my hair, her love still strong even in her weakened state. I sent love back, my heart aching. She wouldn't have much longer now.

The mother had given me not one familiar but infinite—the catch was they only lived a short time—some a couple of weeks, others a month. In the case of this little sweetheart, roughly a year. I wasn't like Iris, I couldn't communicate with animals, but I felt my familiars deeply, communicating with them through emotion.

The door opened and I glanced over as Ren walked in. He strode to a spare seat on one of the couches. Relic tossed him a beer. He caught it and sat back. One of the wolf shifters, Breanne, got up from her seat and strode over to sit beside him. His gaze sliced to me, and I quickly looked away. He'd made his way through almost every female in Draven's pack. Okay, maybe that was an exaggeration, but that's how it felt. I'd threatened to knee him in the nuts so hard he'd black the fuck out if he looked at me again. Sadly, I'd just been running my mouth, making threats I wasn't capable of backing up, which gave me one choice—go back to pretending I didn't notice when he looked at me.

The lights went off and the movie started. Relief filled me. In the dark, I could pretend he wasn't right there, that I couldn't hear Breanne giggle and whisper. Zinny pulled a fluffy blanket over us, and I held it up to Rome. "Want some?"

He shrugged. I tossed it over his lap as well. Zinnia leaned into me, and we settled in with our snacks to watch.

I finished my M&M's and tried to keep my eyes open, but it'd been a long day, not to mention night, sending that creep Stetson to Hell where he belonged. Zinnia relaxed deeper against me, giving me all of her weight, her breathing coming slow and even. I glanced at her. She and Hemlock were both asleep. I tried to stay awake a little longer, but I was so warm pressed against Rome, snuggled between him and Zinny, the fluffy blanket over all of us, that it was a losing battle.

I jolted awake when Violet let out a little cry. Wills quickly fed her, and she instantly calmed, drifting back off—that's when I realized I was lying down, my head on Roman's massive thigh, and he was playing with my hair. I started to sit up.

"You're good, Jaz," he rumbled.

Rome and I were buds, and hellhounds were tactile and protective of females, especially when they were in their territory, emotions or not, mate or not. Nothing about what he was doing meant anything more than he liked the way my hair felt. He'd never tried anything before, and he wasn't now, but for some reason, my eyes shot to Ren like I'd been caught doing something wrong.

He was looking right at me, and his eyes were narrowed. As soon as I caught him out, his gaze sliced back to the movie. I quickly sat up, wiping the side of my mouth. "Sorry I drooled on you," I said to Roman.

"Not worried about a little drool, Jazzy girl," he said, his gaze still on the movie. "You want to keep using me as a pillow, have at it."

I smiled up at him. "Thanks, but I'm good." I sat up and looked down at my sister. She was still fast asleep. I tried not to jostle her. She'd been exhausted the last week. I knew she was sleeping even less than me.

The movie ended a short time later, and while the credits rolled, a hellhound in one of the seats behind us piped up. "So the takeaway from this one is besides good orgasms, a female likes her male to protect her, but also treat her as an equal?"

"Well, yeah," Wills said and elbowed Warrick. "The caveman routine gets old fast."

"Bullshit," her mate muttered. "You love it when I go all caveman in the bedroom, Dove, and don't even fucking try to tell my brothers otherwise."

Laughter rumbled around the room.

Her eyes narrowed, and I saw the moment Warrick realized he'd said the wrong thing.

"Now, Dove..."

"Yes, sometimes a female likes a male to be dominant in bed, as you all know."

Noises of agreement rumbled around us.

"*But* you can't tell me some of you don't like it the other way around from time to time." She winked. "I know War does, don't you, alpha?" There was more laughter, and Warrick scowled. "What you need to remember is, there's nothing you can give us that we can't do for ourselves. When you find your mates, don't assume they'll fall all over you because you have big muscles and sharp teeth."

"We don't just have big muscles, Wills. And I assure you there is one thing they can't do for themselves," Relic said with a wink.

"Oh, I assure you we can," Zinnia said as Hemlock scurried back into her hood and she sat up. "And that way we don't even have to make small talk or stroke your giant...egos."

The females in the room burst out laughing, and there was more grumbling from the males.

"Right, I need to put Vi to bed," Wills said before looking at us. "Catch you both tomorrow?"

"Absolutely," Zinny said, then gave me a nudge. "You ready to head home?"

"Yeah."

Zinny got up with a yawn.

I tried to get up as well, but the blanket was tangled around my legs. Rome obviously felt me struggle beside him because he hooked me around the waist, tugged me forward, then gripped my hips and lifted me to my feet.

I grinned. "Thanks."

"No problem."

"And thanks for the new ink, we love it."

"We do," Zinnia said. "Thanks, Rome."

He shrugged one of his big shoulders. "Anytime. No hardship having a couple hot babes in my chair."

"Idiot." I gave him a shove. "Later."

He flashed his teeth. "Later."

I turned, and *bam*, I was instantly caught in Ren's sights again. I felt his gaze like a lightning strike. I refused to react. What the hell was his problem, anyway? I rolled my eyes, even as my heart pounded like mad. Turning away, I hooked my arm through Zinnia's, and we headed out.

CHAPTER 3

Jasmine

ZINNY and I walked out of the clubhouse and onto the parking lot. It was early autumn, and there was a chill in the air. We weaved our way through the bikes lined up along the front of the building, and I waved to Brick, who got the short straw that was patrol duty on movie night. The hounds looked like a human motorcycle club to anyone paying attention, which worked for them perfectly. If they weren't running in the forest in their hellhound forms, they were on bikes.

Reaching up carefully, I helped the weakened mourning cloak butterfly onto the palm of my hand. After hibernating through the summer, something unique the mourning cloak did in certain areas, she'd ventured out late last month and found me again. We'd spent months together before she'd found a place to hide away during the hotter months, but now she'd reached the end of her life cycle.

My tiny familiars poured every bit of love and comfort they were capable of into me while I had them. I loved them just as much, and it hurt every time I lost one of them. From spring through to autumn, I lost at least one of my tiny friends every week, and in winter, while they lay dormant, hibernating or waiting to emerge when it warmed up, I missed them terribly. I wasn't sure why the mother did this, to them or me, but it seriously sucked.

"Thank you," I whispered to her as she lay on my palm. She gave one last gentle flutter of her wings. "I'll miss you." Then she was gone. A tear streaked down my face, the pain sharp, like it always was.

Zinnia wrapped her arm around my shoulders. "I'm sorry."

"I thought I had another day." I closed my eyes, gathering control, and used my power to soothe the jagged edges of my pain. It helped, which I guess was why the mother had given me this empathic gift in the first place. The weight of their loss would be too heavy otherwise.

The door opened behind us, and Ren walked out, Bree at his side barking out a laugh that had me jolting. I gritted my teeth as they strode past. "Night, *witches*," she called, waving without looking back, and the way she said witches, she totally meant bitches.

I hated her. Zinnia scowled after her.

Ren glanced back right as I swiped the tear from my check and stopped in his tracks. He said something to Breanne, and she looked pissed but headed to his hearse parked on the other side of the lot. He strode toward me, and I knew my eyes were huge in my head.

"Jaz...you okay?" he said in that husky voice of his that lifted gooseflesh all over me.

"She's good, Ren, thanks," Zinny said.

He ignored my sister, his pretty amber eyes locked on me. "You're crying."

A million replies ran through my mind. *Your wolf's waiting. Remember what I said I'd do if you ever looked at me again.* But I didn't have it in me to start something with him, and honestly, there was no reason to. I was in love with a part of him he'd buried so deep, I wasn't sure that male even existed anymore. It was as if the evil spirit who'd possessed him had broken our Ren beyond all recognition, but when he looked at me now, I was positive I saw him. I saw the old Ren, and goddess, it took everything not to rock back.

I felt like an asshole for giving him a hard time at Mags's mating ceremony now. He'd acted like a dick, yes, but that hadn't been him. The male who'd said that shit to me hadn't been the Ren I knew and loved. He was Willow's familiar, part of the family, and he'd be in my life in some capacity for the rest of it.

So instead of the other replies flying around my head, I held up my hand where my butterfly lay and offered an olive branch. "One of my familiars died."

His chest expanded, hands curling into fists, and his intense gaze dipped briefly to my mouth before coming back to mine. No false smiles. Not this time. "Fuck, I'm sorry, Jaz," he said, deeper, rougher than before.

I nodded, expecting him to walk away, but he didn't. His jaw worked like he was about to say something else—

The hearse's horn blasted, and the Ren I'd seen in his eyes retreated, the barrier coming up. He took a step back. "I'm sorry, again, about your familiar, Jaz. Night," he said and walked off.

With my sigils on, I couldn't see them, but I felt them, the souls of the people he'd been forced to kill while possessed. Waiting, always waiting for him to do what he needed for them, to set them free. My heart hurt for Ren and those poor souls.

We headed toward my car.

"So, Jaz, um...what the hell was *that?*" Zinnia said. "There were like sparks flying, and waves crashing, and angels singing." She stopped by the passenger side. "Is there something going on there? Like did you two hook up or something?"

"Nope, we had a fight," I said and opened the driver's door. "Besides our stilted and awkward greeting at Willow's earlier, that was the first time we've talked since."

We both got in. Zinny looked concerned, and that's exactly what I didn't want.

"What did you fight about?"

"He was drunk and being a dick. I told him so. I think he was embarrassed. But we've talked now, so it's all good. No harm done." I opened the glove compartment and pulled out an empty Nerds candy box and carefully placed my familiar inside, then tucked her in the pocket of my hoodie.

I started the car and drove toward the exit. There was no way I was telling my sister what we really fought about. I didn't want her last few days spent worrying that she was leaving me alone to nurse a broken heart.

I felt Zinnia's eyes on me. "I'm glad you're moving past it." She glanced in the rearview mirror, and I did as well. The hearse was behind us. "He needs all the friends he can get."

"Oh, he has friends." I wasn't sure he spent a night alone. Ren lived just down the street from my aunt Daisy's house, in an apartment under Foxglove Funeral Home, his family business. Ren worked there as a mortician.

I glanced in the rearview again. He was obviously taking the wolf home with him. Cool. Whatever, right? He could fuck whoever he wanted. It had nothing to do with me. We reached the house, and I couldn't stop myself from watching his brake lights flash before he turned into the driveway a few houses down.

"Is Mags here tonight or with the crows?" Zinny asked. "I wanted to check if she'd heard anything."

My sister didn't like to talk about Death when she was home, but Mags was now one of his reapers, so she knew what we'd been doing the last month and why. "I think her and Bram are with the crows, but when I spoke to her this morning, they still didn't know anything."

Since Death couldn't leave Limbo, not in his physical form, anyway, he needed someone else to find the souls. Reapers would seem the obvious choice, but they weren't mediums and only saw a soul here on Earth when they were sent to collect them, which meant his reapers couldn't help.

Would he be angry with Zinnia when she went back? Furious that she hadn't found his souls? I'd always respected Zinnia's wishes when it came to him, but I couldn't swallow down my next words. "Does he hurt you, Zinny? Is he cruel?"

She swallowed several times before she turned to me and shook her head. "No, he hasn't hurt me." She squeezed my hand. "I promise."

We went inside and Zinnia headed straight up to bed, but I wasn't tired —not after falling asleep and drooling all over Rome, and not with my emotions so raw after losing my familiar—so I headed to the kitchen to make a hot chocolate.

Stanley smiled when I walked in. His green feline eyes filled with warmth. He was sitting at the kitchen table reading a book.

"Hey, Stan, how's it going?" Stan had been around so long, my and Zinnia's sigils didn't work on him anymore and hadn't for a long time.

"Not bad. We went to the Coven Elders Assembly tonight." He chuckled. "Else was in fine form."

Zinny and I were the only ones who could see Stanley, and that's the way he liked it. He'd made us swear never to tell anyone about him, not even Else. He'd been her familiar and soul mate until he'd been tortured and murdered by Else's evil cousin Edward, when Stan was twenty-one. He didn't want Else to change how she lived her life, something that could happen if she knew he was always with her.

Else had only been nineteen at the time, and losing Stanley had left her heartbroken. She was now seventy-five and had started dating again, like a year ago. Connor was a good guy. He made her happy and thought her grumbling was cute. It made Stan happy that Else was happy, but he was waiting for her, for the time when they could be together again.

To add to the twisted tale, Else's cousin Edward was the one who had possessed Ren, making the whole situation, that was already utterly horrific, that much more awful for everyone.

Nothing was black and white when it came to souls. Some instantly went where they belonged after death—Heaven, Hell, or Limbo—and some, like the ones that surrounded Ren, were trapped here by the person who caused them harm, or by unfinished business, or for a multitude of other reasons. Emotions were a powerful thing, strong enough to send ripples through the spirit world, which is why Edward's victims wouldn't leave Ren. They were trapped until he forgave himself. And some, like Stanley, went to the other side and came back, reassigned as spirit guides or guardian angels rather than being reincarnated so they could stay with the person they loved, which was another reason our sigils didn't work on him.

"Else is always in fine form," I said and grabbed a thermos mug.

Stanley chuckled and came to stand beside me. "She is," he said fondly. "So, you look kind of queasy. What's the skinny?"

"I saw Ren tonight. He spoke to me."

"Far out. Did he apologize?" He sat up on the counter beside me.

"No, the whole thing was kind of weird, honestly." I glanced over at him. "He took one of the wolves back to his place."

He winced. "I'm sorry. That boy is blind to everything but his own pain right now. You can't take it to heart."

Stanley was the only person I could talk to about how I felt. He was also a great listener. "I know, and I get it. But being in love with someone who will never love you back seriously sucks. I wish there was a way..."

"A way to what?"

"Take it all away, these feelings I have for him. To rip them out of me."

"Don't wish that, Jazzy. Love, heartbreak, it's how you know you're alive, and life is a beautiful thing."

I shook my head. "I can't imagine you and Else together. You're such a romantic and she's—"

"Fierce."

"Yep."

He grinned and hopped down from the counter. "I wasn't all sunshine and roses when I was alive, Jaz. I just see things differently now, you know? I don't need to fight or rage. I just need to be here, for Else. Speaking of..." He held his finger to his lips and turned to the door.

A few seconds later, Else limped in. Her soft, silver hair was disheveled, and she was in her fuzzy yellow slippers that made her feet look like giant baby chicks and a matching robe.

"Hey, pumpkin. You and Zinny have a good night? What was the movie?"

"We did. *Romancing the Stone*."

She cackled. "The hounds would've loved that."

"I'm not entirely sure what they thought of it, though the consensus was orgasms are good. I'm sure they had more to say during it, but I fell asleep early on."

She laughed. "I'm not surprised. You and Zinny have been burning the candle at both ends." She motioned to my mug. "You want one of my elixirs to help you sleep?"

"Thanks, Else, but I'm fine. I think I'll read for a bit."

"Okay, pumpkin." She filled her glass. "See you in the morning."

She walked out and Stan waved to me before he shifted into a beautiful black cat and followed her. He only really left her side when she was asleep, and even then he didn't go far.

I finished making my hot chocolate, pressed the lid on the mug, and despite what I told Else, I had no intention of going to bed, not yet.

It may only be early autumn, but it was already chilly, so I tugged on a coat and slipped out the door, grabbing the small gardening shovel sticking out of the veggie patch as I passed.

I tucked the shovel under my arm and sipped my cocoa as I headed down the street. Sliding my hand in the pocket of my hoodie, I wrapped my hand around the Nerds box. She'd been a joyous one, my little mourning cloak, filled with light and warmth. They all had their own personalities and this sweet girl had sent a constant flow of loving energy my way the last month. I was going to miss her so much.

I tried to stop myself from turning toward Ren's place as I passed. The mortuary was closed, obviously, but lights were on in his apartment below. The curtains were drawn, but I saw someone move behind them, then stop. And I realized I had as well, my feet just ceasing to carry me forward. It was Ren. His broad shoulders and tapered waist were perfectly outlined.

Then there was another outline right there with him, so close they'd morphed into one.

I quickly turned away. I didn't want to see, didn't want to know what they did together. I didn't need that in my head, and I forced my feet to keep moving. It was like my heart was constantly being hit by aftershocks, opening new wounds with every one. I'd tried to use my power to heal it, but when it came to Ren, it couldn't even come close. As soon as I smoothed one painful, jagged wound, another opened.

Shoving him from my mind, I focused on what I was doing out here.

The field was just ahead. In a couple of months, all the wildflowers would be gone, and the oak trees dotted around would drop their leaves. We had a field similar to this behind the house, beside our cemetery, but that one didn't have as many trees, and butterflies seemed to love it here.

This was where most of my familiars lived and where I was drawn the first time I lost one of them. I'd been coming here ever since. The moon wasn't completely obscured by clouds, thankfully, helping me see where I was going since my only flashlight was the one on my phone. I made my way to a small clearing, got down on the ground, and dug a little hole, then carefully placed the small box inside and covered it over, returning her to the earth like the others.

Laying my hand on the soil, I closed my eyes and thanked her for all the love she'd given me. Exhaustion overcame me, and I lay down and wrapped my arms around myself, letting the chill breeze drift over me, listening to the night.

I woke with a start and sat up, quickly checking my phone. I'd been asleep for an hour and was chilled to the bone. I dragged myself to my feet, picked up the hand shovel, and headed for home.

Everything was quiet in Ren's place as I approached, the light off now.

"You stalking us, *witch*?" a female voice said.

The glow of a cigarette told me where she was in the shadows a moment before Breanne stepped forward. She was in the shirt Ren had been wearing earlier, her legs bare.

"Nope. I had something I needed to do."

She smirked. "Something that has you skulking past Ren's place late at night?"

"Yes, as a matter of fact, and I wasn't skulking, I was walking."

She stubbed out the cigarette against the wall and tossed it on the ground. "I see you watching us. It's embarrassing. I'm embarrassed for you."

I curled my fingers tight. This female was stronger than me, faster. She could shift into a wolf and use her sharp teeth and claws to kill me easily if she wanted to, but as hard as I tried, I couldn't swallow down my anger. Okay, yeah, maybe there was some jealousy behind it, but right then I was too tired and cold and I didn't care. "As riveting as your sex life is, my walk tonight had absolutely nothing to do with you or Ren. And what's embarrassing is that you think you and he are an *us*. You're one of many, *wolf*, and not even in his top five. Have a good night." I walked away, giving her my back, which was highly stupid, but I was too emotional after burying my familiar and pissed off to think clearly right then.

A growl erupted behind me, and I braced for impact.

"Don't even fucking think about it, Bree," a deep voice said behind me. "Go back inside."

Ren.

Awesome.

Had he heard what I said? I cringed. He had to have heard me. I tried to resist, but I couldn't stop myself from turning back. *Fuck.*

He stood on the road in only a pair of jeans, his hands on his hips, moonlight highlighting every muscle and the thick scars on his chest and arms. I opened my mouth to say something, but nothing came.

What the hell could I say?

I turned my back on him and quickly walked away.

CHAPTER 4

Ren

I woke with a jolt, covered in sweat.

Blood and screams filled with horror and pain, noises a being shouldn't be able to make, filled my head. Their eyes, wide with terror, locked with mine, my roars muffled, trapped, unheard as I watched my own hands slice and cut and tear at their flesh, unable to stop it—to stop *him*.

His voice in my head, like it had been then, telling me to stop fighting him, to enjoy it, that deep down I wanted it. His sick thoughts had been a nightmare on constant loop in my head.

I shoved back the covers and stood, thrusting my fingers through my hair. Breanne stirred. I looked down at her, surprised. What the fuck was she doing here?

I couldn't deal with her right then.

Striding from the room, still naked, I walked out the front door, shifted, and ran. I ran through the field that often had Jasmine's scent drifting through it. It was stronger now, but she wasn't here. She'd gone home.

I shook my head as I ran, trying to shake her image from my mind. I didn't want her in there, not with everything else, not with his voice ringing through my head and the grotesque images of what he'd made me do.

My fox burst into the forest, running hard, trees flying past as the

338

churning in my gut grew deeper, yawning wider until it was unbearable, until I was gasping for breath as I raced through the forest. I'd lived out here for nearly two years after it all happened. There was a small cave close by, and every morning I crawled out of the dark and ran to the same spot.

The red cliffs. When I finally reached them now, I shifted back into my human form and walked up to the edge, gasping, drawing in one desperate breath after the other. I could make it all end. I could stop this feeling, this awful, unbearable fucking torment inside me. No more nightmares, no more blood and screams and horror. No more guilt that I couldn't stop him, no matter how hard I fought.

All I had to do was take another step, just one more, and the four-hundred-foot drop would take it all away. I stared down the cliff face to the rocks at the bottom so sharp they'd tear flesh from bone, reducing a body to pulp.

My fox clawed at the ground, trying to make me step back, before he filled my head with a pair of bright green eyes, like he always did, right before I took the final step. *She needs us,* my usually tight-lipped fox growled through my mind.

She didn't, but it stopped me every time. This unexpected kernel of hope filled me, like a starburst breaking through the darkest night.

He didn't let up, showing me Jasmine and the way she'd looked that day striding across the cemetery, the way she'd crouched down in front of us. *"They want me to tell you, they don't blame you."*

The way she'd taken my fox's face in her hands when I'd tried to retreat and trapped us in place with that unwavering gentle gaze, holding us captive as she'd delivered her message. *"Your guilt is keeping them here, Ren. They can't move on. They can't be at peace until you try to find it as well."*

I stumbled back from the cliff's edge with a roar.

It was impossible, what she asked of me. How did you move past that? I couldn't, and I couldn't jump, not today, so I did the only thing that helped.

You're too weak and pathetic to even kill yourself, Edward's voice echoed through my skull.

I ignored the voice that my own fucked-up mind fed me. Edward's voice. Willow had exorcized him, casting him from me, almost three years ago. He was gone, but my mind didn't give a fuck. I strode to the rotting tree a few yards away, pulled out the blade I'd hidden inside it, and held the tip to my flesh. "Chest to rib." I gritted my teeth as I cut through barely healed scar tissue. "Midsection to hip." Another slice. "Right thigh."

The panic began to ease as the scent of my blood filled the air, as I said aloud and reenacted each precise slice. It was how he started each torture session, those cuts, in that order. My hands and this knife had carved them into innocent strangers. But now, it silenced their screams in my head for a little while. "Collarbone to shoulder." Blood dripped from the cuts to the forest floor. And when I made the final slice, "bicep to forearm," I could finally breathe again.

I dropped the knife and stumbled back, leaning against a boulder, its rough surface cool against my overheated flesh. I was a shifter, I healed fast, but my skin still scarred, and I deserved to wear every one of them. When I caught my breath, I scooped up the knife and tossed it back in the hole under the tree. Suddenly feeling fucking exhausted, I shifted back and ran for home, stopping by a creek when I got close to wash off the blood.

When I finally walked back into my apartment, it was seven in the morning. I frowned at Bree still asleep in my bed, then quickly dressed, shutting a drawer harder than I needed to, and she jolted awake. I'd told her to leave last night after the shit she said to Jasmine, but she'd obviously let herself back in when I was asleep.

"Hey...where'd you go?" Her gaze roamed over me. "I woke and you weren't here."

I pulled on my boots, lacing them up. "Thought I told you to leave last night."

She smiled. "You didn't mean it, so I came back. Why don't you come back to bed?"

"I don't say shit I don't mean."

She sat up. "Did you run off to be with that fucking witch?" she said with a lot of growl in her voice and shoved back the covers.

Jasmine had been coming back from that field last night, after doing fuck knows what. It was dark and she'd been unprotected. My stomach twisted remembering what she'd said before I walked out and stopped Bree from going after her. *You're one of many, wolf, and not even in his top five.*

Jasmine was the only one who'd called me out on my shit, who didn't walk around me on eggshells. *Yeah, and now she just avoids you completely.*

Not surprising after the shit I'd pulled. I knew exactly what she thought of me, how she saw me, and I fucking hated it.

I shoved my phone in my back pocket. "She's got a name, and where I go and what I do is none of your business." Why the fuck was Breanne still here? She knew what this was. She'd made it crystal clear she wanted nothing more from me than sex, and sleepovers weren't part of the deal, and sneaking back into my place was seriously fucked up. I shoved my fingers through my hair. "We got a problem here?"

She made a show of sliding on her panties, a sly smile on her lips.

I scanned her body, searching inside myself for something, any emotion at all, but found nothing. My cock didn't even stir. After my visit to the cliffs, I was back to the way I needed to be—cold, numb, detached. I'd had to find a way to shut everything down, because if I hadn't, I wouldn't be here. I'd still be living wild, my fox in control, letting animal instinct override everything else—or I'd be dead.

Numb worked most of the time, thank fuck, or there'd be no getting through the day.

And when it stopped working, I fucked and I fought to shove back the demons in my head, the self-loathing, to drown out that fucking monster's voice that was so clear sometimes I thought he was still there, and when that didn't work anymore, I went back to the cliffs. A fucked-up cycle that, for now, kept me breathing.

Only the females and the alcohol hadn't really been working, anymore, had they? Not like they used to.

"No problem," she said, her smile dropping, replaced by a scowl. "I just don't want you coming back to me, if you've been fucking that wit... *Jasmine.*" She smiled, flashing her fangs. "I don't do sloppy seconds."

I didn't like hearing her say Jasmine's name.

"Again, what I do and where I go is none of your business. You need to leave." I strode out and down toward the mortuary door at the end of the hall. No, if I was honest, the sex, getting wasted, it hadn't really been working for a long time. But I'd kept it up because the truth was far too fucking terrifying.

Only one thing had been truly working lately.

A pair of jade eyes filled my mind, and my gut clenched so tight I sucked in a breath. Maybe I was a masochist now, because the images my fox kept throwing at me of Jasmine felt like pure fucking torture. Wanting what I could never have, a female I shouldn't even be thinking about but did anyway because just the thought of her was a lifeline, and a seriously fucked-up torment.

I might think my unsuspecting lifeline hated me, but Jasmine wasn't capable of the emotion. She did think I was a "fucking creep" though, and a "slimeball"...oh, and let's not forget the way I made her "skin crawl." Can't forget that part. I'd been drunk when she'd laid that on me, surprising the fuck out of me. I had no idea little Jazzy Thornheart had it in her. I'd never seen her so pissed.

But I'd more than deserved her anger, and I fucking cringed when I thought about the shit I said to her.

She sure as hell wouldn't want my slimy hands on her, and I'd never touch her, not in a million years. All I needed from her were her eyes on me.

It didn't matter if those gorgeous eyes were filled with disgust or anger —or disappointment. I just needed her to look at me, so that late at night I could close my eyes and see them, see her. So I could fall so deep into her eyes that the blood and the pain couldn't reach me.

And I was ashamed to admit I had a fucking entire file of photos of her on my phone, like the fucking creeper she thought I was. While she thought I was texting or watching something on my phone, I took pictures of her. If I wasn't too far gone, like I was this morning, I scrolled through them, and they helped me regain control. Yes, it was fucked up. No, I had no idea what it was about her that soothed the horror inside me, and I realized when I walked in and found Breanne still in my bed, I didn't want random hookups anymore. I didn't want any of it. Besides running to the cliffs and cutting, Jasmine was the only thing that truly helped.

What the fuck did I do with that?

I unlocked the door and walked into the cold room. The only reason I could think of was that she was the one sent to deliver the message to me three years ago, that those souls had chosen her. I didn't know exactly what they'd shared with Jasmine, but I knew enough about her power and how it worked, to know they'd shown her what happened to them, how they'd died—how I'd killed them.

The thought turned my stomach, but it also connected us in some fucked-up way.

Because she knew more about what I did, what that evil fuck had made me do, than anyone else. I hadn't even shared it with Willow. I didn't want that in her head.

No wonder I disgusted Jasmine.

Shoving it all from my mind, I turned on my music and put on my rubber apron. The still healing slices in my skin pulled as I moved and helped keep my mind clear.

I drew back the white sheet covering Mr. Fulton. The witch was in his eighties. He'd died suddenly yesterday night in his sleep. The family was coming to view his body tomorrow, so I needed to get him ready.

"Let's get you dressed and looking good, Mr. Fulton," I muttered and got to work.

A couple hours later, I'd finished touching up his face and had him in his suit—

Something cold, like icy fingers, brushed across the back of my neck. I froze. It definitely wasn't the first time, but this shit was getting more and more frequent. I looked behind me, but, of course, there was nothing there. Gritting my teeth and fighting down the anxiety, I finished getting Mr. Fulton ready, ignoring the cold touches that kept coming.

"Go," I ground out. "Just follow the fucking light already."

Spirits weren't new here. This place got its fair share, but they were transient. They were passing through, if they ended up here at all. I wasn't a medium, but I'd felt them, had seen things all my life living here and so had my parents, it was part of dealing with death every day.

But this, what had been happening to me more and more lately, was something else, and after what happened to me, even with the rune Willow had inked on me to stop a soul from possessing me again, that fear was always there. It didn't help that things were getting worse and I didn't know why. I jolted when invisible, cold hands pressed against my back again, the iciness soaking through my clothes.

No. I shook my head when the thought filled my mind. It wasn't them.

It couldn't be one of the souls Jaz spoke to three years ago, because they were gone. I did what they asked, right? I somehow found the strength to come home, I left the forest. That was as close to peace as I'd ever get. No, this was someone, something else, it had to be. Those souls, they were just on my mind because the anniversary of that fucking nightmare was fast approaching.

It was hard, but I forced myself to continue to ignore it. I turned the music up and got back to work, telling myself over and over I was safe. Possession wasn't possible.

Maybe it was just Mr. Fulton? Maybe he was fucking with me? I hoped like hell it was, the alternative wasn't something I could stomach.

)) ꒰ ⬤ ꒱ ((

I pulled up to the clubhouse. I hadn't been by last night. After preparing Mr. Fulton, I'd shifted and left. I hadn't been in the mood to be around anyone and spent the night in the forest—running, hunting, letting the fox lead and my animal instinct take over, keeping me firmly out of my own head.

But I couldn't be away from Willow and Violet for long. We were witch and familiar. Being away from her all that time when I'd been struggling so bad had only added to the pain. It was early evening, and as I strode toward the clubhouse, I heard the music, nineties dance, the kind of stuff Asher played if the wolf shifter wasn't listening to death metal. Colored lights flashed through the glass windows high along the wall.

"What's going on?" I asked Relic, who was working on his bike out front.

"Zinny's leaving tomorrow. Her cousins are here with some of the wolves. They threw her a party."

The rumble of bikes echoed behind me, and I turned as the rest of the hounds returned from their ride, the ones not stationed around the clubhouse on security detail, anyway.

Warrick kicked down his bike stand, swung his leg over the seat, and started toward us. "Wills was waiting for Violet's daddy to get home so she could join the fun," Relic said.

Warrick was frowning when he reached us. "What's going on?"

"The females are cutting loose," Relic said. "Mags made some potion, supposed to get you wasted and no hangover."

He crossed his massive arms. "Who's in there?"

"All of 'em," Relic said.

"You been in?" War asked.

"Nope. Was told to stay the fuck out."

Grumbling, War strode to the door and yanked it open. I followed, the rest of the hounds striding in behind us. We all stopped just inside the doorway.

Fuck.

"Fuck," Relic muttered beside me.

War shook his head, cursed, then strode across the room and through the door down to the den, and his mate and pup.

Roman and Lothar moved up beside Relic and me and all three of them were grinning.

Dance music pumped through the speakers, and all the females were on the dance floor, bodies and faces decorated with glow-in-the-dark body paint, swirls and colorful designs I just knew Jaz had painted on everyone. They were all barely dressed, hair wild, and obviously fucked up on whatever Mags had given them. More than half of them were tits out, the rest in only a bra.

The Thornheart females were right in the center of it all, Asher with them. Zinnia threw up her arms, spinning, and then Jazzy was suddenly there, bursting from the crowd, her blond hair streaked with glowing pink paint, and unlike their cousins, who wore actual bras, Zinny and Jazzy had matching glowing blue ones they'd fucking painted on. It hid nothing. I was an animal, my sight was excellent, even in the dark, and I could see her tight little nipples perfectly.

I couldn't fucking look away, and I had a strong and sudden urge to tear out the eyeballs of every male watching her dance and laugh and sing, watching the pleasure on her face as she cut loose. She was right here, in this moment. What would that be like? To not think about the past or the future and just be.

I didn't want anyone else to see it. I wanted to greedily keep it all to myself, take a picture so I could look at her like this over and over again.

A hand came down on my shoulder. "Brother, you good?"

Relic's voice called over the music, and I realized I'd been growling, the sound vibrating from the center of my chest.

No, I fucking wasn't. I wasn't fucking good. Not at all.

Jasmine spun then, her blond and pink hair flying around her before she spotted us. Her gaze sliced from the hounds gathered around, then her gorgeous green eyes locked on me. She blinked several times, then she swayed a little, before she straightened her shoulders and started toward me with more than a little roll in her hips.

I couldn't move. There was a design painted on her stomach, swirling around her belly button. I tried really hard, but there was no stopping the way I ate up the sight of her.

She stopped in front of me, tilting her head back. "Ren...why—"

Breanne came out of nowhere and shoved her aside. If Rome hadn't grabbed her, Jasmine would have hit the floor. Jaz pushed away from Rome and charged Breanne, shoving her back. Bree spun on her, and I grabbed for her to hold her back, but then she was wrenched aside, and Asher was standing over her, snarling in her face.

Ash growled low, the sound coming from her chest. Breanne whined and quickly bared her throat. "You lay a hand on Jasmine again and I'll fuck you up, bitch," Ash said.

Ash was an alpha of the Silver Claw pack, and there weren't many in their pack, male or female, who would take her on. She shoved Bree away, who took off back to the dance floor, then Ash wrapped her arm around Jasmine's shoulders and pulled her into her side. "Well, aren't you a scrappy little fucker." She grinned. "But, babe, you gotta be more careful. Yes, Breanne's a screaming bitch, but she has fangs and claws and you don't."

"I don't like her," Jasmine said, still looking pissed off, and her gaze was more than a little unfocused.

"No one likes her, Jazzy," Asher said and chuckled.

Jasmine's gaze lifted, locking on me, and as soon as it did, something went wrong in my chest and my gut and I broke out in a cold sweat.

"Ren does. He likes her, don't you, Ren?" she said.

My mouth was dry, my tongue stuck to the roof of my mouth.

Asher snorted. "There isn't a female Ren doesn't like, babe."

Her lashes fluttered, shutting, locking me out before she turned away. "I need to dance."

"You go dance. I'm gonna kick these fuckers out. Females only, assholes," she said to the males gathered with me.

"You sure you're not sick of dancing?" Lothar said to her. "I got a soft bed and a bottle of whisky in my den. You want, Ash, we could have a party of our own."

"And I've got a vibrator and a bottle of bourbon back at the keep. I'm good," she said, barely sparing him a glance. "Now, all of you, fuck off." Then she strode away to join her females.

"Harsh," Relic said, grinning wide.

The door to the dens below opened and Willow ran out, a huge smile on her face as she rushed to dance, and for a moment, I almost fucking smiled.

345

All I'd ever wanted was for her to be safe and happy, and she was. So fucking happy.

Warrick filled the doorway she'd just walked through, jabbed a finger at us, and then pointed at the exit behind us, silently telling us to get the fuck out, then he disappeared, going back down to look after Violet.

As we were filing out, the hounds grumbling all the way, a new song started. The females cheered and whooped, and I tried not to, but I couldn't stop myself from turning back to get one last look.

And if no one had been with me, I would've snapped a picture of Jasmine in that moment. Head thrown back, blond and pink-streaked hair flying everywhere. Huge smile on her beautiful face.

My memory would have to be enough, but I didn't think I'd have any trouble remembering.

Fuck, no. The sight of her was burned into my mind like another scar.

Another I never wanted to heal.

CHAPTER 5

Jasmine

THERE WAS STILL PINK in my hair. It wasn't as bright, but it would probably take a few more washes to get it all out. I lay on my bed and tried to calm my anxiety. Zinnia was leaving today, going back to Death, going back empty-handed. She said he hadn't hurt her, but she could be lying for my benefit.

I slid my sketchpad and charcoal aside, unable to focus. I worried about her the entire time she was there, and I wouldn't be able to talk to her, not even text or call, for a whole month. I wouldn't know if she was okay until she walked through that gateway in another month's time.

Since drawing wasn't working this morning, I snatched up my phone instead to distract myself while I waited for her to get here. She was doing the rounds, saying her goodbyes. It was selfish, but the goodbyes and seeing my family sad all in one day was more than I could take, so I sat that part out. I clicked on Nightscape to check my notifications, then couldn't help but smile. Asher had posted pics from last night. At least her page was private, so we weren't flashing our boobs to all of Roxburgh.

I flicked through them, then stopped. Breanne with her arms around two other wolves, smiling, laughing. Asher had dominated her last night after she shoved me, but they were pack, family. I hated that she saw right through me to my jealous little heart. The fact that she got to be close to

347

Ren, to touch him, kiss him, talk to him in his room at night, yeah, it ate at me.

I'd never know what that was like, and I hated that I still thought about it, that I still wanted to know. Asher had tagged her, and I clicked on her name like some saddo stalker. Of course, her page wasn't private. She'd love to flash her boobs to all of Roxburgh.

I cringed, hating how bitchy I was being. That wasn't me, and I didn't like feeling this way.

Still, I scrolled through a few pictures, then a few more.

Don't be such a tragic loser, Jasmine.

But I couldn't stop myself. She was gorgeous, her body was perfect. She had all these friends, and the Silver Claw pack gatherings looked like so much fun. My cousin Iris, her familiar, Nia, the sweetest dog in existence, and her mate, Draven, their alpha, were featured in quite a few photos. I'd been to pack land, of course, but I'd never stuck around for one of their parties.

I flicked to the next picture. It was of Draven and Warrick, and Ren was with them. They looked deep in conversation. The next one was a selfie, and she was on Ren's lap. She was grinning, and he was talking to someone beside him.

The next was a photo of a male's bare, ripped stomach, obviously on a bed. There was a scar on his side, and she'd captioned it with a hot face and raindrop emojis. Shifters had their shirts off a lot, and I recognized the scar instantly.

Ash told me that after we'd had our little shoving contest, Bree had warned the other females in their pack to stay away from Ren, that he was hers. Nausea curdled in my belly, and I scrolled away—so quickly that I didn't look where I put my finger.

I froze.

NO!

The like button glowed up at me. *I'd liked it!*

I quickly unliked, but it was too late. She would've gotten a notification. I tossed my phone aside like it was made of lava and jumped off the bed. I wanted to hide under the bed and never come out.

Maybe she wasn't just sleeping with Ren anymore? Maybe they'd started dating? She'd posted pics of him, that wasn't something you'd do if you were just casual, right? I'd been busy with Zinny the last few weeks. I was out of the loop. Maybe...they were exclusive?

In which case, I was the one who was in the wrong. I was the one pining after her male, staring at him like a lovesick idiot. I'd walked by his place late at night, it didn't matter that he wasn't the reason, Breanne saw me, what else would she think? Then I'd walked right up to him last night, under the influence of Mags's potion, so far gone I'd actually been about to ask him *why not me?* The words had been right there on the tip of my tongue before she pushed me aside.

I was the problem, not her.

Me.

My phone dinged from the bed, and I walked toward it like it was a rattlesnake about to strike. I had a DM request in Nightscape. I felt sick as I clicked it open, because of course it was from Breanne.

Hey, stalker, feel free to add that pic to your wank bank. That's the closest you'll ever get to the real thing.

Then there were a whole lot of laughing emojis.

I clicked back out and shoved my phone in my pocket. Would she tell Ren? Of course she would.

"Jazzy?" Zinnia tapped on the door before she eased it open.

I tried to look normal and not like I was going to die of shame and humiliation. "Can I walk you to the gate?" I blurted. I wasn't ready to say goodbye, and I needed to get away from here. "I mean, if it'll be safe for me to walk back out on my own?"

Zinnia usually insisted on going alone. Death made sure she was protected on her hike through the demon-infested forest, but I wasn't sure he'd cover me on the way back. She studied me. "I mean, I can make sure you're safe on the way out, but I'm not sure..."

"Please," I said.

She mulled it over for several seconds. "Okay, fine, but I've got one condition. You tell me what put that look on your face."

"What look?" I said, trying to deny what was obviously plain to see.

She crossed her arms. "Like you crapped your pants in a room full of people."

I opened my mouth to protest.

"And before you even think about lying to me or telling me you don't want to worry me or burden me with your problems right before I go back, don't. This isn't my first rodeo. I've been going to Limbo for a while now, and I come back every time unscathed, don't I? No, I don't like going there or talking about it, because when I'm here, I want to enjoy every moment I have with you, with my family. It's boring there, honestly, so talk to me."

She was lying. I could tell. "Zinny..."

"Talk to me, Jazzy. Don't shut me out. I'm your big sister, so let me do my job." She grinned. "Distract me."

I shoved my feet in my boots and snatched up my jacket. "Fine. I'll fill you in on our hike." I'd do whatever Zinny needed, even if that meant telling her what a dick I'd been the last few months and what a massive idiot I'd just made of myself.

We pulled up to the entrance of Oldwood Forest thirty minutes later. It was at the southernmost end of the larger Roxburgh State Forest, and infested with a whole bunch of demons. Zinnia grabbed her large pack from the back, filled with a few more books, some of her favorite moisturizer and other toiletries, and some more clothes as well. Limbo didn't exactly cater to the living. I'd slipped in some of her favorite treats as well. Skittles, of course, and sometimes a girl just needed chocolate.

She lifted Hemlock off the car seat. "Hop up, Hemy," she said. Hemlock scurried up her arm and into the pack, his little head popping out the top to look around before disappearing inside, to nap.

I locked the car, and we headed into the forest. A lot of the forests around Roxburgh were inhabited by demons, the kinds that couldn't pass as human. Thankfully, humans were naturally repelled by the evil that flowed from the most densely populated areas, and the witches in the city used wards and spells to keep them from the rest. The safe areas were safe because Draven's pack patrolled them and kept them clear.

Usually, we'd try to avoid the demons lurking here, or if I was one of my cousins or Zinny before Death gave her protection, I'd be kicking their asses and lopping off heads left and right. But for this hike, we didn't need to worry. Death kept us concealed or kept the demons away, I wasn't sure which, but they wouldn't give us any trouble. Without Death's protection, though? I'd be demon chum.

"You heard from Mom lately?" I asked after a few minutes.

"Not for months."

"I guess she's still in Paris?"

"Your guess is as good as mine." Zinnia nudged me. "Enough about Mom. Time to spill. Tell me why you looked like you'd just sharted when I walked into your room earlier."

I rolled my eyes. "We're just going right for the jugular, then, no easing into it?"

"Nope, give me the goods."

I sighed. I'd been keeping everything to myself, so she didn't worry, but I realized not telling her when she could see I was keeping shit from her would only make her worry more. "I like someone. Okay, more than like, and while I was stalking his female's Nightscape page, I accidentally liked an old picture of his naked abs."

Zinnia was quiet a second, then she winced. "Shit."

"Yeah."

"We're talking about Ren, right? And that bitch you shoved?"

I stopped in my tracks. "How did you know?"

She gave me a gentle smile. "Jaz, I've known you had a thing for Ren for years. I was hoping you'd tell me yourself, but no. So here we are, you forced me to squeeze the truth out of you."

"You knew?" I started walking again. "I'm so embarrassed."

"What's to be embarrassed about? He's an insanely good-looking guy. Is he a manwhore? Yes. Is he fucked up probably beyond repair? Also yes. But I see the appeal. Just be careful. A male like that will only cause you pain in the long run."

"You don't have to worry about him breaking my heart." Mainly because it was already broken, but there was a more obvious reason. "He's not interested in me. I'm in no danger of him seducing, then dumping me."

She gave me a look I couldn't read. "Just promise me you'll be careful, okay? The darkness surrounding him is thick and cold. The souls who visited you, are they still with him?"

"Some, not all." Some had wandered off, slowly going mad over time, searching for something they'd never find if Ren didn't forgive himself and set them free. Not all mediums saw all spirits. And for some reason, Ren's lost souls had chosen me.

She nodded. "He needs help, and if he doesn't let someone in to give that to him, he's a broken heart waiting to happen."

"I promise you have nothing to worry about, Zin. There's no chance he'll suddenly decide he desperately wants me," I said even as a pang of hurt slid through my chest. "And you're right, his emotions are...turbulent." To put it mildly. My empathic power made it hard to be around a lot of people, which was why I stayed "tuned out" unless it was needed.

She gave me a look. "Have you considered using your healing gift on him?"

"I have, but it's not like I can force him. Wills did mention it. She was going to talk to him, but she never came back to me, so I have to assume he said no."

"Idiot," Zinny muttered.

"Yep." I won't lie, it'd been another blow. I mean, what was he so against? The type of therapy I provided, or that it was me? There was a reason all my appointments were snapped up. What I did worked, and word of mouth from my clients ensured I always had work. "So what do I do about accidently liking that post? Do you have any sage advice for your younger, extremely idiotic sister?"

"Is your name on your Nightscape account?"

"Yes. And she messaged me straight after and said that looking at that picture was the closest I'd ever get to the real thing." My face flushed hot just thinking about it.

"Okay, so basically you only have one option here."

"What's that?"

"Brazen it out. You have no shits to give. It never happened."

My cereal curdled in my stomach. "What if she tells Ren?"

"Same thing. Unaffected. No fucks given." She grinned. "If nothing else, it'll confuse the hell out of them."

We were quiet for a few minutes, and I glanced over at her. I could see the change come over Zinnia the closer we got to the gates. She stood straighter, her expression growing harder, more fierce. She was bracing for whatever would happen when she walked back through that gateway.

"Does he talk to you? Like, do you have conversations?" It seemed an insane question. Did my sister chat over breakfast with Death? *Death.*

Her gaze remained focused straight ahead. "We bargain and verbally fence. I know nothing more about Mors now than I did the first day I walked through those gates." Something moved through her eyes, something I didn't like.

"Are you scared, Zinnia? Are you scared of him?" I waited. I didn't think she'd answer or she'd feed me the same lies she always did to try to keep me from worrying.

"Yeah," she finally said. "I'm terrified of him. But so far, he hasn't hurt me. There's something, it's like...he's watching, waiting for me to do or say something, and the more time that passes, and I don't...the more volatile he becomes."

I wanted to grab her hand and drag her back the way we came, but I couldn't. She'd made a bargain and there was no going back on that. "Zinny..."

She shook her head and forced a smile. "I know after what I just told you, asking you not to worry is an impossibility, but I honestly don't think he'd physically hurt me. He rages and stomps around, but he's never raised a hand to me. If he ever had, no way would I bring Hemy with me."

"And he hasn't...he hasn't forced you to—"

"No, Jaz, I promise. He hasn't touched me."

Relief made my legs shake. *Thank the goddess.*

The small clearing appeared just ahead, a pile of unimpressive rocks and boulders sat in a mound off to the side. We strode over and Zinnia made a small slice in her palm, letting a drop of blood land on one of the stones, then she whispered the words to open the gate.

"Open sesame?"

She chuckled. "No, but so close."

The boulders started to roll, to move and reform.

Zinnia pulled me in for a tight hug. "Be good, be safe, and steer clear of fuck boys, yeah?"

I fought back my tears. She didn't need to see that. I didn't want to make this harder on her than it already was. "You got it."

"Love you, Jazzy."

"Love you, too, Zinny."

She released me, and we turned to the archway the stones and boulders had formed. Limbo was just beyond. Its dark forest was far from welcoming, and the path through it made of skulls even less so.

She didn't walk through right away, though. She waited.

"What happens now?"

"I'm waiting for him. I'm not going through until he ensures your safety home."

With the gate open and Zinnia on the other side, it didn't take long. There was a boom before something huge and black rushed through the trees.

It flew right up to the gate, so fast I stumbled back a step.

Death. He loomed at the entrance, and except for one tattooed hand curled around his long wooden staff, his entire body was concealed under his black cloak.

"Step through the gate." His voice rolled over us, deep and horrific, the sound of a million screams of terror. I wanted to cover my ears with my hands and weep. Zinnia gripped my hand, stopping me from retreating further. He thought she was going to deny him or try to renegotiate, I heard it there in that terrible voice, in the way he leaned forward as if he were waiting for an opportunity to snatch her off her feet and steal her away. His corporal form was trapped in Limbo, though he found other ways to communicate outside it. If he visited Zinnia while she was here, I didn't know.

"I will, but first I ask that you ensure Jasmine's safety out of this forest and back to her car," Zinnia said.

"Come here to me first, then I'll do as you ask."

His fingers were wrapped tightly around the staff, so tight his inked knuckles turned white. He was desperate to have her back. Death didn't like that Zinnia left him, he'd made that clear. He took another step forward and snarled when he couldn't go any further.

"You still don't trust me," Zinnia said. "I made a deal with you. I promised to come here every other month. I haven't reneged and I'm not going to now. Why do you always pull this shit? Does every fucking thing need to be some deal or a fucking bargain? Just say you'll keep my sister safe on her walk back to her car, that's it. No deal, no payment. Just do this one thing for me without a condition placed on it."

He was utterly still, silence stretching out between them.

"If you deny me, I'll have to walk her back through the forest, then come back again—"

"If she continues to search for my missing souls, she has safe passage," he said.

Zinnia blew out a breath. "Seriously? Are you fucking serious right now?" Hemy squeaked from inside the pack but stayed hidden.

Zinny said she was terrified of him, and I believed her, but she was tough and stubborn, and apparently not even Death himself could make her cower. She would keep to her end of the deal, but that didn't mean she'd make it easy on him.

"You failed to deliver the souls, which means the boon is mine," Death said. "Your sister will find them."

"It's fine. I was going to keep looking, anyway." I didn't want Zinnia dealing with a pissed-off Death because she hadn't been able to find them.

"Jazzy, I don't want you putting yourself in danger for him."

"I won't."

"If you want to leave here in a month's time, consort, then those souls need to be found," Death rumbled.

She spun on him. "You can't hold me against my will. You can't go back on the deal we made."

"If balance isn't restored, Limbo will become unstable. Chaos will ensue. Souls roaming where they shouldn't, barriers falling, gates...not opening."

Her fingers curled into fists. "You're Death, for fuck/s sake. Why can't you see them?"

"That's not how it works. Now come, do not keep me waiting."

She ignored him and pulled me in for another tight hug.

Fear had me trembling hard. How the hell was I going to do this? Yes, I'd planned to look, but I hadn't known the stakes then. What other choice did I have? "I'll find them," I said, trying to convince myself as well as Death that I was capable of doing what he asked.

"I know you can do it, Jaz. I know you can," Zinny said. "But you have to promise me you'll stay safe. That you won't do anything risky alone?"

"I promise."

"I will see you in a month, Jazzy. Even if I have to claw my way out of Limbo. I will come home."

She meant it. Nothing could stop her if she made up her mind to do something, not even breaking out of Limbo. "I'll be waiting."

Then she squared her shoulders and strode through the gate, brushing past Death as if he were of no consequence. She turned and waved, a smile on her face for my benefit, then the gate closed and she was gone, the boulders collapsing, rolling back to their pile at the edge of the clearing.

With my heart heavy and full of fear, I headed back through the forest.

354

At least Death kept his word.
I made it back to my car in one piece.

CHAPTER 6

Ren

I DRUMMED my fingers on the arm of the couch. "So...the party got a little wild the other night."

Wills sipped her tea, her lips gently curved while she watched me from the end of the couch. "Yep, though, not as wild for me. I couldn't take one of Magnolia's potions, not while I'm feeding Violet. Which was fine. I just wanted to dance and be with my sisters and cousins. I just...I wanted to be with Zinny."

I had planned to talk to Wills about the spirit I'd felt hanging around, how it was lingering longer, becoming more aggressive. I'd woken last night, the air so cold in my room that I could see it. And when it touched me, it'd burned, but seeing the sadness in Willow's eyes now, I couldn't do it. I couldn't cause her more worry, not today.

"You doing okay?" Zinnia going back to Limbo always cast a dark shadow over the family.

She nodded, but she was lying. "I've been going through our library at home, and Rose has been spending time at the council library. So far we've found nothing that'll get Zinnia out of her bargain with Death. Iris and Mags have been talking to some of the crones in the area. Agatheena told Mags she'd look into it. Hopefully something comes of that."

The deal Zinnia made with Death was that she'd live in Limbo every other month, but that would change to staying there permanently when Jasmine turned twenty-one. That was in nine months. "How's Jasmine taking all this?" I cleared my throat. After Edward talked through me, my voice had never been the same, but when I said Jasmine's name, my already fucked voice went even rougher.

"She's not saying much." Wills shook her head. "When Zinny's here, I see the way Jaz clings to her. It's killing her. I haven't talked to her yet, but Mom said she hiked to the gateway with her this time and saw her off. She met Death—"

"The fuck!" The words exploded from me, loud and growled, and Willow actually jumped. Violet let out a cry from the other room.

Willow blinked at me and put down her tea. "It's fine. Death gave her safe passage back, apparently." She stood and went to get Violet, and I sat there breathing in through my nose and out my fucking mouth so I didn't lose my shit. I'd lived in that forest for almost two years, and the thought of Jasmine in there alone was bad enough, but standing face to face with Death? Fuck no. She was way too fragile, too breakable. So fucking vulnerable.

Willow walked back in, Violet held against her. At the sight of them both, the storm inside me increased. They had Warrick, they were both safe, protected by him, by his whole pack, but as her familiar, the desire to protect Willow and now Violet as well, was a fundamental part of me.

"Vi okay? I didn't mean to—"

"She's fine." She sat back down, and Violet drifted off in her mother's arms.

"That was a pretty big reaction," she said carefully.

I forced my muscles to relax. "You've already been through enough. You're already worried about Zinnia, last thing you need is to be worrying about Jasmine as well." That was all true, but I recognized that wasn't the reason I'd reacted the way I had.

The idea of Jasmine being hurt or put in danger—I didn't fucking like it.

"Zinnia wouldn't have let her go with her if she thought it was dangerous."

I nodded and forced myself to take a sip of my lukewarm coffee. "Yeah, of course."

Willow shook her head, a small smile curling her lips. "Jazzy's changed so much. When you first met her, pink was her favorite color, and she was so painfully shy it hurt to watch her around people who weren't family. Now?" She chuckled. "Well, two nights ago she was dancing in a room full of people in only a pair of shorts and a painted-on, glow-in-the-dark bra. She almost had a throw-down with a wolf, she's covered in tattoos, and she talks to dead people for a living."

I swallowed, my mouth weirdly fucking dry all of a sudden. Jasmine had looked...beautiful...and completely and utterly untouchable.

"She's actually consoling herself over Zinny leaving with another tattoo."

"Yeah?" I gripped the arm of the couch tighter.

Wills pressed a kiss to Vi's little head. "A bigger piece. She drew the rough outline for it a while ago. She finally got it exactly how she wants it. Rome's doing it now."

My thigh muscles clenched, and I had to fight with myself not to stand.

"So what's going on with you? You were gone a couple days."

There was worry in her eyes. I forced the tension from my shoulders and smiled. "Just busy at work." That wasn't entirely true, but I wasn't going to tell her I'd been too fucked in the head to be around anyone.

"I was worried, then I heard about you and that Silver Claw female. Breanne? So I assumed you were with her." Hurt filled her eyes. "I wish you'd told me yourself."

I stilled. Breanne? "Told you what?"

"Is she your mate, Ren? Is that it? You can tell me. I know it's scary and you might not think you're ready, but you deserve to be happy. So if you've found your female—"

"Who the fuck told you that?" The armrest groaned when I gripped it again. Bree sure as fuck wasn't my mate. I didn't have a mate. I didn't want one. I could barely function as it was; how the fuck could I protect and provide for someone else as well.

Wills studied me. "Jazzy said something to Mags. Sounds like Breanne staked some kind of claim over you."

"And she told Jasmine I was her mate?"

Willow frowned. "I mean, I don't know exactly what was said. Jaz called her your female, said she saw her at your place the other night when she was out walking. You guys seem to hook up a lot, I guess we all just assumed—"

"Well, don't. We're not mates. We aren't even friends. We fuck sometimes, but I'm done with that." I shoved my fingers through my hair and stood, pacing away.

"She was with you last week according to Jaz."

Pressure built in my chest, growing tighter and tighter. The need to fucking roar, to join the roaring already vibrating through my skull, damn near choked me. I didn't want Jasmine...fuck, anyone...thinking that shit. My reaction was extreme, even I could see it, and the only reason I was able to swallow the anger down was the sight of Violet lying against her mother, my instinct to protect them so much stronger than my outrage. "It won't be happening again."

"It's no big deal. Be with whoever you want." Willow stood.

"I don't want to be with her. I don't want to be with any fucking one." The confession fell from my lips before I could stop it.

Willow closed the space between us. "Then why are you?"

Fuck. She knew, she knew what I was doing and why. No, she didn't know the details of my time possessed by that twisted fuck, but she knew I used that shit as an escape, because Willow knew me better than anyone. We had a connection that ran deeper than the one I had even with my own parents. "You know why," I ground out.

She cupped the side of my face, and I flinched, then forced myself to stay still when anyone I loved touching me made me want to run like fuck the other way. Holding Violet felt like the sweetest thing in the world, and it made me want to flay my own skin from my body. Hands like mine, the things they'd done, they didn't belong on someone so innocent and precious. But denying Willow, pushing her away again, pretending Violet wasn't here, would kill her, and I couldn't do that to her.

Wills brushed her thumb over my beard. "I've known you since you were fourteen years old, Renny. You knocked on the door, all gangly limbs and boundless energy, and I loved you instantly. My sweet familiar. You'd finally found me. Goddess, Ren, you're my brother, my son, my best friend... my sweet fox, you're a part of my soul, right alongside Violet and Warrick."

I couldn't do this. "Wills—"

"You've come so far...after everything you've been through. You've come such a long way. Don't stop. Promise me you won't stop trying, that you'll keep pushing. I need you. Vi needs you. Do you understand?"

She saw me, right into my very soul, and I suddenly felt as though she'd stood behind me every time I paused on that cliff's edge, every time I almost stepped off.

I nodded, and she leaned into me, her head to my chest, and I wrapped my arms around her, locking my hands together so they didn't touch her, didn't taint her.

"If you leave me, Ren, if you choose to leave me, I'll never forgive you," she said against my chest, proving just how much she saw.

I strode out of Willow and War's place a few minutes later, feeling wired as fuck. Despite my efforts, I was still hurting Wills. She was worried about me, and I didn't know how to ease her fears because I couldn't make her any promises. I'd fight it, the darkness as thick and sticky as tar, for as long as I could, but it wasn't getting easier.

As I strode along the caves, I told myself I was just walking, no destination in mind, but I knew exactly where I was going—to get my fix, my elixir, the antibiotics for the infection festering inside me.

She doesn't want to see you. Why would she want to see a pathetic piece of shit who carves himself up like a psycho? Edward's voice invaded my mind, and I forced it back down deep.

The buzz of the tattoo gun reached me first, a steady hum over low music and murmured voices, over the occasional crack of balls on the pool table. Roman did his work in an alcove off the common room and kept his gear set up there. Nothing unusual about me walking in there. I did it all the time. I hung out here more often than not. No one would think I was there because of Jasmine.

I walked in, and as hard as I tried to play it cool, to not look at her as soon as I entered the room, the pull was too strong. My fucking head swung her way as soon as I stepped foot through the doorway. The pressure in my chest I'd felt when I was talking to Willow returned tenfold as soon as I saw her.

Light flooded the large alcove where Rome was working on her. Jasmine lay on her back on the massage table, feet crossed at the ankles. She wore jeans, and her stomach and chest were fully exposed, except for a thin strip of white fabric covering her nipples. There was new ink already on her stomach and upper chest. Rome was bent over her now, one hand on the inside of her cleavage, pressing on the soft flesh to keep it taut, pulling it outward as he inked something on her breast.

Jasmine lay still, both forearms across her eyes. Her lips were relaxed, and she murmured something to Rome, making the hound grin. The pressure in my chest grew, and the roaring in my head was fucking deafening. I took a step in their direction—

"Ren, brother. Game?" Relic said, his voice having the effect of a record scratch through the noise in my head.

"Yeah."

He passed me a pool cue, and I motioned for him to go first. I'd never played so badly in my life, because all I could focus on was the buzz of that fucking tattoo machine and their murmured voices, interrupted now and then by Jasmine's soft laugher. My fox was clawing to be free, snarling and whining. He wanted to go over there. He wanted to snap and snarl at Rome even though he knew the hellhound could bite his head off with one snap of his teeth.

"You want in on the pit tonight?" Relic said absently.

My fox also knew we were faster, more agile than a hound. "Who's fighting?" Not that it mattered, I needed to blow off some steam. Badly.

"Me, Loth, Fender, Jag, Rome." Relic grinned. "Whoever else is in the mood for me to hand them their asses."

"I'm in."

"You're a glutton for punishment, but I like that about you," he said and took his shot.

The hounds had trained me several years ago, when Willow's role in the family changed and she became her coven's Keeper. She'd been in danger all the time, wasn't mated to Warrick yet, and as her familiar it had been my job to protect her. I couldn't fight my way out of a cardboard box, and because it was impossible for me to stand down, since protecting her was literally part of my DNA, she'd brought me here. It was either that or watch me die trying. The hounds had kicked my ass repeatedly. They'd been hard on me, but fair, and not without mercy. I got a few broken bones, some scars, but I left knowing how to fight really fucking well.

Fender whistled, and I lifted my head as Jasmine jumped off the table, one arm across her chest. There were four butterflies on her stomach as if they were flying down and more flying upward all from a larger one between her breasts; one just above her cleavage, one on her upper chest, one by her collarbone and another on the side of her neck, all different colors and species.

"Looks fucking awesome, Jaz," Relic said.

She grinned, blushing when the rest of the hounds howled their agreement. She checked it out in the mirror Rome had there, then spun to him, beaming, and threw her arms around him. He patted her on the back, then dipped his face into her neck and scented her.

The urge to tear his nose off his fucking face and make him eat it filled me as the roar in my chest grew so intense I had to grit my teeth so it didn't burst free. What the fuck was wrong with me? Hounds were tactile, they scented, they touched, it didn't mean shit, I knew this. Yes, I had a fucked-up obsession with her, a weird connection, but I'd never go there with Jasmine. And yes, I recognized how beautiful she was, but I thought lots of things were beautiful, that didn't mean I wanted to fuck them. She was too young, too fucking innocent, especially for someone like me.

But when Roman started swiping antiseptic cream on her fucking chest, the way he touched her, the way she looked at him—I had to turn away, *this close* to going over there and—what? What did I think I was going to do?

I finally heard her saying goodbye, and I couldn't stop myself from turning back. She had her shirt on again, and for some reason, that soothed us—my fox wasn't baring his teeth anymore, at least.

Her gaze lifted, finding me, and she froze, just for a split second. Her throat worked before she quickly looked away and started for the door.

"Jaz," Rome called.

She turned back, and he tossed something to her. She caught it, lifted it, and laughed. Peanut M&M's, her favorite.

I didn't like that either. Not at all. So much so, there was no stopping my feet from following her. "Catch you later tonight," I said to Relic and told myself I was leaving anyway, when I knew I was full of shit.

I'd tried to convince myself there was nothing going on between Jaz and Rome, but now? They were close, too fucking close. Fuck, were they...were they actually together?

I walked out and it was as if my fox was locked on to her scent like a fucking bloodhound, following her as if his life depended on it.

And I let him.

I walked out into the parking lot in time to see her drive away.

I got in the hearse and followed.

CHAPTER 7

Jasmine

I STRODE into my field at the end of the street and breathed in the cool air. The scent of this place helped soothe me instantly. Walking to my favorite oak tree, I kicked off my shoes, pulled off my socks, and sat down, burying my toes in the earth. Placing my hands down beside me, I let tendrils of magic flow downward. The earth replied, sending vibrations back through my feet and hands, the oak humming softly behind me.

When I felt off-kilter, or alone, this place patched me up, stitched me back together. I'd been coming here a lot since Zinny started spending time in Limbo.

And now that I was alone again, all my fears bubbled to the surface. Somehow, I had to find those missing souls or my sister could be trapped in Limbo indefinitely. Who the hell did Death think I was? I was not my sister. Zinnia was the capable one, the powerful one. Hunting for the souls while she was here had been easy. She led, I followed. I always followed.

Breathe.

You can do this. You have to do this.

I forced myself to focus on the tender skin on my chest and stomach and the new ink Rome had just given me instead of thinking about what I had to do, or what Zinnia was doing now and if she was okay.

I took another deep breath and wriggled, getting more comfortable.

The packet of peanut M&M's crackled in my pocket. I smiled and slipped it out. Relic always had them for me on movie nights. He'd started doing it after seeing Rome give them to me. I liked to snack when I was nervous, and so I brought some along when I got my first tattoo. Now it'd become a tradition between Rome and me. He always had some for me whenever I got a tattoo, even though I wasn't nervous anymore. No, getting new ink helped me get out of my own head, and after saying goodbye to Zinny, I'd needed that more than ever.

I popped a candy in my mouth and closed my eyes. *Think, Jaz.* I needed a next step. Had souls ever gone missing before? If Zinnia knew, she hadn't said. Where would I find that out? We had a library full of our histories, but Death was a god, and in his case more closely linked to demons. I'd need access to a demon library. I knew where one existed, but I'd need help to get to it. I'd need safe passage.

There was a chill in the air, but the early autumn sun was warm against the tops of my feet and ankles.

I kept my eyes closed and tried to focus on the earth and the healing energy it was giving back—but my mind kept wandering.

Ren had been at the clubhouse while I was there. I don't know for how long, but as soon as I saw him my stupid heart had filled with...elation, quickly followed by hurt. Ugh. My heart was an idiot.

I couldn't get out of the den and the clubhouse fast enough. If Ren was there, Breanne probably wasn't far behind, and the last thing I wanted right now was to see the two of them all over each other, or have her bring up that I'd liked that photo to humiliate me.

No, it wasn't Ren's fault that I was in love with him, or that he didn't love me back. It did fucking suck, though. Goddess, if I could take these feelings away, I would, in a heartbeat.

I felt a gentle push against my magic, a little rush of joy, then more, until the energy I felt was like ten overexcited puppies jumping all around me at once. Something tickled my cheek, and I opened my eyes and chuckled. At least ten mourning cloak butterflies danced and dived around me, their happiness at finding me infectious. I held out my arms, and they landed, then took flight, over and over again. Their love for me was instant, beautiful, and utterly pure. My familiars were tiny in size, but their love for me was overwhelming, all-encompassing. I often wondered how it was possible for such tiny beings to love so huge.

One fluttered around my face and landed on my head, and I giggled again, letting their happiness and excitement fill me.

Movement caught my eyes, and I looked across the field. My heart thumped hard in my chest.

Ren stood at the edge, watching me.

And instead of taking off or looking away when he realized I saw him, he strode toward me. My flight instincts kicked in, but I made myself stay sitting, even while my heart galloped faster.

Calm the fuck down.

My new little familiars sensed my unease and immediately tried to soothe me, landing on my skin as if they were giving me a hug, or trying to protect me in some way.

Ren stopped several feet from me, his gaze moving over my bare feet, my arms, where most of the butterflies had landed, then my head where at least two were sitting.

He shoved his fingers through his russet hair. "Hey."

"Hey." I tried to sound unaffected, but it wasn't easy. Being this close, and alone, with the male I loved beyond all reason was hard as hell.

"I was, ah...just going for a walk and spotted you sitting here," he said and rubbed the back of his neck.

His bicep bulged, and my gaze took in the jagged scar there. It looked raw, almost new, when I knew it wasn't. "Right." He must have left the clubhouse soon after me. I'd dropped my car off at the house and come straight here.

"You come here a lot," he said, looking around.

"I like it here."

He took another step closer. "So what kind of butterflies are those?"

"Mourning cloaks."

"They the only kind in this field?"

What was with all the questions? "There are others, but it's starting to get too cold for many of them."

He nodded slowly, his gaze sliding to my chest. "Saw your new ink." He crossed his arms, then uncrossed them. "Wills said you designed it yourself."

This was so freaking awkward. Why was he here? Had Bree told him what I'd done and now he was here to let me down easy? My face heated. "I did, yeah."

"It's cool... Really cool."

"Thanks." The silence dragged out. I couldn't take it. "Ren—"

"So are you and Rome—"

"What?"

We both stopped talking over each other, and when he said nothing more, I made myself speak. "Are me and Rome, what?"

He cleared his throat, his gaze darting around the field before he shoved his hands in his pockets. "Together? You with him now?"

He thought Roman and I were together? Together, together? I studied him. Why was he so stiff? And why was he here acting all awkward and weird? Although there was literally zero going on between Rome and me, I found myself shrugging, like an idiot, because if he thought I had feelings for someone, anyone else, then maybe he wouldn't think I was a giant loser with a crush on him when Bree told him I liked his abs pic. *Cringe.* But then maybe he already knew that I was hopelessly in love with him? As hard as I tried to hide my feelings, the guy wasn't blind. I acted like a damned fool around him, blushing and stuttering, or snapping and snarling. My cheeks felt warm all of a sudden.

His brows went up, and he crossed his arms again, the muscles flexing, his veins bulging. "You think that's a good idea, Jasmine? Rome's way too fucking old for you."

Whoa. What? So now he was going for the concerned friend approach? "You could say Rome is too old for everyone." He was a thousand years old, at least. "I, on the other hand, am twenty, and definitely old enough to decide who I spend time with." I needed to stop insinuating Rome and I were something we weren't, but Ren was starting to piss me off.

"He's gonna hurt you."

I stood, and my little crew of mourning cloaks fluttered around me, sensing my volatile emotions. "Roman's one of the best males I know," I said, telling the truth. The fact there was less than zero sexual chemistry between us was beside the point. "He'd never hurt me."

Ren flinched, but then his jaw hardened. "And when his mate shows up and he tosses you aside like yesterday's garbage? Will he still be the best male you know then?"

"How do you know he hasn't already found her?" WHAT? What the hell was I doing? *Shut up, Jasmine, now!* I mean, I didn't say *I* was his mate. I could be talking about anyone, right?

Shit.

"He's found his mate?" Ren asked, his face going utterly blank, gaze locked on me.

I shrugged again, not answering. "So where's Breanne? You two are usually joined at the..." *Lips? Genitals?* "Hip."

His expression went dark at my question. "Breanne and I are nothing and never will be."

My pulse was going mad, and my palms were sweaty. "She's saying otherwise."

"She's full of shit," he bit out.

Stop talking. "You obviously made her think you wanted more." Apparently, there was no shutting me up.

"I told her what I wanted. She said she wanted the same. We fucked a few times, but that definitely won't be happening again."

My heart slammed into the back of my ribs, stupid, dumb relief filling me. "Okay, well, thanks for the update." In trying to hide my misplaced relief and the unwarranted glee I'd suddenly felt that they weren't an actual item, I went too far the other way and ended up sounding like a sarcastic brat instead of the cool and unaffected I was going for.

He frowned. "It's just that you told Willow that Bree and I were together, and I wanted to...I don't know, clear it up."

"Oh, you did." It was as if some alternate version of me had taken over and I was watching from a distance as I opened my mouth and more venom poured out. "You don't catch feelings. Fucking is just fucking, and if someone is stupid enough to catch feelings for you, you'll dump them like a hot flaming turd? Noted."

He shifted in place, his biceps bunching again, the muscles in his jaw doing a dance as he gritted his teeth.

I felt like a giant asshole. "Ren—"

"Sounds like you got me all figured out, Jaz. I guess we're done here," he said, then strode away, back toward his house.

I inwardly screamed as I watched him go, wondering what the hell had just happened.

>)⟩)●⟨(⟨

Ren

Fire burned in my gut as I strode through the tunnels under the clubhouse and toward the fighting pit. I could already hear the hounds, their howls and cheers at whoever was already fighting. Aggression pumped wildly through me. Images of Jasmine filled my head—the way she'd looked when I'd followed her to that field, her sitting under the oak tree, her feet bare, her blond hair still streaked with pink disheveled around her delicate face, giggling as butterflies fluttered around her.

What the fuck was wrong with me? Why had I followed her? Why did I give a fuck what she thought? But I did, and the urgency to tell her there was nothing between Breanne and I had ridden me the entire way there. I was a fucking idiot, desperate for her approval. Why? I jammed my fingers through my hair and sucked in a breath, trying to gather some control, but then my brain hit me with a greatest hits of what she'd said, and *"Roman's one of the best males I know"* was a personal favorite.

They couldn't seriously be together. She couldn't be Rome's mate. Willow would know, right? But then she'd been so busy with Violet she could have missed it.

I walked into a large cavern. The pit was in the center, dug into the ground, the walls blackened and charred. Hounds surrounded it, watching as Relic and Fender went at it. Powerful blows landed one after the other, smacking against flesh. Blood sprayed the wall as Relic slammed his fist into the other male's face. Fender grinned, spitting out a tooth, and opened his hand, flames igniting across his fingers before he sent a blast at Relic. Snarling, Relic dodged it, then delivered a final blow, knocking Fender on his ass.

The hounds stomped and howled, and Relic walked over and helped his brother up. I searched the room. Rome stood at the edge, shirtless, ready to go next. When the pit was empty, the hound jumped in. Jagger was about to follow, but something came over me, the aggression in me reaching all new heights, and I jumped in before Jag could.

Rome's head tilted to the side, taking me in, not missing what I was giving off. He grinned, amused. "You think you can take me, fox?"

"Not in here to make out with you, hound." I wasn't as big or powerful as the hounds, and I'd never fought Rome before. I'd sparred with him, he'd been at some of my training sessions, most of the hounds here had at different times over the years, but we'd never fought in the pit, not like this. I'd watched him, though. He was brutal, relentless, and like all the hounds merciless in a fight.

I wasn't arrogant enough to think I could take Rome out easily, or at all. But I was fast, and I could shift quickly and cause a lot of damage before I was knocked on my ass. I could make him hurt. Bleed. And I didn't care how much damage was inflicted on me for that to happen.

Edward's laughter rang through my mind. *Rome can protect her. You can't even look after yourself. You make her skin crawl; she told you so herself.*

I jerked my head from side to side, shaking the voice from my head, and focused on Roman. My fox was right there with me, just below my skin, ears pointed, springing on his hind legs, going against every one of his ingrained instincts to flee. Something was driving him to fight as much as me.

Rome's eyes narrowed. "You got a problem with me, pup?"

Yeah, I wasn't hiding anything from him. The hounds used the pit to blow off steam, to keep their fighting skills sharp, and to settle scores. Kicking each other's asses amused them. Now that I was standing opposite the other male, I knew exactly why I was here.

"Yeah, I've got a problem," I said before I knew the words were coming, before I allowed myself to acknowledge what that problem was. "I have a problem with you sniffing around barely legal females."

Roman's chin jerked up. "What the fuck you talking about?"

I don't know where that came from. She was twenty years old, not some teenager; hell, I was only a few years older. I forgot sometimes that I just felt as if I were sixty despite my actual age. The rage in me, that pressure behind my chest, built to unstoppable proportions.

"Jasmine." Her name burst from me in a snarl.

His brows lowered, his amber eyes boring into me, then his lips curled up. "That female's far from a fucking pup, even by human standards. Jazzy's old enough to do whatever the fuck she wants." He grinned, taunting me. "Seems you're worried, fox, that right now...that's me."

My claws burst from the ends of my fingers, and I dove at him, using my speed to my advantage, tearing into his side before swinging and slamming my fist into his jaw. His head jerked back, his lip splitting. I'd taken him by surprise, but I wouldn't get that opportunity again.

He grinned at me, blood smearing his fangs, and punched me in the gut, throwing me across the pit like he was swatting a fly. I flew off the ground, and back at him, punching, kicking, clawing wherever I could get him. He hissed and growled, his fists like anvils smashing into my body every time I came at him.

I spun, punching him in the kidney, grabbed the fist coming at me, and spun back around behind him, slamming my foot into the back of his leg. He dropped to one knee, but only for a moment, before he tossed me like a football across the pit and into the wall, cracking at least two of my ribs.

I ignored the pain radiating through my body, the taste of my own blood, and ran back, time and again. Returning blow for blow. The hound's healing was a lot faster than mine, and his cuts and bruises were already fading. Our fighting techniques were different. I was relying on speed, dodging, spinning, kicking. Roman was all about brute force, using his fists like sledgehammers.

If we both shifted, I'd already be dead. He did use his claws, though, and I hissed when he dug them into my side. Black spots danced in front of my eyes, and I shook my head, trying to clear it, then slammed my fist into his nose. Blood sprayed me before he tossed me aside again.

I staggered back to my feet, about to charge him again—

Warrick was suddenly in front of me, shoving me back. "Enough."

"Not done," I snarled and tried to push past him.

"You're fucking done," he said and all but tossed me out of the pit.

He followed, and when I tried to get back in, he planted a hand to my chest. "You proved your point, you can fight. You fucked up Rome, you made him bleed. But he heals a fuck of a lot faster than you, and if you don't get your wounds looked at now, you'll bleed out and die. Wills will be sad and fucked off at me for not doing what I am now. So go get that shit taken care of."

Rome jumped out of the pit and grinned at me, barely a scratch on him now. "Here for round two when you are, pup," he said, then turned his back, dismissing me.

I took a step toward him. If I had a knife—

My brain screeched to a halt, the rage draining away instantly. The fucked-up direction of my thoughts was enough to stop me from charging after him. I got the fuck out of there.

CHAPTER 8

Ren

I STUMBLED DOWN THE TUNNEL. I just needed to stay conscious long enough to get home.

The door opened ahead of me, and Willow rushed out, her eyes widening when she saw me. Fucking Warrick ratted me out.

"What the hell were you thinking? War said you wouldn't stop." She helped me into their place.

I scowled, while my fox whined, happy to see her, wanting her comfort. "Your mate has a big fucking mouth."

"He was worried you'd bleed out." She shoved me down the hall. "Spare room. Now." Then she rushed off.

Violet's door was open, and I leaned against the jamb. She was in her bed, her little chest rising and falling, so vulnerable, so precious. I'd do anything to protect her, to stop anyone from hurting her—even make her mate, whoever they turned out to be, bleed if I didn't think he was good enough for her. That's why I fought with Rome, right? Because he wasn't good enough for Jasmine, because she was Willow's family and she deserved better.

I looked at the mural she'd painted for Vi. Jaz was kind, caring, and so incredibly talented. Her dad had nothing to do with his daughters, her mom had fucking left her when she was still a kid. She needed people to look out for her, especially while Zinnia was in Limbo.

Something orange caught my eye. It was the tip of a pointed ear, and below it, amber eyes glowed among the leaves.

It was me.

My heart thumped behind my ribs. Is that how she saw me? Hiding, watching? Always at a distance?

I mean, it made sense, that she'd paint me, right? This was Violet's room and I was her mother's familiar.

Wills took my arm and all but dragged me to the spare room. She had a bunch of towels and tossed several over the bed. "Now lie down before you fall down." She handed me another towel. "Hold this to your side. We need to stop the bleeding."

Willow took off again and was back a minute later with her supplies. She winced as she carefully lifted the towel. "He got you deep."

"I'm fine."

"You're not fucking fine. Look at you!" Her gaze moved over me, lingering on the scar across my chest. Pain filled her eyes, but she quickly looked away. Did she suspect? Did she know that self-mutilation was my thing now? The thing that kept me as close to sane as I was capable of getting. She'd never said anything.

"You've fought in the pit before, but you've never let things go this far. Why did you do this?" Her green eyes latched on to mine. "Tell me."

I couldn't. I barely comprehended it myself. I thought I was already as far past sanity as I could go, but it turned out I was wrong. "I just wanted to fight, Wills, it's not that deep."

"Bullshit," she said as she cleaned the deep gouges. "Something's bothering you, I can tell."

"Apart from the *savagely murdering a bunch of people* thing, you mean?" I said, then tried to crack a smile like a fucking psycho.

She didn't smile, she looked pissed. "Would you just fucking talk to me?"

This whole thing with Jasmine, yeah, I wasn't getting into it with Willow. How would I ever explain it? She was Willow's younger cousin, so of course I was feeling...protective, and then there was the connection between us, because of the message she'd given me—and that she knew... she knew what I'd been forced to do to those people because they'd shown her everything. Oh, and yeah, I had pictures of her on my phone that I obsessed over because even when I couldn't have the real thing, her eyes on me stopped me from killing myself—but I'd never touch her in a million years because I was stained with death and blood.

Not that she would ever be mine, because she was Rome's.

Fuck.

I thought about the mural, the way she'd painted me, summing me up so easily. Jasmine saw me, like no one else.

"Ren?"

"I've been feeling a spirit around me...not the normal shit at work. They're not moving along as quickly," I blurted, telling her something I'd already planned to, just not yet. But it was either this or tell her about Jasmine and all the shit with her that even I didn't understand.

She straightened. "How long have you felt them?"

I shrugged. "A couple months, I guess. I don't know why they're lingering, but it's getting worse." I lifted my arm, showing her where one of them had touched me. There was a handprint burned into my skin. "Wouldn't mind some help sorting it out."

"A spirit did that?" Wills asked, worry in her gaze but also a small amount of relief. This was something she could actually help me with.

"Yeah."

"Why didn't you tell me?"

"I wasn't sure it was anything to worry about at first."

"We'll sort it out, I promise. We'll get whoever it is to move along." She swiped some numbing balm over my side and pinched my skin together. "I'll need to sew up these larger slices to stop the bleeding."

I nodded and closed my eyes. Once the soul moved on, things would go back to the way they were. My fox pressed against my skin and whined, telling me I was full of shit.

"We'll get it sorted tonight," Wills said.

›› ›- ◉ -(‹‹

Jasmine

Aunt Daisy and Arthur were out for date night somewhere. Else was in her workroom, which meant so was Stan. And I was curled up on a chair, watching TV and chatting with Mags, who was cuddled up with her crow-shifter mate, Bram.

I just needed a moment to chill after a full day of seeing clients, and fruitlessly searching for Death's missing souls. Unfortunately, there'd been no mention of any recent hauntings or ghost activity in the Roxburgh area on any of the human ghost hunting websites or online groups I'd found.

"Mags?"

"Yeah?"

"When you deliver a soul to Limbo, do you ever see Zinny?" I'd wondered, but I'd never asked before. I don't know why, maybe fear that she might have seen something...bad.

She shook her head, her eyes softening, and held out the bowl of popcorn to me. "I'm usually in and out pretty fast. I always look for her, but that's not really how it works. When I'm there, I'm in that soul's own "personal" limbo. Like the space they occupy there is created from something in their memories. I'm there, but I'm not *there*. Once I pass through the forest and reach the end of the skull path, I'm in that spirit's eternal resting place. Not in Zinny and Death's world, or Limbo as they see it."

I wasn't sure if I was relieved or disappointed. "So I take it you have no leads on the missing souls you want to share?"

Mags shook her head. "No, dammit. The other reapers have been looking as well. Hadeon's had no luck either. You'd have a better chance than us, though. I only see a soul here on Earth when they're ready to move on, same for Hadeon and the rest of Lucifer's reapers. We're not like you, we're not mediums."

"Me and Zinny found nothing. I have a few ideas, though." How I was going to execute those ideas, I still didn't have a freaking clue. "Can we keep Death's warning between us for now? No reason to freak everyone out just yet." My family had tried to help us find the souls when Zinnia first came home, and like us, for an entire month, the whole family had turned over every single stone, searched every bit of information at our disposal, and had come up with nothing. Telling them what was at stake, the possibility of Zinnia being trapped there if I failed, would only freak everyone out when there was nothing more they could do.

"You got it. Mom and Else would lose their minds. You're the expert here, Jazzy. I'm at your disposal. We all are. You need help, say the word."

I didn't feel like an expert, far from it, but I did have a place to start. One that wasn't quite as horrifying as going to the head demon's place of residence, an old, decommissioned asylum, and poking around his bookshelves. "Well, actually I will take you up on that—"

"What's up?" Willow said, walking into the living room.

"Wills, hey, what are you doing here?" Mags asked, as surprised as I was that she was here this time of night.

I couldn't decipher the look on her face. Her green eyes came to me. "I need to speak with Jazzy, actually. Got a minute?"

"Yeah, of course."

I followed her from the room, and the vibe coming off my cousin was seriously tense. She was worried. Maybe even scared. "Everything okay?"

"Not exactly." Her hands were shaking.

"Wills?"

She looked down at her hands, at the way they trembled, and shook them out. "Don't mind me, I'm kinda freaking out, probably for no good reason. It's Ren. He fought in the pit earlier. The way Warrick describes it, he was blinded by rage and didn't care if he got hurt."

I gripped the back of the chair so I didn't react in a way that gave my feelings for Ren away because instant panic filled me as well. "Is he okay?"

She nodded. "Physically, he'll heal quickly, but he's struggling and keeping it to himself again. I finally got out of him that there's a soul hanging around him. He said it's getting closer. It touched him. It marked him, Jaz, burned him. I tried not to let him see how terrified I am. But I'm so scared he'll go fox and run away and I'll lose him all over again. He needs you, your gift. Anything I do will only be temporary, and Ren needs a more permanent solution. We need to know what's really going on. Do you think you can help him?"

Whatever was going on between Ren and I, none of it mattered, not when it came to this. This was serious. The last few years, Zinny had taught me all she knew. This was my specialty. Whether or not I'd wanted this gift, I had it, and I'd learned all I could to master it. "I'll need to assess the situation, but I'm confident I can help him."

Her tense shoulders lost some of their stiffness. "I told him I'd be by tonight."

Nerves zipped around my belly. "Let me grab a few things and we can go."

"It's one of them, isn't it?" she said stopping me. "One of the people he was forced to kill."

"I think so, yes," I said as gently as I could.

She nodded, and I rushed upstairs and gathered everything I thought I'd need, then we told Mags we were heading off for a bit and left for Ren's place. The last time I'd walked past there at night, Breanne had been outside, wearing one of Ren's shirts. Would she be here now?

Wills strode up to his door and knocked before opening it and walking in without waiting. "Renny? We're here."

I looked around. His place was tidy but not overly homey. There was a shirt tossed over the back of the couch and a couple empty beer cans on the coffee table and not much else.

"Hey," he said, distracted as he walked in, and I had to stop my gasp when I saw the damage to his face. His gaze sliced to me. "Jaz...I didn't know...Willow never said..."

Willow's gaze slid from Ren to me and back, worry crossing her face. "Zinny and Jaz are the only witches in the family who have the gifts you need."

375

He thrust his fingers through his chestnut hair. His knuckles were split, still healing, and his battered and bruised face darkened. "Yeah, of course."

Willow noticed as well. "Jasmine won't say anything to anyone about what she sees or hears here. This is just between us, yeah?"

He nodded, and that muscle in his jaw jumped. He was clenching his teeth again. He did that a lot around me, as if he were constantly biting something back, holding something in.

Willow's phone rang and she quickly answered. "What's up?"

Warrick's voice filled the room, Violet's wail right after. She'd hit speaker. "Dove, Vi's messed all through the bed, and I can't find the clean stuff. There's...fuck, there's shit everywhere, and I'm trying to fill her little tub, but every time I put her down, she cries harder."

Wills looked up at us. "Is Relic at the clubhouse? Can he help you?"

Relic was also good with Vi. She liked him.

"He's on patrol."

"I've got this," I said to Wills, because I could tell she was feeling torn. "We'll be fine." Just Ren and me, alone, that won't be awkward at all. I inwardly cringed, thinking about our conversation in the field and what I'd implied. And let's not forget the fact that I'd liked a photo of his bare abs on his girlfriend's Nightscape page.

"You sure?" Her gaze was on Ren.

"I'm fine, Wills. Jaz will sort it out," he said, not looking at me.

He walked her to the door and opened it. Willow stopped, and she studied his face. "You're looking a bit better. Your healing's kicked in."

"I've had worse. Stop fussing."

Her mouth twisted to the side. "I'm still gonna kick Rome's ass when I see him next."

I froze, and Ren stiffened, his shoulders squaring. "No, you're going to say nothing and leave it alone."

She grumbled. "Fine, but I'm pissed off with him."

"I challenged him, not the other way around. And he was just as fucked up; he just heals faster."

I'd lied to Ren, implied Rome and me were an item, then he went to the clubhouse and challenged him?

Wills nodded, but she still didn't look happy. She finally said goodbye to both of us and left. Ren shut the door, and his shoulders were stiff as hell as he turned to face me. There were several questions on the tip of my tongue. Why did you fight Rome? Was top of the list. I swallowed it down, though. I was here for a reason, and that needed to be my main focus.

"So what happens now?" he said, pretending that entire conversation didn't happen in front of me, like the one we'd had in the field was a figment of my imagination.

"You tell me what's been going on and I fix it," I said, doing the same.

I listened while he explained how spirits came and went through the funeral home. "There's always someone here, but in the distance, you know, and it's never bothered me, well, not until..." He rubbed his hands on his jean-covered thighs. "But lately, they're closer."

"You feel more than one?"

"I'm not sure. You can't see them?"

I shook my head. "Right now I'm blocking them." It was as if someone were calling, and I could choose to pick up the call or not. "I can feel them, though. There's definitely more than one." I felt them around Ren all the time. I'd assumed he didn't. But I couldn't decide how much of a risk they were to Ren or to me until I let them reach me again, which meant I'd have to take some extra safety measures. "So you're more aware of...a presence around you?"

"Yeah, they've touched me, a cold hand on my skin, bumping up against me. Then last night..." He lifted his arm, showing me a burn in the outline of a hand. "This happened."

Seriously not good. I schooled my features so I didn't freak him out. They were getting desperate.

He cleared his throat. "Is there a chance they could..." He clenched his fists. "Do more?"

Like possess him? That's what he was asking. I kept all traces of the alarm I was feeling off my face. He was worried enough as it was. I saw the question in his eyes, the question he didn't want to ask, and we both knew the answer, whether he would admit it to himself or not. He knew who was haunting him, just like I did. "Wills inked you with the same rune as the hounds?"

He nodded.

"Can I see it?"

"Yeah." He paused for a second, his gaze going flat, then he reached back and tugged his shirt off, tossing it on the couch.

I gasped, unable to hold it in this time. He was bruised and battered, and going by the darker color at his ribs, he had to have broken at least a couple of them. Wills had obviously stitched the deeper cuts at his side. "Jesus, Ren."

His eyes flashed, gold bursting through amber, his fox staring back at me as well. "It's nothing."

"It doesn't look like nothing." I stepped closer, lifting a hand to touch him before I realized what I was about to do. I quickly dropped it.

"I'm a shifter. I'll be back to normal in a day or two."

"And you did this for fun? You males beat the shit out of each other for the hell of it?" I just didn't get it.

377

"Yeah," he said, his voice impossibly rough. "That's it. For fun."

I shut my mouth, not saying anymore, not asking what I wanted to. He didn't want to talk about it? Fine. The rune was on his chest, just above a vicious scar. One of several scars on his upper body. "This is good, and for most beings, enough, but I think it's best we go a little more heavy duty with you. First, though, I need to see who we're dealing with." I knew, but the question was how far into madness they'd gone.

He studied me. "Okay."

"Can we move the couch?"

A few minutes later, the couch was against the wall, leaving plenty of room for me to set up. Usually it was as simple as answering the spiritual "call" and letting them through, but I needed to try a few things with Ren at the same time, while I gauged the soul's responses and made sure I was using the correct sigil configuration. He stood to the side and watched as I took four black candles from my bag and placed them at each corner of the large rug he had in the middle of the room, then I lit them. Next, I got my salt mixed with dirt from our cemetery.

"When we're ready, I'll need you to lie in the middle."

He nodded, prepared to do whatever I asked without question. Ren had been around witches and witchcraft since he was fourteen. He might not have seen this exact ritual, but he would've seen a lot of others that involved the items I was using.

"So you have the same runes tattooed on you?" he asked.

I poured the salt and cemetery dirt mix around the candles, forming a barrier. "No, I wear sigils. They're stronger, and that's what I'll be tattooing on you." I lifted the one hanging around my neck and held out my wrists, showing him the symbols on my cuffs. "If I had permanent sigils like you will, I wouldn't be able to use my gift."

"So if you take them off..."

I removed my boots and socks. "If I take them off and don't at least hold them, I'm at risk of possession from certain souls. Though I can usually feel if there's that kind of risk. I can feel if a soul is truly evil or wants to do harm before I let them come through."

"And the ones around me?"

I bit the side of my lip. "They don't feel evil as such, but there is an energy that I don't like, so I'll need to take extra precautions when I let them through to speak to them, just in case."

His hands were clenching and unclenching at his side. We were still dancing around the truth, pretending we didn't know exactly who we were dealing with. Maybe he was hoping he was wrong.

"So is your whole place carpeted? No wooden flooring?"

"No, it's all carpet on concrete."

Fucking wonderful. "I can still work with that." I didn't have any other choice. This was where all the activity was happening. Here it had to be. I pulled the mortar and pestle from my bag, herbs, the oils, and more cemetery dirt.

Ren watched me intently.

"To stay safe while I do this, I'll need to coat my skin with a barrier." I'd wanted to get naked with Ren for years but not like this. At least it was warm in here. "Is there somewhere I can prepare?" I did my best to sound unaffected, as if this was nothing, something I did all the time.

"Ah...yeah." He led me down the hall. "You can use my room."

"Thanks."

He left and I quickly mixed the oil, infusing it with the rest of the ingredients. When it was ready, I set the mortar on his dresser and looked around. The navy duvet was pulled up and smoothed out, everything in the room in its place. There were bedside tables on either side, but only one had a lamp. There was a phone charging cord there as well. Ren's side of the bed, which meant the other side was where...Breanne slept, where all the other females had slept. He said he and Bree weren't together, but that wasn't what she was telling everyone who'd listen.

I shoved those thoughts from my mind, and with shaky hands stripped off my clothes, placed them on the end of the bed, and started smearing my skin with the oil. It acted as a barrier, stopping any souls from possessing me, if they tried, when I removed my sigil charms. This wasn't needed very often, most souls weren't a danger, they just wanted to be heard before they moved on, following the light in most cases.

At least I wasn't at risk of blacking out. If I was right, and I was positive I was, I'd met these souls before. I was prepared for what they'd fire at me. Unfortunately, that first time I'd lost consciousness when confronted by souls wasn't the last. Thankfully, I only passed out now if a soul was putting out incredibly strong and volatile emotions and I hadn't prepared for it.

I quickly finished up and then stood there, trying to gather the courage to walk back into the living room completely naked in every possible way. Nakedness wasn't new to me. Witches often had to strip to work certain spells. We worshipped Mother Nature, so it came with the territory. I'd just never done this in front of a male I was deeply in love with, a male who wanted to fuck everyone but me. To say I was self-conscious was a freaking understatement.

Shoulders back, tits up.

Zinnia's voice filled my head—my fearless-as-fuck sister. The way she'd confronted Death, her courage and attitude. She amazed me. I'd always been painfully shy. Yes, I'd been conquering that part of myself more and more over the last couple years, but that didn't mean it wasn't still there. Ren was counting on me, though. He needed me. I could do this. I had to.

I'd wanted to be like Zinnia my whole life, and if she were me, she'd walk into that room with all the confidence in the world. She wouldn't try to cover herself, and she sure as hell wouldn't blush.

I straightened my spine, opened the door, and strode down the hall. Without pausing, I walked into the living room.

Ren turned. "Fuck," he bit out, startled, then froze completely. Well, except for his gaze that sliced down my body and back before quickly darting away.

"I should've warned you," I said. "I thought you knew what I was doing."

"No, I'm sorry. I didn't mean to, uh..." He rubbed the back of his neck. "Look."

I took a steadying breath. "Lie on the rug, Ren."

CHAPTER 9

Jasmine

"So how does this whole thing work? You want to talk to a soul and you just summon them to you?"

"It depends. All spirits are called to one of three places—Heaven, Limbo, or Hell. Once a soul's in Heaven, they can stay there or choose to become spirit guides or 'guardian angels,' and yeah, most can be called on to commune with. Limbo, however, is a little like Hotel California—you can never leave. Spirits in Limbo can't be guides, and they can't be reached by someone like me. Hell, well, that's a little fuzzy. We can speak to *some* of those spirits, but I have no idea how or why that is." I had to assume they had different levels of evil, and access was denied or granted on those grounds. None of the hounds or Willow could tell me, so I assumed it was on a need-to-know basis. "Most souls are greeted with a light, though, that leads them to Heaven. The rest are collected by reapers like Magnolia and taken to either Limbo or Hell." I pulled the rest of what I'd need from my bag. "But some linger, tied to a person or a location. This can be for a lot of different reasons." I held his gaze. "I think that's what we're dealing with here—"

"You don't know, though," he said roughly. "Not until you talk to them."

I shook my head, but inside I was certain these were the first souls who came to me, the ones with a message for Ren, something we'd never talked about since.

Taking a roll of twine and some sprigs of rosemary from my bag, I laid the twine around Ren in a wide circle just outside the salt line, layering up the protection, always, and then muttered a powerful protection spell as I wrapped the twine around each of the four sprigs of rosemary lying at the midpoints between each candle. The herb had many uses, but in this instance I was using it for its cleansing, purification, and, most importantly, its protection properties.

Ren was breathing heavily, his fists clenched at his sides, body so tense that he looked close to snapping, to jumping up and running out of here. I got it; I used to be terrified as well. Now, I refused to let what I was rule my life in a negative way. What he faced was different, of course, but I knew how to ease his fears and help start his healing. Hopefully he'd let me this time.

"It's going to be okay, Ren, I promise," I said as I walked over and kneeled just above his head. Sitting back on my heels, I placed my hands on the sides of his face, my palms on his cheeks, my fingers against his beard.

He looked up at me, into my eyes, purposely not at my nakedness. "What are you doing?" he rasped.

I sent a healing rush into him. The more contact the better, but this was a start and would ease his fears for now. "Calming you down. The calmer you are, the calmer they'll be."

He nodded stiffly.

I smiled, projecting as much warmth and comfort as I could, and gently sent more power through my hands. "Breathe in for me, nice and slow. That's it, now let it out, slowly. Slow it all down. You're safe in this circle. They won't cross over the line; the salt, the rosemary, and candles are warding them off." His eyes hadn't left mine. "Another deep breath for me," I whispered as I slid a hand higher, working my way to his third eye, right between his eyebrows, and massaged there with two fingers while I cupped his jaw with the other hand, giving him a sense of being held, cocooned in warmth and comfort. "How you doing?"

He released a shuddery breath, but his breathing had slowed, his fingers no longer curled in tight fists. "Yeah..." He cleared his throat. "I'm good."

"Awesome." I smiled and slowly slid my hand from his bristled jaw and stood. "No matter what happens, I need you to stay where you are, okay?"

His gaze came to me. "What if they come after you."

"I'm safe. I promise."

He nodded, but he was clearly worried.

There was nothing else I could say to reassure him. I just needed to do what I was here for. So, kneeling outside the circle, I removed the first sigil charm, the one around my neck. "If you see me move in an odd way, don't be alarmed. When souls are unable to pass over, they learn to move things, or touch, which is why you're feeling them. They can get angry, and they can become physical."

"I don't like this," he said and looked as if he were about to stand.

"This is what I do, Ren. Do you trust me?"

He stared at me, his fox swirling in his eyes. "I trust you, but—"

"I've done this before, many times." I undid one of my cuffs and set it on the ground with my necklace. "My eyes will look strange; that's normal as well."

He nodded again, but his entire body was tense.

I took off the second sigil cuff and placed it with the other two. As soon as I did, they were there. The souls rushed forward, faces contorted with anger, the injuries that caused their deaths gaping, festering. Flesh rotting, bones exposed. Their souls were decomposing the same way their physical bodies had...and they were scared and confused and filled with rage.

They shoved at me, yelling, roaring, begging me to help them, to make Ren set them free. Ren may have found the strength to come home, to live in his human form again, but he'd far from forgiven himself. These tortured souls, still stuck here with him, told me that.

They screamed louder, shoved harder. There was nothing I could say, nothing I could do to help them, only Ren could do that, he had to make the choice, but I tried anyway. They were in pain, afraid, going insane. They desperately needed help. They pushed and pulled, yanked my hair, roared in my face. I let them, focusing on remaining calm in the face of their fury.

"I'm sorry," I said. "I'm so sorry you can't leave."

They slapped and punched me, screaming in agony.

"I'll do whatever I can to help you," I said. "I promise." They weren't listening, and the longer I sat with them, the angrier and more violent they became. "I'm sorry," I said again and snatched up my necklace and cuffs. The moment they were in my hand, the souls receded. Their energy was still there, violent and twisted, but they couldn't do as much damage. Although I wasn't sure how much longer that would be true. Their anger had reached a point that finally allowed them to break through, which was why they were able to touch Ren now. Left like this much longer and they'd become even more dangerous.

"Jasmine?" Ren snarled.

He sat up, about to get off the mat. "Don't move."

"Fuck that. You're hurt." He got to his feet.

"Stay where you are," I snapped.

He paused, breathing heavily, his face lined with concern.

"They're stronger right now, and you're their number one target. So sit down until I say you can move."

There was a bruise already showing on my shoulder and one on my hip, red handprints all over my body from their slaps and my scalp stung from the hair pulling, but I was okay.

"It's them, isn't it?" Ren said. "The people I...I tortured and murdered. It's them."

"You didn't do anything to them. It was Edward who did those things. Only him. You were the vessel he occupied, nothing more, and the sooner you believe that, the sooner you can forgive yourself, and they can move on."

He shoved his fingers in his hair. "I can't. I can't fucking do that."

"You have to try. All that you're feeling, the guilt you carry, the intensity of it, is making it impossible for them to go where they need to. And right now, they've never been more drawn to you."

He lifted his head. "Why?"

I didn't want to scare him, but he needed to know. "They've been with you for so long, Ren, but their anger has reached a new level, and the angrier they get at being trapped here, the deeper they slip into insanity, and the more desperate they become, the more harm they want to cause you. It's tipping them into darkness. You've been a vessel before, and those scars are still on your soul. It makes you a target. They've reached a point that if they're given the chance, they will possess you."

"And the scars on my...on my soul, that'll make it easier for them to do that?" he asked, voice raw.

"Yes. If they can't leave, that's the next best thing." I slipped my necklace over my head and secured my cuffs. I motioned to his shirt. "Can I?"

"Yeah...of course."

I quickly pulled his shirt on to cover my nakedness, and when I looked up, he was watching me intently, his fox back in his eyes, the amber and gold swirling as he took me in. I pretended I didn't notice.

He cleared his throat. "So what can I do?"

"You have two options. The first is a kind of exorcism. It's what we do when we have no other recourse. When a spirit won't or can't pass over and has become a danger to the living, the soul must essentially be destroyed."

His brows lowered. "No afterlife, no reincarnation, nothing?"

I nodded.

"No, not that. They've suffered enough. What else?"

I held his gaze. "You have to set them free, Ren. You have to forgive yourself."

>)>●((<

Ren

I stared back at her, into her soft fucking eyes, feeling vulnerable in a way I hadn't with anyone else, not even Willow. "I don't know how."

Somehow, her eyes softened even more. "Let me help you."

"You've seen them, what I...what *he*...did to them, Jaz. You saw. How the fuck do I let that go?"

She shook her head, tucking her long, blond hair behind her ear. "You need to heal. We may not be able to heal the scars on your soul, or on your body, but the emotional ones? I can help you with those. Right now, with that mess of emotion swirling inside you, especially the guilt, it's stopping you from moving forward...of them moving forward. Punishing yourself over and over again for something you had no control over isn't working. It's time we find another way. It's time you let me help you do that."

"I don't expect you to—"

"It's what I do, Ren. It's my gift." She stood and walked to her bag, and despite how fucked up this entire situation was, I couldn't help but eat up the sight of her in my shirt and nothing else. I'd tried not to look, but she'd been fucking naked, her smooth inked skin slick with oil. The sight of her like that would be burned into my mind for the rest of my life.

She pulled out a small book, a marker, and a battery-powered hair trimmer. "For the next few nights, I'll need to come back here to work on your healing and tattoo your sigils. There's also a ritual to keep the souls calm while we're doing that. Then I'll need to come once a week for a while to perform the ritual and repeat a healing session to make sure it sticks." She held up the marker. "But tonight, drawing them on with a tattoo marker will have to do."

Jaz stepped over the string and salt line and back to safety. My relief was instant. My fox calmed as well, no longer whining and growling and pacing restlessly. Seeing Jasmine being attacked by invisible hands was fucking horrific. I'd just been about to leave my spot when she finally stopped it.

She motioned for me to sit again and she kneeled beside me. "So, the scars the possession left you with aren't something that can heal." Sympathy filled her eyes. "But the sigils will hide them and prevent you from being a target for any souls searching for a vessel."

I was broken, marked by what happened in a way that would never leave me, and I was making the souls of the people I had a part in murdering suffer, torturing them even in death. Fucking awesome.

There was one way to stop all of this, though.

It was simple. I just had to take one step, one more step, the next time I was at my cliff, and the pain would be all over—for them, and for me.

"You're going to need quite a few," she said.

"Sorry?"

"Sigils. You'll need a lot of them."

I nodded as her scent washed over me. *Fuck.* It was mixed with mine, while she was still in my shirt. Christ, I barely stopped myself from leaning forward and pressing my nose to her shoulder and breathing her in. Now my fucking fox was whining again, pawing at the ground to get closer to her.

"They'll go along here." She ran her finger across my shoulder, causing tingles to dance all over my skin. "Both sides. One on either side of your throat, here and here. Down your spine, and from the top of your ribs, here..." She pressed a finger to the point just below the center of my chest, and goose bumps lifted all over me. Could she see them? "Down to, well... all the way down." Her face turned pink, and she glanced at the trimmers. "I'll need you to uh...shave."

"And you can do it? The ink?" I asked, my voice weirdly deep, even rougher than usual.

"I can. It's part of my job. Zinny was teaching me before she had to..." She stopped herself, her throat working. "Before she had to leave that first time. Rome finished training me, so I know what I'm doing."

My fox growled at the mention of that male's name, the sound rumbling through my chest. Jaz paused, her gaze darting to mine. I quickly cleared my throat. "And it'll take a few nights?"

"Three or four. The sigils are powerful and your body, and your soul, will need to realign with each session." She licked her lips, and my dick stirred. "One person has to ink all of them, once we start, there's no changing who does it. I know you two fought, but if you're uncomfortable with me doing it, I could bring Rome. He could—"

"No!" The word burst from me in a snarl. "You can do it." My skin felt hot all of a sudden, my muscles tight as hell, and I had to fight not to jump to my feet and pace. I did not want Jaz here with him. I didn't want to see them together. Again, my fox and I were in agreement on that point.

Jasmine ignored my outburst and my fucking odd behavior and popped the lid off the marker. "Okay, then. You ready to get started?"

I nodded, and she opened the book beside her, running her finger down one page, then the next, and seeing her do that had me thinking of how it felt when she did the same to my shoulder. I fucking shivered, more goose bumps lifting all over me. My dick felt heavy and hot as fuck, which was not okay. This was Jasmine. Willow's sweet, little cousin. How the fuck was I hard when I was sitting in a circle surrounded by the souls of the people I'd fucking murdered? How was that possible?

I quickly reached down and adjusted myself when she slid the book out of the way. Yes, she was beautiful and sweet and funny and at times feisty. Yes, there was this fucking weird connection between us, but still, this was messed up even for me.

Then shit only got worse when she placed her hand on my shoulder and started drawing the sigils on my skin. I could feel the heat of her body, where she touched my shoulder was searing hot, and her breath, warm and sweet, brushed the side of my neck as she whispered a spell. The usual urge to pull away, to not let anyone touch me, reared up, but a different, stronger urge to rub against her, to nuzzle, to curl up with her in a confined space and share body heat, was even stronger.

My fox wanted to herd her to our den, to my room, I could feel it. He wanted to press against her and protect her. I breathed deep as she moved to the next shoulder, telling him to calm the fuck down, but his tail just wagged harder, and he pressed closer. I needed to get my dick under control before she started on the sigils that would run down my chest.

She touched my jaw. I jumped.

"Sorry. I just need you to tilt your head to the side."

I did, and she drew a sigil on the side of my neck, then on the other. Her breath tickled my ear as she whispered that same spell over and over, and I bit back a fucking moan. I was in sensation overload.

No one had touched me this much since before I was possessed. When I fucked, I made it clear I didn't want them touching me or I just made them grip the headboard or lifted their arms above them to make sure of it. Every touch from Jasmine was fucking unravelling me, it was pleasure-pain. Agony and ecstasy. The fox wanted more; the male whose hands had held people down, who'd cut and tore and tortured, whose face and chest and arms had been sprayed with their blood and gore wanted to push her away in horror, in shame and guilt.

I gritted my teeth and stayed where I was.

"Can you lie on your stomach?" Jaz asked.

I quickly did as she said and squeezed my eyes closed, letting the images I tried to lock away come forward. My dick went soft in an instant, and I released a shuddery breath. I heard the rustle of pages as she referred to her book again, then she carried on drawing, working her way down my spine.

"Can you...I'll need you to lower your jeans a bit for me, so I can do the last two."

"Right." I rolled to my side, undid my jeans, and rolled back.

Jasmine tugged them down, and I dragged in a shaky-as-fuck breath, all the gruesome images in my head washed away again in an instant as every bit of my focus went to her hands on my lower back as she drew a sigil right above my ass crack.

"Just the chest sigils to go," she said, her voice overly bright. "I'll need you to roll to your back."

Fuck. I wasn't hard, hard, but I sure as fuck wasn't soft either. I rolled over and she handed me the clippers.

"How far down are we talking?" I asked.

She bit her lip and motioned to my groin. "To the top of your... I'll need to do one on...uh, your..." She motioned to my dick. "On the base."

"And I can't do it?" I asked desperately.

She shook her head, her face growing darker. "I'm sorry. It has to be my voice, my spell, and since it's me you want inking the rest of the sigils, then it will have to be me who does them all, or the barrier I've created will have a broken link."

I nodded, and my heart was hammering in my fucking chest. Plenty of females had seen my dick. What was my problem? Having a semi wasn't ideal, but I was a shifter, I wasn't exactly shy. Still, my breath was shaky as fuck as I shoved my jeans lower and quickly used the clippers to manscape. I just kind of shaved to the base of my cock, then tried to gather the hair and shove it in my pocket because this had to be bad enough for Jasmine without her getting one of my pubes in her eye or mouth or fucking breathing one down her throat while she was bent over me.

I handed the clippers to her and lay back, trying to think about anything but Jasmine's hands on me, the sound of her voice as she spelled, the warmth of her breath on my abs as she made her way down my body.

I thought about Mrs. Baumé in the cold room. She needed embalming in the morning. Her family was coming in to dress her in the afternoon, her daughter wanted to do her mom's makeup. The viewing was the next day.

Jaz's hand touched the skin below my belly button, and I stilled, all thoughts of Mrs. Baumé flying from my head as every one of my instincts zoned back on Jasmine and what she was doing, the sound of her voice, her breath. Goddammit, her breath on my skin was fucking with me the most.

My dick wasn't semi-hard anymore, it was hard as steel. I'd angled it down, and now it hurt like a motherfucker. I didn't dare look. I knew what I'd see, a clear outline of my hard-on along my thigh, trying to burst through my jeans.

She drew the sigil just above the base. I breathed deeply. She already thought I was a slimeball, and I was lying here, reaffirming that for her right now. I winced.

"Ren?"

Her voice softly calling my name had me jolting. "Yeah?"

"Like I said earlier, placement is um, really important." There was a pause. "You're ah...angled to the side, this last sigil needs to be in the center."

Could this get any worse? I didn't think so. We were at peak worst, this had to be the summit. There was nothing else I could do but reach down, shove my hand in my jeans, grip my hard cock, and reposition it. "I'm so fucking sorry, Jaz. You must think I'm the biggest fucking creep." She made a sound of denial, but what else could she think? I had to give her some honesty. I couldn't let her leave thinking I was some slimy fucking perv. "I... I don't do touch if I can help it, not anymore. I'm not...used to being touched like this. My senses are all over the place. I'm in stimulus overload, and it's making my body react intensely, and in a way it wouldn't usually. I normally have a fuck of a lot more control than this."

"Ren, seriously, it's okay," she said softly. "Please, don't even worry about it."

I grit my teeth, because her sweet fucking voice only made it worse. "I just don't want you thinking I'm doing this on purpose or whatever..."

Her hand went to my thigh, and then I felt the cool ink of the marker on the base of my hot-as-fuck shaft—then her hand was gone, and with it her warmth, her presence.

"All done," she said.

I opened my eyes, and she was back outside the barrier, already putting everything away in her bag.

"Let me just place these crystals around your house, and say a quick spell. It'll help to keep the souls calm while we figure things out and make those sigils permanent."

She didn't look at me, and her face was bright red. I stayed where I was while she quickly finished up, then headed back to my room. When she walked back out a short time later, she was dressed.

"It's safe for you to move around the house again," she said and hustled over to blow out the candles and gather up her string and rosemary.

"Thanks." I felt like a fucking asshole.

"No problem." She did up her bag and turned to me. "So, just one more thing before I go. If you're still game?"

I lifted a brow. "What's that?"

"Your emotional healing. We can start that now as well. You said touch is hard for you, and I'm sorry to do this now, while you're feeling so over-whelmed, but it'll only take a couple minutes, and I really think we should make a start."

I'd never wanted to do anything less, but if I was going to free the souls around me, then I had to try. "What do I have to do?"

A soft smile curled her pretty lips. "Nothing, just stand there." She walked over, and her still pink cheeks deepened in color. She tilted her head back and looked up at me. "I'm going to wrap my arms around you. You'll feel a warmth move through your body when I use my power. Like when I touched your face earlier, but more intense." She looked awkward and sweet. "Hugging me back is not mandatory. I know that's not your thing, but everyone else I've worked with says it helps."

Jesus. I hadn't had so much contact in a fucking long time. I felt twitchy and restless, and I wanted to retreat. But I also wanted to feel Jasmine's arms around me really fucking badly. I nodded.

Her skin's going to crawl. She doesn't want to touch you. She knows what a monster you really are. They showed her what you did to them. Bet she'll scrub your scent off as soon as she gets home. She thinks you're a slimy fucking creep, remember? Edward's voice filled my head, and I squeezed my eyes shut, trying to force him out.

Jasmine closed the space between us, sliding her arms around me, and pressed the side of her face to my chest. I jerked in her arms, my heart smashing against my ribs.

"It's okay," she whispered.

Warmth washed through me almost immediately, and I curled my fingers into fists at my sides. I didn't hug her back, that would be...too much. Way too much.

"I'm not going to hurt you," she said in that soft, soothing voice.

My heart hammered faster and sweat coated my skin.

"Everything's going to be okay," she whispered next.

Why was she saying that? I jerked again. It was involuntary, but the urge to pull away, to escape this, whatever this was, filled me hard and fast. "Jasmine?" My fucking eyes stung, my emotions going haywire. What the fuck was she doing to me?

"Just a little longer, Ren. I've got you."

I was breathing harder, close to hyperventilating. "Fuck," I choked out.

"Thirty more seconds."

It was too much. I couldn't do this. I couldn't do it.

She started counting down from fifteen.

My muscles spasmed. "Jasmine." It was a plea. There was no missing it in my voice. "I couldn't stop him," I gasped, the words torn from me. "I fought, but I...I couldn't..."

"It's okay," she murmured softly.

The pain it...fuck, it slipped away in a rush, and the sudden urge to hold her back filled me along with a wave of euphoria. There was no other way to describe it. I didn't know what the fuck to do with myself. I fisted my hands tighter to stop from wrapping my arms around her, but there was no stopping my face from dipping lower, from pressing it into the side of her neck and breathing her in. My lips grazed her throat, and a jolt of something powerful slammed through me.

Fuck.

She counted down the last five seconds, then her arms fell away, releasing me. She stepped back, and I sucked in a desperate breath.

"You did amazing," she said, turning away from me. She was shaking, her cheeks damp with tears.

I wanted to ask if she was okay, but my throat was too fucking tight.

She grabbed her bag and slung it over her shoulder, still not looking at me, and I realized she was giving me privacy to get my shit together. "What time do you finish work tomorrow?" she asked, swiping the tears from her cheeks, her body still trembling, her gaze on the floor.

"Six." My voice was fucked, it was all I could manage.

"I'll see you around seven, then?" she said.

I nodded.

Then she was out the door, closing it softly behind her.

I shoved my fingers through my hair and sat heavily on the couch.

How the fuck would I do this all over again tomorrow?

CHAPTER 10

Jasmine

MAGNOLIA AND BRAM got in her car, and I jumped in the back.

"And she definitely knows we're coming?" I asked Mags.

"Yep, I texted Agatheena last night, and she was cool."

Bram snorted beside her. "Still can't believe she took that phone you gave her."

"Me either, honestly," Mags said and grinned. "Though I can be persuasive."

"No shit," Bram said, but I saw his lips curl.

Magnolia and the crone had struck up a kind of friendship. Agatheena Burnside was scary, powerful, and more than your average witch. She was half demon and, like Mags, walked a precarious line between dark and light magic. I guess you could say she'd become a kind of mentor for Mags.

Mags thought the old witch might be able to help me with Death's missing souls, or at least point me in the right direction. I won't lie; I was nervous as hell to meet her. My other cousin, Rose, had met her as well, and she was not in a hurry to ever go back.

Bram started the car and reversed out of the drive, then turned in the wrong direction.

"Are we going somewhere else first?" I asked, leaning around Mags's seat.

"Picking up Ren," Bram muttered. "That forest is crawling with demons. Not taking you both in there without backup."

I froze. "Ren?"

"Bram and Ren know those woods better than most. You'll be safe," Mags said, mistaking my freeze response for concern over my safety.

It wasn't. I knew Ren could kill a demon, multiple demons, on his own. I'd heard the hounds talk about him. My reaction was over the fact that last night I'd drawn sigils all over his body, including the base of his dick, followed by some intense emotion-healing therapy, where I'd been bombarded with everything he was feeling, as if those feelings were my own, and the enormity of that had left me shaken and in tears.

He'd also scented me, and his lips had touched the side of my neck. I hadn't quite recovered from either. I thought I had the rest of the day to get it together. Instead, I had to get my shit together right the hell now.

Bram pulled up outside the funeral home, and Ren jogged out. As he passed the driver's door, he bumped Bram's fist through the open window, then climbed in the back beside me.

I forced myself to act normal. It didn't totally work, though, because my face heated to painful levels. "Hey," I said when he glanced my way.

"Hey," he said and rubbed his palms on his jean-covered thighs.

"Glad you could come," Mags said as Bram headed off.

He flashed her a grin and settled back. Bram and Ren were the same age, and being familiars for the same family, they'd become extremely tight over the years. Mags, Bram, and Ren were more than friends; they were family. After what happened to Ren, he'd distanced himself, but he'd slowly been letting them back in, or at least he'd been trying.

Mags put on the stereo, and I tried to think of what the hell to say. Was I supposed to make small talk now? "Thanks for this. I hope we didn't pull you away from work?"

He shook his head. "It's all good."

"Well, I appreciate it," I said and tried not to fidget.

"I know what's in that part of the forest," Ren said without looking my way. "No fucking way I'd let you go there without me."

I stared at his profile. He made it sound like he was doing this for me, not as a favor for Bram. I didn't know what to say, so I pulled out my phone and pretended I had important shit to do. Well, I kind of did. I spent the rest of the drive replying to clients and confirming and making appointments.

We turned off the main highway and started up a dirt road that took us deeper into the forest.

"I would've thought Rome would be here," Ren said low.

"Why's that?" I asked and inwardly cringed. *Because you implied he was your mate, idiot!*

393

Ren frowned and opened his mouth—

"Hey, Ren?" Mags said, turning down the music, and thankfully interrupting. "Did you ever go out past Bleak River?"

They started talking, and I quietly breathed a sigh of relief. I was a dumbass for implying anything was between me and Rome, but now wasn't the time to clear the air and utterly humiliate myself.

"We'll drive as far as we can, then walk the rest of the way," Mags said a little while later, glancing at me in the rearview mirror. "You'll be fine, Jaz. We got you," she added, obviously seeing the fear on my face.

They were forced to walk because of me. Bram would usually fly Mags to Agatheena's and avoid the danger completely. "I won't lie. I am kinda nervous." That was a complete lie, I was so nervous I wanted to puke. "Wish I had wings like Bram."

Bram's dark eyes stayed on the road. "Asked Talon. He was gonna carry you in, but he got called to a job with my brothers."

A low rough sound had me spinning to Ren. His expression hadn't changed; his gaze trained straight ahead. Had he just...growled? I'd hung out with Bram's brothers a few times—they were good guys. I mean, they were all assassins, but then so was Bram. They were no threat to me. I had to be hearing things.

The road grew bumpier the deeper we drove. Bram did his best to avoid the potholes, but it was getting harder. Finally, he pulled the car off the road—it was more a track at this point—and shut it off. "We'll walk from here."

We all got out. Mags slung her bag over her head, which was no doubt well stocked with face-melting potions, and both Ren and Bram strapped massive knives to their thighs. "Got one of those for me?" I asked, only half joking, while silently freaking the hell out.

"You know how to use one?" Bram asked, not joking in the slightest.

"Ah, no."

"Then no knife for you," Ren said and closed in, kind of crowding me. "Stay close."

I gave him a thumbs-up, even though this was very much a thumbs-down situation and I'd much prefer to get back in the car and get the hell out of this forest, but Zinnia needed me, and I'd do anything to make sure she could come home again.

We headed off in silence, and all three of them surrounded me. Their demeanors changed completely as we walked through the forest. They were on guard, scanning our surroundings, and every now and then Bram would tilt his head in an extremely birdlike manner, listening for any demons that might be coming too close.

This was my first time in this part of the forest. Where I'd gone with

Zinnia was bad, but this place was next level, and the farther we went, the louder it became. Roars and screams and barks, none of them of this world, all of them demon, or some other creature.

"Why would anyone want to live out here?" I said under my breath.

"It has its moments," Ren said from his position beside and a little behind me.

I snorted. "If your idea of fun is running around a demon-infested forest, hoping they don't catch you, drain your blood, and serve it up like an aperitif before eating the rest of you for their main course, then *sure*, this place is like Disney."

His low laugh, deep and rough, slid over me. I barely stopped myself from stumbling and falling on my ass. I hadn't heard Ren laugh in a *really* long time, years, and judging by how fast Magnolia spun our way, neither had she.

"That's some imagination you got there," he said.

That low, raspy voice combined with that sexy-as-hell laugh and I was having trouble catching my breath. "A female's mind is a dangerous place."

He huffed out a breath, still with humor, just less.

"Hell, yes," Mags said.

Bram grunted his agreement and Mags poked him in the ribs, getting a sound out of him I'd never heard before, making Mags and I crack up and Ren emit a low chuckle that I felt in the pit of my stomach.

The fact we were in a demon-infested forest no longer mattered. All I wanted to know was how to make Ren laugh again. "So what's Agatheena like, Mags?" From what I'd been told, she was a recluse and had lived out here for fifty years.

Mags grinned at me over her shoulder. "I could try to describe her, but she truly has to be experienced for yourself."

"Now I'm truly terrified."

"Don't be," Mags said. "She likes me, so I'm pretty sure she won't eat you."

"What?" I stopped short.

Ren ran into me, and his arm automatically hooked around my waist, stopping me from falling on my face. He kind of lifted me, setting me on my feet a few steps ahead, and kept his hand on my lower back for a few very long seconds to make sure I kept moving.

"She's joking," Ren said. "Agatheena prefers demon meat."

"So you do know her?" Mags asked him.

"No, but I've met her."

Mags glanced back at him. "I wondered, with how long you were out here."

Ren's eyes went kind of blank, but he smiled. "She snared me in one of her traps. I talked her out of turning me into stew."

"Holy freaking shit," I whispered.

Ren's eyes lit up again, and he huffed out that sound again that wasn't a laugh, but close.

This news was not great. "So if she's half demon, and she eats demon, that kind of makes her—"

"A cannibal," Bram said.

We all went silent, and that's when I felt the low hum of power. I realized it'd been steadily growing the farther we walked. It was Agatheena, her magic, reaching out to us—

Ren grabbed me suddenly, his solid arm hooking around me again. He pulled me back, stepping in front of me so fast he was a blur. The knife he'd had strapped to his thigh was in his hand a split second later, then it went sailing. A thunk and a shriek followed before a pissed-off, seriously hideous demon burst from the trees, Ren's knife buried in one of its eye sockets.

"Watch her," Ren muttered to Bram and Mags, and then he ran at the demon.

In a blur of motion, he took the demon to the ground, pulled the knife from its skull, and with a snarl decapitated it, turning it to ash. He stood, barely puffing, slid the blade back into the sheath strapped to his thigh, and returned to us.

Bram's head was tilted again, listening for more, and Mags was scanning the trees, a vial in her hand. "Clear?" she asked her mate. Bram nodded.

We started walking again.

"Okay?" Mags asked when she looked back and saw I was close to hyperventilating.

I nodded.

"Sure?" she said.

"I mean, I've never seen anything like that in my life. A demon like that or one having its head cut off, but yeah." I took another deep breath, getting my shit together. "I'm okay."

She winked. "Good, 'cause they only get uglier the farther we go."

"Cool." I shuddered. "That gray, slimy, googly-eyed creep was barely ugly at all."

Ren muttered something under his breath, then he was chuckling again, and I felt as if I'd just won the lottery. I saw Mags and Bram exchange a look.

More demon calls echoed in the distance, noises of creatures even I couldn't imagine what they looked like, and Agatheena's power seemed to grow stronger, as if it were wrapping itself around us, checking us out, testing us. I could feel her wards, and I still hadn't even seen her cottage, but that was a given considering where she lived.

We rounded a massive oak, and then I spotted it. Her cottage was like something from one of the storybooks my mom had read me before she decided parenting wasn't her jam and left. This wasn't the soon-to-be princess's house, though. No, this was the evil witch's house. It blended in with the forest, trees growing all around it, even through it, and the moss-covered stone walls were stained with age.

A worn path came from the bottom of the porch steps and wound its way around trees to the two thick pines standing either side directly in front of us, their branches forming a leafy arch above.

Hanging from the branches, secured by thick twine, were bits of fabric, several buttons, a glove with the thumb cut off. There were also bones and skulls—demon, by the looks of things—some picked clean, some smeared with fresh blood. There were jars filled with all sorts of crap that had my gag reflex working overtime, eyeballs floating in some kind of murky liquid, what looked like fingernails in another, and yet another nearly full with matted hair in a multitude of shades, and then bigger things that I could only assume were organs.

"What the hell am I looking at?" I said as Mags moved up to stand beside me.

"Offerings." She walked around to the side of the tree. "You have your blade?"

"Yeah, of course." I followed her, and she motioned to a knot on the side of the trunk. There was an indent in the middle, and in the very center it was a deep mahogany color, a lot darker than the rest of the tree.

My cousin tilted her head to Bram and Ren, who were watching us closely. "They can't come with us—"

"You're not going in there without protection." Ren said it directly to me.

"You know she's not going to hurt Jasmine," Mags said.

"What I know is she's capable of anything. I've watched her paralyze and disembowel a demon alive for her pot."

Mags frowned. "She's my friend. I'm her guest. She doesn't hurt...or eat...her guests."

Ren turned to Bram. "You're okay with this?"

"Was nervous at first," he said, "but Mags has been here a lot. The crone likes her. Jaz is safe."

Ren's jaw clenched. "I don't want you going in there. Not without me."

I blinked over at him, taken aback. "Um...I need to go in there. She might have information that'll help find those souls. And Mags will be with me." I pulled my blade out and watched as Mags sliced her thumb and pressed it to the dark patch on the trunk, and I realized it was blood that had stained the wood.

"So she knows we're who we say we are," Mags explained before sliding her blade into her pocket.

I did the same. Ren flinched, a low growl emanating from him when I sliced the end of my thumb. He'd seen Willow, her sisters, Daisy, Else, all cut themselves, use blood magic, and I'd never, not once, seen him flinch. Did he think I needed his protection because I didn't have a familiar who could fight? I pressed my thumb to the tree trunk as well.

"You coming or what?" a voice called.

We turned. The old witch stood on her porch, her piercing green eyes boring into me.

"Be right there," Mags called back.

"I need some of your cousin's hair before you can come in," she said, then walked back into her cottage, slamming the door after her.

"My hair?"

Mags motioned to the jar of matted hair. "Yep."

"How much are we talking?" I asked, pulling my knife back out.

"Not much."

I dragged a piece from underneath, at the back, and sliced some off, then popped it in the jar Mags held open for me.

"Right, we're good to go," she said.

"I don't like this," Ren said.

I followed Mags through the opening to the path. There was a light staticky sensation, but nothing else.

"Fuck this," Ren snarled.

He strode toward us, his gaze locked on me.

"I wouldn't do that," Bram muttered at the same time Mags told him to stop.

He only made it to the trees bordering the path's opening. As soon as he reached it, he was tossed back like a pebble from a giant slingshot.

He jumped to his feet and was about to charge it again, I could see the determination on his face, but Bram planted his hand on Ren's chest and shook his head. He was talking, but I couldn't hear what he said because Mags had taken my hand and was leading me up the path.

Mags glanced back at me. "Wonder what's gotten into him?"

"No idea."

She gave me a funny look.

Then we were at the door, and it was flung open. Magic coiled around us, and we were both dragged inside.

"Come on, hurry up," the crone said as we slid to a stop in the middle of the room. I looked around and tried not to show my horror, but I was pretty sure I was failing big-time. There were more jars hanging off the ceiling and walls, and they were filled with...truly disgusting things.

"You trying to catch flies?" Agatheena said to me.

I snapped my mouth shut.

"You seem too squeamish to be a Thornheart, but that's what you are, so stop gawking like a nun in a whorehouse and get your butt over here."

I jumped like I'd been plugged into an electrical socket, but my feet wouldn't move me in her direction. She stood in a small kitchen off to the side, a raven perched on her shoulder, the bird eyeing me with terrifying black eyes.

"She need my blue smoke?" Agatheena asked Mags, flashing yellow, pointed teeth.

"No, she'll be fine." Mags's hand touched my back, and she gently but firmly pushed me forward.

"If you say so." Agatheena's gray hair was wiry and pulled tight in a thick braid, her skin wrinkled and saggy, but her eyes were sharp as they looked me up and down. She huffed, seeming highly unimpressed.

I needed to snap the hell out of it. I was embarrassing Mags and myself. "Sorry, I'm not normally...I just...I don't usually..."

"Stutter like an imbecile?"

My face went up in flames. "Sorry."

"Stop apologizing. And stop looking at Dolores like she's going to peck your eyeballs out." She grabbed three teacups and banged them down on the table. "She only does that if I ask her to."

Jesus. "Right."

"Sit," she said.

We both sat.

"So why are you in such a foul mood?" Mags asked, bravely but unwisely in my opinion.

She filled her teapot with steaming water and banged that on the table as well. "I'm having trouble with a feral shifter. Keeps getting to my traps before I can. Can't make a living if that cockwaffle keeps stealing my demons."

Cockwaffle? "You sell them?" I blurted before I could stop myself. Demons turned to ash when they were killed. Did that mean she sold them alive?

Agatheena took her chair. "Yep. I bind them so they don't lash out, then harvest their organs and bones, mainly."

Jesus, that was grim.

"So what do you want?" she said, pouring the tea.

"Well, we were hoping—"

"Not you," she said, cutting Mags off and pointing a bony finger at me. "This one needs the help, she can do the asking."

Mags stared at her for several seconds. "You really are pissed off, huh?"

She scowled, and Mags gave me a nudge.

I jumped again and ground my teeth. I needed to stop doing that. "Right, well, this is the thing..." Agatheena stared right at me, as if she could see through skin and bone, right to my soul. Mags gave me another nudge, and I barely stopped myself from jumping again and forced myself to talk. "Um, so my sister is Death's consort."

"I know."

"You do?"

"I know everything."

Mags snorted. "I told her."

Agatheena turned her scowl on Mags, and I was glad of the reprieve and quickly rushed on. "Okay, so Limbo and Hell are both missing souls. Death wants me to find them, only I have no idea where to look, and I was hoping you might have an idea where to start?"

"You're right. I do," she said and took a sip of her tea.

"You do?"

"Yep."

I waited for her to continue. She did not.

"Oh, you think you should have that information for free, do you?" she said. "Well, that's not how this works." Agatheena sat back in her chair. "Get rid of the feral, I'll give you the information."

"You want me to kill a feral shifter?" I asked in disbelief.

Her eyes darkened. "Not you. As if you, who probably jumps at her own damn reflection, could kill a feral. No, princess, I meant for your fox to do it. I know him. I've seen what he can do. Get it done. I'll give you what you want."

I frowned. "My fox?"

She rolled her eyes, shook her head, and turned to Mags. "I can't deal with you clueless goddamned Thornhearts today. When you come back to see me, come alone."

Magic snapped around us, and we were lifted out of our seats and, feet hovering above the ground, were thrown with force toward the door. Thankfully, it flung open before I could crash face-first into it.

"When the feral's dead, come back. I'll leave what you need on the tree," Agatheena said.

Then the door slammed behind us, and we were dragged back down the path. Ren and Bram watched, eyes wide, as we were thrust toward them, then dumped outside the wards. I landed on my butt in the dirt. A burst of power followed, letting us know her ward that had allowed Mags and I to pass was back in place.

Ren hooked me under the arms and hoisted me to my feet.

Mags turned to me. "I don't think she liked you."

"What gave it away?" I said, brushing dirt off my ass.

"What happened?" Bram's gaze slid over his mate, making sure she was okay.

"She'll give Jaz what she needs." Her gaze shifted to Ren. "But only if you kill a feral that's been stealing from her traps."

"Me?" he said, looking confused.

Mags looked from Ren to me and back. "That's what she said."

Ren frowned. "I can do it, but I'll need a couple days to track it."

"It's way too dangerous. We don't even know if the information Agatheena has is worth it." I met Ren's amber and gold eyes. "It's too much. You don't have to do this."

His gaze moved over my face, then his nostrils flared and a strange look shifted through his eyes. "Yeah, I do."

CHAPTER 11

Ren

JASMINE HAD BEEN quiet as we made our way back out of the forest, and every now and then she'd cast sidelong glances my way. I didn't blame her. The way I'd acted back there, like doing anything for her was my right, was fucking weird and pushy. But my fox had sprung to his feet and demanded we kill the feral for her, and it came through in a way that was, yeah, intense.

Maybe because her scent had lingered in my place all fucking night, mixed with mine—on my skin, and on the shirt that she'd worn—and it'd messed with us.

It didn't help that she'd just come out of the crone's cottage and I'd been tense as fuck the whole time she was in there. I didn't trust the old witch. I didn't trust many people. Add in the demon-infested forest, a forest I knew well, and I was feeling out of control and overprotective.

I was doing it for Willow. I'd do anything to protect Wills from pain, which meant protecting her young cousin. I didn't need to worry about Mags, she could take care of herself. She also had her assassin mate with her, and Jaz was helping me and I owed her. I'd felt the cold brush of a hand on my arm this morning, but just a whisper, and it'd felt more distant. What Jaz had done for me was working, and I wanted to repay her for it. That's all this was.

I glanced at Jaz now, walking a little ahead of me. She was wearing black jeans and a black, fitted long-sleeved T-shirt topped with a dark denim jacket with black leather sleeves that I knew belonged to Zinnia because I'd seen her give it to Jazzy the last time she was home. Her long blond hair was down, and there were small braids here and there. It always looked a little wild, that tousled just-out-of-bed look.

Jesus.

I quickly shut that thought down.

When she glanced at me again, I got a glimpse of the butterfly inked on the side of her throat. Similar to the live ones she usually had on her shoulder or in her hair, with colorful wings that fluttered, every now and then as she walked. Willow was right, Jaz was different now, not the female I'd first met years ago. She'd been a kid then, always in pink, painfully shy. Whenever I'd tried to talk to her, she'd ducked her head or hidden behind her sister or one of her cousins.

She wasn't that shy, little female anymore. She still liked pink sometimes—my gaze dipped to the hot-pink belt she wore—but now she was a powerful witch, one who wasn't afraid to call me out on my shit, who shoved wolves back and had covered herself in tattoos because they made her happy. A female who spent a lot of her time laughing and dancing and taking care of everyone else, who'd made me laugh when I thought that was impossible. A female who made anyone who got to know her fall at her fucking feet—

Unhinged cackling echoed through the forest a moment before several demons stepped out of the trees, their lizard-like eyes sliding from Bram and I to Jaz and Mags. I grabbed Jasmine's arm and pulled her against me. They were more humanoid than some. Well, they wore clothes at least. Their faces, however, yeah, not so much. Bram pulled his knife and Mags fisted several vials full with deadly potions.

"Leave the breeders, and we'll let you walk out of the forest," one of them said around the thick, drool-covered tusks protruding from either side of his mouth. "You're weak shifters, and you're outnumbered. Hand them over now, or we'll eat you."

Fury burned through me. "Don't recognize me, Husk?"

The demon eyed me, then his chin jerked back. "Fox?"

I wasn't surprised he didn't recognize me. I'd rarely taken my human form out here, only when I needed to fight, and then I'd been naked and covered in blood and dirt. "That's right, and you just threatened our females."

I saw the fear shift through his bulging eyes. I didn't care. He'd threatened Jasmine, and I couldn't let him live. My fox bared his teeth in complete agreement. He needed to die. I grabbed Jaz around the waist, and she squealed in surprise as I hoisted her up into the closest tree. She scrambled farther up as I pulled my knife free and stood under her. "You have two choices," I said. "Fight me now with honor, or show your brothers what a coward you are and run. I promise either way I will end you."

Mags and Bram had moved closer as well, all of us surrounding the tree Jaz was in.

"Come on, coward," I said to Husk. "Let's see what you can do."

He snorted like a bull and charged.

I grabbed him by the tusk as he swiped his clawed fingers at me and slammed his face into my knee, then started hacking with my knife. There was nothing but a red haze after that. All I could see was Jasmine, so soft and fragile, visions in my mind of what these pieces of shit wanted to do to her, and I was lost in my rage. I fought, punching and kicking, slicing and hacking until there were no demons left to kill.

Until the red haze cleared and I stood in a sea of gore and ash. Bram and Mags, with bloody knives of their own, demons with melted, bubbling flesh from Magnolia's potions, dissolving them into nothing, scattered on the ground around us. I looked up. Jaz stood in the tree branches, eyes wide and locked on me. I didn't know what she was thinking, but there was real fear there.

She'd seen me lose it.

And become the monster you truly are, Edward's voice hissed.

My scars itched, my gut caught in a jagged grip, the past fusing with the present. I wanted to turn the knife on myself. I needed it.

"I won't hurt you," I choked out, the words tumbling from me.

She blinked down at me. "I know...I know you won't."

I swallowed hard and watched as she tried to climb down. I lifted my arms automatically, again, like it was my right, like the action was out of my control and driven by pure instinct. And she responded in kind, gripping my shoulders and letting me lift her down.

"Thanks," she said as I lowered her to the ground.

I wanted to pull her in close to me so fucking badly right then. "No problem."

Mags and Bram quickly started off again. Staying in one spot was only asking for trouble. We were close to the car, though, and as soon as Jaz reached it and got in, I took a fucking breath, then backed up several steps.

Bram raised a brow.

"The feral." I needed to run, to work out this tension inside me. I needed some space from Jasmine because I was feeling...fuck...possessive over her in a way that was not okay.

He nodded. "Be safe."

"What are you doing?" Jasmine said through the open window and grabbing for the door handle. "You're going after the feral? Now?"

I held the door shut when she tried to open it, keeping her in the car. "Just some tracking. To find his den."

"On your own? It's too dangerous," she said, trying to shove the door open again.

Again, I stopped her. "I've dealt with ferals before."

Her lips thinned. "What about our appointment later? You can't miss a night."

"I won't miss it. I'll be there." I took a step back when Bram started the car.

"You better be," she said, trying to sound bossy, but all I heard was fear.

She was scared for me, and twisted fuck that I was, I liked it.

)))⬤(((

Jasmine

Ren hadn't missed our appointment. He also hadn't told me what happened in the forest after we drove away, and I was dying to ask. He'd been quiet when I showed up at his place. He was fresh out of the shower, smelling of soap, his hair still damp.

I cleared my throat and dipped my needle in the ink, then continued with the sigil I was working on, just below and between his shoulder blades. It was an important one. They all were, but this was a grounding sigil, one of the main anchors for the rest, and it was more intricate.

He had a really nice back, smooth, muscled, skin tan. *Jesus, focus.* It wasn't easy, not when all I could think about was the way he'd looked fighting earlier, the way he'd fought those demons. *You threatened our females.* My heart had jumped at those words. He hadn't meant *his*, of course. Just the females that were with them. Still, my stupid heart had gone a little nuts, all the same, because I was an idiot.

Goddess, he'd killed so many of them. Mags and Bram had fought as well, but they'd been more...in control. They'd worked together, cutting through the demons coming at them. Ren had hacked and snarled. His face twisted in rage.

"Did you find the feral?" I asked as I wiped away the excess ink, unable to hold it in anymore.

He was quiet for a few seconds. "I picked up his scent. Pretty sure I know where his den is. I'll go back tomorrow."

Fear filled me. "And what will you do then?"

"I've got this, Jaz. He isn't the first feral I've faced off with."

He'd said something like that earlier. I didn't care. Why the hell did Agatheena insist on Ren doing this? "You shouldn't even be doing it in the first place. This is my thing; it has nothing to do with you. That crone is just using this whole situation to her own advantage."

"That's what she does. She's a female, alone, and she wouldn't have always been that powerful or that jaded. She's the way she is because life hasn't been easy. She doesn't ask for help because she probably doesn't think anyone will help. So she does deals. Barters for what she needs."

I huffed out a breath. "Well, now I feel like an asshole."

He chuckled. "You're not an asshole. You worry, that's your thing. But you don't need to worry about me."

I leaned in and started on the next sigil. "I'll never forgive myself or her if you get hurt because of this, because of me."

"Jaz—"

"You don't have to do it, you know. It's too much. I feel terrible." I had to find those souls, but not at Ren's expense. He didn't answer. He'd gone utterly still. I looked down and watched as my thumb stroked his skin. I realized I'd done it several times. I quickly got back to tattooing.

He cleared his throat, and his voice grew deeper. "You need the information, and this is how we get it. With all that you're doing for me, I owe you. And this is something I can do. I want to help."

"I still don't like it." At least with him on his stomach, I didn't have to worry about the fact that I was sitting there completely naked and covered in oil.

"I'm getting that," he said, and he sounded amused again.

He wasn't going to back down, so I shut up and carried on with what I was doing, working my way down his spine. The sigils were a necessity, yes, but they also looked really good on him.

"Just one more to do. Can I lower your pants a bit?" My face heated. He was wearing gray sweatpants and nothing else.

"Yeah," he said and kind of did a plank, lifting off the ground, causing his back muscles to flex.

I bit my lip and slid my thumbs under the waistband and tugged them lower. Nope. Nothing underneath. The top of his butt was also smooth and tanned like the rest of him. Ren was beautiful everywhere. "We'll just do this one, then we're done for the night," I said as I inked the outline. "This one's another anchor sigil. It's really pretty, so intricate. I'm glad I can actually do justice to something like this now."

"Pretty, huh?" he said, and he sounded like he was smiling. "Just what every male wants on his ass."

I laughed. "Better than something hideous, I guess."

He chuckled, and it was husky and sexy and made my belly flip-flop like crazy. "You got me there."

I finished up and was still smiling. "I'll just go clean up, then I'll be back. You can sit up, but stay inside the salt line until I get back." The souls had surrounded us, wailing with despair and fear and rage the entire time I'd been working. I needed to monitor them closely, gauging their reactions, to make sure each sigil was doing what it needed to, which was why I still had to take off my cuffs and necklace and do the naked, slathered-in-oil routine.

I'd done my best to tune them out. It hurt to listen to their suffering, but I didn't tell Ren how bad it was. He asked if they were there, and I said they were, but any more than that I'd kept to myself. He was already suffering enough and doing everything he could to set them free.

I put my sigil necklace and cuffs back on. The souls receded instantly, and I stepped out, over the line, and rushed to the bathroom to wipe off the oil and dress.

When I walked back out, Ren was sitting in the center, his forearms resting on his knees. Every lean muscle was taut, defined, and I had to stop myself from staring too hard.

He rose when I walked in, and I closed the space between us and tilted my head back, trying to be professional, to stop my heart from racing in my chest. "Ready?"

"You're going to...ah, do your healing thing?"

"Yep, you still good with that?"

He nodded slowly. "You think it'll help, and I trust you."

That he trusted me meant more than I could say. It meant everything. I smiled. "And I'll text you a link to an online guided mediation class that's great for beginners, to help you quiet things down and center yourself when I'm not here."

Now he looked skeptical. "Meditation, really?"

"Yes, really. It'll help, I promise. You'll love it." I took a step closer. "Right, let's—"

He brushed his thumb over my jaw, and my pulse went wild.

"You've got some"—he motioned to my jaw—"ink on your face. I was just..." He dropped his hand.

My cheeks heated. "Oh..." I laughed awkwardly and wiped where his fingers had just been, and hoped he didn't see the way mine trembled. "I'm always doing that. I was drawing earlier. Is it gone?"

He cleared his throat. "Yeah."

"Let's get started. I know it's hard, but you can't pull away, okay?"

He nodded again, and I closed the space between us, wrapping my arms around his stomach and lacing my fingers together behind his back, so every part of me that could was touching him. My face was against his chest, and I could hear, feel, his heart banging hard as I sent power into him, seeking out the damage, wrapping around it, not tight, not yet, brushing past it and smoothing it out.

His breathing grew choppy.

"It's okay, Ren," I said. "Everything's going to be okay." His exhales grew almost frantic, and I hung on to him tighter. "I've got you."

I filled him with warmth, with love and affection, as waves of guilt and horror rolled off him and into me. *Oh goddess.* It was as if, for a short time, his pain was my own. I trembled, tears springing to my eyes like the last time, the feeling too big, too overwhelming to hold them back.

"Fuck," he bit out. "Fuck."

I unlaced my fingers and rubbed his back, soothing him as best I could. Most people were calmed by this, my arms around them, and hugged me back, letting the warmth and the healing fill them. People who didn't think they deserved healing responded like Ren. Feeling good, feeling warmth, affection, it terrified them because they didn't believe they deserved it.

"I can't...Jaz. Fuck."

I pressed closer, linking my fingers again tighter, wanting to take all of his pain away so badly and fucking hating that I couldn't. "Don't fight it. Let it in."

"I don't think... I can't..." He growled, his muscles twitching, his body trembling against me.

"Hang on, just a little longer." He was rock solid, so tense it had to hurt.

Then his arms suddenly banded around me, gripping me to him tightly. He shuddered out a breath as his face went to the crook of my neck. My power had won out, for now, and the euphoria was kicking in. He groaned, his lips brushing my neck like last time, but they lingered, and the brush turned into sucking kisses across my skin.

I'd never had anyone kiss me while I healed them. They hugged me, tight like he was now, but this—

Shivers slid through me as his mouth skated along my throat to the underside of my jaw. It wasn't time to stop. I couldn't pull away from him yet. "Jasmine," he groaned, his arms an iron band around me. He trembled harder.

"It's okay," I rasped. "You're okay."

Everyone reacted differently when I healed them. I'd had people feel unexplained rage or resentment toward me, another client had professed his love for me during every session and begged me to go out with him, another had followed me around for a couple weeks, positive I was the love of his life. In all instances, these feelings had worn off when the work was done.

His hand slid up my spine, his fingers thrusting in my hair, his panted breaths against my ear.

Oh goddess.

Ren's reaction was just more...physical.

He tugged lightly, like he was trying to get me to turn to him, while he kissed along my jaw. It was wrong, but this was Ren, and there was no stopping my body from heating, from responding.

The waves of his emotions ebbed, slowly rolling back. He released his grip on my hair and lifted his head from my throat and, still breathing hard, he pressed his mouth to the top of my head.

"Ten seconds," I whispered, and counted down.

Finally, I released him and stepped away, turning away without looking back. He didn't need me staring at him when he was already feeling so utterly vulnerable. I quickly swiped away my tears, still recovering from the intensity of his emotions and of his arms around me—his mouth on me.

"You can move around now," I said, making myself busy picking up the string and rosemary line and packing away the candles.

"You're upset," he choked out, alarm in his voice.

"It happens. Not just with you but with all my clients. I get a bit of what you're feeling, and it can take me by surprise." It was the truth, but I'd never felt anything like I did when I was with Ren.

The color drained from his face.

"Don't overthink it," I said quickly. "What I feel coming from you is nothing that I haven't felt before." Another lie, but I couldn't bear to see the horror and humiliation in his eyes. He had nothing to be humiliated about. I hitched my bag over my shoulder and headed for the door.

"Jaz?"

I turned back, and he moved closer. "While you were healing me, and I..." He shoved his fingers through his hair. "I didn't mean to... I'm sorry, I crossed a line—"

"Don't be. You did nothing wrong. My magic, it's powerful. It affects everyone differently. Please, don't apologize. I promise, I'm not bothered at all." I reached for the door, but Ren reached around me before I could open it.

"I just want you to know that. I'm not...my control...this isn't..."

I turned and looked up at him, into his pained eyes, knowing exactly what he was trying to say. "You're not weak, Ren. You need to know that and believe it. I know it. I feel it, how impossibly strong you truly are."

He stared down at me as if he couldn't register my words, as if they didn't make sense or I were speaking a language he didn't understand.

"You truly mean that, don't you?" he finally said.

"I wouldn't say it if I didn't."

A few strands of my hair were stuck to my lip, and I was about to swipe it away, but Ren beat me to it, our hands bumping. "Sorry." I had no idea why I was apologizing.

"I was just..." He carefully hooked my hair around his finger, brushing it back, then quickly crossed his arms, shoving his hands under his pits and taking a step back.

My face heated, but I pretended I wasn't blushing, that Ren brushing my hair back was nothing, that the kisses he'd just given me were nothing, and I smiled. "I better get going. I have to be somewhere, so I'll see you tomorrow." I started to turn and Ren stopped me.

"Big plans?"

"Um...kind of." Why the hell was my face getting hotter? Ugh.

His lips thinned, his gaze darkening for some reason. "You have a good night."

"Thanks." I walked away and felt his eyes on me until I was out of sight.

CHAPTER 12

Jasmine

I LOOKED up as Mags walked into the kitchen. "Hey."

Thanks to my family's association with a councilor on the witches council, I'd managed to get some names of some very powerful beings in the city who *might* be able to help me. Councilor Trotman had only been able to fit in a meeting with me last night after I'd seen Ren. He'd given me the names on the condition I didn't share where I got them from. I was fine with that.

"Sorry, I hope you haven't been waiting long?" she said.

"Nope, I just got here. No Bram?"

"There's a blood-drunk vampire on the loose." Mags shuddered. "So no Bram, but we can't waste time waiting for him."

I raised a brow. "Did you tell him that?"

She grinned. "Not exactly. You know how he is about me doing shit like this alone, despite the fact that I can kick all kinds of ass. I do have several vials in my bag that can melt a face right off, though, just in case."

"Excellent."

"I mean, it's not like these people are dangerous, right?" she asked.

"Um...honestly, I have no idea."

She chewed her lip.

"I guess we could ask Relic or Rome?" I said, because walking into an unknown situation without backup wasn't smart. I'd also promised Zinnia I wouldn't take any stupid risks.

"Or maybe Hadeon. I mean, yes, the guy's weird, but he lives in Hell, so who wouldn't be?"

Um, hard pass. "Me and Zinnia aren't exactly his favorite people either, and doesn't Bram hate that guy?"

Mags winced. "Good point." She leaned against the counter. "So how many people do we need to drop in on?"

I pulled a crumpled piece of paper from my pocket. "Four."

"I think we'll be fine."

My sister's voice telling me not to do anything without backup filled my head. "What if we take two names each, ask Relic and Rome to tag along, and get it done faster?"

Her mouth twisted to the side. She didn't look happy. "Those hounds can be overbearing. They mistake backup for protection. I don't need protection."

"No, you don't, and Relic knows that. He'll let you lead. I, on the other hand, am no great kicker of ass. I could, of course, use one of those face-melting vials of yours, but I don't like my chances. Zinny's counting on me, and this way we get through the list faster and your mate won't have reason to lose his shit."

"Yeah, I suppose." She rolled her eyes. "Relic's gonna give me shit for this."

I chuckled. "Probably."

She growled under her breath. "Okay, let's do it. You call them, though. I don't want to hear the glee in his voice when you ask."

A short time later, we were in Magnolia's car and heading to the club-house to pick up Relic and Rome.

"Will Bram really be pissed when he finds out you did this?" I asked Mags.

She glanced over at me. "Probably. He's not just my mate, he's my familiar. Can't get much more protective and, yeah, irrational when it comes to my safety than that—or his possessiveness when I spend time with other males. But I'll deal with that later. He thinks a witch should have their familiar with them if there's even a sniff of danger." She glanced at my shoulder, then up to my head, where two mourning cloaks had landed as soon as I walked outside. "But this is the right move." She grinned. "Yours don't exactly have fangs or claws."

I laughed. "Sadly, no. Though they could probably love someone to death if given the chance."

Mags chuckled.

When we pulled into the clubhouse, Relic and Rome were already waiting. They strode over and stopped by the car. Mags rolled down the window. "Get in the back."

Relic scowled. "You can ride with us. We're not all squeezing into that tin can."

"Bram would murder you in your sleep if I rode on the back of your bike, Relic, and you know it."

"He could try," Relic said and flashed his teeth.

"I'll ride with Rome. We're going to have to split up anyway," I said.

Mags reached over into the back seat and grabbed her coat, passing it to me. "You'll need this."

I tugged the list from my pocket and tore it in half, giving her two of the names and addresses.

We'd gone over what we needed to ask on the way here.

"Give me a call if you find out anything useful and I'll come to you," I said.

"Will do."

I got out and Relic took my place, jamming himself into the passenger side. Mags did a three-point turn and tore out onto the street. Relic looked like he was hanging on for dear life. Hounds didn't love cars or letting someone else take control of the wheel.

I chuckled. "Relic looked a little green around the gills."

"Better him than me," Rome said and gave me a little nudge before he headed for his bike.

I loved Rome's bike, it was all chrome and leather, and had a metallic, gunmetal-gray gas tank with chrome skulls on either side. I pulled on Mags's jacket while he started it up.

I was about to get on when the door to the clubhouse opened and Ren strode out. He turned our way and stopped suddenly, his eyes darkening.

I froze under that hard stare, my feet rooted to the spot.

"Get up, babe," Rome said.

I jolted out of my stupor, flicked a wave in Ren's direction, and quickly climbed on. I rested my hands at Roman's hips, and he reached back, grabbed my hands, and pulled them around his waist, making sure I was hanging on tight, and because of his size, that meant my front was plastered to his back and there was nothing I could do about it. I'd ridden with him before and hadn't been worried, but now, with Ren watching, I wanted to pull away and jump right off the back of the bike for some reason.

"Where to first?" Rome asked.

I told him the address, then we were moving, rolling through the gates. As Rome checked the way was clear, I couldn't stop myself from glancing back at Ren. He was striding in our direction, a thunderous expression on his face.

We roared out onto the street, and I shivered, not from the cold air instantly soaking through me but from the look on Ren's face.

A short time later, we pulled up outside the first house on the list. I looked up. The place was tall and narrow and had two levels. It was painted pink with white trim and had wisteria creeping along the narrow veranda. In summer it'd be absolutely covered in gorgeous mauve flowers. It was quirky and cute. When I was younger, this would've been my dream home. Who was I kidding, it still kind of was.

I climbed off and Rome did as well. "You can wait here, I'm fine."

"Not happening," he muttered and swaggered up to the porch and knocked on the door.

I rushed up and muscled in front of him. "If she looks out and sees you, she'll never let us in."

"Females love me," he said with all the arrogance in the world.

I honestly hadn't met a hound who wasn't arrogant, and yes, females loved them, but outside of the clubhouse, most people, male or female, who had even a grain of self-preservation gave these guys a wide berth.

"To anyone looking, you're a seven-foot-tall, long-haired biker with bulging muscles covered in tattoos, and freaky eyes. The only females who love you guys on sight are females looking for a walk on the wild side. The rest of us need a minute."

He grunted and took a step back. "My eyes aren't freaky."

I knocked again. "Yes, they are. You're just used to them." They looked human, yes, but the color changed and sometimes got all swirly, depending on the male. When their inner hounds came closer to the surface, which happened a lot, they flashed red.

"Haven't had any complaints," he muttered.

"'Cause the females you're with aren't looking at your eyes."

He chuckled as the door opened.

A tall, slender female stood there. If I had to guess, I'd say she was in her early fifties. She was stunningly beautiful, had a mass of black curly hair streaked with gray, and dark brown skin. Her rich brown eyes sparkled as she took us in. I wasn't one hundred percent sure what she was. I thought I sensed demon, but there was more as well. Human. I was sure of it. Zara Harris was a demi-demon.

"Can I help you?" she asked in a cultured British accent.

"Hi, are you Zara?"

"Who wants to know?"

"I'm Jasmine Thornheart. You don't know me, but I was wondering if we could have a chat?"

"About?"

"Soul summoning. We were told it's your expertise. I'm hoping you can help us?"

She held my gaze and her head tilted to the side. "You're a medium as well."

Somehow, she knew what I was just by looking at me. "I am."

"Then why do you need me?"

"The souls we're looking for aren't showing themselves to me."

Her gaze slid to Rome, taking him in from head to foot. "And who's this." She liked him, there was no missing it. A lot.

"This is Roman, my friend."

She held out her hand. "Roman, nice to meet you."

He took it. "Call me Rome."

"Come on in." She opened the door wider for us to follow her inside.

Rome nudged me, and I looked up. "Told you."

I rolled my eyes, and he chuckled as he followed me in.

Zara made us tea. She was open and honest about her gift, but unfortunately wasn't able to help me.

I left the house twenty minutes later with a stash of herbs that I'd been struggling to find and one of the candles she made. Rome left with her number. She'd slipped it into his hand before we walked out.

I really liked the female. She'd told me to come by anytime, and I was actually contemplating it. She was one of those people who hid nothing, and you felt it. She was who she was, and she was extremely cool.

Rome started for the bike. "Where to next, Jazzy?"

I fished out the address as my phone dinged. I quickly checked it. A client I'd been trying to connect with could finally see me. I had a message for her that was important but sensitive, and not something I wanted to give her over the phone. Part of the job, for me at least, was being there when you delivered the kind of news I needed to deliver to her. It was irresponsible to hit someone with something potentially devastating when you had no idea where they were or if they were on their own.

"I actually have to be somewhere else. Can we pick this back up later this afternoon, if you're free?"

Rome frowned. "Something up?"

"Just a client I need to see. They don't live that far from here. I'll walk."

"I'll take you."

I hitched my bag. "I'm good. It's literally just a few blocks away."

"How long you think you'll be?"

I shrugged. "Probably a couple hours."

He flashed his teeth. "I can work with that, I'll just"—he looked back at the cute pink house we'd just left—"find something to keep me occupied until you're ready."

I shook my head and rolled my eyes. "Well, you have fun, and I'll text when I'm done."

"You need me before that, call, yeah?"

"Will do."

Rome winked and strode back up to Zara's veranda, and I headed off down the street. I realized after several blocks that I'd underestimated the distance. I texted to let my client know I'd be a little late, and they replied with an apology that something unexpected had come up and asked to reschedule again. *Dammit.*

I quickly replied and shoved my phone in my pocket. Now what was I going to do? There was no way I was going back to Zara's house. The last thing I wanted to do was interrupt her and Rome—if what I thought was happening was happening. Which meant I had at least two hours to kill.

I pulled the piece of paper from my pocket and typed the address for the next person on my list into my maps app. It was literally a block away. I headed off again. I wasn't going to go in, but no harm in doing a walk-by. I pulled the paper back out as I walked and checked the name again.

Xavier Rush. I'd met the male before at Rose and Ronan's place. He was a dhampir as well, someone Ronan had met during some business dealings. They'd become kind of friends. He was a little odd, but then Ronan had been as well when we first met him. Ronan was a good male. He wouldn't be pals with the guy if he was a homicidal maniac, right?

It started to drizzle, so I walked faster, and my two little mourning cloaks fluttered from my head and landed on my shoulder, sheltering under my hair. I zipped Magnolia's coat right up to my chin and pulled my hair forward so they were protected from the wind and rain.

I rounded the corner and rushed down the narrow street, checking numbers on mailboxes, then spotted it. Xavier's house was a massive brownstone, four levels high, with dark gray trim and a shiny black door. The rain came down harder, and I rushed across the street and up the stairs. Rome might be pissed when I told him that I'd come here, but I'd met this guy before, I'd even had a brief conversation with him.

I was about to knock when the door opened and a female walked out. There was a wide smile on her lined face, a look in her eyes as if the heaviest burden had been lifted from her shoulders.

"Whatever you're here for, you've come to the right place," she said and walked away.

I watched her go. It was impossible to miss the warmth, the happiness radiating from her. I *felt* it.

"Can I help you?"

I spun around. Xavier stood there, his lips curled up on one side, his cool lavender eyes moving over my face. "I'm not sure, but I hope so."

"We've met before. Jasmine, yes?"

"Sorry, yes. I'm Rose's cousin. We met at her and Ronan's place a few months ago."

"I remember." He smiled.

His eyes drew me in, and I momentarily forgot what I was doing. He was handsome, there was no missing it, I'd thought as much when I first met him. His hair was a deep brown and had a wave to it. It was combed back and seemed to sit perfectly around his chiseled face. He was tall and lean but muscled from what I could see. His jacket and trousers strained around his biceps and thighs.

"You said you needed my help?"

I jumped again, my face flaming hot at being caught checking him out. "Oh...right." I laughed, and it came out a weird kind of giggle. "I heard you're a specialist when it comes to metaphysical barriers?" Similar to Ronan's ability, all dhampir seemed to have some kind of metaphysical blocking ability, though not as many were as powerful as Ronan. Xavier's power was different, from what Councilor Trotman said. Apparently, he could search nooks and crannies on metaphysical planes, but couldn't create his own.

"I am, among other things. Would you like to come in?" he asked.

"Please, if you have time to talk?"

He opened the door wider and motioned me inside.

I walked in. The floors were hardwood and gleamed. Wainscoting matched the floors and the rest of the walls above were a rich cream. Twin curved staircases rose from the grand foyer on either side of the room, leading up to the second floor. There was a delicate and expensive-looking side table with a marble statue of a female looking into the distance, her body draped in silk, on top. I'd never seen anything like it. "Your home is stunning."

"Thank you. It's been in my family for several generations. I've lived here my whole life." He motioned to a door on the right.

"You collect antiques?" I asked as I walked into the beautifully furnished room.

"I do."

I guess you'd call it a formal living room. Damask silk fabric covered the couch and chairs, there were gorgeous pieces of furniture, vases, statues, and a rug that I assumed cost more than my car. "I don't know anything about antiques, but everything is just...beautiful."

"That's very kind of you. Please, take a seat."

I sat on the love seat, and Xavier sat across from me in an armchair.

"Thanks for agreeing to talk."

"Of course."

"When I asked if you were a metaphysical expert, you said among other things." I was extremely curious about the male now that I was here.

"Yes," he said and didn't elaborate.

"The female who just left, she said you helped her?" I was being nosy, but I wanted to know. The happiness that flowed from her when she left was...intense. "Can I ask how you helped her?"

"I don't usually discuss my clients with other people, Jasmine. The service I provide is...delicate. But I guess in this instance, I could share a little of what I do. I assume someone told you of my ability to travel through realms? Yes, it sounds exciting, but there isn't much call for it." He grinned, and his eyes seemed to swirl as he took me in. "If I were a great explorer, maybe it would be something I'd enjoy, but I prefer to be here."

"I don't blame you. Your home is amazing."

"I'm glad you think so." He tilted his head to the side. "To explain what I do, I'll need to give you a little backstory. Like all dhampir, or at least those not stolen and used for their powers, I was raised by my human mother. She was cold, though, held her emotions close, I assume to protect herself from her own trauma—I later found out her parents were...extremely unkind to her. Thankfully, she kept me around. Had she not, I would have ended up emotionless. But it was through my mother's cold demeanor, her neglect, that I discovered what I could do."

If a dhampir was separated from their human mothers at an early age, they lost the ability to feel emotion, which was what happened to Ronan and his sister.

"I'm sorry you went through that. It had to be tough growing up that way," I said, not sure what else to say. He seemed like a nice guy, and no one should have affection withheld or be ignored like that. My own mother had been restless and absent, but she loved us. In her own way.

"That's very kind of you to say, Jasmine," he said. "But it was a long time ago now."

He obviously didn't want to get into his emotions, we barely knew each other, but I was used to caring for people's emotional well-being. It was my job, and it came naturally. I shifted the conversation back. "So what is it you can do?"

"As you know, dhampir are born with an array of blocking powers. No two are the same, but they can be similar. As a child I learned I could block certain emotions I was feeling, put up a wall to completely protect myself from anything...unpleasant I was feeling. Compartmentalize, if you will. As it grew stronger, I could do it for others, for short periods of time, and now, after years of practice, I can locate intricate emotions, localize them and build walls, completely cutting off those feelings permanently."

I stared at him stunned. "And that's what you did for the female who just left?"

"Yes." His gaze seemed to draw me deeper. "She'd grieved her mate for a very long time. The weight of it was more than she could bear. It was stopping her from living, from moving forward. So I concealed that pain from her."

I blinked several times, trying to absorb the enormity of that, of what he'd just done. "Will she still remember him?"

"Yes. But the longer the walls are intact, the longer those feelings of grief will be starved and eventually wither and die. Now she can remember the good times without the pain. She can be happy."

"That's an impressive gift." Extreme but impressive.

Could something like that work for Ren? Possibly, but I doubted he'd go for it, and he had me. I'd heal him, it'd just take a little time. I definitely couldn't do something like that. Take away the way I felt about something or someone. Then I remembered telling Zinnia I wished I could take the way I felt for Ren out of my body. Maybe I could understand why someone would contemplate it, but that had just been words, said when I was feeling particularly low. I'd never actually do it.

"Your gift is impressive as well, Jasmine, I can feel it."

I smiled and looked away from the intensity of his lavender eyes. "I'm no slouch."

"What can you do exactly? I'd love to know."

"I'm a medium. I communicate with the dead. I also have the ability to heal emotional scars via touch, which is why my sessions usually end with a hug. Receiving messages from loved ones who've passed on can be painful. I do my best to ease that pain before they leave me."

He stilled, his gaze penetrating. "As I thought. Impressive."

I smiled. "I guess we're kind of in the same business, we just have different forms of treatment. Sadly, it doesn't help my sister, or Death with his problem."

"Death?" He frowned. "What problem is that?"

"Missing souls."

He sat forward. "Missing?"

"The body count to soul ratio there isn't adding up. Death and Lucifer are both missing souls."

He sat back, looking surprised. "That's astounding."

"I was wondering if there was something you could do to help find them. If maybe you had the ability to sense them in this realm or others?"

He shook his head. "Unfortunately, no. If only I were that powerful. And your sister's somehow involved."

"My sister is Death's consort. It's this whole messed-up situation."

"Indeed."

"Anyway, thanks, Xavier. If you think of anything, or of someone else who might be able to help, could you call me?"

"Of course."

I stood, and he did as well. He slid his phone from his pocket, typed my name into his contacts, then handed it to me. "Can I ask, the butterflies in your hair? My curiosity has gotten the better of me."

I quickly typed in my number and handed it back. "My familiars," I said and smiled.

"Really?"

"Yep."

"But their lifespan... I'm sorry," he said quickly. "I understand the relationship between a witch and their familiar, or familiars in your case, is very close."

"It's okay, and you're right. At any one time, depending on the time of year, the number of familiars I have can range from none, while some hibernate and others wait to emerge, to hundreds. That kind of loss is extremely hard." I lifted my hand to one of the sweet little souls with me, and she fluttered to my hand. "At the moment, there are only mourning cloaks around. These two have been with me for just over a week now."

"And you feel a connection to them?"

"Yes, very strongly. Their love is...overwhelming at times, especially when I have two hundred of them flying around me." I chuckled. "But yes, our connection is as strong as any other witch and her familiar, which is why it hurts so much when they go."

His mouth tipped up to the side. "If it ever becomes too much, I'd be happy to help you with that."

I shook my head. "Thanks, but they deserve to be mourned. I love them just as fiercely. I'd be afraid that would change if I never felt their loss."

"Very wise."

"Well, thanks again, Xavier. It was fascinating talking to you."

His lips curled up and his eyes warmed. "You as well, Jasmine. Maybe we could...do it again sometime?"

I paused. "Talk?"

"Well, yes. Over dinner perhaps?"

My face heated. "Like a date?"

His smile widened, and I got a flash of fangs. A little shiver slid down my spine. "Yes, like a date."

"I'm not sure... I mean... I don't know."

"I'll let you think about it. In the meantime, if I think of anything that could help you, I'll let you know."

CHAPTER 13

Jasmine

It was later than I'd intended when I was finally on my way to Ren's place, but after my disappointing day, hitting wall after wall in my search for the missing souls, then meeting up with Rome, who was pissed with me for going to Xavier's alone no matter how many times I told him there was absolutely no danger, I'd been running late.

I'd asked Rome if he was going to see Zara again, and he'd looked at me like I was insane. "Was just a hookup, Jazzy," he'd said. "She's a nice female, but she was just a way to pass the time, and I was that for her as well."

Harsh but true. Now that Warrick had found his mate, a lot of the hounds, especially the really old ones, were getting restless. They wanted what their alpha had, and I didn't blame them for it.

After that, I met up with Mags for a debrief. She'd gotten the same amount of leads as me—in other words, none at all.

And now I was on my way to Ren's place, and trying to get my head in the game when all I could think about was Zinnia and how she was counting on me, and I was failing her miserably.

Hitching my bag higher, I walked the short distance to the funeral home, across the parking lot, and down the external steps to Ren's basement apartment. Music played low inside, so I knocked harder than I usually would.

The door swung open and Breanne stood there. She smelled of alcohol and cigarettes. As soon as she saw me, she scowled. "What the fuck do you want?"

So much for him and Breanne being done. He obviously couldn't stay away from the wolf, no matter what he'd said to me. Pain sharp and ugly swamped my chest. I gave myself a mental slap. *Get it the fuck together.* "I'm here to see Ren."

"Hey, I've got a better idea!" she said in an overly bright and high-pitched voice. I assumed it was her attempt to imitate me. Her eyes flashed wolf. "How about you fuck off instead?"

I so wasn't in the mood for this shit. My temper skyrocketed, but I fought it back. "I don't know what your problem is with me, and I honestly don't care. Whatever it is you think I'm here for, I can guarantee you're wrong."

"I think you're here to beg my male to fuck you like the pathetic little *bitch* you are," she snapped. "Well, you can't have him. For one, he doesn't want you. And for another, I'm here to give it to him the way he likes it."

Ouch, that fucking hurt, way more than it should. This entire thing fucking hurt, but that was my problem, not Ren's. Still, I wasn't some emotionless robot, and holding in my anger was *hard*, especially after the crappy day I'd had. "I'm so happy for you both, you deserve each other, but—"

"Jaz?" Ren moved in beside Breanne. "Ah...hey."

"Hey. I'm sorry if I'm interrupting something, but we have to do this tonight, you know, like we arranged yesterday." I sounded pissed, snappish, and seriously judgmental. I didn't want to be any of those things, and that pissed me off as well.

He smelled of alcohol as well, and I was seriously thankful they were both fully dressed, unlike the last time I saw Breanne here. "Yeah, right. Sorry, I lost track of time. Come in."

"You're asking her in?" Breanne snarled.

He turned to her. "This'll take a while."

"I'll wait."

He shook his head. "No, you'll go."

She stared at him for long seconds, her lips curling, fury burning in her eyes. "If I leave, I won't ever come back."

Ren said nothing, just stood there.

She growled so loud, I jumped. Then she disappeared back into his apartment and grabbed her jacket, bag, and a bottle of vodka. "Your loss, asshole." Then she stormed off.

Awkward silence filled the space between us.

He rubbed the back of his head. "Sorry about that."

"What the fuck, Ren?" I said before I could stop myself. "You knew we were doing this tonight. What the hell is wrong with you? I can't believe you've been drinking."

His eyes narrowed. "I wasn't aware I had to run every minute of my day by you."

I stared at him. Was he serious? Yeah, he was drunk, or at least on his way, but really? I shoved down my anger. Arguing with him was a waste of time and energy. "Let's just get this over with." I strode into the living room, dumped my bag on the couch, found my candles, and set them out on the rug.

I sensed Ren walking in behind me and ignored him, going back to my bag and getting out the salt and cemetery dirt and laying out my line, followed by the string and rosemary, and setting them out as well, while saying my protection spell. The mortar and pestle were next. I put them on his table and angrily pounded together the ingredients for my soul-repelling oil. The souls would get riled when I started tattooing his sigils again, and I needed to make sure they continued to work, which meant I still had to remove my sigil charms and protect myself with oil since they were so volatile. Ren watched all of this but still said nothing.

Yesterday, in this very room, he told me that Breanne meant nothing to him, that he was done with her. He'd also kissed my neck, which I knew had nothing to do with me and everything to do with my power, but humiliatingly, I thought about it on and off all day, and the way I'd made him laugh, because again, I was an idiot. And when he'd seen me with Rome this morning, there'd been this look on his face? He hadn't liked it. Why I didn't know, but it obviously wasn't because he wanted me for himself, something I'd secretly hoped.

He was still quiet, and I could see out of the corner of my eyes that he had his arms folded, a stubborn damn look on his face now, which was probably why instead of going to his room to strip, I did it right there.

What I was trying to achieve, I wasn't one hundred percent sure. He obviously saw me as nothing, barely a female, not desirable, not anything at all, so why hide? Did I think this would change his mind? Put a crack in that armor, make him sorry for choosing literally everyone over me, or make him feel shitty for hurting me over and over again. No. Because he didn't even know he was doing it.

Still, it made me feel better somehow.

I stripped down to my bra and panties, then without pausing took them off as well. It was hard, but I ignored his sharp indrawn breath and got busy smearing oil all over my body. He didn't avert his gaze. I felt his eyes on me the entire time, probably because he was drunk and I was throwing my naked ass in his face. "Get on the mat, Ren," I said as I smeared oil over my breasts and down my stomach.

He didn't move. "Jasmine—"

"Now," I bit out. "And take your shirt off."

He growled low under his breath but did as I said, and my stupid belly quivered at that rough sound. I covered the last of my skin with oil, grabbed my bag, and stepped into the string line with Ren.

I quickly removed my necklace and cuffs, placing them outside the barrier. I'd felt the souls pressing in as soon as I walked in the house. I was positive the sigils I'd selected for Ren were the correct combination, but I needed to know for sure. They stood around the string line, moaning and screaming, begging me for help, but it was more distant than it had been. The sigils I'd already done were definitely working. I tried to tune them out now, to not feel their pain and fear, and to focus on what I had to do. It wasn't easy.

I checked the sigils I'd drawn on his skin with my tattoo marker. They'd held up well. I took out the box with my portable tattoo machine. It was small and light but did the job.

Ren tilted his head my way. "Jasmine?"

His low, raspy voice lifted goose bumps all over me. "Eyes straight ahead," I bit out.

He did as I said and thrust his fingers through his hair. "What you walked in on—"

"I didn't walk in on anything. I arrived at a mutually agreed upon time for our appointment, since I'm providing a professional service and all. And you know, doing a favor for Willow, but instead I get insults thrown at me by your *friend*. I'd say I was sorry for interrupting your party with Bree, but I'm not. My time is important. In case you've forgotten I have souls to find."

"You didn't interrupt anything."

"No? She seemed to think so. Since, apparently, I'm a bitch, and the only reason I'm here is to beg *her male* to fuck me."

"What the fuck?" he snarled.

"Don't act so surprised. You either want her and you're denying it for some reason—while, by the way, treating her like crap—or you're using her to get off, giving the female mixed messages, and generally being a dick."

"Jaz—"

"When you invite someone over to drink vodka with you, someone you bone on the regular, they're going to have certain expectations." I was being a bitch, like Bree accused me of, but I couldn't stop myself.

"I didn't invite her here."

Oh sure. "It's none of my business."

"You seem pretty worked up, Jasmine, throwing a lot of shit at me about it, so I should get to defend myself. No, I didn't invite her here. I've had a shitty fucking day, and she showed up with vodka and I wanted a drink." He took a steadying breath. "I shouldn't have let her in, but I...I wasn't thinking clearly. It won't happen again."

"Like I said, it's none of my business." I finished getting my tattoo machine ready, filled my little ink cup with ink and added a few drops of the potion I'd mixed before I came, and stirred it carefully. "I'll start with your shoulders. It'll be easier if you sit up straight." He was sitting on the floor with his forearms resting on his knees.

He did as I said, and I gasped. His scars looked raw, goddess, almost fresh. I reached out. "Ren, what happened to you..."

He grabbed my hand, stopping me from making contact. "Nothing." He held my gaze, his tone a demand that I don't ask him any more about it, that I ignore what was right in front of me. Our eyes stayed locked, and his fox swirled behind his. "It's nothing," he said again, breaking the silence.

I nodded and pulled my hand out from under his. "If you say so." Then I turned on the tattoo machine, dipped it in the ink cup, loading the reservoir, and angled closer. "Try not to move." Then I started tattooing while I recited the same spell I had the night before, over and over again.

An hour passed without him saying a word, and I was glad for it, then he said out of the blue, "You painted me."

I stilled.

"My fox, anyway, on Violet's wall."

He'd seen it. "Yep. You're important to her. You're Willow's familiar," I said, telling him the truth. Yes, he'd belonged there, but that wasn't the only reason I'd painted him. I'd seen his eyes in my mind and envisioned them in that leafy corner, and there'd been no stopping me. I started spelling again, killing the conversation, and thankfully he let it go.

It took me several hours to do his shoulders. It'd taken longer because this set was a lot more intricate. I'd also needed to monitor the souls closely as I went. They were furious, not at Ren but at me, which meant I was using the correct sigil configuration like I thought, and now that I was using magic ink, the souls could feel it, the distance growing between them and Ren, and not in the way they wanted. They were still stuck with him, only now they couldn't get to him quite as easily, and when I was done, not at all.

I turned off the tattoo machine and shook out my hand. "That'll do for tonight. I'll be back tomorrow and hopefully get the rest done then. If we could start earlier, that'd be good. It'll take a few more hours, but I want to get this finished." My voice was hoarse from spelling for hours.

"Right," he said and turned to me, keeping his gaze above the neck. "Thank you, Jaz, for this."

I nodded and quickly put on my necklace and cuffs. The souls drew back, then vanished from view. Calmer again now. "Stay there while I get a towel to wipe off this oil."

I went to stand, but he grabbed my arm. "I'm sorry I was an asshole."

"Are you?"

"Of course I am." His gaze searched mine.

I wondered what he saw when he looked at me. This male confused the hell out of me. I'd made Ren think I was with Rome, and he picked a fight with him. He saw me with Rome this morning, and he'd looked at me in a way that I couldn't read but had twisted my belly in knots. Then I get here tonight, and he was with Breanne, almost like he was trying to hurt me. "Why did you invite Breanne in, Ren?" I said, finding courage I didn't know I possessed.

"Like I said, she had vodka," he said roughly.

"And that's it? No other reason?" *Like trying to make me jealous?*

As I sat there, looking into those wild eyes, his expression as closed off as it ever was, I knew I was wrong, that I'd read into things, seen things that weren't there because I wanted it to be true so badly, and my face heated.

His nostrils flared. "No other reason."

I nodded, feeling stupid. If there was another reason, it wasn't to make me jealous, it was to sleep with Bree. Goddess, I was an idiot. "If you could gather everything for me, that'd be great," I said, snatching up my clothes and leaving to clean up.

When I walked back out, he had his shirt on and the candles were sitting on the coffee table, the string and rosemary gathered beside it. He'd packed my tattoo machine as well, and it sat by my bag. I strode over and put everything inside the bag, then turned to him.

My belly was in knots, and the last thing I wanted to do was pull him into my arms and hug him. Well, I did, despite everything, which was why this sucked so much. *You're a goddamn professional, act like it.* I looked up at him. "I'll try to make this as painless as possible," I said, attempting a lame joke and forcing myself to relax.

"Jaz, about earlier. We made a time. I shouldn't have let Bree in."

"Let's just forget about it. I'm sorry for being a snappish shrew. I had a weird crappy day as well." I forced a smile. "Now, I just need you to stand there and think of England while I do my thing."

He frowned. "What?"

"It's a British saying. Don't worry. Let's do this." I stepped closer and wrapped my arms around him. The hot, hard wall of his chest pressed against mine. His arms stayed at his sides like last time, at the beginning anyway, and I wrapped myself around him and poured my powers into him, seeking out his emotional wounds. I gently wrapped around them, doing what I could to add to the foundation of healing I'd been building.

His body grew hotter, his muscles twitching, trembling. "I've got you, Ren," I said softly. "Everything's going to be okay. You did nothing wrong. It wasn't your fault." The words came to me again, the words his damaged emotional state told my gift he needed. He shook harder, telling me I was right.

"Fuck," he croaked. "Jaz—"

He tensed, and I knew like last time, it was a lot for him. He was moments from pulling away. "Just a little longer." A tidal wave of pain and fear, of guilt slammed into me, more powerful than last time, and I bit back my cry of agony.

I whimpered and held him tighter. "You're almost there."

"Fuck," he said again, trembling so hard it had to hurt.

My gift coiled tighter around his emotional wounds, pouring into them, smoothing over some of the jagged edges. Not enough to make a huge difference yet, and Ren might not even notice, but it was a start. A step in the right direction. I thought about the way he'd laughed in the forest. Or maybe it was already helping.

Tears swam in my eyes, my throat aching from fighting back a sob, then it happened, the agony began to recede, and like last time, Ren groaned. He was breathing harder.

"I can't...I can't stop," he said and wrapped his arms around me, one sliding into my hair and tipping my head back. "Jaz, fuck." His mouth slammed down on mine.

He kissed me.

He kissed me deep, his tongue sliding against mine hungrily. I was locked in his arms, my head held in place by his fist in my hair, so all I could do was surrender to it—give him the release he needed in that moment. This kiss, his hunger, it wasn't about me, I reminded myself. It wasn't for me. This was a reaction to the way my power made him feel and the alcohol he'd shared with Bree, that's all.

But, goddess, it was so good...and so wrong. I could taste the vodka he'd been drinking, and I wanted to shove him away and pull him closer at the same time. This was torture.

"I'm sorry," he panted against my lips. "But I need to..." He kissed me again, his arms a tight band of muscle around me.

I didn't fight it. Humiliatingly, I didn't want to.

Finally, he lifted his head, panting.

I released him and stepped back, my self-preservation instincts still intact, even if my common sense had left the building. "All d-done."

His gaze went to my lips, and without thinking, I wiped the back of my hand over them, needing the taste of him gone, needing to pull myself back together.

He flinched. "I'm sorry. I...fuck, I shouldn't have done that. I forced myself on you. I didn't mean to... I couldn't stop."

"It's...it's okay, I'm okay. My magic, is strong, things happen." I'd had more than one client become confused about their feelings for me, the ones that needed multiple sessions could sometimes grow attached.

He watched me for several long seconds, and I could tell he wasn't sure what to do or say. "I made you cry again," he rasped.

"That's all part of it as well," I said and brushed the tears from my cheeks.

His hands were trembling. "You sure you're okay?"

"Positive." I smiled up at him and hoped it wasn't as shaky as it felt. "I should get going—"

"Please, not yet. After that...I ah...can you just stay for a little longer?"

I wanted to run away, but what he was feeling after such intense emotions wasn't unusual.

"I ah...went out again earlier, tracked the feral for a few hours. He's claimed a large territory while he's been out there, and he moves fast." He rubbed the back of his neck. "I'm still working out his patrol route, but I should be able to corner him soon."

"You did?" Now I felt even more of an asshole. "Thank you. Really. You shouldn't even be doing it. Agatheena had no right to ask—"

"Don't need to keep thanking me, Jaz."

"Right."

"You have any luck today?" he asked, fidgeting, seeming unable to keep still. Not surprising after that session.

I was far from okay, but I had to show him I was because that's what he needed. "No, actually. Nothing. My next move is paying the demon leader a visit at that creepy old asylum he lives in."

"What?"

"He has a library I need access to." These were the demons who could pass as human, who didn't eat humans and who followed the rules.

"No. No fucking way. That place is too dangerous," he said.

"I wasn't asking for your permission, Ren."

He was still shaking, and he shoved his hands in his pockets. "I know. But that place, it's dangerous."

"I'm aware. I was hoping Chaos could organize something for me." Chaos was a Knight of Hell and demon hunter. He'd brokered the conditions the demons in the city lived under, and he was an ex and good friend of Willow. But since I was trying to keep Wills out of this so she wouldn't

428

worry while her hands were full with Violet, I couldn't ask her to call Chaos for me.

"Do you have Chaos's number?" he asked, like he was reading my mind.

"Well, no, and I don't want to worry Willow right now—"

"And Warrick hates the knight, which means the other hounds aren't fans of the guy either. Not sure Rome would like you calling him."

I frowned. "It has nothing to do with Rome."

"I take it he'll be going with you? You'll need someone at your back. That asylum is a seriously fucked-up place."

"You don't need to worry about it. I have it covered."

"Right." His jaw tightened. "Your voice is wrecked from spelling. Let me get you a drink before you go?"

I just wanted to get the hell out of there. He wasn't the only one shaken by our session. The residual from his emotions was still working its way out of me, and I was struggling not to cry. Though, if I was honest, it was more than that. This whole thing was taking a toll on me, one that was getting harder by the day. "I have somewhere to be—"

"The clubhouse? Rome waiting for you?" he asked, doing more of that jaw clenching, and he pulled his hands from his pockets and crossed his arms, his forearms bulging.

I ignored his question, for reasons unknown. No, that was a lie. My reaction to seeing Bree here with him tonight had been extreme. She already thought I wanted Ren, I didn't want him thinking it as well.

The out-of-control kisses we'd just shared weren't helping my cause, but I couldn't handle the humiliation. I was already feeling too raw. So I didn't correct him. I let him believe whatever he wanted without confirming or denying it. "I'll see you tomorrow," I said, then walked out.

And didn't even jump, much, when I heard him growl viciously behind me before he closed the door.

CHAPTER 14

Ren

I SIPPED my coffee and sat back. Relic was in the chair beside me, telling me about the problems he'd had with his bike and what he thought was wrong with it. I hardly heard a word. All I could think about was Jasmine and if she'd come here to the clubhouse last night after she'd been at my place. After I'd kissed her like my world was about to end and she was the only thing that could save me.

I'd fucking kissed her, and nothing could have stopped me.

She acted like it was nothing, like it was just part of the job, which had sent my possessive instincts through the fucking roof. Were her other clients kissing her, touching her? My fox snarled. No, that wasn't okay. We had to make sure that wasn't happening. We had to put a stop to that if it was.

Like I had a right to demand she do...or not do...anything.

She'd said she had big plans, and she'd been fucking blushing, her face bright red. She'd left my place, the taste of me still on her lips, and she'd come here. Where else would she be going? She'd left me standing there trembling, fucking knees weak, body on fire after she'd decimated my emotions, after she'd let me hold her, kiss her, and she hadn't looked back. She said it was her power making me feel this way—she was wrong. I'd felt this way for a long fucking time. Her power just drowned out all the noise, all reasons I couldn't have her for a few minutes, and heightened the reasons I should.

When that high had hit, Jasmine was mine. Every part of me roared she was mine.

Until she pulled her power back and left me shaken and restless and confused.

I tapped my fingers on the table, unable to keep still. Was Jasmine here every night with Roman now?

I'd almost expected him to come to my place last night, to fuck me up. He had to have scented me on her. He had to know I'd kissed her. Unless Jasmine had washed me off, washed away every trace of what we'd done.

I wouldn't blame the male if he had come for me. If I were Rome and had a female like her, I'd want her with me every night as well, but Roman wasn't right for her, no fucking way.

"Did Jaz come by the clubhouse last night?" I said before I could hold it in any longer.

Relic shrugged. "Don't think so." Then he studied me more closely. "Why? What's going on?"

"Nothing. She's been helping me with some stuff at work, was going to ask her about it, but she's not answering my text." A lie, all of it, but I was positive Relic was part bloodhound, and if the male caught the scent of weakness, like me having some weird fucking thing for Jasmine, he'd stick his nose in my business. If he knew I'd spent most of the night looking at pictures of her on my phone like a fucking psycho, he'd never let me live it down. "So you think it's the carburetor?" I asked, getting him back to the previous conversation.

He jumped straight back in, and I tried really hard to listen, but images of a naked Jasmine, coating her smooth inked skin with oil, kept slamming into the back of my skull. *Fuck.* I should never have let Bree in. She'd showed up with a bottle, and I knew she wanted more. I'd had no intention of giving it to her, but I knew what she wanted. My head hadn't been right, far fucking from it.

After I'd seen Jaz and Rome that morning on his bike, her arms around the hound, plastered to his back, something had snapped inside me. I'd walked away, straight into the woods, shifted, and ran straight to my cliff.

I'd stood at the edge, the cool air on my bare skin, the wind whistling around me as if it were telling me to take that last step, to jump, to stop the awful fucking feeling inside me. Jasmine had been mine, in my head, she'd belonged to me in some twisted, weird, fucking way. We had that deep connection, she and I, like no one else. Yes, she thought I was an asshole most of the time, and yes, that connection was because of the people I'd murdered while I was possessed, but it was something.

It was fucked up, but it was something for me to hang on to. It was mine.

She'd been mine.

Now she had that with Rome. No, she had a fuck of a lot more than that.

She had no idea she was the reason I'd never taken that last step. And she'd never know the reason I'd stepped back from the ledge yesterday and used a knife on my skin to work through my pain instead was because I knew I'd see her that night.

That was the reason I'd still be here tomorrow morning, and not on the bottom of that fucking cliff, because I'd see her tonight as well. So yeah, I'd spent the night going through my pictures of her. Anything to still feel connected to her and to stop the images of her and Rome together from invading my head.

The door to the rooms out back opened and shut. Not the private dens below ground, but the rooms in the back of the main clubhouse, where the hounds hooked up with humans and others they didn't want knowing about their inner sanctum. I looked up as a hound walked out, a female wrapped around him, her long blond hair a mess around her shoulders. They were making out as he carried her toward the exit on the other side of the room.

I recognized the hound's boots, the chrome skulls on the sides, like his bike. Rome. I sucked in a breath, and my fox lost his shit, charging forward, snarling and growling. I barely kept my seat.

I felt Relic's gaze slide to me, hearing the growl rumble from deep in my chest.

There it was, right the fuck in front of me. Rome and Jasmine. Something I'd never wanted to see. Fuck no. I wanted to scratch my fucking eyes out. She lifted her head and laughed.

I froze.

Not Jasmine.

Some other female. Human, not witch.

I stood so fast, my chair scraped behind me and fell over. He was fucking around on her? He had her, he had Jasmine, and he was fucking some random chick instead? *What the actual fuck.* That piece of shit! If Jaz were mine, if she wanted *me*, if I wasn't so fucked in the head, I'd never let her go. No other females would exist. Hell, they already didn't, not in any real way, and she wasn't even mine.

I slammed my mug on the table.

"Yo." Relic frowned. "What's up?"

I ignored him and started across the main room as Rome walked his female toward the door. I didn't know what I was going to do—no, fuck that, I knew exactly what I was going to do. I was going to slice the tendons in the backs of his legs, and as soon as he was down, I was going to kick the fuck out of him until he was unconscious. He leaned in and kissed the female again—

The door opened before they reached it—and Jasmine walked in. *Fuck.* I walked faster to get to her, waited for the pain to hit her eyes, the betrayal.

She smiled. "Hey, Rome. Hey, Brandy." Then she carried on past like she didn't give a fuck that the male she loved, her mate, was stepping out on her.

I slammed on the brakes, stopping in my tracks.

She didn't care.

Because they weren't together.

She'd lied to me. My fucking legs almost buckled underneath me, and I switched directions without thinking, going after her. She'd just finished punching in the security code for the dens, and I came up behind her and opened the door, making her jump. She spun round, eyes wide.

"Jesus, Ren. You gave me a fright," she accused and scowled up at me.

"You lied to me." Her head jerked back. "You said you and Rome were together, that you were mates," I said, firing my own accusation at her.

Her brows shot up. "No, I didn't."

"Yeah, you did."

"No, Ren, I didn't. Think back to our conversation. You made assumptions. I didn't confirm or deny anything. That's not lying, that's omitting information, because it's none of your damn business."

"You've come here the last two nights, you said—"

"I said nothing like that at all. I spent most of last night doing research on past soul disappearances at home, and the night before that I met with Councilor Trotman."

"Trotman?" No, she hadn't said she was coming here, had she? I'd thought up the absolute worst scenario and made it truth.

"Shit, I wasn't supposed to tell anyone he helped me," she muttered.

I dragged in a deep breath because my lungs burned from holding it. My hands were shaking, and there was a feeling in my gut I hadn't experienced before in my life, a feeling I couldn't have, not about this female. Not her. My gaze moved over her, her beautiful, perfect face, those full lips, those wide green eyes. Her sweet little body that I'd seen bare, twice now. My gaze lifted, and there were two butterflies on her hair.

I'd never wanted to kiss anyone more in my life.

And she was right. She'd implied, but she'd never confirmed it. "I saw him with Brandy, and I almost—"

"You almost what?"

"I thought he was stepping out on you, that he was gonna hurt you."

"And that's your business how?"

I was breathing hard, trying to think, to find the right fucking words. But I didn't know what to say, what the hell I was doing. Still, when she spun away, yanked the door open, and strode through, I followed her, down the stairs and into the tunnels.

She stopped and spun on me again. "What, Ren? What do you want?"

"You implied...and I thought...I thought..." The words flew from me, and I choked them back.

"You thought what?"

That I'd lost you.

We stared at each other. I was breathing hard, as if I'd been running all fucking day, and without my say-so, my gaze dipped to her perfect lips.

They parted, and she drew in a startled breath. "Ren."

The door opened and Rome and Relic started down the stairs, shattering the moment. I took an abrupt step back, as if Jasmine were my worst nightmare and not every one of my wildest dreams. But then my possessive instincts went haywire again as Rome drew closer, and I grabbed her arm and towed her down the hall, away from them, and into the room I kept here, where I stayed sometimes, shutting the door behind us.

She looked around, her gaze going to the bed, the small dresser with clothes I kept here as well. "What's going on?"

What the fuck was I doing? Why had I dragged her into my room and shut her in? *Because you want her to yourself. You want to shut her in here with you and never let her leave.*

"Ren." She licked her lips, and I was fucking mesmerized. "My power, when I use it like I am with you...it can be confusing, can make people feel things that aren't—"

"Have you talked to Chaos?"

She frowned at my sudden change of subject, but I couldn't hear her tell me what I was feeling wasn't real. I couldn't. Convincing her it was the truth was pointless. I couldn't have her, no matter how much I wished otherwise, I wasn't fit for any kind of real relationship, especially not one with her, because Jasmine deserved everything, and I had nothing to offer her.

"No, not yet. I don't want to hassle Wills with this. I know Warrick and Chaos's relationship isn't the best but was hoping to catch Warrick today, see if he could put me in contact with the knight."

"I'll call him. Chaos is a friend. Let me set this up for you." I stared her down, because I knew how stubborn she was, and I wasn't taking no for an answer for this next bit. "And I'll take you to the asylum."

Her lips parted. "No. You don't need to do that."

"You need help, yes? I can help. Your familiars aren't useful in this instance. You need protection. Plus, I owe you." I crossed my arms so I didn't reach for her. I wanted her arms around me again. It was agony, but I craved it. After only a few sessions with her, I craved her touch, when touch had been something I couldn't stand, still couldn't stand from anyone but her.

"You're already repaying me by hunting down Agatheena's feral."

"And I'll be doing this as well," I said, making sure I left no room for argument.

"You won't take no for an answer, will you?"

"No." I held her gaze. "If you go alone...or with anyone else, I won't be happy, Jasmine."

She blinked up at me, and I could see her fighting her temper. She wasn't a fan of my tone or what I'd just said, but she also knew I wasn't backing down. "If you insist." She blew out a breath and crossed her arms. "Thank you, I guess."

›)⊃●(((

Jasmine

"So, like, how safe are we here?" I asked as we walked past demon businesses, clothing shops, bars, and cafes, while passing actual demons on the street. Their gazes followed us, their eyes giving them away, something otherworldly shining through.

Ren's hand was suddenly on my lower back as he scanned the street. "No one's going to hurt you, Jaz, because if they try, I'll gut them right here in the street."

I looked up at him, and my mouth went dry. He meant it. He looked like he had in the forest when we left Agatheena's, right before he killed all those demons. "But we have safe passage to the asylum, yes?"

"Chaos cleared it. We'll be fine."

This part of the city was where demons who followed the rules lived. The Knights of Hell monitored them and had a close relationship with their leader, a demon named Rune, a male chosen by Lucifer to keep all those living in this city in line.

"What do you think Rune's like? I mean, he's in charge of all the demons here, so he has to be kind of terrifying, right?" I rubbed my arms, goose bumps lifting all over them.

Ren ran the tips of his fingers down my spine, then back up, like he was trying to offer comfort but didn't want to touch me fully. "It'll be fine."

It just made me feel even jumpier, setting my nerve endings off into little spasms and making it hard to focus. After what he said during our first session together, I knew Ren avoided touch. I'd seen females on his lap, their hands on him, but now that I thought about it, he always moved their hands away, with a forced laugh or a movement that would dislodge them, and unless he was really drunk, he kept his hands to himself.

Knowing that now, I could look back and recognize the discomfort on his face during those times. Is that why he drank so much? The fact that he'd touched me in the forest to make me feel safe and the way he was touching me now, trying to comfort me despite how uncomfortable it had to be making him, said just how much I hadn't been hiding my fear either time.

"I'm glad you're here," I said, wanting him to know how much I appreciated him, despite my resistance.

He was still scanning the street. "If you came here without me, Jaz, I would've followed you, anyway, only I would've been pissed."

My gaze shot up to him. "Are you serious?"

"Deadly."

"You would've followed me?"

"Yes."

He was still looking everywhere but at me, scanning our surroundings for trouble. "Why?"

"Because you're not the shy little female I first met. You've got all this attitude, venom when you feel like spitting it, but you don't have one single thing to back all of that up with."

"Yes, I do."

"Jasmine, you don't."

"Relic and Mags taught me some moves."

His lips actually curled.

"What?" I bit out.

"A few moves won't do shit against a rabid demon," he said, glancing my way before going back to searching the surrounding streets.

"Are you saying I'm weak?"

"No." His fingers did another swipe down my spine, making me shiver. "I'm saying your attitude could get you in trouble, and I'm going to make sure that's not going to happen."

I was getting more pissed by the minute. "First, I'm not an idiot. I would never do anything I thought was truly dangerous. And second, you can't watch me every minute of every day, so how will you know if I'm doing something you deem dangerous or not."

"I won't, but I can discourage it."

"How?"

436

"A good spanking is excellent for a quick attitude adjustment." As soon as the words left his mouth, he kind of froze.

My mouth dropped open. "Spanking?"

I expected him to back down, to apologize, instead he turned my way, the gold flecks in his eyes brighter. "Yes, a good spanking works wonders."

My mouth opened, closed, then my face heated, and I knew it must be glowing bright red, a mix of outrage and, goddess, excitement. "You wouldn't."

"Try me."

"You don't get to tell me what to do," I said, sounding like a sullen teenager, but I was dumbfounded, and angry, and highly turned on, which was confusing as hell.

"There it is," Ren said, pointing at something, as if the conversation we were having wasn't anything out of the ordinary.

I turned to look, and dread washed everything else away. "Jesus." I'd tried to imagine a nearly two-hundred-year-old insane asylum, but even my imagination hadn't conjured anything like this. It was as if they'd plucked the building from old England and dropped it in the middle of Roxburgh. It'd been called Sunnydale back in the day, but there was nothing sunny about this place. The stone walls were dark with a slick moss, the windows topped with pointed arches like a cathedral. It was massive. I couldn't even guess how many rooms this place had.

We walked through the gate and into a large garden area at the front where I assumed patients would've been allowed out to sit on fine days, and made our way toward the wide heavy, wooden doors. This place had been decommissioned in the early 1980s, and I couldn't imagine how awful it must have been in this place for its residents.

I stumbled back when I felt the press of several disturbed souls.

"Jaz?" Ren asked as the sound of sliding metal on metal reached us through the door.

"There are restless spirits here, a lot of them." I could feel them, but thanks to my sigils, they were kept at a distance.

"You gonna be okay? We can leave?" His hand, still on my lower back, gripped my shirt, fisting it as if he wanted to tear me away from here.

"I'll be okay," I said. "I just wasn't expecting it."

The door opened, and Ren straightened. His arm slid around me, and he pulled me back, shocking the hell out of me. He was touching me again.

"Who the fuck are you?" the demon at the door said, head up, scenting the air.

I opened my mouth to speak, but Ren got there first. "We're here to see Rune."

"He's busy, and you'd be wise to get the fuck off his territory. He's not a fan of shifters."

I shook myself out of my stupor and pulled out of Ren's hold. "Chaos organized this meeting with Rune. He's expecting us."

"Name?" the demon snapped.

Ren said our names, and the demon pulled out his phone, tapped the screen, put it to his ear, then barked out a few words I didn't really understand before he shoved it back in his pocket. "Let's go."

He strode back inside, and we followed.

A shudder instantly rolled through me as we walked across the threshold. This place was worse than I thought. The old linoleum was stained and cracked, everything was cold and stark, and the smell was indescribable. Like hospital, but mixed with a whole lot of other things that turned my stomach. As we passed doors, I could feel the emotional echoes of the people who'd lived here. I shuddered again, and when the press of the spirits trapped here pushed harder, causing icy tendrils to slide over my shoulders and down my back, my hand shot out and I grabbed Ren's.

His fingers flexed around mine, and his gaze sliced down to me.

"I'm sorry," I said and quickly pulled my hand away.

"This way," the demon said, rounding a corner and heading toward an ancient-looking elevator.

Ren said nothing as he took my hand again, holding it firmly. My heart raced, and I couldn't look at him. How many times had I imagined doing this? Holding his hand like this. But in my wildest dreams we'd been walking on the beach or down the street, not through an asylum filled with demons and tortured souls.

The demon hit the up arrow. "Top floor," he said. "Don't wander around. We won't be responsible for what happens if you go somewhere you shouldn't."

"No worries there," I said as the doors slid open and Ren led me inside.

He hit the button for the top floor, and the doors slid closed again. "You doing okay?" he asked.

"Yeah, I'm fine. Sorry, I'm just feeling a lot here, and it kind of freaks me out." I loosened my hand around his, attempting to let his hand go. "I'm okay now."

He looked up at the numbers ticking over as we climbed higher but kept his fingers firmly around mine, not letting me go. The elevator bounced to a stop. "I've got you, Jaz, okay?" The doors slid open.

I didn't know what to say. I was feeling seriously breathless and a little dizzy from everything I was feeling, from Ren holding my hand, from the spirits here and the emotional echoes bombarding me from the past. "Thanks," I said. It was all I could get out.

We stepped into a small foyer. There was only one door we could go through, so we walked up to it, and I knocked.

The sound of heavy footfalls echoed through the door, and I had to stop myself from taking several steps back the closer they got. Ren moved so he was standing mostly in front of me, his grip on my hand tightening.

Finally, the door swung open, and if I hadn't already been bracing for some kind of impact, I would've jerked back and fallen on my ass.

A demon filled the door, towering over me. I looked up into his other-worldly eyes, a color between yellow and green. Power oozed from him, heavy and thick, and made my belly tremble.

"Jasmine," he said, his voice resonating through me.

"Uh...um, yes, that's me." I needed to pull it together. This guy was a pal of Lucifer's for fuck's sake. Showing weakness to a male like this was a really bad idea.

He stepped back, opening his door wider, his pale, terrifying gaze sliding over me. "Come in, lovely." His gaze slid to Ren. "You can wait out here, fox."

"Where my female goes, I go," Ren bit out. *His female?*

My gaze shot to Ren. He was pissed.

"Yours, is she?" Rune said.

"Yeah," Ren snarled. "And she doesn't leave my side."

Rune dipped his head, his face close to my neck, and he breathed in deep, then made a rough sound. Ren jerked me back with a growl. Rune grinned, flashing a set of fangs very much like a vampire, even though that wasn't what he was. "I don't smell you, fox." He looked down at me. "You smell like innocence and fear. An intoxicating combination."

My face went up in flames, humiliation filling me. My gaze darted to Ren and back up to Rune. "I don't care who you are, you don't get to scent me. Ever. Understand?"

"Jasmine," Ren said low, tightening his hold on me.

Rune grinned wider, a long, vibrating rumble rolling from his chest. "Oh, lovely, yes. I like you very much."

"The feeling is not mutual. I find you kind of sleazy, actually," I bit out, letting my humiliation run my mouth, then slammed it shut. *Fuck.*

"You're brave as well, little witch," he said. "Thankfully, for you, I like that as well."

"How about you take a fucking step back," Ren snarled.

Rune looked up. "You're starting to annoy me, fox."

I needed to get it together and this meeting back on track before Ren started a fight. "Chaos brokered this meeting for a reason. Can we stop all this...weirdness, and get down to it?"

Rune chuckled. "Yeah, lovely, let's get down to business."

Ren growled again.

The massive demon stepped away from me. "It's your lucky day," he said to Ren. "As delicious as she smells, I don't fuck with virgins."

Oh my goddess. NO. He did not just out me like that. My humiliation flamed higher as I followed him into what was obviously his apartment.

I didn't look at Ren as I took in my surroundings. Rune had made the top floor into one huge studio space. There were lots of windows, and it felt very different from the rest of the building.

"It used to be a rooftop garden. They walled it in sometime in the 1950s," Rune said as if he could read my mind. "So, lovely, little Jasmine, what is it you want from me?"

"Access to your library."

His brow arched. "Why?"

"Death is missing souls."

"And I should care, why?"

"He isn't the only one. Lucifer's missing some as well. Ask him if you don't believe me."

Rune studied me for several long seconds. "And you think you can find them?"

"I have to, my sister's depending on it."

He straightened. "All right, lovely, you want access, I'll give you access."

Relief flooded me. "Thank you—"

"But you have to do something for me in return."

Ren grabbed my hand again. "She's not doing a damned thing for you."

"Yes, she is. Or she'll leave here empty-handed."

CHAPTER 15

Ren

"WHAT DO you want me to do?" Jaz asked Rune.

I fucking hated this asshole.

"You're a medium, yes, lovely?"

"Yes."

He nodded. "You feel the souls here?"

"I do."

"I need you to get rid of one of them. He's surpassed malevolent and taken a turn into violent poltergeist territory. I need him gone. He sticks to the fourth floor, a space I need and haven't been able to use since we moved in here."

"No fucking way," I growled. "Not happening."

Jasmine placed her hand on my forearm, silencing me with a single touch. "This is what I do. This is part of my job."

"Good," Rune said. "Get rid of him and you'll have free rein over the library." His lips curled up. "Any time, day or night, you're welcome to stop by."

Jaz blushed. "I appreciate it." She looked around his apartment. "Do you have a room I could use?"

"You don't have your things with you, for protection," I said, trying to stop her from doing this.

"My bag's in the car. I have what I need in it. Could you get it for me?" she asked, then turned back to Rune. "I need somewhere private to prepare."

"Bathroom?"

"Perfect."

"I'm not leaving you here on your own," I said, staring down the demon eyeing her like a juicy fucking steak. Despite what he said, he wanted her.

"He's friends with Chaos. He's not going to hurt me," Jaz said.

"Yeah," Rune said with that fucking smirk still on his lips. "Me and Chaos are buds, she's safe with me. There's a lock on the bathroom door if you're worried."

Chaos was not this asshole's bestie. I knew that much.

"Please, Ren. I need to do this."

Fuck. "When you're locked in the bathroom, I'll go get your bag." As if a lock could actually stop this fucker.

"Do you have a robe I could use? And some gauze would be good as well," she asked Rune.

My hackles shot up.

"Gauze is under the sink. But no robe. Would one of my shirts work?"

"Thanks. Yep, that'll work."

No. No fucking way. "Use my shirt." I'd walk around shirtless, I didn't give a fuck. For some reason my fox would not tolerate another male's scent on her. Neither of us could.

"It'll be easier with something that opens at the front. It's fine."

Rune grabbed a shirt from the back of a chair and handed it to her, his eyes dancing when he looked my way. He'd worn it. He was purposely giving her a shirt covered in his scent. I stared him down, struggling to breathe through my rage.

"Ren?"

My gaze sliced to Jaz.

"My bag."

"Lock yourself in the bathroom," I said again, and she hustled to the room Rune pointed to and shut herself in. I heard the lock engage a moment later. I turned back to the demon. "You touch her and I'll fucking kill you."

"Big talk for a little fox." He flashed his teeth. "You have no idea what I'm capable of."

"I don't care. You hurt her. I will find a way to end you." I strode out the door.

》》◐《《

The smell of Jasmine's blood hit me as we got into the elevator. It was mixed with Rune's scent, and my already hostile fox lost his mind. "You're bleeding." I grabbed the front of the shirt she was wearing, about to yank it open.

She gripped it tighter at the front, her eyes widening. "Ren," she snapped.

I spun on Rune who leaned against the elevator wall. "What the fuck did you do to her."

"He did nothing. I did it to myself," Jaz said, bringing my attention back to her.

"What?" There was too much danger here, too many unknowns, and my protective instincts were off the charts. Add in whatever the fuck this was, and I was close to losing it completely. That's when I spotted the blood soaking through the white shirt she had around her body, at her stomach, her upper arms. "What the fuck did you do, Jasmine?" I growled.

She frowned at me. "A poltergeist of this strength requires extra measures. Protection glyphs."

"You carved them into your skin?" I said in disbelief.

"They're not deep, and it's nothing Else's balm can't heal. I've done this before several times."

"You carved up your own skin," I said, my breathing weird, heavy. She should never do that. Never suffer that. She was perfect and clean and good. Only monsters like me carved up their own skin, only those who deserved it. "That's not right. You shouldn't...you shouldn't do that."

She studied me. "You've seen Willow cut herself hundreds of times."

Jasmine looked genuinely puzzled, and I realized how I sounded. Like an overprotective mate. I needed to calm the fuck down. Being here with all these demons was fucking with me, that's all this was. "I just saw the blood and reacted. Sorry."

Rune chuckled behind me, and it was hard, but I ignored the asshole.

The elevator stopped with a ding, but the doors didn't open.

"We rigged it this way. Didn't want anyone on the fourth floor who wasn't supposed to be there," Rune said. "Whenever you're ready, lovely, say the word and I'll open the doors."

"Oh, I thought there'd be somewhere I could..." Her face darkened.

She'd mixed up some of her oil in the apartment, which meant she needed to strip off and cover herself in it like she did when she was with me. I'd take that fucking demon's eyes out before I let him see her like that.

She removed her sigil necklace and cuffs and put them in her bag. "I'm going to need you both to turn around, please, gentlemen. I need some privacy."

443

Rune arched a brow but did as she asked. "So what am I missing out on?"

I turned my back as well but kept him in my periphery. If he so much as peeked, I'd kill him.

"I need to cover myself in the oil I made upstairs, so the spirit can't possess me," she said as the scent of the oil intensified in the small space. Which meant it was warming against her skin.

Rune groaned. "So you're telling me, you're behind me, naked, and rubbing oil all over your body?"

"Yes."

He made a purring sound. "All glistening and slippery?"

"Um..."

"You're positive I can't watch?"

I snarled.

"Positive."

Rune chuckled again.

"Right, all done."

"What if you get into trouble?" I said, fear a gnarled knot in my gut.

"I won't," she said.

"I'm not shutting this door after you," I said, close to snatching her up and getting the fuck out of there.

I heard her rummaging around. "Fine, but I'm putting down a salt line, it's mixed with cemetery dirt so it's pretty potent. You'll be safe behind it. If the spirit does try to get to you, and the line thins, leave before it breaks. I'll follow when the job's done."

"Not leaving you behind, Jaz. Not fucking happening."

"Open the door," she said without answering me. The doors slid open. "And, Rune, please get Ren out of here if you have to."

I snarled again.

›)❍(‹

Jasmine

I stared into the corridor and tried to keep my breathing even. Unlike the other parts of the building I'd seen, this floor had been left untouched. There was grime on the floor and walls, doors hanging off hinges. The hall was lined with several gurneys, worn leather straps dangling down their sides. I took another step and hissed when I stepped on broken glass.

"Jaz?" Ren called.

444

"Just some glass on the floor," I called back and kept moving.

I hadn't told Ren quite how dangerous this was. I'd dealt with poltergeists before, but never alone, always with Zinny. I knew what I was doing, though, and it wasn't like I had any other choice. We had no leads. The feral was still on the loose and, who knows, he might have scented Ren and left the area. Even if Ren found him, Agatheena might never give me the information I needed. I didn't know how long I had before Zinnia was trapped in Limbo for good, and the demon library might actually have some answers.

A crash came from the other end of the hall, and I headed toward it, whispering the spell I'd need to send the soul where he belonged, letting it build and slowly swirl around me. I needed the magic to grow in strength, to gain momentum, especially since it was just me.

I peered through the window in the next door. There were papers scattered around the room. An office. Pushing the door open, I cautiously walked in. The emotional energy in the room was dark, sadistic. Whoever had used this office had saturated it in their ill intent, in their cruelty and the pleasure they took from it. There was an overturned filing cabinet, a hole in the wall where it once stood. Files spilled out from the obvious hiding place. I picked one up, flinching in horror when I saw what was inside.

The pictures were old, in black and while, and they turned my stomach. What was documented here was not just images but written in careful detail was pure, unmistakable evil. Torture. The other files I picked up were the same. This creep had worked here, was charged with looking after the patients in his care, and instead he'd abused them, running secret experiments on them, torturing them over and over again.

Another crash came from out in the hall. I dropped the files and walked back out, glaring back toward the elevator when I saw Ren and Rune both watching me. Ren's face was contorted with fear, and Rune's was utterly unreadable. I turned away and carried on. If I wasn't quietly freaking out, perhaps I'd be embarrassed that I was naked again. But right then that was the last thing on my mind. I walked to the next door. It was stainless steel, no window this time. The emotions coming from that room lifted the hair on my arms and sent icy claws down my spine.

I increased the pace and volume of my spell. "What is evil must not walk among the living. Hell, take this soul so dark, remove it from the mortal realm, never to return." The poltergeist was behind that door. I felt him. He was excited. He knew I was coming, and he wanted to hurt me. Gripping my knife tighter, I flicked out the blade and sliced the final glyphs into my forearms.

Ren's snarl echoed down the corridor, but I didn't dare break concentration and look his way.

I let the blood slide down my arms and onto my feet, letting it strengthen my powers as the spell swirled faster and faster within me. My hair whipped around my shoulders from the force of it, and I lifted my arms and cried it out again, then aimed my hands at the door. It flew open, crashing into the wall, and I walked in.

The poltergeist stood beside a gurney and smiled wide when he saw me. There was some kind of contraption that sent ice through my veins on one side and an electrotherapy machine beside that. There was also a table covered in knives and other things he used to cut his patients. A hand drill for the lobotomies he performed on them while they were still awake, and another table with horrifying things he'd obviously used only on his female patients, in his "study" of the reproductive systems. All of it without consent or anesthesia or pain relief of any kind.

"Welcome," he said. "Please climb onto the table."

I stared him down, repeating my spell again and again, louder, until I was screaming it, my hair flying around me.

His twisted features contorted further, and he flew at me. I stumbled back but didn't stop my chant, didn't slow. He roared when he realized I was protected and he couldn't possess me.

Hadeon was going to be pissed I was calling on him so soon. "Hell, take back this soul so dark, remove it from the mortal realm, never to return," I cried, over and over again.

Light and heat swirled beneath the ghost, the ground jarring with a boom before Hadeon appeared. He snarled and spun to me, then paused and slowly turned back to my poltergeist who was now frozen in place. "Well, now, aren't you a piece of shit," Hadeon said to the ghost, then he grabbed the evil fucker by the throat and dragged him screaming to Hell.

I collapsed against the wall. He was gone. It was done. Shoving the door open, I walked out into the corridor.

I didn't have time to brace before they came at me.

Souls, his victims, so many of them. They came at me all at once, the ferocity of their anguish hitting in a torrent. They didn't want to harm me. They didn't want to hurt anyone. They were terrified, and that terror was so great, so overwhelming, there was no stopping what was about to happen, something that hadn't happened for a very long time.

I lifted my gaze to Ren, but I couldn't warn him. There was no time to explain. He saw the look on my face and started running toward me.

Everything went black.

)))·◉·(((

Ren

. . .

I sprinted down the corridor, dropping to the floor beside Jasmine. Her body was limp, her face without any sign of life. I knew that look, I saw it every day. "No," I snarled. "Jasmine!" I pressed my fingers to her throat. Nothing. Not even a weak pulse. "No. No no no. Don't go, butterfly. Don't you fucking dare leave me."

I scooped her up in my arms and ran for the elevator. "Call a healer. She's unresponsive."

Rune stared down at her, and his head tilted to the side.

"Fucking call someone," I roared, clutching her to me and slamming my hand on the button for the ground floor. I pressed my ear to her chest. This couldn't be happening. Her heart wasn't beating. She wasn't breathing. She couldn't be dead. Jasmine couldn't be dead.

I looked up at Rune, snarling when he touched her forehead.

He shook his head. "She's not dead."

"She's not breathing. Her pulse—"

"Have you ever heard of catalepsy?"

"What? No, what the fuck are you talking about? She needs a healer. Now."

Something swirled in Rune's yellow-green eyes. "She's not dead. Her condition, whatever this is, is similar to catalepsy in humans. Something back there triggered it, but she will wake up." He hit the button for the top floor, and as soon as we hit the ground level, the doors closed again and we were on our way back up.

When the door opened again, I followed Rune back into his apartment, Jasmine's lifeless body clutched to me. "Are you sure?"

"Her mind's still active, as if she's in a dreamlike state. I'd get nothing if she was dead."

I sat on the couch and brushed her hair back from her face. "Wake up, butterfly. Open your eyes for me. Come back to me, baby." My fox whimpered and clawed at my subconscious before releasing a mournful howl, calling to her, trying to get her to reply, not understanding what was happening.

I don't know how long I sat there, holding her to me, begging her to come back to me. Light dimmed and night fell. I forgot Rune was even there until the lights switched on. I looked up as he disappeared into the bathroom, shutting the door. The shower came on a minute later.

She'd been out for hours. What if he was wrong? What if she was gone? My heart shredded in my chest.

I looked back down, and Jasmine blinked up at me. Her wide green eyes unfocused, confused. "Ren?"

I released a shuddering breath. "Christ, Jasmine." I crushed her to me. "I thought you were dead. I thought you were fucking dead."

"I'm okay," she said croakily.

"What the hell happened back there?" She licked her dry lips, and I had the strong urge to crush my mouth to hers.

"I-it hasn't happened for a long time. I thought I'd be okay—"

The bathroom door opened, and Rune walked out in pants, no shirt, flashing his inked and branded chest, grinning when he saw Jasmine awake. "You're back, lovely."

"Glad to see you're not distraught over my possible death," she said to him, trying to straighten in my arms.

Which was when I realized she was naked against me with only Rune's shirt covering her nakedness. I tugged it down to make sure it covered her ass.

Rune grinned. "The fox was distraught enough for the both of us."

Her gaze darted back to me. "I'm sorry, you must have been..." She chewed her lip. "I'm sorry," she said again.

"You're okay. That's all that matters. How are you feeling?"

She sat up, and I was forced to let her go. She stood and I held out my hands to catch her if she fell, but she seemed sturdy on her feet.

"I'm fine. There are never any lasting effects." She tightened the shirt around her oil-slicked and cut-up body. "I'll just grab a quick shower, then you can show me the library?" she said to Rune.

"I take it that means our poltergeist's gone?"

Her expression hardened. "Yes, to Hell, where he belongs." Then she strode to the bathroom. "I'll be quick." Then she shut the door.

I stared after her. I was shaking. She'd recovered, but I sure as fuck hadn't. I'd never forget the way it felt to hold Jasmine's lifeless body in my arms.

How the fuck was I going to go back to normal after this? Be alone with her again tonight, let her touch me, wrap her arms around me?

How was I going to ignore this feeling inside me, the fucked-up voice inside my head, god, roaring through my skull, telling me that Jasmine was mine.

Mine.

CHAPTER 16

Jasmine

REN LAY STILL as I bent over him, tattooing the finishing touches to one of his sigils. His abs clenched. Jesus, his stomach was roped with muscle. My fingers accidentally brushed his side, over the scar there, and he shuddered. I was trying to make as little contact as possible, but it was hard. I repeated my spell, holding his skin taut, and inked the flick at the bottom. I may not be an actual tattoo artist like Rome, but I was an artist, and I was going to make sure the sigils I'd inked on Ren looked good.

"You sure you're okay?" Ren asked for about the tenth time since we started.

"I'm okay, Ren, honestly. It's like nothing happened." After I woke, Rune had shown me the library. It hadn't been nearly as impressive as I'd imagined—I thought he might be holding out on me, honestly—definitely not as vast as ours, but he had let me take a bunch of books on loan, and I'd be poring through them as soon as I got home. I needed a freaking breakthrough like now. If I had to exorcise a hundred twisted poltergeists, I would if it ensured Zinnia came home.

"For you, maybe," he said, and it was obvious he'd said it through gritted teeth.

I moved to the next spot, just below his belly button. "I am sorry I scared you. I wasn't prepared for all those souls. I've never felt anything like it." His abs tightened again under my hand as I started the next sigil, and I tried not to notice that this time, he wasn't hard. Not that I wanted him to be, right?

Of course not.

But my head was basically hovering over his junk, which meant last time hadn't been about me at all. He'd explained why he'd reacted that way, but still...at the time I'd wanted it to be about me, that he'd wanted me. It was stupid. It shouldn't make me feel less, or unattractive, but it kind of did, even though I knew wanting me, especially when I held him, healed him, was a twisted side effect of my magic. And so was the possessive way he'd been acting, the protectiveness. He was confused, and the sooner this was over and done with, the better for both of us. Being this close to him wasn't good for me, was messing with me, even though I knew the truth.

I glanced up. His eyes were squeezed closed, the fingers of both hands in tight fists, and color slashed his cheeks.

"Is it hurting?" As soon as I spoke, goose bumps lifted across his stomach, right where my breath had brushed his scarred skin.

"I'm good," he said, not looking at me.

"Ren?"

"Yeah?"

"You look in pain."

His nostrils flared. "I'm good, Jaz."

"I don't believe you. Look at me," I said.

His chest expanded, then his eyes opened, dipping down and hitting me. His gaze was dark with bursts of gold flecks, swirling, intense. The fox was back. "I'm good, Jasmine. Not in pain." He made sure to hold my gaze and not look at my nakedness when he said that.

A swooshing sensation dipped low in my belly, and I had to drag my eyes from his. "Good." When I looked back down, there were more goose bumps—he also wasn't soft anymore. Nope, he was hard as hell.

He'd looked at me, and he'd gotten hard.

My face heated when I realized that's why he'd been concentrating so hard. I was about to ink a sigil on the base of his dick. He'd been trying to stay in control, now he'd lost it completely. *Shit.*

It had nothing to do with me, being touched was overwhelming him, he just wasn't used to it, that's all. He was a guy with a healthy sexual appetite. I was a naked female smeared in oil. Even if I was a mess, bruised from my fall with cuts that were still red and raw, I was bent over his dick. Of course he'd get hard.

I could be anyone.

I thought I'd lost you.

He'd said it when I woke up. I'd been unconscious before that, but I'd heard his voice off and on. I was pretty sure he'd called me butterfly, his voice rough and filled with fear. I tried not to think about it and focused on finishing the sigil.

Now for the next one. My face grew even hotter. "I just need to, um... your jeans."

He lifted his ass and pushed them down like he had when I did his back. "Enough?"

"Yep," I said way too brightly, trying to cover my embarrassment. The thick base of his cock was right there, the denim forcing it to angle down, which had to hurt in his current state. "I'll try to be quick."

He grunted.

I glanced back up and he had his eyes closed again, his arms crossed over his chest. "Just two more," I said and started on the next one just above his dick. I outlined it, then carefully filled it in, wiping away the ink as I went. I finished it in record time, then paused to load up with ink and gather my courage.

"Okay, last one. Ready?"

He grunted again, his breathing shaky as I leaned over him and started spelling. I pressed my needle to the base of his dick. A thick vein ran down the middle, and it was getting in my way. "Sorry, I just have to..." I inwardly cringed as I used the thumb of my other hand to kind of press on it, moving it as I worked. "There's a...a vein and I need a smooth, um..."

"Don't talk, Jasmine," he growled out. "Do not fucking talk."

Now he was *pissed* at me? "So sorry if my voice offends you—"

"Not offended, Jaz. Your warm breath on my cock is the problem."

"Oh." I slammed my mouth shut, my cheeks so hot now my freaking eyes watered. Somehow I managed to recite the spell, while trying not to breathe on him too much, as I worked the tattoo gun. It wasn't easy, not when I was fighting the instinct to push his jeans down farther. Not when I wanted to shove them all the way down and let his cock spring free to ease my curiosity. He smelled of soap and musk and the forest. My nipples tightened, and I bit my lip and did my best to stop the pervy direction of my thoughts and get this done.

"The outline's done," I said and used my cloth to wipe away the extra ink.

A shiver rolled through Ren, and my gaze shot up to him again.

"Finish it, Jaz," he bit out.

"Right."

"And don't fucking talk."

Oops. I forgot. I changed my needle so I could fill in the outline and dipped it in the ink spiked with my potion. I pressed it to the silky skin of his cock, and he shuddered again. I wanted to ask if he was okay, but I bit my lip and stopped myself. I had to keep wiping away the extra ink so I could see what I was doing, and every time I did, he jerked.

On the next swipe, he growled low. Tingles lifted across my scalp and down my arms.

Holy shit, he was really hard now. It had to hurt, having it forced down like that, not to mention my needle working over it. Shame burned through me when I was forced to squeeze my legs together to ease the intense throb there.

I finally did the last little bit, quickly swiped away the ink, then straightened. "All done."

His arms were still locked over his chest, and he was breathing in and out shakily, as if he were trying to slow it down.

"You okay?" I asked.

"That all of them?" he said instead of answering.

Most likely because it was a stupid freaking question. He wasn't okay. How could he be? This whole situation was fucked up to the extreme. "Just the two on your neck, and then we're finished."

He nodded, reached down, and cursed as he yanked up his jeans. "I'm fucking sorry, Jaz. You shouldn't have to deal with that shit. I thought I had it under control, but you're fucking beautiful, and you were touching me, and you're naked, not that I'm looking," he quickly said. "But I know you are, and every one of your breaths against my skin felt...and I...and your hands on me, and fuck...I'm making it worse."

You're fucking beautiful.

My stupid, hopeful heart sped faster. Ren thought I was beautiful? "It's okay," I said. "You don't need to explain. If you could just sit up. We'll get the last two done."

He rubbed his hands over his face and nodded.

Ren

She moved up beside me, and I could feel the warmth radiating from her bare skin against my side. She wasn't touching me, but it was as if she were pressed against me so damn tight, her warmth soaking right through me.

Dammit, I'd had my dick under control until she'd made me look at her. The only place I could look was her eyes, and as soon as I had them locked on mine, my cock had stiffened. I wanted to reach down and squeeze it, badly. It felt like it was going to be torn off shoved down the leg of my jeans the way it was. But there was no way in hell I was going to adjust it in front of her. She had to think I was the biggest fucking pervert.

This was when Edward's voice would usually invade my mind and tell me I was making her skin crawl just being this close to her, but it never came—and I realized it hadn't for a while now. And then the heat of Jasmine's skin seemed to intensify, and all my attention was back on her.

I tried not to look, and I didn't, but when she leaned forward, pressing the needle to the side of my throat, I could see the flash of color from the tattoo on her chest in my peripheral vision, the way her soft tits swayed as she moved. I sucked in another fortifying breath and closed my eyes. I tried to zone out as she did the first one, but the fox could smell her blood still, and I could still remember the way she felt in my arms, the fear, the roar of *mine* through my head. She swiped the ink away and more goose bumps lifted across my skin.

"One final sigil to go, then I'll get out of your way. You won't have to see me again for a week." Her warm breath brushed my skin once more, and it took everything in me not to shiver again.

I hated the thought of not seeing her again for another week. Yes, doing this with her was torture, but it was...it felt good as well. She thought I was a manwhore and an asshole, and more than likely a pervert at this point, but being this close to her, just the two of us— Christ, these past several days had done more for me than anything else had since I was possessed.

The thought of not seeing her tomorrow night? I hated it. Yeah, I might see her at the clubhouse, or when I was hanging out with Willow, but it wouldn't be the same, I wouldn't have her to myself, and I knew every day until I could be here in my living room with her again, just the two of us, would feel like a fucking eternity.

She moved to my other side, dipping her needle in the ink, then got started. I closed my eyes and tried to focus on anything but the feel of her fingers curled around the back of my neck. Her thumb pressed to my skin like she had the base of my cock, but this time to hold the skin taut, not to press down a bulging fucking vein because blood was pumping hard and fast to my engorged cock—and still was with her so near.

Minutes ticked by. "I just need to fill it in."

Her soft voice had tingles dancing all over me. Then she was back at it, filling in the final sigil, whispering her spell. The soft sound of her voice repeating the words over and over again was a torment, Heaven and Hell all rolled into one. I needed her to stop for my own fucking sanity, but I thought I'd die if she did. I'd hated touch for so long after what happened, and now I was addicted to it, to Jasmine's touch. Only hers.

The longer she worked, the closer to the end we got and the more I dreaded its arrival.

"All done," she finally said, still in that soft voice.

Her hand was curled around my throat as she wiped the excess ink from the final sigil. "You suit them, you know. They look really good."

"Yeah?" I turned to her and realized my mistake too late.

Our eyes locked, our faces, *our mouths*, so close, and every one of her soft breaths now brushed my lips instead of my throat. Our gazes held. She blinked, her soft green gaze bright and startlingly beautiful. A scent reached me—arousal. Jaz was turned on, pussy wet.

Fuck. I gasped in a breath that only made it worse. I looked away and quickly stood.

She stood as well, and like last time, she grabbed my shirt, pulling it on. Her head was dipped. "We need to do your healing, then I'll leave you to the rest of your night."

How the fuck was I going to survive it? "Sounds good."

Not looking at me, she stepped into me, wrapping her arms around my waist. She hadn't cleaned up and changed first, like she usually did, and with how thin my shirt was, I felt every one of her curves pressed against me, soft and warm. Her power slid through me, gentle but persistent. I kept my hands at my sides, fingers fisted so fucking tight my knuckles felt close to splitting. She murmured her words of encouragement, like last time, but I was lost in the feel of her, of her power, a jumble of thoughts and sensations, in her addictive scent.

The emotions swirling inside me were drawn away, her power sliding through my body as if she was stroking me, soothing me from the inside out. I sucked in breath after breath as it was all taken from me. For a short time, those awful feelings were gone.

The euphoria built, slow and steady, and I started to shake.

"Ren?"

Her voice washed over me, and I stared down at her. My arms were locked around her small waist now. I didn't remember doing it, but I was holding her tight to me. *Let her go.* I couldn't fucking do it; like the last two times, I couldn't let her go. My gaze dipped to her luscious mouth. So pretty. So fucking inviting.

She blinked up at me and licked her lips. "Ren?"

I swallowed hard. "Yeah?"

"When you thought I was with Rome, that we were seeing each other, you didn't like it, did you?"

I gritted my teeth. We couldn't go there. I couldn't tell her how I was feeling. I didn't fucking understand it, not really, and nothing could ever happen between us, nothing beyond this. I'd only hurt her, and I'd run off the edge of that fucking cliff before I ever did that. But still, my arms remained locked around her, not letting her get away, holding her to me.

"And when you thought I was dead..."

"I can't talk about that," I choked out. "I can't fucking think about it, not yet—"

She reached up, cupping my jaw, and shook her head like she was shaking something loose. "What you're feeling, it's okay. You don't...you don't want me. I know it's the magic."

No. It was her. It was Jasmine. "Don't," I rasped, but at the same time, I leaned into her touch. "Don't stop."

"Ren," she whispered, breathing harder.

Her gaze dipped to my mouth and back up.

She wanted to kiss me too. She wanted *me*. I could fucking smell it.

I couldn't make myself release her. I couldn't turn away. I needed to taste her again. Just one more time. Just once more before this ended, before she left me without her for a whole fucking week.

My fox pricked up his ears and edged closer. I was trapped by her warmth. It radiated from her body, her eyes, her soul. Jasmine was pure warmth, and I was drawn closer like I was in the grip of hypothermia and she was the only thing that could save me.

"Please," I finally rasped, pleading with her. I wanted to taste her again so badly, but I was in control this time, and I needed her to want it as well. I needed her to kiss me.

"Please what?"

"Kiss me, Jasmine. I need you to kiss me."

"Ren—"

"Please."

Trembling, she slid her arms around my neck. She licked her lips, her gaze searching mine, then finally she lifted to her toes, and I dipped my head closer to hers, her lips a mere breath away, waiting, desperate for her to close the distance between us.

Her cheeks were deep scarlet, so sweet and shy and beautiful, then she finally pressed her mouth to mine.

My mind went blank. There was nothing, no one, just her and me and the taste, the feel of her mouth on mine. I tried to stay still, to keep my hands to myself, but I snapped. Every moment I'd spent with her had slowly worn me thin. I was at breaking point, and knowing this was the last time, the last kiss, I broke in half—no, I fucking splintered apart.

My arm hooked her around her waist tighter, the other delving into her long blond hair as I hoisted her higher, the shirt she'd put on slid up, and my hand met hot and slippery bare skin. I groaned against her lips and opened my mouth over hers, kissing her deeper. Her sweet, little tongue tangled with mine, the urgent sounds she made driving me fucking wild.

"You taste so fucking good, butterfly," I rasped against her lips. She hooked her legs around my waist, her bare pussy grinding on my hard cock through my jeans, and I hissed and quickly reached down to adjust my hard-on.

The side of my hand slid across her slippery flesh, and I almost came in my jeans. She ground down harder. "Touch me...please."

If I touched her pussy, I'd throw her on the couch and fuck her. This felt so fucking right, but it wasn't right. She was all but naked, and this was moving too fucking fast. Her fingers were in my hair, her mouth so hot and sweet and perfect.

I wanted her so bad I shook, but I couldn't do this.

Images of blood and gore flashed through my mind, on my hands, hands that were sliding over Jasmine's body, hands that were tainted and wrong and evil.

Someone knocked on the door, and I pulled away, panting.

Jasmine froze, blinking up at me.

"Ren, it's Mom!"

"Shit!" Jasmine cried and flew out of my arms. She snatched up her clothes and ran from the room. The bathroom door slammed a second later. I didn't need to worry about having an erection in front of my mother. It deflated all on its own at the realization of what I'd just let happen, again. But this time, I'd let shit get out of hand. I quickly grabbed a shirt from the clean laundry I'd dumped on the chair, yanked it on, then strode to the door and opened it.

"Mom, hey."

She beamed at me like she always did when she first saw me and, like always, that look was quickly followed by concern.

"Have you been eating enough, honey?"

"Yeah, of course."

"How about sleeping? If you don't get enough sleep—"

"I've been sleeping. I'm okay." She worried, but she was usually more subtle.

She bit her lip and nodded, her eyes glossy. What was going on here?

Then it clicked into place. Tomorrow was the anniversary of what happened to me. I wasn't the only one who dreaded this time of year.

She looked past me to the candles, the salt, the string and herbs set out on the mat, and frowned. "What's going on, Renny?" Her gaze flew to my throat, to the sigils she could see there. "Ren?"

"Everything's fine. I promise."

"Hi, Mrs. Macanroy," Jasmine said, walking into the room.

Mom's gaze slid to Jaz, and she beamed. "Oh, Jasmine! I assumed it was Wills here. It's so nice to see you. How've you been, honey?"

Jaz smiled, her cheeks still pink, her mouth darker and swollen from our kiss. A yearning filled me, and I wanted to yank her back into my arms and finish what we'd started. I wanted to claim her, bite her, mark her. I felt dizzy and overheated. My skin was clammy and my fucking gut ached.

Ours.

My fox didn't say much, but his voice echoed through my mind now. *Only ours.*

I froze. *No.* He couldn't mean what I thought he did.

Claim mate. Bite. Mark.

My lungs seized and my heart slammed with force against the back of my ribs.

"Oh, am I interrupting, is this...is this a date?" A smile so wide it hurt to look at covered my mother's face.

"No," I said quickly, not wanting to get her hopes up, and locking my fucking knees so I didn't fall on my ass as what my fox said rang through my skull. "Jasmine was just doing some ink for me."

The concern was back. "Are you okay?"

"They're just simple sigils," Jasmine said. "For general well-being," she added.

Mom frowned, then looked up at me and forced a smile. "Well, that's good."

"So did you need something, Ma?" I asked when she stood there, the worry taking over again.

"I thought tonight was the night we were going over the plans for the renovations. If you're busy, maybe we can do it tomorrow? It'll have to be early, though. I have an appointment with the designer at lunchtime."

I'd forgotten our plans completely, but if she left me here with Jasmine now, I wasn't sure what I'd do. Either fuck her, or tell her to leave and hurt her, and I wasn't sure which would win out right then. "It's all good. If we don't do it now, we won't get a chance in the morning." Mom didn't need my help with this, but she liked to include me since my parents insisted it was my business as well. Tonight's visit wasn't really about that, though. No, it was about the three-year anniversary of her son being possessed and going on a killing spree, and her needing to be close to me, to reassure herself I was okay.

Jasmine quickly moved around the living room, grabbing her things, still blushing like crazy, and I shoved my hands in my pockets so I didn't reach for her when she walked over to us. She smiled at Mom. "Nice to see you again, Mrs. Macanroy."

"Call me Sally, honey," Mom said and walked into the living room and began unloading color samples and bits of fabric onto the couch.

Jasmine smiled up at me. "I'll leave you to it."

I nodded, my throat so fucking tight I wasn't sure how I was managing to still talk. "Jaz..."

She shook her head and smiled brighter, her eyes lit up and filled with happiness. "I'm fine. You hang with your mom. We'll talk later, okay?"

I nodded.

Her gaze darted to my mother, who wasn't paying us any attention, organizing everything and laying more stuff out on the coffee table, then back to me. She lifted to her toes, curled her fingers around the side of my throat, pulled me down, and pressed a quick kiss to my lips, making my heart thump hard. She dropped back down, grinned wider, then spun away and ran up the stairs and onto the street.

My fox whined, then growled, and the urge to run after her, to grab her and drag her back was so intense, I took a step after her.

"Renny, what do you think?" Mom said.

I slammed on the brakes and forced myself to shut the door.

And every step I took, taking me farther away from her, the more my fox lost his shit.

Fuck.

CHAPTER 17

Jasmine

Mr. Jenkins held my hand tighter than I thought possible, seeing as how frail he was. A tear slid down his weathered cheek, and he shook his head. "My granddaughter told me to make this appointment months ago, but I was a skeptic and an old fool." He smiled and another tear streaked down his face. "That was my Nelly, no if, ands, or buts about it. No one knows what you just told me, only her and I."

I squeezed his hand in return. I worked with a lot of humans, they made up eighty percent of my business, and I loved that I could give them this peace of mind. A message from a loved one to ease their fears and their hearts. "I'm so glad I could help you today," I said softly. "Nelly loves you so much, I can see it radiating from her." She'd crossed over two years ago, ascending straight to Heaven. I'd tapped into her energy as soon as Mr. Jenkins walked in.

Tell him he has to stop sitting in that living room and get out of the house and enjoy himself. Tell him to use the money in our holiday account and go on the cruise we always planned.

Her voice echoed through my mind, her features soft, but her tone no-nonsense. I chuckled. "She wants you to get out of the house and enjoy yourself. She said you're to use the money in your holiday savings account and go on that cruise the two of you planned to go on."

His lips quivered and more tears fell. Often in situations like this, the tears weren't sad ones, but came from relief, from the confirmation that their loved ones were okay. Add to that the intense emotions that came from truly knowing there was something more after death, that death wasn't an end, that it was just moving to the next part of your journey...it was a lot to take in. Mr. Jenkins was feeling all of that now. He also missed his wife terribly.

To have that kind of love—

Tender new shoots of hope grew, unfurling inside me. Ren felt something for me, he did. This time, it felt different. He'd had more control. He'd kissed me because he wanted to last night, not because of my power, I was sure of it.

If his mother hadn't arrived when she did, I didn't think we would have stopped at kissing. I'd tried to convince myself the way he looked at me all the time was nothing. I told myself it was something else, because how could it actually be what I desperately wanted it to be? He'd never made a move.

For so long, he'd coped with what happened to him through alcohol, by giving himself to any female who wanted him. By not caring about himself.

But he'd changed. The fake smiles were coming less often. He'd actually laughed, and yes, he was also moodier, more aggressive—jealous—and no, they weren't great emotions, but they were something other than indifference, and that had to be a good thing. He was allowing himself to feel whatever it was he was feeling, and maybe that included the way he felt about me?

I thought about our kiss, the way he'd said my name. The way he'd growled against my lips. My toes curled in my shoes. I'd never experienced anything like that in my life.

I ended the session with Mr. Jenkins, giving him a tight hug, pouring my healing powers into him, wrapping them around the part of him that looked back fondly on his time with his wife, and smoothed the jagged edges. He'd stifled it, all his energy going to his pain, so I worked to heal it, to revive that part of him, and bring it renewed life.

Mr. Jenkins left, and I took one of the books I'd borrowed from Rune's library from my bag to look through while I waited for my next client. I hadn't found anything useful yet, but there had to be something. Please, goddess, let there be something.

As I turned the pages, my anxiety surged, that I couldn't do this, that I'd fail Zinnia.

My next client arrived, and she'd just sat down when my phone chimed. I excused myself and quickly checked who it was. My knees actually went weak when I saw Ren's name on the screen.

Can you come by tonight?

Maybe some would play it cool, leave him hanging for an hour or so, but I wasn't cool. Why would I wait? This was the male I was in love with, with every fiber of my being.

Still, I managed to find some self-control and instead of writing back and saying, *OMG! Can you believe we freaking kissed last night? It was the best kiss I've ever had. I love you so much I think I might die.*

I went with: *Sure thing. What time?*

Ren: *I finish work at six. Any time after then*

Again I reined it in and replied with a very cool: *See you then*

I scanned our messages, nearly vibrating with excitement and happiness. It was happening. It was actually happening between us.

I shoved my phone away and went back to my client. Somehow, I had to get through the rest of my appointments without self-combusting.

The day went way too slow, but at five fifteen I was blowing out my candles and packing everything away. I grabbed my bag, stuffing my demon book back in, locked up the small room I rented for work, and took the narrow stairs to the street. I waved to Beth in the shop below through the window of her flower shop and headed to my car.

My phone beeped as I climbed in, and I slid it from my back pocket so fast I almost dropped it. Not Ren this time. It was a number I didn't recognize.

Have you thought anymore about dinner?

Xavier, it had to be. I wasn't the kind of person to string someone along, not that I'd been in the position to string anyone along before, but still. There was only one person I wanted to have dinner with.

Sorry, Xavier, I'm kind of seeing someone. It's new.

His reply came a minute later.

My loss. If I think of anything to help you with your missing souls, I'll be in touch.

Me: *Thank you.*

))》●《((

Brushing my hands over my hips and smoothing out the fabric of my dress, I tried to steady my nerves when I headed for Ren's place. The sun had set, and I could see lights shining from inside. Taking a steadying breath and gripping the bottle of wine I'd swiped from the cupboard, I walked up to the door and knocked.

I could see his shadow moving behind the door's frosted glass. He stilled for a moment, hovering there. My smile slipped a little when he didn't instantly open up. I stared at his silhouette, and he was obviously staring at mine. Was he going to leave me standing out here? Cold dread washed through my veins, and I gripped my bottle of wine tighter.

Please. Please open it. Please let me in.

He moved suddenly, and the door swung open.

His gaze sliced down my front, hit the wine in my hand, then came back up. His gaze stayed on mine a moment, then he looked away and opened the door wider. "Come in, Jaz."

The rest of the good feelings that I'd been floating on all day splintered at his tone, at the look on his face. Something was wrong. *No. You're imagining it. Stay positive. Everything's fine.* That kiss meant something to him as well, it did.

We walked to the couch, and he motioned for me to sit. "We should talk."

No. A voice in my head screamed. *NO. Please no.* I stupidly ignored that, too, not ready to believe what every cell in my body was telling me, not ready to let the energy rolling off Ren to penetrate.

"Have you had any trouble now that the sigils are all done? Felt any souls around you at all?" I asked, stalling, desperate to not have this conversation.

He shook his head. "Everything's stopped, like you said it would. Thank you for that, Jaz, truly." He shoved his fingers through his hair. "But that's not why I asked you over."

I held up the bottle of wine. "Would you like a glass?" I stood and headed for the small kitchen. Ren watched me as I took down two glasses, my hands shaking. I opened his kitchen drawers, searching for a corkscrew, but there wasn't one.

Ren strode over and slipped the bottle from my hands, setting it aside. "Jasmine, we need to talk—"

I spun on him. "No, we don't."

A look crossed his face, telling me he'd rather be anywhere but here.

A sane person would take the hint and retreat, would try and save face. I didn't feel sane in that moment. Far from it. "Don't do this. Please." The last was whispered, pleading.

He looked pained, awkward. "You're...god, so beautiful, Jaz, so fucking gorgeous, and sweet, and funny and fierce. I care about you, I do, but what happened last night—"

"Was perfect. Was the only thing that's felt right in a really long time," I said, throwing my heart on the floor in front of him, begging him to pick it up, to take it and keep it for his own.

"I wanted you last night, I did, badly," he said roughly. "But this can't happen between us."

I was breathing hard, shaking. "Why?"

462

"You know why. I'm not fit for any kind of a relationship."

"But this is different, we'd be different. I could help you, we'd be good for each other," I said, close to begging.

"Butterfly," he said gently. "I'm sorry."

I grabbed the edge of the counter so I didn't collapse on the floor right alongside my bleeding heart. "You want me and not just last night. You want me now. I know you do. Why are you pretending there isn't something between us?" *Something huge. Something real.* "Why are you lying?"

The muscles in his arms tightened. "Any male would be lucky to be with you, Jaz, and I mean that, but it's not going to be me."

I closed the space between us. My guard had shattered when he'd kissed me last night. There was no throwing it back up now. I felt as if he were tearing me limb from limb. This couldn't be happening. I loved him. Goddess, so much. I fisted his shirt at his stomach, pressing in close, and looked up at him. "I want you and you want me," I said, fighting the sob crawling up my throat. "Tell me, tell me you want me too. Stop lying and tell me."

Ren winced, actually winced. Pity filling his eyes. "Don't make this any harder—"

"Say it. Tell me you don't want me."

"Jazzy."

"Say it!"

He sucked in a breath, his nostrils flaring. "I don't. Not the way you want me. I'm sorry. I'm really sorry, Jasmine. I'm not capable of that, of having a...a relationship with anyone, not anymore. I never should have—"

I shoved away from him, shaking my head, his words wounding me more than anything else ever had, and in a way I knew I'd never recover from.

I looked up at him and fought down the tears. I'd already humiliated myself enough in front of this male. I straightened my spine, my hands to his chest, and looked him in the eyes. I was about to say, *If you send me away now, you will lose me forever. Do you understand? If you don't fight for me now, I promise you, there will never be an us. Never.* But my power reached out instinctively, moving through him, and I felt his torment, and just how broken he was. I knew it already, of course. He was emotionally scarred to an extent that no amount of work on his own would heal him.

He needed help. And I was the only one who could do it.

What I was doing right now, it wasn't fair, not to him, and not to myself. He needed me to help him heal, not beg him to love me like some pathetic fool. Not make everything he was already suffering so much harder. Goddess, I was so fucking selfish. I knew what he'd been through, and still all I was thinking about was myself, what I wanted, what I needed. I loved him too much to do this to him.

I shook my head and choked down my pain. "You must think I'm a desperate idiot. Goddess, I'm so sorry." I forced a laugh and took a step back. "No, you're right, of course. This"—I motioned between us—"would be a horrible idea."

He searched my gaze, and his jaw tightened. "Jasmine—"

"It's fine, Ren. Honestly. I lost my head there for a moment." My heart felt as if it had been mangled in my chest, but I forced a deprecating grin. "I thought we could have some fun, but mixing business with pleasure is never a good idea, right? Can we just forget this happened?"

His gaze searched mine, then he nodded. "If that's what you want."

"It is. Right, I have to take off, but I'll be in touch so we can sort out a time for your next session."

He stood impossibly still, watching me closely. "Okay."

I walked around him and strode blindly toward the door, my heart hammering in my chest. I walked through the door and up the stairs as calmly as I could, hoping he didn't see how hard I was shaking, then as soon as I reached the top and was out of sight, I ran, like I could outrun what had just happened.

Whatever hope I'd had, had turned black, had shriveled and died. It was bitter and cold and so wrong I wanted to claw at my skin, at the center of my chest and the organ pounding so desperately there. It still called for him, still demanded I go back, even now.

CHAPTER 18

Ren

I STRODE out onto the street and watched Jasmine run like hell away from me. She'd tried to backtrack, to pretend she didn't care, that she'd only come for some fun, but she was lying.

My heart was pounding like it was trying to liberate itself from my chest.

Fuck, when I answered the door—the look on her face, the hope, the excitement. Everything she felt for me had been right there, open and real and so fucking raw.

And I'd smothered it, killed it.

I'd hurt her.

Oh fuck.

I bent at the waist, gripping my thighs, and dry heaved. Everything inside me was rebelling against what I'd just done. My fox was losing his shit, shredding the ground beneath his paws, howling in pain.

She was ours, our mate, and I'd rejected her. I pushed her away.

A weak, tainted piece of shit like you has no right touching a female like that. Edward's voice echoed through my mind. My broken mind bringing him back as if he'd never left.

Images of the newspaper article I'd seen this morning, crumpled up and tossed on the floor of my father's office, flashed through my mind. A piece written about the families of the victims, *my victims*, three years later. Their faces...how they felt about their loved one's killer still on the loose...

My skin crawled.

Letting her go was the right thing to do.

I had to move. I couldn't stand here, and I couldn't go back into my place. Not when all I could see now was Jasmine standing there, so beautiful, eyes filled with pain, not when her scent had filled every inch like she'd always been there. I strode down the street and through the field, then into the forest. I didn't dare shift, not right then, not when we both wanted to go after Jasmine so badly. If I let animal instincts take over, my fox would take us straight to her.

Christ, the pain in her eyes was all I could see. I could feel it. Her pain had felt like a kick to the backs of the knees. It'd taken everything in me to stand fucking upright in the face of all that pain. I should never have kissed her, touched her. I should have fucking resisted. I could tell myself that, but it'd been impossible. I'd been drawn to her so completely that resisting wasn't an option, and now I'd made everything so much worse.

A demon snarled up ahead, and I pulled the knife from my boot and kept running. It stepped out in front of me, and I attacked, taking out all the pent-up agony and rage I was feeling. I sliced and sliced, a sound coming from me that could only be described as a disturbed wail before I finally removed his head. After that I heard no more demons as I ran toward my cliff.

The demons in these forests knew me well. I'd lived alongside them for long enough. They knew what I could do, and they'd learned to stay the fuck away from me. The sound of rushing water echoed ahead, and I pumped my arms harder, sprinting faster. It'd be better for Jasmine, for everyone if I was gone. If I dove off the edge of that cliff. I gasped for breath, struggling to process what just happened back in my kitchen, what I'd just done.

Oh fuck.

What had I done?

What I had to. I was stained with blood. A monster.

A monster who was still torturing the innocent people he'd killed, their souls unable to rest because of me, because of how fucked in the head I was. A monster who hurt everyone around him.

You're a weak, pathetic coward, Edward's voice snarled. I punched the side of my head and roared. "Shut up!"

He wasn't there. He was gone. That was my own voice.

And it was right.

I ran and ran until sweat poured off me, until the cliff finally came into view. I dug my heels in deeper, my breath puffing in and out faster. I looked straight ahead, focusing on the night sky, and raced for the edge.

Almost there. It was almost over—

A heavy weight slammed into my side, knocking me back several yards from the edge. I spun with a snarl, and came face to face with a giant hellhound. Warrick.

No one was stopping me. I jumped back up and sprinted toward my goal a second time, but he moved quickly, tossing me away from the edge again.

I stood, panting hard. "Get the fuck out of my way!" I roared.

Warrick shifted, his golden eyes burning into me. "Not letting you kill yourself. You're not doing that to Willow and Violet. And you're not doing it to me, to your brothers."

"Why the fuck are you here? Just go."

"We stopped by the house just as you took off. Your scent, brother...it's not right. What happened?"

We?

Willow stepped forward, out of the shadows, her gaze locking on mine before she strode right for me.

"Don't," I bit out.

She ignored me and kept coming, wrapping her arms around me. I didn't want her comfort, couldn't take it. I pulled her arms from around me, stumbling back, and tore my shirt from my chest, hands shaking, and went for the tree. I pulled out the knife and made the first slice. It was the only thing that would stop me from losing it completely in that moment. The relief was instant.

"Ren," Willow cried out and tried to run to me.

Warrick snagged her around the waist and hauled her into his arms. "Let him."

"What? No!" She struggled, but Warrick held her tight.

"He needs it."

He knew, somehow Warrick knew. I recited the positions of each slice like a mantra, remembering each slice I'd made in an innocent person, shaking, bleeding. My shame, my brokenness on display in all its horror for Willow to see. Something I'd never wanted. Something I would have done anything to prevent. But I couldn't stop. It was the only way to ease this fucking awful feeling inside me, the only way.

When I finished, blood slid down my body, pooling at my feet.

Willow's sobs filled the night, while Warrick held her upright, holding her tight in his arms.

I thought I'd already hit the lowest I could. I thought I'd been there. I'd been so fucking far from it.

"Why?" Willow whispered.

I looked over at her, the numbness setting in. "It's the only thing...that makes it okay."

"Makes what okay?"

"Living."

CHAPTER 19

Jasmine

I CHECKED MY PHONE AGAIN. Still no reply from Mom. It was the middle of the night, but I was still awake, the awful feeling in my gut wouldn't go, not after what happened with Ren.

Paris was five hours ahead, it'd be early morning there, but still I hoped she'd answer. I needed my mom, for once I needed her, but as usual she was never available, not for me, and not for Zinny.

We'd never been enough. I tried to tell myself different, but it was the truth. She'd taught me a lesson, and I'd been too stupid to learn from it.

Words mean nothing, actions speak the loudest.

Mom told us she loved us, but she left us behind, and she barely called. She'd forgotten both my and Zinny's birthdays last year. Ren had shown me he didn't want me, that he wasn't interested in me, by being with a constant stream of females right in front of me, never giving my feelings one single thought—because I was so far off his radar, I was on another planet to him.

He'd shown me, time and again, and I'd ignored it, desperate for him to love me. I'd known he'd only kissed me, touched me, because of my magic, because his emotions had been thrown into chaos. And yet I'd convinced myself we had something real.

And I'd forced him to say it.

Tell me you don't want me.

I don't. Not the way you want me. I'm sorry. I'm really sorry, Jasmine.

It was more than I could bear, this pain. Even when there'd been no cause for it, I'd had hope. That's what love did, it lied to you. It turned you into a blind fool, the unrequited kind anyway. Deep inside, in the part of me I'd tried to ignore, I'd allowed myself to imagine us together, because anything else felt so wrong.

Voices drifted up from downstairs.

Willow's voice, and she sounded upset.

A muffled sob came next, and I shoved the covers off, rushed out to the hall, and started down.

"Oh goddess," Aunt Daisy said, cradling Violet close. "I thought he was doing better."

There was a low rumbling voice. Warrick.

I stopped on the stairs, not wanting to intrude, and because I knew instantly who they were talking about.

"So did I," Willow said, and she sounded defeated, heartbroken. "Warrick stopped him, but if we hadn't followed him, he would've done it. He would've...jumped off that cliff."

I gripped the banister, my heart seizing in my chest.

"How many times has he almost jumped off that fucking cliff and I had no idea?" Willow said. "I should have been with him, especially today—"

"Today?" Daisy asked.

"It's the anniversary of when he was possessed, the first day Edward forced him to kill. There was this...this big fucking write-up in the *Roxburgh Times*, interviews with the grieving families, the faces of all the victims, a *serial killer still on the loose* angle. When I saw it, I rushed to Ren's, but he'd already taken off." She made a strangled sound. "Goddess, Mom, he cut himself, he...he mutilates himself..."

"He's been doing that a while," Warrick said. "Those scars, he never lets them fully heal."

Daisy sobbed.

I went back up the stairs feeling sick to my stomach. I hadn't realized what date it was. I'd been worrying about myself, about my feelings, when Ren had been suffering. I could help him heal, but this would never end for him, it would never go away.

Ren was broken, and he needed me. But I couldn't give him that at the expense of my own sanity. I wouldn't let him keep suffering, but if I didn't do something to stop this pain in my chest, I wouldn't be any use to him.

I'd been desperately trying to heal myself, to smooth away the jagged edges of my own pain, but the wounds were too vast, too deep. They were scars now, thick and raw and there was no healing them.

He needed me, but I couldn't do it, not like this. Not when I couldn't breathe, couldn't walk and talk and live in a world where he was while I loved him, knowing he didn't love me back.

This had to be over.

It had to end.

I wouldn't let Ren hurt himself anymore.

I loved him too much for that.

>)>·◑·(·((

I stared up at the brownstone, the vintage lantern above the door making its shiny black surface gleam.

All I could think about as I sped here in my car was the face of the female who'd walked out of that door the last time I was here. The peace, the joy, the *relief* that flowed from her.

I wanted that. I needed it. I needed to be free of this pain. I couldn't take it another moment. I wasn't strong enough to help Ren as long as this agony was inside me. I wanted it gone. I wanted this feeling inside me gone. For good. And the only way to do that was by putting up a thick, impenetrable wall and blocking it off, suffocating it. Killing it. For Ren's sake, and mine.

I jogged up the stairs and knocked before I could change my mind. I was on a pain Ferris wheel, and this was the only way of getting off that ride and staying off it for good.

The door opened and Xavier stared down at me, a frown lowering his brows. "Jasmine? You've been crying. Is everything all right?"

I barely realized I was crying, no, sobbing. My throat hurt and my eyelids were tight and puffy. Goddess, this was humiliating. "I need your help in a...a professional capacity," I said, my voice shaky and broken when I was trying so hard for it to come out strong.

"Come inside, let me make you some tea and we can talk."

I shook my head. "I don't want to talk, I want this"—I pounded my fist to the center of my chest—"gone. I want it gone."

Placing his hand on the small of my back, he steered me inside and into the same room where I'd met with him the last time I was here. He sat me down and crouched in front of me. "What, Jasmine? What do you want gone?"

My lips quivered, and I squeezed my eyes closed, trying to catch my breath when another sob was right there. I felt weak and pathetic, but that small bit of hope, that kiss, it crumbled the wall I'd built to protect myself and there was no getting it back up. I needed someone else to do it for me. I needed Xavier to do it for me. I grabbed his hand in both of mine, my eyes locked on his steady, cool gaze. "I'm in love with a male who will never love me back, and I want you to take it away, Xavier. Please, can you lock it away?"

His gaze didn't falter, but he didn't say anything either. He just stared into my eyes. Again, I felt drawn in, held in place, like he was looking inside me. I let him. I opened myself up and let him see it, all of it.

Finally, he asked, "You're positive there's no hope?"

"None. I've endured this...this feeling for so long. I've watched him with other females. Seen him try to drink his own pain away. He doesn't...he doesn't want me...he..."

Say it. Tell me you don't want me.

I don't. Not the way you want me.

His words echoed through my skull again, and I bit my lip to hold in an agonized cry. My throat was raw from fighting it. He didn't want me, but he did need me. After what I heard Willow say, I had to put him first, over my own pain. Mine was nothing to his. This was the only way. I wouldn't let Ren take his own life. Nothing was more important than that. "He doesn't want me. He told me. Please, will you help me."

Xavier stood and slid his hands in his pockets. "You understand how this works? If I do this, it can't be undone."

"I understand," I rasped. "Does that mean you'll do it?"

He studied me for several long seconds, then nodded. "If this is what you truly want, who am I to deny you."

I dragged in a breath, it felt like the first one since I ran from Ren's house. "I don't have any money with me, but I'm good for it. Whatever your price—"

"No payment." He held out his hand. "Come."

I took it and let him lead me from the room and down a wide hall. He opened a door at the end and flicked on a light, then carried on down a set of steep stairs and along to another door. He opened it and led me into a large room. This was the basement, but it didn't feel like one. The lighting was warm and the walls were emerald green. Shelves covered in books took up most of the wall space and, getting a closer look, I saw they weren't the kinds of books found in your average library. These were old, and I felt the whisper of power flowing from them. Magic. There were several globes and an old-school blackboard with symbols drawn in chalk, variations of the same one.

He led me to the edge of the room, then moved a chair to the side before he rolled the mat back, revealing the hardwood floor. There were intricate symbols painted on the wood in white, laid out in a hexagon. Symbols I'd never seen or used before, not in my family or coven and not in any books in our library.

"What are these," I asked, looking up at him.

He looked down at them as well, his head tilted to the side as if he hadn't really looked at them in a long time, not with fresh eyes. "They're symbols I created, well, modified. They help to boost my blocking gift and enhance my ability to pinpoint with absolute accuracy the location of the particular emotion that I need to seal off."

"They're beautiful," I said, telling him the truth. To do this, to create these, Xavier saw things in a way a lot of people didn't, couldn't.

His lips lifted on one side in a small smile, but those intense lavender eyes stayed the same, cool and unaffected. "Thank you. They took me a very long time to perfect."

I motioned to the blackboard. "Are those others you're working on?"

"Yes." He frowned at the chalk drawings. "I'm getting close, but they still need work." He turned back to me. "Please, take a seat."

He motioned to the chair he'd just moved and I did as he said, a flurry of nerves making my legs shake. I sat and watched as he strode to the other side of the room and proceeded to remove his jacket, followed by his shirt. He folded each carefully and placed them on a desk. He toed off his shoes and removed his socks, then turned to me. His pale, hairless chest was rigid with muscle, and the same symbols on the floor were tattooed on his chest and stomach in the same arrangement in red ink.

My heart hammered harder, but I made myself stay where I was. I had to do this for Ren, and for me. I was no good to him in my current state. I couldn't help him while I was hanging on to such intense feelings for him. He didn't deserve my anger. He'd done nothing wrong. I'd pumped him full of magic, had filled him with so many emotions he'd avoided in so long, and it had made him feel something that wasn't real. It had confused him. He never would've kissed me otherwise.

"What happens now?" I asked.

Xavier stepped into the hexagon. "Now, I take your pain away."

I wanted that, so badly. "What will it feel like?"

"It won't be painful, if that's what you're asking. You may feel a little pressure while I build the walls, some get a mild headache afterward, but only for a short time, and nothing more than that." He lowered himself to the floor and crossed his legs. "I need to go into what looks like a trance while I find the source of your distress. Right now, while you're feeling it so acutely, it shouldn't be difficult, but it helps if you think about the source of your pain—in this case, the male you love. It'll broadcast the location of those emotions louder for me."

"Okay." That wouldn't be hard. Ren was the only thing in my head in that moment.

Xavier closed his eyes and rested his hands on his knees.

I did what he asked and let it all tumble through me. The cemetery several years ago, legs shaking as I walked over to give him his message. That instant connection snapping into place between us because of it. Watching him with other females when he finally stopped living in the forest and came home. Our fight, the one where I called him names, letting my own hurt feelings control me. The kisses, the way he'd held me to him so tight, making him laugh in the forest. The look on his face when I arrived at his place tonight. The way he'd looked at me when he told me he didn't want me.

My heart clutched in my chest as if it were happening all over again, and I fought the sob trying to crawl up my throat—

A pressure in my head had me sucking in a startled breath. No, it wasn't painful, but it was weird. Xavier was in my head, shuffling through my emotions. I breathed through it, through the odd sensations and the pain of my unrequited love for Ren.

I stayed focused on him, replaying that last kiss over and over in my mind, the look on his face, the things he'd said, and until this moment, the emotional pain had only grown more acute with every replay. I let it play out in my head, and again, and again, and each time, it grew less painful. With each run-through, I stopped feeling what I had during those encounters, the emotions becoming muted, and the physicality of it becoming more pronounced.

Until finally—that's all there was left.

The pressure in my head eased, and I felt Xavier withdraw.

I breathed slow and easy, searching for it, for Ren, for my love for him, but it was—gone. All of it. There was nothing there. I thought about him and felt nothing but sympathy for his predicament. There was still attraction, but no emotional connection.

No pain.

It was gone. I was free.

I wasn't in love with Ren anymore.

CHAPTER 20

Ren

THE FERAL HAD MOVED DEEPER into the forest. I kicked a pile of bones and searched the area around me. I'd been out here every night for almost a week.

I hadn't seen Jasmine since I hurt her and she ran from me. She was due to come back to heal me the day after tomorrow. But there was no way she was coming back, not now. Not after what I did.

I headed back the way I came. I'd been avoiding any place I thought Jaz might be, and it was fucking killing me. She was my mate. I knew that now with every part of me. She was mine, and I fucking craved her—her voice, her warmth, her touch, her mouth. Now that I'd had those things, being deprived of them was a new kind of torture.

I couldn't be the male she deserved, though. It didn't matter how much I wanted her, I was no good for her, no good for anyone. But I could do this. I could help find these souls and make sure Zinnia came home. For Jasmine.

It took another thirty minutes, but I finally reached Agatheena's cottage. Smoke drifted from the chimney, the door firmly closed. I couldn't walk up and knock, so I did the only thing I could, I called her name. I was no doubt attracting every demon in the forest, but I didn't care, this was fucking important.

Several minutes later, the door finally opened and Agatheena walked out. "You trying to get killed, fox?" she said as she started down the steps.

"I need to talk to you."

She rolled her eyes as she slowly made her way toward me. "Figured that much out for myself."

A demon burst from the trees behind me and I spun, flinging my blade and burying it in the demon's neck. I stalked over, hacked off his head, dusted the ashes from my hands, and walked back.

Agatheena watched me with that shrewd gaze. "You kill the feral yet?"

"You know I haven't." The witch knew every damn thing.

"Then not sure why you're hanging around my front gate caterwauling," she said, looking at me like she was sizing me up for her pot.

"I give you my word, I will kill it. I'll kill anything you want me to, just give me the information Jasmine needs now."

"Manners are free and yet you seem to have forgotten how to use yours," she said.

I ground my teeth. "Please."

She eyed me, then shrugged. "Fine." She pulled a vial from her pocket and tossed it to me through the barrier between us. "Your blood, fill it. Not risking you going back on your word."

I sliced my arm and filled the vial, pushed the stopper in, and tossed it to her. "I won't go back on my word."

She put it in her pocket and tilted her head, looking at me in a way that I didn't like, not at all. "Taking this information to her won't earn you forgiveness, you realize that?"

I wanted to tell her to mind her own damn business, that she didn't know what she was talking about, but she saw right through me. "I don't expect forgiveness. I just want to help her."

"That's good, because you're too late."

My fox's ears pricked at the eerie note to her voice, the look that shifted through her eyes. "What's that supposed to mean?"

She shrugged a bony shoulder, her eyes flashing red, her demon side coming through. "Only that you missed your chance."

The old witch was fucking with me and enjoying it.

She pointed to a glass jar hanging off the tree. There was a small piece of folded paper inside it that hadn't been there before. "There's your information. Get that feral taken care of." Then she turned and headed back up the path.

I stared after her, my heart in my throat. *You're too late.* Those words echoed through my mind and kept on doing so as I took the piece of paper from the jar, shoved it in my pocket, and headed for home.

·)·)·)·❀·(·(·(·

This was the last place I wanted to be.

The line to get into The Vault had been down the street. Thankfully I knew the bouncers, and they'd let me through. I'd been trying to find Jasmine, to give her the message from Agatheena, but she wasn't home or at the clubhouse. Warrick said some of the hounds had come here, Iris, Mags, and Rose as well. Jasmine would be with them.

It didn't happen often, but there was a band playing tonight. The vampire cover band played older music and were a favorite around the city, which meant the place was packed. I worked my way through the crowd, but it wasn't hard to find who I was looking for. The hounds stood head and shoulders above everyone else. There were a lot of pack members from Silver Claw here as well. Bram stood to the side, talking with Ronan and Draven. Bram's three brothers, Payne, Rook, and Talon, were with them as well.

The band was playing, so I knew exactly where I'd find Jasmine. I searched the dance floor. She and Rose with their pale blond hair made it easy to find them in the crowd. They were at the edge, so Iris, Mags, and Rose could stay close to their mates.

The song ended and I started toward them. Jaz had turned and was talking to Rome and Relic, a huge smile on her face.

"Hey, Roxburgh, you wanna get *Close to Me*?" the singer called out.

The crowd cheered as they started playing The Cure song. Jasmine did a little jump and grabbed Rome's hand. The big male grinned down at her and shook his head. I could see him mouth, "I don't dance, Jazzy," from here.

A growl tore from my chest. I didn't want her near Rome. No fucking way.

You threw her away.

Because I didn't have any other choice. That didn't change the way I felt, though.

She danced anyway, right in front of Rome, still holding his hand, moving around him while he stood there with a fucking huge grin on his face. Jaz laughed and sang and moved between Rome and Relic as if they were living, breathing fucking poles for her to swing around.

My fox wanted to break free, and my claws pressed against the tips of my fingers. Before I could reach them, Bram's brother Talon was there. He took her hand and led her out onto the floor, the cocky crow pulling her into his arms, laughing and dancing with her, with my Jasmine.

Mine.

I planted my feet to the floor, not knowing what the fuck to do. I wanted to kill him, tear him limb from limb, but I'd given that right up. I'd given her up, and there was no going back, so I watched them, rooted to the spot, not sure what the fuck to do, feeling like I was dying inside.

I may have given her up, but I needed her to look at me. Selfishly, I still needed that from her. I wanted her eyes on me. I missed it, craved it. I needed it. I'd been without it for almost a week.

As he spun her around, her gaze finally found me. Usually, I'd see a change in her. A multitude of emotions would flash through her beautiful eyes, because she'd felt the pull toward me like I had toward her. But this time, there was nothing. Her gaze skittered over me like I was anyone else. There was none of the hurt or disappointment I'd seen before she left my place a week ago.

There was just...nothing.

›)) ◗ ◖ ((‹

Jasmine

Talon laughed when I spun around him. All I was feeling in that moment was happiness, a release, blowing off some steam after a week of reading from the demon library, of combing Nightscape for any reports of unusual spiritual activity, of driving around aimlessly and walking the city with my sigils off hoping they'd just pop out and show themselves, and coming up with absolutely nothing—and that sense of freedom, just for a couple of hours, didn't change when I spotted Ren across the room. The pain didn't come. The feeling of wanting him so bad it was like an open wound was gone.

He was just Ren.

My cousin's emotionally scarred familiar. Someone I'd known for a long time. A male I cared about the same way I cared about Roman or Relic. I wanted to help him, the same way I would anyone who came to me suffering and in need of my brand of healing.

I'd been avoiding him this week, afraid that when I finally saw him it would all come rushing back. But it didn't. The constant longing, the awful pit in my stomach was gone.

Throwing up my arms, I tilted my head back and sang at the top of my lungs, the relief pouring from me.

The song ended, and when the next started, everyone rushed toward the stage. It was a crowd favorite. I'd seen the band play before with Mags a couple months ago. The lead singer was hot, and when he sang this song, everyone went wild. I was pushed back, and Talon stopped me from falling, catching me with an arm around my middle.

Iris and Rose had moved back as well, standing with their mates. Mags was scowling beside me, trying to see. Then Bram was there, grabbing her and lifting her onto his shoulders. I looked up, jealous, she'd have a perfect vantage point from up there.

Talon bumped my arm, then motioned at himself and pointed upward. I grinned and nodded. He gripped my hips and tossed me onto his shoulders as well. Mags laughed and grabbed my hand, right as the drums kicked in and everyone started losing their minds. The crowd was singing and jumping around, and I danced on Talon's shoulders, belting out the lyrics at the top of my lungs. The room was so hot, and I noticed several of the wolves had taken their shirts off, dancing in their bras. I had on a sports bra that looked more like a top. Screw it. I tugged my shirt over my head.

Talon held up his hand. I gave it to him, and he tucked it in the waistband of his jeans.

Tomorrow, I'd get back to my search, but tonight, I'd take this small reprieve from the constant worry over the missing souls, and Death, and bring my sister home.

Mags looked over at me, grinned, and pulled up her top. Bram reached up and grabbed the bottom of it, yanking it back down. I cackled, and she scowled and tried again. Next minute, Mags was pulled down, tossed over Bram's shoulder, and his hand came down on her ass as he carried her toward one of the dark corners. No doubt to make out.

I wanted to make out with someone too. I glanced down at Talon's tattooed hand on my knee. He was hot. There was no doubt about it. He had intense black eyes and a wickedness about him that was incredibly appealing.

The song ended, and I looked down again, surprised to see Ren was standing in front of him. I hadn't even seen him come over. I always used to know where he was if he was in the same room. Right now, his face was all twisted up and he looked pissed off. I couldn't see all of Talon's face, but I thought he might be smiling.

I tapped his hand, and he looked up. I motioned for him to put me down. He gripped my waist and lifted me from his shoulders, then hooked his arm around my neck.

I looked between him and Ren. "What's going on?"

"Can we talk?" Ren said, his eyes blazing.

I glanced at Talon. He winked.

"Does it have to be now?" I kind of wanted to kiss Talon. He was cute, something I hadn't really noticed before. I mean, I'd noticed, I just hadn't cared.

"Yeah, it has to be now." Ren grabbed my hand, yanked my shirt from

Talon's waistband, and towed me across the floor to an empty table in the corner.

"What's going on?" I asked.

He thrust my top at me, and I blinked down at it.

"Put it on, Jaz. There are creeps all over this fucking club staring at your tits," he growled out.

"What?" I looked around. "No they're not, and my tits are covered."

"Believe me, they're looking."

I took my top back, but I didn't put it on. It was hot and there were people wearing a lot less than me. "I don't know what this is about, but I'm here with my friends. I've had a shitty fucking week, and I need this. If this isn't important, I'm going to head back." I took a step away from him, but he grabbed my wrist, stopping me. "What is it, Ren? Jesus."

"I spoke with Agatheena. She gave me the info you need."

I stilled. "She just gave it to you?"

"I swore I'd get the feral. She took some of my blood, deal done. I was going to kill it anyway. No big deal," he said, his gaze dipping below my chin, and his lips peeled back in a snarl before they slid back up.

His words weren't matching the expression on his face. He was wound tight and pissed off. The veins in his forearms and biceps were bulging, and his eyes were nearly glowing.

"Well, can I have it?" I said, starting to worry that my healing wasn't working. He should be starting to feel it, a change in his emotional well-being, but if anything he seemed more tense than usual. Ren had a lot of healing to do, though, and sometimes the process made people act out of the norm.

"It's back at my place." His gaze locked on mine.

"Oh, well, I'll just get it tomorrow when I come by for your healing session." I glanced back at the dance floor when the next song started. I loved this song.

"So you're still coming over tomorrow, then? I wasn't sure after...what happened."

He studied me, and I gave him a measured smile. "I'll be there. I haven't been at home crying over a broken heart, I promise." Not anymore. If my heart was broken, I had no knowledge of it, not anymore, and that's the way I liked it.

"I hurt you," he said. "And I feel fucking shitty about it, about how I handled everything."

"Don't worry about it. I'm completely over it."

"I don't believe you," he said, looking even more pissed.

I frowned. Now I was getting pissed off. "Well, believe it."

"The way you're acting...the way you're looking at me like I don't exist..." he said, stepping closer. "The way you're throwing yourself at Talon, taking your top off in front of all these males? Are you trying to make me jealous? Is that what this is?"

I stared at him in disbelief. "You didn't want me, Ren, and that's fine because I can tell you with one hundred percent honesty..." I held his gaze. "I don't want you, either, not anymore." He flinched, and I felt bad, but I ignored it and carried on. "I care about you. You're Willow's familiar, you're a friend, but I promise you, that's all you are to me. You definitely haven't influenced my actions tonight. I just want to enjoy myself."

He looked, goddess, lost. I gentled my voice. "I want to help you, Ren, more than you know, but you need to get a handle on your emotions. I know it's confusing, the type of healing we're doing. It can make you think or feel conflicting things. You wouldn't be the first client I've treated that started to feel, I don't know, possessive over me or whatever. Or imagine some kind of deeper connection. The fact we've known each other a long time, only makes it more confusing."

"That's not what's happening here," he said.

"If you say so." Of course that's what was happening here. He was behaving like some protective older brother. "How much have you had to drink?"

He planted his hands on his hips. "Nothing. I'm not drunk, Jasmine."

"I'm sorry if you're struggling at the moment. Maybe you should be with Willow right now?"

His brows shot up. "What? I'm fine."

I smiled. "Okay, well, that's really good. I'm going to head back. You have a good night. I'll see you tomorrow," I said and walked away.

He was acting this way for the same reason he'd kissed me during our sessions: he was going through a massive emotional upheaval. He would get past it. With more healing, he'd get well again.

He just needed time.

CHAPTER 21

Ren

I OPENED the door and Jaz stood there, her bag over her shoulder and a barely there smile curving her lips. Her hair was down and tousled in a way I wanted to sink my fingers into, and she was wearing makeup, more than she usually did, her gorgeous green eyes surrounded by charcoal and her full lips deep red. "Hey, Ren," she said and walked in.

"Hey." I studied her, still surprised she actually showed up, but she seemed...fine. More than fine. And when she turned to me, her gaze was warm but nothing more. There was no anger or sadness. She looked at me like I could be any one of her clients. Something unpleasant curled its fingers in my gut. Something was seriously off. "Are you okay?"

Her features rearranged into surprise. "Of course." She waved me forward. "Because your sigils are done and we're only working on your emotional healing today, we won't need any warding. Let me just quickly change out the crystals, it'll keep the souls calm, then we can get started."

"Sounds good." I watched as she rushed around, picking up the crystals she left last time and packing them in her bag. I couldn't take my fucking eyes off her. She took out a small pouch with new ones and walked around laying them out while spelling, muttering the words under her breath.

When she was done, she walked over to me and tilted her head back. "You ready to get started?"

"Yeah, sure." Was I ready for her to wrap her arms around me? No, I fucking wasn't. I'd craved it, wanted her hands on me all week, and now that I knew Jasmine was supposed to be mine, I wasn't sure I could do this and let her go again afterward. How could I do this and not kiss her? I hadn't been able to resist the other times, but I had to. The reasons we couldn't be together hadn't changed.

"Cool. Let's do this, then I'll be out of your way," she said.

I didn't want her out of my way. I couldn't have her, but I needed her close. I needed her. Jesus, this was hard, confusing. What did I do with these conflicting emotions? "You don't need to rush off," I said. I wasn't trying to give her mixed signals, but I was feeling fucking desperate.

"I actually do. I've got somewhere I need to be." She pulled her phone from her pocket and checked it. "In half an hour as a matter of fact." She slid off the light coat she was wearing and draped it over the back of the couch.

I let my gaze leave her beautiful face and slide down the rest of her body. My mouth went dry and my hands immediately curled into fists. She was wearing a black dress, one that clung to her body and every one of her sweet curves. A couple of silver necklaces rested on the mounds of her soft breasts, and she wore silver bracelets that jangled as she moved. Her legs were bare, and she was wearing lace-up boots with a chunky heel. Add the hair and the makeup and she looked edgy and sexy as fuck.

The grip in my gut turned into jealous fury. "Hot date?" I said, and somehow I kept all that I was feeling out of my voice, or at least I hoped I did.

She glanced up at me, and her cheeks had turned pink. "Something like that."

My fox lost his mind, and I grabbed the back of the couch to stop myself from leaping over it, pinning her to the wall, and demanding she tell me who. I wanted to tear the fucker to pieces, whoever he was. I couldn't stop myself asking, "Rome?"

Her brows shot up, then she chuckled as if I wasn't over here internally having a rage seizure. "Roman and I are friends, nothing more. You know that. He's like...a brother." Her cheeks darkened further. "I was a dick for giving you the impression that there was ever anything more between us." She shook her head. "So no, not Rome."

"Then who?" I asked, because I had to know.

She chuckled again and tucked her hair behind her ear. "No one you know. I'm nervous enough, let's talk about something else. Like Agath-eena's message, for example. I'm desperate to know if she has something that can actually help."

There was not one thing I would rather talk about than who this male was and where I could find him alone later tonight so I could fuck him up. Because this wasn't fucking happening.

I was the stupid fucking asshole who'd rejected her, though. I didn't get to decide who she dated.

"Right, yeah, of course." I shoved my hands in my pockets because my hands were shaking like hell from rage and regret and this awful feeling that I'd made a terrible mistake. "It's just one word. I don't know what it means, never seen it before, so I'm guessing it's a clue. I'll give it to you after we...do the healing."

"She's not making it easy, then? Yeah, she definitely didn't like me," Jaz said, then rounded the couch and took the last few steps until we were almost touching, but not quite.

I shook harder, and there was no hiding it.

"You okay?" There was concern in her eyes.

The shy, longing looks she always gave me, that I'd told myself were something else, were gone. Feelings I only now realized she'd had for me, because she'd felt what I had, that connection, one mate recognizing the other. Or at least she had. Apparently, I'd destroyed anything she'd felt for me completely. And no, I wasn't okay. "Yeah, this healing thing, it's intense, that's all."

She nodded. "I know." Then she wrapped her arms around me, pressing her soft, warm body the length of mine. Her face to my chest. Warmth immediately flowed from her into me, but it felt different. Everything was different. Before, I'd felt as if she were part of me, somehow. Now there was a distance between us, and I hated it.

"It's okay, Ren. Everything's going to be okay," she said, her voice soft, soothing.

Still, that distance persisted. I shook harder, a restless feeling, an ache in the center of my chest burrowing deeper. Something was missing.

"I've got you," she said.

Again, without realizing I was going to do it, my arms curled around her in return, and I held her tight, desperate for what was gone, whatever it was that was missing.

"That's good, Ren, let it fill you," she murmured.

I squeezed my eyes closed and wished this was how it could be, that she could be mine, that I wasn't this broken mess—

Something shattered inside me.

She stilled. "Ren?"

"Yeah?" I choked out.

Jaz rubbed my back. "You're hurting, I can feel it. There's a...a new scar."

She was the new scar, and it felt so big, it eclipsed everything else.

Another rush of warmth washed through me, and my legs almost fucking buckled. "All good, Jaz. Guess when old shit heals, new shit comes up."

"I guess," she said, sounding unconvinced.

The euphoria hit, and it took everything I had not to bury my face against her throat and fill my lungs with her scent—to take her gorgeous face in my hands and kiss her breathless.

The time passed way too fast, then she was counting down the last ten seconds and I had to force myself to loosen my hold on her, to release her when her arms finally fell away, letting me go.

Like always, she gave me space to feel what I was feeling after the intensity of a session, only this time what I was feeling was something completely different. "Jaz, are you all right?" I asked, when I saw her dab at her eyes, her hands trembling slightly. She soothed my pain, and I made her cry.

She smiled and nodded. "Yeah, all good."

The urge to pull her close and comfort her grew fiercer. "I'll go grab the note," I said and quickly walked away before I did something I shouldn't, then took the few moments in my room to try to get my shit together.

When I strode back out, she was in her coat, ready to leave. I didn't want her to go, though. I wanted her to stay. I handed her the note.

"Thanks." She opened it and frowned down at it. "Halcapio." She looked back up at me. "What does that even mean?"

"No idea."

She blew out a frustrated breath. "Cool, thanks for nothing, Agatheena. I'll show Mags, maybe she's heard it before." She shoved the note in her pocket and smiled up at me. "You're making great progress. I hope you know that. I don't know how much you feel yet, but I saw it during the session. Your original wounds are looking so much better." She frowned. "This new one that appeared—"

"The new one doesn't have anything to do with what happened. I don't want it gone. I want to keep it." I never wanted the sting of giving up Jasmine gone. Never.

"Are you sure about that?"

"Positive."

She nodded, her gaze searching my face like a doctor would their patient. "Right, well..." She aimed her thumb over her shoulder. "I need to head off. If I don't see you before then, I'll see you in a week's time."

"If you find out what the note means, let me know, yeah?"

"Sure thing," she said, then walked out.

I gripped the back of the couch to stop myself from following her, because if I saw her with someone else right now, I would kill them.

I would end them right in front of her, and there'd be no coming back from that.

>>>●<<<

Jasmine

Xavier sipped his whisky, his very nice lips tilting up on one side. "So, any luck finding your souls?"

"Unfortunately, no."

He sat back. "I'm sorry to hear that."

"Not as sorry as me." I thought about them constantly, so much so, I'd started dreaming about them, about finding them, about Zinnia stuck in Limbo forever, about her calling my name.

He inclined his head. "I can see how much that distresses you. Let's change the subject to more pleasant things? How was your dessert?"

I smiled at his attempt to make me feel better. "Amazing. I've never had anything like it." Xavier was handsome and extremely charming. He was an intelligent guy, well read. Interesting. He also could wear the hell out of a suit. I really liked talking to him. I wasn't nervous around him, which was surprising. I was shy by nature, yes, that had improved over the last few years, but going on a date? I should be a sweaty, blushing mess.

"This is one of my favorite restaurants," he said. "I really wanted to share it with you."

I sipped my wine. "I'm glad you did." I studied his features, his contained expression. "So why did you ask me out?"

His brow arched. "You don't know?"

I shook my head and smiled. "Nope. Only you know that. I'm a medium not a physic."

"Well, let me enlighten you, then, Jasmine. First, you are stunningly beautiful. Honestly, after you left the first time you turned up on my door, I wasn't able to forget about you."

Okay, now I was blushing. "That's...really nice of you to say."

He chuckled. "I tell you I think you're astoundingly hot and you think I'm being nice?"

"It's nice to hear it," I said and had trouble holding his gaze all of a sudden. "You're not too bad yourself."

"I'm glad you think so."

His voice had grown deep, husky. I wasn't sure I was ready for what I heard in his voice, but I didn't hate it. "And you're not put off knowing that I was in love with someone else?"

He leaned forward, resting his elbow on the table. "No, because it's gone. This male who held your heart has been banished from it. Which means there's now room for you to fall in love with someone else."

This male was smooth. He knew all the right things to say. That wasn't necessarily a bad thing, but I hadn't been around too many males this well adjusted or controlled. All the males around me, besides Arthur, tended to be volatile. "I'm not sure I'm in the market for love just yet," I said and tried not to fidget under his direct stare.

"No one goes out looking for love. It finds us whether we're expecting it or not." He grinned, and I got a flash of fangs. "That's what I'm told anyway."

"You've never been in love?"

He took a sip of his drink, then shook his head. "No, I never have."

"I'm sorry."

"I'm surprised you feel that way, even after the pain you suffered?" His gaze dipped to my mouth and back up. "And don't be sorry. Everything happens for a reason, yes? My time will come if it's meant to."

"I hope that's true. I like to believe we're not all wandering around like idiots, making the same stupid mistakes over and over again."

His grin widened. "It's a nice thought."

"As for love. Yes, my feelings were unrequited, and I may not feel it anymore, but I haven't forgotten the storm that would whip up inside me whenever I saw him. The excitement, the stupid, useless hope." I screwed up my face. "I guess deep down I'm a romantic...or a sadist."

He chuckled again, and his head tilted to the side. "And have you seen him since?"

"Yes."

"What did you feel?"

"It was gone. The storm had passed completely. I care about his well-being, but that's all. No more excitement, no hope for more. No pain thinking about him with someone else." I'd felt none of that earlier when I went to his house. It was an odd feeling. Was I relieved? Absolutely. But there was a small part of me that missed it.

"I'm glad," he said. "I hated seeing you in so much pain."

An hour later we were sitting in Xavier's car outside my aunt's house. "I had a great time tonight, Jasmine. I'd love to see you again sometime."

"I did too." And I meant it. "And I'd like that."

His deep lavender eyes dipped to my mouth before he reached out and gently cupped the side of my face, leaning in. Did I want him to kiss me?

There was no reason to stop him, right? I leaned in as well, and his lips brushed mine softly before he lifted his head.

"I'll be in touch," he said.

I opened the car door and got out. "Night, Xavier."

"Good night, Jasmine."

I shut the door, and he drove away. My fingers lifted to my mouth and I stared after his car as it turned the corner. He'd kissed me. I tried to decide how I felt. I mean, it was...nice.

A scrape came from my right, and I spun around. Ren stood there. He was in gray track pants and running shoes. His shirt was off and tucked into the waistband of his pants. His eyes glowed gold from the shadows, the moonlight highlighting his muscles that were glistening with sweat. Before, seeing him like that would have had my knees trembling. Now? Well, that hadn't really changed. Ren was still beautiful. There was no denying it. But it was just lust, nothing else.

He was panting. "Good date?"

"Yeah, it was."

He planted his hands on his hips. "That was him, the car that just drove away? Xavier, Ronan's friend?"

"Yep."

"You seeing him again?" he asked.

"Probably, yeah."

His chest expanded sharply and a growl rolled out. "He touched you."

"If he did or didn't, is my business," I said, because he couldn't keep doing this, playing the overprotective big brother or whatever this was.

"I can smell him on you, Jaz. He put his hands on you." He took a step closer.

My pulse sped up. "I'm not sure why it matters to you?"

"I'm just making sure it's what you wanted?"

His gaze glowed brighter. His behavior was starting to piss me off. This was why I'd been so confused, this was why there was always this stupid bit of hope I couldn't shake. I hadn't been able to see it clearly before, so blinded by my feelings for him, but I saw it now. "That's not your place. You don't need to look out for me. I have plenty of people doing that already."

"Jaz." He took another step closer, his voice impossibly rough. "Last week, what I said... I hope you're not seeing this guy because—"

"He's not some rebound from you, if that's what you're implying. You don't need to worry about my feelings. Yes, I care about you, I do, but not like that. I want you happy and healthy, but I'm not harboring any secret hope of you one day becoming my boyfriend." *Not anymore.* "I'm over it, Ren. Like completely. I don't need to be another thing you feel guilty about, okay? Don't think about it anymore, please. I'm not."

His head dipped, his abs flexing with every panted breath he took. "You're completely over it," he said under his breath. "Right."

"I'm just gonna head inside. I still have some books to go through from the demon library. I've been searching for some reference to what halcapio means."

He nodded. "I'll help."

I blinked up at him. "You don't have somewhere else you'd rather be?"

"No. Not in the mood to drink, and I'm too wired to sleep. May as well do something productive."

There was no real reason to say no. And if the answer was in one of those books, we'd find it faster with two of us. "Okay, sure."

He followed me inside, tugging his shirt on before we walked into the house, and headed to the kitchen. Stanley was sitting on the counter when we walked in and grinned at me when he saw Ren.

"I'll leave you to it," he said and winked before he walked out.

I put the kettle on and pulled down two mugs. "Tea? Coffee? Cocoa?"

"Coffee, black, thanks."

I made the drinks and put them on the table. "I'll just get changed and grab the books. Be back in a sec."

"Where are they?"

"Up in my room. I'll show you."

He followed me upstairs. I'd taken Rose's old room when I moved in. It had its own bathroom and was one of the bigger bedrooms. We walked in and I pointed to two stacked piles on the floor next to my desk and art supplies. Ren grabbed an armful and headed downstairs. I grabbed a pair of yoga pants and a hooded sweatshirt and went into the bathroom. I bumped the door with my hip and dumped my clothes on the counter, then quickly washed my face, took off my boots, and stripped off my dress.

"That all of them?" Ren asked, his voice close.

I spun around and he was standing there, staring at me. I thought I'd bumped the door closed, but there was a decent gap.

He bolted from the room.

My face heated. I mean, he'd seen me naked more times than I'd like to think about, but it didn't matter. I was in my underwear, pretty pink lace bra and panties. Did he think I'd been hoping Xavier would see me like this tonight? I hadn't, I just liked nice underwear. *Why do you care what Ren thinks?* I quickly got changed and headed back downstairs.

"I didn't mean to look," he said when I walked in.

"It's not like you haven't seen it all before." I was trying to make light of things but it just made everything more awkward.

I sat and pulled the first book off the stack, and Ren grabbed the next.

We read in companionable silence for several hours, and more than once I'd been so absorbed I'd forgotten he was even there. Ren had made us another coffee and a snack, and we discussed some of the weird things we found. It was nice actually. I would've found this impossible before, concentrating on reading with him right there. I would've been hyper focused on him. Not anymore.

Several hours and three cups of coffee later, I finally found something. I scanned the page, then looked up at Ren. "I've got it."

"What does it say?" He got up and moved around beside me, scanning the page I'd been reading over my shoulder, then straightened. "Fuck. That can't be good."

No, it most definitely was not.

CHAPTER 22

Ren

Rune sat back on his leather couch, shirtless, trousers undone, and sipped his morning coffee. A female rushed out of his bathroom. She darted glances his way, but Rune was staring at Jasmine in a way I did not fucking like.

The other female scooped up her shoes and headed for the door.

Rune's gaze slid from Jasmine and the pile of books we'd returned and focused on his retreating companion. "What are you forgetting, Kelsey?"

She stopped and turned back. He said nothing, just waited. She rushed back to him, and he reached up, fisted the back of her hair, and pulled her down for a hard kiss. The female whimpered. I glanced at Jaz, and she was bright red.

My little female couldn't hide how she was feeling. She never could. I'd just forced myself to ignore it, until now. Now that she didn't seem to care in the least about me anymore.

She's not yours.

I'd decimated any feelings she'd had for me a week ago, which was seriously bad timing, since I wanted her now more than ever. Now that I felt the changes inside me, the way her healing was pulling me from the shadows and into the light. No, I'd never recover from what that monster made me do, I'd never forget, but I didn't feel as if I were drowning, suffo-

491

cating in a sea of horror and despair anymore. I could fucking breathe again.

I hadn't been to my cliff since the night I hurt her and Willow and Warrick followed me there. I hadn't thought about going there or the difference in the way I'd been feeling, until last night when I sat with Jaz poring over books and managed a whole twenty minutes without remembering. Without seeing blood on my hands, or hearing the sound of agonized screams. Something had definitely shifted inside me, and it was because of Jasmine.

She licked her lower lip, and I wanted to pull her to me and kiss her. I wanted to beg her to let me kiss her the way Rune was devouring the female wriggling on his lap.

Jaz shifted, her gaze darting to me, then away.

Rune finally let her go. "Back in bed," he said low, gritty.

The female rushed to do as he said, and the massive demon turned back to Jaz, now with an obvious fucking hard-on. "Care to join, little witch?"

I barely choked back my snarl.

"I'll pass, but thank you for your kind offer," she said with a humorless smile and a good dose of sarcasm.

"I promise you'll like it," he drawled.

"And I promise I'll slit your fucking throat if you say shit like that to her again," I growled out.

Jaz spun to me, a frown on her pretty face. The three mourning cloaks that had been sitting on her shoulders, fluttered around her head, giving her away. I'd pissed her off. Again. "Maybe you should wait downstairs," she said to me.

That wasn't happening. "I'm not leaving you with him."

"You've interrupted my morning," Rune said. "If you're not going to join in, then get to the fucking point."

"Halcapio," Jaz said. "Defined in the demon physiology book I borrowed from your library as one who consumes living souls for subsistence. What can you tell us about soul eaters?"

His silver gaze narrowed. "Why?"

The book hadn't given a huge amount of information, just a few lines. "Because we think that's what's happened to the ones we're missing," I said.

"Impossible. There are no Drar here," Rune said.

"That you know of."

His silver eyes flashed red. "I would know."

"Would you?" Jaz said. "There's no chance one could have slipped through?"

He stood, sliding his hands into his pockets and paced away. If there was a soul eater, also known as a Drar'toth demon, then that wouldn't be good for Rune. Lucifer was his boss, he was missing souls as well, and it was going on right under Rune's nose.

He turned back. "I'll put some feelers out."

"What can you tell us about the Drar'toth?" Jaz asked. "Are they humanoid in appearance?"

"Yes. They're also a solitary breed. Live alone. They're always hungry. Food doesn't satisfy, but they gorge on it between souls, trying to satiate their hunger. They run hot, something they bask in when they're in Hell, but not here. Hellfire and the sun or artificial heating are not the same. They have trouble regulating their temperature here."

"So they'll be sweaty and drinking and eating a lot?" I asked.

"Yes."

"And the souls, what happens to them? Is there a way to free them or are they lost forever?"

"You can free them, or what's left of them, by killing the soul eater, but they're not easy to catch or kill. They absorb knowledge from the souls they devour. So they know how to blend in among humans, and depending on the souls they ate, they can be deadly and highly intelligent."

Great.

"You'll let me know if you find them before us?" Jaz asked.

He studied her for several long seconds. "If there is a Drar in this city, it's probably best you leave it to me, little witch."

My fox's hackles lifted, and his lips peeled back with a snarl. Jaz's gaze sliced to me when the sound crawled up my throat. We didn't like the demon implying we couldn't protect our female.

"I can't just sit back and do nothing," she said.

"You won't have to," I said. "I'll be with you."

"You think you're capable of taking on a Drar'toth, fox?" Rune said.

I grinned. "I'm capable of a lot of things, demon." Grabbing Jaz's hand, I tugged her from her seat and led her from the apartment and toward the elevator.

We got in and her hand slipped from mine. I wanted to snatch it back, so fucking badly.

"So you still want to help me?" she asked, studying me.

"Yes." No fucking way would I let her do this alone. I couldn't let her even if I wanted to, which I did not.

"You don't have to, you know? I can ask Rome or one of the other hounds." She chewed her lip. "Look, things got complicated between us for a minute there, but you don't owe me anything, Ren." She looked up at me, unflinching, nothing but sincerity in her eyes. "I shouldn't have let things go as far as they did. I'm sorry for that, really I am. Please, don't blame yourself."

Now she was acting like she'd somehow taken advantage of me? "I want to help you. It has nothing to do with what happened between us." *Don't say it.* I couldn't hold it in, though. "I know I said some things to make you believe otherwise, but I did want to kiss you, Jaz, badly."

She didn't believe me. I could tell by the look in her eyes.

The doors slid open. "You're confused," she said, striding out and down the corridor. "The intensity of our sessions has been messing with you. Like I told you, you're not the first person I've worked with to feel things that aren't there. One client begged me to go out with him repeatedly, another followed me for a couple weeks, positive I was the love of his life, then it wore off and they moved on."

She'd had a fucking stalker? I fought down the urge to find these males and choke them out. Barely containing my rage, I kept pace beside her and pushed the main door open. We walked out into the crisp autumn morning air. I needed to shut the fuck up, but I couldn't. There'd been this shift inside me. Now that I could see more clearly, I felt...different, more in control. "I'm not confused," I said. "I knew exactly what I was doing. Yes, your powers broke through to the part of me that'd been holding me back. But those feelings had always been there. Whatever you think happened between us, you need to know I wanted it as well."

She stopped and turned, blinking up at me. "You said you didn't want me, and you meant it."

"I was scared of the way I felt about you. I should never have said that, I should never have—"

"Whatever you're about to say, don't." She shook her head. "You only think you felt something for me, and you're wrong. You've suffered for so long, Ren. I've helped you get relief from that pain, that's all this is. You're misinterpreting gratitude for something else." She shook her head. "I don't think you should help me with this."

I bit back a growl. If I kept pushing, she'd back away completely and get someone else to help. "Okay, maybe I am a little confused," I said, lying. I wasn't fucking confused. Jasmine was mine, but she wasn't ready to hear it. "Let's just...put all of that stuff aside for now, yeah? Zinnia getting home is the most important thing. So let me help you."

⇾⇾⊱●⊰⇽⇽

Jasmine

I eyed him. Before my visit with Xavier, I would've jumped on the things he'd just said. I would've believed every word and not seen the truth. It was nothing more than transference; he was associating all the good things he felt during our sessions with me just like my other confused clients. It wasn't *me* he wanted, it was the way my powers made him feel. He hadn't been interested in me before we started his healing and now, suddenly, he thought he was. It seemed clear to me.

I should tell him no, but I could tell by the look on his face, no matter what I said, he was determined to help. "Fine. But if you make googly eyes at me, you're done."

He grinned. "No googly eyes. I can manage that."

We strode down the street, passing demons like this was totally normal. It was hard to compare these demons with the ones who lived in the forest. On the outside at least, they seemed like an entirely different species.

Ren unlocked the hearse, and we got in. The engine rumbled to life, and the three butterflies on my head fluttered down to rest on the back of my hands. They were sending warmth and love through me, a lot of it, as if they were trying to comfort me. I wasn't sure why. I didn't need comforting. It was like they were seeing something I couldn't.

"I'm okay," I said to them as their wings rose and fell slowly. There was another rush of love. "I promise." I looked up and Ren was watching me. "They're comforting me for some reason."

"Yeah?" he said as he pulled out onto the street. "Why?"

I shook my head. "No idea. I'm assuming it's from being around all those demons." I lifted my hand, and they crawled back onto my hair. "So where do we think a soul eater would hang out?"

"How many all-you-can-eat restaurants are there in the city?" Ren asked. "Cheap ones. If you spend all your time eating, drinking, and overheating, it can't be easy holding down a job."

I grinned and pulled out my phone to search for all-you-can-eat places nearby. "I'm going to go out on a limb and assume he'd hang near demon territory. It'd just be instinct, right?"

"Makes sense."

"Joe's All-You-Can-Eat Home Fry is just a couple blocks away."

We walked into the restaurant a short time later. It did not smell great. It was dark and dingy and the decor didn't look like it'd been updated since 1982. "Hungry?" I said to Ren when he screwed up his face.

His lips twitched. "Tempting, but I'll pass."

The wall by the entrance was covered in pictures. Joe's Home Fry Challenge was written in block letters and tacked above pictures of customers with plates scattered across their table. All but one of them looked ready to barf.

We checked the rest of the place out, but I wasn't sure what we were doing here. How this would help? The demon wasn't just going to wave us over and show himself, even if he was, by some miracle, here at this precise moment. But it wasn't like we had anything else to go on.

We walked into Jumbo Jim's Seafood Bizarre twenty minutes later. "Joe, now Jim, who's next?" This place wasn't much better, but it at least looked clean and was definitely busier.

"Johnny. Has to be," Ren said and grinned.

I wish he'd stop grinning at me all the time. I mean, I was happy he was happy. But it gave me a weird feeling. Thankfully, that feeling was not swoony and lovey-dovey, that was impossible. It was something else, and I didn't like that either.

"Jim's got his own wall of people trying to give themselves a heart attack," he said, motioning to the wall above the bread and condiments table. Jim's Gut Buster Showdown.

I scanned the pictures. "Same green-around-the-gills expressions."

"Except this guy," Ren said. "He looks pretty happy with himself."

I took a closer look. "That guy was on Joe's wall as well. Everyone else looked ready to toss their cookies, except him. He has more empty plates than any of them. The dude looks like he won the lottery and is ready to go back for more."

Ren leaned in to take a closer look. "Definitely looks like he's enjoying himself."

It was probably nothing, but I snapped a picture, anyway.

We didn't linger long and headed to the next place. Sapphire Cabaret.

"A strip club?" Ren asked when we headed for the main door.

"Yep, but a lot of the reviews mention their buffet. Apparently it's cheap for all you can eat and the food is good." I smiled at the doorman as I walked in and Ren grabbed my hand, surprising me. "What are you doing?"

He was scanning the room, jaw tight. "This place is full of horny humans. You need to stay close."

I tried to pull my hand free, but he gripped it tighter.

"Ren, it's fine."

"Humor me."

The grip he had on me, it wasn't like I had any other choice.

Sapphire's had their own all-you-can-eat challenge, only here you got to eat off one of their dancers, and yep, they had pictures as well. "There he is again." The plain-looking male sat at a table, face shiny, a naked female lying in front of him, covered in grease and what looked like gravy and a few dregs of mashed potato. There was a green bean under one of her naked boobs. I pulled out my phone and compared pictures to make sure I was looking at the same guy. "That's definitely him." He was average build, average looks, the type of guy who'd blend in easily with a crowd. I scanned the picture again, then looked back up at the one on the wall. "Huh."

"What?"

"Same date. Look." I showed Ren the picture I'd taken. It had January 12 written under the photo and so did the one on the wall here. "This guy stuffed himself full at Jim's, then came here and did it again."

"Dude's got a serious appetite," Ren said before tightening his grip on my hand and leading me to the bar. He waved over the barman.

"What can I get you?"

He held his hand out for my phone and aimed the picture at the guy. "We're looking for someone. There's a picture on your wall. Does he come here often? Do you know his name?"

The guy leaned against the bar. "Might know his name, but I'm finding it hard to remember just now."

Ren growled, yanked his wallet from his back pocket, and pulled out a couple bills, sliding them over. "How's your memory now?"

The guy grinned. "What do you know, it's all coming back to me." He pocketed the money. "Guy's name's Frank, don't know his surname. He comes here every Thursday night without fail. Sweaty guy. Freaks some of the girls out, but he pays well. Sits by the air-conditioning vent near the buffet table and stays there for a few hours, eating until he's stuffed, then leaves."

"You know anything else about him? How to contact him?" I asked.

"Nope. Now you want a drink or what?"

Ren shook his head and turned to me. "Think we might've found our guy."

"We'll have to come back tomorrow."

"Looks that way." The next song began and a female walked out in a thong and started dancing around a pole. "Let's get the hell out of here."

I laughed at how uncomfortable he seemed. "You don't want to stay for the show?"

"Not even if you paid me," he muttered.

"Hey, sweet thing, how about a private dance," a male voice said before someone grabbed my hips and pulled me into them. My back met a hard, round belly and a sweaty, fleshy arm came around me as he ground his dick into my ass.

Before I had a chance to even try to get away, Ren's fist shot out, throat-punching the other male. The guy's arm fell away, and he hit the ground a second later. With a snarl, teeth bared, Ren kicked the gasping human in the ribs, then grabbed my hand and towed me from the room.

"You could've killed him," I said as we walked out onto the street.

"I don't give a fuck. No one touches you, Jasmine. No one. Understand?" His chest shook with violent breaths.

I blinked up at him, confused and seriously unsettled. I got that he was protecting me, but what he'd just said, the way he'd said it... This was getting out of hand. "You need to calm down," I said when his gaze kept sliding back to the door we'd just walked through, as if he wanted to go back in there and finish what he started. "He was just some creep. It's over. Done."

"I want to go back in there and break his neck," Ren growled. "I want to make him fucking bleed." He paced away and back.

I grabbed his hand. "We need to go." He looked on the verge of giving in and doing what he'd just said.

He didn't budge, like he hadn't heard me. "What he did, the way he... rubbed against you?" A look of disgust covered his face. "I should cut his fucking dick off. I should gut him and watch him bleed out. I should—"

"Ren. Breathe." I grabbed his face to get his attention, because he was still looking at that door with murder in his eyes. "Ren," I said with more force. His gaze slid to me, and his eyes flashed. "Let's go, okay? We need to go. Someone might've called the police. We need to get out of here."

His fierce gaze dipped to my lips. "Jaz." He swallowed, his Adam's apple sliding up and down. "Butterfly," he said roughly.

I tried to step back, but his fingers thrust into my hair, then his mouth crashed down on mine.

CHAPTER 23

Ren

OH FUCK.

Yes, this is what I needed. Jaz's warm curves pressed to mine, her soft lips. She was all I wanted, all I needed. I was so in love with this female. So insanely in love with her, I couldn't think straight.

I'd been in love with her for a long time, but I hadn't allowed myself to feel it, to recognize it. I hadn't believed I deserved it. That male had touched her and I'd seen red and everything fucking snapped into place.

Edward had possessed me, poisoned me with his evil, broken me, but Jasmine was putting me back together, piece by jagged piece.

I groaned against her mouth—

Then I realized she was utterly stiff in my arms. Her lips were pressed tightly together. I tried to coax her to kiss me back, but she kept her mouth firmly closed.

My fox growled, the sound vibrating in my chest. She shoved at me, hard, and that was when I realized it wasn't the first time.

I loosened my grip on her, and she yanked her mouth from mine. "No, Ren," she bit out. "Let me the hell go."

Oh fuck. "I'm sorry, I thought—"

"That I'd want you to kiss me? Making out with the first female you see when you're struggling to deal with your emotions isn't working for you anymore, Ren. I thought you were starting to see that." She stepped back.

"Jesus." She dragged the back of her hand across her mouth as if my kiss disgusted her. "Let's just get the hell out of here."

My heart smashed against my ribs. "I'm sorry," I said, feeling fucking wrecked. Looking at the coldness in her eyes was a slap in the face. My fox whined, confused. Why didn't our mate want us anymore? Why wouldn't she look at us like she used to? I wanted to snatch her back in my arms and kiss her until the female I knew came back. Because Jasmine had never looked at me like that, not as long as I'd known her.

That warmth was completely gone when she looked at me now. A couple weeks ago, she'd wanted me. Now. She didn't.

"I'll take you home."

She strode off ahead to the hearse.

You missed your chance.

Agatheena's words echoed through my head.

I'd fucked up so badly. I'd truly lost her.

A piece of shit like you never deserved a female like that, the voice in my head hissed, Edward's voice. Self-loathing filled me. He was gone, but echoes of his evil, his poison remained.

We drove in silence, because I didn't know what the hell to say.

When we stopped outside the house and Jasmine got out, I felt her pulling away even more.

There had to be something I could do to fix this.

And I knew who had the answers.

⋅⟩⟩⟩ ◉ ⟨⟨⟨⋅

Panting, I stood over the feral's body and called to Agatheena. He'd put up a serious fight, I was bloody and battered, but the job was done. She wanted proof, I had her proof. I just hoped she gave me some answers as well. After I'd dropped Jaz home, I'd come out hunting.

Agatheena knew what was going on with Jasmine, why she'd changed. Something was seriously wrong and I needed her to tell me. The small but fierce witch appeared on her porch, squinting down at me. "He still warm?"

"Yes."

She waved a hand. "Good. Bring him here."

The low hum of her magic vanished. She'd dropped the ward so I could pass. Grabbing the feral's hind legs again, I dragged him down the path to the cottage.

"Around the back to my shed," she said, coming down the stairs to lead the way.

I followed her along the side of the house and around the back. She waved her hand again, and the door to the small shed flung open. I

500

followed her in, and lamps on the walls ignited, lighting the space. There were hunks of meat already dangling from meat hooks. I wasn't sure what kind, but there was a bloody pile of clothes in the corner.

"Hang him there," she said. "Upside down."

With a grunt, I lifted the massive feral wolf, forcing the hook through flesh, and stepped back. The witch shuffled up, took a vicious-looking knife from the wooden bench beside her, kicked a bucket under the feral wolf shifter, and slashed his throat. Blood immediately spilled from the deep slice.

She walked back out and I followed her, the door slamming behind us.

"I'll be in touch if I need you for anything else," she said, dismissing me.

"I need to ask you a question, something you said about Jasmine."

She climbed the stairs to her cottage and turned back, eyes narrowed. "And what was it I said, fox?"

"That I'd missed my chance, that I was too late. Why did you say that? You know something, don't you?" I was trying to keep the desperation out of my voice and failing badly.

"I know many things that you don't."

I ground my teeth. "Jasmine's changed. I want to know why."

"You sure about that?"

"Yes, I'm sure. Fucking tell me."

"You may regret asking for the truth, fox. The truth isn't always easy to swallow."

I swallowed down my snarl. "Tell me. Christ, she used to look at me like, like—"

"Like she was in love with you?"

My breath shuddered. "Yes." My hands shook at what I saw in her eyes. "And now, when she looks at me, there's—"

"Nothing?"

"Yes."

"It's simple, fox. Jasmine has been in love with you since the first time she met you. She continued to love you, even while she was forced to watch you drown your pain in booze and other females, knowing there was nothing she could do, knowing that you'd never be hers. After you rejected her, her pain was unbearable. It hurt so much, she knew the only way she could help you heal was to let that love go. So she did. She let you go the only way she knew how."

I was going to be fucking sick. "She let me go? What does that even mean?"

"It means she doesn't love you, not anymore." Her eyes flashed red. "Unrequited love's a bitch, fox, but I think you're finding that out for yourself."

Then I was airborne, Agatheena's magic snapping around me, gripping me powerfully before dragging me back down the path and launching me out of her property. I landed hard on the ground as her cottage door slammed shut.

I stood there, breathing hard, feeling sick to my fucking stomach.

Jasmine had let me go.

>>●<<

It was late afternoon when I got back, but instead of going inside my place, I felt a pull in a different direction, as if something had wrapped around me. The hum of magic. Jaz. I knew it was her, and I doubted she even knew she was doing it.

It grew in waves that took my fucking breath way.

Waves of distress.

I spun around and ran in the direction she was pulling me—the field down from my house where she spent a lot of time. As I hit the edge, I spotted her. She was on her knees, her body bent forward, her hands out in front of her, and she was sobbing. I ran for her, scanning the field, looking for the danger.

As I got closer, I slowed down and sucked in a breath. "Jaz?"

She looked up at me, eyes red, cheeks wet with her tears. "Who would do this?" she sobbed. "W-who. Why?"

In her cupped hands were several butterflies, the mourning cloaks she always had with her, and others. At least fifty, all dead, lay lifeless around her. *Fuck.* "What happened?"

"They were poisoned. S-someone came here and used p-poison on them."

I crouched beside her, not sure what to do but desperate to comfort her. "Why don't you put them down, Jaz. Let me get you home."

She shook her head. "No, I have to bury them. I'm not leaving them like this. They loved me, Ren. They loved me so much. They loved me like no one else ever has. And now they're gone. Someone hurt them."

"Tell me what to do to help, and I'll do it," I said, feeling fucking helpless. I wanted to pull her into my arms, but she wouldn't want that from me. She was my mate, and I couldn't even comfort her when she was in pain.

She looked up at me, and the agony in her eyes cut so fucking deep. "A box. I need a box."

"Okay. Don't move, I'll be right back." I sprinted home and grabbed the shoebox still sitting in my room from the new running shoes I'd bought and grabbed a spade from the small garden shed we had behind the main building, then rushed back.

Jasmine was where I left her, tears still running down her face. She was talking to her little dead familiars, her pain so acute I felt it as if it were my own, burrowing into my chest.

I placed the box down beside her and opened the lid. The tissue was still inside, and I quickly smoothed it out.

Jaz gently placed the butterflies in her hands on the bottom, then carefully picked up one closest to her off the ground.

"Can I help?"

She nodded.

I watched how she did it and tried to be just as careful as her. When the bottom was covered, I folded over another layer of tissue and we slowly collected the rest, until we had them all. She placed the lid on and picked it up. I followed her across the field, and she pointed to a spot by an oak tree. I dug the hole she needed, and she placed the shoebox inside and covered it with dirt, then she placed her hand on top and closed her eyes.

When she looked up at me a minute later, her lip was quivering, but there was anger in her eyes now as well. "I won't let anyone else hurt them."

I swallowed hard, struggling with seeing her like this and not sure what the fuck to do. "What do you have in mind?"

"I'm warding the field," she said and strode to the edge.

I went after her. "You can't do that, Jaz. This place belongs to someone else, you ward it and things will get messy." No one knew who owned it, but it'd never been fenced and no one had ever seemed interested in building on it. Which meant anyone could wander onto it. But it was still someone else's property.

Another tear streaked down her face. "What if they come back, what if—"

"If they come back tonight, I'll stop them," I said. "I'll stay there. I'll make sure they're safe."

She blinked up at me, her eyes like glittering emeralds. "You'd do that?"

I tucked her hair behind her ear. "Of course." Usually when I touched her, she'd shiver or her eyes would get this soft, dazed look in them. Now there was only gratitude there, pain, but nothing else, not for me, not anymore. Agatheena was right.

Then she collapsed, her grief too much. I scooped her up before she could hit the ground and pulled her into my chest. I pressed my lips to the top of her head. "I've got you, butterfly. Let it out. Let the pain out."

She sobbed against my shoulder, and I felt the turmoil and pain rolling off her, slicing through me. That the mother would do this to her, give her familiars like this, so fragile and unable to live a long life, that Jasmine would love with her whole heart only to get it broken over and over again was cruel. It was fucking torture, and I hated that fucking evil bitch for it.

I carried her down the street, and she clung to me the whole way, sobbing against my chest. There was no reason for anyone to spray pesticides in that field. Unless whoever owned it was finally going to do something with the place, and they'd used some kind of weed killer to clear the field? That was the most likely scenario. I needed to find out who owned that land. This couldn't happen again. I wouldn't let it.

When we reached the house, the front door opened and Else limped out, her face etched with worry. "Is she hurt?"

I shook my head. "Someone used poison in her field."

Else made a pained sound. I didn't need to explain, she knew what that would mean for Jaz's tiny familiars.

"Take her up to her room. I'll get one of my calming elixirs," she said and headed to her and Magnolia's workroom.

I carried on upstairs to Jaz's bedroom and looked at the bed. I didn't want to put her down. I wanted to keep her in my arms, but I promised to guard her field. I doubted anyone was coming back, but I wouldn't let her down again. If it gave her peace of mind, I'd fucking stay there every night.

Pressing a kiss to the top of her head, because I fucking had to, I laid her on the quilt. She curled in on herself, and all I wanted to do was get onto that bed with her and hold her in my arms. Else walked in, and I crouched down in front of Jasmine. "I'll make sure no more of your familiars are hurt, Jaz. I promise."

She stared blindly ahead, lost deep in her pain.

Else moved in, and I forced myself to step back, to turn and leave.

It was getting harder and harder every day.

What the fuck was I going to do?

CHAPTER 24

Jasmine

"How you doing?" Mags said, easing the bedroom door open.

I looked up from my phone. Xavier had texted, asking me out again, but I wasn't sure I wanted to. No, I knew I didn't. He was a nice guy, handsome, but I just wasn't feeling it. I was also still feeing emotionally drained and fragile after yesterday. I'd spent the night with my magic focused inward, healing the wounds yesterday had left me with. It'd taken hours. A wound that deep needed a lot of work and still wasn't completely healed, that kind of pain never was, but it was at least bearable. Even so, I definitely wasn't in the mood to be around anyone who wasn't family. "I should be used to the pain of losing them by now, but it never gets any easier. And yesterday, what happened...with so many of them at once..." I swallowed the lump forming in my throat.

It was early morning and I was sitting on the end of the bed. I needed to get up and get my shit together. Tonight we were going after a soul-eating demon, and right now I was struggling to work up the energy to go downstairs and eat breakfast. Magnolia climbed up beside me. "I can't imagine what it's like for you. Why the hell did the mother do that?" She shook her head. "It's fucking cruel." Her gaze went to the comma butterfly on my hand. "And who's this?"

"He was at my window this morning. Like the mourning cloak, his species can handle the cooler weather a lot better than some." I looked up at my cousin. "Somehow, he found me."

"He's beautiful," Mags said, her gaze searching mine. "Else said Ren brought you home?"

"Yeah." He'd carried me the entire way.

"He's at your field now, you know. He's been there all night."

Warmth curled in my belly. "He said he would, but I didn't think he'd..." What did I think? "That was nice of him."

Mags smiled gently. "You think he's just doing it to be kind? He obviously cares about you, Jazzy, a lot. You don't stay up all night in a field for just anyone."

"We're friends," I said, and I guessed that was true now.

"You sure it's not more than that?" she said, studying me closely.

"It's really not more than that," I said.

"If I had a friend who looked at me the way Ren looks at you, Bram would gut him." Her eyes danced, her lips curling deeper. "You like him, Jaz, I know you do. You've had a thing for Ren for forever. This is a good thing, right?"

I hadn't planned to tell anyone what'd happened between Ren and me, but this was Mags. She loved me and Ren, and if she got involved now, thinking she was helping, things could get seriously messy. "We kissed," I said to her. "Several times. I made it clear I wanted more, he made it clear he didn't. Yes, he's protective of me right now, attentive, and despite what he says...and does, things that might suggest he feels otherwise, it's not what you think, it's my power making him act this way, not me. You know I've had other clients misinterpret their feelings toward me. He's started healing, and his emotions are all over the place. He didn't want me before we started, and once I'm done and everything calms down, whatever it is he thinks he's feeling will fade away, just like it did with the others."

She blinked several times. "You hooked up," she shrieked. "And you're only telling me now?"

"It's over, I didn't see any reason to—"

"Well, you were wrong. You hook up with someone, *with Ren*, the male you have been freaking in love with for years, you tell your favorite fucking cousin."

I thought I'd kept my feelings a secret, obviously not. "How I felt doesn't matter. It's over. I'm fine."

"You're fine? *You're fine.* Bullshit." She rubbed her temples. "You two have been circling each other for fucking years. You convinced yourself it was one-sided, but it's not. The longing fucking looks across the room, the yard, the cemetery, the forest, you name a location and you two have eye-fucked. It wasn't missed by me, or anyone, honestly. Whatever he said to you when he pulled back, he was lying. He's scared, guilty, doesn't think he's worthy, insert all the negative self-talk here, and it's on repeat in that male's head. He told Bram he's tainted, that he can't get the blood off his hands no matter how hard he scrubs them. You know, you've seen his emotional damage. But one thing I do know without a shadow of a doubt? He cares about you, a lot. He's just scared shitless."

She was wrong. "It's my power," I said again, almost desperately.

"It's not. I know he's done a fucking terrible job of showing you. The alcohol and the females certainly didn't help, and if any other male did that, then laid a hand on you, I'd chop it off. I'd tell you he was a player and to run for the hills, but this isn't just some male, this is Ren. My sister's sweet, loving, protective familiar. A male we've known since he was four-teen. He was drowning, the booze and the one-night stands were a coping mechanism. A crutch. He hasn't been to the clubhouse to party since you started working on him, you know that, right?"

I shook my head. "No, you're wrong." A sick feeling twisted in my belly.

"I'm not. Jaz, I'm not wrong—"

"It's too late," I said, cutting her off. I couldn't hear another word. She was wrong. Ren didn't want me. He didn't.

"It's not. It's never too late."

"It is." I held her eyes. "I did something. Something to lock them away."

She stilled. "Lock what away?"

"My feelings for him. I don't...I don't love him, not anymore, and I never will again."

Mags flinched. "You didn't."

"It hurt, Mags, so much. He told me...he said...he said he didn't want me. It was unbearable, but he needed me. He needed me to help him heal, and I couldn't do that with all that pain. So I let him go so I could be what he needed."

"Jasmine...what the hell have you done?" She gripped my shoulders.

"He was hurting himself, over and over again. He tried to take his own life. I couldn't let him do that, I couldn't."

"How did you do it?"

"The how doesn't matter. It's done."

A tear streaked down Mags's face. "And there's no way to reverse it?"

"No."

She pulled me into her arms and hugged me tight. She said no more, because there was nothing else to be said.

I stared at the wall, that feeling in my stomach, the twist, gripped tight. I didn't know what it was. I shouldn't feel anything when it came to Ren. Certainly not regret or sadness over what I did. The love I had for him was gone, right? How could I be sad over something I didn't want, that I wasn't capable of wanting anymore?

›)›●‹‹‹

I couldn't stomach breakfast and headed down the road to the field instead. My new friend sat on my shoulder, fluttering his wings gently as I walked. It was midmorning, Ren would be at work now and I wanted to check the damage. If I'd lost others through the night, they'd need to be taken care of.

"You stay on my shoulder, sweet boy," I said, and he fluttered his wings.

He may not be able to understand my words, but he could read my emotions, and I knew he'd stay where he was until my apprehension, my fear over what I'd see was gone.

I walked through the old fence and stopped in my tracks. Ren sat under my favorite tree. There was a wild fox and two tiny cubs beside him. He was murmuring low, and the mother came closer, bringing her cubs with her. She butted her nose against his hand.

"Hey, mama," he said as she took something from his fingers. "That's a good girl."

His gentle, husky tone gave me familiar flutters low in my belly.

I tried not to freak out. It was fine. He was a good-looking male, that hadn't changed just because Xavier had walled in my feelings for him, and he was being kind to animals. I could appreciate both of those things. He'd never stopped being attractive to me. I still *liked* him, I still thought he was...hot, I just wasn't *in love* with him.

He glanced up and something shifted in his eyes before a highly attractive smile curled his lips. The fox spotted me, too, and loped off into the trees, her cubs following. Ren stood. "Hey."

"You're still here." I walked over to him.

"I said I'd keep them safe," he said, searching my face. "How you doing, Jaz?"

A zip of electricity shot through my belly, then slipped lower. Not good, not at all. "Thank you, for doing this. Knowing you were here last night, it helped a lot. And I'll be okay."

"I'm glad."

"So what species is your new friend?" he asked, motioning to my shoulder.

"He's a comma butterfly, smaller than the mourning cloaks but, sadly, he'll only be around for a couple more weeks, a little longer if I'm lucky, then he'll go off to hibernate." Sympathy filled his pretty eyes, and I looked away. "Usually I can handle their loss a lot better. Yesterday was...a shock. It wasn't the end of their life cycle. Someone had cut it short."

"I spent the night doing research on my phone. I know who owns the field. I'll make sure no one comes back and sprays poison here."

"How?" I scanned the wide field. When the street was subdivided, this large field had been bought but never developed. It bordered the forest and now felt like it was part of it.

He crossed his muscled arms. "I'll talk to him."

"You'll talk to him?"

His lips quirked up on one side. "I can be persuasive."

He was smiling more. Did he realize that? And they weren't fake smiles clouded by shadows, they reached his eyes. "You think just talking to him will work?"

"Trust me. In the meantime, I called Ronan. He's on his way. He's gonna block the trees they sleep in. By the time he's finished, whoever sprayed poison won't be able to see them. It'll be like they're not there."

I smiled, huge, and had to fight the sudden urge to throw my arms around him. "Thank you, Ren. Seriously. Thank you so much."

His gaze fell to my lips, and he pulled in a shaky breath. "Anything for you, butterfly."

There went those damn zaps in my belly again, accompanied by a warm, soft feeling in the center of my chest. It was gratitude, that's all. He was being kind, and I appreciated it. One friend appreciating another. Then why the hell was I blushing? I hadn't blushed around him since before I went to Xavier for help.

"So what time are we going to the Sapphire tonight? I mean, if you still want to help me." Had Xavier messed up somehow? Had he, like, left a crack in one of the walls he'd built or something, because there were feelings, definite feelings starting to brew inside me. Not the same as before, nowhere near what they were before, but there was something there.

"I'll come by around nine and pick you up."

I stuffed those feelings down deep. "Sounds good."

CHAPTER 25

Jasmine

THE SAPPHIRE CABARET was a lot busier than it had been the night before. There was a group of guys here for a bachelor party and several other groups of guys in suits dotted around the room, while big burly males stood by the doors, scanning the crowd and making sure no one misbehaved.

"Stay close," Ren said as we headed for a booth across from the all-you-can-eat buffet, putting a whole room between us and it.

I slid in first, and Ren followed.

No one was eating, but going by the steaming hot food, the buffet had just been replenished.

"He'll be here soon," Ren said.

My gaze slid to the door. "Get it while it's hot."

"Exactly."

A female stopped by the table and took our drink orders.

Ren's body was pressed to my side, and it made my belly feel kind of weird, so I shuffled over an inch. "So I did some more research, and Drar'-toth demons can make a soul last months."

"How's that possible?"

"They ingest them, but feed off the souls slowly until there's nothing left."

"This guy has to be leaving corpses all over the city. Why haven't the knights taken him out?" he said, looking down at me, studying my face intently. "This demon, he's dangerous, Jaz. We see him, you stay back, okay?"

"I have no desire to get close to him," I said, ignoring the look in his eyes. I saw real fear there, fear for me. "And as for why the knights haven't taken him out? Maybe he hasn't been here long. There's no way they would've given a Drar permission to live here, they're far too dangerous. He had to have escaped Hell another way. This guy has adapted quickly, takes only what he needs, gorging on human food between souls, and the bodies he leaves would appear unharmed. No fang or claw marks, no blood and gore, just a body. Nothing to alert the knights that something was up."

Another female stopped by the table. She leaned over it. "You want a dance, handsome?"

She was eyeing Ren, and I gripped the table, alarmed when the green-eyed monster stirred and lifted her head. There was no way I was jealous. Impossible. Who Ren let dance all over him made no difference to me.

Ren barely glanced her way. "No, thanks."

"What about your girlfriend?" she said, leaning further over the table, her gaze coming to me.

"I'm not his girlfriend," I said, far too loudly, and Ren stilled beside me. "No dance, thank you."

She shrugged and strode away, then thankfully the drinks arrived because my face had flushed hot as my mind raced. I sipped my drink and purposely didn't look at Ren. I could feel his eyes on me, and I wanted to squirm. He was studying me as if he were trying to see inside me. Could he see the way I was internally freaking out? I really hoped not.

"There's a guy at the buffet," Ren said. "He just handed a wad of cash to the barman we spoke to yesterday. He went straight to the table to load up his plate."

A guy in a shiny gray suit was leaning over the table, piling spoon after spoon of mac 'n' cheese onto his plate. "How much money?" I asked.

"A lot more than you'd pay for one meal."

"This must be Frank." When the pasta was piled dangerously high on his plate, he added four rolls on top and hustled to a table, sat down, and proceeded to eat, or more, devour everything on it, almost in an uncontrollable frenzy.

"That shit's definitely not human," Ren said.

"Nope. I guess a lot of places would bar someone who showed up all the time and consumed more food than should be humanly possible. They wouldn't make any money out of it." His face was greasy, and he had what looked like sores around his lips. His hair was slicked back and his dark eyes darted around the room as he scooped up mouthful after mouthful of food with a shaky hand. There were food stains on the lapels of his jacket and on his white shirt, I could see them even from here, and given the way the dancers screwed up their faces and avoided him, I had to assume he didn't smell that great either.

"Frank obviously likes it here if he's willing to pay extra instead of hitting another spot," Ren said, curling his fingers around his glass.

We watched as the guy glanced up at one of the dancers between mouthfuls, his spoon actually pausing for the first time as he watched her move around the room. "He has a thing for one of the females."

Ren followed my gaze. "I think we've found our demon."

For the next three hours, we watched as he all but cleared the buffet table, basically all on his own, then sat back to nurse a drink while he watched his favorite dancer work the room, give lap dances, then perform on stage. No other female seemed to catch his attention.

He watched her as she headed for a door in the back, then got up and followed—until one of the bouncers cut him off, shaking his head.

The demon's face turned red, but he strode back across the floor and out the main doors.

"Let's go," Ren said, grabbing my hand.

We walked out onto the street. Frank hadn't gotten far. He was standing at the edge of the building, beside an alleyway, waiting. He slipped back into the shadows when someone appeared at the entrance.

It was the dancer he'd been watching. She was in street clothes and sneakers, her shift obviously done for the night. She looked around, then strode down the street. Frank followed, and we followed Frank.

"What's he going to do?" I said as we kept pace. "What if he hurts her?"

"I won't let him," Ren said.

Shit.

The dancer turned a corner ahead of us, and the demon rushed after her. We had to stay back so he didn't see us, and when we rounded the corner, the dancer was at the door of an apartment building. She walked in, the door closing behind her. "Where is he?"

"He can't have just disappeared."

The apartment building was on a corner, and we rushed across the street and down the other side of the building. Nothing. He wasn't there either. "Where the hell did he go?"

A noise came from above us, and I glanced up and grabbed Ren's arm. He looked down at me and I pointed up. Ren tilted his head back. "What the fuck?" he mouthed.

The demon was on a fire escape, two floors up. He was peering through a window, his pants around his ankles, his hand moving fast as he jerked off.

"We need to stop him," I whispered.

Ren pulled me aside, into a shallow alcove in the wall, where the street-lights didn't reach. "After tonight, she won't ever have to worry about the asshole again. But I can't take him out yet. We need to follow him. After what you said about his feeding habits, we need to make sure he doesn't have anyone locked up somewhere."

Ren was going to kill him; it was the only way to free the souls the demon devoured. Still, the idea terrified me. Frank groaned low above us. I cringed.

"So um...have you had any more trouble at your place? Are the souls still quiet?" I whispered, trying to ignore what Frank was doing. I also needed to know. I felt them with him, but they were different, so much calmer. Even more than I would have expected.

"No more cold patches or touches," he said and moved closer. "Thanks to you."

"I'm really glad I could help," I said.

"I've been um...meditating, like you said, and Rose gave me the name of a counselor." He looked uncomfortable. "She offered online sessions, and I've done a few."

I blinked up at him through the shadows. "You did?"

"Yeah," he said low. "I want to let the guilt go, Jaz. I want to help the souls move on." His throat worked. "And I don't...I don't want to feel this way anymore. I don't want this awful fucking jagged rock right here." He pressed his closed fist to the center of his chest.

I wanted that for him, too, above anything else. "I'm proud of you." I smiled up at him. "I want that for you as well, you don't know how much."

"I wouldn't even be able to take those small steps if it wasn't for you, for all the ways you've helped me."

"Seeing that pain leave your eyes, seeing you smile again..." My voice was husky with emotion. Locking away a part of myself didn't feel like much of a sacrifice knowing this was the outcome. I wouldn't have been able to continue to do my job properly if I'd been nursing my shattered heart. "It's all I wanted."

His eyes softened, and he moved another inch closer—

A groan reached us and I looked up as Frank orgasmed. Something I could have gone my entire life never seeing or hearing. He quickly pulled up his pants, and Ren curled an arm around my waist, pulling me deeper into the alcove. Frank jumped to the ground, something no human could do without injury, and headed off down the street.

"Let's go," Ren said against my ear, making me shiver, then taking my hand again, and we followed after him.

›)‍›)‍●‍((‍‹

Ren

"This is recon only," I said to Jasmine, who had a seriously determined look on her face. "Once we find where he's bunking down, you need to leave."

Then I'd do what needed to be done. No fucking way was I letting her get close to this monster.

She's already with a monster. That's why she stopped loving you. She knows what you truly are, sees it when she tries to heal you, and it disgusts her. Edward's voice in my head piped up, trying to drag me back down, to destroy all the work Jasmine had done, the work I'd done. I forced his voice out of my head. I couldn't let him win.

She doesn't love you, not anymore. Agatheena's voice joined in, echoing through my mind.

"I don't like that idea," she said. "Not one bit. Who knows what that creep's capable of."

My fox bristled. Did she think we weren't strong enough to protect her? "But I know what I'm capable of," I said, and my voice was rough as hell.

"I know you're strong, Ren, and I know you can fight, but this guy is a demon. He literally just jumped two stories to the ground like it was nothing."

Her hand, so small and soft and warm in mine, was another reminder of how breakable she was. "I know I'm a fox, not a hound like Rome, but I can protect you just as good as he could." My words came out a snarl.

She blinked at me. "I know that."

What the fuck was I doing? Talking myself up like I'd ever be good enough for her. Did I really think that would change her mind? That she'd suddenly want me again? I didn't want her to change her mind, right? It was a good thing she didn't want me anymore, that she didn't love me, and I needed to remind myself of that when I was with her and every instinct in me roared to make her ours.

Love wasn't a cure. I could love her, and she could love me, but that didn't change the fact that I would never be the male I was before. Yes, I was doing a lot better, but my mind was still broken, and my soul would forever be scarred. I wasn't what she needed, mate or not. "Sorry, I'm on edge. You're right, we don't know what he's capable of, which is why I want you far away from him when I take him out."

"It's okay. I get it," she said. "He's taking the next street."

He disappeared, turning ahead of us. I kept hold of Jasmine's hand and walked quickly after him as quietly as we could. But it wasn't a street he'd turned down, it was an alley, and something groaned from the shadows. "Stay behind me."

I took a step into the darkness, and glowing red eyes opened from the depths, locking on to me. Frank was looming over a human, a homeless male going by the makeshift shelter he was slumped beside.

"He's feeding," Jaz said, her voice shaking.

Frank dropped the other male, leapt across the alley, and scrambled up the side of the wall like fucking Spider-Man. We ran to the human male on the ground, his face was gray, the life washed from him, already gone. "It's too late."

"We can't let him get away," Jaz said, looking up to the top of the building.

"He'll need to come back down." I leaned in and scented the dead male's shoulder where Frank had gripped him. It was hard with the scent of unwashed human trying to overpower it, which was probably why Frank chose the target he had, but it was still fresh enough that I could pick it up. "I need to shift. I'll be able to pick up his scent easier."

Jaz nodded as I quickly stripped and handed her my clothes. "Stay close, my fox is quick, and once he catches Frank's scent, he'll take off. If you lose me, get somewhere safe and call Bram and Mags."

She nodded.

Her eyes widened as I shifted, my joints popping, bone and muscle reshaping. I was big for a fox, bigger than any in the wild. If anyone saw me, hopefully they'd assume I was a dog. I expected him to take off instantly, but instead, my fox nudged Jaz, pressing his snout into her palm. She gave him what he wanted, running her hand down his back.

I gave him a mental nudge, and he finally trotted to the dead male, scented him, then turned, and nose to the ground trotted from the alley and down the street. Jaz jogged along beside us. The streets were quiet, but they weren't empty. My fox ignored the looks he was getting, though, focused on finding our target. He turned another corner and slowed, scenting a small area more thoroughly. His ears pricked up, and I felt the spike of adrenaline rush through him.

He had the demon's scent.

He took off, and I heard Jaz's feet on the pavement as she ran after us. I wanted her to leave, to go somewhere safe, to stay back. But she didn't, she stayed with us, and though my fox was constantly aware of Jasmine, he was also focused on finding his target, of showing Jaz how clever he was.

He carried on through a parking lot behind a tire shop. There were old tires in the back, stacked up, and he sniffed around them until he picked up the scent, then took off again. A brick building loomed behind it, every single window in the abandoned building had been broken, the walls graffitied. The demon was inside.

I shifted, and Jasmine handed me my clothes. I pulled them on quickly. "You need to go. You're not coming inside."

"You need me," she said and pointed to the brick wall in front of us. "That symbol isn't just graffiti, it's an alarm, it'll let him know you're coming, and that one"—she pointed to another—"that one will cause sickness if you pass, stomach pain, violent shakes, vomiting. I can neutralize them, but there could be more inside."

I ground my teeth. "I don't like this."

"I'll stay back." Her gaze held mine. "I trust you to protect me."

Fuck. "You need to stay behind me at all times."

"I will."

She strode to the symbols Frank had spray-painted on the wall, pulled her knife from her pocket, and sliced her palm. I hissed, the scent of her blood setting my fox off. The scent of her blood fucked with both of us. He snarled, searching for danger. I did my best to calm him, to reassure him our mate was okay, but he was pacing and on edge.

I wanted to snatch up her hand and stop the bleeding immediately but forced myself to stand back while she spelled under her breath, then pressed her blood-soaked palm against the demon symbols. It sizzled, acrid smoke drifting from her. Jaz tensed but didn't make a sound, then she moved to the next and did the same.

When she was done, she curled her hand against herself. I strode over and took her wrist, lifting it.

"It's nothing."

I ignored her and carefully uncurled her fingers. Her skin was blistered and raw. "You're burned. We need to dress this." My fox howled, hating she was injured, that we'd let her hurt herself.

"I'll take care of it when I get home, besides, there could be more inside," she said.

The thought of her doing that again made me want to snatch her off her feet and carry her away from here. But Frank had seen us back there. He knew what Jaz looked like, and I wasn't leaving until he was nothing but ash.

"If shit gets dicey, you run, okay? Get the fuck out of here as fast as you can."

"I will."

The way her gaze darted from mine, I was pretty sure she was lying. *Fuck.* "Let's go. Keep your hand on my back so I know where you are at all times."

She nodded and, on quiet feet, I led her into the dark building. There were massive old machines filling the enormous space. The place smelled metallic, of oil, and broken glass crunched underfoot as we crossed the concrete floor.

We made our way carefully, and were nearly to the other side, when Jaz fisted my shirt and tugged, stopping me. I looked at her over my shoulder, and she pointed to the floor at the end of one of the machines. It was nearly impossible to see in this light, but it was there. A symbol.

Jaz quickly lowered herself to the floor and rolled under the machine, the scent of her blood came next, then the hiss of her flesh and that same acrid scent. She rolled back out and slid under the one beside it, another hiss, more of that scent. I felt helpless, following her as she checked the rest of the machines.

I knew she was in pain. I felt her distress. The connection between us that I realized had always been there felt different now, somehow stronger, but also muted in a way that didn't feel...right.

She finally rolled out from under the last machine, and I took her good hand and helped her up, unable to stop myself from pulling her into my side. I needed to touch her, to feel her close. I pressed my mouth to the top of her head. "Okay?" I whispered.

She nodded. Another fucking lie. She trembled, and the palm of her hand looked as if she'd dipped it in fucking boiling oil. The fact she wasn't crying in pain spoke of her strength and determination, two things I already knew about this female.

I placed her good hand against my side, needing to know she was with me, and moved to the doorway in front of us. I peered into the darkness, listening. My fox pricked his ears. Nothing but silence came from the shadows.

Sliding my knife free, I stepped through, Jasmine right behind me.

It was a small room, an old office perhaps, but nothing else. I pulled out my phone and used the flashlight. No other doorways, no exit.

"Are you sure he came this way?" Jaz whispered.

I nodded and walked to an old storage shelf. "His scent is stronger in here." He definitely came into this room. I shone my phone at the floor. There were marks in the dust from the narrow wheels under it.

I turned off the light, shoved my phone in my pocket, and reached for the shelf but Jaz stopped me with a hand to my bicep, pointing to the other side. Another fucking symbol.

I clenched my teeth. I couldn't watch her go through that again, but she was already whispering her spell. She pressed her blood-covered and blistered hand to the symbol and pain etched her beautiful face, her skin leaching of all color. She shook from it, and I moved in behind her and wrapped my arms around her, wishing I could absorb the pain, take it from her. Smoke rose, the sizzle and scent of her burning flesh reaching my nose. But she didn't pull away, she finished her spell, breaking its dark magic before finally dropping her hand and collapsing against me.

I turned her to face me, and tears glistened on her cheeks. I brushed them away. My mate was crying, my precious female was burned, in pain, and I couldn't do anything to ease it. "I'm sorry," I choked out. Useless words, and not just for her physical pain, but for the pain I'd caused her over the years while I'd been lost in my own. Blind, dumb, deaf to everything. So focused on getting through one more day, just one, that I hadn't seen anything around me, or anyone.

She wiped her face on her shirt and smiled crookedly at me, cracking my chest down the middle.

"I'll live," she said, her lower lip quivering.

I gripped the back of her head and pressed a kiss to the top of her hair, knowing that's all she'd let me do, all I'd let myself do, but still needing that contact so fucking badly. "You ready?"

She nodded. "Yeah, the pain's subsided some."

That was her third lie of the night. The pain was still there in her gorgeous eyes, but I nodded and eased the shelf forward. More darkness greeted us behind it, but there was a flicker of light in the distance, lower than the level we were on. The basement.

"Stairs," I said against her ear and placed her hand on my back again before slowly, carefully, making my way down. I wanted to leave her up here, but if he doubled back and found her alone—no, I couldn't leave her alone in this place.

As we reached the bottom, music drifted out of a room to the side. There were shelves and other clutter down here, and we slipped into the room. The sound of Frank humming along to the music reached us. I peered through one of the shelves.

He was doing a weird fucking little dance as he stripped off his clothes. He tossed his jacket aside, then his shirt, before shucking his pants. His skin was sweaty, more scabs like the ones around his mouth at his joints. He straightened with a groan of relief, and Jaz grabbed my arm, her nails digging in.

Holy fuck. His greasy skin writhed. Souls moving beneath it. Hands stretched his flesh, fingers splayed, faces, mouths open in silent screams. They were trapped inside him. He spun in a slow circle, swiveling his hips, singing along with the song playing.

I took Jaz's hand, placed it on one of the shelves, and mouthed *stay here.* She nodded.

My best bet was taking this fucker by surprise. He strutted about, still dancing, singing, swinging his flaccid dick around like he was hot shit. No doubt on a high after just feeding.

He dance-walked farther away. The humming stopped, there was a clang, like pots and pans being moved around. He couldn't still be hungry.

I eased closer, saw a flash of naked skin, then it was gone. A crash came from behind me, a shelf toppling over. *Fuck.* He knew we were here. I sprinted for Jasmine, but it was too late.

Frank had his arms locked around her, his scabbed, sweaty face pressed against hers, grinning wide.

"You hurt her, you die screaming," I snarled, taking a step closer. My heart was in my throat. I knew I loved her, but right then I realized my whole fucking world was in that soul-sucking demon's arms.

"Imagine, if you will," the demon said in a weird voice that resonated through the room. "Her sweet, juicy, vibrant soul writhing beneath my skin. Imagine it screaming in agony as I feed off her slowly, piece by delicious piece, until there's nothing left of her. Until every last trace of your female ceases to exist."

Jasmine's lips were moving, spelling, and the demon hissed and slapped his hand over her mouth, then opened his. Jasmine's muffled scream came next. He was devouring her soul.

I ran at him but hit an invisible barrier. He grinned and pointed up. There was a symbol painted on the ceiling right above him. Some kind of protection or barrier.

Jaz flailed in his arms, trying to get away while I lost my mind, slamming into the invisible wall over and over again. Frank howled suddenly. Jasmine had her knife buried in his thigh, and with a cry, she dragged it up, slicing his leg wide open.

The demon's arms fell away from her with a howl, and he stumbled back. As soon as he stepped a toe over the symbol, the barrier dropped, and I pounced. I yanked him away from Jasmine and unceremoniously started hacking at the piece of shit. He rebounded fast, though, punching me in the ribs with the force of a wrecking ball.

My ribs shattered, and he knocked the knife from my hand. I wrestled him to the ground, hissing when he sunk his teeth into my arm. He was incredibly strong and fast. Jasmine dove on his back, her little knife plunging into his back over and over again.

Fuck. I slammed both hands against his ears, and he screamed as I plowed my fist into his face. Snatching my knife from the ground, I slashed his throat. Blood sprayed me, and ignoring his gurgled screams, I sawed through his thick skin and hardened bone.

Finally, his head gave, rolling with a thud to the floor. A second later he turned to ash.

Jasmine landed on top of me, ash on her face, and in her hair. Then the screams of dozens of trapped souls burst into the air, a frenzy of fear and pain, and Jaz curled around me, holding on tight.

I wrapped my arms around her. "You're okay," I said against her hair. "I've got you." Words she'd said to me, to make me feel safe when I'd been so fucking lost.

One by one, the souls' mournful screams came to a stop.

We couldn't see them, but the reapers must be here, taking the missing souls where they were always meant to go, reestablishing balance.

Jasmine gave me all her weight, and I rubbed her back. "Jaz?"
Nothing.

I lifted her head. She wasn't breathing, and every bit of life had drained from her face completely. "Jasmine!"

CHAPTER 26

Ren

I CARRIED Jasmine to her room, thankful everyone was in bed. It was close to morning, but I had no idea what the time was.

Laying Jaz on the bed, I shut us in and crawled up beside her and pulled her against me, holding her tight.

This was the same thing that happened at the demon compound, this wasn't what it looked like, what it felt like, I knew it, I felt her...fuck, her life force inside me. My fox howled inside me, calling for her to wake up. Jasmine was going to be okay. She wasn't leaving me. I just had to hold on, hold on to her.

I lay there holding her lifeless body as time ticked by, until the sounds of the family waking, going down to the kitchen for breakfast, drifted up from downstairs. They didn't know we were here, and I wasn't getting off this bed to tell them, not until Jasmine woke up.

She'd been out for hours last time, but this was definitely longer.

"This is the second time you've done this to me, butterfly. Made me think I lost you." I pressed my face into her shoulder and breathed in her scent, curling around her more tightly. She felt cold. Fuck, she was so cold. I tugged the quilt at the end of the bed over her. "That's enough now, Jaz. You can wake up now, baby." I shook her a little as panic filled me. "Wake the fuck up, Jasmine. Wake up now."

521

Not a sound, no movement, nothing. The gaping hole in my stomach and behind my ribs was unbearable. Living without her wasn't an option.

She's okay, I reminded myself for the millionth fucking time.

Because Jasmine was here, her life force, right there in the center of my chest, burning bright.

I rolled her to her back and cupped her beautiful face. Her skin was pale, had lost all color, all life. I didn't know how long this thing could last, but I was seriously starting to freak out. "Jaz, please, I need you to come back to me." I pressed a kiss to her forehead, her cheek. "Come on, butterfly, wake up." My eyes stung, and my chest felt as if there was a boulder on it. "Come back to me, Jazzy."

There was a tapping at the window. The curtains were still open and early morning sun filtered through, backlighting tiny flappy wings. Butterflies, so many of them, trying to get in, to get to her. I got off the bed and opened the window. Maybe they could reach her when nothing else could. They flew to her instantly, a multitude of color surrounding her, covering her, pouring their love into her, calling her back.

A witch needed her familiar. They needed each other. If anyone could get through to her, they could. I dragged a chair to the side of the bed and sat, taking her hand in mine, and then I prayed. I prayed to the goddess to bring her back to me.

Her hand jolted in mine. My head shot up.

She blinked several times, and the butterflies covering her all took flight, fluttering and dancing above her. "Ren?"

My eyes closed and I bent my head over her hand again, pressing my mouth to her skin, feeling it warming beneath my lips. Her other hand brushed the back of my head.

"Ren?"

Relief pumped through me with such force, I shook. Her fingers flexed against mine, and I lifted my head.

"W-we did it, didn't we? We freed the souls. It's over," she said, a small smile curling her lips.

I nodded and released a shuddering breath. "For a minute there..." I tried to calm my pounding heart. "I thought...I thought I might lose you."

"I'm sorry... I—"

"I love you," I choked out, unable to hold in those words another day, another moment. "I'm in love with you, Jasmine."

She stared at me, her eyes wide, then she started to shake her head.

"Don't tell me I'm wrong or that it's because you've been helping me and I'm confused. I know what I'm feeling. I fucking know. You are mine. You're fucking mine, Jasmine." There were a lot of reasons why I should keep this to myself, that I should let her go, but I needed her. I'd tried to fight it, but I couldn't do it anymore. Living without her wasn't an option. It just wasn't. And whether she would admit it or not, she needed me as well.

Her lower lip quivered. "I don't...I can't—"

"You loved me, you did." I held her tighter. "I'll make you love me again."

"You can't," she said, her voice filled with anguish. "You can't fix it. I don't..." Her throat worked. "I care about you, so much. You're my friend, but I can't...I can't love you the way you want me to."

Why the fuck was she saying this? My fox paced, confused. He didn't know why our mate didn't want us. He wanted us to take her home to our den. He wanted to claim her, bite her, mark her. She was ours, but she was denying us. "I know I hurt you, but I'll fix it. I can fix it."

Her fingers curled around mine. "You did nothing wrong. It's me. It was me. I wish it was different, Ren, I do, but I can never love you—"

The door flew open and Mags rushed in. "I got here as fast as I could. I had to deliver the souls. I was there, you were on the floor...thank the goddess you're okay."

Mags ran to Jaz, and I stepped back, retreating. Shaking so fucking hard my legs felt unsteady under me. She couldn't mean that, but she did. I saw it in her eyes. I felt it. I fucking felt it through the bond she was denying.

She could never love me.

She didn't want us.

›⟩❯❯●❮❮‹

Jasmine

Ren walked out the door, and I stared after him, utterly frozen.

"Jazzy?"

"Ren said he loves me," I whispered as my tiny familiars settled around me.

Magnolia stared down at me, her eyes wide, filled with things I didn't want to see right then. "Oh, Jaz."

"He can't mean it. He can't," I said, trying to convince myself I hadn't seen the truth of his feelings shining at me in his gorgeous eyes.

"I think he meant it," Mags said gently and sat in the chair Ren had just been in.

"What have I done?" I choked.

"There's definitely nothing you can do—"

I shook my head. Xavier said it couldn't be undone, more than once. He

523

told me to make sure it was what I wanted. I never in a million years thought Ren would ever fall in love with me. It had been an impossibility in my mind.

Mags sat forward. "And you really don't feel anything for him, nothing?"

"Nothing like before. I want him to be happy. I recognize how handsome he is, I'm still...attracted to him." I'd tried to ignore it, but that was something that had never stopped, even after what Xavier did. "I like him, a lot, but I don't love him. It's just not there anymore. It's gone." My love for Ren was trapped behind impenetrable walls, and there was no busting them down.

Mags grabbed my hand, her gaze filled with sympathy. "I'm so sorry."

"He'll get over me, he will, and then all this...it'll just be a bad memory."

Magnolia nodded, but she didn't look convinced.

She left, and I got out of bed and stared out the window. As I did, something rose up inside me, a strange feeling, a yearning that I couldn't decipher, that I didn't understand. It reminded me of when I was a child and Mom would send us here during school holidays while she took off on another adventure.

And even though I'd loved it here, and my family, I'd missed Mom terribly.

I felt homesick, I just didn't know what I was homesick for.

CHAPTER 27

Ren

My fox whined and pawed at the ground. He'd been doing it all day. He wanted us to go back to our mate, to bring her home where we could keep her safe. He didn't understand why she didn't feel the bond, and neither the fuck did I.

I'd never heard of it happening before. When a fox found his mate, when that lightning struck, there was no mistaking it. The male felt it first, yes. But as the bond grew in strength, his female felt it, too, and Jasmine was my female. I knew it with everything in me, but still she was indifferent.

Agatheena's words slammed into my skull.

"It's simple, fox. Jasmine has been in love with you since the first time she met you. She continued to love you, even while she was forced to watch you drown your pain in booze and other females, knowing there was nothing she could do, knowing that you'd never be hers. After you rejected her, her pain was unbearable. It hurt so much, she knew the only way she could help you heal was to let that love go. So she did. She let you go the only way she knew how."

What the fuck did that even mean? How did you just let it go?

My muscles ached to run, to run to my cliff; my palm itched to grip my knife to ease the throb of my scars, something I hadn't felt for a while thanks to Jasmine, but I'd been fighting it back all day. I didn't want it back. I didn't fucking want it.

I paced across the room. Going there now would undo all the work Jaz had done. All the work I'd done. I needed to stay strong, to keep my head.

I wasn't giving up on her, I couldn't.

Someone knocked at the door. It was late, and I strode to it, hoping it was Jaz on the other side, but knowing it wouldn't be.

Bram stood there. "You got a minute?"

"Is it Jaz? Is she okay?"

He studied me. "She's fine. Can I come in?"

"Not really in the mood for company, brother," I said, shutting the door and following him into the living room.

"I know," Bram said. "But you got me, anyway."

"Mags told you what happened?"

He nodded. "Just got back from a job or I would've been here earlier."

There was only one reason Bram was here, he was worried what I might do. "I'm alright," I said. Was I convincing him or me? "You don't need to babysit me. Yeah, my mate just told me she didn't fucking want me, but I don't plan on swan diving off the edge of a cliff, not tonight anyway. I'm not giving up that easily."

"Mate?" Bram straightened. "She's your mate?"

I rubbed my hands over my face. "Yeah. I didn't know, not until she started helping me. Deep down, somewhere, I know I did, and that's why I stayed away from her, because I couldn't fucking bear to be near her as tainted and fucked up as I am, and because I was afraid. I'm still fucked up, and I'm still afraid I'll fuck things up and hurt her, but I want her more than anything. I need her. She's everything. She's—"

"I know. I know how you feel," Bram said. "I know what she means to you. I had no idea she was your mate, though. Does she know?"

I shook my head. "She doesn't want me. She doesn't feel it."

Bram shoved his fingers through his hair. "There's a reason for that."

I gripped the back of the couch. "What did she do?"

His jaw worked as if he were wrestling with something.

I knew this male well. We'd grown up together. Something seriously fucked up was going on. "What the hell is it? Tell me."

"If I'd known what this was, between you and Jaz, I would have spoken up sooner."

I had no idea what he was going to say, but my friend was a male of few words, and he didn't get involved in shit if it didn't involve Magnolia. For him to speak up now meant it was something serious, something he couldn't ignore. My fingers dug deeper into the couch, and my fox paced.

"I know what it's like to be in love with someone and think there's no hope. I didn't think it was my place to tell you after Mags found out, if I'd known—"

"Fucking tell me, Bram."

"She went to someone, I don't know who, someone with powers and asked for help."

"What kind of help?"

"Help with her heartbreak, over you, and they did something to her...to stop her loving you, Ren. That's why she doesn't feel it, she can't."

I struggled to fucking breathe. I'd hurt her that much, so much she'd done something to break free from me, to cut me out of her like a piece of rot. I didn't blame her after the way I ignored her, flaunted other females in front of her—rejected her.

Fuck. She'd been living in pain as long as I had and I hadn't seen it, so caught up in my own.

Maybe I should walk away, leave her alone, let her be happy without me. But she was ours, our mate, and I couldn't let her go.

I grabbed my keys and strode out the door. Bram shut it after us and strode down the street with me. It was late, Jaz would be asleep, but I couldn't wait.

"What are you gonna do?" Bram asked as he kept pace beside me.

"Fucked if I know, but she's mine. I can't just walk away. There has to be a way to fix this." The alternative was too fucking awful to consider.

We walked around the back of the house.

Bram clapped me on the back before heading for his tree house, and Mags, in the backyard, and I used my key to get into the house. It was silent. Everyone was asleep. Walking into Jaz's bedroom in the middle of the night was probably a terrible idea, but it was as if I were being pulled to her by an invisible force. My mate was here. Where she was, I needed to be, whether she felt it as well or not.

I took the stairs and stood outside her closed door, my breathing shaky as fuck, my gut a sack of jagged fucking rocks. But I needed to hear her say it. I needed the truth. I gripped the door handle and eased it open. The curtains were open, the moon casting shadows across the walls, the tree outside the window making them sway.

Jasmine was sitting up in bed, her knees drawn up, her arms wrapped around them, her eyes wide and on me. I didn't say anything, shutting the door behind me, and stared back at her across the room. She was utterly breathtaking. Her blond hair was a sexy mess around her face, her tattooed arms bare. She bit her lower lip, and her eyes drifted shut for a moment before opening again, except now they glistened with tears.

"You know, don't you?" she whispered. "You know what I did?"

I took a step closer. "That you loved me, and now you don't? That you had someone destroy what you felt for me because I hurt you so much that you couldn't bear the pain another moment?"

"You didn't know you were hurting me," she choked out.

"You didn't tell me."

"I thought it was the best thing for both of us. It hurt to be around you, but I wanted to help you. You needed that from me, more than anything else. I didn't think...you said you didn't want me, and I believed you." She bit her lip again. "I never thought—"

"That I'd fall in love with you? That after you helped me and I could see clearly again through all the blood and pain and horror, that I'd finally see you? That I'd see my mate?"

She jolted, her entire body rocking back. "What?"

"You really didn't know?" I stepped closer. "Christ, Jaz, that new wound that opened up inside me, while you were healing me? That was you. That was wanting you so fucking badly, but forcing myself to give you up when that was the last thing I wanted to do. That was giving up my mate."

She stared at me wide-eyed through the shadows.

"You are my mate, Jasmine. My female. My reason for breathing. You've been my reason for a long fucking time, even before I knew. It was your eyes I saw when I stood at the edge of a cliff and imagined stepping off, it was your eyes that pulled me back, time and time again. I just didn't know why, not until you wrapped your arms around me and everything clicked into place. The truth. What we are to each other."

She was trembling so hard I could see it even through the shadows. "I didn't know."

I closed the space between us, unable to stay away from her another moment. "I know I hurt you. I fucked up, but please, butterfly, fix this. I need you, Jaz. I fucking need you."

Tears streaked down her face. "I c-can't. I wish I could, but it can't be fixed." She sobbed. "I'm so sorry. I'm so sorry I did this to us. I'm so s-sorry—"

"Who did it?"

"It won't change anything."

"I'll make them fix this, I'll—"

"You can't."

"This can't be it."

"I'm sorry," she said again.

This couldn't be happening. It couldn't be true. My world had narrowed to her. Without her I was nothing. Something snapped inside me. I grabbed her shoulders. "Love me back," I demanded, pleaded. "Please, butterfly. Please love me back."

"I can't," she sobbed.

I held the side of her face with one hand and curled my fingers around the side of her throat with the other. "You're mine. You're fucking mine, Jasmine. I won't let you go. I'll make you love me again. No matter how long it takes." I brought my mouth down on hers, needing her taste more than anything else on this planet.

She fisted my shirt, but she didn't push me away. "I'm sorry," she said against my lips. Our panted breaths mingled, then she tugged me closer and kissed me back. "I'm sorry," she said again, then lay back, taking me with her.

Trembling, I covered her, kissing her deeper, harder. I should get the fuck up and leave, but I couldn't do it. My mate was kissing me, touching me, and I was lost, completely fucking lost. Her hands slid down between us, tugging at my belt, sliding down the zipper, then her hand was on me. I groaned into her mouth.

She wriggled, tugging off her panties, then her thighs were hugging my hips. The head of my cock brushed over hot slick flesh, and I tried to lift my head, but she hooked her arms around my neck and pressed her forehead to mine. "It's okay," she rasped and lifted her hips.

I slipped inside her, just the tip, and I shook harder. "Jasmine?"

"It's okay," she said again.

I was too fucking weak to resist. My mate might not love me, but she wanted me. Her pussy was primed for me. I pushed forward, and her nails dug into my back with a cry. "Yes," she whimpered. "Please."

Mouths still touching, breathing each other's air, I slid deeper, unable to hold back. "Oh fuck," I groaned. She was so fucking tight and wet and impossibly hot.

Her hips lifted again, taking me deeper, her nails scoring my back, and I couldn't restrain myself. I started to move. We shook and rocked against each other, and I pinned her down more firmly with my body, lifted my knee for better purchase, and slid deeper. She cried out against my lips, her pussy squeezing me so damn tight, fluttering and clenching around me. "You feel so good, Jaz. So fucking perfect."

Her feet locked behind my back, and she strained against me, arching. Her mouth opened, and I covered it with mine, smothering her screams as she came for me fast, trembling. Her pussy gripped me fucking tighter, and I finally had her under me. There was no holding back, no finding an ounce of control in that moment. I thrust into her, utterly lost but somehow finding the strength to pull out at the last moment and grind my cock between our bodies, coming on her stomach instead of inside her like I desperately wanted to.

We lay there panting, still clinging to each other. Both of us were still dressed, our clothes damp with sweat and stuck to our skin. I kissed her neck, her jaw, and looked down at her beautiful face. She stared back at me, and there was a guarded look in her eyes that I fucking hated. "This isn't...I didn't come here for this, I—"

"It's okay," she said again, her fingers brushing my jaw. "It felt right. Please, don't question it."

"What happens now?"

She shook her head against the pillow. "I don't know." Her gaze searched mine. "I wish this changed things..."

She trailed off because it didn't, not for her. I was so in love with her my heart felt as if it might burst, but nothing had changed for her. Not one thing.

"I wanted to...to give you this before I leave," she said, staring at my chin.

It was like she'd punched me in the stomach. "Leave?" I grabbed her chin and shook her. "A pity fuck before you leave me? That's what that was?"

"No, it wasn't like that. I wanted you. I never really stopped wanting you that way, even after..."

"Even after you took what was mine and cut it out of you? Even after you stole our future from us and tossed it away. And now you're going to bail. Leave me here like I don't exist?" I snarled. "Find someone else you can love? Is that it?"

She pushed at my chest, and I had no choice but to get off her even though it was the last thing I wanted to do. I stood, stuffed myself back in my jeans, and did them up. Jasmine sat up, returning to the position she'd been in when I walked in here. Knees up, her arms wrapped around them. I could smell us, our come, the tinge of blood because my mate was a virgin until a few minutes ago, and instead of tending to her like my fox and I both wanted to do fucking desperately, she was pushing us away.

"I did that, and I'll own it," she said. "But I truly thought you'd never love me back. I never would have done what I did otherwise. I'm leaving for you, to make it easier on you. I don't want to hurt you, Ren. You've been hurt enough already. You should be with someone who can love you like you deserve."

I was breathing hard, my blood pumping through me so fucking fast I felt dizzy. "Let me make one thing perfectly clear. I'm not giving up on you, on us. Not fucking ever. You leave me, I will follow you. I will always follow you."

Then I turned and walked out the door, before I snatched her from that bed and kept her anyway.

CHAPTER 28

Jasmine

"I HATE SEEING you like this, Jazzy girl," Stanley said from his spot at the end of my bed.

I dragged my hand across my face, wiping away my stupid tears. "I hurt him, Stan, so badly. I never wanted that. I did it because I loved him, because I didn't want to hurt him, and I did it anyway."

He dropped down to an elbow, lying across the mattress. "You didn't know he was your mate. It's not your fault, sweets." Sympathy filled his eyes. "And that male was so closed off, there was no way you could've known."

There was an ache between my thighs, reminding me of what I did with Ren. I'd wanted him. I'd never stopped wanting him that way, but all I'd done was make it worse. I'd meant it to be a goodbye, I guess. But giving myself to him like I did had been selfish, and I'd made everything worse.

"Do you like him?" Stan asked.

"Yes, of course."

He smirked. "You obviously think he's hot."

My face heated. "Obviously."

"Maybe you don't need to love him to be with him, not at first? You're mates, that connection has its own magic. That bond can break spells and fight evil, it can bring people back to life and heal wounds...it can even break down barriers. I don't know much about foxes or how they mate, I assume by marking? Do you know for sure that mating properly won't change things between you? This Xavier guy blocked your love for Ren, but does that mean you can't fall in love with him all over again? Plenty of people have mated first and fallen in love later. Not everyone knows their intended mates for years before they're thrown in their path. Iris and Draven are a perfect example of that."

I blinked over at Stan, my heart doing a giant thump in my chest. "I... don't know."

"Well, before you pull up stakes and leave us all in the dust, don't you think you should find out?"

I chewed my lip. "You think he'll want to try?"

He gave me a look like I was a complete idiot. "Uh...yeah. You're all he's thinking about, Jaz, I promise you that." He tilted his head to the side. "I know you don't feel it anymore, but do you remember how it felt to be in love with him?"

Pain sliced through me. "Yes. It hurt like hell."

"Then maybe this is a good thing? Maybe it's a way to start fresh." He climbed off the bed. "I'll let you mull that over, and I'm gonna go check on my girl. I can hear her singing in her workroom. You know I love it when she does that." He winked and walked through the door, heading down to be close to Else.

If there was ever proof of how strong the mating bond was, all I had to do was look at Stan. He'd stayed by Else's side for over fifty years.

I shoved back the covers and strode to the shower. The mating bond *was* a powerful thing. Maybe this could work. Maybe all hope wasn't lost. I wanted him still, I cared about him a lot. That was a good start, right? I didn't want to live my life without my mate, and I didn't want Ren to either, to suffer because of what I did. I had to at least try.

》》)●《 《《

Asking Ren if he wanted to try to make this thing between us work wasn't something you did over the phone, but when I came by the funeral home, there'd been a whole lot of cars parked out front. Someone was having a viewing or a service, which meant Ren would be busy.

I'd gone back to the house, and with no missing souls to hunt, I'd had the whole day to think about what I'd say when I saw Ren. I still wasn't sure how to approach this. The only thing I could do was just lay it all out and see what he thought, but the nerves in my belly were off the charts.

When I finally walked back to his place, it was getting dark. He would've finished work a few hours ago. I'd wanted to come sooner, but Aunt Daisy needed some help at the cemetery harvesting.

My nerves were insane by the time I knocked on Ren's door, but nothing but silence came from inside. I walked back up the stairs.

"Looking for Ren?" Mr. Macanroy was walking out of the funeral home. He was tall and lean with the same russet-colored hair as Ren.

"I am, yeah. Do you know when he'll be back?"

He slid his hands in his pockets. "He went for a run a while ago, but I'm sure he'll be back soon."

"Oh, okay. I'll come back."

"I was actually hoping I'd see you, Jasmine," he said, stopping me. "I've been wanting to thank you for what you've been doing for Ren. He's changed so much...we're seeing glimpses, more than glimpses of our boy, the way he was before..." His amber eyes, so like Ren's, softened. "Just seeing him smile again...thank you, Jasmine."

"I'm glad I could help, but it wasn't just me. He did the work."

He pressed a key into my hand. "Go in and wait for him. He won't mind."

"No, I shouldn't—"

"It's fine." He gave my hand a squeeze and left.

I stood there for a minute, not sure what to do, but then a fat, cold raindrop landed on my cheek, then another and another, then the sky opened up. I ran down the stairs to his front door, unlocked it, and rushed inside.

Ren's scent filled the space, and I unconsciously breathed deep. I loved the way he smelled. It instantly made me think about him pressed against me, his weight, the sounds he'd made. I shivered. It'd been good, really good. Who was I kidding, it was amazing. I had no idea it'd be like that, that connection, that chemistry. That had to count for something, right?

I walked deeper into the living room and stood there, not sure what to do with myself. Yes, I'd been here a lot lately, but I didn't want to invade his privacy. In the end, I sat on the couch.

I tried to busy myself by flicking through Nightscape, but I hadn't slept after Ren left my room the night before, and as hard as I tried to stay awake, it didn't take long for the tiredness to take over. I resisted, but something about being here, and Ren's scent, being around his things, had me struggling to keep my eyes open.

>>➤●◄<<

I startled awake when something cold hit my arm.

I looked up.

Ren stood over me, hair wet, water dripping down his bare chest. He was wearing jeans that he must have just pulled on because they were dry, unlike the rest of him. He stared down at me, his chest heaving.

"You're, ah...your dad let me in," I said, suddenly feeling awkward and shy.

"I see that," he said, glancing at the key on the coffee table.

"I was going to wait outside, but then it, uh..." My gaze dipped without my say-so, taking in his wet, bare chest, and for some reason seeing all the sigils on him, the ones I'd tattooed on his skin, had my skin flushing hot. "Started raining."

"You can come here whenever you want, Jaz." His gaze moved over me, and his nostrils flared. "My mate can come and go as she pleases."

My mouth went dry. The way he was looking at me, the intensity, was something I'd never seen before. He looked wild, on edge, like he was holding himself back.

"We're not mated yet," I said, and it came out a husky whisper.

He quirked a brow. "Yet?"

I licked my dry lips, still trying to decide the best way to word this. "Last night, after you left—"

"After I left you last night, I came here and tried not to tear the walls down, then when nothing else would work, I sat where you are now and looked through all the pictures I have of you on my phone, taken when you weren't looking, some when you were. I've got a whole file of you, Jasmine, that I look at when I need to calm the storm inside me. Pictures, because the real thing was out of my reach. I had that, needed that, needed you, and somehow I didn't work out what you were to me until it was too fucking late."

He had pictures of me? I forced myself to focus on what I needed to say, but it wasn't easy, not after what he'd just confessed, and not with the way he was staring down at me. "You were right, the things you said before you left."

"Which things, Jaz?" Gold flecks burst through amber, his fox swirled in his eyes, staring out at me.

"When I did what I did, I took something from you as well." I was finding it hard to breathe normally. "No, I didn't know what we were to each other then, but I do now, and I'd like to try to fix it. I don't know if it's possible," I rushed out, "but a friend of mine reminded me how powerful the mating bond is, and that anything's possible between mates."

His stomach muscles clenched, and the veins in his forearms bulged. "What are you saying, Jasmine? You want us to mate?"

"Um...that was suggested, but I don't think we should go that far, if...if it doesn't work, I don't want you tied to me and suffering."

"If what doesn't work? I'm still not sure what you're suggesting, butterfly?"

My belly went all zippy and flippy-floppy when he called me butterfly. "That we stay...close, that we try to develop the mating bond. You feel it. Maybe I'll start to as well and—"

"You'll fall in love with me again?"

"Yeah. Maybe."

He leaned forward, gripping the cushion above me with one hand and the arm of the couch with the other. "How close are we talking, Jaz?"

"Well, um..."

He leaned in more. "This close?"

I nodded.

"How about this close?" he said and came closer still, his mouth hovering above mine.

I nodded again as electricity shot through me.

"Closer?" he said with a whole lot of growl in his voice.

"Yes—"

His mouth slammed down on mine, and he hooked a muscled arm around my waist, hauling me off the couch. I wrapped my arms around his shoulders, my legs around his waist. This was dangerous, so damn risky. If this went wrong, if it didn't work, I could hurt Ren all over again, badly. But I owed it to him, to both of us, to try. I had to at least try. I may not be able to feel the love I'd had for him before, but I still remembered the wild fantasies, the dreams I'd had, the images I'd played through my mind over and over of the two of us together.

I wanted him, I wanted this to work. I wanted to love him again, but this time without any of the pain and sadness. I wanted to know what it was to love him without holding anything back. I wanted to love him this time, knowing he loved me in return.

His tongue delved into my mouth, and he carried me through the living room and down the hall into his bedroom. He lowered me toward the mattress.

"Not here," I blurted as everything seized inside me. "Not where you brought..." *All the others. Not where I saw you with Bree through the window.*

He hitched me higher, and the bedside drawer opened and closed, then he was striding back into the hall. He opened the next door. It was a small room with a set of weights in the corner and a couch against the wall. He sucked on my mouth, there was no other word for it, like he couldn't get enough of me, then stood me on my feet. He quickly tossed the couch cushions aside and pulled on a nylon strap, unfolding the bed. Then he grabbed a couple duvets from the closet behind him and tossed them on the foldout.

He turned back to me, grabbed me before I knew what he was going to do, and tossed me on top of it.

"Better?" he asked.

"Yes."

"Good." Then he was on top of me, kissing me again, deep and insistent. I thrust my fingers through his damp hair, wanting more. Goddess, the male could kiss. Not that I'd kissed a lot of guys, but none of them had come anywhere close to this.

He did the mouth-sucking thing again and lifted his head, staring down at me. "How you feeling after last night, baby? You sore?"

My face went hot again. "A little achy, but it's not so bad now."

His jaw clenched. "I should have been more careful. I should have looked after you when we were done."

But I'd ruined things, and he'd left.

"It's fine. I'm fine."

He shook his head. "It's not. But I'm going to look after you now, Jazzy. You trust me, don't you?"

I did. I'd seen all of him. I'd wrapped my arms around him and seen every part of his soul, the pain, the anger, the scars, and the crippling guilt. But not one part of him was bad. Ren was a good male, so incredibly good. Under all those awful shadows crowding him, surrounding his soul, was a warm, gentle light. His true nature, the sweet fox I'd known as a kid. "Yes, I trust you."

His gorgeous eyes seemed to grow brighter, and an animalistic sound rumbled through his chest. He gripped the bottom of my shirt and lifted it over my head. "I'm gonna take care of you, so good. So fucking good, butterfly." My bra came off next, and he lowered himself down on top of me, kissing me sweet and gentle this time. "You're so beautiful, so fucking perfect," he said as he trailed kisses along my jaw. "So warm. Every part of you. I just want to take care of you, protect you." He kissed along my jaw. "I want to give you everything you need, make you feel good. I want all of it, Jaz, all of you."

He wasn't holding anything back. Ren was laying it all out for me, and it was exhilarating and terrifying. I would have done almost anything to hear those words from him a few weeks ago. And I won't lie, it felt nice, really nice to hear them even now. I could almost believe the feeling welling up inside me, but what I was feeling was a memory. Those feelings were gone, and I'd be doing us both a disservice by believing the lie my brain was trying to tell me.

You didn't just fall in love that easy. It wasn't going to be so simple. Wanting it and actually having it were two very different things. This was lust and affection for a male I'd known since I was just a kid, that's all I was feeling in this moment.

He sucked my nipple into his mouth, and I arched beneath him, a groan leaving me as I gripped his hair tighter. Ren wasn't in a hurry, he licked and sucked and toyed with me.

"Wanted to do this for so long," he said, holding my other breast in a firm grip. "Night after night, you naked in my house. Fucking torture, Jaz. Having you wrapped around me, kissing you, holding you, then letting you leave?" He tilted his head back and held my eyes as he licked the taut peak. "I fucking hated it. More than once I had to stop myself from following you, from snatching you up and carrying you back to our den."

I shivered at the way his voice had grown more gravelly, like his fox was blended with it. He kept his eyes on me as he spread my thighs. I shivered again when his hands slid to my sensitive inner thighs. His thumbs moved in circles over my jeans, up and down but not high enough, not where the ache had deepened and I was so damn slick. He kissed between my breasts, over the tattoo there, then down, sucking kisses over my feverish skin until he reached the waistband of my jeans.

I was panting now, squirming. He held my eyes as he popped the button and dragged down the zipper, a question in his eyes. I nodded. Yes, I wanted whatever he wanted to do to me. Badly.

I lifted my hips, and he dragged my jeans down my legs and tossed them on the floor, then his hand, fingers splayed, slid up my thigh and rested on the top of my pussy. He licked his lips and, over my panties, dragged his thumb along my slit.

"So fucking wet, butterfly. Jesus." He watched what he was doing as he pressed his thumb deeper, adding more pressure, grinding it against me. I whimpered, and he looked back up at me. "You don't even know how long I've been wanting to taste you. I hurt this sweet pussy last night, and now I'm going to worship it."

Oh fuck. I was close to combusting. I watched as he hooked his finger around the fabric plastered against my aching flesh and dragged it aside.

"Fuck," he groaned. "Fucking look at you," he said, his voice a low growl. He leaned in, his eyes lifting to mine, and he tasted me, a soft lick that had me trembling.

His tongue was hot against my swollen, slick flesh and I couldn't take my eyes off him. His had drifted closed, and he did it again, his muffled groan filling the room. He gripped the sides of my underwear and tugged them down my legs and tossed them aside, then he was back. He gripped my legs, his hot, rough-skinned hands roaming my inner thighs, squeezing and holding me wide as he lapped at me again.

"Fuck, baby."

"Ren..."

His mouth covered my pussy then, his lids fluttering as he tasted every inch of me, a look of bliss on his stunningly handsome face. I wanted to watch, but I couldn't hold myself up any longer, not when he sucked on my clit and gently slipped one of his thick fingers inside me. My ass lifted, arching against his mouth, wanting more, needing more.

But he kept the same pace, building the sensations in slow, steady waves that made me gasp and rock my hips, lost to the pleasure building inside me.

"You gonna come all over my hand, butterfly?"

I whimpered again. "Y-yes."

"Yeah, you fucking are," he growled.

He slid in another finger and increased his pace, finger-fucking me deeper. "Shit...ahhh..."

"I wanna feel my mate's pussy squeezing my fingers. Give it to me, Jasmine. Give it to me now."

I screamed and rocked uncontrollably against his hand as I came all over his fingers like he told me to. When I collapsed back, panting and trembling, he climbed off the bed and shucked his jeans. His long, thick cock jutted from his muscled body, and he curled his fingers around it, stroking slowly as he came back to me, between my spread thighs.

"Need to fuck you now, baby. Need it so fucking badly," he choked out.

"Please," I said, my voice husky from my screams.

He grabbed something off the floor, a condom. He tore the foil and rolled it on. I couldn't believe I was doing this, that we were doing this. It could all go so fucking badly, but I wanted him. My desperation to feel him inside me again surpassed everything else.

He covered my body with his, his skin so scalding hot. I wrapped myself around him instantly, wanting him as close as he could get to me. His kiss was hungry, urgent, and I returned it with the same. Maybe this would be enough, maybe I didn't need to love him. I liked him, cared about him, wanted him beyond all reason, craved him. Maybe that could be enough.

And then I couldn't think anymore because he reached between us, taking his cock in hand, and rubbed against my slick opening.

"Tell me if you want me to stop," he said. "If you're too tender."

I nodded, but that wasn't going to happen. I felt empty in a way I never had before. Emptier than the night before in my room.

He pushed inside, just the head, and I dug my nails into his shoulders. The stretch a little sore but mostly magnificent.

"Okay?" he asked, staring down at me.

I nodded again, and he gave me more, forcing a wanton groan from me.

There was that dull ache, but the pleasure far outweighed it. I spread my thighs wider, my hands sliding down to his ass, and I lifted my hips.

He growled and rocked, filling me with every inch of him. I looked down between us, and he did the same, and we both watched as he slid out, then thrust back in. The sigil I inked on the base of his cock disappeared inside me, and something about that was so incredibly hot. Ren growled.

"Oh fuck," I rasped. "More."

He hooked an arm under my hips, the other delving into my hair, this thumb sliding along my jaw. He held my eyes as he slid out and thrust back in. My lips parted, noises coming from me I'd never made before, unable to hold any of it back with his eyes locked on mine. They silently demanded I hold nothing back, that I give him everything I was capable of giving him, and I had no choice but to obey.

His mouth took mine, swallowing my cries and feeding me his groans and growls as he fucked me harder, faster. It didn't take long before he had me gasping, my next orgasm rushing up on me. My inner muscles clamped down on him, and he lifted his head, still sucking at my lips, tasting my tongue while he watched me lose it completely. When my pussy gripped him again, he started fucking me faster, and I flew to pieces, crying out and shaking under him as I came again.

"That's it, baby. Fuck. That's it," he growled.

A moment later he throbbed inside me, his entire body shaking, his muscles jumping as he pounded into me, coming with me. Sharp canines extended from his top jaw, and the sight, the thought of them puncturing my flesh, of him marking me, just made me come harder.

I knew he wanted to do it, his fox shone from his eyes as he ground into me, as he trailed the sharp points along my shoulder and shook even harder, from holding himself back, from fighting the instinct roaring inside him telling him to do it.

"I'll never get enough of you," Ren rasped against my ear. "Not fucking ever, butterfly."

CHAPTER 29

Ren

I GASPED, my hips thrusting forward, pushing deeper into my precious female's mouth. Water sprayed my back and dotted her face as she looked up at me, eyes hot as she sucked me hard.

We'd spent the last week staying close. Really fucking close.

I hadn't let her spend a night away from me since I found her here. I'd had her in every room of the house except my bedroom. But I had plans to make her comfortable in there, and I was starting on that when she left for work this morning.

I cupped her gorgeous face, sliding my thumb around her stretched lips. Nothing had ever felt this good. Everything we did together was the best I'd ever had. Fuck knows how I'd resisted biting her, marking her, mating her, like I was desperate to.

"Fuck," I groaned when she cupped my balls and massaged. Her other hand moved between her thighs, rubbing her clit, getting off on sucking me. The sigil she'd inked on my cock close to her lips but not making it into her mouth. "You close, baby?"

She whimpered and nodded. Her eyes were wide, and as she stared up at me, I hated that I still saw the distance there, the disconnect, but I did. She wanted me, got hot for me, she *cared* about me, but when her lids fluttered, closing for several seconds, then opened again, I got hit with a sadness in those green eyes, fuck, an apology. Because she knew exactly what I saw, what I searched for every time her eyes met mine.

I didn't want that from her. Shit, I couldn't look into her eyes and see that. I fucking hated it. I didn't want pity, never from her. I shifted, about to pull out. I didn't want it like this.

But then she swirled her tongue around the head of my cock and sucked it down deep with another whimper. I wasn't prepared, and the needy sound sent me over the edge. She knew I was about to come, and like the other times she'd taken me in her mouth this week, she gripped my hips and didn't let me retreat, letting me come down her throat.

Panting, I pulled out of her mouth, hooked her under the arms, and pressed her against the wall. Swiping her hand from between her legs, I thrust two fingers inside her. "If I see pity in your eyes when we're getting each other off again, butterfly, I'm gonna spank your sexy ass until it's bright red."

At my growled words, she cried out, coming hard for me. Her hips rocked against my fingers until she was done, then she fell against me, wrapping her arms around my shoulders. I held her up, kissing the top of her head, then straightened and tilted her head back so I could kiss her swollen, sweet-as-fuck lips. "You hear what I said? Don't want you thinking about anything but how good you feel when we're together. That's it, nothing else."

She wrapped her arms tighter around me, her head to my chest. "I wasn't thinking about anything else." She was lying. She might not be able to feel the mating bond between us, but I did. Yeah, it was muted because of the block, but what she was feeling still flowed to me.

"I love you," I said. I couldn't hold it in, it had to come out.

I'd said it every day, and I'd keep saying it. One day soon, she'd say it back. I believed that. I had to believe that. Then I squeezed her ass and swatted it, making her laugh, taking the tension away when the seconds stretched out and I knew today wouldn't be that day.

I'd asked her again who fucked with her mind, but she wouldn't tell me who blocked her love for me, like she knew that as soon as she did, I'd go after them and tear them apart. I'd make them fix it even if they died trying. She was right. No one should be able to fuck with people's emotions that way, even if she had asked for it.

We got out of the shower and I hooked a towel around my hips and grabbed the other before Jaz could so I could dry her off. We may not be officially mated, but my fox didn't care. We needed to take care of her. Bathe her, feed her, protect her, and make her come as many times as she could handle, and today when she left for work, we'd make sure our den was perfect for her as well. We'd make sure my room was completely different, that she was the only female to see what was in it, touched the things in it—new paint on the walls, new bed, new bedding. New bedside tables and two new dressers were arriving this afternoon as well, one for Jaz. And I was going to put the bed on the opposite wall so the room looked nothing like it did now.

"So you'll be gone all day?" I asked as I rubbed the towel over her shoulders and arms. My gaze slid to her mouth. God, her mouth was addictive. I wanted to kiss her all the fucking time.

"Yeah, I have a busy schedule. A couple new clients as well, and things always take longer with newbies." A smile curled her lips. "You know I can dry myself."

"Where's the fun in that?" Jesus, I wanted her again. I wrestled my need into submission. It wasn't easy.

I finished drying her, which was more torture for me than her because everywhere I trailed the towel, I wanted to taste her skin afterward. She smelled different now. My scent was all over her, and both my fox and I loved that as well. It filled me with pride, made me feel fucking ten feet tall

She headed to the small room we'd been sleeping in, and I followed, pulling on a pair of jeans, then hovered at the door, watching her dress. "You want anything in particular for dinner?" I asked, eating up every smooth, inked inch of her.

She glanced up at me. "Mags wants to hang out. Have a girls' night, so I'll stay at home tonight."

I gripped the doorframe tighter, and my claws punched through the tips of my fingers. "Will I see you tomorrow?"

She seemed distracted and nodded absently as she tugged on her boots, then proceeded to gather all her things that had accumulated over the last week, stuffing them in her bag so there'd be nothing left of her except her scent. I didn't like it. My fox clawed at the ground, growling his displeasure, but there was nothing I could do. If I pushed her, she'd retreat. She was already scared she'd hurt me, that if this didn't work, she'd have to leave and it'd fuck me up. She was right, of course, but I couldn't let her know that.

We'd had a healing session last night, and I knew she'd seen how big my feelings were for her. She hadn't said anything, but she'd been quiet afterward, at least until I'd tugged her ass to the edge of the couch, yanked down her panties, and ate her pussy until she screamed out my name.

Some might call what I did avoidance, but they'd be wrong. I just didn't want her getting in her own head about us.

She hitched her bag over her shoulder, and the little comma butterfly that'd been hanging around her lately fluttered around her head as she tilted it back to look up at me. "I better take off."

I nodded as I gripped the side of her neck and used my thumb under her chin to keep her head tilted back, then I bent down and kissed her, hard and deep, before hooking her around the waist and holding her close so her body was pressed to mine, branding her with my scent as best as I could. While she was away from me, I wanted everyone to know she was taken. I couldn't mate her, so this was the next best thing.

I lifted my head a little and gave her another small kiss, then another, then forced myself to step back when what I wanted to do was toss her on the foldout and fuck her over and over again until she loved me back.

Her face was pink and her lips were puffy again. "Fuck," I said low.

"What?" She licked her lips.

I groaned. "I'm two seconds away from tossing you back on the bed, butterfly."

She grinned, pressed a kiss to my bare chest, patted it, then stepped around me. I followed her to the door, trailing her like a sad fucking pup. She opened the door and looked back at me.

Her smile softened. "You know...you're the best male I've ever known," she said.

I didn't know what to say. There was this look in her eyes I couldn't read.

"I just...I wanted you to know that," she added, then she flashed me another smile and walked out, closing the door behind her.

›››●‹‹‹

Jasmine

I stared up at the house, so tall and forbidding. The look on Ren's face, the tone of his voice when he told me he loved me again this morning and I couldn't return the sentiment was branded on my mind. I was hurting him, and I couldn't do it anymore.

I took the steps and knocked, wrapping my arms around myself, feeling chilled even though it was warm today.

The door swung open. "Hey," I said, like an idiot, not entirely sure of the reception I'd get.

Xavier tilted his head to the side. "This is an unexpected surprise."

"Sorry to just show up at your door like this." I hadn't fully decided I was going to come here until I walked out of Ren's place this morning. But despite what Xavier said, that this couldn't be undone, I had to try. He was my only hope.

543

"Do you want to come in?"

"Please."

He stepped back, and I walked inside.

He motioned to the living room, and we took our seats. Sitting back, he crossed his legs and sighed, a look on his face that said he was far from happy. "I assume this isn't a social call?"

I'd offended him when I turned him down, obviously. "About what happened between us. It wasn't you—"

"No, then what was it?" he asked, and his voice was colder than I'd ever heard it. "You're just not a fan of money and power? You don't like presents or being treated like a princess? Or being flown all around the world? I could have given you anything you wanted, Jasmine. Anything."

This whole arrogant routine was new. "I'm sorry if I hurt you—"

"You didn't hurt me. You wasted my time." He tapped the arm of his chair impatiently. "And now you're here wanting something else from me, yes?"

I shifted in my seat, guilt filling me. "I'll pay you whatever you want."

"And what is it you want, little witch?" He sat forward, eyes narrowed. "What made you come here this morning, reeking of another male, an animal no less, mouth still swollen from...well, it's not hard to guess. What made you think you could walk in here and ask anything of me after you led me on, then brushed me aside like nothing?"

I didn't want to be here. Everything inside me was telling me to get the hell out of this house, but he was the only person who could help me, if it was even possible at all. He said it wasn't, that he couldn't reverse what he did, but I had to try. "I really do like you, Xavier. There just wasn't...a spark between us, you have to know that. You had to feel that as well. And I...I think I know the reason for that. Ren, the male I came to you about, well, it turns out, he's my mate, and what I did...it was a terrible mistake."

"The fates may have selected you for him, but that doesn't mean their choice was correct."

"It was, Xavier, I know it was the right choice. I need to know, is it possible...if I spend time with him, if I try to strengthen the bond between us, can I fall in love with him again?"

"That's what you've been doing? Why you smell of him?"

"Yes." I didn't like the way he was looking at me. He looked angry.

"No," he said without flinching. "Even if you mated with him, let him mark you, nothing would change. You can like him very much." His brow arched. "You can lust after him, but I think you worked that out for yourself. But no, there can never be love, not for him."

Oh goddess. "There has to be a way to reverse this. Please, Xavier. Please, there has to be something you can do—"

"I've always believed people should stick to their convictions." His gaze slid away, his jaw pulsing like he was grinding his teeth. "I told you what would happen. I told you it would never be undone, and now you're here begging me to undo it." His face was stone, but something had shifted in his eyes. "You disappoint me, Jasmine. I thought you were different than the rest. I thought you were a female of your word. But you're just like all the others, like her, aren't you?"

Would never be undone. He didn't say *couldn't.* Not this time. "Who are you talking about? I'm like who?"

He stood suddenly and paced away. "You truly want the barriers removed, despite all the pain your love for this male caused you?" he said, his back to me.

"Yes."

He paused. His hands were balled into fists, his knuckles white under the strain. "Is love truly worth it, the risk of all that pain, do you think?"

"Yes, absolutely. I didn't think he could ever love me back, but I was wrong. When it's real, Xavier, when it's returned, there's nothing else like it," I said, ready to fall at his feet and beg him to help me. "Is there anything you can do? Anything?"

"When your sister and Ronan found each other...I was surprised," he said, ignoring my question. "A male such as me with a female, not to just sate a base need but because he held affection for her. Because he...loved her." He shook his head. "I didn't think it was possible. Not after all he'd been through. If he can find that, then a male like me, a male capable of those kinds of emotions should be able to as well, shouldn't he?"

"Yes." I stood and moved closer to him. "I absolutely believe there is someone out there for all of us, Xavier."

His gaze sharpened, filling with a determination that had me taking a step back. "Doing what I'm about to ask of you is...going against my own convictions. Convictions I've lived by for almost all of my life, but I've been contemplating it for some time. Then I met you and began thinking more seriously about it, about what my life would be if only I'd allow myself to truly experience it. To move forward, though, I need someone like you to help me. If I do as you ask, you will do something for me?"

"You can do it? You can remove the barrier?" Hope fired through me.

His lavender eyes were so dark now they looked black. "Not easily, and at a great cost to me. Are you willing to pay a great cost in return?"

"What do you want me to do?" I'd do anything to be with Ren, to give him all of me. I was desperate. This week with him had been one of the best of my life, but every day he told me he loved me was like a slice to my soul. I was hurting him, not being able to give him that in return, and it was killing me.

"I have walls of my own. Walls I built as a child, some to protect myself." His gaze hardened. "Some my mother forced me to build. They limit me, restrict me. They stop me from being the male I was born to be, from finding the happiness I find I now crave. Whether that's a female of my own, or something else entirely, I'll never know if I stay as I am. I want the walls gone, but to break them would be dangerous, without help." He stared me down. "Which is where you come in. I need you to use your healing abilities on me to repair the damage done by..." His jaw pulsed. "By my mother, and the wounds breaking the walls down would leave, and in return, I'll remove the walls I built for you."

There was no need to think about it. I wanted that part of me back. I wanted my love for Ren back. "I'll do it. I'll help you."

"How long will it take? To get me through the worst of it?" he asked.

"I won't know until I see the damage," I said, not willing to give him any time frames. Depending on what he had locked away, it could take months of coming here to work with him. "It could take some time."

He took several steps closer. "Can we speed up the process with more intensive, more frequent sessions."

"It's possible, but I wouldn't advise it. That kind of healing shouldn't be rushed—"

"But it can be done?"

"Well...yes. I suppose."

He cupped the side of my face, and when I tried to jerk back, his other hand shot up and grabbed the other side of my head, holding it firmly between his hands.

I tried to pull away again. "What are you doing?"

"Ensuring you don't renege on our deal. You will stay here until it's done."

"No...I can't do that." I tried to pull away again, to fight him off, but he wouldn't let me go. Pain burst through my head, and it felt as if my entire body was thrust to the side.

"Yes, you will."

Everything went dark.

CHAPTER 30

Ren

I DRAGGED the old mattress from my bedroom and carried it outside, then hitched the new one up from the back of the hearse and carried it inside and to my room.

The paint was dry. I'd had a fan heater blowing in here all night. The blue walls had been replaced with a deep sage-green color, the closest I could find to Jasmine's eyes. I loved it. Tearing off the plastic, I tossed the mattress on the bed frame I'd pushed to the opposite wall, and the two new dressers I'd ordered had arrived earlier. I'd put one where the bed used to be and the other by the door. I'd also grabbed some new curtains from the store. I didn't know about that kind of shit, but the gray ones the shop assistant told me to get looked pretty good.

The dryer beeped; the new sheets and duvet cover were dry. They'd smelled too chemically straight out of the bag, and my fox hadn't liked it. I didn't know what time Jaz was coming over, but I wanted everything perfect when she did. I wanted her to walk in here and feel like she'd stepped into a brand-new room. Ours. No trace of anyone else. Honestly, I couldn't even remember anyone else. Those drunk nights, burying my pain in whoever wanted me, had dissolved into nothing, into a bad dream long forgotten, replaced by Jasmine.

I grabbed all the trash from the new bedding and scooped up the mattress plastic from the hall, then carried them out to the dumpster. After one final look around the room to make sure everything was perfect, I got started on dinner. I'd been without her an entire night and never wanted to spend another one away from her again. Jaz never said she'd be here in time to eat, but I liked feeding her. She always seemed to get hungry around midnight as well, usually after I'd made her come and she'd napped for a little while. She'd get up and stand in front of the fridge in one of my shirts and pick at whatever she could find. I fucking loved watching her eat before she came back to bed, then fell asleep, sated and full. It eased my fox and me both.

I had a chicken in the oven and was chopping tomatoes for the salad when my phone beeped. Wiping my hands, I grabbed it from my pocket.

Jaz. My stomach instantly tightened, my heart fucking swelling in my chest. How the fuck had I not seen exactly who she was the minute I laid eyes on her? It felt impossible that I hadn't known.

I quickly tapped the message open.

Butterfly: I'm sorry, Ren, but this thing between us just isn't working out. I'm leaving. It's the best for both of us. You'll see. Please don't come looking for me.

I blinked down at those words, scanning them over and over again, as if they'd reshape and reform into something else. But they didn't. *This thing between us just isn't working out.* I read it again, and again, trying to get it to make sense, because everything inside me said it didn't.

But it was right there. She'd typed out the words, her nails tapping against the screen like they did when she sent a text. Nails that had scored my skin, fingers that had glided over my body, thrust into my hair and held me to her as if she were afraid I'd pull away.

I thought about yesterday morning, the way she'd looked up at me in the shower. The look in her eyes that had been a blade in the chest, that distance, that look of pity. Affection, not love.

I grabbed the edge of the counter when my legs fucking buckled beneath me.

Jaz had left.

She was gone.

Still, I sprinted from the house and out onto the street and didn't stop until I ran into the house and up to her bedroom. I shoved open drawers. Her stuff, it was still there. It was all still there. I fisted my hair. What the fuck was going on?

"Ren?" Mags stood at the door, sympathy in her eyes. "She messaged you?"

"This doesn't make sense, all her stuff—"

"She asked me to pack everything up, that she'd come for it sometime soon."

"When?"

She shook her head. "She didn't say. I'm sorry...goddess, Ren, I'm so fucking sorry."

The door opened and Willow walked in. Violet was asleep in her car seat, and she handed the seat and Violet to Mags, then strode toward me. I stumbled back. I couldn't do it. Willow was my witch, my best friend, I was her familiar, but I couldn't do this. If I let her comfort me, if I let this pain inside me take hold, I'd fucking shatter all over again—and this time there would be no coming back from it.

Willow stopped and held up her hands as if she were trying to soothe a wild animal about to bolt, and I realized my claws had punched through the ends of my fingers, that my canines were extended, and with every one of my panted breaths, my fox's growls resonated through my chest so loudly I wasn't sure I could speak, even if I had the words.

"Jaz just needs some time. Give her some time. You two have been pushing things pretty hard this week. She's just spooked, that's all," Willow said and took another step closer. "The bond between mates is stronger than anything. Block or not, she'll come back. I know she will."

Willow was wrong. Whoever it was who created the block inside her, had a power stronger than the mating bond. My mate fleeing from me and asking me not to look for her was proof of that.

Fur sprouted across my chest and stomach, my thighs. My fox was taking over. The last time he managed to do that was after Edward's evil spirit was exorcised from my body and the knowledge of what I'd done had been too much.

My fox dulled the pain. He didn't understand complex emotions and was all about instinct. He was the reason I'd survived as long as I had without Jasmine's healing touch.

He snarled and exploded forward, taking over my body and making it his, and I surrendered to it, letting him.

"Ren!" Willow called.

But we were already at the bottom of the stairs and out the door, flying along the street toward the forest.

You are the best male I've ever known. I just...I wanted you to know that.

She'd said those words to me before she left yesterday, and I'd been too stupid to realize she was saying goodbye.

›››●‹‹‹

Jasmine

549

. . .

My head throbbed as I blinked into the darkness. Where the hell was I?

The last thing I remembered was talking to Xavier.

He'd grabbed me, held my head, then everything went dark—

I quickly sat up. I was still in his house. Still in the living room where I'd been talking to him. There was no sign of Xavier now, and dim light filtered in through the large windows, the night filled with stars. Had he taken the walls down in my mind, is that why I'd passed out? But I didn't feel any different. I stumbled to my feet and walked out of the room. The lights were on in the foyer. I looked at the clock on the side table. It was after ten. Ren would be worried. He'd be wondering where I was.

I rushed to the door, every instinct in me screaming to get the hell away from here as fast as I could. I gripped the door handle and yanked the door open—

A scream tore from me, and I stumbled back.

Nothing.

I was looking out at nothing.

No stairs, no path, no houses. No street. There was only darkness.

Nothingness.

"I wouldn't walk out there if I were you. You might never make it back."

I spun around. Xavier was walking toward me. He looked wrong, as if I were looking at him through heat waves on a hot summer day. He kept coming, then stepped through the strange distorted-looking air, stopping in front of me.

"What the hell is this?" I said, backing away from him, putting more space between us.

He slid his hands in his pockets. "You're in my world now, Jasmine. And in my world, no one can see or hear you, and you can't leave it unless I allow it. This is where you'll remain until you finish the work you're here to do."

"What the hell are you talking about?"

"I told you when you first came to see me that I wasn't an explorer of realms, that I preferred it here. Well, I created my own realm. It's exactly like my home in every way, except no one can ever find it."

Ronan could create alternate realms—their home was in one—and apparently so could Xavier. "You don't need to keep me here. I promise I'll help you. I'll come back as many times as you need. I will. But I can't stay here. I have people who love me. My family"—*Ren*—"will be worried about me. They'll come looking for me."

He stared at me, his eyes terrifying in their utter lack of empathy. "They won't find you. No one can until I choose it."

"What about Ronan?"

"Why would he ever come looking for you here? Ronan thinks that when he developed his emotions, he became like me. He thinks my emotions have always been as developed as his now are. He also sees me as a friend. He'd never think I could do anything like this."

His words slid over me like ice. "*Thinks* you've developed emotions?"

"I'm good at imitating them. Although I'm not completely without them. I was, after all, raised by my human mother. I'm definitely not a victim of my specie's defect, losing them completely through maternal abandonment. No, my lack of emotion is due to my own actions. I omitted the extent of the blocks I've created in my mind, which is why letting you leave isn't an option. If we start and you decide not to come back, there is a chance I could lose my mind all together."

"I wouldn't do that."

"I can't risk it," he said simply and without sympathy. "We'll begin in the morning." Then he strode away through the quivering wall between realms, leaving me there and ignoring my screams to let me out.

CHAPTER 31

Ren

MY APARTMENT FELT COLD.

I quickly chugged back my coffee and dumped the mug in the sink. I'd only been gone a couple days, but it felt as if all traces of life in this place had faded to nothing. I got back from Philly late last night, but it'd been a fucking waste of time. I thought she might have gone home. She and Zinnia still owned a house there, but Jaz hadn't been back, and none of her friends there had seen or heard from her.

Shoving my feet in my boots, I grabbed my keys and walked out, got in the hearse and headed down to Daisy's, parked and walked into the house. Everyone was already here, and they'd all been searching for Jasmine frantically.

Iris looked up when I walked in, her familiar, Nia, at her side. "You look exhausted."

I didn't need sleep, couldn't sleep, not until Jasmine was home. "Any news?"

She shook her head.

Warrick leaned against the wall, Draven and Ronan there as well. Bram stood behind Mags.

"Nothing," Rose said. "None of us have heard from her since she asked us not to contact her for a while."

The last two weeks, I'd called and texted her repeatedly, and she hadn't picked up or replied, not once, which I guess should be expected if she was trying to get away from me, but then why had she asked her cousins to give her space? For the first few days she'd written them back, even if her replies had been stilted and distant. But for the last week there'd been no word from her at all. Wanting space or not, that wasn't Jasmine. She put others first, always.

I shook my head. "No, fuck this, she wouldn't do that shit, not to any of you."

I'd tried to trace her phone and so had Bram's brother, the male was good with that kind of thing, but not even he could find her.

She'd vanished completely.

"Zinnia's due back in less than a week," Mags said. "She wouldn't miss that, she'd be here."

Jasmine always spent the days before organizing something for her sister—a party, a girls' night...fucking something—then she'd wait for her to walk out of the forest. She wouldn't miss that. The fact she wasn't here now, planning her sister's homecoming, said more to me than anything else could. No matter what she thought about me, she wouldn't ignore everyone else, and she wouldn't miss the opportunity to make a fuss over her sister coming home.

Iris stiffened. "You think something else is going on?"

"None of this feels right," Rose said, her face going pale. "But I just assumed..." Her gaze slid to me.

They'd all thought the same thing, that she was staying the hell away from me, that she needed time to herself to heal.

"No, you're right. This isn't about her needing space, she wouldn't let us worry like this. Something's seriously wrong," Mags said. "I think someone or something is stopping her from contacting us."

Daisy grabbed Art's hand. "Who would do that?

"Fuck." Willow stood. "And she definitely said nothing during your sessions, anything, some kind of clue of where she could be?"

I shoved my fingers through my hair. "If she had, I would've said."

"Shit, I know," she said, her hands shaking. "I'm just...fuck."

I glanced at Mags. She nodded. They needed to know everything.

"There's something you don't know," Mags said. "She wasn't just looking for those missing souls because she wanted to help Zinny, she was searching because when they were at Limbo's gate, Death demanded Jasmine find them, he said if she didn't, there was a risk Zinnia could be stuck there."

"Goddamn it," Else said.

"She knew there was nothing anyone else could do, so she kept it to herself. Only me, Bram, and Ren knew about it. We did what we could to help."

"While she was looking, she talked to some powerful people," I said. "And I just have this feeling..."

"You think someone she talked to did something?" Willow said, the horror in her voice, on her face, almost sending me over the edge.

"I don't know." I didn't know fucking anything and I was on the verge of losing my fucking mind. The mating bond, the connection between us had been growing and strengthening by the day when she'd been here, but now? "She's still alive, I feel it, but it's...the connection's muted." Similar to the last time she passed out, but so fucking faint now it terrified me. I clung to it, like I had that night in her bedroom. It was my lifeline, because if I could still feel it, no matter how faint, it meant she was still alive. She was still breathing—she was still with me.

Bram nodded, the other males in the room nodded, grunted, obviously knowing what I was describing from having mates of their own. It didn't matter that we weren't officially mated, I'd spent enough time with her, holding her, kissing her, inside her, that we were connected on a deeper level.

"Family's everything to her," Daisy said, lips quivering. "She wouldn't just leave...oh goddess."

No, she wouldn't; not even to escape me. If she could come home, she would have, I was positive of that.

"We're still hunting for her," Warrick said. "And we won't stop until she's home."

The hounds were born trackers, with abilities that went beyond using scent to find their target, and so far, they'd had no luck either.

"I know we assumed she was concealing herself, but I think wherever she is, there's some kind of power masking her," Willow said.

"I think you're right," Mags said and stood. "Me and Bram will head to Agatheena's. She might be able to help us."

The witch boasted that she knew everything; I only hoped she felt compelled to prove it, because Jasmine was in trouble. I knew it down to my bones.

"We need to widen our search," Iris said.

Draven nodded. "I'll get the pack to search the forest. If she's in there, we'll find her."

"And I'm gonna hunt down every person she's been in contact with over the last couple of weeks," I said.

"Everyone keep in contact," Willow said.

I nodded and walked out.

I would find her. I would bring her home.

·)))·●·(((·

I stared down the street at the massive brownstone. My second stop. Zara Harris, the female Jaz and Rome had met with, assured me she hadn't seen Jasmine since the day they stopped by her place. She seemed believable enough, but I didn't trust anyone.

I'd spent the last two days going through Jasmine's client list from the last couple weeks. It was easy enough for Talon to hack her online booking system. I'd tracked every one of them down, but no one had set off any major alarm bells.

I focused back on the house. I'd been here for several hours now, watching. I'd met Xavier several times. We'd briefly spoken, once at Ronan's place, but other than that, I knew nothing about the dhampir—except, of course, that the fucker had been interested in Jasmine and had taken her out on a date. That he'd kissed her. The steering wheel groaned as I gripped it tighter. I didn't know much about Xavier's powers, so I'd called Ronan to get any info he had on the male. He said Xavier was private, he'd never told Ronan what he could do, but it was known in their circles that he could travel through metaphysical planes, but Ronan wasn't sure if he could create his own. Ronan and his sister, Luna, were both extremely powerful. Ronan could block entire streets, could create entire realms that existed inside another, and could move around completely undetected, which meant, Xavier could be capable of fucking anything. He also ran a business from his home, but Ronan didn't know what that business entailed, again, because the male was private.

I scanned the front windows. I didn't fucking trust him, and not just because he wanted Jasmine. I just, I didn't like the guy.

A female rushed along the street, and I sat up straighter when she took the stairs to Xavier's front door and knocked. She seemed jittery, nervous, her hands shaking. When no one answered the door, she checked her watch, then knocked again, harder this time.

It was coming up nightfall, and there were lights on in a couple of the front rooms. I'd assumed he was home.

Her shoulders slumped when there was still no answer. She turned, about to leave when the door was wrenched open. Xavier stood there, rumpled, a harried look on his face.

I couldn't hear what they were saying, but the female looked upset. Finally, he shook his head, and shut the door. She covered her face with her hands, shoulders jolting with her sobs.

Grabbing a small pack of travel tissues from the glovebox, I shoved the car door open and jogged along the street and through Xavier's front gate.

The female looked up and sniffed. "If you're here for an appointment, don't bother, he just cancelled mine."

I held out the tissues. "Are you okay?"

"No." She took the one and used it to dab at her eyes. "I was really hoping to get this over with today."

"Yeah, me too," I lied. "I can't believe he's cancelled."

Fresh tears slid down her cheeks. "God, I'm a mess. Do you have a broken heart as well?" She flushed and bit her lip. "Sorry, I shouldn't have asked that."

I stilled. "No, it's fine. And yeah...I do." I forced myself to appear calm, instead of grabbing her and demanding to know what the fuck she was talking about. "So do you know how it works?"

She shook her head. "Not really. I found out about him through a friend of a friend. I just know it works. I never knew blocking someone's emotions was possible." Her face fell. "God, I just want it over with, you know?"

I nodded, my heart fucking racing.

Blocking emotions.

"Anyway, thanks for the tissue," she said and scurried past, heading down the street.

My fingers curled into fists. It was Xavier. He was the one who'd locked away Jasmine's love for me, who'd fucked with her mind.

I took the stairs and banged on the door, fighting down my rage. When Xavier didn't answer straightaway, I banged again, harder.

The door was yanked open when I pounded on it a third time and the male filled the doorway, the scent of lemon floor cleaner and bleach drifting out behind him, as if he'd doused the place in that shit. His gaze hit me, and something shifted through his deep lavender eyes. "What do you want?"

My fox's hackles lifted instantly. We really didn't fucking like this male. I wanted to barrel past him, to barge into his house and call for Jasmine. I wrestled my anger and fear down. "You're a friend of Ronan's. I'm Ren, his sister in-law's familiar." I held his gaze, not letting him look away from me. "Their cousin Jasmine's my mate."

He blinked several times, rapidly, but otherwise didn't move, didn't react. "Okay," he said. "And I will repeat. What do you want?"

"Can I come in?"

"No. Say what you're here for, then leave. I'm busy."

I wanted to grab him by the throat and fling him aside. "You know Jasmine."

"Yes, I do." His head tilted to the side. "We dated."

"You had one date, and then she realized she just wasn't that into you...

since she already had a mate, something she didn't recognize because you'd locked away her ability to feel it."

"I blocked the pain your rejection and neglect caused, at her request," he said.

"And then you swooped in and tried to take her for yourself."

"Is that why you're here? To stake some kind of claim? Because you're wasting your time. Jasmine turned me down when I asked her out again. Jealousy is unnecessary."

I wanted to plow my fist into the asshole's smug face. "The reason I'm here is because she's missing, and she hasn't answered any of my calls or texts."

"Unsurprising, since she feels nothing for you."

It took all my strength not to stagger back a step. I ignored his verbal strike. "Are you sure you haven't seen her?"

"Are you suggesting I've somehow lost all cognitive recognition?"

"No, I'm suggesting that you're hiding or withholding something from me for some reason, and I strongly suggest that if you have seen or heard from my mate, you tell me right the fuck now."

"I assure you, I have not. And if I had, the decision to contact you or anyone, for that matter, would entirely be hers."

Then he shut the door in my face.

Every instinct in me roared to get inside, that he was hiding something. I felt for the buzz of magic, something I was more than familiar with, but there was nothing, and no wards either. I'd seen a human security system, though, a panel inside by the door, an alarm. I strode back to the hearse and got in.

Then I pulled my phone from my pocket and hit Willow's number.

"Any news?" she said before I could say a word.

Wills had been struggling with Jaz's disappearance, all her family had. But Willow had Violet to think of, and she was limited to how much time or how far she could go searching.

"No news. But I've got this...shit, it's more of a gut feeling than anything else. It's probably nothing, but I...I can't seem to let it go..."

"Jasmine's your mate. Your instincts are invaluable. Listen to them. Do you need me to come to you?"

"No, I'm on my way to you now. I need your help with something."

"I'll be waiting."

I disconnected and started the hearse. I just needed to pick something up from Willow, then I was coming straight back.

Xavier had to leave sometime.

›››●‹‹‹

Jasmine

The door to the basement room opened again and Xavier walked back in, the strain of our session today was still etched on his face.

"Who was at the door?" He'd left me in this room several hours ago. I was just thankful he'd kept me here in the "real world" for a little while instead of his metaphysical, monstrous one. He'd showered and changed, but that was the only difference I saw in him since he left to see who was banging on the door.

"A couple clients. I sent them away. Let's get back to work."

I didn't want to. I didn't want to delve into Xavier's pain again, not yet. It was too much, too awful, but when the session was over for the day, he'd put me back where no one could see or hear me—and where monsters hid in dark hallways.

The small comma butterfly fluttered over to me now and landed on my shoulder, offering me comfort. The little guy had tracked me here before Xavier trapped me in this house, and somehow he found me. I'd been feeding him water and overripe fruit from the food Xavier had given me.

"Ready?" Xavier said.

There was real fear in his eyes. "Yes." He was seriously struggling but determined to do this no matter the cost to him, or me.

The first barrier he dropped was two weeks ago, during our first session. It had been intense, to put it mildly. The emotions had been so strong, they'd almost knocked me over.

He obviously needed time to recover, but he insisted on doing this as fast as possible. I wanted this over as well, so I could go home to my family, to Zinnia who would be home in a matter of days—to Ren. But that meant my magic was almost constantly drained, leaving me weak, and fucking defenseless.

Xavier was a desperate male, emotionally unstable, confused and conflicted, and right now he was capable of anything.

I wrapped my arms around his waist and had to stop myself from shuddering. I didn't want to touch him, be near him—I didn't want to be anywhere near what was inside this male. Something lurked deep, something that sent ice down my spine, and I'd been getting closer to it with every wall he dropped.

But I had no choice, so I poured my powers into him. It flowed through every part of him, seeking out the biggest wounds. Xavier had lived in this house all his life, and he'd compartmentalized his emotions like an internal replica of his home. He'd locked unwanted emotional responses in different "rooms" of his mental house. There were blind spots and rooms I couldn't even get close to, and behind those thick barriers, Xavier was still the little boy he'd been when he'd built them. So vulnerable, so scared, and so incredibly sad.

Within moments, I was shaking. The emotions of the little boy were agonizing, and tears immediately sprang to my eyes. "Do it," I rasped.

He shuddered a moment before his arms wrapped around me, and he dropped the walls, exposing another emotional wound.

I whimpered and held him tighter. "You're a good boy, Xavier. Y-you did nothing wrong. You didn't deserve to be punished."

He gasped, and his arms tightened around me, so tight it was painful.

"You didn't deserve it," I said again.

He made an inhuman sound, like a wounded animal, and I braced. His nails elongated, digging into my sides through my shirt, making me cry out.

Another wall dropped.

Oh goddess. It was bad. I thought I'd find abuse or neglect, but what I found was something else entirely.

A longing for blood, for death, a need to hurt and torture, flooded me. Pushing back against my powers was the desire to kill, so strong inside him, it was like riding a raging tide.

This was Xavier. This was his true self. Evil in its purest form flowed from him into me. I cried out again, trying desperately to heal the wounds he'd exposed, but terror made it impossible to do what I needed to. This was what his mother had forced him to wall in—the sadistic monster that he truly was—to protect herself and those around him.

He was panting, and the way he hissed, the strange sounds he made, I knew his fangs had extended.

"Yes," he snarled. "Fuck."

I tried to push away, but he held me with inhuman strength. His fangs scraped along my shoulder, tearing the fabric. "No!" I screamed. "Don't...p-please."

A dark chuckle rumbled through him, then he struck. His fangs pushed through the flesh at my throat and agony fired through me. It hurt, oh goddess, it hurt worse than anything I'd ever endured. A dhampir's bite, like a vampire's, could give pleasure or pain. He chose this, he chose pain.

If this was the end, I was glad he chose the latter. I'd take pain over pleasure from this monster every single day if I had to endure it. The last time I experienced pleasure was with Ren, and that's how I wanted it.

He pulled more deeply from my vein, and I tried to scream, but the sounds wouldn't come. My vision blurred and my head spun, my limbs growing heavy and weak.

559

He pulled his fangs from my throat suddenly, his tongue rasping across my flesh. "You want to feel the love you have for your mate again, witch?" He pressed his mouth to my ear. "Then I'll give it to you."

I did. I wanted to feel my love for Ren again, so badly I ached, but the damage the block coming down would create would be vast. I'd seen it in Xavier, and I wasn't strong enough to heal myself, not like this. But I didn't care. If I was going to die, I wanted to do it loving my mate.

"Are you afraid of the pain?" He tilted my head back and stared down at me. My blood smeared his lips. His lavender eyes were black now that he'd fed.

I shook my head.

He brushed my hair away from my face. "Liar. I can hear your heart beating. It hurts, but you can heal yourself, Jasmine. I know you can. I've watched you do it."

He'd watched me?

"You look confused. Let me enlighten you. When I was trying to discover if you could help me, I decided to do an experiment, to see if you could use your gift on yourself. So when you were tucked up in your bed, I went to your favorite field, the one you often go to, the one you told me about on our date, where your tiny familiars live, and I poisoned them."

I whimpered, and a tear streaked down my face. He'd done it. He'd killed them. Even when the walls inside him had been intact, locking the monster in, the evil had seeped out of him.

"You're such a pretty little thing, even more so when you cry. I had planned to free you after you healed me, but now I think not." His head tilted to the side. "I finally know my own mind, Jasmine." He tapped the side of his head. "It's all in here now, just how it was before Mother forced me to lock it away, back again in glorious vivid color, down to the minutest detail." He grinned, flashing his sharp fangs. "And I know exactly what I want to do with you. Should I tell you?"

I wanted to pull away, to shake my head, but I'd lost too much blood, all I could do was lie helpless in his arms.

"I want to make you suffer in every way it's possible to make a being suffer, for no other reason than the pleasure it will give me. I want to feed from you until you are close to death. I want to fuck every hole in your emaciated body, torture you to the edge of death, then bring you back from the brink, and do it all over again."

I managed a pathetic jerk in his arms.

"Are you game, little witch?"

"N-no. Please, please let me go." I knew begging was pointless, he probably enjoyed it, I'd seen inside him, but my will to live didn't give a fuck about common sense.

He made a tutting sound and gripped the sides of my head. "Being trapped here will hurt all the more while you're missing your mate, won't it, Jasmine?"

His power pulsed inside my head, seeking out the walls he'd created, and a moment later—they crashed. An emotional wound tore open inside me, and I screamed.

My body jerked to the side, and he tossed me back into the alternate reality he'd created, still in the same room inside his house—but where no one could ever find me.

CHAPTER 32

Ren

XAVIER JOGGED down the stairs at the front of his house, got in his car, and sped off.

I watched the car until it turned at the end of the street and disappeared from view. The house was dark, no movement coming from inside. He'd turned off all the lights when he left, which I hoped meant he planned on being gone a while or, better yet, all night.

Xavier said he didn't know where Jasmine was, but there was something about him that set my fox off, something inside me that told me I needed to be here. I sure as hell didn't trust that male. Staying tucked in the shadows, I pulled my phone from my pocket and hit Willow's number.

"You there?" she said.

"Yeah, and I've got my opening. Still not feeling any magic. There definitely aren't any wards, just the security system."

"Piece of cake," she said.

Tugging the hood of my sweatshirt up, I ran across the street. I hadn't told Willow the address or whose house I was breaking into because she'd be here in a heartbeat. Yes, she could look after herself, but being her familiar meant her safety was my priority. It didn't matter that she didn't need my protection, that she never really had, but that instinct never went away, and she knew better than to force me to divide my protective instincts between her and Jasmine. If my female was in there, worrying about them both could cause me to make a mistake.

"Cakewalk," I said, my heart beating faster as a surge of anticipation, of urgency filled me.

"Now I want cake," she said.

"When don't you?"

"Good point. You sure the house's empty?"

"It's empty." I'd been watching the place for hours, and no one else had come in or out until now.

"Okay, this is just your straightforward, run-of-the-mill B and E. Don't loiter. Don't fuck around in one room too long. Keep your ears pricked. You need to be scenting constantly—"

"I got this, Wills." Her fear for me was bleeding down the line.

She was quiet a beat. "I know you do."

I rushed up the steps. "I'm at the door," I said low, scanning the street.

"You know what to do," she said.

Yeah, I did. I picked the lock easily, then shut the door behind me. No sounds, no movement greeted me. I quickly got out the vial, popped the cork, poured Willow's blood onto my palm in an X, then hovered it above the security panel. "Ready."

The hum of magic from Wills's blood was instant. She recited the spell, and I repeated it. As soon as I finished, the small red light flashing on the panel died.

"It worked." We'd never tried anything like this. We'd heard of it being done, the witch–familiar connection acting like a kind of conduit. Familiars were often sent in by their witches to do tasks for them, especially animal familiars, since they could go places undetected, but we'd never tried.

She sighed in relief. "Thank fuck. Let me know when you're out."

We disconnected, and I shoved my phone away and walked deeper into the house. If he knew something about Jasmine that he wasn't telling me, I'd find it. My fox's ears were up, listening for any sign of life in the big, old house. I sniffed the air, searching for her scent, but I wasn't getting anything, not under a layer of floor cleaner and bleach. No one used that much of the stuff unless they were trying to mask something—or someone.

I headed for the stairs. I'd start at the top and work my way down.

I wasn't leaving until I'd searched every single room in this house.

›)*⦿(‹‹

Jasmine

. . .

I wrapped my arms around my knees tighter, shivering, my muscles seizing as waves of agony radiated through me. If I didn't die from the emotional wound Xavier had torn open when he released my feelings for Ren, then he'd make me suffer when he came back.

There was no escape from this world he'd created.

In this realm, it was as if I were in his mind. The rooms where he'd locked away the most vulnerable parts of himself in his psyche, where he kept his deepest fears, were locked here as well. He had walls so thick in his mind I couldn't get through, but here, in this realm, those rooms were guarded by monsters, dark shadows with sharp teeth and claws.

I didn't know if he knew they existed. I had to assume he avoided those places here the same way he did in his mind. The house was big enough that he'd never have to go to those rooms, in this realm or the one he occupied.

A creak came from outside the door. I stilled.

Oh goddess, he was back.

I dragged my upper body off the floor and somehow struggled to my feet. The handle rattled, followed by the sound of metal on metal, the handle turning again—the lock clicked.

I stumbled back several steps, fear, adrenaline spiking so high black dots danced across my eyes.

The door swung open and the light flicked on.

Ren.

I ran to him.

›)›●(‹‹

Ren

I walked deeper into the basement room. The walls were covered in bookshelves. Old books by the looks. The guy liked globes, and there was a blackboard with chalk drawings on it. Symbols of some kind. A mat had been rolled back and there was a sigil configuration on the floor.

I stayed clear of whatever that was painted on the floor and pulled out my phone, taking pictures of it and the blackboard. I'd never seen anything like them. I took a few more of the room, then shoved the phone back in my pocket. Striding to the desk, I searched the drawers, then moved to the shelves. There was nothing here. Nothing that would lead me to Jasmine, anyway. Why the fuck was my gut telling me this was where I should be?

The urgency tightened in my chest. "Jasmine?" Her name fell from my lips, desperation making me say it again, louder this time, then again—until I was roaring her name, not caring who the fuck heard me.

›)›●(((

Jasmine

A sob escaped as Ren lost it, calling my name until his voice was raw.

I lifted my hands to his face, but they went right through, like he was a ghost. "I'm here. I'm right here."

He looked straight ahead, looking through me. His chest heaved as he stared unseeing right at me. "Where the fuck are you, butterfly?" he choked. "I need you to come home to me."

With the walls inside me gone, the love I felt for him flowed through me and straight to him. "I'm here!" I cried out again, willing him to see me.

With a curse, he turned away, walking out the door. I ran after him, out into the hall, trying to make him see me, hear me. He shut the door after him, locking it again. His head tilted, and he listened for a moment, the house still utterly silent, then he kept walking. I ran in front of him—and he walked right through me.

"Ren! Look at me." He stood by the security panel, pulling a vial from his pocket. "Please, Ren."

He smeared blood in an X on his hand and lifted it, hovering over the keypad, then muttered a spell. The light above it began flashing again.

"No...no, don't leave. Don't leave me here."

He looked back, looking through me again, then yanked the door open.

"Ren! Don't leave me!"

He walked out and shut the door behind him.

I banged on it with all my strength, but he didn't hear me, he didn't come back. I ran to the window and watched as he tugged up the hood of his sweatshirt and strode away.

My legs gave out. I sat there in a heap on the floor, not sure for how long, staring into the darkness, fighting the monsters in my own mind, the ones telling me that there was no way out, that I should just give up. Fighting the still gaping wound inside me that Xavier had made, too weak to repair it.

No.

Ren would come back. He would. He'd find me. I had to believe that.

I just had to stay alive.

The nudge of a soul reached me. It didn't mean me any harm, but it was persistent.

Pushing myself to my feet, I took off my necklace and cuffs and placed them on a small table. A woman appeared in front of me. She was tall, her dark hair streaked with gray and pulled back in an elegant bun. She was wringing her hands, fear in her eyes.

I knew who she was instantly. "You're Xavier's mother."

She nodded and moved back, waving her hand for me to follow. Not all ghosts could verbally communicate, some could only show me things. I followed her up the stairs to the second floor, to the room at the end of the hall. It was locked. She pointed above it, and I reached up and found the key above the doorframe.

She walked through the door, and I quickly unlocked it and followed.

The room was feminine, adorned with lots of mauve and pink. This was one of the rooms Xavier avoided in his mind, a room he never went to in the real world or here in the one he'd created. I walked deeper into the bedroom and tripped on something. I looked down and bit back my cry. A skull, an old one by the looks. Feeling sick to my stomach, I got down on my knees and looked under the bed. Several bodies, clothing hanging off their bones, were stuffed under it. Xavier's mother nudged me, and I got up and followed her to what had once been her dressing room. It was large, dust- and cobweb-covered clothes hanging off the racks.

And on the floor were more bodies.

So many.

I stepped over the remains of humans and animals. Dead bodies that had been left where they fell to rot, their bones and clothing all that remained of them.

Images flashed through my mind: Xavier's mother showing me what happened here, what Xavier was, what he did. All of it. Everything channeled through me like a horror movie.

I grabbed for the wall, sick to my stomach.

These were Xavier's kills. Before his mother forced him to lock away his sadistic cravings, this was where he brought his victims. It would have been so easy. One moment they would have been in his home, the next, hidden by his power, confused, alone.

Until a little boy with black curly hair and wide lavender eyes found them. A little boy who looked sweet and innocent but was anything but. He'd lead them to this room. His mother's room, a replica of it at least, that he'd created and used as a dumping ground in his own special playground.

More images flashed through my mind; his mother was trying to help me. Showing me where I needed to go.

"Thank you," I said.

He avoided this room, but I wasn't safe in here. There was only one place he wouldn't be able to find me. I had caught a glimpse of it during one of our sessions.

Xavier had a complete blind spot—his conscience—and it'd been walled off so thoroughly in his mind that he had none to speak of, which was why he'd spent most of his life mimicking others and their emotional responses. He hadn't liked the way his mother made him feel when he did bad things, so he'd made sure he didn't feel it anymore. He'd locked it in the attic of his psyche, before he'd even created this secret realm he'd trapped me in. After he'd locked that part of himself away, the true monster he was came to being. Over the years, he seemed to have forgotten about the attic. I doubted he even thought about it at all when he'd created this alternate realm. The biggest risk was that it might not exist here at all, but I had to try.

To get to it, though, I'd have to pass the monsters he had guarding the top floor and the other rooms he kept walled off.

His mother turned toward the door, then back to me, panic in her eyes.

Xavier was home.

The sound of a car door closing outside jolted me into action.

I had two choices: stay here and endure Xavier's torture and hope I survived long enough for Ren to find me, or somehow get past the hall of monsters on the top floor and make it to the attic, if it even existed here at all, and hope Xavier couldn't find me.

The door opened and closed downstairs.

Adrenaline spiked, giving me the surge of strength I needed. Xavier's mother waved toward the door urgently.

"Thank you," I said to her again, then spun away, out of the room, taking the next two flights of stairs as fast and quietly as I could.

I looked up to the fourth-floor landing. The darkness up there was dense, suffocating. My magic might've been all but drained, but I was a witch, a Thornheart, and I sure as hell wasn't weak.

I thought about Zinnia, about Willow, and Mags, about Rose and Iris, and Daisy and Else. All of them warriors in their own way. I may not know how to fight these monsters physically, but I was clever and resourceful.

I rushed back down to the third floor. I didn't have much time. Xavier would be going down to the basement to check on me soon. Flinging doors open, I searched until I found what I needed. Then I rushed back up the stairs.

It was now or never.

When I reached the fourth-floor landing, I held up the candles I'd found in one of the bedrooms and drew on my weakened magic, whispering the spell to light them. Fire flared. The candles were thick, real beeswax, and they cast a decent pool of light around me.

A scuttling sound came from just ahead, followed by claws being dragged along the wood paneling lining the hall. I was still weak, my legs unsteady, something the fear and adrenaline pumping through me wasn't helping. This was a long shot, but in fairy stories, dark equaled bad, and light, good. No, the world wasn't that black and white, but to a child, that was truth, that was why Xavier had monsters protecting the most vulnerable parts of his mind in darkness.

An adult might have created locks, steel walls, or buried them deep underground. But Xavier had been a child when he created the barriers in his mind and this alternate realm in his house—somewhere he could be himself, where he could do the terrible things he craved before his mother found out what he was.

And what was a child scared of? Monsters, under the bed, hiding in the shadows waiting to pounce.

"Jasmine!" Xavier bellowed downstairs.

Fuck.

I took a step forward into the dark hallway, holding one of the candles behind me and one in front, so I was surrounded by a ring of soft light. Oh goddess. I could hear the monsters moving around me, surrounding me. I held the candles higher and stifled my scream.

One of them slithered in front of me, the light from the candle casting shadows on its hideous face. Its pupils blew wide from the light, and it hissed, lifting a bony arm to protect its eyes.

"Get back," I said. "Let me pass."

It didn't move. Jagged teeth filled its wide mouth, its eyes huge in its gaunt face. I could feel another close behind me, could hear it breathing, could smell its sour breath. The one in front of me lifted a dirty claw-tipped finger, arm outstretched. It breached the light around me—

With a shriek and a hiss, he scuttled back.

I was right. Light hurt them, scared them. I took another step forward, chancing a quick look behind me. The others were gathering closer, but stayed back after seeing what happened to their friend. As I advanced, the one in front moved back.

Something swiped at my ankle, slicing flesh, and I bit my lips to stop from crying out.

I needed more light. I lifted one candle high and lowered the second. I could feel blood trickling down my leg. There was another quick swipe on the other side, where the shadows were thicker. I kicked out and made

568

contact with something. It growled and snapped its teeth. I couldn't let go of the candles, and I had to walk carefully. If the flames went out, I was screwed. So far they hadn't figured that part out, and I was praying to the mother that they didn't.

I was close to the end of the hall, where I assumed the attic stairs would be—if there were any at all. The monster in front jerked forward, teeth flashing. I waved my candle at it, and it slithered back out of the light. Something stood against the wall ahead. A ladder. It was misshapen and narrow, but it led up to a manhole in the ceiling.

The monster in front of me slid to the side to escape the light, joining the monsters behind me. I turned so my back was to the ladder. Almost there.

When I finally bumped into the wall, I carefully placed the candles on the floor so the light formed a wide circle around me. "Stay the hell back," I said and gripped the ladder with a hand behind me, stepping onto the first rung backward. It was awkward, but I wasn't giving them my back, not yet.

One of them swiped at me with a snarl, still staying clear of the ring of light. The candle flame wavered perilously. His black, red-rimmed eyes watched it do this, and he waved his massive clawed hand at it again. It disappeared for a moment, then flared back to life.

The monster looked at me, and I was positive it smiled.

Fuck.

He swiped at it again and the flame went out, dousing one side of the ladder in shadow. I spun and scrambled up the narrow rungs, screaming when it was wrenched to the side beneath me. I didn't look down and shoved open the attic door above me. It swung open as the ladder was wrenched from the wall. I grabbed the lip of the opening just in time, dangling and kicking my legs as the monsters below jumped for me, their claws scratching, gouging, their growls and hisses deafening.

With a cry, I dug my toes into the holes left from where the ladder had been attached to the wall and hauled myself up. Then with the last of my strength, I lifted the trapdoor that was lying on the attic floor and slammed it shut after me and shoved the steel bolt across.

Silence filled the room.

I spun around, searching the small space. Dim light came through the only window. I was above the peaked roof at the very top of the house, a tiny little attic room all on its own. It didn't seem to be connected to the rest of the house. I could make out a large wooden trunk against the wall and bed in the corner with an upturned crate beside it. A wooden truck with chipped blue paint sat on top, and there was a stack of papers inside the crate and crayons scattered around it. I grabbed the papers.

Xavier had drawn these when he was a child. His mother had shown me images of him up here. I looked through the pictures, and my stomach turned over. Drawings of death, red crayon spurting from a stick-figure cat's stomach. Decapitated people.

Monsters like the ones in the hall.

I'd been right. They were a creation of his child's mind, then manifested in the realm he'd created. But this room felt different. The hum of Xavier's power was gone. The air didn't move like heat waves rising from scorching sand. If I was right, and he'd blocked this room from his mind completely, then he definitely might not know this attic was here anymore. And if he didn't know it was here, perhaps I'd left his realm? Could this tiny little blind spot in his psyche be safe?

The bolt in the trapdoor rattled, a low growl echoing from below.

Or not.

Fuck.

I rushed across the room to the wooden trunk and heaved and shoved and finally got it on top of the door. I had no idea if that would hold, but it was all I could do.

I straightened and turned.

Then it hit me. There was *light*. It was dim, yes, but light all the same.

I rushed to the window and looked out. No blackness. No nothing. It was still before dawn, but the street, the houses, they were all there, but there was also no getting down from here, not when I was four stories above ground.

I was out of Xavier's prison, but now I was in another one. If I had time to regain my strength and my magic, there was a lot I could do, but flying or telepathy wasn't one of them. "Goddamn it."

Something moved beside me, and I spun around. The comma butterfly had found his way to me. His orange wings fluttered madly. I felt his love, his relief at finding me again. He'd been with me a while now, and he wouldn't have much time left before he needed to find a place to hibernate or he'd grow weak and die. He'd already been with me longer than should be possible. I held out my hand, and he landed on my palm.

"Hello, my little friend. I'm so glad you're here." He may not understand the words, but he understood the feelings that went with them. What I was about to attempt was a long shot, but it was all I had. He'd been with me when I was with Ren; he knew what I felt when I was around him. I thought of Ren now, letting those feelings flow from me—of course what I felt now was so much bigger, so much more, but the vibrations would be the same. "Bring him to me," I said. "Find him." It would take him at least a day to make it home, maybe longer.

His little wings fluttered again, and he lifted off my hand.

"Thank you," I whispered and watched as he flew through a broken

panel in the louvered air vent above the window and disappeared—hopefully, to make the long journey back to Ren.

All I could do now was wait and hope like hell that he understood what
I wanted him to do.

That he had enough fight left in him to get to Ren and bring him to me.

CHAPTER 33

Ren

THE CEMETERY WAS quiet and oppressively dark even though we were only a few hours from dawn.

Willow, Iris, Rose, Mags, Daisy, and Else all stood in a circle. They'd been like that now for most of the night. They were calling on their ancestors, asking for help, for anything that could lead them to Jasmine.

Else was shaking, losing strength. She couldn't do this for much longer, and going by the desperation in their voices as they chanted, and the pain on their faces now, they weren't getting the answers they wanted.

I strode away. If I didn't move, I'd fucking roar, or tear something to pieces. They didn't need to see me like that. I'd caused that family more than enough worry over the years. Jasmine was their family, but she was my mate, and I needed to bring her home.

Another day had passed, though, with no news. The hounds, the wolves, Agatheena, they all had nothing. I burst into a run, needing to burn off the rage, the fear inside that I'd never find her, that she was lost to me forever. She'd put me back together, and whether she wanted me or not, I would bring her back. Somehow, I would find her.

Chest heaving, I stopped and paced back and forth, only realizing in the moment that I'd come to Jaz's field. I dropped my ass under her favorite tree, for no other reason than she'd been here. I pulled out my phone and worked my way through every picture I had of her, and fuck it hurt. I ached for her. Her absence was a crater in my chest. Squeezing the phone tight, I closed my eyes and again prayed to the mother. I wasn't a witch, but if anyone could help, it was her. She didn't answer, of course, she never did.

My breath burst from my lungs when something flowed in the center of my chest.

Jasmine.

What the fuck? I narrowed my focus to where I felt her, where the mating bond pulsed inside me steadily.

It flared again. I didn't fucking move, didn't breathe—

It happened a third time.

I shot to my feet. That feeling, it wasn't muted, not anymore. She was using magic to reach out to me, she had to be. "Fuck. Fuck!" My female needed me, was calling me, I was sure of it, and I had no fucking clue where to look. I paced, my body primed to run, but I had nowhere to go. I made myself breathe. *Think.*

I swiped my phone open again and scrolled through the pictures I'd taken at Xavier's house. That fucking house. There was something about it, something off. My instincts still told me that's where I needed to be. I hadn't looked at the pictures since I got back yesterday. Now I searched each one, enlarging them, studying every inch, looking for something... fucking anything.

I zoomed in on the next one. I'd taken it in the basement room. What the fuck was that?

Something tickled my cheek. I swiped at it and tried to make the image bigger. Was that? There was a shadow, a shadow that looked—

I zoomed in again. The unmistakable outline of a cheek came into focus, a chin, lips. I knew those lips, that chin, I'd run my fingers over that cheek. It was faint, ghostly, like looking at a faded reflection in a pane of glass.

Jasmine.

But not a ghost, because I felt her. She was alive.

Something brushed my cheek again. I tore my gaze from the screen. A small butterfly darted and dived around my face. What the hell? It was dark, butterflies weren't out at night. It fluttered and swooped around me, not stopping. It was the same kind of butterfly that had been with Jasmine the last time I'd seen her. I was sure of it. It was darting away, then coming back, then darting away and coming back, like it...like it wanted me to follow.

My heart pounded harder in my chest. Was this really what I thought it was? Could Jaz have sent one of her little familiars to find me?

The butterfly darted around me again, flying away, then coming back. I held out my hand, and it landed. "I know where we're going." I cradled the butterfly in my hands and ran for my place and the hearse. She was in that fucking house. He was keeping her there and using his powers to hold her prisoner. That had to be it.

I jumped in the hearse, and the butterfly stayed on my hand as I started the engine and roared out onto the street. I needed to keep my cool or I'd wreck the fucking car. *Fucking focus.* I was getting her out of that house, and if I had to kill that fucker to break her free, I'd do it.

If he'd hurt her...

I gripped the steering wheel tighter.

Then I'd draw on all the twisted fucking shit Edward had forced me to do when he'd possessed me. I'd risk it all, even my sanity, and I'd get her back.

I'd make him bleed.

I'd make him scream.

And I wouldn't stop until I had my mate home safe.

The drive to the house felt like an eternity. I had no plan, but I knew I couldn't just storm in there like I wanted to. If I did that, he could vanish with Jasmine. He could take her away, hide her behind another of his blocks, and I'd never find her.

Parking the hearse a block away, I got out, pulled on my hooded sweat-shirt, and followed the little butterfly to the house. Sticking to the shadows, I stood across the street. All the lights were on, and my fox tensed, tilting his head to the side, listening.

Xavier was raging. The butterfly danced around my face, trying to get me to follow. I ducked low and sprinted across the street and down the side of the house. Peering through the window, through the lace curtains into the living room, I spotted him. Xavier's face was red with fury, and he was screaming Jasmine's name. He paced away, then back, then called for her again. His hands and chin were stained with blood. My claws punched through the ends of my fingers, my canines descending.

I told myself she was okay...because she had to be. If she wasn't, he wouldn't be raging like he was.

He couldn't find her. Somewhere, somehow, she was hiding from him in his own house.

I forced myself from the window and let the butterfly guide me. He darted up, flying higher until I lost sight of him in the darkness. *Fuck.* I strained, trying to see. The clouds parted, and light from the nearing dawn cast a dull light across the side of the house. There. He was swooping and swerving, struggling, then he rounded the corner back to the front of the house. I eased around the corner, looking up in time to see him disappear through the vents above a single window at the very top, in the small peaked tower in the middle of the roof.

Something moved behind the window.

A shadow.

Jasmine.

It had to be. She was in there. I knew it with everything in me.

The bond between us bloomed then, so big and bright and beautiful.

I ran around to the side of the house, searching for a way to get up there. I couldn't go inside and risk him trapping me as well, or finding her. These old Victorians usually had a way to escape in case of fire.

Around the back, there was a narrow steel ladder attached to the side of the house above the porch. Jumping, I grabbed the edge of the porch roof and swung up, then walked as quietly as I could across the roof. The ladder was rusted, neglected. I gave it a strong tug and, thankfully, it held. I scrambled up the next three stories as fast and as quietly as I could, not wanting to linger on the old thing.

My fox retreated, not a fan of heights, but he didn't go too far. He was as desperate to get to our female as I was. Everything inside screamed for me to run to her, but I couldn't. I had to balance carefully on the ridge to make my way to the front of the house.

When I finally reached it, I crouched down, gripped the edge of the roof and dropped over the side, planting my feet on the window ledge.

The window opened, and I swung into the room, landing with a thud on the wooden floor. My hand went to my knife as my eyes adjusted to the darkness.

Then I saw her.

Jasmine stood several feet away, staring back at me, eyes wide. "You found me," she rasped, her lips quivering.

Then she ran at me.

⁂

Jasmine

My body collided with Ren. One of his arms locked around my waist, and the other went to the back of my head. He dropped his face to the side of my throat and breathed deep, scenting me, his fox rumbling in his chest when he exhaled.

"Thank fuck," he growled, his muscles trembling.

I fisted his shirt, holding him to me, afraid to let him go, afraid this wasn't real and he wasn't actually here. Tears stung my eyes, then spilled over.

Ren slid his fingers under my chin, tilting my head back. His gaze searched mine, then a shuddering breath fell from between his lips and I knew he saw the truth of what I felt for him shining back. He saw my love for him burning bright.

"Butterfly," he said hoarsely, then his mouth was on mine, kissing me with a hunger and desperation, so sweet and fierce that my heart ached. His big hands held my face, breath puffing from his nose, our lips fused. He dug his fingers into my hair, kissing across my cheek, along my jaw. "You're okay," he rasped. "You're okay, baby." He said it over and over, I knew to reassure himself as much as me. Finally, he lifted his head. "We need to leave."

Taking my hand, he started toward the window. Rain tapped against the roof. I tried to limp after him as another gush of blood trickled down my leg, a cry falling from my lips.

"You're bleeding," he said and crouched beside me before carefully taking my foot in his hands. He hissed as he studied my sliced-up feet and ankles, the gouges along my calves. Fury rolled off him. "Xavier did this?"

I shook my head and motioned to the trapdoor. "No, his monsters."

"Demons? There are demons in this house?"

As if I'd called to them, their roars echoed from below, the trunk lifting an inch off the ground before crashing back down. I jumped, my nerves shot from an entire day and night of listening to them.

Ren pulled his knife free, growling.

"Not demons. Creations of Xavier's mind. They've been here since he was a child. His mother's spirit came to me, she showed me everything. This was where she put him when he did…" I shuddered. "Terrible things. He's a sadistic monster, Ren, and his mother was afraid of him. Eventually, she made him lock away that part of himself. This house, at least the alternate reality he created within it, is exactly how he's compartmentalized his emotions. All the rooms on the top floor are where he's locked away the things he doesn't want to deal with. It's all up here, and up until a couple days ago, so was his bloodlust and desire to inflict pain."

"He released it?"

"Yes. That's why he had me here, to help him heal the wound left when he dropped each internal wall. When I wasn't healing him, he threw me into the realm he'd manifested as a child, a duplicate of his house."

Ren frowned. "But Xavier's raging downstairs looking for you. Why can't he find you up here?"

"Because he locked away all memory of this room and the pain it represented when he was a child. It's a blind spot to him, which is why it doesn't exist within his invisible realm. This room is outside of it, and why you were able to find me."

"Jesus."

"Up until yesterday, when he released his true nature, he hadn't tried to hurt me, but as soon as he let that wall drop, he changed...and I, I knew I had to find a place to hide."

"I'm going to fucking kill him. Right after I get you out of this place." His fingers trembled as he gently cupped the side of my throat. "There's no way you can climb out of here like this, though. And I won't risk carrying you, not while the roof is wet and slippery."

"And the moment we go through there"—I motioned to the trapdoor in the floor—"we're back in Xavier's fucked-up little world with the monsters he created." More roars and growls came from below. "They only exist in his realm. They shouldn't be able to pass through into this one, but I didn't want to risk it. They're afraid of light, it hurts them, but there's nothing up here we can use, and I left my candles at the bottom of the ladder."

His eyes blazed, his chest expanding with his rough breath. "You could've been killed."

"But I wasn't."

He strode to the trapdoor and the trunk on top, about to shove it aside. "Wait here."

I grabbed his arm. "I'm not even sure they can be killed."

He shoved his fingers through his hair. "I want you out of this place right the fuck now." He checked his front pockets, then the back. "My phone. Fuck. In my rush, I left it in the hearse." He looked up at me. "If the only way to get you out of this room is through the house. I'm not leaving you here, not even for a moment. We'll use the daylight to our advantage."

"But if we go through the house, we'll still be stuck back in Xavier's hidden realm."

He flashed me a grin. "Xavier knows you're here somewhere, but he sure as fuck won't be expecting me."

The idea of Ren taking on Xavier terrified me, but I also knew what Ren could do. My pulse raced. "It's almost dawn."

The gold of his eyes glowed in the dim light. "There's just enough time to tend your wounds." He cupped my chin, running his thumb across my lips. "Then I'm getting you out of here and taking you home."

CHAPTER 34

Ren

I scooped Jaz up and carried her to the bed in the corner of the room, crouching down in front of her. Blood still seeped from some of the deep scratches. Her wounds badly needed dressing. What they really needed was one of Else's or Mags's balms, but for now I would do what I could to keep them clean.

I checked my knife strapped to my thigh. The monsters below us were scratching and crashing into the trapdoor, making the trunk jump, desperate to get to Jasmine. And it was only a matter of time before Xavier remembered this place with all the shit he'd done to his head the last two weeks. Jasmine wasn't safe. I reached back and tugged off my shirt, then used my knife to cut it into strips.

"You'll get cold without your shirt," Jaz said, as always worrying about everyone else before herself.

"I'm good, baby. I run hot." I grinned at her, trying to remove the worry from her eyes. "Pretty sure you already know that. Woke up every night you were at my place with these ice blocks you call feet tangled with mine."

Her lips curled up and some pink hit her pale cheeks. "Fine, you got me there."

I carefully wrapped a strip of my shirt around her calf, another around her ankle, then her foot, tucking it under. "Not too tight?" She shook her head and watched as I did the same with the other foot. "That's all I can do for now." And I fucking hated it. Every one of my instincts demanded I get her to safety and have her wounds properly tended, then find her food and feed her. I couldn't do any of those things.

The shadow on her face vanished as the sun finally rose higher, light glinting off her blond hair.

It was time.

·)·)·)·●·(·(·(·

Jasmine

"Stay behind me," Ren said as he gripped the iron ring that would open the trapdoor. "If things go wrong, you run back here and lock yourself in, okay?"

"Okay," I lied, because he needed to hear it.

"You're lying," he said, eyes narrowing, seeing right through me.

I cupped his jaw, leaned in, and kissed his gorgeous lips. "If something goes wrong," I said against them, then lifted my head, "there's no fucking way I'm leaving my mate and running to safety."

His eyes flared, a rumbling sound coming from his chest. "Say it again."

"My mate," I whispered.

His eyes drifted shut for a moment and he breathed deep for several seconds before they opened again. "That's right." He took my chin in his fingers. "Mine." He flashed his teeth. "So how the fuck did I not know how stubborn you are? It's literally a trait of every female in your family."

I grinned. "Thank you."

His gaze went to my mouth, and his eyes darkened. "I will protect you, Jaz, and sometimes you might not like the way I do it, but you're mine, and you come first always, even if me doing what is necessary fucks you off." His gaze dropped to my smiling lips. "And even if you're being cute."

I planted my hands on my hips. "Are you saying you'll make me do what you want?"

"I'm saying, if shit goes wrong, even if I'm bleeding out, I will pick you up and throw you back up here whether you like it or not."

My cousins had shared how possessive mated males could be, and no, he hadn't marked me yet and made it official, but that didn't seem to matter. Going by the arrogant line of Ren's jaw and the steel in his eyes, he wasn't joking. I also knew arguing would only make him more determined. For now, while he was like this, I needed to tell him what he wanted to hear when it came to this stuff and work around it. That sounded better than lie to his face, but he was out of his mind if he thought I'd hide up here while he bled out. "And I'm the stubborn one?"

He grunted.

Yep, he'd gone full cavemen. "We'll cross that bridge if we get to it."

"Jasmine," he growled.

"Fine," I lied.

He growled again and shook his head, because yes, he knew exactly when I was feeding him a bunch of crap. "Stay behind me," he said again and opened the trapdoor.

The snarl of monsters reached us before we saw them, followed by their shrieks and the sounds of them scuttling back as the morning light from the attic flooded the section of hall below us. Ren gripped the lip and swung down, then motioned for me to follow. Snarls echoed around us, the monsters now hiding in the shadows, watching, waiting for an opening, for a chance to get to us.

I did the same as Ren, dropping down, and he caught me, placing me carefully on my feet. I searched for the candles, but they were gone. *Shit.*

Ren spun suddenly and kicked the door closest to us open, more light flooded in from the room, forcing the monsters to retreat and allowing us to move forward. He kicked open door after door, flooding the hall with more and more light. Until we were almost at the end. Ren kicked the last door open, but there wasn't enough light to reach the stairs, and definitely enough distance for the monsters to pounce.

I yanked off my sweater. "Stand back."

"What are you doing?"

"Creating light." I held my sweater out in front of me and whispered the spell to create fire. My sweater ignited, and spinning it like a lasso over my head, I grabbed Ren's arm and made a break for the stairwell. The monsters shrieked and swiped at us but dove for the darkness, pressing themselves into the corner.

As soon as we hit the landing, their growls and howls stopped, and I tossed my burning sweater on the floor.

Ren stomped the fire out. "Nice work." He hooked me around the waist and kissed me. "Now you need to hide, and I'll deal with Xavier."

"If you call for him, he'll have warning. I need to be the one to get his attention."

"Not fucking using you as bait, Jasmine."

"Yes, you are." He shook his head, and I wrapped my arms around his waist and tilted my head back, looking up at him. "You won't let anything happen to me. It's our best chance and you know it." His fox flared in his eyes, he was about to tell me no. "I'm doing it, Ren." I didn't have an inner animal, but like he said, I was a Thornheart and stubborn as hell, and I made sure he saw that in my eyes.

He cursed. "You don't get anywhere near him. You call him and you get the fuck back and leave the rest to me."

"I can do that."

He grabbed my hand again, and we crept down the stairs. The closer to the bottom we got, the louder Xavier's ranting became. There was a crash, and he roared. When we hit the bottom of the stairs, Ren motioned to the living room, and we slipped along the wall and rushed in.

Xavier lay on the floor outside the realm he'd created. He was shirtless, sweating and shaking, obviously struggling badly with his new exposed emotions now that he'd been left to live with them for a full day and night, and desperate for me to heal him.

Ren stood behind the wall beside the door to the living room. Grabbing my arm, he pulled me to him and kissed me. "I love you," he said, staring into my eyes, like he had so many times, knowing I couldn't say it back, and not knowing if I ever could.

Cupping his whiskered jaw, I held his gaze in return. "I love you, too."

He sucked in a sharp breath.

I smiled up at him, gave his hand a squeeze, and stepped into the doorway, staring out at Xavier's distorted figure. "Looking for me?"

His head lifted, and with a growl, he shot to his feet. Shaking, he strode straight for me, moving from one realm to the next as if it were nothing. His fangs had elongated, his features inhuman with pain and also hunger. "You've been a very naughty little witch, Jasmine, hiding from me," he said panting.

"I know it's crazy, but the idea of letting you torture me to the point of death only to bring me back from the brink and start all over again wasn't really something I was in a hurry to experience," I said.

He stopped, his lavender eyes so pale and bright and full of twisted rage that I wanted to step back, retreat. "You shouldn't be able to hide from me, not in my own world. I searched everywhere for you. Tell me where you were?"

He took a step forward, and I took one back into the living room so I was even with Ren. I could see a tiny bit of apprehension in Xavier's eyes. He didn't know how I'd evaded him, and he was obviously afraid if he came at me, I might vanish again. "You have blind spots, Xavier. Places in your mind you've walled off. Did you know your mind is just like this..." I held my arms out. "Like your home. And the emotions you're afraid of, you've walled off so thoroughly that the rooms are blind spots. Spots that are completely outside this hidden world of yours."

"You escaped?" he asked, his eyes narrowing, then shook his head. "You think I'm fucking stupid? If that were true, you wouldn't be here."

"When you were a little boy, you did lots of bad things, didn't you? Things that scared your mother."

He stilled, completely, unnaturally.

"You scared her, disgusted her so much that she'd lock you in a room to escape you."

"No," he snarled. "You're wrong."

"You made up monsters, hideous creatures that you imagined protecting you, monsters that would kill anyone who tried to stop you from doing the sadistic things you loved to do."

"I don't know what the fuck you're talking about."

"I can show you, if you want me to. They're on the fourth floor, Xavier. They've been up there a very long time."

He was breathing heavily.

"Do you ever go up to the fourth floor, Xavier?"

He frowned. "No."

"Did you even search for me up there?"

His chest heaved and he started to shake, confusion, rage twisting his face.

No. He hadn't. "Why? Why do you think that is?" I needed contact usually to work my magic, but I reached out for him now and slid the tendrils of my power around him, not enough he'd notice but enough to press at the wall in his mind, the wall he'd locked all those memories behind.

He shook his head. He didn't have an answer. He didn't know why he avoided the fourth floor, and now the memories were pressing against that wall while I pushed with my magic from the other side.

"You were a bad boy, Xavier, and that's where bad boys go."

He roared and charged me.

I stumbled back as he ran at me, and Ren exploded from his hiding spot, knocking him to the ground. He went at Xavier like a wild beast, his fists connecting with the dhampir over and over again.

Xavier was taken by surprise, and blood spilled from his nose and ran down his chin. He roared and swung back, missing, then tried to shove Ren off. But Ren wouldn't be moved. They rolled across the floor, Xavier's mouth open, fangs extended, trying to bite and tear at Ren, who shoved him away. Xavier jumped to his feet and staggered. Ren pulled his knife free and charged the other male.

Xavier's eyes flared bright purple, and he threw a hand up. Ren was thrown out, outside the barrier of Xavier's realm. Still in the same room, but not here. Not with me anymore.

"Run, Jasmine!" he roared, unable to see or hear me but knowing I could still hear him.

Through the distorted air, I watched him spin away and run for the front door. I knew exactly where he was going—to the attic, to get back in.

I retreated and sprinted out the door, agony shooting up my legs. The sound of Xavier pounding after me echoed on the wooden floorboards, his gait off. He was injured.

I ran up the stairs, using the railing to pull myself along, leaving a trail of blood as I went. He was closing in on me, so close.

"Jasmine!" he roared. "Come back here."

I hit the fourth-floor landing and backed up as far as I dared to the shadows and the snarling monsters. Their growls rose higher as they moved closer. Xavier swung around the corner, his face contorted. He slowed when he saw me standing there.

A snarl came from behind me, and his gaze sliced from me to the shadows behind me.

"Do you recognize them, Xavier? Your monsters?" I said, trapped between them.

"I don't..." He shook his head. "What are they doing here?"

"You put them here. I can help you remember," I said, pressing deeper into the wall when he took a step closer. I reached out with my magic, letting it build and grow. I'd had the night to recover, and I was close to full power.

Xavier moved closer still, and the monsters' frenzied snarls grew in volume when they saw him. They wanted him, wanted to get to him. Xavier had created them, then he'd abandoned them here, and they were angry.

Xavier grabbed for me, and I knew it was coming. I latched on to him, wrapping my arms around him with all my strength, pouring my power into him, aiming it all at the attic wall in his mind. He groaned from the force of it, grabbing for the wall to hold himself up. My magic had finally had the chance to recover and he was momentarily weakened by the force of it.

I knew the moment it won out, when he stopped trying to shove me away and wrapped his arms around me instead, so tight I thought he might actually crush me.

He groaned again, then struck, burying his fangs in my throat. I screamed, but I didn't let go. I needed to stop him, and the only way to do that was to break down every one of his emotional walls—before he drained me completely.

I cried out again and slammed the last of my magic into him, and it was like dominoes. As soon as the thickest wall in his mind came down, the rest followed, crashing down one by one, opening wound after wound, wounds I would not be healing.

He screamed and pulled away from me, his fangs tearing my flesh as he did. I fell back, pressing my hand to my throat. Xavier stumbled to the side, gripping his head, and that was close enough.

A black leathery-clawed hand grabbed his shoulder and yanked him into the darkness.

Xavier screamed, a bloodcurdling death rattle that sent ice down my spine.

The world shifted, the distortion that had surrounded me vanished. The realm Xavier created dying along with him.

Then Ren burst from the hall and gathered me up in his arms. "Butterfly," he choked, pressing his hand to the wound at my throat.

It was finally over.

Then those words took on an entire new meaning, because Ren was alone. I realized for the first time in three years, there were no souls with him.

He'd finally let go of his guilt.

"They're gone," I choked out.

"What?"

"You freed them, the souls, you did it. They're gone, Ren. You set them free."

CHAPTER 35

Ren

"I'M OKAY," Jasmine said again.

As soon as we'd gotten out of Xavier's realm, the hounds had picked up her scent. By the time we got to my place, everyone was here. My small apartment was overcrowded with Jasmine's family, our family.

Daisy grabbed her again, hugging her so tight Jaz squeaked. Else had cleaned out her wounds, and dressed them, including the one at her throat. Watching Jaz in more pain had been fucking hard to bear, but none of us knew what kind of shit was on those monsters' claws. Her wounds would need to be closely monitored and Else had given us strict instructions before she slathered Jaz in balms, while Mags had given her spoonful after spoonful of potions and tonics.

I watched her now, a tired smile on her face, and my fucking heart clenched.

She loved me.

Jasmine loved me.

And right now, my female was exhausted, especially after losing so much fucking blood, but there was no way she'd say so. No, that's what I was for.

I pushed away from the wall. "Time to go, everyone. Jaz needs her rest."

Else turned to me. "I'm not leaving. She needs looking after."

"Love you, Else, but I'm kicking you out. All of you. I can take care of my mate."

Bram chuckled low beside me, and Mags nudged him to be quiet.

Daisy beamed. "Yes, we should go. Ren's got this."

Draven, Warrick, and Ronan collected their mates, and Relic and Rome said their goodbyes. Daisy and Art and Mags and Bram followed, and Else left last after giving me a list of instructions.

"I'll call if we need you," I said to her and pulled her in for a hug.

She wrapped her arms around me in return and nodded, then lifted her head and held my face in her hands. "Take care of each other," she said, then left.

I closed the door, and turned to Jaz.

She was watching me, a small smile on her lips. "You can take care of your mate, huh?"

"Yeah, I can," I said and strode over to her, scooping her up in my arms. "Doesn't matter that we haven't made it official, butterfly, it's a done deal." I carried her down the hall and into our room. She froze in my arms, twisting to take everything in.

"Everything's new." I pressed my nose to the side of her throat and breathed in her scent. "We wanted our female to have a den that was all hers."

"I can't believe you did all this," she said, then she shook her head. "No, I can believe it."

Leaning forward, I carefully eased her to her back on the bed. "I'd do anything for my beautiful, precious female. Anything."

"I know."

I tugged off my shirt and climbed into the bed with her and we stared at each other through the dim light. "The block he used to lock away what you felt for me..." I rasped. I knew the truth, I could see it in her eyes, she'd said the words. But I needed to hear her say it again. "It's really gone, isn't it, butterfly? You...you love me again?" My voice sounded as desperate as I felt, and I didn't give a fuck. Jasmine knew me like no one else, she'd seen every part of me, I didn't have to pretend to be anyone else but the male I was with her.

She cupped the side of my face. "The block's gone," she said, her voice a husky whisper. "And everything I felt for you is back, and it's so big and so wild and, goddess, all consuming." Her eyes danced and glistened. "I'm so desperately in love with you, Ren, it's kinda ridiculous. And somehow, I love you even more now than before, when I thought that was impossible." She traced my lips with her thumb. "Does that answer your question?"

"Yeah," I said, my fox rumbling his approval through my chest. My heart pounded. "And in case you were in any doubt? I'm so fucking in love with you, Jasmine Thornheart, I don't know what to do with myself. I've loved you a long time, even before I allowed myself to see it. You're the reason I'm still here. You're the reason I woke up and chose to live one more day. It was your eyes in my head, your face, your voice, that pulled me back from the ledge every time I stood there. You are literally my reason to walk this earth, and I promise I will never, ever hurt you again."

A shuddery breath fell from her lips, then she thrust her fingers into my hair and pulled me to her, kissing me fiercely. She tasted fucking perfect, like autumn and home.

Her fingers dug into my flesh, her movements restless against me. She grabbed at the front of my jeans, trying to tug them open, and I took her hands and lifted them, shaking my head. "Butterfly, you're still too weak from blood loss—"

"I don't care, I want you."

"Baby—"

"I need you, Ren. Please," she choked out.

And I needed her. No way was I strong enough to stop this with her looking at me like that, with that tremble of need in her voice. "Okay, but first, I make you come."

She growled under her breath.

Christ, she was cute. Fucking shaking, I slid my hand down the front of her pj shorts. Else and Daisy had helped her shower and change before they sorted her wounds when we got here. "You'll get me, but not until I've tasted you." Her hips lifted, her panted breaths prickling goose bumps across my shoulders and down my arms, my stomach muscles were so fucking tight they were close to cramping.

She wriggled her hands free and weakly tried to shove her shorts down for me.

I grabbed her wrists again and held them more firmly. I wanted her hands on me badly, but just the warmth of her touch was enough to snap my control. Touch was still overwhelming at times, but not in a bad way, not with Jasmine. I shook my head and chuckled when she growled again. "You're injured, butterfly. You have to promise you'll stay still and not hurt yourself, or we can't do this."

"I'll stay still," she said in that same breathy, husky voice, and my cock throbbed harder. "Now, take my damn shorts off."

I grinned. "As you wish." I carefully peeled them down her legs, stopping at her knees.

"Ren," she gritted out.

"Can't get them any lower than that without hurting you or messing with the bandages." Else said Jasmine had to be extremely careful for the next two days, no bumping them or fucking with the dressings. I slid my hand up the side of her pj top, over her ribs. Goose bumps lifted across her skin, and her stomach trembled. "But I can work with you like this. Trust me."

She wrapped her arms around my neck, looking into my eyes. "I do, with every part of me."

I kissed her again deeply, then fucking shaking, I curled my hand around one of her breasts, squeezing. I played with her nipple as my tongue slid over hers, kissing her over and over again, small sips of her perfect lips, then devouring her with the full force of my hunger.

The scent of her pussy was driving me to madness. Trailing kisses across her jaw and down her throat, I sucked her tender flesh, marking her skin, and as I slid my hand down her belly, her legs parted as far as they could, which wasn't far. Her hips rolled, and I growled, fighting with my hunger for her, barely stopping myself from tearing the shorts from her body completely.

I gave her what she wanted, what I needed. I covered her slick pussy with my hand and slid my middle finger along her slit, pressing deep. She whimpered, and I circled her tight opening, teasing us both before gliding higher. She gripped my forearms, her nails digging in. Her lids were heavy, her lips swollen and parted, and when she bit the lower one and rolled her hips against my hand, I almost came in my fucking jeans.

"You close already, baby?"

"Yeah."

I jerked her top up with my other hand and yanked down the cups of her bra, then sucked a tight little nipple into my mouth as I slid two fingers deep inside her. Jaz fisted my hair with a cry. I fucked her with my fingers, while I worked her clit with my thumb. She tightened around me, and I lifted my head to watch.

She sucked in a breath, then screamed.

Oh fuck. Her pussy felt so good clamping down on my fingers. She was so fucking gorgeous straining for me, her beautiful eyes dazed and heavy with desire. When she quieted, I kissed her again while I tugged my jeans open and shoved them off, my cock was so hard I couldn't take it any longer.

"Roll to your side, baby," I said, helping her so her gorgeous round ass was aimed at me. I wanted to slide inside her so badly, but I wanted her taste on my tongue as well. Getting off the bed, I kneeled beside it, gripped her ass, spreading her, and dragged my tongue along her pussy from behind, groaning.

She pushed back against me, wanting more, and I gave it to her. I wanted to spread her legs wide so badly, but I wouldn't risk jostling her and hurting her, and I doubted she had the strength right then to do much more than lie there and let me pleasure her, which was more than fine with me. I sucked and licked her until she was dripping and rocking and begging me to fuck her.

I had decent self-control, but not now, and never with Jasmine. She destroyed me with a fucking look, broke me down with a plea. I was hers to command. I wanted to worship her for the rest of our lives.

She sobbed. "Please, Ren. Please."

"Shhh, butterfly, I'm gonna take care of you." I got up on the bed, and she tried to roll to her back, but I stopped her, keeping her on her side. She watched as I fisted my cock, then gripping one of her ass cheeks, I held her wide and slid the head through the center of her soaking pussy lips. "In this position, it's gonna feel like too much at first, so I'm gonna need to take it slow."

She bit her lip and nodded, her cheeks dark, her chest rising and falling fast.

I tilted my hips forward, the head sliding in. Her hand shot back, and she grabbed my thigh, her nails digging in. I leaned over her, holding the side of her face. She looked up at me, a sob falling from her lips as I slid in another inch. I gritted my teeth, holding myself back when all I wanted to do was thrust inside her to the root and claim her, bite her.

"Okay?" My voice was nothing but a growl.

"Y-yeah."

"Not too much?" I slid in another inch, then back.

She whimpered, and her eyes fucking dazed. "Yes, but I...I like it. Oh goddess...please. I want it."

She was killing me. "You want more, mate, I'll give it to you. You want your male to claim you, don't you, Jasmine?" I snarled, snapping the words, animal instinct taking over. "You want your male to make you his."

"Yes, do it. Make me yours."

There was no stopping me now, now that I had her in my arms, now that I was finally back inside her, now that she loved me again. I slid in deep, planting myself fully inside her, and she turned from me, crying out. I needed to see her face when I claimed her, so I gripped her chin so she couldn't look away, making her look at me, then I started moving, unable to go easy or slow.

I fucked her deep, hard. I wasn't going to last long, no fucking way. Not when she was everything, fucking everything to us and we were finally going to make her ours. We were going to mark her, and love her, and take care of her for the rest of our lives.

I slid my hand lower, curling my fingers around her throat, and leaned in, dragging my nose along her jaw to her ear, breathing her in, scenting my mate, a scent that was already branded on my soul. A scent I would recognize for the rest of my life, a scent that would lead me to her in the next so I'd make her mine all over again. "Gonna give you my mark, butterfly." I slammed into her with a grunt, a growl quickly following as I kissed my way down her throat.

One of her hands curled around the back of my head, holding me to her, as if I'd ever pull away, then her other hand took one of mine, linking out fingers. I kissed and sucked the skin between her neck and shoulder and my teeth sharpened, my canines extending. My fox threw his head back and howled his approval as I bit down on her flesh.

Jasmine screamed, her pussy clutched me so fucking tight, over and over, as she came for me, and with a snarl, I came with her.

I slammed into her, the taste of her pussy and her blood on my tongue filling my senses. I owned every part of her and she owned me.

I finally slowed my thrusts and gently licked and kissed the mark I'd given her, and Jasmine shivered. When I lifted my head again, she brought my mouth to hers, kissing me.

"You taste that, Jasmine Thornheart?" I said against her lips. "That's mine," I growled. "All mine."

Then I got into bed beside her, wrapped her in my arms and held my mate while she drifted off to sleep.

CHAPTER 36

Ren

JASMINE WALKED into the living room, and I studied the way she moved. It'd taken her a week to regain her strength after Xavier almost drained her of blood and nearly another two weeks for the wounds on her legs and feet to heal, but the scars were still there. Fading, but still fucking there. I forced down the out-of-control feeling inside me that came with that memory, along with the desperate desire to go back in time, drag Xavier from that shadowed hall, and finish him myself.

I studied Jaz again. My mate was stubborn and incredibly strong, add in the fact she never complained and had that caring and loving nature of hers, always choosing to put others first, which meant she often forgot to take care of herself. Good thing she had me to do that now.

"You sure you're okay going for a walk?" I asked her again.

Her lips curled up. "Yes, Ren, I'm sure I can handle a short walk. You seriously need to chill."

"Well, that's not happening. I will never be *chill* when it comes to your health and safety," I said, and my fox added some growl to my voice, making sure our mate knew we were in accord on this matter.

She grabbed my hand and towed me through the door and up the stairs to the street. "Both of you can relax. I'm more than fine. And if you think you have a hope in hell of stopping me from going to my field, you're completely crackers."

"Crackers, huh?"

Her smile brightened, lighting up her eyes. She'd been desperate to get out among her butterflies for the last week, but I'd not been ready to let her out of my sight. I still wasn't. "We've been mates for nearly three weeks. When does this newly mated, crazy protective streak start to calm down again?"

"Calm down?" I laughed, it was low and gritty and seriously dark.

Jaz's brows shot up. "Mags said you guys go a little loopy and a lot caveman when you first mate, but then—"

"But then nothing, butterfly. Every day that you're mine, the need to protect you grows fiercer, right along with the bond between us." I grinned. "That isn't gonna change, so you'll just have to put up with me fussing over you."

She stopped and wrapped her arms around my middle, smiling up at me. "I think I can handle it."

"I'm glad to hear it."

"I feel pretty protective over you as well," she said. "Bree better steer clear of me for a while."

My stomach sank. "You know you have nothing to worry about. Those other females, they're not... Fuck, Jaz, I don't remember any of it. That part of my life, it doesn't exist anymore—"

She pressed her finger to my lips, silencing me. "I know. I don't feel threatened. I trust you completely. But I also don't like the thought of you with anyone else." She grinned. "Sadly, you didn't come to me a sweet little virgin, and this mate thing isn't only making *you* loopy, so prepare for your female to stake her claim on you whenever the urge strikes."

"Yeah? And how do you plan on doing that?" I said, knowing where she was coming from, because even though Rome was just her friend, I still wanted to tear the male apart whenever they were in the same room.

She slid her arms from around me, took my hand, and started walking again. "Well, I thought I'd keep it simple. Making out with you *a lot* will probably do the trick."

"Most definitely. At every opportunity."

Her laugh was light, beautiful. "That was my plan."

We walked through the gates of the field, and every part of her lit up. I'd been waiting to tell her something for a while, and now was the perfect time. She laughed and spun around as butterflies surrounded her, landing on her. Her breath hitched as her little familiars showered her with love and affection, and she gave them the same in return.

"I've missed you," she said, then sat in the middle of the field, her arms outstretched, talking to them, her pleasure and joy infectious.

I watched her, couldn't take my fucking eyes off her. She was the most exquisite creature I'd ever laid eyes on. She was everything I'd ever dared hope for and never thought I'd get.

Jasmine was my salvation. She'd saved me, by loving me. She saved the souls who'd been trapped with me. She'd helped me to finally set them free.

When she looked back at me, I walked over and sat on the ground beside her. "They missed you, and they didn't even know you until now."

"Yes," she said. "And it's the same for me."

"I get it. When I finally let you in, it was like a part of me I didn't even know was missing was returned to its rightful place."

She moved, and her little familiars took flight, fluttering above her as she climbed onto my lap, straddling me. Her arms slid around my neck. "You're the love of my life, Ren."

"And you, butterfly, are mine." She kissed me, and I held her tight and kissed her back. "I thought maybe we could have our mating ceremony here, what do you think?" I asked when we came up for air.

Her cheeks grew pink with delight. "I mean, it'd be perfect. This is one of my most favorite places, but wouldn't we have to get permission from the owner?"

"I'm asking her now."

Her chin jerked back, and a cute little frown shifted her features. "What?"

"The field's yours, Jaz."

"What?" she said again, her brows shooting up.

"I thought perhaps we could build a house here. Over there." I pointed to a spot on the other side of the field. "We won't disturb your butterflies over there or the other insects and animals who live here, what do you think?"

"You bought this field?" she whispered.

"Yeah."

"When?"

"After I found you here sobbing, after..." I didn't finish that sentence. Neither of us wanted to think about that time, or who did it. "I wanted to be able to protect it for you."

A tear streaked down her cheek. "Thank you." She kissed me again, then peppered more all over my face.

I swiped away her happy tears and grinned. "Is that a yes?"

She laughed. "That is most definitely a yes." One of her hands cupped my face, the other gripped the side of my neck, right over the sigils she'd inked there. "Thank you for trusting me with your heart, Ren," she whispered. "I promise I'll protect it with everything I have."

I cupped her beautiful face in return. "Thank you for trusting me with yours, butterfly, and I promise you, if anyone tries to hurt it, or take you from me again, I will burn their world to the ground until there's nothing left but ash."

EPILOGUE

Jasmine

Four months later

MUSIC DRIFTED THROUGH THE HOUSE, along with the sounds of my family's laughter. The house had been built in record time, mainly because it was small, but it was truly everything I'd hoped for. We'd planned it carefully, neither one of us had wanted to disturb the little ecosystem here, and there was room to expand when the time came.

Which meant the house was quirky and unique and I adored it. Bram and his brothers had helped Ren build it, since they had experience, they'd all built their own homes, and Bram's tree house behind my aunt's place was exactly the style I wanted.

"Sit down, those ankles are looking kind of puffy," Mags said to Iris.

"They are not," Iris said and looked down, then cursed when she couldn't see over her round belly. She was only five and a half months along, but with twins on the way, she was well and truly showing.

She lifted a leg out in front of her. "They're fine."

"They're not," Wills said from her spot on her mate's lap.

"I'll sit when I want to sit," Iris said, a stubborn look on her face.

My cousin had been struggling with the whole taking-it-easy part of her pregnancy. Draven strode over, picked her up, and set her on the couch.

595

Then he sat beside her so he could pull one of her feet into his lap. "Time to rest those cute, puffy little ankles," he said.

"Draven," she growled. "I want to dance, not sit here like an invalid." Nia trotted over and rested her head on Iris's belly.

"Rest now, and you can dance later," he said and started massaging.

Her eyes rolled back, but she kept the stubborn look on her face. "Fine. But only for a little while." She ran her fingers through Nia's soft fur.

Draven grinned but was wise enough to turn away so she didn't see him.

Mags stood with Bram, his arm draped around her shoulders. She was telling him something and he was smiling. Rose was standing in front of Ronan, his arms were around her waist, and they were talking to Art and Aunt Daisy, who was holding a sleeping Violet. Else and Connor were sitting on the couch sampling the finger foods, and Stan stood behind her with an amused look on his face, listening to her tell some story that had Connor bark out a laugh.

My gaze slid to Zinnia. She stood alone, staring out the window. She had to return to Limbo in a few days and she was trying to hide it, but I knew she was scared. We'd found the missing souls, but we were still running out of time. In five months, I turned twenty-one. If we didn't find a way to get Zinnia out of her deal with Death by then, I'd lose her. She'd be trapped in Limbo with him forever.

Ren's arms slid around me from behind, his chin resting on my shoulder. "We'll find a way," he said, reading my mind. "The females in this family can overcome anything." He kissed my neck. "We're proof of that."

I covered his hands with mine, linking our fingers. "I know, but it feels... it feels like I'm already losing her."

"Whatever happens, you'll never lose her. Your sister won't go down easy. She'll always find a way back to you."

Ren was right, but Death wasn't just some demon or monster that could be slain. He was a god, and in his eyes, Zinnia was his. He'd never back down. He'd never let her go.

The music was turned up, and Mags grabbed Zinnia's hand, dragging her into the middle of the room. Wills joined her, and Draven lifted Iris to her feet because there was no stopping her. Else and Daisy joined in as well.

I turned in my mate's arms and kissed him. "I love you, Ren. And I love our home."

He grinned down at me. "I love you, too, butterfly. Now get out there so I can watch my mate dance."

I laughed and spun away, running to dance surrounded by my family.

Right now, we were all safe, and we were together.

I was going to hold on to that for as long as I could.

A PROMISE OF ASHES

))) ● ((‹

Zinnia

I whispered the words and stood back as the boulders shifted, rolling and reshaping into a tall, wide arch.

I'd said my goodbyes last night, and I didn't have it in me to do it again this morning. Jaz would be pissed when she woke and found me gone, but she'd understand.

Leaving her always sucked, but knowing she'd found her mate, that she was loved and protected, definitely helped while I was away.

A wolf howled in the distance. Ash. I knew her howl, and she said she'd be on patrol this morning. She'd no doubt picked up my scent. Throwing back my head, I howled in reply, giving it my best shot, anyway. Others in her pack joined in. Their howls of farewell, lifting goose bumps across my skin.

I shivered and turned towards the gate; if I loitered out here too long, Death would come for me, and that was the last thing I wanted. I wasn't ready to see him, not yet.

Hitching my pack, I stepped through the gate and onto the path of skulls—

"Zinny!"

I spun around. Jaz stood there, Ren at her side, a bloody knife in his hand, and a grin on his face. My brother-in-law had left a trail of demon ash to get her to me.

My stubborn sister lifted her hand, and I smiled, not wanting her to see my pain or fear, and lifted my hand as well.

"I love y—"

The gate shut, vanishing in front of me, cutting my baby sister off, and locking me in Limbo.

I forced myself to turn away, from everyone I loved, and start walking. The path to Death's home was long and winding, but as long as you didn't veer off it, avoiding the dark forest either side, it was safe.

As I walked, I rebuilt my defenses, shutting everything down, my fears, my sadness, my rage—still, I wasn't prepared for the terrifying awe when I rounded the last bend. I never was.

The huge black, stone castle, jutting up from the ground always managed to steal my breath and make my knees tremble.

I walked up its wide steps, to the massive arched doors that swung open for me.

"Mistress, we've been anticipating your arrival," Egon said.

I smiled. "Hey, Egon." When I first met the male, I'd gone for my knife. Thankfully, he hadn't taken offence. Egon was a horned demon. His skin was leathery and deep green. His eyes were scarlet and he had pointed, shiny black horns.

"Your room is ready, Mistress," he said.

"Thanks. I'll head straight up."

"Would you like me to bring you a small repast? Dinner is still some hours away."

I shook my head. "No, thank you. I think I'll just unpack."

He dipped his head. "As you wish." Then his scarlet eyes met mine. "The master requests you to seek him out after you have settled."

"I'm not sure why he always insists I do that, he knows exactly when I get here." Egon said nothing, just waited for me to give him the answer he needed. "But yes, I'll find him."

Relief filled his eyes, and something else that set me on edge before he rushed off.

I headed up the wide, black staircase to the second floor and wall sconces lit the way, making the stone gleam. My chamber was almost at the end of the hall. Mors slept in the room beside mine. I'd never been inside, but I imagined it as some kind of twisted, torture chamber, full of things that would make your stomach churn.

I dumped my bag on my bed and all I wanted to do was get under the covers, close my eyes, and sleep for the next month. But if I didn't go find Death now, he'd come looking for me, a dark shadow, in robes that moved like they were a living, breathing thing, those blue eyes glowing from beneath its hood, full of anger.

If he was here at the castle, he was either with his brother, Somnus, or in his study. Still, I knocked on his bedroom door first. When there was no reply, I took the stairs to the next level. Somnus's bedroom door was closed. If Mors was with him, the door would be open. The study it was.

The heavy wooden door was open when I reached it, a fire crackling from within, causing light to dance across the wall. The clink of ice told me he was inside. Power flowed to me then, wrapping around me, pulling me forward, telling me he knew I was there. The fear that always came when I was with him, filled me now and there was no stopping it. I let him draw me into the room—

Then froze, a gasp forced out of me before I could stop it.

Death stood in front of the fire, a tumbler in a tattooed hand.

But there was no robe.

I'd been coming here for a year and a half, and I'd never seen him without it.

He was shirtless, in only a pair of black trousers. His body was hairless, what I could see of it, anyway, from his tattooed skull to his waist. In between the ink, his skin was pale, and he was lean and cut with muscle. His head was dipped, looking into his drink as he swirled it. I still couldn't see his face.

"You came," he said, his voice rolling over me like thunder.

Words he said every single time. It took me several attempts to reply. I was having trouble catching my breath. "L-like I had a choice," I said, like I always did, but this time my voice shook.

He carefully placed his glass on the mantel, and turned to me, firelight dancing across his features.

I took an abrupt step back. Mors was...terrifying, his features etched by violence, and carved by death—and so utterly beautiful, it was hard to look at him.

His face was free of ink and he had a prominent nose, high cheekbones, a strong jaw, and sensual, dark crimson lips.

"Your robe?" I rasped.

"I no longer require it," he said, shaking me to my core with that terror-filled voice.

"You don't need it?" What the hell was that supposed to mean? I wanted it back. This, seeing him like this, it was too much. Way too much.

He shook his head, eyes boring into me. "I'll see you for dinner, consort. Make sure you're there on time."

I barely suppressed my shiver.

The way he said it, made it sound like I was the main course.

A BOND IN FLAMES

THE THORNHEART TRIALS

BOOK #6

AUTHOR NOTE

I can't believe we've reached the end of The Thornheart Trials Series! A Bond in Flames is my fortieth published book and one that I'm super proud of! I love this vast, dark and twisty world, and I hope you do too, because I have so many stories I want to write in and around Roxburgh... and in case you missed it, the hounds are coming next and Relic is up first!

As for Zinnia and Death's story... let's just say they led the way and I followed. Like all my stories in this world there are dark vibes and themes, and I also play fast and loose with Greek and Latin mythology—in that, I take little bits of what I want, leave the rest, and twist it to suit my characters and stories—and A Bond in Flames is no different.

But most importantly, I want to thank you so much for coming along on this journey with me! I've been writing and publishing for over ten years, and I appreciate every single reader who has taken a chance on one of my books. It honestly means everything to me. I wouldn't still be here without you!

Yes, this is the last book in The Thornheart Trial Series, but it isn't the end, there is so much more to come!

PROLOGUE

Zinnia

Rose looked into the mortar. "Will there be enough?"

"That's just for you." I took the blade from my pack, sliced both palms, and smeared blood all over my naked body.

My sweet cousin's eyes widened. "What will that do?"

I flashed her a grin, refusing to let her see my fear. "Boost the hell out of my power... and make me look badass. I'm coming face-to-face with Death. I plan on making a memorable first impression."

She stared at me in disbelief. "But your soul... you need the oil."

"My soul is going to be just fine. It's going to be okay, Roe, I promise," I lied. This was far from fine, but there was no other choice, not for me, not anymore.

Rose quickly finished covering her body with the oily potion, and I took her hand.

The pile of stones rumbled behind us, and we spun around as the ground shook, the earth rolling beneath our feet as if it were trying to force Rose to let me go. Her hand slipped in my blood-covered one, but we linked fingers, holding tight.

The stones rolled, reforming, revealing skulls, as if the bones had been fossilized in each one, empty eye sockets and jaws hanging wide. When they stopped, we were staring into a gateway—right into Limbo.

It was dark on the other side, shadowed, cold. A thumping sound echoed in the distance, rolling through the portal. It was a slow, steady beat, growing in volume until I felt the thump in my bones.

Death.

Rose trembled.

He was coming for her.

She squeezed my hand. "What should I say?"

The wind became violent, her blonde hair whipping around her lovely face. I squeezed her hand in return. "Let me do the talking," I called over the raging storm.

The rumbling sound was constant now, the icy blast making it hard to draw breath.

Then I saw him.

A shroud of moving shadows. He kept coming until he stood on the other side of the gate, so tall, he towered over us. I watched, unable to breathe as he lifted the twisted wooden staff in his hand, glowing with power, and thumped it one last time against the ground.

The wind stopped in an instant, the world seeming to still around us.

I gasped for breath, and I felt Rose's fear spike higher. I tightened my hand on hers. I'd seen Death once before, when he came to me in a nightmare and turned my world upside down. He had to be close to seven feet tall and was completely concealed, except for a thin, tattooed hand gripping his wooden staff and blue eyes that glowed from beneath his hood.

We waited as that frigid glare moved between us.

"I told you to come alone," he said to Rose.

The deep way his voice resonated, arctic and terrible, washed over me, invoking a multitude of emotions—grief and heartbreak, loneliness and despair, but worse, oh goddess, the pure, raw horror. It took everything in me not to fall to the ground, shaking and sobbing.

I had to be strong, though, for Rose, for my entire family. "I'm afraid you can't have her," I said and hoped like hell he didn't hear the waver in my voice.

Rose moved closer to me, and I held on to her tight.

Death studied me for several long seconds. "And you think you can stop me from taking what I'm owed?"

"If you take Rose's soul, you'll be interfering with a bargain between Lucifer and her sister's mate. Lucifer granted immortality to the Thornheart sisters if they mated. Rose is mated. She can't die."

Rose spun to me, shocked.

Death grew larger before my eyes, his grip on the staff so tight, the wood creaked.

I pushed on, refusing to back down. I couldn't. "If you make an enemy of Lucifer, there'll be a war. You'll disturb the balance between the four realms."

Death made an inhuman sound that sent spikes of terror through me. "She doesn't need to die to enter my world, witch. I can take her as she is. Her soul will still be mine."

"Rose's brother-in-law is Lucifer's alpha hellhound, a male he considers a friend. Do you think Lucifer will let that stand?" I said, trying to sound as strong as I could in the face of his immense power.

"The bargain grants her immortality, not where she'll live out eternity. Lucifer will have no grounds to start a war."

His voice made me want to cover my ears and scream.

"Come here, Rose," he said to my cousin.

She turned to me, shaking, teeth chattering. "It's okay."

Death held out his hand.

I held on to her tighter.

"It's okay," she said again, taking a step forward.

I pulled her back. It was time.

"You did all you could, but you can't stop this. No one can," Rose said.

Gritting my teeth, I turned from her and back to Death, my heart beating fast. I wanted to run the fuck away from here so badly; instead, I stared into his cold gaze. "It's not Rose you want. It's me."

Rose spun to face me. "What?"

Death stilled.

"You've been searching for me for a long time, but I made sure you couldn't find me. I hid, using this." I lifted my arm, showing him the tattoo. "I'm the one you want, the one you've been waiting for." Releasing Rose's hand, I stepped forward. "You came to me in my dreams when I was fifteen years old. You told me who I was, what you wanted from me, and I ran. Do you remember?"

Death said nothing, his tall frame stilling under his cloak.

"I woke up after that first visit from you, and I refused to go back to sleep until I found a way to keep you out of my head. It cost me, but I did it."

Death leaned forward, still in his realm, but right at the edge. "Who are you?" he demanded.

Scooping up my blade from the ground, I pressed it to my forearm and, with a cry, sliced the small tattoo from my arm, removing the mark I'd worn on my skin for the last thirteen years. "Your birthright. I was born to be your consort, Mors," I said, using Death's true name.

He jerked back, then flew forward again, hand outstretched, but unable to reach me.

"Zinnia, no," Rose cried.

I turned to her, holding my cousin's horrified stare. "I've been running from this for a long time. He was drawn to your soul because of me. I need to make this right, to protect our family and our coven."

"Don't do this," she choked.

"You were willing to sacrifice yourself for your coven, Roe. And so am I. It's the only way."

"Come to me, consort," Death said, so deep and menacing, it chilled me to my core.

I straightened my spine and turned to him. "Your consort must enter Limbo willingly, and I will go with you, but I have a condition."

"Name it," he said.

All his focus was on me now, as if Rose no longer existed.

"Zinnia, don't do this. There has to be another way," she said.

"I have a sister who needs me, and I won't abandon her. I'll come with you, but only if I'm free to move between realms."

"No."

"That's my condition."

He was silent for several long moments. "Each time you visit, you must remain with me for at least one lunar month before returning to your realm."

"Then I want a lunar month here as well."

Death made a sound raw and violent. "I will agree, but only until your sister's eighteenth birthday. After that, you will remain here with me."

"Her twenty-first birthday," I countered.

He shook his head, about to argue.

"If you agree, I'll leave with you now," I said.

He was quiet for a moment, then finally inclined his head. "But know this, consort, if you fail to return to me, the bargain is void. I will come for you, and when I have you back, I'll never let you leave."

"Understood," I said. "And if you refuse to let me leave, same deal, the bargain is void. And I promise you, I'll find a way to escape, and you'll never see me again."

"Don't do this," Rose sobbed beside me.

I closed the space between us and pulled her into a tight hug. "I knew this day would come, Roe. I can't hide anymore. It's done." I looked into her eyes. "Take care of Jazzy for me, and Hemlock. It's only four weeks, and then I'll be back."

"Thank you," Rose choked out.

I tucked her hair behind her ear. "I want a party when I get home, okay? Something to look forward to."

"You've got it," she whispered.

"Consort," Death said, making me jolt.

I stepped away from my cousin, grabbed my clothes, shoved them in my pack, and turned to Death. He held out his hand as I strode up to him. "Pass on the hand holding. I'm not a fan of PDA," I said, then turned back to my sweet cousin, blew her a kiss, and walked through the archway and into Limbo.

The gate closed immediately, locking me in.

I was naked and covered in my own blood. A moment ago, I'd felt powerful—not now. Now I felt vulnerable and alone, but there was no way in hell I was showing the god staring down at me that. Death stood tall on the path of skulls, a path that disappeared into the dark forest surrounding us. He was concealed by his cloak that moved around his body like a living shadow.

Dropping my pack, I quickly pulled on my clothes and shoved my feet in my boots, then looked up at him. "Well?" I said, when he said nothing. "I assume we follow the path?"

"Do not veer off it."

At the sound of his voice, my knees almost buckled under me. Somehow, I locked them before I fell to the ground and screamed. "Awesome. Let's get going, then." I strode ahead and immediately wished I hadn't as creatures I couldn't make out darted along beside us, disappearing into the forest. Branches cracked as if something large was moving through the trees close by. Shrieks and strange mournful howls from animals I did not recognize echoed around us. And Death himself, right behind me. Goddess, I felt him there every step of the way.

I didn't think it actually took that long, but with Death looming behind me, it felt like an eternity before we rounded a bend and a huge black stone castle came into view. It jutted up from the ground, imposing and dreadful, and it took everything inside me not to just *run*. Even though there was nowhere for me to go, the urge to run was almost impossible to resist.

We walked up its wide steps, to the massive arched doors, and they instantly swung open. A horned demon stood there. His skin was leathery and mottled green. His eyes were scarlet, and he had pointed, shiny black horns. I grabbed my knife.

"No," Death rumbled behind me.

My knife was snatched from my hand.

"Egon is my servant. You will not harm him."

Egon backed away, staring at me in an odd way, a look in his eyes that I couldn't read. Death kept coming, still close behind me, directing me to a wide black staircase without a word.

My stomach was in barbed knots when we reached the second floor. I was his wife for all intents and purposes, and I'd made a deal to be with him. Nausea churned in my stomach.

You can survive this. Whatever happens next, you have to survive this. Jasmine needs you.

Wall sconces lit the way, making the stone hall gleam, and macabre shadows danced along the walls. Something scurried in the dark, and I had to bite back my shriek.

Death stepped in front of me, forcing me to stop suddenly. I stared up at him, fear in my throat so thick, it damn near choked me. Those glowing blue eyes watched me from under his hood as he reached out and shoved the door open beside me.

"Your quarters," he said, and with every word, his voice vibrated with a rage that I didn't understand. "This is where you will sleep. You may move freely throughout the castle. If you go outside, always stick to the path." The words he said didn't match the fury in his voice, which rolled off him in heavy waves. "There is no escape and nowhere to hide. Running is pointless. I will always find you." Then he turned and walked away.

CHAPTER 1

Zinnia

Eighteen months later

A ROAR ECHOED down the hall, and I shot up in bed. It was deep and filled with agony and sent ice shooting down my spine. Hemlock scurried onto my lap; my familiar was the fiercest little rat in existence, but even he found those roars of pain unsettling. I ran my hand down his back to soothe us both.

The sound of Death's bedroom door opening was closely followed by the heavy thud of his boots as he strode past my room and down to his brother.

Somnus, his twin and the personification of sleep, lived in the castle as well. I'd yet to see him awake, though, and sometimes, like tonight, he roared and made awful noises for hours, as if the god were being flayed alive in his dreams.

He was also how Death first visited me when I was just a teenager, so it was a good thing he stayed asleep because the god was not one of my favorite people.

Hemy ran up my arm and tucked himself against my neck. There'd be no sleep tonight for anyone, not with Somnus having one of his episodes.

Sliding my hand under the pillow, I grabbed my knife, scooped up

Hemlock, and slipped out of bed. Easing the door open, I checked that the way was clear, then rushed down the hall.

Somnus's door was ajar, and I could hear Death's voice rumbling low from inside. Just hearing him talk used to make me tremble in fear and horror. Yes, there was still some fear, and on occasion, I was overcome by the volatile emotions that he was able to evoke in me, but I'd been coming and going from this place long enough now that I'd managed to gain some control over my responses to him. Well, I had until I arrived back a week ago. I'd gone to the library to let him know I'd returned as instructed and found Death *without* his cloak. I'd never seen him without it before and it wasn't something I'd ever forget.

"You came," he said, his voice rolling over me like thunder.

Words he said every single time. It took me several attempts to reply. I was having trouble catching my breath. "L-like I had a choice," I said, like I always did, but this time, my voice shook.

He carefully placed his glass on the mantel and turned to me, firelight dancing across his features.

I took an abrupt step back. Mors was... terrifying, his features etched by violence and carved by death, and so utterly beautiful, it was hard to look at him.

His face was free of ink, and he had a prominent nose, high cheekbones, a strong jaw, and sensual dark crimson lips.

"Your robe?" I rasped.

"I no longer require it."

He'd said it in that deep, terror-evoking voice, shaking me to the depths of my core, and offered nothing more. After eighteen months of not knowing what he looked like beneath that dark shroud that covered him from head to foot, it had been a major shock, and it was still taking some getting used to.

Before the cloak came off, all I knew was the brutal intensity and raw power that poured off him. I hadn't been able to see the way he watched me or, goddess, feel the lightning strike when his glacial gaze pierced right through me. Every time that stare locked on mine, it caused shards of ice to shoot through my chest and down to my gut, and since finding him like that, I'd felt as off-balance as I had the first time I'd come here.

The god was inscrutable, watchful, stubborn, infuriating, and confusing as hell, and I didn't know him any better now than I did that first cold, wintry night he'd brought me to his castle. In fact, somehow, I knew him even less.

Doing my best to ignore the constantly moving shadows and the weight of a multitude of invisible eyes watching me, I darted into the library, shut the door, and climbed into the massive leather chair that sat in front of the always-blazing fire. Curling up, I dragged the fur that Egon left draped over the wide arm for me across my lap while Hemy scurried down from his spot tucked against my neck, settling in under it as well. I didn't know what it was about this room, but spending time in here was the closest thing to peace I'd found inside this castle. Maybe it was all the books, the smell of leather, that reminded me of home, of the library in Aunt Daisy's house or the rows of spell and recipe books in Aunt Else's workroom.

The book I'd been reading was still in its spot, on the deep mahogany table beside the chair, and I picked it up—

Somnus roared again, so loud that the windows rattled. Hemlock trembled, and a cold chill skated down my spine.

I covered Hemy's back with my hand to calm him. I hadn't known if it was safe for him here in Limbo the first time I came, so I'd left my tiny familiar at home. It'd been extremely hard on both of us.

But this was my life now.

Even though my family at home in Roxburgh was still desperately trying to find a way to get me out of this bargain, I knew there was no escape.

And deep down, I thought they did too. Jazzy's twenty-first birthday would be here before we knew it, and my visits home would end. I'd be trapped here in Limbo with Death, in this castle, for the rest of my life.

I ran my fingers over the scar on my forearm, where I'd cut out the markings given to me by a demon—a different bargain that had kept me hidden from Death for thirteen years until I couldn't hide anymore. The price I'd paid for it was immense, but even then, deep down, I'd known my reprieve was only temporary.

In the end, it had all been my choice—protecting my cousin, my coven; leaving my sister; and coming here. Yes, an impossible one, but a choice all the same, and one I'd make again and again.

That meant I had to make my peace with it, with saying goodbye for good, with never seeing my family or Jasmine ever again.

>>**◆**<<

I woke to the clink of ice against crystal.

Blinking the sleepiness away, I lifted my head from the arm of the chair, and my heart immediately leaped into my throat before I snatched up my knife.

Death stood in front of the fire, a drink in hand—watching me.

I sat up straighter. My body had instantly sensed the threat and reacted before my mind fully had a chance to engage. His gaze dipped to the knife now gripped in my hand, his brow lifting. I shrugged. What did he expect?

He was shirtless, as he often was now, in only a pair of black trousers that sat low on his hips. I tried not to stare at the shadows the fire created on his skin or the way they danced over the taut ridges of his muscled chest, but it was hard. That smooth, hairless, inked body was as beautiful and terrifying as the rest of him. The very thought of touching him was so utterly absurd and wrong and frightening, it was laughable. It'd be like petting a beast capable of eating you whole or swimming in lava or touching the sun—unthinkable.

He took a sip of his drink and ran a hand over his tattooed skull.

I waited for him to say something; he didn't.

Death looked tired.

The room was still dimly lit, but it was morning. There was no sun here in Limbo; there was the illusion of one, though, and light filtered through the arched windows.

"A little early for that, isn't it?" I said, eyeing the amber liquid in his glass instead of looking directly at him. I couldn't take the silence any longer, not with all that turbulent energy radiating from him.

"You didn't sleep in your bed," he said, ignoring my comment.

"What gave it away?"

He ignored my sarcasm. "Why?"

"Because I didn't want to." Hemlock poked his head out from under the fur. He'd become bolder around Death lately, and I'd noticed a look in his cute, beady eyes that was beginning to look alarmingly a lot like worship when he gazed at our jailer.

"Somnus kept you awake?" he asked.

"He kept the whole castle awake." If it wasn't Somnus screaming in his sleep, it was Death playing his piano—dark and mournful songs that I'd never heard before and made you want to curl in a ball and sob. I shoved the fur aside and stood, holding Hemy to me. "I need a shower."

"You will eat first. Meet me in the dining room in fifteen minutes."

I paused, fighting down my natural instinct to tell him to go fuck himself and his orders, but I'd been there and done that, and it'd gotten me nowhere, so I bit back what I wanted to say and carried on toward the door.

Are you just going to roll over and stop fighting?

No, I wasn't. I would never stop. If I wanted a goddamn shower first, I'd have one. I turned back to tell him so and froze.

Death had his back to me, facing the fire. He held the fur I'd been wrapped in all night in his hand—and it was pressed to his face.

I spun and darted off on silent feet. Death hadn't touched me, not in all the months I'd been coming here, even though he called me his consort. After that first night when nothing happened, I'd been relieved. Then, as the months drew on and still he didn't demand more from me, I'd actually started to feel... even more off-balance. Yes, I was thankful, but if not that, what did Death want from me? Why was I here?

Then he'd gone and taken off the cloak, after all this time, and I had no idea why or what it meant, but it had to mean something, right? And now he was smelling the fur I'd slept with?

I rubbed my arms, now covered in gooseflesh, and rushed into my room, shutting myself in.

The room he'd given me was large and filled with antiques and trinkets. It was like someone had just gotten up and walked out, leaving everything behind. It also had its own sitting area, but I didn't use it. I wasn't sure why, only that I got this odd, queasy feeling when I did and an ache in my chest that I didn't understand, which was why I preferred the library.

I sat Hemy on the bed that was shoved in the corner like an afterthought, snatched up some clothes, and quickly showered. I may be his prisoner, but I wasn't going to just give up and obey every one of his unreasonable demands. Still, I didn't linger. I needed to make a stand, but I didn't want to make him angry either.

Death was already sitting at the massive black lacquer table when I walked in.

He eyed me over his mug, gaze sliding from head to foot and back. "You ignored my order."

"Are you surprised?" I said and sat, smiling at Egon when he put a cup of tea in front of me, just the way I liked it, smelling of the fragrant herbs I'd grown.

I'd planted the herbs I needed in the kitchen garden. I was a witch— being without my herbs wasn't something I could tolerate. Death hadn't said anything when I'd brought a bagful of seedlings my third month coming here and made room for myself in his grounds. It was bad enough my medium powers were greatly hindered here, which was not surprising. I was in Limbo, after all. There was no need for souls to communicate with me; I didn't even know where the hell they were. Honestly, I had no idea how this realm worked. Thankfully, my magic was still okay.

"No," he said, his long, thick, tattooed fingers curling tighter around his mug. "I'd be more surprised if you actually did as I asked of you, consort."

"You don't ask—you demand. In case you haven't worked it out yet, I don't like orders." I smiled at Lyle, Egon's adult son, when he placed my overnight oats beside my tea. "Thanks, Lyle." He gave me a quick grin and hustled back to the kitchen.

"Eventually, you will learn my way is best," Death said. "In all things."

"Well, that's not going to happen," I said, scooping up a spoonful of oats and shoving it in my mouth. Something moved through his eyes; they kind of brightened, or maybe I was imagining it.

"Since we missed our evening drink, we'll make up for it now. I'll go first," he said.

Dammit, I'd hoped he'd forgotten. I shook my head. "You went first last time."

Death had pulled on a shirt—it was black—but he'd only done up a couple of buttons, so most of his chest was visible. It was as if he didn't like wearing clothes or could barely tolerate them. I wanted a better look at his tattoos, but I didn't want to stare. I'd caught glimpses of them but not a good look—again, because staring was not something I wanted him to catch me doing. The only one that was easy to see was the star that covered most of his chest. The center of it was decorated in swirls that created the appearance of shadows and light.

He sat back in his seat. "Your answer the night before was unsatisfactory. So I'll go first."

"And you gave me the same answer you do every time," I fired back.

"Because, so far, that has been the only answer required."

Our nightly drink took place in the library and consisted of us each asking the other a question. I'd refused when he'd first proposed it. The last thing I'd wanted was to spend any more alone time with Death. When I'd denied him, he'd raged for hours, throwing an epic tantrum. Then, when my cousin Magnolia had inadvertently pissed him off during her trial, I'd been forced to barter with him. The only way to save her from his wrath was to let him have his way. So I'd reluctantly agreed to question time.

From the moment I first came here, he'd been angry and intense and volatile. He still was, but since I returned a week ago, the anger wasn't rolling off him in hot waves like it had, and the volatile energy had calmed as well. It was still there but not as bad as before. Again, I wasn't sure why. This Death was different from the one I left the month before, and I wasn't quite sure how to deal with him.

I defied him—something I'd done since I first came here—but the Death sitting across from me now wasn't furious because I was bickering with him. He seemed almost... intrigued.

There had been questions I'd wanted to ask him but hadn't dared. I'd kept them simple for a reason. But without all the unhinged rage, I decided to try my luck. "Fine. I'll let you go first, but I get two questions."

He sat his mug down and rested his lightly clasped hands on the table. "Very well."

I was taken aback by his easy acquiescence.

The blue of his eyes grew darker and then stormy, the calm I stupidly thought I saw vanishing before my eyes. "Tell me, wife, how many males have you fucked?"

Inside, I flinched; outwardly, I showed nothing, or at least I hoped I hadn't. This was a turn I hadn't anticipated—not at all. I shrugged. "Does it really matter?"

"Yes."

"I'd have to count."

"I'll wait." He stared me down.

I tried not to squirm. What the fuck was this? Was this some kind of trap? Was he hoping for a virgin bride? I had no reason to lie, and I wouldn't, but this could be a good way to test this newish version of Death. I sat back and pretended I was having a hard time remembering, counting on my fingers. Was it stupid to rile Death? Absolutely. Had I been doing it anyway since I came here? Definitely. Finally, I sat forward and winked. "Less than ten."

"I want a number."

"More than five. I will say, my number would be a lot higher if I hadn't been so busy looking after my sister and working all the time. I've had more offers than I can count."

He set his mug down slowly. "Are you mocking me?"

"Of course not." I scooped another spoonful of oats. "Seven," I said, giving him his answer and shoving the oats in my mouth.

Fury etched his terrifyingly beautiful face, turning it utterly sinister. He didn't like that.

I gripped the edge of the table so he didn't see my hands tremble and forced a smirk. "Am I too much of a whore to be your consort now? By all means, send me back and forget I exist."

Darkness began to swirl around him. His cloak was made of moving shadows. Right now, they were barely there, but I saw them. His cloak gave away his moods—the more volatile he was feeling, the darker it became, wrapping around him. "Ask your questions," he said, voice filled with quiet menace.

I refused to be intimidated, even if I was trembling inside. "From what I understand, your mother created you and your brother rather than birthing you, turning you both into gods. Is that true?" My question obviously took him aback as well. He was used to my simple, no-stress questions. Nox, his and Somnus's mother, was the personification of night. I had yet to meet her, and from what little information I'd been able to find about her, that was a good thing.

"Yes," he said.

The passage I'd read said she'd created him and Somnus from light, that he'd existed before his godly status. "What were you before she made you a god?"

He went utterly still, studying me so closely, I had to fight not to whimper.

"A star," he finally said and stood.

I stared at him, unable to hide my surprise. "Like you were part of the universe?"

"Yes," he said. "I have something I need to attend to, if you'll excuse me," he said, then strode away, the dark shadows of his cloak flowing heavily around him as he left the room.

CHAPTER 2

Zinnia

I PLUCKED a sprig of rosemary from my hair while I smeared on lip balm. I'd been outside all day working in my garden. The seasons here... well, there weren't any—not here at the castle, anyway. It was different every day. Today the air had been dry with an icy bite to it, and my lips felt windblown and swollen.

The light was gone outside now, and I preferred to be indoors when that happened. Too many noises I did not like came from the woods around the grounds when night fell. I glanced at the silver clock on the wall; it was intricately tooled, delicate birds and foliage all over it. It was one of my favorite pieces in my room—it was also time to get a hustle on.

Scooping up Hemy, who'd been watching me from the top of my dresser, I put him on my shoulder. He pressed his little body against my neck as we walked out. "Let's go face the music."

If I'd known Death would force me to make up for our missed question time this morning, I would have hunted him down last night and forced him to do it when we were scheduled to, because twice in one day was not something I ever wanted to contend with again.

As always, the shadows and harsh whispers followed me as I rushed by. They were souls, or at least some kind of reflection of them from around Limbo, their voices echoing down the hall, their emotions like a heavy cloud. They haunted the halls, and I'd tried many times, but I couldn't reach them, couldn't communicate with them—with any souls at all when I was here. I was more than a little curious about the souls here and how this realm worked, but no one had offered to share.

Death's voice rolled from the library, followed by Egon's far gentler one, answering.

Death had made himself scarce since we ate this morning, when things took a weird turn with the whole what's-your-number question. He'd been pissed when he left. I really hoped he was in a better mood tonight, because I was tired, I missed my sister and my cousins and aunts, and the thought of sparring with him this evening had me feeling weary to the bone. It was all we did, but no matter how tired I was, I would meet him barb for barb. You gave Death an inch? Well, I didn't want to know what him taking a mile entailed.

Taking a fortifying breath, I knocked on the door. Death's gaze slid to me when I walked in, and I felt it like a lick of fire up my spine.

"I'll stay with him, my lord," Egon said, dipping his head and rushing from the room.

Death turned to the sideboard, and the *tink* of crystal came next.

He was pouring our drinks, which was all part of the ritual, I guess. I wasn't sure why he'd wanted this so badly.

I sneaked a glance over at him. His black shirt clung to his massive upper body, open to just below his pecs, giving a flash of the star tattooed on his chest. On closer inspection, I realized there were two more inside it —one slightly smaller, the same shape exactly, and another, much smaller one among the intricate swirls in the center. Small but bright. He lifted his gaze, and I quickly looked away.

"You smell like your garden," he said when he closed the space between us and held out my drink.

Oh, cool. He was smelling me again. That wasn't unsettling at all. "No flies on you tonight, my dark, malevolent one," I said with a smirk, trying to hide my discomfort, but couldn't meet his eyes.

This was the part I dreaded the most during our usual question time, taking the glass from him without our fingers touching. I usually just grabbed it on the top and bottom, avoiding where his hand wrapped around it. I wasn't sure why, but I couldn't do it. Touch Death? Not fucking likely, but tonight, he stood beside me, facing the fire as well, and instead of turning to face me when I did, he stayed where he was. His hand engulfed the glass, and his pinky was tucked under it. There was no taking the glass from him without my fingers touching his.

"You think me malevolent?" he asked, still holding out the glass.

Goddammit, I had no choice but to take it, or I'd draw attention to the fact that I was quietly freaking out at the prospect of my fingers touching his. "Aren't you?" *Three, two, one.* I grabbed it, and my breath was slammed from my lungs when his rough, warm skin seared mine. His gaze sliced to me, and the one-two smack of power had me staggering back.

"Sit down," he said without concern or explanation.

I all but fell back onto the leather chair. "You did that on purpose," I bit out.

He sipped his drink. "Did what?"

"Forced me to touch you. Gave me a bump of your power." Why lie? It was obvious at this point, and my avoidance of touching him couldn't have been lost on him.

He studied me. "You're stronger than I expected."

"You were testing me? Why?" He didn't answer, just stared at me. I refused to squirm as the silence stretched out. "You won't tell me?"

"It's time for us to begin," he said. "I believe it's my turn to go first."

No, he wasn't going to tell me; in fact, he was going to ignore what I'd asked completely. "You know I'll only ask you when it's my turn."

"You will not," he said. "You will ask something else."

I stared at him, and it was so incredibly hard, but I didn't look away. "Then I'd strongly suggest you don't ever do that again. I agreed to come here, but I didn't agree to be your entertainment or whatever the hell that was."

"The males you fucked, consort, were you in love with any of them?" he asked, as if I hadn't spoken at all, jumping into what was obviously his question for the night.

What the actual hell was this? Death seemed to be in the midst of some fucked-up metamorphosis, from a cloak-wearing, staff-thumping, rage-fueled monster to what stood before me now. He was all god, there was no mistaking it, but at times like this, there was a humanness to him that took me off guard. I sipped my drink, trying to decide how to answer. "I've believed myself in love many times."

He stilled, then placed his glass on the mantel above the fire. One moment he was there; the next, he was looming over me, his massive, tattooed hands on either side of me, gripping the arms of the chair. "Did you give your heart to any of the seven males you lay with, wife?"

"You're really hooked on that number, huh?" I said absolutely unwisely and despite my pounding heart, but I wasn't the kind of female to let a male walk all over me, not even Death himself, it seemed—not without a little fight, anyway. His scent filled the space between us, and it was like nothing I'd ever experienced before—dark, rich, and smooth, heady in a way that made you want more. It was too much, like everything else about him. Having him this close was like facing off against a fire-breathing dragon, and I tried so hard, but there was no controlling my body's deep trembles.

"Breathe," he said roughly.

That's when I realized my lungs were screaming for oxygen, and I gasped in a much-needed breath.

"Now, give me my answer," he said, studying me.

I was all but panting. "No, I have never truly given my heart to any male," I choked out. "And I never will," I added for reasons unknown.

His gaze slid over my face, and I felt it like the lick of the dragon's tongue. His eyes did that thing they had at breakfast earlier, almost brightening. "I believe you."

Then slowly, too slowly, he straightened, reclaimed his drink, and looked back into the fire as if none of that had just happened, while I sat there panting and trembling and trying to get my shit together. I wanted to make him squirm. I wanted to throw him off-balance like he seemed to be enjoying doing to me today.

Hemy gave me a little nudge, then pressed against me, sensing my unease and trying to soothe me. I drew strength from him. He may be tiny, but his love for me, his loyalty, was mighty. I licked my windburned lips and looked up... and caught Death looking at my mouth. I cleared my throat, and his gaze slowly slid up, locking on mine. It would be so easy to look away, to lose the battle of wills between us. He may be stronger, his battle plan more forceful, his arsenal far better equipped, but I was just as relentless. My attack was more subtle, yes, but I had no intention of waving the white flag anytime soon, no matter how exhausting this fight was.

"Tell me, my lord, am I the only consort you've had?" Someone had used that room before me, a female, and I'd wondered....

His glass paused on the way to his mouth, and he stared into it. His jaw tightened slightly. "No."

I stilled. "How many? I want a number," I said, throwing his words back at him from earlier that day.

"More than one and less than ten," he said, doing the same as I had.

What the hell did that mean? And where were his other consorts now? "What happened to them?"

"You asked your question, and I gave you your answer," he said.

"That was a non-answer—"

A roar of agony rattled the castle walls. Death slammed his glass on the mantel, spun, and strode from the room. I didn't know what possessed me, but I shoved off the chair and rushed after him. This was different. Somnus's roars of pain sounded different—goddess, horrifying and more... desperate.

Death shoved open the door to his brother's bedroom. Egon was at

Somnus's bedside, using a cloth to wipe his face. Blood slid from the sleeping god's eyes, nose, and ears, dripping onto the white linen pillow beneath him, staining it scarlet.

"He's gone too long," Egon said, his hand trembling as he tried to swipe away more of the blood.

Death moved closer and cupped his brother's face. He said something low and guttural in a language I'd never heard before. Somnus's eyes snapped open suddenly, and I gasped. They were black and glossy with distant stars, like staring into the night sky.

"*Frater*," Death said, accent thick and in that same guttural voice. Somnus stared blindly ahead, and then his eyes closed again. Cursing, Death looked up at Egon. "Prepare my things. It's time."

I looked between them. "What's going on? Time for what?"

Death turned to me. "You'll need to pack for at least a week, but pack light."

"Pack?"

"We leave in the morning," Death said and strode from the room.

>>>●<<<

There was a soft knock on my door.

I opened it, and Egon walked in carrying a set of leathers—body armor—black with deep burgundy patches at random spots.

"The master wanted me to give you these," Egon said and placed them on the chest at the end of the bed.

"He wants me to wear those when we leave tomorrow?"

"Yes, my lady." He dipped his head and turned to leave.

I got in his way. "Why do I need to wear body armor, Egon?"

He shook his head, his glossy horns shining in the lamplight. "It is not my place to say, my lady."

I'd told him to call me Zinnia more times than I could count, but he refused. "Wherever we're going, it's dangerous?"

He wouldn't meet my eyes. "It will be a... a difficult journey, yes."

"Egon—"

"I must finish packing for my lord," he said and rushed out the door.

If Death was going on some dangerous quest, why take me along? To him, I was just some weak mortal. A witch, yes, but mortal all the same. He was a god; I'd just slow him down. I rubbed my arms. He'd been playing his piano earlier, and the song had been so achingly sad, I still felt unsettled from listening to it. When he played, it was as if the whole castle stopped, as if everyone was caught up in his song, pulling emotions from those who listened and breaking their hearts into a million pieces.

623

It was agony.

Shaking out my hands, I tried to let go of it—the feelings his song had stirred in me along with the concern over this trip he was forcing me to take with him—and paced the room. I strode to the window and looked out at Death's night sky. Stars twinkled down as if I were back home, but I wasn't staring up at the same sky as Jasmine; no, Death had created it when he created this realm.

Movement caught my eye in the garden below.

I stepped closer to the window. He was down there. His chest was bare, and his smooth skin glowed while deep shadows highlighted every ridge and muscle. His head was tilted back, his gaze aimed to the heavens, while his lips moved.

Was he praying?

I moved closer to the window to get a better look and gasped. The shadows covering his body moved, reforming his appearance. They transformed him, his face reshaped by darkness into a skull, his chest and arms, a skeleton, and his eyes were black, as if reflecting the night sky, just like Somnus's had looked earlier.

He jolted suddenly, and his eyes cleared, the shadows moving and reshaping, his face and body returning to what they were before. I quickly stepped back, my heart beating hard in my chest.

Whatever I'd just witnessed, I got the feeling it was a sign of things to come.

I needed to be ready for anything.

CHAPTER 3

Zinnia

THE LEATHERS WERE sturdy but well-worn. Whoever owned them before me had obviously kicked ass because they were scarred and patched in a bunch of places. From the inside, you could see most of the damage was from clean slices, most likely knives or swords. If I was wearing what amounted to armor, then there was a chance I'd be fighting, so I'd strapped several throwing knives to my waist and my larger knife to my thigh. I also had a few of Magnolia's nasty potions with me—one that was straight to the point and melted the face off a creature in seconds, and another that caused temporary confusion, hallucinations, and blindness.

I walked out of the castle and had to fight not to suck in a sharp breath.

Death stood at the foot of the stairs, wearing heavy boots and worn leather like me. It molded to his tall frame, and dressed like that, goddess, the already large male was massive and even more imposing. I thought about the way he'd looked in the garden—utterly transformed, his features skeletal, his eyes aimed at the sky while his lips moved rapidly, speaking to... only he knew who—and shivered. He'd never looked more like the God of Death than he had last night. My gaze trailed over him now; yeah, there was no mistaking who he was right now either. His shoulders looked even broader this morning, his long, lean body hugged to perfection in all that black. His muscle wasn't bulky. If I had to describe Death, I'd say he had the body of an extremely tall Olympic swimmer: long muscles, agile, fast. His movements would be smooth in a fight, gliding from one move to the next—

"Ready?" he asked.

I jumped, not prepared for that voice. I never was.

"As I'll ever be." I carefully lifted the strap of the small bag I'd borrowed from Egon over my head as I descended the wide stairs. The bag was small and made of a soft but thick felt, perfect for Hemlock to stay warm in. I carried my pack in my hand. Hopefully, I had everything I'd need since I'd packed light as instructed. "So who did the leathers belong to?" I asked him.

His gaze swept over me, from the boots to my wavy red hair that I'd braided down my back to keep out of the way. "A warrior," he said.

"A friend of yours?"

Something moved through those crystal clear, glacial eyes. "No."

"Lover?" My belly twisted in an uncomfortable way for some reason.

He didn't answer, which was answer enough, wasn't it? I was wearing his ex-lover's armor. Realization struck. "She was your consort?"

"Yes."

What did it matter to me? Still, I felt kind of weird wearing something that had belonged to a female he once... cared about? Loved? Then again, who's to say he loved her? I was his consort, and we sure as hell weren't in love. "Where is she now?"

"Dead."

He was doing that thing he often did, watching me in a way I didn't understand. The way he replied, leaving things unsaid, as if he was waiting for me to figure out the punch line on my own when there was no way I could. "How did she die?"

"Gruesomely."

I couldn't read him at all, which was nothing new. "You don't seem very upset about it. Was she consort number one or number ten?"

He said nothing.

I jerked back. "Do all your consorts die gruesomely?"

"Not all." He held my gaze. "Some a little more peacefully."

Well now, wasn't this a new and horrifying discovery. "And how long do you expect me to last?"

"That is entirely up to you, consort," he said, then held his fingers to his lips and whistled.

He'd actually answered several questions without asking for anything in return. A crashing sound came from deep in the forest. "What the hell is that?"

"Our transportation."

The trees at the edge of the forest, several yards away, shuddered, followed by the sound of several large branches cracking; then two giant monsters burst through.

"Holy fuck." I stumbled back, but Death grabbed me, his fingers curling around my wrist and holding firm, and then he tugged me forward. I jolted as electricity bolted through me. Still, it was less shocking than it had been in the library. I could breathe at least. He called out to the beasts in that same language, in that same low, guttural voice he'd used with Somnus.

They slowed, stopping in front of us.

Their skin was thick like a rhino's but mottled black and gray. They had long, thin, muscular legs and claws like razors. Their heads were elongated, birdlike, with lower jaws that jutted forward and mouths that were full of sharp teeth and fangs like a wildcat.

Death said something to one of them, again in that language I didn't understand, before he turned to me. "She won't hurt you unless you mistreat her. She understands verbal cues." He still held my wrist, and even through the leather, I felt his touch pulsing through my arm.

I tried to pull away, but he turned to me, and his other hand came up fast, wrapping around my throat in a firm hold. I gasped and grabbed his wrist, trying to get him off, to pull away, but there was no dislodging him.

Was this how I died? Death having some random psychotic break and choking me to death?

"They only understand one language," he said, voice low as he held me, gasping and thrashing, immobile in his grip. "Stop fighting me."

I realized when I gasped in a desperate breath that I could breathe. At least he wasn't trying to cut off my airway. Warmth filled my throat, and little sparks danced down to my chest.

He dipped his face close to mine. "Now when you speak to her, she'll understand you." He was right there, closer than he'd ever been to me before. Goddess, I'd actually felt his warm breath against my lips.

Blinking, I tried to fight the pull, but I was sucked into his gaze, like a black hole dragging my soul from my body. He didn't need to cut off my breathing; I was holding my breath all on my own.

He released my throat suddenly, and I gasped in another lungful of air, but the reprieve was short-lived because he gripped my waist before I knew what he was about to do and hoisted me onto one of the beasts.

What I wanted to do was jump right the hell back off. I was disoriented and freaking the fuck out, but I had to get it together. No, I wasn't a warrior, but I was no slouch either. So instead of letting him see how rattled I was, I scooted forward on the beast to the only place I could sit comfortably, where there was a natural groove behind her shoulders. Death wrapped a girth belt around her belly, just behind me, and strapped on my pack, then slid on leather bridle-like headgear over her beaky jaw, secured it, and handed me the reins.

I gripped them while Death ran his hand down her long nose. "Thank you, Zuri, for your service to my consort and me. I know being away from your loved ones will be painful, but you and your family will be rewarded for your sacrifice."

I heard the words as he said them in another language, but this time, I understood them. "That's her name? Zuri?"

"Yes." He ran his hand along the larger beast on the other side of him. "And this is her mate, Raze," he said as he secured Raze's girth strap, then tied his wooden staff to it. He slid the bridle on before swinging himself up onto the beast's back. "Let's go," he said, and Raze started walking.

Zuri instantly followed her mate, moving up beside him, so close that my leg kept brushing Death's. I tried to steer her away, to put more distance between us, but she wasn't having it. *Awesome.*

Death rode toward an opening in the forest.

"So where are we going?" I asked, because the silence was making me jumpy. I glanced at his staff. "And why do you need that?"

"My staff has many purposes, including a weapon."

"You're Death, what do you need with weapons?"

"I'm never without my staff. We're also going to the Outer Realm, beyond Limbo, beyond everything, and I need a weapon because my powers will be significantly weakened there," he said.

Fear coiled deep inside me. "Going there kind of sounds like a seriously dumb thing to do, then."

"Perhaps, but it is necessary."

"Why?"

He stared straight ahead, and his strong jaw tightened, the muscle there pulsing several times as if he was grinding his teeth. I didn't think he'd answer, but then he glanced my way. "Because Somnus has been asleep too long. It's why he suffers, why he's in pain. He's fighting it. If I don't wake him, he'll fall into an eternal slumber, never to return."

Obviously not good for Somnus or Death. "Why won't he wake?"

Death looked away from me again. "Because time moves differently in the dream realm, and his task there is of the greatest importance. He can only leave for a short time before he must return, but he must leave. He must wake occasionally, or he never will again."

This journey was obviously dangerous, so what the hell did he think I could do? Why was he making me go with him? "And there's something in the Outer Realm that can wake him?"

"No. What we need is in the Night Realm."

His mother's realm. "So we're going there as well?"

"Yes."

"How long will it take to get there?"

"It will take two days and nights to pass through Limbo's forests and reach the gateway to the Outer Realm. How long it takes to reach our destination after that will depend on what is waiting for us on the other side."

"We could die?" I said, filling in the blanks.

"You could. I can't die—I'm a God—but I could be seriously injured and out of commission for a very long time."

Fuck. "I'd rather not die, if it's all the same."

"If you do as I say, you'll be fine. Now hold on tight," Death said, then patted Raze. "Run, my friend."

The beast took off, and Zuri bounded forward. I jerked back, almost coming off, and yanked on the reins to right myself, then hung on like hell. They were massive and ungainly, but they could move.

Death kept that pace for the rest of the day, and by the time we stopped for the night, I was exhausted. My thigh muscles ached and cramped, my back hurt, and my fingers were stiff from gripping the leather reins so tight.

Death jumped down as if we'd been riding for minutes, not hours, and removed Raze's girth strap and bridle. I groaned, dragging my leg over Zuri's back, and kind of slid to the ground. My legs buckled under me, but before I could hit the dirt, Death was there, his arm hooked around my waist, stopping me from falling.

"You need to work on your stamina," he said roughly.

The coarseness to his voice lifted goose bumps all over me. I quickly pulled away, clinging to Zuri's girth strap while the blood pumped back through my muscles. "I'm not used to riding all day, that's all. I'm not weak."

He stepped away from me. "If you say so."

I gritted my teeth and barely resisted picking up a rock and tossing it at his head. I removed Zuri's girth strap and bridle and hung them over a branch, watching as she and Raze trotted off into the forest to eat and rest.

Wordlessly, Death led me to the mouth of a cave that cut into stone at the base of a tall cliff. It was getting dark, but there was still enough light that when I looked up, I could tell it was hundreds of yards high.

"What is this place?" I asked as we walked in. I stopped in my tracks. "Whoa." There were candles already going, and an ornate fireplace was carved into one of the rock walls. A small kitchen was on the opposite side, a wooden table and four chairs beside it, and a large bed on a four-poster iron frame sat back, recessed in the stone. Dark fabric hung down the sides, tied back by leather cords, and the bed was draped in black velvet. Everything smelled clean and fresh, as if someone still lived here and had just done a spring clean.

"This was my home when I first created this realm," Death said, surprising me.

I spun to him. "You lived here? How long for?"

He shrugged a broad shoulder. "I can't recall. A long time." He opened his jacket hurriedly, sliding it off, and instantly rolled his shoulders as if he had been desperate to remove it. He turned to the entrance as he tugged off the shirt he wore underneath, visibly relaxing. The entrance vanished, just from a look, and now stone covered it—trapping us in. His gaze slid to the fire next, and flames immediately ignited in the hearth. "Sit. We'll eat."

I looked around again, for a door, for an escape, if I needed one, but there wasn't one. I was trapped in a cave with Death.

"Consort," he said, jolting me. I tried not to look panicked as I turned back to him. "Sit. Eat."

When I turned back, the table was set, plates piled with food at either end. "Neat trick," I said and managed to walk to the table without collapsing again. Sitting at the table, I took Hemy from his bag and set him on the table beside me. He blinked up at me, still drowsy. He'd slept all day. "You hungry?" I looked down at my plate. All my favorites were there. Slow-roasted beef, gravy, crispy potatoes, green beans, and glazed carrots. I put a couple carrots and a potato in front of Hemy and poured some water into a saucer.

Death's boots thumped against the stone floor, echoing through the room, and somehow, I managed not to jump, but my nerves zipped across my belly as he drew closer, then pulled out the chair opposite. I glanced up as he sat. His plate looked the same as mine, but he had twice the amount of beef. There was a pitcher with water and a mug, and a glass of wine as well. I took a fortifying sip. It hadn't escaped me that there was only one bed, and the idea of lying on it next to Death was more than I could even contemplate.

"Stop staring at your food and eat it," he said, voice low. "You'll need to keep up your strength."

I picked up my cutlery and sliced off a succulent piece of beef. "For all the fighting I'll be doing?"

His gaze dipped to my mouth, watching as I slid the fork past my lips. "I don't know what awaits us. We need to be prepared for anything." He shoved food in his mouth, his biceps flexing, then took a gulp of wine. "Where we're going, demons are rampant, but you're a warrior. I've seen you fight. It's nothing you can't handle."

I lowered my knife and fork. "You think I'm a warrior?"

"I know you are. My consort wouldn't be anything else," he said as if it were obvious, a fact, then lowered his gaze back to his food.

I sat there, kind of frozen, surprised he saw me that way and, yeah, pleased that he recognized my abilities and didn't see me as some weak female. "So all your consorts were warriors?"

"Not all warriors wield a sword."

This was true.

"Eat, Zinnia," he rumbled, not looking up, and the oxygen was punched from my lungs.

I quickly shoved a piece of carrot in my mouth so he didn't feel the need to look up again, but my heart was pounding wildly in my chest. He never called me by my name. Ever. It was always *consort* or occasionally *wife*. I took another sip of my wine and tried to get it the hell together while he ate across from me.

Finally, he wiped his mouth on a napkin and sat back. "Do you have a question for me tonight?"

I nodded, swallowing my last mouthful. I'd asked him multiple questions today, and he'd answered most of them. I didn't remind him of that, though.

"Good, but I have one for you first," he said.

I rolled my eyes. "Fine. I'm too tired to fight with you about it tonight."

"Why would you fight with me? It's my turn," he said, and his eyes glittered in the candlelight.

"Sure it is, Mors," I said, firing his name at him. If he was doing it, then so was I.

He stilled, unnaturally so, his eyes darkening. "I told you what would happen if you spoke my name again," he said. "Did you forget?"

Fuck. I had. I was full and warm from the fire and the wine and growing sleepier by the minute, which was why I was more relaxed than I'd ever been around him before. "I guess I did."

"You realize you must do whatever it is I ask? You vowed, and a vow cannot be broken."

In other words, I'd fucked up big-time. "What do you want?"

"I'll tell you when the time comes," he said.

Awesome, that didn't sound ominous at all. "Fine, not much I can do about it now, right?" I was doing my best not to let him see how freaked out I truly was. How the hell could I forget? He was watching me closely. Maybe he was waiting for the freak-out? Well, I wouldn't give him the satisfaction. "So what's your question? I'm as ready as I'll ever be."

His massive, scarred hand curled around his glass, and he took another sip of his wine, dragging it out, trying to torture me with suspense. "If you had the means, would you kill me?"

Okay, I hadn't expected that one. Was that Death's way of asking if I liked him? Yes, I'd kill you, equals no? No, I wouldn't kill you, equals yes? Despite everything, I didn't hate him. I wasn't naïve enough not to understand that there were bigger things at play here. He hadn't chosen me to be his consort any more than I'd chosen him, and going by his actions since we made our deal, I wasn't so sure he even wanted me here. It felt more like he needed me than wanted me. So no, I didn't hate him. "No, I wouldn't kill you."

He abruptly sat forward in his seat. "Why?"

I automatically jerked back; the intensity flowing from him had skyrocketed. "You get one question, remember?" Again, I was struck by how different he was. He was more... animated, and he seemed to possess more than one emotion. He wasn't just angry all the time like he had been before.

He ground his teeth, then visibly forced himself to relax, his big shoulders losing their rigidity. "I remember. Ask your question."

After all that had happened at this dinner alone, I should go for an easy one, but I couldn't stop the question that was forming in my head from coming out of my mouth. "Do you miss them, grieve them... your past consorts?"

No, he didn't like that question, not at all. His face had turned to stone. He didn't want to answer it, but we'd made a deal, and he had to. A low, rumbling growl came from him, and I barely managed to hold my ground and not jump from my seat and find a hole to shove myself into.

"If I allowed myself to truly feel the weight of their loss, I would never sleep come sunset, and I would never leave my bed come sunrise." Then he stood suddenly and strode to the hearth, giving me his back.

Shock had me glued to my seat. Again, Death had surprised me. He'd cared for them, and he'd lost them, all of them.

"You should get some sleep. Take the bed," he said without looking at me.

I jolted from my chair, scooped up Hemy, and did what he said without a word.

We'd done more than enough talking for tonight.

CHAPTER 4

Death

THE CANDLELIGHT and shadows made her red hair look like dimming embers. Her face was to the side, her thick lashes resting against her cheeks. My consort was just as fiery in temperament, possessed a warrior's heart, and had the kind of beauty that could bring the strongest of gods to their knees.

But I would not fall.

I would not let sadistic hope infiltrate my heart. I knew better. Still, I approached the bed to get a closer look, drawn by a higher power, by a force I had no control over. Resisting her wouldn't be easy, but if I let myself fall again, Nox would only take pleasure in my inevitable destruction; it was all she had left.

I'd bartered for our nightly question time because not only did I want an excuse to learn all there was to know about her life, but I craved her nearness and the sound of her voice. I thought I might actually be addicted to her sexy husky laugh, when she had occasion to, though that only usually happened when she was with Egon or Lyle.

And though I knew I shouldn't, that it was dangerous beyond measure, I climbed in beside the female sleeping soundly in my bed. I may not have hope, but this little witch was still my guiding star, and not getting closer to her was like asking the wind not to blow or the snow not to fall.

Just tonight.

I'd sleep beside her only tonight.

>)⟩●((‹

Zinnia

Wrapping the fur around her shoulders, she walked to the hearth. The fire crackled, light dancing on the stone walls. Anticipation moved through her while she waited for him to come home. She missed him when he left and counted the hours until he returned.

But tiredness eventually won out, and she got into bed.

She woke as his palm drifted up her thigh. Shivering, she covered it and brought his big, tattooed hand to her lips, kissing his scarred fingers. "I missed you, my love."

I woke with a jolt, gasping in a breath. It was dark, only a small candle glowing from somewhere deep in the room. My eyes were desperately trying to adjust while my heart still raced, and my belly, it felt... strange.

That's when I became aware of the massive male lying under me. I was draped over a wide chest, my hand resting on ridged abdominal muscles, skin molten and smooth. Death's intoxicating scent filled my lungs, and my body buzzed with electricity.

I broke out in a sweat.

I was lying on him, draped over his body like I had a right to be here. I was frozen in place, wanting to pull away but too scared to move in case I woke him. My nerve endings itched, and my belly squirmed. I couldn't take it; I scrambled back, but I shouldn't have been worried about waking him. His eyes glittered in the candlelight, not blue but black, the night sky in their depths, and they weren't cold; they were hot, smoldering.

"What... what are you doing?" I choked out.

"I was sleeping."

"You can't just get in here with me," I fired at him, freaking out so bad, I was breathing hard.

His lips peeled back. "That's where you're wrong, wife."

Oh goddess. "You look... as if you want to...."

"How do I look, little witch? Tell me." His voice was nothing but gravel, resonating through me, over me.

"Like you want to ..." Punish me. Hurt me.

Suddenly, shadows swirled around him, thick and heavy, and the room filled with a deep and horrible dread. Darkness moved around his face, reshaping it, gathering at his eyes and cheeks, his nose, transforming his face into a skull, into Death. His hand shot out, and I scrambled out of his reach.

It paused midair.

"Mors?" I said. Yes, it was stupid to say his name again, but something was wrong, and I needed to get through to him somehow.

Rage blasted from him, like a furious storm, and I wrapped my arms around myself.

"I will not harm you," he roared, his words and his tone a total contradiction. It wasn't the first time he'd done it, and it was unsettling as hell.

Then he climbed out of bed, and his cloak settled around him as he stormed across the cave. A door appeared, swinging open, and he strode out before it slammed behind him.

I stood there frozen, staring after him for several seconds. At least until the adrenaline drained from me and that awful heaviness left the room with him. My legs shook, and I flopped back on the bed. What the hell was that? And not just the weird way Death was behaving.

That hadn't just been a dream; it was more... an apparition, a manifestation? Maybe my medium powers weren't totally smothered here? What I'd seen, it was like one of the visions I had when I communed with a spirit, when they wanted to pass on a message, and the vision I'd just received was here in this cave. Did one of his consorts die here? Is that who I saw? I only saw it for a moment, but that had been Death's hand she'd kissed. No one else had hands like he did.

I tried to go back to sleep, but I lay awake for hours; my mind wouldn't shut the hell up. I had too many unanswered questions. Who was that with him in the dream? Why was she reaching out to me now? If she was one of Death's consorts, how did she die?

Somehow, I'd managed to drift back to sleep, because when I woke again, it was to the smell of bacon and coffee.

Shoving back the covers, I scooped up Hemy and got out of bed. Death was sitting at the table, facing the hearth. He was leaning forward, his elbows resting on his knees, a mug of coffee in his hands, and he was staring into the unlit fire.

I stood there, not sure what to say.

"Come and eat," he said, not looking my way. "We need to leave soon."

Cautiously, I walked over. I wasn't sure what to expect. I could say nothing about what happened last night and pretend he hadn't done what he had, but I wasn't going to do that, not anymore. I'd been coming here, to Limbo, for a long time, putting up with his mood swings, and if what he said was true, and he had no reason to lie, all his consorts died, which meant I might not have all that much time left. So what the hell did I have to lose? Yes, he scared the hell out of me at times, but again, dead girl walking over here.

"You want to tell me what happened last night?" I asked as I pulled out one of the chairs and sat. I put Hemlock on my lap. "'Cause I have to tell you, it was fucking weird." There was a mug of hot coffee in front of me, and I sipped it as he straightened and turned in his seat to face me. And go me! When his blue eyes collided with mine, and there was a good amount of fury in them, I didn't shudder *or* pee myself. "Don't look at me like that. I've put up with your mood swings for eighteen months. I'm not going to cower before you anymore," I said and snatched up a slice of bacon, broke off a small piece, and gave it to Hemy. My hand was hardly even trembling when I shoved the rest in my mouth. Again, go me!

"I don't recall one instance of you cowering before me, consort. You have snarked and battled your way through every one of our conversations. You have conveyed your disdain for me with every encounter. You leave my castle with glee when every cycle of the moon has passed and return with a thundercloud over that head of fiery red hair when your time with your family has ended." He shook his head, and his lips actually twitched. "But cower? No, there has been no cowering, little witch."

I was momentarily stunned, and I shoved another piece of bacon into my mouth while I rallied. "Will I live long enough, do you think, to truly know you? I can't help but wonder, because you are not the male I first met. You're constantly changing."

He quirked a brow, and the blue of his eyes deepened, darkness swirling from within. "How so?"

He knew exactly *how so*, but he was trying to intimidate me, daring me to say it out loud... testing me. "Your moods, for one," I said, taking some toast and smearing it with butter, then spooning scrambled eggs on top. "You raged all the time when I first came here."

"Did I now?" he said.

A little shiver slid through me, but I ignored it and pushed on. "You also hid under your cloak, skulking around the castle like a pissed off, moody shadow." I bit my toast and chewed, looking across at him. "It was like you were trying to scare me off, which was kind of surprising considering how desperate you were to get me here. Why is that?"

He just stared at me.

"Your intimidation tactics won't work on me, not anymore. The way I see it, my days are numbered. The worst is already coming, probably sooner than I'd like." I shrugged, even as the thought of never seeing my family again twisted brutally in my gut. "There's nothing you can do or say now to scare me, so why don't you just answer the damn question?"

He ran his hand over his tattooed skull, making his biceps bulge, then sat forward in a deceptively relaxed pose. Like we were just two normal people shooting the shit over breakfast. "What did you expect me to do?" he asked instead of answering.

I noted, with not a little unhappiness, that he hadn't contradicted my premonition of my own rapidly approaching demise. "Honestly? I thought you were going to force me into your bed and make me your sex slave. I am your wife, right? Essentially. I thought you'd want to consummate this unholy union, then try and breed me until I eventually died a shriveled, used-up old crone." I scooped another forkful of eggs into my mouth and watched with satisfaction as his expression, always so stoic—except when he was raging, that was—shifted into genuine surprise. I mean, I was exaggerating. I hadn't expected him to attempt to breed me until I died or make me his sex slave, but I hadn't really known either. I had, at the very least, assumed he'd force me into his bed, and I was more than thankful he hadn't.

Then he'd gotten into bed with me last night and looked at me like he wanted to make a meal of me. In that moment, terrifyingly, I knew he'd wanted me, and that seemed to just piss him off more.

His fingers tightened around his mug. "You thought I would repeatedly rape you and force you to bear my offspring?"

I shrugged and sipped my drink. "Yeah, kind of."

He shot to his feet, the chair crashing to the floor, making me jump, and then he paced from one side of the room to the other. He turned back to me now with those shadows swirling around him, his eyes darkening, his face transforming.

I opened my mouth to say something. I wasn't quite sure what, but I needed to defuse the situation somehow because what was coming off him wasn't... good.

But before I could, he spun away and stormed out of the cave.

Well, shit, perhaps I'd pushed him too far? The god's moods swung on a dime. You never knew what you were going to get. What I wanted to do was stay right the hell here, but I didn't think it was wise to make him wait, not now. So I quickly finished my coffee, put Hemy in his bag with some breakfast, and headed outside.

Death stood with our beasts. He'd already put on their girth straps and bridles and was tying a water bladder to Zuri.

I was stuck with him, with no escape for at least a week. I needed to rein it the hell in or this trip would be unbearable. Biting my lip, I walked over to him, fighting my nerves. I was going to have to apologize, wasn't I? Goddammit. "I'm sorry," I muttered. "I thought you were—"

"The kind of male who would force himself on a female?" he snarled low, still with his back to me.

"I'm sorry," I said again. "But in my defense, you are a god. Some of you guys have a pretty bad rep, even you have to admit that."

He turned to me, his eyes so bright a blue, I startled. "You're right—we're all sick, evil monsters," he said, and there was definitely sarcasm in his voice.

That was also new. Right, time to change the subject. "So how far are we riding today?"

He closed the space between us, so close now, I had to tilt my head all the way back. "About the same as yesterday," he said, then curled his fingers around my waist.

My breath punched from my lungs, and then I was in the air, tossed up onto Zuri's back, and he was already walking away before I realized what had happened. I let out a shaky breath and tried to get my shit together while he swung up onto Raze.

He glanced my way. "Try and keep up." Then he told Raze to run.

Zuri took off instantly without me having to tell her to, and I held on for dear life as we bounded through the forest at full speed.

Toward what? I had no idea, but I got the feeling wherever we were going—whatever came next—would change me in ways I couldn't even imagine.

CHAPTER 5

Zinnia

WE STOPPED FOR A QUICK LUNCH, but other than that, we'd ridden hard all day. Night was falling, and the air had chilled. I rubbed my arms as Zuri slowed, following her mate's cues, then stopped in a clearing in the middle of nowhere. Howls and cries echoed in the distance, lifting the hair on the back of my neck. I slid down off Zuri, managing to stay upright all on my own this time, and pulled my knife free as I scanned our surroundings.

"We're getting close to the gateway," Death said.

"Are those sounds coming from the Outer Realm?"

He shook his head. "Occasionally, creatures—demons—get through."

"Is that how Egon came to be here?"

"Yes. There's no real way to stop them. Egon regularly takes out a hunting party and culls the more dangerous breeds."

"Do I need to be worried? Will they hunt us?" Our little cave last night had been like a five-star accommodation, because, looking around now, there was nothing here, no cave, no cabin, no place to hide.

"It depends on the creature. While some will sense me and stay away, others will see me being here as a challenge."

"Why the hell would they think that?"

"They are Nox's followers. She won't want me in her realm, and she'll try and prevent it."

I turned fully to face him. "Your mother doesn't like you?"

"Nox hates me and my brother," he said and pressed his hand to one of the largest trees near us, looking up.

"Why?"

He tilted his head back, and his eyes rolled back as he muttered under his breath. A ladder rolled down from nowhere. "Up you go. I'll take care of Zuri and Raze," he said and waited for me to jump to it.

"I don't need you to protect me, you know? I'm not the kind of witch to hide while danger lurks beneath me—" He hooked a strong arm around my waist and all but tossed me halfway up the rope ladder. "What the hell are you doing?"

"Saving time," he said and turned away to take care of our mounts.

So goddamn arrogant. I spun away and climbed up the rest of the way. It was a tree house, kind of like the one Magnolia lived in with her crow-shifter mate, Bram, but not as big. The room was a large circle, with soft clay-colored walls and an open fire in the middle, already going, the flue disappearing up through the peaked roof. A bed was to one side, shaped to fit the wall, and there was a low table on the other side with cushions around it and more along the wall to sit on. Everything was bright jewel colors, and the place had a warm and cozy feel.

I found it hard to believe Death just came up with this out of thin air.

He popped up through the floor, pulled the ladder up after him, and the hole in the floor vanished, sealing us in. "No escape, huh?"

"No way for a demon to get in while we sleep," he said.

"And what if I need to pee?"

He motioned to a doorway with a colorful piece of fabric hanging over it.

Awesome, he'd be able to hear me. "The demons can't actually hurt you, though, right?"

"The closer we get to the gateway, the more I can feel my powers weakening." He turned to the low table, and this time, he needed more than a look to make food appear; he closed his eyes and held his hand above it.

His mother wanted him powerless when he was in her realm or close to it. Didn't she sound just lovely.

We sat on the ground on cushions, and I loaded up my plate with rice and beans and lamb. I took a sip of my wine. "This looks amazing. If you can do this, why have Egon cook?"

"He likes to do it."

"Take care of you?"

"Yes."

Death cared about Egon, considered his feelings, wanted him to be happy. "He's your friend."

He grunted and stabbed a piece of meat and put it in his mouth, and as soon as he'd swallowed it, his gaze came back to me. "Why wouldn't you kill me if you had the means?" he asked, picking up the same line of questioning from the night before.

I'd really been hoping he'd forget about that, but the male had the memory of an elephant. There was no reason to lie. "I don't hate you. I never really did. When I was younger, I was scared, so I hid from you. But I figure, you didn't specifically *choose me* to be your consort, and this whole... thing, whatever *this* is"—I glanced between us—"was out of your control as well. So how can I hate you for it?"

The muscle in his jaw jumped, but he said nothing.

I took another sip of my wine. "My turn." I could ask what exactly *this thing* was. He demanded I be here in Limbo with him, but I had no idea why. I didn't think asking that right now was a great idea, though. "What's with this place?" I asked instead, deciding to appease my curiosity.

"What do you mean?"

"I live in your castle. This place is the complete opposite of that. This is not you."

"No, it's not me, but it was the first thing that came to mind, so I recreated it."

"Recreated? Who lived here before?"

"You asked your question, and I answered it," he said and carried on eating.

I studied him. "It belonged to one of your consorts, didn't it?"

He said nothing.

Which meant, why yes, yes, it did. "So what was this place? Did she build it here in Limbo? Or was it something she lived in before she became your consort, and if so, how do you know what it looked like?"

Still, he said nothing, and then a thought occurred to me: was this where they spent quiet time together? Like a night away from the castle, just the two of them... the Limbo equivalent of a dirty weekend?

A weird feeling swirled in my belly, and without my say-so, my eyes slid to the opulent bed, big and draped in soft, richly colored fabrics. I swallowed audibly in the utter silence that had engulfed the room. I was right. Somehow, I knew I was right. I mean, the bathroom didn't even have a proper door. This place was for people who had no boundaries, no inhibitions, and were completely at ease around each other.

I turned back to Death and noticed he was watching me closely.

Clearing my throat, because it felt impossibly tight all of a sudden, I carried on eating, but Death didn't look away from me, not once. If anything, he grew more intense, and the energy he was throwing off was filling the room. Goddess, goose bumps had lifted all over me. I licked my lips nervously.

Death made a low sound that shot right through me, and I took a swig of my wine.

"So what time will we reach the gate tomorrow?" I said because the silence, the tension, felt like a rope pulled taut and about to break at any moment.

He snapped out of whatever this was and unfroze, the tension dialing *way* down. "If we leave early, we should be there before midday."

I nodded. "I'll need to prepare before we leave. If there's a chance I'll be fighting, I need my magic at full power, and an extra boost would be a good idea as well. I'm not ready to die quite yet."

"You can have as much time as you need," he said. "Do you need to perform a spell or some kind of ritual?"

Whenever he talked to me like this, no deals or bartering or demands, like he could be anyone, just your average Joe asking questions—well, except for that voice—I was always taken aback, but I knew better than to let my guard down. Not with how fast his moods shifted. "Yeah, a simple ritual. I'll use blood to increase my power."

"Do you want me to kill something for you?" he asked in his destroyer's voice, but somehow, it came out like crushed velvet.

It slid over my skin, and I barely suppressed my shiver. Jesus, the way he said it, so intimate, as if he were whispering dirty things in the dark.

This was a different version of Death, again. This transformation hadn't been slow and steady; no, he just seemed to have suddenly changed when I came back, and every day that passed, this new side of him was making an appearance more and more. He was giving me more "human" vibes and less of the vengeful God of Death. Though that was still there as well, it just wasn't all he was now. He was... more.

I cleared my throat again. "Ah... no, thank you. That won't be necessary. I'll use my own blood."

His gaze shot up from his food. "No," he said so loud, I jumped.

I frowned at him. "I'm a blood witch, you must know that?" I held up my hand and showed him my scarred palm. "How do you think I got this? I mean, when I first came here, I was covered in my own blood, so this can't be a surprise to you."

"You are not to cut yourself, not anymore," he said, his eyes darkening, burning into me.

I stared at him, not backing down despite the tremble in my belly and the way the hair on the back of my neck stood up. "Cutting and magic go hand in hand in my coven. It gives us strength and increases our power. It's what we do, and it's who we are," I fired back at him.

His fingers curled into a tight fist. "You test me, consort. You push me at every turn, but I will not concede to you on this. You will not win."

What I wanted to do was scream in his face, just release all the rage and fear I was feeling in that moment, but somehow, I knew that would be the absolute wrong thing to do. Instead, I forced it down, and then I reached out and covered his clenched fist with my hand. It was rough, his skin scarred and hot. Power sparked from him to me, and it was hard to keep holding on, to keep my breathing even, but I didn't let go and made myself look deep into his eyes so he'd see the truth of my words as I said them. "If you take this from me, you may as well kill me now. This is not a battle for you to win or lose. Without my magic, I am nothing. I don't exist. I won't be Zinnia Thornheart anymore. Without my magic, I won't be me, and that's not something I ever want to face." I shook my head. "I'm here, and I'm not going anywhere. I've accepted that this is my life now—what's left of it, anyway—but you have already ripped me from the people I love most in this world, and you need to know that I won't let you take this from me. Whatever the cost, I won't let you take this from me as well."

The hand under mine was pulled away, and then it shot out, curling around the side of my throat, not tight, similar to the way he'd held it outside the castle before we left. Then his hand slid higher, his long, thick fingers sinking into my hair, shocking me. "Always so fucking stubborn," he rasped.

I stayed completely still, breathless, as his thumb touched my chin. His gaze dipped; he was no longer looking into my eyes but watching what he was doing as he slowly slid his thumb higher, his rough skin scraping mine, until the very tip brushed the bottom of my lower lip. His gaze was focused on that connection and nothing else.

A shaky breath punched out of me at the look on his face while he touched me.

He blinked, as if knocked from wherever he'd just gone, and looked up at me. "You may practice your magic then. Stubborn little witch." Then he finally released me.

I sank back in my seat as if I'd been unplugged from an electrical socket, my body still buzzing and my heart pounding.

Death strode across the room. The trapdoor reappeared, and he kicked the ladder back down and jumped to the ground after it.

I took another shaky breath and tried to get my heart back under control.

>>◦●◦<<

She turned in strong arms, sliding her hands over wide shoulders.

"Do you want me to fuck you, Aster?"

"Yes," she whispered.

Firelight danced over his bare skin, making the tattoos on his flesh come alive. She trailed her hands up his stomach and over his chest. They were slender, beautiful hands. He rolled her to her back, his long, thick fingers curling around her throat. "My precious Stella."

She wrapped her legs around him, and he slammed inside her—

My eyes flew open, my body hot and coated in a fine layer of sweat. The room was warm, too warm, and I blinked up at the ceiling. A vision, not a dream.

Aster.

She'd been with Death in this tree house, and she may or may not be the female I'd dreamed about the previous night. Why were they showing me these things? If I could use my medium power to its full potential here, I could call them to me and ask what they wanted.

Was it a warning of some kind? Had Death killed them? Was that what they were trying to tell me? Not to get close to him, not to let him in, or I'd end up the same?

It was still night; I could tell by the sounds the insects made outside. Pushing myself up, I shoved back the covers, then bit my lip. Death had come back sometime while I'd been asleep. He'd arranged himself on the larger cushions. His upper body was kind of propped up; one hand was behind his head, and the other, resting on his abs. With his arm back like that, I could see the tattoo that ran all the way down the back of it more clearly. He had two of them, another identical one on the other arm. Inverted torches. The death of the flesh, and the eternal life of the soul— that's what they meant. The one I could see was beautiful, flames licking down his forearm to his wrist.

It looked so real, like if you reached out and touched it, you'd feel cold steel or the heat of the flames.

My gaze slid over the rest of him. He looked the same as he did in my vision: his skin, golden in the firelight, the dancing flames moving over the dips and valleys of his muscled body, the way his tattoos almost looked alive in the dim light.

He was devastatingly beautiful.

Something in my lower belly tightened, and I bit my lip again. I didn't want to be attracted to him, especially now, when I thought about what those visions could mean, but I guessed it was inevitable, right? He was essentially my mate; an attraction; whether you wanted there to be one or not, was part and parcel with that whole thing. A higher power had brought us together; fate had chosen me for him, and him for me. The only difference here was, Death could have more than one consort in his lifetime.

What happened if I didn't die an untimely death? Would the consorts keep coming? Would I end up the head sister wife of Death's polygamist family? His hand slid lower, and he groaned in his sleep. I slammed my legs together when unwanted lust, caused by that sound, zipped right through my belly and landed between my legs. *Shit.*

My gaze trailed back up his body, over his square jaw and that strong nose, to his dark lashes resting on his cheeks. The male had perfect bone structure, but then he was a god, so what did I expect—

His eyes opened, locking on mine.

My heart thumped against my ribs. "I just... I woke, and you... you were snoring," I blurted, lying through my teeth while my face went up in flames. "Keep it down," I snapped and rolled over so I was facing the wall and could hide my humiliation.

Silence rang out for several stunned seconds, and then I thought—though I had to be wrong—I heard a low laugh before the room went silent again.

CHAPTER 6

Death

SHE'D BEEN in a trancelike state for the past ten minutes. She sat with her hands pressed to the forest floor, eyes closed, lips moving rapidly, spelling. The knife was on the ground beside her, and I had to grip Raze's girth strap to hold myself back when she finally opened her eyes, picked it up, and sliced her forearm. The scent of her blood hit me instantly, and the darkness rushed forward, confused, enraged, the shadows afraid we were losing her.

That she was being taken away from us already.

The shadows fed off my emotions, and I couldn't fight down all that was warring inside me, couldn't hold them back. The weight of my cloak fell around me, and the world turned gray and misty as the shadows gathered at my eyes, transforming the rest of my face.

Her blood dripped down her arm and pooled on the ground, absorbed into the earth, becoming part of my world, part of me. I'd never felt anything like it; heat trickled over my shoulders and back, sliding around my hips and down my cock. My eyes rolled back in my head.

What the fuck is happening?

She did it again, slicing the other arm, then closed her eyes and tilted her head back, muttering her spell over and over. I could *feel* the power move through her, because it was moving through me now as well. More blood hit the ground, sinking into the dirt, and I gritted my teeth so I didn't groan when the warmth washed over me again, down my chest, my stomach—

Fuck.

I fought not to go to her, gripping the leather strap tighter.

"Are you okay?" Her voice drifted over to me, and the shadows instantly receded, her voice soothing them, reassuring them. She was alive. She was okay.

I wasn't. I was far from fucking okay.

"Yes," I bit out and somehow managed to stay where the hell I was.

She nodded, watching me closely, but I could tell she didn't believe me. It seemed I was incapable of hiding anything from her. Taking out a small pot from her bag, she scooped out some of its contents and smoothed it over her cuts, then bound them with linen and slid her jacket back on. "All done."

Zuri bumped Zinnia with her snout when she reached her, and my consort ran her hands down the beast's neck. "I'm okay, sweetheart," she said. "I promise."

The gentle voice she used didn't help the way I was feeling right then, so I closed the space between us and tossed her up onto Zuri's back. She made a sound of surprise, then scowled at me. "We need to leave."

"Well, I'm ready when you are."

I swung up onto Raze, and we headed off. I tried to focus, to prepare for what was to come, but all morning, visions of her lying in bed in that tree house, looking at me from across the room, kept infiltrating my mind. The way she'd been looking at me, there was lust in her eyes. I could barely resist her as it was. If she ever decided to act on those feelings, I was fucked, because there was no resisting her. What she didn't know was that I was hers to command.

She was my queen, and I existed to bow at her feet.

To worship only her.

》》◐《《

Zinnia

The gateway's power was like a giant magnet—the closer we got to it, the stronger its pull.

Zuri was restless beneath me, jumpy and nervous. I ran my hand down her neck. "It's okay, sweet girl," I said. "You can go home soon."

We wouldn't be riding them past the gate. We'd be traveling on foot once we entered the Outer Realm.

The forest grew darker the closer we got to it. I shivered. It felt as if night was falling when it was barely after midday. I studied Death; his wide back was rigid as he searched our surroundings.

How the hell had we gotten here? The first time he'd come to me, I'd been fifteen, and he'd terrified me—so much so, I'd refused to sleep until I was sure he wouldn't invade my dreams again. How did we go from that night to now? To me traveling through realms with him on the back of a beast.

The memory of that night rushed forward unbidden.

A voice whispered through my head, then another.

I felt awake, but I wasn't.

"There she is, brother. I found her for you."

The owner of that voice was nowhere to be seen. I was in a forest, dark and dense. I spun around, searching the trees. "Who's there?"

Electricity clawed over my skin, like tiny talons clinging to my flesh. Dread sliced down my spine, and the veins on either side of my throat felt as if they were struggling to pump blood fast enough. I felt dizzy and out of breath.

Shadows moved among the trees, and I tried to step back, but I couldn't move. My feet were locked in place, thick roots twisted around them, holding me fast. I shook my head furiously. Why wasn't I waking up? I needed to wake up.

The shadows swirled more furiously, twisting closer.

No, not shadows.

Oh goddess, it was a massive black robe, the hood up, concealing the being underneath. It moved as if it was alive. It came closer, and I fought harder, but there was no escape.

"Do not fight." A voice drenched in sorrow and agony and rumbling with earth-shattering rage rolled over me.

I froze, terror locking every muscle in my body.

Death.

Somehow, I knew who he was.

He stopped in front of me, bright blue eyes piercing me from beneath his hood. "You belong to me," he said in that horrifying voice. "On your eighteenth birthday, I will come for you, consort."

I stared at him in terror.

"You will belong to me, serve me... love me."

I wanted to scream, to cover my ears and curl up on the ground. The dread and despair that filled me made me want to die. If I had a knife, I would've slit my own throat then and there. I'd never felt this way, this hopeless, this depth of emptiness. Oh goddess, it hurt.

I tried to shake my head, to say no, but my body was locked solid, utterly immobile. I felt a hot tear streak down my ice-cold cheek while my mind screamed, the sound trapped inside me, unable to leave my mouth.

His arm lifted, a bony hand about to cup my face—

I jolted awake.

Jasmine stood over me, her face wet with tears. "You were screaming. I thought you were dying," she sobbed.

I pulled my baby sister into my arms as Hemlock scurried up my arm and curled around my neck, hissing in my ear, letting me know he was scared as well, looking for the danger. "I'm okay." I shoved back the covers. "Go back to bed, Jazzy. I just had a bad dream, that's all," I lied.

She nodded, her eyes wide and filled with fear. "Something's wrong."

I wrapped my arm around her narrow shoulders. "I promise I'm okay. I just... I remembered I had a paper due tomorrow. I dreamed Mr. Anders was chasing me with a knife, demanding I give it to him. Go back to bed. I'm gonna make some coffee and get it done." I couldn't go back to sleep, not when Death might be there waiting for me.

She nodded and yawned. "Don't ever scream like that again," she muttered and headed to the door.

"I won't," I said, which was useless since I had no idea I'd been doing it.

Jasmine wandered out, and I snatched up my phone and searched the word consort.

A wife, husband, or companion.

I shot to my feet. No. Never. I would never be his.

Zuri stumbled, jolting me back to the here and now, and I ran my hand down her neck to soothe her.

In the end, the fates had gotten their way, like they always did. There'd be no escaping my destiny, and there never had been. When I thought of the price I'd paid to conceal myself from him—I shuddered. I hadn't known. Even after what was stolen from me was gone, I still hadn't understood the magnitude of it.

I shook off the memories, not wanting to go back there, to what happened three days later in that grimy little house, or think about those dead yellow eyes that haunted me still on my darkest days.

Zuri tilted her head to the side, and I felt the tension in her body as unease built behind my chest; something was seriously off. We were still in Limbo, but I felt it—the Outer Realm was seeping through the gateway and polluting this part of the forest. What the hell would it be like on the other side?

Death continued to scan the area around us. He felt it as well.

"We're close, aren't we?"

With a growl, several demons burst from the trees and attacked Zuri. She shrieked in pain, and Raze spun around, roaring. I jumped from her back, before she bucked me off, and went after the demons biting and slicing her with their claws. I pulled out my knife and stabbed the one closest in the eye, about to spin him around and stab him in the throat—but then Death was there. He still had powers, even if they were diminished, but instead of making them go *poof*, he grabbed the one I'd stabbed. His hand and forearm turned black—something I'd never seen before—and as soon as he touched the demon, blood spilled from the creature's mouth. Death gripped him under the chin and wrenched his head back, tearing it clean off with a snarl.

Another came at me, and he slashed its throat with his staff, kicked it in the sternum, and went down with it. He pulled a knife from his boot, and gripping the demon's face with that black hand, holding him down, blood oozing from between his fingers, he hacked its head off, and it turned to ash.

Death finished off the rest before I could even get to them. The touch of Death was real, and I'd just seen it in action.

When the last demon disintegrated at his feet, he strode to me, his gaze slicing over my body. "Are you injured?"

"No, I'm fine." I quickly checked on Hemy. He was curled up, trembling, and I held him in his bag close to me. "I'm so sorry, baby," I whispered.

Death closed in. "It's only going to get worse. Let me send him back. Egon will look after him."

I hated being parted from Hemlock—he was my familiar, and it physically hurt to be away from him—but I would never forgive myself if something happened to him. He was terrified, and it broke my heart to see him like this. I nodded and scooped him up. "Egon is going to take good care of you until I get back, okay? You know he loves to give you treats." Hemy squeaked, then gave me a little hiss, not happy, not wanting to be away from me either. "Do you have enough power this close to the gateway?"

Death nodded.

I kissed Hemlock on his fuzzy little head and handed him over.

Death gently took him, cradling him in his big, tattooed hands. Hemlock looked up at him wide-eyed as Death closed his eyes, head tilted back.

One moment, Hemlock was there; the next, he was gone. When Death opened his eyes again, they were bright, glowing. "Egon has him. He knows what to do."

Zuri whimpered. She was bleeding badly, and Raze was pressed to her side. "Is she going to be okay?"

"As long as they leave now so Raze can tend to her wounds—his saliva has powerful healing properties," he said and strode over to them. "You may go now, my friends. I'm sorry your mate was injured, Raze. When she has recovered, come to the castle, and I'll make sure you have all the food you need and clean wool and cotton for your nest."

Raze made a low sound and leaned into Death when he ran his hands down the beast's side. We quickly got our bags, removed their bridles and girth straps; then Raze nudged his mate, and they loped off into the forest.

"We need to keep moving." Death scanned the trees surrounding us. "There could be more demons close by."

Slipping on my pack, I tightened the leather straps, then secured my hunting knife to my thigh and motioned ahead. "Lead the way."

We walked quickly and quietly through the dense forest, and every now and then I heard the crack of a branch or a distant howl. "They're stalking us."

He glanced down at me and nodded. "We'll be harder to detect once we pass through the gate with my power so diminished. We should hopefully get a head start before they work out we're there."

"So what are we doing when we get through? Is there something we need to collect, something that will wake your brother?"

Death continued to look ahead. "His physical body is in my castle, but his dream-self is in our mother's realm. It's the only way he's safe from her there. We need to go to the location his dream-self resides and call for him to wake." He tilted his head to the side, listening, and I did the same, but then he carried on.

"Why is his... dream-self there in the first place?"

"He guards something there that only he has the ability to protect."

"What's he guarding?"

He paused, just for a moment. "Something precious."

That pause was enough of a tell that I knew he wasn't going to share more than that—not yet, anyway—but there were also a whole bunch of holes in that story, not just what this "precious thing" was.

We carried on without too much trouble after that. At one point, Death spun around with a snarl, pounding his staff on the ground, and whatever had been following us changed their mind and stayed back.

The trees were dense here, and when we broke through to the other side, I saw it. The gateway. It was stone, similar to the gate out of Limbo, but this was made of glossy onyx, flecked with silver, like tiny stars.

Coldness, dread, evil seeped through the gateway as I stared at it. "I can hold my own, but I'd be lying if I said I wasn't afraid."

"I won't let you die," Death said, his voice resonating through me.

I swallowed, my throat impossibly dry all of a sudden. "Promise?" I smirked up at him, as if I could hide just how scared I was.

"You have my word."

Then Death took my hand, and we stepped through.

CHAPTER 7

Zinnia

We entered into darkness.

"This way," Death said, voice low, tugging my hand and leading me into a forest of jagged obsidian. Lightning flashed through the night sky while thunder rolled repeatedly in the distance.

Hisses and growls came from somewhere behind us.

Death spun around and cursed. "Run."

He didn't need to tell me twice. "Go, I can keep up." He was fast, really fast, veering left and right through towering rocks. Pumping my arms, I shadowed his every move, afraid I'd fall and impale myself on one of the vicious-looking rocks poking out of the ground like giant stalagmites. The growls grew louder. "They're gaining on us," I called.

Death spun around suddenly, hooked me around the waist, flung me over his shoulder, and took off, just as a horde of something loud and angry exploded around the edge of a wide rock behind us. I hung on to him as he sprinted over boulders and tore around the jagged towers of stone that seemed to have burst through the ground.

Lightning flashed bright, turning night into day, giving me a good look at what was chasing us.

Holy fuck.

Their mouths were hanging open, drool streaming behind them as they chased us, moving faster than should be possible on all fours. Death's powers were all but smothered here, but my magic still burned bright inside me. I couldn't call on nature, to shake the ground beneath our feet or call on the wind, because we weren't in the Earth Realm anymore; we were somewhere else, somewhere Mother Nature wasn't.

So instead, I sent my power at them with a roar from deep in my gut, blasting them with a wall of magic. It had strengthened after cutting, after spilling blood, and several of the creatures flew back, smashing into the sharp rocks, but there were more coming. I called on the fire inside me, and it manifested, flames dancing above my palms. With another cry, I fired it at them—not easy while I was bouncing on Death's shoulder and close to throwing the hell up. Several were tossed aside, engulfed in flames and screaming, but there were still more.

I had hoped to save Magnolia's potions, but now seemed like a good time to use one. I shoved my hand in the side pocket of my pack. There were several different vials, all different shapes. I finally found the one I was looking for—the long, thin one. I tapped Death's back. "Let them get closer," I yelled.

"You better have a good plan," he yelled back but instantly did as I said and slowed.

If I weren't facing a horde of bloodthirsty monsters, I'd probably wonder why he so easily did what I asked, without question, but I was, so instead, I egged them on. "Come on, you ugly fucks," I yelled. "Catch me."

One of them roared, spittle flying everywhere and flashing their long, piranha-like teeth. They bounded toward us at full speed, and my heart pounded in my ears as the huge demonic creatures got closer. It roared again, so close to us now that I got a clear view of its tonsils. There were five of them left, and their eyes were wild and filled with hunger. *Just a little closer.*

The one at the front leaped, snapping its teeth barely a yard from us. The rocks had become less crowded. I needed to do it now, before the creatures had a chance to spread out. They snapped and bounded closer—

I tossed the vial hard, smashing it against the rocks beneath their feet. It shattered, the potion and its toxic fumes covering them. Their roars turned to shrieks as their flesh melted, dissolving, leaving only bone as they all but turned into piles of goo behind us.

Death spun around. "Fuck," he said roughly, lifting goose bumps all over me. "That'll do it, little witch."

Silence surrounded us. We'd gotten them all—at least, the ones chasing us.

"So, um... you wanna put me down now?" I said from my position still dangling over his wide shoulder.

His hand pressed against the backs of my thighs and applied pressure as his other hand went to my back, and he carefully eased me down. He did it slowly, too slowly, and my front dragged all the way down his chest.

We were close, too goddamn close.

"Nice work," he said, looking down at me.

I cleared my throat. "I'm glad you approve. My cousin's potions are vicious." I stepped back, and his hand, still resting on my back, slipped away.

He seemed to lean forward, his eyes darkening.

"So now what?"

His chest expanded sharply. "Now we walk. Stay close."

I had to power walk to keep up with him, and every now and then, he'd tilt his head and listen for anything else following us. The terrain changed as we went, the rocks becoming even more sparse now, and I'd spotted the odd vine of an ivy-like plant curling around boulders and crawling along the ground.

Lightning flashed over us, forking through the dark sky, followed closely by ground-shaking thunder that felt as if it rolled right through me. "Is it always dark here?"

"It never used to be, but it is now."

"Because of your mother?"

"Yes."

"When will we reach her realm?"

"In a few days," he said, scanning our surroundings.

"Will we see her while we're there?"

"Not if I can help it." When he spoke about her, the shadows instantly gathered around him.

Ahead were trees; they were sparse, but as we got closer, I could see they shimmered, like they'd been sprinkled with fairy dust. "It's beautiful."

"Don't touch anything unless I do, and definitely don't eat anything," Death said.

Awesome. The vines I'd seen were thicker here, and some had grown up the tree trunks. I rushed to keep up with Death, who hadn't stopped. As we traveled deeper, I realized the vines had flowers, and they unfurled, opening and closing as we got close, like stars blinking in the sky. "What are these?"

"They're deadly," Death said, "like most things here. The Outer Realm should be more of a no-man's-land, relatively safe to move through and ruled by no god, but over centuries, Nox has been slowly claiming it for herself. Now it's like an extension of the Night Realm—always dark, the lightning, the plants and trees, and now crawling with her demons and other creatures. It used to be all rocks here, like the ones we ran through, but my mother is greedy, and she knows taking the only buffer that exists between us will anger me."

Based on the way Death had described his mother, it seemed Nox had created a world as toxic as she was. "She sounds bored. Time to get a life."

Death's gaze sliced to me, and his eyes did that brightening thing they did sometimes. "Yes, it is."

We carried on walking, and the trees went from sparse to a dense forest. I stayed close to Death. It was impossible to avoid everything with how thick the forest had become, and my leathers were the only thing protecting me from the noxious plants around us.

A weird hooting sound came from above, and Death stilled immediately. One moment, I was beside him; the next, he'd pulled me in close to him, and we were surrounded by darkness, by shadows. His cloak had settled around us.

"Be still," he rasped.

I blinked up at him, trying to breathe with his arms around me again, with him so impossibly close, and with those blue eyes glowing down at me in a face that now looked like a skull. The shadows hadn't just covered us; they'd gathered around his face, turning him into the god he was. Again, I tried to breathe, but being this close to him while he looked like that? Yeah, I was having some trouble.

The hooting came again, closer this time.

One of his large, tattooed hands came up, and he took hold of my jaw. He dipped closer, his face only a couple of inches from mine, and shook his head, telling me to be quiet. My heart smacked against my ribs with force. I opened my mouth, but I couldn't drag in the oxygen I needed. What I felt coming off him... it was nothing like I'd ever experienced—the darkness, the anguish, the rage, and all that banked power, locked down against his will, unable to be accessed. It wasn't gone, though. No, it was still very much there, writhing under the surface.

And alarmingly, it wasn't just fear I was feeling all of a sudden. My nipples tightened, and a pulse throbbed between my thighs.

The hoot came a third time, but it was in the distance now.

"Breathe," he said huskily.

Finally, I was able to drag in a ragged breath.

"And again."

I stared at him, unable to look away from those glowing eyes and that shadowed face as I drew in oxygen like I'd never breathed before. My head spun, and my body was still thrumming. Goddess, I was so hot and achy.

"What was that?" I whispered to break the unbearable tension.

"An owllike creature that can tear a face off with one swipe of his talons. He's Nox's pet, and she can see through his eyes."

"That doesn't sound good," I said, still whispering. "Do you think she knows we're here?"

"Possibly."

I licked my lips as nerves coiled impossibly tight in my belly. "Your cloak... I thought your powers didn't really work here."

His glowing gaze studied me closely. "My cloak isn't a power," he said, still perilously close. "It's part of me. We are one and the same."

The mournful hooting sound came again, and it was far in the distance now. Still, he didn't take the cloak away, keeping us ensconced in his camouflage, turning us into shadows.

His breathing grew rougher, and he wasn't moving away. His arms were still around me, and his hands were hot against my back.

"Who's Aster?" I blurted. Ever since I dreamed about her last night, I'd been wanting to ask.

He flinched.

"One of your consorts?"

"How do you know that name?"

The roughness to his voice tore a shiver from me. "She came to me while I slept. She showed herself, offering me a vision of her... and, ah, you while we were in the tree house."

"What do you mean showed herself?" he bit out.

"I'm a medium, communing with the dead is what I do. I didn't think those powers worked in Limbo, but somehow, she showed me a... a memory of the two of you."

"What were we doing?" His eyes bored into me.

I wished I'd kept my damn mouth shut, but he wasn't going to let it go, not until I shared what I saw, because he never let anything go. The fact we were so close, still under his cloak, and he looked like... *that* while my traitorous body burned for the terrifying god holding me made it all the more humiliating. "You were... making love."

His nostrils flared, and a growl rolled from his chest.

I didn't dare tell him it wasn't the first one that I'd seen or that I'd started to wonder if the consorts that came before me were trying to warn me of something. "She showed me. I didn't ask for it. She—"

"Stop," he growled out, so much banked rage in that one word.

I swallowed convulsively, my mouth impossibly dry. He'd loved her. He'd loved Aster, and he'd lost her, like the rest. "I'm sorry. I didn't mean to cause you pain."

He released me suddenly, and the cloak vanished, the shadows going with it. "We need to keep moving."

I nodded and followed as he strode off, wondering what the hell just happened. I felt that way a lot when I was with Death.

We didn't speak much after that, and in the darkness, I lost track of time and place. I had no idea how long we walked for—long enough my feet ached, anyway. Finally, we broke through the trees, and the landscape changed again. The only constant here was the thunder and lightning, and when the next flash forked through the sky, it gave me a better look at what was ahead. It was wild and vast; there was rugged coastline and the sound of a turbulent sea along with the squawk of birds, or at least birdlike creatures, echoing in the distance.

"We'll rest for the night," Death said.

"This place is way too exposed. We should keep walking," I said, even as my feet screamed in protest.

Death lifted his staff, pointing to something in the distance as more lightning flashed.

There was a glossy black tower, thin and tall. A beacon of pale light glowed from the top, aimed out to the furious black ocean, like a demonic lighthouse. "Does anyone live there?"

"Yes."

"Will we be welcome?"

"No, but they will let us in," he said and started for the tower.

CHAPTER 8

Zinnia

DEATH BANGED on the black wooden door.

This place seriously gave me the creeps.

Heavy footsteps, slow and ominous, came from behind it, and I had visions of Frankenstein's monster standing on the other side. I wasn't ashamed to say that when the door slowly creaked its way open, I stepped a little behind Death.

A short male with long, wispy gray hair that reached his waist and gray skin only a shade darker stood there, scowling at us. "My lord," he said with distaste.

"We require a room for the night, Horace."

His beady red gaze sliced to me, then back to Death. "But of course." Then he disappeared back inside, and we followed.

Horace wasn't a breed of demon I'd ever seen, but every instinct in me said that's what he was. His feet were disproportionately large to his body. His legs were strong and muscled, but his body was wiry and misshapen. His features were somewhat humanoid but bulbous and exaggerated in a way that gave him away, and of course, there were those red eyes.

"He doesn't seem happy to see you," I said to Death under my breath. "Will he rat us out?"

"He can't, at least in theory. This tower is supposed to be a sanctuary, a safe place for travelers to rest before sailing the Night Sea."

I spun to Death as Horace stepped behind a small reception desk and grabbed a key from the wall. He handed it over. "Do you require a repast, my lord?"

"We do," he said.

No, thanks. Whatever this guy was serving, I wasn't eating. Of course, with Death's powers basically out of commission, there would be no pulling a five-star meal out of thin air.

"I'd also like to hire a ship for our passage tomorrow," Death said.

"We're going in that ocean?" I asked, unable to bite back my horror.

"Yes." He pulled two gold coins from his pocket and handed them to Horace. "I want your best." He took out another coin and held it up. "And I want provisions, enough for two days, and the ship better be seaworthy, and the crew trustworthy, demon, or I will come back here, no matter how long it takes me, and I will torture you, flay the skin from your flesh and the meat from your bones, and I won't stop until you are ash. Do you understand?" Horace grabbed for the coin, and Death pulled it out of reach. "Do you understand?" he said again, his earth-shattering voice making Horace wince.

"Of course, my lord."

"Do not *of course* me. I know your tricks. I've been on the receiving end of them more than once, and I know that despite your post here, you are my mother's lapdog. That will not save you if you fuck with me or my consort." Then Death tossed the extra coin at the demon, snatched the key from the desk, and strode toward the stairs.

Horace's red gaze was burning with fury when it slid to me. I quickly spun away and rushed after Death.

He took the stairs two at a time, obviously angry as hell.

"You've had some issues with Horace before, then?"

His lips curled back. "You could say that."

"What kind of issues? Not like ship stuff, right?"

"Yes, ship stuff. It ended up at the bottom of the ocean."

Fuck.

"Well, after the warning you gave him, I don't think you'll have any trouble this time." I freaking hoped not, anyway.

Death grunted. Not reassuring at all.

"By the way, when were you going to tell me about this little sea voyage? 'Cause I have to tell you, I'm not much of a fan of boats and wide-open ocean... like at all."

"I know," he said, "but you'll be fine."

"You know? How?" I said when he finally stopped outside one of the rooms and slid in the key.

His hand stilled, just for a split second, but then he turned the key and shoved open the door. "I know a lot of things."

Great, another room with one bed. Like seriously? "Can we get another room?" I eyed the huge bed. On second thought, he could have it. It looked like it was made out of charred bones from creatures of unidentifiable origin, if the skull in the center of the headboard was anything to go by. At least there was a fire going against the wall, because it was cold and miserable.

"No. We stay together, especially here." He hurriedly undid his jacket and slid the heavy leather off, tossing it on the back of a chair. He wore nothing underneath it, and this time, his back was to me, so when he rolled his broad shoulders and flexed his arms, I watched the way the muscles bunched, making the inverted torch tattooed down the backs of both his arms move and the flames dance.

Seeing him like this was so... weird. He was the God of Death, and I was forced to spend time with him in a way only—well, possibly ten—other consorts had. He'd obviously had intimate relationships with the others, at least some of them. The very idea of taking things there with him was... not something I could even truly contemplate.

Not only was it way too intimidating, but that didn't seem to be what he wanted from me, and I certainly didn't want that from him.

Then I thought about the way my body had reacted while we hid under his cloak, and I inwardly winced. I had no control over my reaction; it didn't mean I wanted to go there with him. Maybe that's why the others had died. The kiss of Death. Once you let him into your pants, you'd signed your own death warrant. "You don't like wearing a shirt or a jacket, why?" I asked.

He turned to me. "I've spent very long periods of time in only my cloak, so it takes time to get used to clothing again."

That made sense since, up until a week or so ago, I'd never seen him in anything but his cloak.

There was a knock at the door, and Death strode over, opening it. Horace rushed in, pushing a trolley. There was food crammed on top of it, and surprisingly, it didn't smell terrible. The demon left it by the fire, then hurried off without a word.

I eyed it. I'd planned to give the meal a miss, but I was starving now, and I needed to keep up my strength. "Is there anything here that you need to warn me about?"

"It's safe," he said, picking up what looked like a turkey leg and biting off a hunk of meat.

"Safe isn't what I asked." I picked up an orange and started peeling it.

"I'm more concerned with what that is," I said, motioning to the leg he was tearing into.

"A bird. Not one you would know, but still a bird. It tastes like chicken."

Okay. It wasn't an orange I was peeling, but it had a deep red flesh and looked super juicy. "I'll take your word for it." I took a bite. *Nope.* Grabbing my napkin, I spat out the offending piece of fruit. "What the hell is that?"

Death's lips actually curved up on one side, and the effect was, well, nothing short of devastating. "A centeen egg."

"A what?"

"It's a kind of giant insect. Their eggs are enjoyed like caviar here."

I gagged and scrubbed the napkin over my tongue. "Jesus, that's disgusting."

A low sound rumbled from him. My gaze shot up. He was—holy shit, he was laughing. If I thought the grin was devastating, then Death laughing was... life-altering.

I tried not to stare, stunned, as he took a loaf of bread and tore it in half, then used a knife to scrape out some flesh from the centeen egg and spread it across the bread. "If you eat it the right way, it's quite delicious."

"Like hell it is." I grabbed my wine, which was thankfully good, and swilled it around my mouth. "I'll be tasting that until the day I die, and thankfully, according to what you've told me, I don't have long to wait." I smirked and grabbed a piece of bread without bug eggs on it. "How will you remember me? The most annoying consort you've ever had—"

"Don't." He slammed his hand on the table.

I jumped, tossing the piece of bread in my hand in the air, my heart flying into my throat. He was breathing hard, his nostrils flared, his hand curled into a tight fist.

"Don't," he said again, with less force but with a whole lot more feeling.

His blue eyes were burning into me, conveying a lot of things that I didn't know what to do with. I didn't know what to say, where the hell to look. "I'm sorry," I rasped, finding it hard to find my voice. "I... I didn't mean to upset you."

He was breathing hard, that fist still clenched tight.

"I was just joking around, okay? I do that when I'm freaked about something. It annoys my sister as well."

Still, he said nothing. What the hell was his problem, anyway?

"You really are pissed off?" Now I was getting pissed. "Well, that's kind of selfish of you, honestly. It's my head on the chopping block. I think I have a right to deal with it however I like."

He stood with a snarl. "Do you want to die, is that it? Do you have a fucking death wish, consort?"

"No, but I am one of a *long* line of consorts, and you told me yourself that most have died pretty fucking gruesomely, so forgive me, but something like that is kind of hard to forget."

He leaned forward, planting his hands on the trolley between us. "Then don't fucking die."

I stared up at him. "I'm definitely going to try not to, Mors, but my odds don't sound that good," I fired back at him.

"All you have to do is stay close to me, and you'll live. It's not hard."

"You make it sound so easy, but obviously, it's not, or consort number one would still be here with you, right? Or is that not how it works? 'Cause you sure as hell haven't tried to help me understand."

He ground his teeth. "There are things I can't tell you, things I want to tell you... so..." he growled. "So fucking badly. But I can't, so your only hope is to trust me."

I scoffed. "Right? Easy. Trust the guy who obviously does not trust me in the slightest. You make deals and barter with me because you don't trust I'll keep my word, yet you want me to just give you blind trust without even attempting to earn it?"

He straightened and paced away, his hand running over his tattooed skull. His back moved with the way his chest heaved. Where the fuck had this come from?

"If you want me to trust you, why don't you tell me what the hell is going on?" I said. "Why are you so pissed off right now? It can't just be about what I said."

He spun around. "You saw me in your vision, in your dream, with... with her. Tell me, Zinnia, what you saw."

I'd seen him with possibly more than one "her" but I knew the one he was talking about—the one he'd called Aster. I swallowed, my throat dry. "You were..."

"'Making love' were the words you used. Try having that, *feeling that*... then reaching for it over and over again and having it taken from you. You dying, little witch, isn't something I want to even fucking think about." Then he snatched up his bag, turned, and strode into the bathroom, slamming the door after him.

Leaving me sitting there utterly stunned and, again, seriously confused.

I lost my appetite after that, and when he finally came out of the bathroom, subdued and smelling like soap, I grabbed my own bag and locked myself in the bathroom as well. I took my time, having a long, hot shower. My muscles ached, and I didn't smell the freshest after days of riding and walking.

As I dressed, pulling on a pair of shorts and a soft T-shirt, I thought about Hemlock. Egon would look after him, but I missed him so damn much. Where would he sleep tonight? Shaking it off, I forced myself to open the door and walk back out into the room. The only light was coming from the fire. Death was in bed, one arm behind his head, his eyes closed. The chair would have to do. I started toward it.

"Get in the bed, Zinnia."

He'd said my name again. "I'll just take the chair."

"You've called me by my name three times now."

I spun to face him. "Seriously?"

"Seriously," he said, his eyes still closed. "I'm calling the first one in."

"You're going to make me sleep with you?"

"I'm going to make you sleep in a comfortable bed and get a decent night's rest before we face the Night Sea tomorrow, and I know you're too stubborn to do anything I ask, so I'll make you do it."

I huffed out a breath. "Why are you like this?"

"Get in the bed."

"You're an asshole, you know that?" I was pretty sure I saw his lips curl up again.

"Shhh now, I'm trying to sleep," he said.

I stared across the room at the hideous bed made of bones and the god lying in it and tried to freaking breathe.

"If you're not in this bed in five seconds, I'm coming to get you."

That spurred me into action. "Fine," I muttered and rushed across the room, because again, Death always meant what he said.

Shoving back the covers, I climbed up, staying as far over on my side as I could without falling out, then dragged the heavy comforter up to my chin.

There was no way I was going to fall asleep. No way.

CHAPTER 9

Zinnia

SHE KISSED *her way across Death's stomach, grinning at him. "You're beautiful, you know that?"*

"The only thing beautiful in this room is you, my precious Stella."

A growl came from outside the tower, and she shivered. "I don't like this place."

His fingers delved into her hair, and he tilted her head back. "As long as you stay close to me, you'll be safe."

She smiled again. "I know, and I insist on repaying you for your protection."

Death flashed his teeth. "And how will you do that?"

"Watch," she said and kissed his chest again.

I blinked into the darkness, my skin tight, my belly swirly. I was hot; my skin was burning up, probably because I was draped over Death... again. This time, with the way my lips tingled, I had the horrifying feeling that, like the female in my vision, I'd been kissing his chest—

Long fingers delved in my hair, fisting, tilting my head back.

Oh fuck.

My gaze sliced up to Death, and he stared at me in the shadows, his blue eyes glittering. "I tried to wake you," he rasped.

It felt like I'd only closed my eyes for a moment, but I'd been asleep for hours. It was early morning. I licked my lips nervously, trapped, locked in place by that gaze. A part of me was still in my head, feeling what she had, as if this weren't real.

"Were you having a vision?" he asked.

His deep otherworldly voice moved through me, making me tremble, and I became more aware of where I was, and how incredibly hot and smooth his skin was. How hard his body was beneath mine. He was wearing pants, but I felt his solid thighs flex beneath me.

The female, he'd called her only Stella this time, was right—he was beautiful. The God of Death was awe-inspiring in every way, and she'd gotten to touch him, to kiss him.

You're touching him, and I'm pretty sure you kissed him as well—his chest, anyway.

He massaged my head gently, and I almost freaking purred.

"Zinnia?"

Goddess, the way he said my name. I shivered again. I felt mesmerized, like he was the witch and not me, and I was fully under his spell. "Yes?"

"Were you having another vision?"

I nodded, and my chin grazed his chest. My nipples hardened immediately. "Um... yeah."

Why aren't you moving? Move.

He continued to massage my scalp, and I was trapped by his sorcery, frozen in place.

"What did you see?"

I didn't know what these visions meant, but there was no use hiding this one, I'm sure he'd figured out what it was about for himself. Was the female I saw in bed with him here in the tower the same one I'd seen in the tree house? Did he call all his consorts Stella? "You were with a female." It came out a whisper. "She was on top of you."

"Like you are now?" he asked in a velvety tone.

"Yes."

The space between us felt electric, the room closing in, as if the world around us had vanished and he and I were the only two beings who existed.

"What else?"

"She was kissing your chest, and you were fisting her hair."

His fingers twisted, then curled, tugging lightly, and humiliatingly, a moan slipped past my lips. "Then what happened?"

Get off him. Move. "She was... being playful and offered payment for your protection."

His nostrils flared. "How?"

"She, um... she kissed your chest again..." His eyes narrowed, and he licked his perfectly formed lower lip. "And then I... I woke up."

A heaviness fell between us, and the tension grew, kept growing until I had to fight not to squirm on top of him. His gaze was on me, moving over my face, and the urge to lift higher, to slide up his body and suck that lower lip into my mouth was almost overwhelming.

His chest was rising and falling faster while he watched me, waiting. He knew what I was thinking, and he was waiting for me to make the first move.

Don't. Don't do it. Kiss of Death, remember?

I shouldn't, but still, I pressed my hand into the mattress, about to slide up his body, to risk everything to get to that mouth—

A loud knock had me jolting and shoving away from him.

Death's lips peeled back with a low snarl before he shoved back the covers and strode to the door. The muscles in his back shifted, flexing, his biceps bulging when he clenched his fists before yanking the door open.

Horace stood there, and his eyes widened when he looked up at Death.

"What?" Death snarled.

"Your ship is ready and equipped with enough provisions for your journey," Horace said, a slight tremble to his voice. The demon definitely wasn't as brave this morning in the face of Death's fury.

"We'll be down when we're ready."

Horace bowed as he backed up. "Of course, my lord."

Death slammed the door and turned back to me as I slid out of bed.

"Get back in the bed, wife," he said, his tone fierce.

Goddess, I felt that in my belly and lower. I was about to laugh at his arrogance, but the hunger in his eyes, the power of a god demanding he be obeyed, gave me pause. My go-to of escaping awkward situations with humor or being a straight up smart-ass definitely wasn't the way to go in this instance.

Easing away from the bed, I shook my head. "No, I won't be doing that."

His head tilted to the side, his glittering blue gaze tracking me. "What did you say?"

Death was like two different beings—the new, more human side of him had been dominating, but then the other, the scarier version of Death, would make a surprise reappearance, like now. This was the Death I'd met when I first entered Limbo. The rage-filled, demanding god.

"Take a breath," I said, probably unwisely. "Think about what you're saying."

"You called me by my name, consort, three times—"

"And what? Now you're going to use one of those times to force me to fuck you?" I fired at him, all thoughts of trying not to piss him off further flying out the door. "You'd really want that? For the first time we have sex to be because you forced me?"

He blinked, his heaving chest stilling for several beats, and then he

666

shook his head, like he was trying to shake something from his mind. "I would never force myself on you," he said, the shadows starting to swirl around him. "You are my consort. I protect you. I'll never harm you." His nostrils flared as he dragged in another breath.

"Glad to hear it. Whatever that was that just happened a moment ago, you need to rein it in. I'm here with you because I have no choice, but I'm not powerless. You said it yourself, I'm a warrior, and I will fight to protect myself, even against you, and even if that means it kills me." Which it would; there was no beating Death.

The shadows swirled more fiercely, and one side of his face had transformed, now a skull, with the other side unchanged; he had one glowing blue eye, but the other was a black void. He took a stilted step forward, and it took everything in me not to stumble back, but somehow, I held my ground as he strode across the room.

I tilted my head back when he stopped in front of me. I tried to say something, but my voice wouldn't work as his hand came up. Still, I flinched.

He made a rough, wounded sound, and then gently, so gently, his fingers brushed under my chin, across my cheek. "Forgive me, Zinnia," he said, the power of his voice making my knees weak. "I would never harm you. I am... not myself here."

I locked my damn knees and searched his pained expression. He was sorry, tormented by what just happened, and I couldn't bring myself to punish him more when he was obviously punishing himself. "I forgive you." I shoved my hands into my pockets. "And I believe you."

He nodded, obvious relief in that one blue eye; then the shadows swirled again, dissipating, and he dropped his hand. "Gather your things. We need to leave."

>)) ● (((

The dinghy creaked as Death rowed us away from the shore and toward the black ship anchored and waiting in the Night Sea. Horace sat behind me, not saying a word.

The water was as black as the ship, the only contrast from the white foam when the waves broke.

"How long will it take to reach the Night Realm?"

Death pulled the oars through the water, the veins in his biceps popping. "Tomorrow night, when we reach land."

The ship was getting closer, and I could see the crew watching from the deck. "How dangerous is it?"

"You will be safe as long as you stay close to me," he said, the same thing he'd said to me before, and the same thing he'd said to the Stella I'd seen in last night's vision.

We reached the ship, and a rope ladder was tossed down. Death held it and motioned me forward. I climbed it quickly, and the demons on board stood back, keeping a respectable distance when I reached the top, but all of them were looking at me as if their last meal had just boarded the ship. No way was I turning my back on them, and it was hard not to pull my knife free under the weight of all those hungry eyes.

The rope ladder creaked, and the sound of the oars knocking the side of the boat reached me. I refused to turn and look, but I knew Horace was rowing away, leaving us here. The thump of Death's boots hitting the deck echoed behind me, and the demons quickly dropped their gazes.

Death handed our bags to one of them and turned to another. "Anchor up," he said to who I assumed was the captain of this ship—a ship that looked as if it would be more at home at the bottom of the ocean. The demon called the order, and the rattle of a heavy chain came as the anchor came up and a massive black sail dropped. The old ship groaned as wind filled the tattered sail, and we started moving.

The demons rushed off to do whatever it was they needed to do, and I turned and gripped the railing, watching as the land grew more and more distant. I had no idea what was coming, but dread filled me, growing deeper the farther from shore we got. The demon captain called orders, Death now at his side, and his crew called back, their collective voices filling me with more dread.

I wanted the hell off this ship already, but I didn't want to reach land either. The gods only knew what Nox had in store for us.

CHAPTER 10

Zinnia

THE SHIP SEEMED to lift completely out of the water before crashing back down. Rain and wind battered us as the ocean churned, throwing the ship around like it was a rubber ducky in a hot tub.

We went up again, and my stomach dropped as we slammed back down. My feet slipped from under me as water washed onto the deck. I grabbed for the railing as a strong arm locked around my middle, and I was hauled off the deck and dragged back under the small eave above the door that led down below. The door swung open behind us, and Death reached back and yanked it shut.

"Thanks," I said and tried to move out of Death's hold.

He tightened his grip. "You're not going anywhere, little witch," he said close to my ear, making me shiver. "No fucking way I'm letting you get swept overboard."

"I'm fine. I'm just more of a land lover," I called over the wind. "In case you hadn't figured it out." I'd spent the first couple hours throwing up over the side, much to the amusement of the crew.

"Yeah, I got that," he said, still way too freaking close.

The way his voice affected me made my face heat. Thankfully, in this position, with him behind me, he couldn't see his "warrior consort" blushing like a besotted teenager. I didn't want to want him, but with every day that passed, lying to myself got harder—because I was definitely feeling things, or my body was, anyway.

The ship rolled again, and I managed to bite back my scream, just. "Can this thing capsize?"

"It's just a storm. It'll pass."

"That didn't answer my—" Something moved in the darkness, rising out of the sea, then diving back down, something huge. I grabbed Death's forearm locked around my waist. "There's something in the water."

"Where?" he yelled over the furious wind.

I pointed just as it rose out again and gnashed long, sharp teeth, then dove back down. The ship jolted sharply, but this time, it wasn't the storm. "Oh fuck."

Death brought my hand to one of the beams beside us before releasing me. "Don't let go," he said as he took off his jacket. "Knife," he said to me.

"What?"

"I need to slow it down, or he'll put a hole in the hull," he yelled.

And we'd sink. "What are you going to do?"

"If he's bleeding, he'll be more concerned with other predators on his tail than sinking us." He slid the knife from the sheath strapped to my thigh, then pulled his own from the side of his boot.

"What the hell are you doing?"

He signaled something to the demon captain. "I won't be long," he said to me. Gripping both knives tighter, he ran to the ship's railing, jumped up onto it, then dove into the sea.

I rushed to the edge just as he surfaced, then dove back down. "Holy shit." I searched the water, waiting, but he didn't surface again. Clinging to the railing, I ran around the edge of the ship as it jerked and lilted to the side, groaning and crashing down against the waves throwing us about. Death was immortal, but even he couldn't survive the jaws of a monster like that.

It was so dark, the ocean nothing but swirling obsidian, and I couldn't see anythi—

The monster rose with a roar, then dove back down—then nothing.

I ran around the ship again, hanging over the edge, desperately searching for Death. A hand landed on my shoulder, and I was shoved back from the edge. I spun as one of the demons pulled me toward the door that led below the ship, the bastard's yellowed teeth sharp and its bullish face curled in a sick grin. "No, Death can't die, but coming back after being minced up by that monster out there will take months, maybe even years. He'll have forgotten all about you by then."

Another demon joined him. "I got her first. You owe me," he said to his buddy.

This wasn't happening. No fucking way. Death had my big knife, but my small one was just as lethal. Twisting from his hold, I pulled it from my boot as I spun around and slashed. He grabbed his throat, roaring as blood sprayed from the severed artery. Spinning back, I kicked his leg out from under him, and he hit the deck. More demons gathered around to watch as I smashed my boot down on his ribs, cracking several of them, then pulled his own knife from the sheath at his hip, a nice big one, and used it to saw off his head, tossing it overboard before it had a chance to turn to ash.

Another came at me, the crew laughing and egging him on. Thank fuck Hemy wasn't with me right now. If these demons had hurt him... just the thought fueled my rage. The demon lunged at me, and I ducked, spun, and shoved the knife into his side. He screeched as I wrenched it up, then back down, spilling his guts all over the deck. I shoved my elbow into his throat, spinning back to slash it open. The blade's serrated edge was so sharp and brutal, it half decapitated him with one swipe. I yanked his head back and hacked through his spinal cord and vertebrae, severing his head, and he turned to ash as well.

The next demon stepped forward. "She's mine," he spat.

I was conserving my magic. If I had to take them all out one by one, I would, but I wasn't using my powers until I absolutely had to. I wouldn't risk draining myself too soon. I lifted the knife—

Death bounded over the railing. He was covered in blood, deep gouges across his chest, and the fury on his face when he took in what was happening would have given me pause if I wasn't so fucking relieved to see him. "No, demon, she's mine," Death roared, so fiercely, I stumbled back.

He strode forward, grabbed the demon in front of me by the throat, and tore his head from his body with his bare hands. The demons around us dropped to their knees, their heads bowed, their fear obvious. Death spun to the captain, who was on his knees as well. He grabbed him by the throat as well and lifted him, shoving him against the mast. "You allowed your crew to attack my consort," he said in a voice that had more than one demon pissing themselves and several more openly weeping.

It was full of all the things that the God of Death could deliver—horror, pain, terror.

"Has it been so long since I entered the Outer Realm that you forget who I am, demon?" he roared. "Have you forgotten what I'm capable of?"

"No, m-my lord," the demon stammered.

Death's hatred swirled around him, the shadows transforming him into the vision of his name, his face a skull, his cloak whipping about. He moved fast, slamming his fist into the demon's chest. His hand had turned black when he pulled out his beating heart and shoved it in the screaming demon's mouth before he tore him open, emptying his insides out all over the deck to slide around in the ash already there from the two demons I'd just killed. Death got in his face. Holding the demon's gaze and ignoring his muffled screams, Death gripped his throat tighter.

The demon shook his head frantically, his eyes pleading for mercy, but Death had no mercy to give and tore his head from his body, tossing it on the ground before he turned to ash as well.

Finally, he turned slowly, his cloak whipping around him in the storm. "If any of you look at my consort, I will kill you," he said, and then he pointed to one of the demons standing out of the circle—the only demon who hadn't been cheering when they'd all surrounded me. "You're the captain now. Keep your crew in line."

Then he took my hand, shoved the door open, and led me below deck.

⟩⟩🌑⟨⟨

Death shoved the door open to one of the rooms and pulled me in.

"Stay here," he said and disappeared.

Mounted lanterns flickered against the walls. There was a table against one side of the small room, an old steel tub down from that, and a bed on the opposite side. I flicked back the covers and inspected the worn cotton sheets. They looked clean. Risking it, I leaned in and sniffed. They smelled clean. I assumed we had Horace to thank for that. Though I wasn't sure I'd get much sleep tonight, not when the entire crew was after my blood—or something even worse.

The door opened again, and Death strode back in, a demon rushing in behind him carrying two buckets of steaming hot water. He dumped them into the tub and rushed off again while Death unloaded his armful of food on the table. Bread, cheese, and a bottle of wine.

I said nothing and neither did he as the demon returned and dumped more water in the tub, another demon behind him with his own buckets. They came and went until it was three-quarters full, and then Death told them not to come back and slammed the door and locked it.

"Those scratches on your chest, they look really bad," I said and closed the space between us. I lifted my hand, and he stepped back.

"They're full of poison," he said. "I need to soak the wounds in hot water now, or they won't heal properly."

"Could the poison actually kill you?"

He shook his head. "It could make me sick, though."

"Well, get in the tub. What are you waiting for?"

His gaze swept over me. "Are you hurt? Did they hurt you, Zinnia?"

He was using my name more and more, and it was an assault to every one of my senses each time he uttered it. "I'm fine. I should've expected it. I'm the idiot who dropped her guard."

He did another sweep of my body. "You're not an idiot." Then again, from head to toe. Finally satisfied I was okay, he nodded and sat on one of the chairs.

"It's kind of you to say, but we both know that's a lie."

He made a rough sound and pulled off his boots, kicking them aside. Then he stood again, his hands dropping to the buttons of his pants, and he undid them—and shoved them down.

Holy shit.

He didn't turn away. He stood there in all his slick, hairless, naked glory. I tried not to look; I really did. My mouth went dry. "Looks like I can cross shy off the list," I said and tried not to sound as breathless as I felt. Goddess, I knew he was beautiful, but I was seriously struggling to breathe. He was just all finely sculpted muscle and tattoos. No female could look at him and not be... affected. *You're still staring.* Yes, yes, I was. I pulled out one of the chairs and sat at the table as he stood by the tub. His hand changed color— pale gray, then deepening until it was black again. He held it above his chest, and the slashes oozed, a black substance bubbling to the surface. He swiped his hand down, and the poison splattered on the wooden floor before evaporating.

"So the hand of death does more than just straight up murder, then?" I said as he climbed into the tub.

"It does."

The polite thing to do would be to sit with my back to him, but I refused to show weakness. He knew what he was doing, and I wouldn't give him the satisfaction of letting him see he'd gotten to me, and I would not freaking blush. It's not like his was the first cock I'd seen. Was it the most perfect? Yes. The biggest? Hell, yes. But I was no shy little virgin, and I refused to act like one. It didn't matter who he was.

Breaking off a piece of bread, I topped it with cheese, then poured us both a glass of wine. "How long do you have to soak those wounds?" I asked and glanced up again. He was sitting in the tub, facing me, of course. He'd want to see if he'd gotten to me. The tub was pretty big, but his knees were forced to bend a little and spread wide.

He had his head tilted back, resting on the edge. "Until I feel all the poison's gone. I should have gotten most of it, but with my weakened powers..." He shrugged. "Could take a few minutes, could be an hour— depends how deep its claws went."

"So what else does the hand of death do?"

"Besides what you just saw? Not much. Mainly just the whole straight up murder thing."

"Nice," I said, ignoring the stupid flutters in my belly at the way he was looking at me. "You want some food?"

His head lifted, and those mesmerizing blue eyes locked on me. "Please."

I made him a cheese sandwich and grabbed his wine. He tracked me as I walked over to him, and I did my best not to ogle him as I handed him his wine. He drank it and gave me the glass, then took the sandwich.

"Thank you," he said. "You can go first tonight."

Of course he hadn't forgotten. No matter the circumstances, the evenings were question time. I took my seat again and popped a piece of cheese in my mouth while I contemplated my question. One kept circling my mind. It was a dangerous question and probably not the one I should ask considering our circumstances, but I wasn't sure I could help myself. "I should get two questions tonight. Your crew just tried to make me their sex slave, so you owe me."

His hand exploded out of the water and gripped the edge of the tub like he was about to bound over the side. "Do not remind me of that. We still need to make it to land, and if you talk about what they were going to do to you, Zinnia, I will get out of this tub and slaughter the entire crew. Do you know how to sail a ship? Because I can't do it alone."

He meant it. Vengeance burned in his eyes. He was fighting it, the need to slaughter every one of them. "I won't mention it again, promise." I pretended to zip my lips. "So that's a yes on the two questions?"

"Yes, but I get two as well."

I guess he had jumped into the ocean during a storm to fight a giant sea creature, so it'd be rude not to agree. "Fine."

He smirked.

Goddess, that smirk was dangerous. I tapped my lips and mulled over the best way to ask my question while he waited patiently. I cleared my throat. "How many times have you made this trip with one of your consorts?"

His nostrils flared. "Twice."

"Twice? You've had an unverified number of consorts. How could it only be twice?"

"Is that your second question?"

Was it? "I don't know."

"Well, while you decide, I'll ask you one. During the times you've been away from me, have you fucked anyone else?"

The vein pulsed at the side of my throat. He was obsessed with my sex life, and the way he'd been looking at me when he asked that... goddammit, I was having trouble breathing again. "*Anyone else* implies that we're already fucking," I said, for reasons unknown.

674

He bared his teeth in a way that should be terrifying but didn't scare me anymore. "Answer the question, wife," he said, using my title as if it held all the weight in the world.

As if that title actually meant something. As if me being with another male would actually be a betrayal. "Would you truly be angry if I had?"

The steel tub bent under his hand. I'd take that as a yes.

"Answer the question, Zinnia," he growled.

"No, I haven't been with anyone since I revealed who I was to you."

He visibly relaxed.

"Why do you care?" I said before I could stop myself. "You don't love me. You didn't choose me. I was chosen for you, just one of, well, possibly ten random other females to darken your castle steps. I don't get it."

His jaw tightened. "That's obvious, but what you need to understand is, you are mine, Zinnia. You are everything I want, all I want. I have no use for any other female, no desire to be with anyone but you. You don't need to *get it*. That's just the way it is."

I stared at him, stunned, for several seconds. "So what you feel, it's like a mate bond?"

"Yes, it's a lot like that. Which is why being parted from you is... hard." The tub buckled further under his hand. "And why the thought of you with someone else..." His lips peeled back. "I don't like it."

I was stunned. I had no idea. He'd never shown it—well, not until the last week or so. Until he'd just spelled it out, I'd had no idea what he was thinking or feeling. "I feel sorry for you then," I said into the silence. "This must truly suck. I don't know why your consorts keep... dying or why fate has an endless supply of us lined up for you, but it has to be painful to feel a connection like that to someone, then have them taken away over and over again."

Something shifted through his eyes that I couldn't read, and then his head tilted to the side. "You feel sorry for me? You think you're going to die in the near future, but it's me you're concerned about?"

I shrugged. "Don't get me wrong, I don't want to die, not yet. But I have family waiting for me. Loved ones who will welcome me with open arms when that time comes. This... it's endless for you."

"Don't," he said roughly. "Do not accept death as the outcome. Do as I say, and you will live."

He was delusional. The odds were not in my favor. The way he was looking at me, the pain and desperation, the need for me to believe it, to be the exception, was hard to look at. I was a realist, though. Whatever the fates had in store for me was what would be. No, I wouldn't go down easily, but I needed to come to terms with the possibility of my reality.

"Right, next question," I said, not wanting to talk about my death anymore. "Did you sleep with all your consorts? You're old as hell. You wanted my number, but I'm assuming yours is pretty freaking high." Where the hell had that come from? I was trying to lighten the heavy mood that had fallen over the room, but now it sparked with electricity.

His chest rose and fell as if he was trying to steady his breathing. "Not quite as old as Hell."

"Answer the question."

"No."

"Because you didn't want to, or because they didn't live long enough?"

He said nothing.

Nope, not feeling overly reassured by the whole *don't accept death as the outcome* thing. My gaze dipped to his chest. "The poison out yet?"

"Yes." His gaze darkened, the shadows beginning to swirl around him. "My turn."

My stomach squirmed, and that look in his eyes, I felt it. Goddess, did I feel it. "Shoot."

"Do you want me to fuck you, Zinnia?"

My body instantly responded. A pulse throbbed deep inside me. So many things were flying through my head right then. He was beautiful; he wanted me and only me. I was his consort and I would be until my last breath, and if things went the way they usually did for Death, that would be coming sooner rather than later. I'd lived my life to the fullest, as best as I could, anyway, with the responsibility I'd had. And I realized, looking over at him, I wasn't about to stop now. "Did your consorts die because they kissed you? Slept with you?"

"No," he said.

He could be lying, but I didn't think so. His pain was too real. He didn't want to lose me; I saw it, felt it. "You're overwhelming, Mors, in so many ways. The idea of surrendering to you, of letting you have me in that way, it's too much. So no, I don't want you to fuck me, not yet."

He flinched, but besides that, he didn't move, every muscle in his body rock solid. "I understand—"

"I haven't finished," I said and took a steadying breath while my heart tried to leave my body. Apparently, I was a masochist, and I'd decided to give in to it completely. "No, because the first time we do sleep together... I'll be the one fucking you."

CHAPTER 11

Zinnia

DEATH ROSE FROM THE WATER.

Every muscle on his lean body was taut, his veins popping from his smooth, inked skin. He was breathing heavily, and the shadows around him swirled faster. "Come here, Zinnia."

His voice rolled through the room like thunder, and my knees almost gave out. I shook my head. "If you want me, it has to be on my terms."

With each of his exhales, a growl rattled his chest. His stomach was roped with muscle, his thighs bulged, and his cock jutted from his body, hard and thick and long and, goddess, intimidating.

Death looked every bit the god he was, and he was looking at me as if he was on the verge of insanity from his hunger—*for me*. I wanted him so badly, I trembled all over. But this was Death. I was no coward, but he was, shit, too much... of *everything*. "I have to call the shots this time... and you have to let me call you Mors without holding it against me. I'm not calling you Death while we're in bed."

"I agree to your terms," he said. "Take your clothes off."

An unexpected laugh burst from me. "You've waited this long, so how about you find a little patience?"

"Impossible." He stepped out of the bath, water dripping from his body.

"Tell me what you want, and I'll give it to you. Anything your heart desires —it's yours."

This was another new side of Death. Yes, he'd been giving me glimpses, but this was next-level, and the more he showed me, the less afraid I became. I reached up and undid the top button of my jacket, working the rest until the heavy leather slipped from my shoulders and hit the floor.

Death watched my every move like a predator waiting to pounce on prey.

I dropped my hands to the buttons of my pants; he took a step forward. I stepped back, lifting my hands. "No."

He snarled.

"I come to you."

His fingers curled, clenching and unclenching at his sides as he watched me shove down my pants. "Is the water safe? Is there poison in it?"

"You don't need to wash," he said, baring his teeth. "I like you like this."

"Covered in sea salt, sweat, and demon blood?"

"Yes."

"Is the water safe?" I asked again, even as my belly went wild with nerves and excitement.

"The poison evaporates when it leaves the body. It's safe."

"Good." I dragged off my shirt and then removed my underwear. "Step back," I said. "At least four paces."

He growled low but reluctantly did as I said, tracking me as I walked to the bath and got in. He was barely holding himself back; I could see it in the way his muscles twitched and his breathing grew heavier with every passing second.

"Your body is perfection," he said. "Fuck, female, I want to lick every inch of you."

I lifted my gaze, letting it move over him as I slid the soap over my skin. "I like the way you look as well." Understatement of the century.

He stood straighter, a pleased light flashing through his eyes. "Cup your breasts for me. Play with your nipples. Do it," he said.

This was going to be a challenge; gods didn't like to be told what to do, but that was the only way this was happening. Still, I did as he asked, cupping my heavy and achy breasts. "I'm only doing it because I want to and not because you told me to. I'm in charge here, remember?"

"Will you ride my face, little witch?" he said, his hands still fisted at his sides. "I'll fucking beg you for it, if you like? I'm desperate for a taste of you, Zinnia. You have no idea how much."

Death had a dirty mouth, and yeah, it was working for me—big-time. "Are you in pain?"

"Yes."

678

"You can stroke your cock if you like." A vision of Death stroking himself filled my head, and my inner muscles clenched.

"If I touch my cock now, I'll come, and the next time will be inside my wife's sweet little cunt."

I flushed hot all over, so turned on, my next breath shook out of me. "Go to the bed and lie on it," I said.

He gave me another flash of his teeth, a look that said he was frustrated and entertained by my demands all at the same time. He strode to the bed and sat. His head dipped so his eyes were shadowed by his brow. "You need to know that after you fuck me, Zinnia, I will have you my way. I'll claim you so often and so deep that even when I'm not inside you, you'll feel me there. Every single day."

I was trembling now from how much I wanted him. It was getting seriously hard to hold my composure. Every word he said was stripping away my armor. This was probably a terrible mistake, but if my mortal life was reaching its end, I was making the most of every moment, even if it scared me. I knew what was about to happen between us—for me, at least—would be life-altering, soul-searing, earth-shattering, and I'd be a fool to pass that up.

"Lie back," I said and mentally gave myself a pat on the back when my voice didn't tremble like every other part of me was.

He lay back, his abs tightening as he did, then slid his hands behind his head. His gaze slid over my chest—what he could see of it above the water, anyway. "Now what, wife?"

Jesus, now he was being cocky? Or, at least, he was trying to be. He was still trying to maintain some kind of control. I got the feeling he hadn't been in this position, letting someone else lead, many times in his long life. He'd called me wife sparingly in the past, choosing consort more frequently, probably because wife seemed more intimate, more claiming, and considering when he chose to use it, he felt the same. I licked my lips because they were dry as hell. Had there ever been anything in existence as utterly beautiful, as awe-inspiring, as Death, hard and naked, lying on his back and waiting for me to have my way with him?

I rose from the water, and the cocky look on his face vanished. He ate up the sight of me, his cock jerking against his flat stomach. I grabbed the clean towel draped over the back of a chair, and slowly, carefully, dried myself off. "That feels better," I said and dropped it.

"When was the last time you were fucked, little witch?"

"It's not question time right now, Mors."

His nostrils flared. "When we're together like this, you can call me by my name, and I can ask you as many questions as I like."

Fair enough, I guessed, but talking about me sleeping with other males wasn't really something I wanted to get into right now. "Do you really want to know the answer to that?"

"Yes. Tell me."

I moved closer, standing at the end of the bed. "A couple years ago, I guess." I shrugged. "I've been busy."

"Who were you with?"

"No one special, just some guy I met while I was on the road. It used to get lonely, and he was nice. We had fun," I said, trying to get across how little the encounter meant.

His eyes darkened, the blue swirling with black. "I want to tear his limbs from his body."

Well, shit. I needed to turn this back on him and make him see how hypocritical he was being. I could guarantee he hadn't had any dry spells. "What about you?" I asked, taking a deep, steadying breath and climbing onto the bed. He tracked me as I crawled up beside him, his hands slipping from beneath his head.

"Keep your hands where they are," I said, and he growled again. "Answer the question. When was the last time you had sex?"

"A very long time ago, with my consort, before she was taken from me," he said, then, ignoring my order, reached out and slid his fingers down my cheek. "I've been waiting a very long time for you, Zinnia."

He was telling the truth; there was no doubting what I saw in his eyes and on his face. "Why?" I whispered, my throat tight with an emotion that surprised me.

"Because I didn't want anyone else."

None of this made sense. Could he only be with females destined to be his? Or was he just that into monogamy? There was so much I didn't know and desperately wanted to, but now was not the time to ask. Now, I was going to be the first for Death after what could be hundreds of years of celibacy. Curling my fingers around his wrist, I took his hand from my face, put it back behind his head, then grinned at him. "Well then, my lord, I'm about to rock your world."

A grin broke out across his face, and it was like it had the force of a thousand stars behind it, its impact like a sucker punch to the sternum. "Show me what you've got," he said, and there was no missing the teasing note to his voice.

My heart crashed into my ribs like a car in a head-on collision. "Well now, that sounds like a challenge."

His grin slipped. "Now, Zinnia—"

"Did I tell you I liked to take things slow?"

He growled. "We'll go slow next time."

I tutted and cupped his square jaw as zaps of electricity shot through me, making me squirm. Kissing Death had been on my mind a lot. At first, it had been unimaginable, but now? Goddess, he had those utterly perfect lips and the thought of it, the temptation, had become too much to ignore. "Making out really gets me in the mood." I was about to make out with a god. I'd laugh and scream—both at the same time—but I was too turned on in that moment to do anything but try to remember to do the whole oxygen thing.

"You're already in the mood. I can smell it. Your cunt is hot and slick and more than ready for me," he said through clenched teeth. "Kiss me, but do it while you fuck me."

The please went unsaid, but it hung between us. Death didn't beg, despite what he said earlier, and he'd get no mercy here, not tonight. For the first time since I started coming to Limbo, I was the one with all the power, and in this, I needed it.

Sliding closer, I lay beside him and pressed my naked body to his. I was trembling, but there was nothing I could do about that. "Don't move," I rasped as I leaned in and pressed a kiss to his jaw. "Stay right where you are."

He hissed. "Do you enjoy torturing me, little witch?"

"Doesn't this feel good? Having me pressed against you?"

"You know it does." He was panting now.

"Then stop complaining and let me kiss you." I lifted up to my elbows, so I was looking down at him, and studied his handsome face. "You have perfect lips. I've thought about kissing them a lot."

"Zinnia," he said, his voice full of raw hunger.

I dragged my nose along his throat and kissed the corner of his mouth. "You smell really good, like dark spices." He was shaking as well. Goddess, he was perfection. I pressed my mouth to his, and he groaned against my lips, then jolted as if he was about to pounce, but I reached back and grabbed his wrists, reminding him to keep them where they were.

Slowly, I ran my lips over his, reveling in their firm warmth, then dragged my tongue along his lower lip, desperate to taste him. My body was on fire, my nipples impossibly hard against his chest, and the pulse between my thighs was so damn deep, I couldn't stop myself from sliding on top of him, from straddling his hard body as I opened my mouth to slide my tongue deep into his mouth. He groaned again as his tongue slid against mine.

My hips rocked all on their own, working my pussy against his hard stomach, while I made out with Death like it was the end of the world, and I guess it kind of was—my world, anyway.

His skin was scalding hot against mine, and there was no way he couldn't feel how wet I was now. Kissing him was addictive. I could stay where I was all day and just kiss while rubbing up against him, but my body was screaming for more.

"Up," Death growled against my lips. "Sit on my face. Let me taste you."

I lifted my head a little and stared into his otherworldly eyes. "That sounded like an order."

His gaze seared mine. "Please."

His plea rolled through me, making me shudder, and my pussy clenched hard with need. Death never begged for anything, but he was, for me. How could I deny him? Why would I want to? Licking my lips, I slid higher.

"Yes," he said. "That's it."

I kept going until I was sitting on his chest.

"I'll need to hold you steady," he said.

His hand was out from under his head and wrapped around my waist before I could tell him no. He lifted me like I weighed nothing, putting me where he wanted me, and all thoughts of stopping him from touching me flew from my mind when he opened his mouth over my pussy and dragged his tongue through my center.

His deep moan was so incredibly sexy, my hips rolled on their own. He gripped me tighter, holding me down on his face with more force, and my head dropped back as he used that tongue with the kind of skill only a male who'd been alive since almost the dawn of time could have. I was shuddering and sweating, crying out with every skilled swipe of his tongue and every suck of those perfect lips.

I tried to hold back, to make it last, but I couldn't; I came with a scream. Death locked his arms around my hips, holding me down on his mouth, sucking and feasting on my pussy as I came against his lips.

When I collapsed, he dragged me down his body, thrust his long, thick fingers in my hair, and took my mouth in a claiming kiss that had my world spinning. I'd had every intention of being the one in control, but I didn't try to stop him when he worked his legs between mine and forced me to spread wide with his bent knees, or when he hooked me around the waist, just above my ass, and lined the head of his hard cock up with my opening.

I expected him to slam inside me, but he didn't; his entire body trembled, but somehow, he held back. "You need to control how much of me you take. I don't want to hurt you, but after seeing you fight those demons, after almost losing you, after how long I've waited for you, the force of the hunger I'm feeling is dangerous, and I would rather die before hurting you... so please, my perfect, feisty, beautiful little witch, put me out of my misery and fuck me the way we both need it."

CHAPTER 12

Death

ZINNIA WRIGGLED HER HIPS, her hot, slick pussy scalding the head of my cock. My arm banded around her tighter, and she whimpered. "You're going to break my spine, Mors, and then no one will be fucking anyone," she said, panting.

I quickly let up my grip, which felt impossible in that moment, but somehow, I did it. I wrapped her wild red hair around my fist and sucked and kissed the skin along her throat, her shoulder. Gods, I wanted to take a fucking bite out of her, that's how deep my hunger went. I wanted to suck and bite and crush her to me. None of it was enough; nothing would bring her close enough to me.

Throughout my life, I'd been tipped into madness of the darkest and most twisted kind, but nothing had ever made me feel as out of control as this moment. I'd waited for her for so long, so long I'd been without my consort, and now I would finally claim her. Gods help anyone who tried to take her from me. Not this time. This time, I would keep her; this time, she would stay.

She squirmed against me, her hips wriggling, working the head of my cock inside her. I gritted my teeth, breathing hard, trying to stop my heart from exploding out of my chest and my hips from slamming up. "That's it, nice and easy," I said, the opposite of everything I was feeling. But my precious consort came first, in everything. My wants and needs, my desires, they all came second to hers. She thought I was the one in control, that I controlled her, but nothing could be further from the truth—I was her servant.

She was my queen, and I would worship at her feet until the end of time. All she had to do was trust me.

Believe in me.

Stay with me.

Want me.

She whimpered again, but this time because she pushed down, taking more of me inside her.

"*Oh fuck,*" she gasped and rocked her hips, the wet sound of her cunt making me insane as she worked the inch of my cock she'd managed to take, letting it stretch her before taking more. "You're too big," she moaned, then took more, sinking her teeth into my shoulder.

I almost fucking came. Gripping her ass, I barely held on to my sanity. "You were made for me, Zinnia. The fates chose you for me," I growled out. "We will fit together, I promise you." Her pussy, tight and scalding, swallowed more, and I locked my muscles so I didn't thrust upward. "Feel good, little witch?"

She rolled her hips again and took more. "I-I think I'm losing my... my mind," she said with another roll, right there with me. "Oh goddess, you're... it's..." She shuddered. "Fuck," she hissed and started rocking on top of me. Each time she took more, her needy sounds grew, until she had every hard inch buried inside her. "Mors," she groaned my name like a cry for help.

"It's okay, Zinnia. Relax..." She moaned against my throat as she carefully rocked her hips. *Fucking hell.* My eyes rolled back. "That's it. Now show me how good it feels. Show me," I said, gripping her hips and encouraging her to move again.

She wrapped her arms around my head, and then her mouth came down on mine, feeding me her needy kisses and panted breaths while she started to move. "Yes," she whimpered against my mouth. "So good."

I let the reins slip, just a little, and lifted my hips, desperate to get closer.

"Oh fuck," she said; then my little consort completely lost control. My sweet, feisty witch moved faster, giving me everything she had until she was begging me for more.

Gripping her hips, I gave it to her. I pulled her down as I thrust up, filling her deep. The feel of her wrapped around me, of her holding me so tight, of her wanting me, was so sublime, she had me spinning. Gods, I was back in the night sky because my precious consort had me seeing the stars.

"Mors," she moaned.

My name on her lips had my hips snapping up, meeting hers with force, making her cry out. I'd be worried I'd hurt her, but she was so wet that I was gliding in and out of her with ease, and her moans hadn't stopped and were full of pleasure, not pain.

Then Zinnia sucked my lips one last time and sat up, planted her hands on my chest—right over the stars tattooed there—and swiveled her hips. No, she definitely wasn't in any pain. Her head fell back as she took from me exactly what she needed.

I watched her in awe. "Take what you need," I growled. My wild, willful consort. My beautiful warrior. A female of power and intelligence, of beauty and warmth.

She was everything.

She was mine.

And I would not lose her. I wouldn't survive it, not this time.

She was fierce, lost to her pleasure now, and the sounds she made as she gave in to it sent shivers all through me. She cried out—a raw, wild sound that I would never ever forget—as her pussy clamped down hard on my cock. I had to hold on to her hips as she bucked and cried out, falling against my chest while she rocked mindlessly, lost in her pleasure. Wrapping my arms around her—one arm over her back, and the other on her ass—I locked her to me, and then I fucked her, thrusting my hips up hard to meet hers again, while she trembled and cried out, still coming for me.

There was no more holding back. "Yes, that's it, my precious Stella," I groaned and came hard inside my beautiful little wife, my Stella, my everything.

I thrust into her until I was spent, until we both lay there panting. I gently fisted her soft, warm hair and lifted her head, in need of her kisses badly, but she turned away, then tried to slide off me. I tightened my hold on her.

"Let me go, Death," she said, no longer using my name and making it clear she was not just pulling away physically. She was going to distance herself from me again.

No fucking way. Not after that. She couldn't pretend she didn't feel for me some of what I did for her, not after what we just shared. "Look at me," I growled.

She turned toward me but averted her eyes.

"You're angry with me. Did I hurt you? Did I—"

"I get it, you've had a lot of consorts, and I'm most likely heading toward total annihilation in the very near future. This is... whatever the hell it is, but would it hurt you to get my fucking name right while you're inside me? This Stella, she was obviously your favorite or whatever, but even the dude I had a one-night stand with remembered my fucking name."

I froze. I had said that, hadn't I? *Idiot.* "I've never had a consort named Stella."

She rolled her eyes. "I literally heard you say it in my visions twice."

I swallowed, my mouth dry, hating that I'd hurt her. "Stella means star," I rushed out. "When I say my Stella, I'm saying my star."

Her gaze dropped to my chest, to the intricate stars tattooed there, then back up. "So you what? Call us all the same term of endearment so you don't fuck up?"

"No. You are my consort, my guide, my light, my sun. That's just what you are. You are my little witch, but you are also my Stella," I said, trying to make her understand. I wanted to explain, to tell her everything, but I couldn't; doing so would mean losing her for certain. So I waited and hoped like hell she accepted my explanation.

She chewed her lip. "So this is another one of those bigger-than-me, dawn-of-time things that I'm never going to understand? Gotcha. Fine, whatever, but I've had visions of you with one, possibly two other females, so I know this isn't some grand love, and we're just fucking to kill time, but in all those visions, you called her... or them Stella, so I'd rather you didn't call me that again, thanks."

We weren't fucking to kill time, and even she couldn't believe that bullshit. And as for grand love? She had no fucking idea, but she would. "I'll try my very best not to call you that again," I said.

She eyed me for a moment, then finally, thank the gods, relaxed back against me. Her warmth instantly put me at ease. I slid my hand down her back, and she shivered. Yes, I liked that.

"You need to do better than try, my guy," she said. "Because if it happens again, it doesn't matter if I'm riding you like a rodeo bull, if you call me that name again, there will be no happy ending for you. I'll leave you to buck it out all on your own."

I stilled. "A rodeo bull?"

"You heard me," she said and wriggled against my side, getting comfortable.

A grin spread across my face, so wide, my cheeks hurt.

She paused in her wriggling and lifted her head. Her breath burst from her lungs. "What the hell are you grinning about?"

"You entertain me, little witch. I haven't been this entertained in a very long time."

"I'm glad I amuse you," she said, trying to be sarcastic, but her lips were twitching.

"I'll be your rodeo bull anytime, by the way."

She snorted. "Like there was ever any doubt."

The laugh burst from me before I knew it was coming. Zinnia startled, and I laughed harder, wrapping my arms around her and holding her to me.

›)›●‹((‹

Zinnia

Gripping my sword, I slashed at the bloated, foul-smelling demon swiping red-tipped claws at me. I shifted my body to protect my back; my leather armor creaked as I slashed again.

They kept coming. I was on my own. There were too many. I stumbled back, closer to the rocky cliff. Oh gods, there was no way out of this.

The demons closed in, one grabbing me by the throat while another snatched something from my back, something I needed to protect, something precious. The demon released my throat, then slammed a fist into my stomach.

I stumbled back, and then I was falling, falling toward the sea and jagged rocks. My screams turned into a roar of fury. This did not end here. They would pay for this—

With a gasp, my eyes flew open a moment before I hit the rocks.

My heart pounded in my chest, the familiar ache more intense than ever before, because instead of making me watch the scene unfold, whoever that was, she'd put me in her shoes. It was as if that were happening to me. Something tickled my cheek, and I reached up to brush it off, my fingers coming away damp. I realized tears were pouring down my face, likely from the lingering feeling of my entire world being ripped from me in that vision. Goddess, it was suffocating. Death was still beside me, breathing slow and steady. I needed air; I needed to shake the vision. I had no idea what his past consorts were trying to tell me, but the more they showed me, the more real they felt.

Easing out of bed, I quickly dressed, grabbed my knife from where Death had put it earlier, and slipped from the room. I wasn't worried about the crew attacking me, not now that Death was here, and even if one of them did, they were lacking in skill and, as I'd proved earlier, not overly hard to kill.

Rushing up the steep stairs and onto the landing, I shoved the door open and stepped out onto the deck. I dragged in a desperate breath, letting the sea air fill my lungs, before I strode to the railing, sucking in another frantic breath.

Her pain, whoever she was, had been like nothing I'd ever experienced. She'd been filled with so much fear and heartbreak and rage. Her world had been snatched from her along with the people she loved with a fierceness that I felt to my soul, that I understood.

The revenge in her heart had been white-hot.

Was that what she wanted, what they all wanted? Revenge?

Against who? At first, I thought they were warning me about Death, but I didn't believe that now. The female in that vision had loved him. Had all of them felt that way?

The thought had me gripping the railing tighter. Had they all fallen in love with him?

Did I truly think I would be the exception? That I'd somehow resist him? I wrapped my arms around myself. Did I really think I could outsmart the fates? That I could prove them wrong? I wasn't better or smarter or stronger or in possession of greater self-restraint than the females who came before me. I knew I wasn't. Death was a god, and I was a mere mortal; there was no resisting this pull I felt between us, not when it grew in strength every day.

Goddess, the way he'd touched me, held me, the things he'd said, the way he'd wanted me—I'd never experienced anything like that in my life.

His laugh when he'd wrapped his arms around me, holding me tight to him, had been heart-stopping—

A rough hand clamped hard over my mouth, and an oddly shaped body slammed into me from behind. I tried to fight, but there was no getting out of the demon's hold. He pulled his hand away, but only long enough to stuff a dirty rag in my mouth.

"Over you go," he said against my ear, then tossed me over the side.

I flailed, bracing, preparing to hit the water.

Instead, I was snatched from the air and shoved into the bottom of a dinghy. The demon who'd tossed me over the side quickly made his way down the rope ladder and got in as well. I didn't recognize either of them; they weren't crew. Someone else had sent them.

One of them started rowing while the other secured my wrists and ankles and tied a gag around my head, trapping the rag in my mouth. I couldn't spell, and I couldn't reach for my blade; I was fucking helpless.

The demon rowed for a while, and I wondered where they were taking me. We were too far from shore, but then I saw it, another ship, black and huge, camouflaged in the darkness.

Someone moved around on the deck, another demon, their misshapen shadow striding to the railing and watching us approach. They kicked down the ladder and stepped back.

Whatever this was, it was bad.

The eerie *coo* of an owl echoed overhead.

Really fucking bad.

CHAPTER 13

Death

I JOLTED AWAKE.

It was quiet—too quiet.

My arm shot out across the mattress. Nothing. It was empty.

No Zinnia.

Only cool sheets. She'd been gone a while. Bounding out of bed, I stormed out of the room, not giving a fuck that I was naked, and leaped up the stairs and onto the deck. "Zinnia!" My roar echoed through the night, causing the demons asleep up here to startle awake. "My consort! Where the fuck is she?" I demanded.

"I haven't seen her," one of the demons said as he scrambled from his pallet.

Rushing him, I grabbed him by the throat and shoved him against the mast. "Where the fuck is she?"

He shook his head, trembling, the smell of piss reaching me. "I-I promise. I haven't seen her. I didn't do anything."

Shoving him away, I strode back the way I'd come, jumped down the stairs, and kicked every cabin door open, yanking back covers and flipping beds. She wasn't here. I knew it deep down; I felt her absence like a festering wound in the center of my chest. The same as when she left me,

689

when she left Limbo to go back to her family for a month, and I was left counting down the fucking weeks, days, hours, minutes until she returned.

She was gone, but she hadn't left me. Someone had taken her, and when I caught up with them, I would tear them to pieces, until they were nothing but bloody chunks of meat wriggling on the ground.

"Everyone, up!" I bellowed. "Get me to the docks, now."

⇾⟩⟩⟩◦⟨⟨⟨⇽

Zinnia

The captain of the *Fetid Slug*, Sig—I mean, it was as if the ship had been named especially for him—sidled up to me again, like he had been with increasing frequency since I got here, and pressed his face to my throat, sniffing deeply. He made a weird, excited little noise.

"Does she still smell like his lordship, Sig?" one of the other demons asked excitedly.

"Oh yesssss, and her cunny is still ripe from his tupping. His seed marks her," the captain said.

It took everything in me not to gag. That this creep was smelling me and, by the looks of it, getting off on it was more than I could stomach. "Bring your nose anywhere near me again, and as soon as I get the chance, I'll slice the fucker off." They'd at least removed the gag. They seemed to be amused by my threats. Little did they know, they weren't just threats. I would deliver every one of them, slowly. Unfortunately, there was some kind of ward on the ship, and my magic was bound tight.

Another demon dropped to his knees and crawled closer.

"Back the fuck up," I snarled.

He ignored me and kept coming. If my legs weren't tied to the chair, I'd kick the ugly fuck in the face. I jerked and fought, but it was hopeless, and he dragged his bulbous oily nose along the leather of my pants all the way up, until he was pressed between my thighs, and dragged in a deep breath.

"Oh yes," he said and laughed excitedly. "His lordship has used her. The scent of his seed is strong. She is the right female. The mistress will reward us."

They all giggled their weird fucking giggles, eyes flashing with glee.

"When I tell *his lordship* what you just did, asshole, he'll tear your face off and feed it to the fishes," I snarled. "That is, if there's anything left of it when I'm through slicing your ugly fucking face to ribbons."

They laughed again, uproariously.

Sig picked up a piece of my hair and pressed it to his nose, breathing

690

deeply again. "You are a weak female. Your words are stupid. Your threats are false and make us laugh."

"And your breath smells like shit and makes me want to puke," I said, probably foolishly, but I didn't give a fuck at this point. I was usually good at controlling my temper, my emotions. I'd had to be with a mother like mine, and with my line of work, you learned to lock it all down. So when I did lose it, when I let that side of myself take hold, it was hard to get control back, and these ugly pervs had pushed me so far past my control, there was no coming back.

Sig's face darkened with rage a moment before he balled up his sledge-hammer-sized fist and slammed it into the side of my head.

)) ● ((

When I regained consciousness, I was being jostled, carried unceremoniously by the demon who'd sniffed my crotch and one of his buddies. It was dark, and I blinked, trying to clear my fuzzy vision. He'd hit me hard, and the side of my head still throbbed.

We were off the boat and moving across rocks and stones toward a massive temple surrounded by forest—the same kind of forest as the one we'd walked through in the Outer Realm. The towers on either side of the temple looked like the demon lighthouse we'd stayed in.

It wasn't hard to guess who was so desperate to meet me that she'd had me abducted off our ship.

I tried to fight, but it was no use; I was still trussed up and gagged again.

The massive stone doors swung open as I was carried toward them. The demons strode inside and continued on through an enormous entrance-way. The tile floor was black obsidian with flecks of opal. Everything else was dark and cold. The only light was coming from a giant chandelier made of bone and huge charred antlers from some kind of otherworldly creature.

Another set of double doors opened as we approached, and I was carried into a room full of demons, and other creatures I'd never seen before in my life. They all went silent as I was brought in and dumped on the floor. The crotch sniffer undid the ropes around my wrists and ankles and tugged off the gag as the crowd gathered around, looking at me as if I was the oddity in the room. I tried to flex my magic, but the temple had the same ward, binding my powers here.

My hands and feet throbbed as blood rushed back, and it was hard, but I dragged myself to my feet. I was more than outnumbered, but that didn't mean I'd give up. No, I'd make as many of them bleed as I could before they took me down. I slid my blade free, gripping it tight, and turned in a slow circle, waiting to see who struck first.

Several of the demons laughed, one of them jerking forward, trying to scare me. I slashed fast with my knife, surprising him, and sliced through the side of his face, splitting it open. He shrieked and bared his bloody teeth, about to lunge.

"Enough!"

A voice echoed through the room, and it had the same kind of resonance as Death's. I locked my knees and turned to face Nox as the crowd parted to let her through.

"What do you want?" I said through gritted teeth, bracing for anything. I couldn't win, but that didn't mean I'd just lie down and die.

There were hisses and gasps around me at my question. Perhaps addressing a goddess the way I had was considered rude, but so was being kidnapped and knocked out.

"Forgive her. She is a witch and ignorant. She means no offense, I'm sure," Nox said as she finally emerged from the parting crowd.

She was tall and willowy, her skin like mother-of-pearl, her hair a glossy black waterfall down her back. She wore a long, flowing black gown in a sheer fabric, and her hands were folded in front of her, tipped with long, pointed black nails.

She blinked, staring at me with large black eyes, no white to be seen. It was the same way Death's and Somnus's eyes looked when they changed, looking like the sky on a starry night. On Death, it could be unsettling; on Nox, it was terrifying.

"I honestly don't care if you're offended," I said. There was no surviving this. If Nox wanted me dead, I was sure she could click her fingers, and I'd be splattered all over the marble floor. I wasn't going to bow down to her.

"I can hear your weak little mortal heart pounding in your chest, witch. Best you speak to me with respect, or I will rip it from your chest and crush it in my fist." She smiled, revealing bright white teeth. "But none of us want that now, do we, Zinnia?"

"I have no idea what you want."

Her eyes narrowed, but she smiled wider. "Oh, you are delightful, so full of fire, even when it can be so easily extinguished."

"The fact you can easily kill me isn't lost on me. You're a goddess, and as you pointed out, I'm a witch, one who has her powers currently bound by you. I know I can't win here, but if you think that scares me, you're wrong. I've faced fiercer monsters than you before, and if I die today, I will do it fighting."

Nox blinked at me, then threw her head back and laughed. The peanut gallery joined in, laughing with her uproariously. When her chuckles finally died down, she wiped away an invisible tear. "My dear, I only wanted to meet my son's consort. He can be..." She waved an elegant hand through the air. "... so possessive of his things."

"I'm not a thing."

"Of course you aren't, dear." She smiled wide again. "I want to get to know you, that's all. You've arrived just in time for dinner, so we can sit and talk." Her gaze slid over me, her mouth twisting with distaste. "We dress for dinner here," she said, then waved her hand toward me, and my leathers were replaced by a long black gown, my weapons vanishing. I looked down at myself. The dress brushed the floor, and the lace was like a delicate black spiderweb that covered nothing. My naked body was totally visible beneath. The gown was old, extremely fragile, and smelled slightly musty.

I ran my hands carefully over my hips, and a strange feeling filled me— a weird kind of excitement, a rush of happiness. I was getting something off it, vibrations from the past, from the female that had worn this before me; there was no other way to explain what I was feeling.

"Something wrong, dear?" Nox asked.

I looked up. "Give me back my things."

She ignored me and glided forward, toward a massive table. "Sit, Zinnia, it's time to eat." I had no choice but to follow. She sat, and a demon rushed ahead and pulled out a chair. I reluctantly took my place beside her. Was she going to kill me by poisoning my food? Poison could be nice and fast or slow and drawn out. Nox wouldn't enjoy clean or fast. She'd want to take her time; she'd enjoy my screams of pain. I grabbed the steak knife beside my plate and gripped it tight.

Nox glanced my way and shook her head with a tittering laugh. "Are you going to stab me with that, witch?"

She said *witch* with mockery in her voice, as if I were so insignificant, it was hilarious, and I supposed I was to her, but the demons still gathered around, sizing me up, were another story. "If any of your friends come any closer, they'll be losing an eye."

She chuckled again, then clapped her hands, and the food was brought out.

"Are you planning on poisoning me, goddess?"

She gave me a sidelong glance. "Poison? How very boring. No, my dear, the food is quite safe."

"You would say that."

She shrugged one elegant shoulder. "Suit yourself. Go hungry if you must."

I would be. No, I didn't really think deadly wolfsbane in the soup or hemlock baked into the bread was her style, but I wasn't going to take her word for it.

"So how have you been getting along with my son?" she asked after swallowing a spoonful of wolfsbane soup.

"Why don't you ask him that yourself when he gets here?" I said, because Death would be coming, and he would be furious when he arrived. "I'm sure he's worked out who snatched me off our ship."

Her smile turned indulgent. "Mors can be rather possessive, can he not? An independent female such as yourself must be finding it hard to adjust." She broke off a small piece of hemlock bread and popped it in her mouth. Then she held out the basket. "Are you sure you won't have some? It's very good."

"I'm sure, thank you."

"Did you know there were others before you?" she asked, turning on her seat to face me.

Bitch. "I did, yes."

She did her tittering laugh. "Of course you did. Do you think you're different? That you'll be the exception, Zinnia?"

"Why not?" I said, because I knew it would annoy her. She liked to be the most arrogant monster in the room, but I could be arrogant as well. If nothing else, it'd amuse me to piss her off. "I'm no goddess, but I am a powerful witch, and your son likes me very much. He doesn't seem that fond of you, though, for some reason. Why is that?"

The amusement in her eyes vanished, quickly replaced by vicious glee. "Do you want children, Zinnia?" she asked, ignoring my question.

Every part of me stilled. She knew. She knew my deepest, darkest secret. "I'm not sure. I haven't really thought about it."

"You probably should. My son has always wanted a child—a lot of them."

Nausea swirled in my belly. "We haven't talked about it," I said, trying to stop my hands from shaking.

Her black eyes bored into me, sinking deep. "Perhaps you should, dear." Then she turned, her gaze sliding to the main doors a moment before they flew apart, the wood splintering into shrapnel.

Demons ducked for cover a moment before Death strode in, expression like thunder. He was shirtless, his leather pants straining over his thighs. His stomach was taut, and the fist of one hand was clenched around his staff as shadows swirled, gathering around him, turning into his cloak. My heart thundered in my chest at the sight of him. His face was transformed, the shadows turning it into a skull, but instead of dark eye sockets, his blue gaze glowed out from under the hood of his cloak. "Zinnia!" he roared.

Nox waved her demons forward, and they instantly and stupidly ran at him.

"It's better if he blows off some steam before we converse," Nox said to me, completely unaffected. "He seems agitated."

He looked ready to tear the temple down around us. The demons ran at him, and he smashed his fist into the first one's head, crushing his skull. He spun his staff, slamming into them as they attacked, slicing and hacking them to pieces, but they kept coming, essentially committing suicide, one after the other, blindly doing as Nox bid them.

Death was smeared with demon blood and ash, veins bulging, jaw clenched, rage rolling off him. It didn't seem as if mutilating a roomful of demons and other creatures was helping calm him down; in fact, it seemed the opposite to me.

I stood so he'd see me over the chaos, and his gaze sliced to me instantly. He strode toward me, swiping demons out of his way with one brutal swing of his staff after another, until he reached me. He didn't spare his mother a glance; he hooked his arm around my waist and hoisted me up so I was partially over his shoulder.

"So sensitive," Nox said with a sigh. "You always were my sensitive boy."

Death's grip on me was bruising and kind of humiliating, but I didn't say a word or try to get down, not when fury sparked off him like a live wire ready to set everything in his path on fire.

"You know why we're here, and if you try to stop us, if you come near my consort again or have your demons follow us, I will slaughter every demon in your realm. You know I can, and you know I will."

Her lips pursed, and the look in her eyes turned nasty. "You're wasting your time with this one—you know as well as I do. She's not fit to rule beside you, my son. She's as weak as the others." She tilted her head, a look of fake sympathy rearranging her features. "Maybe next time?" She stood and lifted her hands palm up, and shadows began to swirl above them, so thick and dark, it was like she held the night in her hands. Power snapped from her, making the hair on the back of my neck stand up. "Let me end this for you now. Let me end this before you grow attached to her and you're hurt when this ends as badly as the rest."

"No," Death roared as he slammed his staff onto the floor. The marble cracked, a fault line snaking across the entire room and out of sight. "You are not the only god in this room. You may have limited my powers here, but I am not powerless. Attempt to take her from me and see what happens. You're not as strong as you once were, whereas I grow stronger with every passing day. Make a move to hurt her, and I will destroy you."

Malice lit her face, but she dropped her hands. "It was only a suggestion. I care about you, you must see that?"

"Do not follow us," he snarled, ignoring her bullshit, and pointed a thick, tattooed finger at her. "I'm warning you now, and I won't do it again—I will strike you down." He strode from the room into the massive entrance hall, then out the doors.

As soon as we were outside, he lowered me to my feet. "Are you injured?" His eyes narrowed. "Your face. They hit you?"

"I'm fine."

His fury ratcheted back up. "I told you, more than once, do not leave my side."

He was roaring again. "Stop yelling at me," I bit out.

"It seems it's the only way to get you to listen to me. 'Do not leave my side' means exactly that, or are you hard of hearing?"

I scowled. "If I wasn't before, I am now. Lower your damned voice. If you said, 'stay by my side because my megalomaniac mother will send crotch-sniffing demons to abduct you,' then I would have stayed in bed and ignored my need for fresh air."

"What? They did what?" he roared again, then spun back to the temple doors, about to storm back inside.

I grabbed his arm. "I'm fine. And I'm pretty sure you decapitated the offending demons back there already, so punishment has been meted out."

Death's gaze sliced down my body and back, and a strange stillness moved over him. His brows lowered. "Take that off."

"What?"

"The gown, take it off." He didn't yell this time; no, his voice was low, tight.

There was a note to his voice I'd never heard before. "My clothes are back in the temple."

"Take it off, Zinnia, now." Then he grabbed the front of the dress, holding the delicate fabric in his hands... and tore it off my body.

"What the hell are you doing?" I tried to cover my nakedness as he stared down at me, nostrils flared, panting like a furious bull.

His hand shot out, and using his weakened powers, he summoned my leathers and knives from inside. They appeared in his hands. "Cover yourself."

If I weren't cold, I'd ignore him and stay naked just to piss him off. "What the hell is your problem?"

"Put them on," he growled.

"You're an asshole, you know that?" I said as I snatched my clothes from his hands and quickly pulled them on.

Death watched me the entire time, his gaze sliding over my bare skin until I was finally covered. Then he tilted his head back and made a strange throaty sound. A moment later, a creature appeared at the edge of the forest in the distance and headed straight for us.

It was similar to Zuri and Raze but also not. It was stockier, its legs thicker. It trotted over and stopped beside Death.

He ran his hand down its side. "Thank you for your service," he said, then grabbed me around the waist and tossed me up before he swung up behind me as well.

Then the beast took off.

CHAPTER 14

Zinnia

WE RODE FOR SEVERAL HOURS, picking our way through the forest before, finally, we came to a small clearing. A stone building sat in the middle, not huge, but still a decent size. It was made of glittering steel-colored marble with vines wrapped around the columns on either side of the entrance and partially over the roof.

Death jumped down from the beast, grabbed me around the waist, and hauled me off after him. He'd been quiet the entire ride, barely saying more than a few words.

At first, I thought it was about his mother and what just happened and the fact he thought I'd disobeyed him, but now, I wasn't so sure. The rage that had radiated from him had receded, and something else had replaced it. Something that felt a lot like melancholy.

"What is this place?" I asked, standing beside him.

"Somnus and I spent most of our time here as children. I created it when I was very young. It was safe, warded, impenetrable by anyone but him and me and those we chose to grant admittance."

I studied his profile. The night sky swirled in his eyes, but again, there was no anger. They were wide, as if he was about to face something that frightened him. "Not even Nox?"

"Not even her."

So even as children, they'd avoided their twisted mother. "You created it? When you were just a child?"

"Yes."

He said no more and seemed to go somewhere else for a moment. I touched his arm. "Why are we here?"

"This is where Somnus is. His dream-self, anyway."

"Why would he come here, back to this realm, so close to Nox, even while he's asleep?"

"I'll show you," Death said and took my hand, leading me to the tall main doors.

They were damaged, the marble chipped and gouged. "Someone's been trying to get in."

Death's eyes swirled, and I felt his fury return. "Yes, but breaching them is impossible."

Whatever was in here had to be something important or powerful for Nox to be so desperate to get in. "That must piss Nox off."

"It does, but still she tries, and the fact Somnus and I have a temple in her realm and still she's denied admittance infuriates her."

Death slid my knife from the sheath strapped to my thigh, then sliced his forearm. He handed the knife back to me, then, dipping his finger in the blood dripping from the wound, drew a symbol on the door. The door rumbled, and a moment later, it swung open.

Taking my hand again, he led me through the massive doors, and I saw that the slice on Death's arm had already healed. The doors closed behind us, and I took in the room. Inside was vastly different than outside. Everything was pristine, lush couches and cozy blankets, vibrant colors.

"Did you and Somnus choose the furniture?"

"Yes, when we were very young. This was a refuge from our mother, so we made it as comfortable as we could. We created every piece in this temple," he said absently.

"You were powerful even as a small boy." Something was seriously wrong with Death; he didn't just give away information like that.

His hands hung loose at his sides, but they curled, his fists tight. "When you're a terrified child, it's amazing what you can accomplish."

My heart broke for him and Somnus. "You were here a lot?"

"Sometimes, we were in here for months, and sometimes, years at a time."

"Years?" I choked out.

The veins bulged in his forearms. "Nox created us because she was lonely. She wanted to know what it was like to love someone besides herself, but after we were born, she quickly returned to her default of using everything and everyone for her own gain. She sold Somnus regularly, bartered her small son in exchange for power." His lips curled in disgust, his eyes bright with fury. "She let other gods sleep beside him, let them piggyback off his power. He didn't have full control over it yet, so he didn't know how to distance himself from it. He was forced to see the twisted shit they did in the Dream Realm to others, and sometimes, they turned their twisted shit on him." His nostrils flared. "I made it so she couldn't get near him anymore, and as punishment, she stifled my powers in her realm so she'd always be stronger."

I felt sick to my stomach. How could she do that to her own children? "I'm so sorry. She really is a monster."

The muscle at the side of his jaw tightened. "More than you know."

He carried on through the main room and down a short hallway. Right at the end was another closed door. Death pressed his hand to it and whispered words I couldn't hear.

The door swung open, and he stepped inside.

I followed but abruptly stopped, definitely not prepared for what was in there. I expected an altar dedicated to Somnus or something like that, some artifact that we could take back to the castle to wake his brother in Limbo; instead, there was a little girl.

Death walked to her side, staring down at her. He kept his features hard, but again, somehow, I felt his emotions and just how wild they were in that moment.

She was very young, maybe two or three years old. "You have a sister?" I whispered and joined him. My breath caught. She was utterly beautiful. Her hair was long and glossy black like Nox's, her skin the same shimmery mother-of-pearl. "Why is she here? Why isn't she with her mother?"

"Her mother doesn't know she exists, and that's the way it must be for now," he said, voice low.

"Doesn't know she exists? How? And if Nox doesn't know she exists, then why is she trying to break into the temple?" I glanced up at him.

He ran the backs of his fingers down the child's round cheek. "It's complicated."

"How long has she been here? How old is she?"

"She's been here in stasis for a very long time. In human years, she is but three years old."

"Why is she like this? Why is she being kept asleep like this?"

"This was a punishment, part of a curse, and there is only one way for it to be broken. Until that happens, she must stay here, and Somnus stays with her in the dream world, protecting her, taking care of her so she is not alone or afraid, until she can finally wake again."

"A curse? So there's no way we can take her from this temple?"

"No, not without breaking it first."

He didn't elaborate, which meant he couldn't tell me.

I couldn't take my eyes off the child lying there. "Are you able to talk to her through Somnus like you did me? In the dream realm?"

"No, she is blocked from me in every way. Only Somnus can reach her."

I didn't think I could despise Nox more. I was wrong. "What will happen to her when we wake him? Who will protect her in the dream realm?"

His jaw tightened again, and his hand actually shook as it hovered over the little girl's cheek. "There are places she can hide. Somnus will ensure she's hidden before he rises from his slumber. It will be only a few days, and then he can return to her."

"She must be so scared," I choked out, thinking of Jasmine when she was that little and my responsibility, and of baby Violet. I don't know what came over me, but I reached out and cupped her tiny, little face, leaning in close and smoothing my hand over her hair. "It will be okay, little one," I whispered. "Your brothers will keep you safe." My heart squeezed. "What's her name?"

"Marigold."

I glanced at him, but he wasn't looking at me or his tiny sister; he had moved to a small statue beside her bed. "Your knife," he said and held out his hand.

I took it from its sheath again and handed it to him. This time, he sliced through his palm and squeezed his fingers into a tight fist, letting his blood drip down the small statue while muttering words in a different language.

Death's head was back, his eyes closed, and power rolled through the room, shaking the ground. I grabbed onto the side of the bed so I didn't fall.

Finally, he opened his eyes, swiped his thumb through the blood pooled in his palm, and pressed it to Marigold's forehead.

"While you walk the Dream Realm alone, let my blood be your protection, let it shelter you, guide you, comfort you," he said in a low, raspy voice.

Then he stepped back, and the power pulsing through the room dropped, returning to how it was when we walked in. "You still have power in here?"

"Enough."

"Now what?" I asked when Death said nothing more.

"Now we go home. Somnus will wake in the next few days, and I'd like to be there to greet him." His gaze slid to me, and his eyes were back to black, flecked with distant stars.

He studied me in a way that made me uneasy. I glanced at Marigold, then back at him. "Is there something else you need?"

He shook his head. "Wait for me in the great room. I'll be out in a moment."

I nodded and hustled out of there, but I couldn't help but glance back before the room was out of sight. Death had dropped to his knees beside the bed, the child's hand held in his massive, tattooed, and scarred ones, and his head was bowed. He was talking, but there was no way I could hear what he was saying. I quickly turned away, feeling guilty for watching such a private and obviously painful moment, and did what he said.

When I walked back into the great room, I spotted a set of wooden animals. They lay on a small table by one of the couches, and I imagined two little boys in this place, playing with toys, sheltered within these walls. They'd been here sometimes years at a time. Were they always alone? What the hell was wrong with Nox that she didn't care for them or protect them? They were gods, yes, and I had no idea how children with that kind of power were raised, but this was wrong any way you looked at it.

After meeting Nox and seeing the way Death loathed her, I doubted she'd ever cared for them the way a mother should.

When Death walked into the room, he was back to being somber and contemplative. Leaving Marigold behind had to be incredibly difficult.

We walked back through the massive doors and outside. "How long has it been since you've been with Somnus awake?" I asked to try and take his mind off his pain, to remind him that he had something to look forward to.

He lifted me onto the beast, then swung up behind me. "Thirteen years."

Thirteen years ago, I'd been just fifteen years old. "When Somnus found me? Is that the last time you talked?"

"Yes."

His arm wrapped around me, and he fisted the beast's knotted mane. "Sleep if you need to. We're not stopping until we're back at the ship."

Then the beast lowered its head, and we took off, galloping back toward the Night Sea.

The closer we got to the ship, the more Death's mood deteriorated. He wasn't speaking, and the shadows swirled around him constantly now. A profound sadness and that anger, so much anger, burned from his chest behind me and went right through me, settling in my gut. I found myself wrapping my hands around his forearm, my thumbs sliding back and forth in an attempt to soothe whatever was going on with him.

When we reached the ship, Death ushered me down to the cabin, then headed back up, and I heard one demon scream followed by Death roaring threats. I waited for him to come down after that, but he didn't.

A demon knocked on the door an hour later carrying buckets of water.

He filled the tub, then left. I quickly washed and changed into a pair of tights and a T-shirt, but despite Death telling me to sleep, I couldn't; it was impossible when all those volatile emotions inside him were so raw and real to me.

I lay in bed, stared at the dark and moody sky through the small round window in the opposite wall, and pressed both hands to my chest to try and ease the ache. Goddess, I had this hollow feeling inside me. I didn't know what was causing it, but I needed it to stop.

It wasn't because of Death; it was something else. Though, I kind of felt like he was avoiding me. I shouldn't care, but I did. So many things had happened during this trip that could have him feeling the way he did, but it felt as if he was directing the force of his emotions at me when we'd ridden —that he was angry at me. But why? Yes, I went up to the deck without telling him and got myself kidnapped, but that didn't warrant that kind of fury. It had to be something else.

I was still mulling all this over hours later, when the door opened and closed. Death walked to the tub, stripped off, and climbed in, barely looking my way, but when he did, his nostrils flared and he ground his teeth.

Any doubt I had about my hypothesis vanished. He was most definitely pissed at me.

Words flew around my head as I tried to think of what to say. Despite how long I'd been coming to Limbo and how things had changed between us this last week, I didn't know him, not really. How could I? He was as old as time, a complex god, and he told me nothing.

He also didn't owe me his trust, and I hadn't earned the right to hear his deepest and darkest secrets, like he hadn't earned that from me. Which meant there was only one thing I could do. Shoving back the covers, I got out of bed and walked over, stopping at the foot of the bath.

"Go back to bed," he said, his gaze locked on the edge of the tub.

"Look at me."

His lips peeled back, but he did as I asked. His eyes were still black as night, like his mother's eyes, not a bit of white showing. "It's my turn," I said.

"Not tonight, witch."

Not consort or wife, not little witch, just witch, as if he was trying to put distance between us.

"Yes, tonight. We made a deal. This is what you demanded, so we'll do it."

His eyes flashed. "No, we will not. Now go back to bed."

He stood abruptly and snatched the towel, roughly drying himself off, then slung it around his waist.

"You're angry with me, why?"

He growled.

"Mors—"

His growl exploded in volume. "Do not... call me that. We are not in bed, witch, so you do not call me by my name."

For some reason, that hurt a lot. It was almost as if... as if he hated me in that moment. "Why are you angry at me?" I asked again. He turned away, and I grabbed his arm.

He swung back, pulling from my hold. "I told you to go back to bed."

"Since when have I done anything you've told me?" I fired back.

"Never, not one fucking time." He ground his teeth again. "You did this, you caused this..." He stopped himself.

"Tell me what I did." He was breathing hard. "Death, tell me what the hell is up your ass, because I've got to tell you, this tantrum of yours is starting to piss me off."

"Is that right?"

"You're not just angry, are you? You're angry at me?"

His face contorted. "Yes," he yelled.

"Why?"

He shook his head, his fingers in brutal fists, the veins in his arms and neck popping. "That is something you have to figure out for yourself."

"You can't just tell me?"

"No."

"And what if I can't figure it out?" I asked. All that volatile emotion pouring off him was too heavy a burden to carry.

He took two steps toward me, closing the space between us, and grabbed my arms. "You have to, do you hear me? You have to because I can't do this anymore. I can't fucking do this again."

I stared up at him. "Do what? I don't understand."

He cursed so loud and full of anguish, I flinched. When he saw me do it, another growl rumbled from him, and he hauled me off my feet. "You're not afraid of me, little witch."

It wasn't a question; it was a demand.

"No," I said and hooked my arms around his neck, pressing my body close. "I'm not."

"Fuck, you piss me off," he snarled, then twisted my hair in his fist and slammed his mouth down on mine.

Our mouths weren't in a dance, moving together; no, they were dueling. "You piss me off more," I said, digging my nails into his shoulders hard enough to draw blood.

He growled. "You disobey me again, and I will lock you in my bedroom and never let you out." He shoved me against the wall. "No, I think I'll do it, anyway."

I hissed, "No, you fucking won't."

My shirt was yanked off over my head and tossed away. "You think you can stop me?"

I bit down on his lip and tasted blood. "I can try, and I think you know me well enough now to know I won't stop until I win."

He swiped his tongue over his lip, coating it in blood, then yanked my head back and thrust it in my mouth, kissing me hard. "I have nothing but time, female," he said against my lips.

My legs were around his hips, fighting to get him closer while making him work for it at the same time. "You're a confusing, arrogant pain in the ass."

He shoved his hand down the front of my tights, into my underwear. "Turns out confusing, arrogant pains in the ass make your cunt wet as fuck."

"And it turns out infuriating, disobedient witches make you hard as hell." I yanked the towel away, and the long, hard ridge of his cock dug into my stomach.

The sound of fabric ripping came next. "They were my favorite tights, asshole."

"I'm about to stuff your pussy full of your favorite cock, so I think you'll get over it," he said, maneuvering me like a rag doll, then shoved my panties aside.

"How do you know yours is my favorite?" I fired back, even though we both knew I'd never had better, that no one had ever made me feel the way he had in this cabin.

He laughed, and it was dark and arrogant; then, he slammed inside me.

I cried out, the invasion too much but exactly what I needed. "*Oh fuck.*"

The smile dropped from his face as he slid out, then thrust back in. "When I'm finished with you, I will be the only lover you remember. The rest will cease to exist. How long did you feel me after, little witch, when I fucked you the first time?"

I hadn't stopped. I'd still felt him before he filled me a moment ago. "G-goddamn... ah, arrogant."

He pressed his forehead against mine and thrust inside me again, then held there. "You were made for me, inside and out, and the first time I claimed you, I ruined you for every other male for the rest of your life."

The rest of my life could be only a matter of hours or days, so I guess he was right. I didn't say that, though. When I talked about that, it angered him, and I currently had as much angry Death as I could handle. "You... th-think so?" He still hadn't slid back out; he was still deep inside me, doing this subtle swivel of his hips, and goddess, it felt so fucking good. I was close to coming from just that. My pussy started clutching at him desperately.

"I know so, and if another male comes near you, I will tear him into tiny pieces, but not before I've made him scream for mercy."

I couldn't hold back; my pussy clamped down on him, and I cried out, coming for him and moaning his name.

"That's it, wife, moan for me." Then he lifted me away from the wall, pulled out, spun me to my front, shoved me down on the bed, and, dragging my ass in the air, slammed back inside me. His hand went between my thighs, and one of those long, scarred fingers slid over my clit while he pounded into me from behind. I came again, screaming this time, mindlessly clawing at the sheets.

His big body covered me, one hand curling around my throat, his mouth coming to my ear as he fucked me hard and fast. "You are mine, Zinnia, and I won't fucking lose you, do you hear me? I won't," he said the last part in a way that resonated though the room like an oath.

All I could do was make an incoherent sound as the God of Death claimed me in the most primal of ways over and over again.

CHAPTER 15

Zinnia

WE WERE FINALLY on the last leg of the journey, and I gripped Zuri's reins as she galloped through the forest. She'd healed while we were gone, but Raze had been sticking close to his mate since Death called for them after we walked through the gateway back into Limbo.

He nudged her every now and again, making her move where he wanted her, to keep her from edging too far ahead or putting any kind of distance between them at all. Zuri would make this high noise and shake her head in frustration, overwhelmed by his dominance. I got how she was feeling; the last few days, Death hadn't left my side.

I glanced over at him. He'd invaded my life at fifteen years old, and had been completely unaware of how terrified I'd been of him or that the way he went about it had sent me down a dark path, driving me to go to extreme lengths to avoid him. I'd lost something precious as a consequence, far more than was fair, and that was before I'd been forced to leave my family and come here. After all of that, after all I'd lost, I never dreamed I'd actually like him. That I might actually enjoy his company—but I did.

The castle finally came into view, and Death galloped up to the stairs, his anticipation at seeing his brother awake for the first time in so many years palpable. He swung off Raze, and I eased off Zuri, stretching my aching body. Death had made good on his promise; he'd taken me at any opportunity, deeply and thoroughly, and there wasn't a moment, not since the first time we were together, that I hadn't felt him with me, inside me.

And I wanted him. Goddess, I wanted him all the damn time.

Shivering, I focused on taking off Zuri's girth strap and glanced up when the doors swung open and Somnus strode out. He should be frail from never moving, never eating, only sleeping, but he wasn't. He looked every bit the god he was.

Death grinned wide, taking the steps two at a time to greet him. I couldn't take my eyes off them as they embraced, as Death said something to him low. Their connection was obvious, the love between them unmissable.

When they released each other, Somnus looked over at me. I lifted a hand in greeting, feeling awkward, not wanting to intrude on their reunion, but I also kind of knew him as well. He'd been here the entire time I had, even if he'd been asleep. He smiled, but it was strained.

Death strode back to me. "Come and join us."

I shook my head. "You two have a lot to catch up on, right? Like thirteen years' worth of gossip to share. I'm going to take a bath, snuggle with Hemy, and have a nap. I'll join you afterward." Death had regained his control somewhat since losing it completely on the ship, but I could tell it was a battle. He didn't want to be angry, but it was still there.

"Okay, but don't stay away too long," he said and pressed a sweet kiss to my lips before he strode back to his brother, and they disappeared inside.

I'd said thanks to Zuri, and she and Raze had just trotted off when Egon hustled out, his horns glinting in the light. Hemlock was on his shoulder, and he squeaked, making excited noises when he saw me. I scooped him up and held him close. "I've missed you, my sweet baby." He wriggled and squeaked some more, trying to get as close as he could to me, and I giggled when he tickled my neck.

"Thank you for taking such good care of Hemy. He's happy, so I'm happy."

"No thanks necessary, I assure you." Egon took my bag. "I thought you might like a bath, my lady."

"Are you saying I stink, Egon?"

His lips twitched. "Never."

"Well, I do, and I'd love one."

"Good, because I've drawn one for you," he said.

We headed inside. "Have I ever told you that I love you?" I said and hooked my arm through his. "Because I do."

He didn't profess his love back to me, but I did see the corners of his lips curl up, and he patted my hand. "I am exceedingly glad you're home safe."

"You and me both. Were you bored without me?"

708

He made a rough sound that was absolutely a laugh. "Oh, most assuredly. The castle was a sad and lonely place without you stomping around and bickering with his lordship."

"Stomping? I do not stomp."

His lips twitched again. "Of course not."

"Or bicker."

"Never."

"Smart-ass."

"Possibly."

I laughed then, and it felt really good. "Just so you know, you're my favorite."

"Second favorite, surely," he said.

"Maybe."

The slight lip curl became a full, fang-flashing grin. The demon had not missed that something had changed between Death and me.

"Shut up," I said, then couldn't hold back my own grin, because I wasn't... unhappy. For the first time in all the months I'd been coming here, I wasn't desperately missing home. Yes, I was confused and scared of the things I was starting to feel, plus a whole lot of other things, but I wasn't unhappy. I thought I might actually be the opposite, which just made me all the more terrified.

We walked into my room, and Egon put my bag on the trunk at the end of the bed.

"Lyle made you a mug of your favorite tea. It's waiting for you by the tub. Would you like a light repast brought up?"

"No. Thanks, though, Egon. I'll wait for dinner. And I deeply appreciate the tea."

He smiled and dipped his head, then walked out, closing the door behind him. I sat on the edge of my bed, pulled off my boots with a sigh, and wiggled my toes while Hemy had the zoomies on the mattress around me. I undid my leather jacket and let it slide off my shoulders. Next, I shucked off the pants and let out another sigh of relief. Striding to the dresser, I pulled out some clean clothes, and my gaze caught on the knickknacks sitting on top.

I picked up a silver thimble; it was worn inside, with tiny dents from needles pressing against the tip. Someone had used it regularly. Without realizing I was doing it, my hand went to the center of my chest, rubbing at the ache that came out of nowhere. That seemed to be happening a lot. Some of the pieces on the dresser and around the room had to be ancient, and some were probably just a century or two old. There were things all over this room, little oddities, keepsakes—a random book still open face down on the table by the chair next to the window, a delicate bedside clock inlaid with jewels, small dried-up pots of paints, and several paintings of the view from the window or the garden that were executed with passion and pleasure, but even I could see they were by someone who only painted as a hobby.

Only now, right in this moment, did I realize what they were.

They were small pieces of the females who had come before me. Each of Death's consorts had left something of themselves in this bedroom.

One day soon, would all that remained of me in this castle be some trinket left behind?

More than likely.

No, I wasn't going to just give up. I wasn't going to let someone end my life, or whatever had happened to the females before me, without a fight, but I had accepted that death could be the eventual outcome of this journey fate had sent me on, whether I liked it or not.

))) ● (((

"How are you enjoying Limbo?" Somnus asked as he tore another strip of meat from the bone he was holding.

Somnus had been quiet, distracted, and his leg jiggled almost nonstop. He hadn't said much since I sat, instead choosing to devour everything on the table like a man who hadn't taken a bite in thirteen years.

"Does anyone really enjoy Limbo?" I said, grinning as I cut off a small piece of carrot and handed it to Hemy, who was perched on my shoulder.

Somnus glanced at Death, not looking amused by my little joke in the slightest. "A person can enjoy any location as long as they are in close proximity to those they love."

He was also protective of his brother.

"Yes, that's true. It's hard being away from my family a month at a time. I have a younger sister—"

"Who is newly mated, yes? She does not need you to be there for her like she used to," Somnus said. "I understand the hardship of being absent from the lives of my family, of being parted from them, but sometimes, we need to do what's best for ourselves as well as others."

I stared at him, surprised that when he did finally choose to speak, it was to essentially scold me for not being excited enough about being here with his brother. "That's true. When did you last do something for yourself, Somnus? As I understand it, you've spent centuries— longer?—trapped in the Dream Realm to protect your sister. No, I still don't fully understand all the ins and outs of your situation..." I glanced at Death. "Because no one will tell me, but you're not really practicing what you preach." Was that a

710

dickish thing to say? Probably, but I wasn't a fan of being judged by someone who knew nothing about me.

He blinked over at me several times. "I am immortal. I have been alive since almost the dawn of time and will continue to live when we reach the end. I have many lifetimes ahead of me. My time with Marigold in the Dream Realm is but a blip in my lifetime. Best you consider the situation you find yourself in closely, or you will end up—"

"Somnus," Death growled.

He froze, then blew out a breath and slumped back in his seat. "Apologies, both of you. I'm not... I'm not myself. I'm anxious to get back to Marigold."

"It must be hard being away from her," I said.

"It is. Thankfully, I have a... a friend, Pascal, who can check in on her from time to time." His gaze went to Death. "I trust him with my life," he added, reassuring his brother.

"Are you sure, Som?" Death asked, looking tense.

"I've never been more sure of anything."

Death held his brother's stare, then nodded.

I took a sip of my wine. "So, how do you know so much about me and my sister?" I asked Somnus.

He looked up from loading his plate with more mashed potatoes. "I have access to every living being in every realm in existence. Dreams, nightmares—they come to everyone. I was searching for you, and then one night, there you were."

I turned to Death. "How does it work? How did you reach me in my dream that first time?"

Hemy pushed closer to me when he sensed my emotions shift, my little familiar trying to comfort me. That time of my life was not something I liked to look back on. Death was studying me in that way of his, like he could sense it as well and was trying to reach inside me and learn my secrets.

He had his elbows on the table, his hands linked together in front of him. Darkness swirled in his eyes. "If I sleep beside Som, as long as we're touching, I can tap into his powers, and he can point me in the right direction."

I looked away, down at my food, when Somnus asked him a question, changing the subject. But I couldn't shake the memories of that time, of what happened next. The night the God of Death came to me—a terrified kid, only fifteen years old—in my dreams and told me I belonged to him.

How I'd struggled to stay awake afterward so he couldn't reach me again. I'd taken potions to keep myself awake until I was delirious and desperate. Until I'd finally learned of a demon who could help me. Then I'd made a choice in fear and delirium that ended in me losing something precious, something that I could never get back and could never be undone.

I stumbled to the demon's door and knocked.

His name was Fluke, and it had taken me three days to find him. Three days of drinking coffee, of using forbidden potions and elixirs to fight off sleep. If my family knew I'd come here, they'd be furious, but this demon was my only chance. "You said on the phone you can help me?"

The demon's muddy yellow eyes looked me up and down. "You are Death's consort?"

"That's what he says." The demon was old, powerful. He'd been around so long, his skin looked thin and almost translucent. His eyes were cloudy, and the fangs that curved around his chin had blackened. If I weren't so exhausted and scared, I would've probably peed myself. But what waited for me in my dreams, my future, if the demon couldn't help me was far worse.

"What's your fee?" I asked, my words sounding slurred from exhaustion and the potions still in my system.

He opened his door wider. "Come in and we can make a deal."

I needed to get this done quickly. Mom was gone again, and Jaz had been staying with a friend. I hated being away from her for more than a couple of days. I followed him in, and he led me to a tall bench, motioning to it. I sat, and he walked to a shelf and pulled down a small bottle. The liquid inside was black or maybe deep red, it was hard to tell in the shadowed room.

"This is the blood of the goddess Nox. She is the night and Death's mother. This cost me deeply to acquire, and if you want my help, you must be prepared to pay a great price."

"Whatever it is, I'll pay it."

"Then lie on the bench and lift up your shirt," he said as he closed the space between us, excitement dancing in his eyes.

"What are you going to do?"

"Take something you do not need. Now do it, or leave and await your fate."

I would never leave Jazzy. She needed me. And I would never belong to Death, and I sure as hell would never love that monster. I had no choice but to do as the demon asked. I lay on the bench and lifted my shirt. He stalked over and kneeled on the floor beside me.

"Once I take payment, I will mark you with the blood of Nox. Only her blood has the power to conceal you, and the only way for Death to find you will be if you cut the markings from your skin, do you understand?"

I nodded, my heart racing wildly in my chest.

Pulling up his sleeves, he rubbed his hands together, his translucent skin glowing the faster he rubbed. Then he pressed one to my bare stomach, pushing and grinding his palm. I screamed and thrashed, but leather binds snapped up like snakes and wrapped around my arms and legs, holding me down. White-hot agony burned through me as his hand pushed through, disappearing inside me. Shadows danced at the edges of my vision—and then the pain was too much. Everything went dark.

When I woke again, only a few candles flickered around the room. I looked down at myself. My stomach looked as if nothing had happened, as if the demon hadn't shoved his hand through my skin and into my body. My forearm stung, and I lifted it. There was a small tattoo-like marking there.

"You're awake finally," the demon said, and I quickly sat up, almost unbalancing and falling.

I looked back down at the tattoo. "What did you do?"

"The deal is done. You are now concealed from Death for all eternity."

I struggled to my feet. My stomach ached, and I felt weird. "What did you take from me?"

He motioned to a jar on a table beside me. Something fleshy floated in pink-tinged liquid. "I've given you your life back. That is a powerful thing and requires something equally as powerful as payment. I restored your life, and now you will never be able to create it. I took your womb, child."

"Zinnia?"

Death's voice pulled me from the horror of that memory, one I chose not to revisit, ever, but tonight, for some reason, I hadn't been able to shake it off.

"Where did you go just now?" he asked, studying me closely.

I forced a smile. "Sorry, I must've zoned out. Tired, I guess. I didn't sleep earlier like I'd planned to." I was trying to hide how that memory affected me, but Hemlock was totally giving me away. He was pressed into me, nuzzling my jaw, pouring as much love and comfort into me as his little soul had to give.

"Egon," Somnus called. "Bring the ambrosia, my man. My brother and I have much to discuss."

I smiled at him. "Looks like you're in for a big night. I'm going to head up to bed." I stood, but Death grabbed my hand, stopping me from walking past.

"Are you well?" His gaze moved over my face again. "You seem unsettled."

"I'm fine," I lied. "I just need a good night's sleep, that's all."

"And you'll be in my bed while you do it. Tonight and every night from now on. When I come up later, that's where I expect to find you."

"How very presumptuous of you," I said, raising a brow.

"This was inevitable. If you try to defy me, I will come for you and put you where you belong," he said, and darkness flashed through his eyes again.

This side of him hadn't been present as much, not after we left the ship and headed for home. I recognized it for what it was now—fear that I would reject him, deny him. He chose force, to bend me to his will, rather than ask and risk me saying no. That was something we were going to have to talk about, but I was too tired right then, and we had an audience.

So instead of giving him the attitude he expected before he inevitably made me do what he wanted, I decided to skip that part and, instead, cupped the side of his face, then leaned in close. His eyes widened, and I relished his surprise. It wasn't often I got one over on this powerful male. "All you had to do was ask, my lord," I said and pressed a soft kiss to his perfectly formed lips.

He made a delicious gruff sound as I straightened and walked away.

"Night, Somnus," I called.

"Good night, Zinnia," he called back, sounding a lot cheerier than before.

CHAPTER 16

Zinnia

IT FELT weird being in Death's huge bed on my own. It felt weird being in his room, period.

The fire crackled against the opposite wall, and that at least gave the place a bit of warmth, but here now, on my own, I was feeling out of place —insignificant.

I stroked Hemy, who had curled up beside my pillow, and that helped. But there was this niggling feeling inside me that wouldn't go away, that I didn't like much at all.

I'd never had low self-esteem or let insecurities get the better of me. I'd always been confident in who I was, how I looked, my place in the world. I'd basically raised my sister on my own since our mother was more absent than not. I'd protected Jasmine, taken over her care full time when Mom left to travel the world and barely looked back.

So I knew who I was. I was Zinnia Thornheart, Jasmine's big sister, and a powerful witch and medium. I'd liked being her—loved it, in fact. Being a god's consort? One of possibly ten other females? Nope, that had never been on the cards. So no, I'd never had low self-esteem, but I needed to know where I fit into all of this. With him? I'd definitely never be his one and only love; he'd possibly loved them all. I wasn't the jealous type, but it was an odd feeling being one of so many and possibly not his last consort either—there would be more after me, possibly many more. I guess that was no different than meeting someone and knowing they had a bunch of exes. It was normal, right?

Again, I wasn't the jealous type, but something was developing between us, something wild and huge and unstoppable, and I couldn't help but wonder if this was what it was like for him with all of them.

"I'm being an idiot," I said to Hemy. He hissed his disagreement. "You're just saying that because you love me." He squeaked, and I scratched his tiny chin. "Thank the goddess I have you, my sweetheart." Because now that we were back in the castle, I was feeling off-kilter. I wasn't sure what my role was anymore, what I was supposed to do.

Death was into me, that much was clear, and I was seriously struggling to come to terms with the fact that after eighteen months of coming here, I was now suddenly into him as well, like in a seriously big way.

The door opened, and he strode in.

His gaze sliced to the bed as soon as he walked in, and when he saw me, he grinned.

Not his normal grin. I'd never seen this grin; it lit up his entire face. "You're pretty drunk, huh?" I said, sitting up and leaning against the headboard.

"Not at all," he said, and the way he said it made it obvious that he was totally drunk.

"How much ambrosia did you and Somnus drink?"

He sauntered over, kicked off his boots, and then reached back, pulling off his shirt before tossing it aside. He stared down at me, eyes glinting. "I like seeing you in my bed, little witch, very much."

I laughed softly. "I can see that."

He flopped down on the bed beside me, then scooted over and wrapped his arms around my waist. "Fuck, I love the way you laugh. It's husky and so incredibly bewitching." I was still sitting, but now, with his big body wrapped around me and his head in my lap, I was stuck out of the covers.

I looked at the huge, tattooed god in my lap, his face relaxed in a way I'd never seen before, and my chest warmed. When was the last time he'd allowed himself to be this vulnerable?

"I like your laugh as well." I ran my hand along his shoulder, massaging.

He groaned, then dragged the sheet under him back and curled his hand around my bare thigh. "And I love your smooth skin." He pressed his nose to it. "And the way you smell, like honey and your garden and the night sky."

Now my belly was all swirly. "What does the night sky smell like?"

"Clean and crisp... overwhelming, breathtaking," he muttered. "What do I smell like?"

I blinked at his question, not expecting it at all. "Well—"

"And if you say death or some variation of it, like decay or rot, I'll tan your lovely ass."

Another laugh burst from me. "That does sound like something I'd say."

"Because I know you, my sweet Stella. I know all of you," he said, and there was a little more slur to his words.

Stella. Yes, it meant star, but I still didn't want him calling me that, especially when I'd had visions of him using that name affectionately with other consorts. There was no point calling him out on it while he was like this, though, and I didn't want to argue with him either, so I answered his question because despite him using that name, I was enjoying seeing Death like this—relaxed. Open. "Right now, you smell like leather and ambrosia and power," I said, giving him his answer.

"How does power smell?" he asked, turning my question back on me.

"Like endless shadows, vast and wild." I traced his lower lip. "Overwhelming, breathtaking."

He grinned. "Copycat."

"It's the truth."

He made a sound of agreement. "You always tell the truth, don't you, love?"

My heart kind of paused when he called me that, then exploded back to life. "I try to."

"Will you leave me?"

I was stunned silent for a moment, then quickly rallied. "I can't. We have a deal, remember?"

"But if you could, would you leave?"

I stared down at his profile. "If you'd asked me a couple of weeks ago, I would have said, yes, I would leave. Now... I'm not so sure."

He smiled, but his eyes stayed closed. "You're falling in love with me."

I had another of those heart explosions. "Again, you are being presumptuous. You're the most annoying male I've ever encountered. How could I ever fall in love with you?"

He chuckled at my sarcasm. "I have no idea, but you will."

"And will you fall in love with me?" I asked, while my heart tried to crawl into my throat.

He laughed again and shook his head against my lap as he held me tighter, as if I'd said something absurd, and I hated that sharp and unexpected disappointment filled me.

"I'm already in love with you," he murmured.

I froze.

717

His fingers dug deeper into my thigh, massaging, marking my skin with his long, scarred fingers. "That's why you can't leave me. I won't recover if you do, not this time."

He'd lost everyone, and in a couple of days, Somnus would be gone again as well. "Mors—"

His eyes opened, and he rolled to his back, looking up at me, holding me captive with that bright blue gaze swirling with shadows. "If you leave me, if you go and never return to me, there will be no coming back from the cloak. I'll let it consume me. I will retreat into it, and I'll never see you again."

He'd revert to the Death he was when I first came here, when he first came to me. The way he was looking at me, what he'd just said, it was too intense... too much. "I bet you say that to all your consorts," I said, trying to lighten the heaviness that had fallen over us.

His gaze searched mine, the darkness overtaking the bright blue, and all traces of humor, of softness, left his face. The shadows thickened around him.

My mouth went dry. What he wanted, what he was asking of me, was too much, too soon. "Death?"

He sat up suddenly and got off the bed.

"Death—"

"Rest. I have some things I need to do," he said, and then he walked out.

I stared after him, confused. He was angry with me again; I could feel it. What the hell did he expect? So much was changing so fast. Did he expect to profess his love for me and I'd fall at his feet? That I'd say it back? I wasn't ready to do that, and who knew if I ever would be? I was still trying to get my head around this whole thing—the parts I understood, anyway.

I wasn't where he was—I just wasn't. And honestly, I didn't think he was truly there either. He didn't love me, not yet. It was too soon. This was the fate thing making him think he felt that way. I cared about him. Goddess, I wanted him, but love? No, because falling in love with him, careening toward a fate that would more than likely see me losing him anyway, was the most terrifying thing I could imagine right now.

Sliding back down the mattress, I tugged up the covers. Hemlock snuggled in against me and instantly fell asleep. I, on the other hand, lay there for hours listening for Death's footfalls in the hallway, wondering where he was and just how hurt and angry he was with me.

›)›❂(‹‹

Death lay on his back, one hand behind his head, the other resting on his stomach. He was asleep, so still and so utterly gorgeous. I glanced over at

Hemlock; he'd gotten sick of my wriggling during the night and was on the chair across the room by the fire, fast asleep.

I turned back to the male beside me. I wasn't sure what time he came in. I hadn't heard him, but he must have been gone several hours at least because I'd been awake that long.

My body was pressed to his side, and I wasn't sure if I'd sought him out while I'd slept, restless from more visions of the females of his past streaming through me, sending me a message that I hadn't yet figured out, or if he'd pulled me against him when he'd returned.

Considering how we left things last night, I was assuming it was the former.

I appreciated his attempt at honesty last night. Even if he'd been drunk when he said all those things and even if I didn't believe he truly felt that way, I hated that I'd hurt him. Death had suffered a lot in his long life, and I didn't want to be another wound on his soul. He didn't deserve that. But he was expecting too much from me way too soon.

That didn't stop me from feeling guilty, though. Leaning deeper into him, I rested my hand on his stomach and kissed his chest. His skin was so smooth—no hair, just taut, smooth skin over lean, hard muscle. I slid my hand down his hairless stomach, wrapped my hand around his hard, smooth length, and stroked slowly.

Death made a rough sound before his eyes blinked open. He sucked in a breath. "Fuck," he said when he released it.

"You were just so tempting lying there, I had to touch," I said, kissing his stomach. "How are you feeling this morning?"

His fingers delved into my hair. "Like I want to wake with you pressed against me every morning," he growled.

I shifted, moving down his body, and his legs parted, giving me room to slide between them. "I've been wanting to do this for a while."

He shoved his pillow higher behind his head and looked down, watching me. "You going to suck me, wife?"

The way he said that, dear goddess, my pussy clenched. "That was the plan."

"Then don't let me stop you. I've stroked myself to visions of this, of you right there, licking those perfect, full lips, with eyes eager and hungry."

I squeezed my thighs together. "You have?"

"The things I've imagined, Zinnia—the rough, the slow and intense, the raw and fucking dirty—it's kept me sane and driven me to madness all at the same time."

The web of veins from his lower stomach down to his cock stood out in relief, his cock hard and thick against his flat stomach. I licked my lips. "I've had a few thoughts myself."

He reached down and cupped my face, sliding his thumb over my chin, across my lower lip. Hungry but okay to wait for me to do as I pleased. "I'm sorry I walked out last night," he said. "Sometimes, the way I feel... the things I want to tell you..." He shook his head. "I get... frustrated."

"I noticed." Like on the ship, how angry he was that I didn't know whatever it was he was so desperate for me to figure out. "Are you sure you can't just tell me whatever it is you want me to know?"

"Yes," he said, then fisted my hair, finally losing patience. "Suck me, my consort, before I lose my sanity."

"Your wish, my lord, is my command." Then I wrapped my mouth around the head of his cock and sucked him down as deep as I could, which wasn't far. His groan sent tingles of pleasure through me, and my inner muscles clamped down again.

Taking the base of his cock, I stroked as I sucked and kissed, as I teased him with my tongue, until he was panting hard, and then I took his smooth balls in my hand and massaged.

Death did an ab curl, hooked me under the arms, lifted me, spun me around, and planted me back on top of him so I was facing away. Then he gripped my hips and dragged me back until I was straddling his face. His tongue lashed my pussy, and I cried out, rocking against his mouth as I reached for his cock again and sucked him into my mouth. I could only just reach now with the height difference, and I could only suck the head into my mouth, so I used both hands to stroke the rest of his length while I sucked him as best as I could.

His tongue was relentless, working me the way he knew would get me off fast. I sucked him harder, rocking and moaning around his cock. Then he shoved two fingers inside me and sucked my clit, and I groaned, sucking him harder while I came against his mouth. His cock pulsed hard, and his hips lifted, thrusting deeper into my mouth as he came for me.

I collapsed on top of him, and he lifted me again, turning me back around like a rag doll and curling me into his side.

"Rest, love," he said, his lips against my hair. "When you wake, I'll fuck you and worship you until you pass out again."

"Sounds good," I said, wrapping my arm around his middle.

I drifted off to Death's chuckles.

CHAPTER 17

Death

"So how does Limbo work?" Zinnia asked while she braided her hair.

I hadn't taken my eyes off her once. Everything about her fascinated me. Everything she did, everything she said. My obsession with her somehow grew with each passing day, despite trying to keep control of my feelings, despite knowing how dangerous it was. Now wasn't the time to fall, but it was too late—I already had. Thanks to Somnus and his ambrosia, I'd told her as much.

Nothing I'd said to her had been false, I just wished I hadn't said it, not yet. She wasn't ready to hear it, that much had been obvious, and again, thanks to the ambrosia, I hadn't been able to school my emotions when her avoidance of my declaration inevitably came.

I hadn't mentioned my feelings for her since, and neither had she. The last two nights we'd fucked in my bed and laughed and talked about things that were light and amusing, not only avoiding what I'd said to her, but also the things she wanted to know that I couldn't tell her.

Right now, she was trying to distract me from my pain. Somnus had returned to Marigold and the Dream Realm last night, and there was no telling how long it would be before I spoke to him again.

No, that depended wholly on the female watching me expectantly now. She had no idea just how much rested on her shoulders. If she did, if she

721

knew the truth, she would probably run like hell from me, and I'd never see her again—or worse.

"What do you want to know?" I asked and stroked my hand down Hemlock's back. I watched the play of emotions moving across Zinnia's face and the way she chewed her pretty lower lip. It was still puffy from my kisses earlier.

If I lost her now...

Her familiar nudged my hand for another pat, stopping me from falling into that dark, hopeless pit, and I brutally shoved those thoughts aside.

"Where is everyone? Like, this place is full of spirits, and I know when a soul comes here, they're assigned their own kind of... personal Limbo, right? But where are they?"

I scooped Hemlock up and held out my hand. "How about I show you?"

She put down her brush and strode over, taking my hand with a grin. "Are we going on a field trip?"

I chuckled; I'd been doing that a lot lately. I'd forgotten what it was like until I found her and she'd pulled me from the cloak slowly but surely, without even knowing she was doing it. It had been so long since I'd had occasion to laugh, to feel happiness, to feel anything but rage. I didn't think it was going to happen, that again, it wouldn't happen, but it had. Zinnia had brought me back.

"Yes, a field trip." I loved the feel of her hand in mine; it was small and smooth and warm.

All she had to do was hold it back and not let go, and we would make it.

Just trust me, and finally, we'd make it to the other side.

›››·◉·‹‹‹

Zinnia

Death led me from the castle and along the skull path, the one I followed when I came and went from Limbo. We walked until we reached the edge of the forest. Hemlock had stayed perched on Death's shoulder the entire time, which amazed me, honestly.

I gave his head a little scratch, and he squeaked, letting me know how happy he was, so I left him where he was.

"Which way?" If we took the path that went to the left, it would lead us to the gateway to my home, but there was a path that went right as well. I'd never explored it. It was less trodden, narrow, the skulls not as compacted down, leading into the thickest part of the forest.

"Right," he said, and since this path was only wide enough for one person, he pulled me forward so I was in front of him.

"This is where my reapers bring the souls," he said as he walked.

It was cooler in here, under the thick canopy of the trees, the scent of loam much heavier. Finally, we reached a clearing and stopped. "Now where do we go?

"Nowhere. We're here. This is where they are," he said.

"What do you mean, here? All of them? How?"

He lifted a hand, and his cloak appeared, shrouding him as he waved his palm in front of me.

The clearing transformed to a cottage with a woman sitting on the porch singing while she knitted. He waved his hand again. A man busking on a city street. *Again.* A woman on a beach walking her dog. *Again.* A wolf shifter howling mournfully in a dark forest. *Again.* A man playing violin in a concert hall.

I heard them all, felt them; the souls were bright and so incredibly vibrant.

Again and again and again, Death waved his hand, showing me the souls locked in Limbo, in the place they'd most wanted to be for eternity.

Finally, he lowered his hand, and his cloak vanished.

"That was..." Shockingly, I felt tears gather in my eyes. "I felt them," I whispered. "My ability to communicate with the dead, it's... bound here, well, except for the visions I've been getting, but I haven't been communicating with them. It's all one-sided." Having his past consorts trying to tell me something that I didn't understand was so goddamn frustrating. "But just now, I felt those souls. When you showed them to me, I felt each and every one... I heard them."

He cupped my face, brushing the tears from my cheeks. "It hurts you not to use your power?"

"It's a huge part of who I am, you know?" I shook my head. "It's what I do, how I help people. When I'm here, I feel... like I have no purpose, like I've lost a part of myself."

He swiped his thumb over my cheek again. "I'm sorry, Zinnia, I truly am. It won't... it won't always be this way..." The muscle at the side of his jaw pulsed. "If you... things won't be..." He cursed.

"What? Tell me."

He drew in a breath as if he was trying to regain control. "I can't."

"Or you won't?" I stared up at him.

"This is one of those things that you have to figure out for yourself."

Frustration filled me. "How the hell am I supposed to do that? You've given me nothing, no clues, no hints. Not one damn thing."

"That is where you're wrong," he said roughly.

I growled in frustration. "So what happens if I do figure everything out? What happens then?"

"Good things, little witch, really fucking good things."

I dropped my head so it rested against his chest. "So no pressure then?"

He chuckled low, his fingers sliding into my hair and massaging my scalp. "I believe in you," he said and kissed the top of my head.

His attempt at trying to keep things light, to pretend he wasn't tense, failed, because like I had been for a while now, I felt it. He was more than tense. There was this deep hollow feeling inside him, a feeling of total hopelessness. It was cold and lonely and desperate. No one deserved that. I hated that Death lived with it. Goddess, it must be torturous.

Lifting my head, I held his magnetic gaze. "I promise you, Mors, I will do everything in my power to do what it is you need me to." I didn't know if we would stay together, if I'd grow to love him the way he said he loved me, or if this thing between us would last—if I'd even survive it—but he didn't deserve to live a life missing a part of himself, and that's what this was, what I was feeling. It was like Death was missing a part of his soul, and I wouldn't stop until I helped him get that back. I thought about what he said to me after he'd been drinking ambrosia, about what would happen if I left him, and my heart squeezed tight. I pressed my hand to his chest and smiled up at him.

"I know you will, love," he said, not holding back, not asking for more from me, but not hiding the way he felt about me either.

He believed me, but he was afraid to believe *in me*. I felt that as well. "What you need to know about me is, when you become my friend, I will fight for you with everything I have."

"And am I your friend, Zinnia?" His eyes glinted, but he wasn't making fun of me; he truly wanted to know.

"You are most definitely my friend." Which astounded me after all we'd been through, but it was the truth.

He tucked my hair behind my ear. "I don't know what I did to deserve that honor, but I am privileged beyond measure."

He was serious. There was no sarcasm in his voice, no rancor or doubt. He truly felt that way, and it broke my heart to know that Death had been so lonely for so long. Taking his hand, I started back toward the castle. "You know what?"

"What?"

"I'm going to cook your dinner tonight. Do you like dumplings?" I glanced at him.

A smile curled his lips, and my heart did a dramatic flutter. "I'm not sure."

"Do you want to find out?" I asked.

"I'd love to."

›››❯◗●◖❮‹‹‹

Death wiped his mouth with the napkin and sat back. "That was exceptional."

"Well, there's more where that came from because I looked after Jazzy on my own most of the time, and we ate a lot of bland food, cheap and easy, so when we went to stay with our aunts in Roxburgh, I asked Else to teach me to cook. We spent a lot of time in the school holidays cooking for the family. I loved it, which is another reason I love a big garden."

"Where is your mother now?" Death asked, and there was a coldness to his voice that had me straightening in my seat.

"Last I heard, she was in Paris, but she could have moved on by now," I said. "It's fine. She does her thing, and we do ours."

"She abandoned you when you were children," he said, his voice deepening.

"She was around when we were young, just not when I was old enough to be responsible for Jazzy. She does love us, but having kids just wasn't her thing."

His gaze slid to the stairs and up, to where Somnus slumbered.

"Don't even think about it."

"About what?" he asked, all innocence.

"About sleeping in your brother's room tonight and paying my mother a visit in her dreams."

His jaw tightened. "I just want to talk to her."

"No," I said, "you will not."

He shrugged. "Fine, if you're so against it."

"I am."

He inclined his head.

"So how about dessert?"

His gaze darkened. "I know what I'd like for dessert."

My body heated instantly. "Well, you can hold that thought, because first we're having chocolate mousse."

"Sounds almost as delicious as what I had in mind—"

The door from the kitchens opened, and Egon rushed out. "Excuse me, my lord, but I must speak with you."

Death stood. "What is it?"

"Something that requires your immediate attention," Egon said, giving him a look.

"I'll be back as soon as I can. Stay here," Death said to me and rushed from the room.

))>●(((

He'd been gone for hours.

Egon said he had something important to deal with but wasn't saying what. He'd also looked kind of freaked out.

They may want to hide whatever this was from me, but I could still feel Death. His concern, his frustration, his pain and anger were being broadcast to me like I was tuned into his frequency. It was as if he was calling to me or reaching for me, and I couldn't just wait there for him when I was positive he needed me somehow.

Quickly dressing in my leathers, I strapped my knife to my thigh and ordered Hemy to stay in the room, then rushed downstairs. Once I was sure the coast was clear, I slipped out of the castle. Egon would try to stop me, but I would not be stopped.

Pressing my fingers to my lips, I called for Zuri. She trotted out of the forest a few minutes later on her own. I expected to see Raze right behind her, but he wasn't there. When she stopped in front of me, I ran my hand down her long nose. "Is Death with Raze?"

She jerked her head.

And they'd made her stay behind as well. "Can you take me to him, sweet girl?" I didn't have a bridle, but I didn't think I'd need one; she'd be able to track her mate without my guidance.

She bent her front leg, lifting it, and jerked her head again, offering me a boost up. I quickly hoisted myself up, then held on tight, wrapping my arms around her neck. "Take me to them, Zuri."

She took off at speed, the cool wind stinging my face and whipping through my hair. Nerves filled me; something wasn't right. No, something was terribly wrong. Zuri burst through the tree line and into the forest, and darkness closed in instantly. We rode at breakneck speed, dodging trees and jumping over fallen logs. My fight-or-flight instincts grew more desperate the deeper we went and as we got closer to wherever it was Zuri was taking me.

A drawn-out cry echoed through the forest, eerie and mournful, like a banshee's wail. It was the sound of someone lost, hopelessly searching for something. Zuri slowed to a trot, tilting her head to the side, listening. I searched the shadowed forest around us—

Something rushed at us, and Zuri reared, throwing me from her back. I hit the ground hard and, gasping, quickly rolled to my feet. I pulled my knife from its sheath and frantically searched the area around us.

Another cry filled the night, louder, closer. I stood beside Zuri. "It's all right," I said, and she snorted and stomped restlessly. I turned to hoist myself back up when something flew toward me, digging long nails or claws into my side, cutting into my flesh as they passed. Then they were gone, too fast for me to see what or who it was.

I hissed, covering the wound. I pressed my back to Zuri and held my knife out in front of me.

They flew at me once more with another swipe of their claws, tearing into my thigh this time, and then they were gone again. "Show yourself," I called. I tapped Zuri's front leg. "Let me back up, Zuri."

A strange, repetitive, high-pitched sound came from the shadows to my right, and I spun back.

"Come out and let me talk to you. I won't hurt you," I said, which was laughable. The only one getting hurt right now was me.

The sound came again, lifting the hair on the back of my neck.

They sped across the clearing again, and this time, the claws sliced across my cheek. "Fuck." I needed to get back on Zuri and get the hell out of here, but she was nervous, dancing away, torn between running and her instinct to stay and protect me. I tapped her front leg. "Let me up, Zuri," I said again. "Come on, sweet girl."

Her eyes were huge, but this time, she lifted her leg, and I gripped on to hoist myself back up—

Something slammed into me, knocking me back to the ground. "Fuck." I quickly rolled to my feet again. "Fucking show yourself, asshole," I called, in pain, scared, and pissed the hell off.

A branch cracked to my left, and I twisted toward it. Something moved in the shadows, slow now and in an odd, stilted way. My instincts took over all else, telling me to run, but there was no outrunning whatever this was.

They stepped closer, closer still, then finally into the clearing.

Zuri shrieked and reared.

Holy fuck. This was no demon or other creature, and it wasn't a lost soul either.

What stood before me had to have been brought to life using the foulest of magic or the kind of power I quaked at the thought of. A female walked awkwardly toward me. Dirt stained her rotting, tattered clothes, skin hung from bone, and her long blonde hair was stringy around her skeletal face.

One moment, she was two yards away, walking as if her bones were about to snap, and the next, she was in front of me, her skeletal hand wrapped around my throat, gnashing her blunt teeth. I shoved my forearm against her bony throat, the smell of rot stinging my nose.

"G-give... it to me," she said disjointedly.

"What do you want?" I growled out.

"Give it to... me."

"Back the fuck up, and I'll give you whatever the hell you want."

She jerked forward more viciously, and I strained to push her back, then slammed my palm against her skull and fired my magic into her. She flew backward, slamming into a tree, but was back on her feet, and in a blink, she was in front of me, snapping her teeth. I did it again and again, hitting her hard with my magic, but she got back up every single time. I gave her more and more, until I felt my powers begin to weaken; she was draining me. *Fuck.*

She rushed back, and I shoved my arm against her throat again and smashed my fist into her jaw repeatedly to try and dislocate it. If she couldn't bite me, I only had the long, sharp nails to contend with. She shrieked, her head jerking forward, jaw snapping at speed. I punched her again, and one side of her jaw drooped, only a piece of rotting flesh holding it in place.

"Alga, stop!"

Death's voice echoed through the forest around us. She froze instantly, forgetting about me completely, and turned.

"That's it," he said roughly. "Come to me." She was at his side a second later. He wrapped his arms around her. "You shouldn't be wandering," he said.

"N-no... D-Death," she said. It was garbled, disjointed.

"It's okay now. It'll be okay."

"H-help... Alga," she said.

"I will," he rasped as he held her face in his hands and looked down at her. He smiled, kindness shining in his eyes—but then he tore her skull from her shoulders, and her body collapsed, falling in a heap at his feet. He dropped her skull with the rest of her bones, breathing hard.

"Mors—"

"I told you to stay at the castle. She could have killed you," he said.

"Who is she?"

He looked up at me. "Go back to the castle, Zinnia."

"I'm going to need you to explain what the fuck just happened here."

He held my gaze. "Now." His voice was filled with fury. He was not going to tell me anything, not one damn thing.

Movement on the ground caught my eye. The bones, they were reforming, the head rolling back to the neck, the jaw clicking back in place. "What the fuck is she?"

He strode to me, grabbed my hips, and tossed me onto Zuri's back; then he took her face in his hands. "Take her to the castle, and do not stop. Do you understand, Zuri?"

She shrieked the affirmative, then took off through the forest, flying back toward the castle.

I turned back in time to see Death shove Alga's reforming bones into a sack and carry her away.

CHAPTER 18

Zinnia

I woke in bed alone, the sound of the piano drifting up from downstairs. He was back. Blinking up at the ceiling, I fought down the dread inside me. I'd lain awake for hours, waiting for Death to come back, to explain what the hell happened in those woods, to tell me who Alga was and what she was searching for.

Pushing back the covers carefully so I wouldn't wake Hemlock, I got out of bed and walked out into the hall. Would he even talk to me? I had to try, because right now, my brain was struggling to understand what I saw out there or what any of it meant. I rushed along the hall, the shadows dancing along the walls as if they were swaying to the music. The song was achingly sad; goddess, it was heartbreakingly beautiful.

My footfalls were silent as I made my way down the stairs and across the main hall.

The room beyond it was dark still—only light from an artificial moon filtered in through the tall windows.

Then I saw him.

His bare, tattooed back, head dipped while his strong hands moved over the keys.

Emotion poured from him, so enormous that despite everything, it pierced my soul. I stayed where I was, listening as he played his mournful

729

song, watching as he felt every note. When the song finished, he sat there, utterly still.

"Come here," he finally said, voice low.

He'd clocked me as soon as I came down the stairs; of course he had. I felt his words in the pit of my stomach, his deep voice rolling through me, pulsing inside me. As soon as the command left his lips, I was moving across the marble floor.

I stopped beside him, and he turned to me, waiting for me to say whatever it was I was going to say, and I could see in his eyes that he wasn't going to give me the answers I wanted. "One of those things I need to learn on my own?" I said instead of all the things I wanted to say.

He shook his head. "One of the things you never need to know."

I had no idea who Alga was, but he'd been gentle with her—at least until he tore off her head. He was the God of Death, and she'd most certainly been dead. "She wasn't a soul. She was... something else."

"She was," he said.

"Is she part of some fucked-up skeletal army? I've seen the way you look when your cloak is called forth, when the shadows cover you. You change—you are Death. Somehow, she's part of that, isn't she?"

"There are a lot of things you don't know about me, about my world, and a lot you will learn over time. There are other things, though, little witch, I pray you never have reason to learn." Taking my hand, he tugged me closer and cupped my cheek over the slices I'd cleaned and dressed when I got back. He stood, crowding me. "Where else are you injured?"

"My side and my thigh. I washed and dressed where she clawed me. I have my healing balm with me. It's fine."

"Are you in pain?"

"They're not that bad now. I have a potion that helps with pain, and it kicked in a while ago."

He studied me, trying to see if I was telling the truth. "You could have been killed," he rasped.

"I wouldn't have gone down easy," I said, now sounding breathless.

He gripped my hips, avoiding the slices on my side, and lifted me, planting my ass on the piano. His hand went to my throat, not gripping it, his open palm pressed to the base, and then he slid it lower, as low as he could go without his skin leaving mine.

I was in a pair of shorts and an old, stretched-out T-shirt, and the neck hung low. His palm sat directly over my heart. "You're so warm," he said roughly. "Your heart, it's beating almost frantically."

"You tend to have that effect on me." I lifted my hand, pressing it to his bare chest, right over his heart and the stars tattooed there. It was pounding, hard and fast.

"You have the same effect on me, love." His other hand gripped my uninjured thigh tight. "You always have."

"Even when you were stalking around, cloaked and full of rage?"

He licked those gorgeous lips. "Yes."

Hot, rough-skinned fingers slid up my thigh, then over my hip before gripping the worn fabric of my shirt tight. He dragged it up, forcing me to lift my arms. He dropped it on top of the piano beside me, and my nipples puckered as soon as the cool air hit them. Without taking his eyes off me, Death lifted a hand, aiming it at the door behind him, and invisible hands swung it shut with a loud click.

Then his hands were back on me, gliding, massaging, moving over my bare skin. He watched where they traveled, as if what he was doing was the most enthralling thing he'd ever seen.

"I don't think you realize how important you are to me, Zinnia. You don't get it, and that's not your fault. But believe me when I say, if something had happened to you today..." He looked up, darkness swirling. "I would have torn it all down. I would have burned so hot in my fury and grief that there would have been nothing left but stardust."

I swallowed, trying to process what he was saying. I couldn't. "You can't say things like that... you can't—"

"It's the truth. Do you want me to lie to you?"

I was struggling to take it all in, to focus, because his hands were still moving over my body, making my skin warm and tingly, making my breasts ache and causing a deep throb between my thighs. He carefully but forcefully pushed me back so I was lying on the piano's cool surface. His hands slid down my belly, and then he tugged my shorts and underwear down my body and tossed them onto the piano with my shirt.

"Spread your legs for me," he demanded softly.

I did as he said, instantly obeying. I should stop this after what he'd just said, after that declaration, but I couldn't bring myself to do it. I wanted whatever he was offering with an intensity that made me quiver. Resting his hand low on my belly, he dragged his thumb through my slick pussy, sliding it up and back. I was fully exposed, naked, and sprawled out in front of him. Death seemed content to take his time touching me.

"You can't imagine how good it feels buried deep inside you," he said and pushed the tip of his thumb inside me. "You don't know this, my precious consort, but I am your humble servant. Anything you desire, all you need to do is ask, and I will bend and twist, I will contort my world to make it yours as well."

My hips rolled. "Mors..." I said, even though I had no idea what to say next. What could you say to that? I had a god in the palm of my hand, but not even he could save me from fate, from death, if that's what was destined for me—just like the rest of them. But while I had him, while he was mine, he would worship me, and I would worship him.

If anyone deserved happiness, it was the male watching me like I was the brightest star in the sky.

"But it seems no matter what I say, you refuse to allow me to protect you." He slid his thumb the rest of the way inside me and kissed the inside of my thigh. "Outside this castle, if you are not with me, if you are off the path that I already told you not to wander from, you are at risk... yet you left the safety of these walls and ventured into the forest." He grazed his teeth along my skin, then nipped me. It wasn't hard, not enough to really hurt, but I gasped. "How many times do I have to say it? How many times do I have to ask you to remain at my side or in the safety of these grounds?" He looked up at me. "Do I need to punish you to make you do as I say, is that it?"

I moaned as he slid his thumb from me and replaced it with two fingers. "Y-you needed me," I said, quickly losing the ability to think or speak logically.

"Did I now? How do you know that, little witch?"

"B-because..." My hips rocked against his hand, trying to take more, to take those long, rough fingers deeper. "Because... I felt you. Your pain, your anger. I felt it here." I pressed my hand to my chest. "I just... I just knew, and I had to find you."

He stilled for a second, and I whimpered in protest. He started moving again, fucking me with his fingers, as shadows swirled around him, as his cloak manifested. "Then let me make something clear." He leaned forward. "Unless I ask you to come with me, you will remain here." Half of his face transformed, turning it into half a shadowed skull, half the male I was growing to care for more than I knew how to understand or process. "If you risk your safety again, your punishment will be a lot worse than the one I'm about to give you."

"What are you...?"

He lifted me, flipping me over. The stool scraped against the floor as Death planted my knees on it, and then he grabbed the back of my neck and forced my upper body down. My hands slammed down against the keys, making a chaotic, tuneless sound. He shoved the stool farther in and changed my position so my forearms were on top of the glossy black grand piano.

Then, leaning over me, he pressed his bare chest against my back, his arms bracketing me. His cloak brushed against my bare skin, and the power flowing through it lifted sparks all over me. I was in sensation overload.

One of his hands left my view, and a moment later, it was on my ass, squeezing. "Are you ready?"

"W-what are you...?"

His hand came down, hard.

I cried out and tried to bolt upright, but he held me down. "Mors—"

"You refuse to listen to me, so now I have to punish you," he said roughly, then spanked me again.

Humiliation burned my cheeks. "Don't you dare do it aga—" *He did it again.* I hissed, outraged, as his hand came down on the other cheek.

"You will learn, and you will obey me," he said against my ear as he massaged where he'd no doubt just left a massive handprint.

The burn sank in deep, and I squirmed.

"Hmmm, I'm not sure you've quite learned your lesson yet."

"Don't," I said, but my protest was weak because, goddess, it felt... I squirmed again, and my inner muscles throbbed, clamping down. It felt good.

He shoved my thighs wider. "One more," he growled.

This time, when he spanked me, his hand was low, slapping my pussy, but instead of crying out, I groaned, dropping my head to my forearms. Death covered my body, and having his skin against me, the feel of his hard body pressed to mine, was like having a craving I hadn't even known I'd had satisfied. He was hard; I could feel his cock through his pants pressed against my tender flesh.

"I need you," I gasped. "Please."

He dragged his nose up my throat. "Fucking you is a reward, love, and you haven't earned one, not yet." His staff appeared in his hand beside me.

"You want me," I managed, pushing back against his hardness.

"More than you will ever comprehend, but I've also had thousands of years to master my control, and if making you understand the severity of your actions means I walk around hard as fuck for a day or two, then that's what will happen." His cloak surrounded us, like a dark, warm cocoon. "I'm not a sadist, though," he said as he dragged his hand down my bare back, his roughened skin lifting goose bumps all over me. "I will deny you of me, but I also won't leave you wanting. Your needs are paramount always."

I pressed back against him more firmly. "Then don't deny me," I said, so hot and wet and achy, I was close to begging.

He kissed my shoulder. "I'll make you come, love, and it will feel earth-shattering." He pressed his mouth to my ear. "But nowhere near as good as when your male, the god who owns you, who is the master of your cunt and the owner of your heart, is buried deep inside you." He nipped my shoulder. "But that's the point. How will you learn without consequences?"

"Arrogant asshole..." The insult died on my lips as he kissed his way down my spine.

"I have reason to be arrogant, and you know it."

Something warm and smooth slid along my pussy, gliding over my opening, then up to my clit. "What... what is that?" I groaned.

"Did you know my staff is part of me?" His mouth came back to my ear. "I feel what it feels. It's alive in my hands, like another arm or leg or..." He pushed the tip of his staff inside me, the smooth wood hot, yes, as if it was alive.

"Oh gods," I breathed, dropping my head to my forearms, panting, desperate for more.

He pushed it deeper, and I felt every knot and twist of the gnarled, worn wood as it filled me. "If the conditions are just so, I can come just stroking it," he said, panting against my throat. "You feel... so good. So fucking good, Zinnia."

He slid it out, then back in, and I cried out.

"I'm going to make you come now, love, so hard that you'll make a mess all over my piano stool. Are you ready?"

I was only capable of making sounds—desperate, needy sounds, like an animal, a creature that only existed for Death and the pleasure he chose to give me.

He fucked me with his staff faster. His front was still pressed to my back, his cloak surrounding us. I knew his face was at least half his skull mask, and the thought only turned me on more. He was breathing heavily in my ear as he slid his hand down my stomach and started circling my clit just the way I liked it. Simultaneously, his staff hit me at the exact spot that had me quickly spinning out of control.

"Mors... *Oh fuck...*"

"You're dripping, love. Your juices are sliding down my staff, soaking into the wood, filling every divot and channel, marking it with your hunger, giving me a part of you for eternity." He groaned. "I feel you too now, love. I can feel how badly you need to come, how good you feel right now. How much you want your god inside you."

I sobbed. "Yes, please. Mors... please."

His hand left my clit, then came down on my ass, hard, before it was back at my clit, spanking me there as well. I screamed and came, spasming around his staff while he soothed my clit with firm pressure, circling, rubbing, prolonging my orgasm.

"I won't give in." He pressed his hard cock against my bare ass, the fabric of his trousers rough against my tender flesh. "Because I won't lose you. And until you prove to me that you won't put your life at risk, I won't fuck you. Understand?"

I collapsed against the cool surface of the piano, breathing hard, and shuddered as he slid his staff from my body. It vanished, and he scooped me up in his arms. His cloak was still draped over him, and it hid his eyes.

His face was all skull mask now, all Death. I snuggled closer, sliding my hand over his chest, and stared up at him, into the shadows of his hood, where not even the blue of his eyes glowed anymore. He meant what he said. He would deny us both until I proved myself the obedient little consort and did as he said.

"I get you're worried, I do." How could he not be after what he'd been through? "I promise I won't take any more risks, okay? But you can't expect me to stay locked up here when you're away from the castle."

"I expect you to stay here where it's safe unless I'm with you," he said.

"That's what I just said."

"No, it's not. I won't ever lock you up."

"What you're suggesting sounds pretty confining if you ask me."

"Which means the punishment stands." He held me closer. "It pains me as much as it does you to do this. Denying you goes against every part of me."

I flashed him a grin. "Oh, it pains you much more, my lord, and if you think I'm going down without a fight, you are sorely mistaken."

CHAPTER 19

Death

GROWLING, I rushed down the stairs, across the wide entrance hall, and into the kitchen. "Where is she?" I barked at Egon. I felt her close, but she wasn't inside the castle.

He looked up from chopping vegetables and pointed his knife toward the door that led to the back garden. Of course that was where she was. My heart thumped wildly in my chest. She spent hours out there every week, tending her herbs; I should have known that was where she'd be. Still, my heart refused to slow until I saw her for myself.

Shoving the door open, I strode out to the gardens. The oxygen was punched from my lungs the moment I saw her.

She was on her hands and knees, her wild red hair tied back in a messy knot on top of her head. She was singing low, something I'd never heard before. The kind of music they probably listened to at the hellhounds' compound or the wolf shifter keep or while she was with those twisted fucking crows. Where all those males no doubt watched her, wanting her.

My fingers curled into tight fists just thinking about their eyes on her.

Hemlock poked his head up from behind one of the bushy herbs, and Zinnia chuckled, making my heart fucking squeeze.

The last few nights had been unbearable. I told her I was punishing her

736

for her carelessness over her safety, and I was, but it was me who was suffering. Especially since she was taking every opportunity to tempt me.

I rubbed at the ache in my chest. The thought of her leaving me in a week's time for another month twisted my insides. Every time she came back, the month passed by faster than the last.

It always caused me pain when she left, but this time, above all others, felt the worst. So much had changed between us this last month, and I'd actually contemplated breaking our deal and forcing her to stay, but I never broke my word; it was part of the foundation of who I was. Not to mention, forcing her to stay would not only push her farther away from me, it would be breaking her trust, and she'd never forgive me.

I also could never hurt her in that way.

Biting back a groan, I took her in. My body had reacted to the sight of her instantly. Gods, I wanted to lift her from the garden, pull her into the small orchard behind it, and claim her all over again, but I couldn't, not yet, not until she understood how important her safety was. She'd teased me about it again while we'd eaten dinner last night, making light of it. I didn't know why she insisted on testing me, but if she made light of something so important, how could I trust her to heed my warnings?

She glanced up then, spotting me, and stood.

I strode toward her. She was irresistibly beautiful, and her soul, it shone through her eyes, so bright and warm. It was all I needed—those eyes on me, that glimpse of her soul—and I was home.

I was no longer alone.

I missed you. The words lingered on my tongue, but I didn't speak them. I'd seen her less than an hour ago, but the way I felt about her, it surpassed love or any descriptive word for the emotion. What I felt for her surpassed explanation. "Your garden looks healthy," I said instead of all the other things flying around my head and filling my heart.

"Checking up on me?" she said, dusting her hands off on her jeans.

Yes. "No. I was simply passing by and saw you." She was looking at me as if she didn't believe me. I brushed my hand over a particularly bushy plant. "So what's this one for?" I asked, trying to change the subject.

No other being made me feel this mortal, or what I assumed it felt like to be mortal, than the female staring up at me, her lips quirked up on one side. The last three weeks, the shadows had receded more and more. It'd been so long, so long in the darkness, consumed by rage, I'd forgotten who I was. Until Zinnia. Until she drew me from the cloak and touched my soul.

"Do you really want to know? Or are you just trying to cover up that you were, in fact, checking up on me?"

She was making fun of me again, and I liked it. I was also interested. I was interested in every part of her. "I want to know." Hemlock poked his head up again, squeaked, and lifted onto his back legs. I scooped him up. The tiny rat seemed to like me. Zinnia watched as I placed him on my shoulder, and he tucked himself in close, but she didn't comment.

"Okay... well, this one here is licorice. I use it in a few of my healing tinctures. The root is good for an upset stomach, for example," she said and pointed to the one beside it. "This one, on the other hand, will give you an upset stomach if used... irresponsibly." She smirked. "So watch yourself, my lord, or you may find yourself making frequent and urgent visits to the bathroom."

"Are you threatening me with diarrhea, little witch?" I said and fought a grin.

"Possibly."

"Threatening your consort is never a good idea, especially when he's a god." I tilted my head to the side, studying her pretty lips. "Do you require more correction, do you think?"

Her face flushed, and my body heated with hers. "That would be a no, thank you. *Correction* doesn't work on me. I have my own mind, and no amount of spanking from you will change it."

"Apparently not." I took a step closer. "It will make you come very hard, though, won't it, Zinnia?"

She grinned wider. "Tell me, my lord, exactly how blue are your balls? Still planning on holding out to teach me a lesson, or have I been punished enough?"

She enjoyed mocking me, playing, teasing, and I liked that as well, even if I feared she didn't take the reason behind my actions seriously. "My balls are fine, thank you, love. I have my hand and images of you riding my cock locked away in here." I tapped the side of my head. "So I'll survive just fine." It was a lie. I was suffering so goddamn badly. "But if you're struggling, a quick blood oath will put this all behind us, and I'll happily spend the next few days in bed curling your very pretty toes."

Her smile slipped. "I'm not doing that."

I wanted to fucking snarl, to demand she do it, to drop to my knees and fucking beg her to let me keep her safe. "Why?"

"You really don't get it?"

"I really don't," I said and had to fight back the growl in my voice.

She planted her hands on her hips. "Because I'm your consort, Mors, we're supposed to be partners... even if the power dynamic is so unbalanced, it's ridiculous. And even if my time with you here is most likely limited, I will not be bound by oaths and forced to obey you like a prisoner, not anymore. Why can't you understand that?"

I understood it, but history told me not to believe in good intentions or

738

promises from those I loved. When someone cared for you in return, risking their lives for you was nothing. It didn't matter that I was a god and she was mortal. She'd already shown me she was prepared to walk into an unknown, dangerous situation when she thought I needed her. Things had progressed. She felt my emotions when they were elevated or I was distressed—something she'd already proven—which was why a blood oath was more important than ever.

The look on her face, though, was one I recognized well. She would not back down, not yet, and if we carried on with this conversation, she would only end up even more angry with me, and I didn't want that. I wanted her smiles and her teasing. I wanted her blushes and her soft looks. So fool that I was, I chose to change the subject back to her garden. "I will attempt to," I said, lying through my teeth. "This garden, it's really important to you, isn't it?"

She stared up at me for several moments, knowing exactly what I was doing and deciding if she wanted to call me out on it or let the subject drop. She blew out a frustrated breath but went with the change of subject. "Creating a garden is the first thing a witch does when she moves to a new home, especially when she's mated or married," Zinnia said. "On our mating or wedding day, we're given a small pot with a vervain plant in it to start our new garden."

"Why that herb in particular?"

"The leaves of the vervain and its tiny purple flowers can be used to protect against evil spells and negative energy. It can also be used to purify our homes and has many medicinal uses. Vervain represents home and family—love." She tucked her hair behind her ear. "When a witch takes it out of the pot and plants it in her garden, though, is the most significant."

"Explain," I said, searching her face, struggling to read the look in her eyes and hating that I didn't know what she was thinking.

"We only plant the vervain in our new gardens when it feels like home. That one herb provides us with nearly everything we need to take care of and protect our families... so we only plant them when we're sure that's where we are, with family. When we're with the people we choose to love."

I looked down at the plants flourishing in her garden. "Which one is vervain?" I asked.

She was silent. I looked back up.

Her gaze held mine. "I don't have one."

I swallowed abruptly. Of course not. Of course she didn't have one. Words escaped me as she stared up at me.

"We didn't have a mating ceremony, Mors, and my family didn't send me off with my new husband holding a tiny pot of vervain after an epic party. That's not what this is... This is no love story for the ages."

My heart physically ached at her words.

You have no idea, little witch.

The answer to all of this was mixed up in those words. She had the answer to how this ended, how it could end, but she just had to surrender to it, to let me in.

She just had to choose me.

CHAPTER 20

Zinnia

THERE WAS a soft knock at the bedroom door. "My lord."

Death jolted beside me, waking instantly. "What is it?"

He'd been restless in sleep the last few hours, and I'd been lying here awake, frustrated and contemplating my situation.

"We've had another breach," Egon said in a hushed, urgent voice.

Death stilled completely. "Fuck."

I felt his eyes on me, and I kept mine closed. Whatever this was, he didn't want me to know. I felt it. The tension was a dense wall between us. The way he eased off the bed, trying not to jostle me, told me I was right.

Death wanted my trust while he kept so many things from me. He quickly dressed and slipped out of the room.

I could just lay here and do nothing, stay in the dark and blindly do as he instructed, or I could do what I always had and protect my soul and my heart and choose the truth—whatever it was.

I'd rather be faced with all the horrors and ugly parts of a person, see all their scars on full display, than live in ignorance for my own comfort. Pushing back the covers, I quickly dressed, shoving my feet in my boots. Hemlock scurried across the bed, squeaking at me. "You have to stay here, okay? It's too dangerous." He hissed, then turned his back to me and wriggled under the covers, showing me he was not happy.

Better that than something happening to him.

I slipped out into the hall. At night, the whispers of the souls here were louder, as if the darkness amplified their thoughts and feelings. Ice slid down my spine as I rushed along the hallway. It felt as if they were right behind me, their mouths to my ear, telling me their secrets, their regrets— the darkest marks on their souls.

When I reached the bottom of the stairs, I stuck close to the wall. Death was talking with Egon. The demon nodded at whatever his lord said, then strode away, and Death spun and walked out. With the coast clear, I rushed across the room and eased the door open, slipping out.

Death was striding down the skull path, shrouded in shadow. I hung back, following at a distance, using all the magic I had to try and conceal myself from him. It wouldn't last. I could only summon a thin and fragile barrier that would wear thin, then dissolve completely from the strength of his power, but that was okay. It just needed to hold long enough for me to learn what the hell was going on.

He lifted his hand, and a path appeared through the trees, one I'd never seen before. We were close to where I'd been attacked by Alga. Where I'd seen Death remove her head, then carry her wriggling corpse away in a sack moments later.

An awful shriek came from up ahead—the same awful sound I'd heard from the undead female while she'd circled me, swiping at me, clawing me.

The shadows thickened before his cloak swirled around him, his staff appearing in his hand a moment later. He didn't pause but kept walking as the shriek came again. We carried on for a little longer, and then Death stopped. I quickly stepped off the path and pressed my back against one of the large trees. Leaving the path was risky, but I had no choice. I didn't want him seeing me, not before I knew what this was. Sliding my knife free, I hung back and watched.

Death turned to his right and said something, his voice low, rough, and then he held out his hand. Bony fingers appeared first before one of the undead stepped awkwardly from the forest beside the path, its movements jerky and disturbing. Its clothes were hanging off bones draped in old skin and tendons. She took Death's hand.

"Come now," I heard him say. "You know you're not supposed to wander."

As they passed a tree with sparse foliage, light from the faux moon shone down on her. She had her skeletal face upturned, looking at Death, and from what I could see of her hair, it had once been black and wavy.

Death didn't remove her head or shove her in a sack like the last one we encountered; no, he was talking to her, his low voice drifting back while she said the odd, garbled words and walked jerkily at his side. As if they were going on a midnight stroll together.

What the fuck was this?

They carried on for several yards, and I followed, keeping a good distance between me and them. Then they stopped, and I realized the path had ended. Death cupped her skeletal face—then pressed a sweet, soft kiss to her bony cheek before he straightened, lifted his staff, now glowing with power, and iron gates appeared. Shrieks filled the night, moans, garbled voices calling for him. As if he had some undead army behind that gate that worshipped him.

Had I been right? Had Death amassed some fucked-up undead horde? With his evil bitch of a mother and her army of demons right next door, I guessed it made sense for him to amass his own, but no matter how you looked at it, this was wrong. It was twisted and cruel. If he had done this, then he wasn't the male I thought he was... hoped he was, not at all.

Nausea gripped my stomach as he opened the gate and the undead female stepped through. As soon as she had, he pulled it shut, and the gate vanished.

Death turned then, and I had two choices, either hide and run through the forest, hoping I'd beat him home or—

I dropped the gossamer thin barrier of my magic that remained and stepped out of my hiding place and onto the path. I wasn't the kind of female to hide or run, not when the danger concerned someone I cared about, consequences be damned.

Death went still.

"Who's your friend?" I asked, legs braced, waiting for the impact of his anger.

He started toward me, his cloak flaring out behind him as he walked, his staff gripped tight in one hand. The volatile emotions rolling off him were *intense*, and it took everything in me not to step back as he strode right up to me, towering over me.

"Your new girlfriend?" I asked, refusing to cower under that ferocious glare. "I guess it makes sense that Death would be up for some necrophilia."

His nostrils flared. "Go back to the castle, Zinnia."

"You're not going to tell me who that was?"

His blue eyes glowed down at me. "No."

I ground my teeth. "Mors—"

"Do not speak."

What I felt coming off him was wild, unstable—goddess, a raging storm. My knees almost buckled under the weight of all that was pouring off him. I didn't understand it, what caused him to feel this way, but it was horrible.

"Talk to me. What's going on—"

"Go." He said it softly, but it was as if he'd roared it.

I flinched and backed up when the storm grew more violent. Pushing him right now would be a serious mistake, so I said nothing more and walked away.

He said he wanted me as his consort, he said he loved me, even if I hadn't actually believed it, but he constantly shut me out. I understood his trepidation, and I knew he couldn't tell me anything, but living with so many secrets between us wasn't going to work. His expectations were too high. He wanted too much from me without any of the trust and without giving me even a glimpse of the payoff. He couldn't even promise me a life.

The foundation I thought we'd been building, the closeness we'd slowly developed, had already been on shaky ground after his demand that I obey him. Now, after tonight, it was crumbling, slipping away beneath my feet.

Because it was built on nothing.

I glanced back over my shoulder. He hadn't moved, his dark gaze following me as I strode away. I got another wave of all he was feeling, and my knees almost gave out beneath me a second time. The anger inside him was breathtaking, and it was aimed at only one person—me.

›)›●(((

Death didn't come back to bed after that. I'd lain awake, waiting, but he never came. He wasn't at breakfast the next morning either. I checked Somnus's room but found only the slumbering god.

"Where's Death?" I asked Egon when I walked into the kitchen.

He glanced up from the silver he was polishing. "He's busy with an urgent matter."

"What urgent matter would that be?" I leaned on the table.

"My lord has a lot of responsibility in his realm. Sometimes his attention is required away from the castle," Egon said and started polishing again.

"His army of the dead? Is that what has his attention?"

Egon stilled for a split second, then continued polishing. "I'm afraid I don't know what you're talking about, my lady."

"You do, because you came and got Death last night when one of them escaped."

He kept his head down, polishing the silver jug in his hand like his life depended on it.

"I followed him, Egon... I saw one of them. She's the second I've seen." I planted my hands on the table. "Please tell me what the hell's going on here."

Egon blew out a breath and placed the jug on the table. "You know I can't tell you, Zinnia," he said, using my name for the first time. "I wish I could tell you all you need to know, I truly do." His fingers curled tight around the rag he was holding. "You have no idea how much, but I can't. For many reasons—reasons I pray to the gods you learn, and soon."

I ground my teeth. "Death tells me I have to work it out for myself, yet I'm not allowed to wander around on my own or ask anyone else questions. How the hell am I supposed to figure out whatever it is he wants me to figure out when I'm being hobbled at every turn? I go back home in three days, Egon. That's another month away, and another month closer to my sister's birthday. I'm going to be trapped here with a god who is so angry with me, for reasons he won't share, that I'm starting to feel dread when I'm around him." I planted my hands on my hips. "What the hell does he want from me?"

"The answer is a simple one," Egon said, holding my gaze, beseeching me to read his damn mind.

"Only it's not," I said. "Nothing about this situation is simple."

I spent the rest of the day in my garden with my herbs. It made me feel closer to Jasmine, to my cousins and aunts, to my coven.

And I needed them now more than ever.

>>>◐((<

Death wasn't at dinner that night, and he didn't come to bed. He was absent at breakfast for a second day as well. Egon said nothing, but he seemed stressed.

I, on the other hand, was pissed.

After I'd watered my garden, I went up to Death's room and gathered Hemy's and my things and moved them back to my room. If he was staying away to avoid me, I'd make it easy for him.

When dinnertime finally came around, I left Hemy napping by the fire and headed down to the dining room. No Death. I sat and thanked Egon when he filled my glass with wine. Like the last three meals Death had missed, his place was set, which made it clear he wasn't communicating with Egon either.

I was hungry. I'd barely eaten the last two days, but thanks to my anger, my appetite was back.

The sound of the main doors opening and closing echoed through the castle.

I turned to the door, and a moment later, Death appeared. His gaze sliced to me as he strode toward the table.

My heart leaped in my chest. *Do not give him the satisfaction.* Forcing myself to freaking move, I scooped up some mashed potatoes and shoved them in my mouth.

"I hope you didn't rush back on my account," I said and stabbed some beans with my fork and shoved them in my mouth as well, then grinned to piss him off when he took his seat opposite me.

"I've had things to do," he said as he dished himself a plate of food.

"Oh, me too. While you've been gone, I've been super busy taking all my things out of your room and packing for my trip home."

He said nothing, didn't even look up as he started eating.

"So are you going to tell me where you've been?"

"No."

"Awesome." I took a sip of my wine and sat back. "Question time, big guy. Tell me, why are you angry with me? What have I ever done to you? I think I deserve to know that, don't you?"

He chewed his mouthful. "You already know."

I snorted. "The fuck I do."

He lowered his knife and fork. "Maybe if you stopped talking and started fucking thinking, you'd work it out."

I stared across the table, confused and hurt and pretty sure my anger was close to matching his. "I can't read your mind, Death. You're going to have to help me out a little."

He slammed his fist on the table. "I can't."

It was as if he was reverting back to the Death he was when I came here. So full of darkness and rage. "Why do you even want me to? The anger I feel inside you now, it's almost as if... as if you hate me," I said, as an awful, gripping feeling in my stomach tore through me.

His nostrils flared. "Think," he said with quiet violence rolling from him and ignoring what I'd said completely. "Fucking think," he roared and slammed his fists on the table again, this time knocking over his wine.

I blinked across the table at him. For the first time in a very long time, I was filled with fear and dread. The full force of the god he was, was reflected in his face and his voice. It wasn't him I was scared of, but the thoughts and feelings he was capable of evoking in others. I'd stopped feeling it, the horror and woe, the soul-gripping fear and heartbreak that Death was capable of making others feel, but I did now, and humiliatingly, tears filled my eyes. The feelings he was summoning in me were so strong and awful, I wanted to curl into a ball and weep. "This isn't going to work," I forced out past trembling lips.

He glowered at me. "What?"

"Release me," I said, shaking so hard that he had to see it. I hated that as well.

"Never," he snarled.

"I found a way to hide from you before," I choked out. "I can do it again."

His gaze swept my face. "You will not. You try it, and I will drag you back here and never let you leave."

"Isn't that what you have planned already? Never letting me leave? Trapping me here in this hell with you until I die brutally?" I shook my head. "I'm not going to accept that. I'm not yours. I don't belong to you, and the fates can go and fuck themselves. I've given up enough because of you. I won't give up my life as well."

He sat forward. "You think you know what it is to suffer? You know nothing of loss."

I didn't know this version of him. This wasn't just anger; this was cruelty. He was trying to hurt me. To push me away even while he desperately tried to hold on. "No, you're right. I don't know the loss you have. How could I? I'm a mere mortal, not a god with an eternity of living behind him. But I do know loss, I know fear, and I know heartbreak."

He sneered. "What have you lost? Enlighten me."

My heart was racing, and I was trembling so hard now, my voice shook. "When I was fifteen years old, still just a child, a powerful god invaded my dreams and told me I was his—"

"I already know this story, little witch. Don't waste your breath," he bit out, a nasty smirk curling his lips.

"I was so scared," I said, pushing on, "that I took dangerous amounts of forbidden potions and elixirs to make sure I stayed awake. I didn't want the terrifying god to come back. I was afraid he'd hurt me, but most of all, that he'd hurt my sister, so I searched for help, and eventually, I found it." Death was staring at me, his eyes black, no blue left; not even the night sky was reflected in them, just pure blackness, but he didn't interrupt this time, and I had no intention of stopping. "I wasn't thinking clearly with the potions and the lack of sleep. I was delirious, confused, afraid. I heard of a demon named Fluke who could help, so I went to his cottage."

Death snarled and sat forward. "What did he do, Zinnia?"

"He got me to lay down. He drugged me and shoved his hand in my stomach. The pain was so bad, I lost consciousness. I don't know exactly what happened when I was out... not good things, I know that much. My entire body hurt when I woke with the markings on my arm." I ran my hand over the scar where I cut the mark out so Death could find me. I glanced back up at him. "I'm pretty sure he took more than my womb that day as trade." Death shot to his feet with a roar, his chair flying back and crashing against the floor. I stood as well. "So yes, Mors, I know loss."

"Fluke belongs to Nox," he said as he grabbed the end of the huge wooden table and flipped it, tossing it halfway across the room. "I will kill him. I will make him scream. I'll find a way to destroy my mother. I will make her wish for death."

Of course Nox, that twisted bitch, had a hand in what happened to me. She'd seen me coming. She'd found me when Death had. I could rage about the unjustness of it all, like Death was, but it was too late. It was done. One truth remained, though. "We're not good for each other," I said.

He was breathing hard. "You're not leaving me."

No denial—he knew I was right. "I've been here for a lunar month. I leave first thing in the morning. While I'm gone, I want you to decide if this"—I motioned between us—"really is what you want. If all this pain and anger you're feeling is really worth it to trap me here, when it's obvious neither of us want this. You don't love me, Mors. You don't. What you're feeling is a lie, a manipulation, a byproduct of the fates' meddling. Love isn't forcing someone to be with you... not when you've made it clear you despise me more than you truly want me."

"You're wrong," he choked out. "You don't understand—"

"Then make me understand. Give me something... give me anything."

He stared across at me, mouth gritted shut, eyes burning into me, but he said nothing.

His hands were tied.

Still, disappointment filled me as I turned away and strode from the room.

CHAPTER 21

Zinnia

I GLANCED at my bags by the door as I got into bed. Hemlock was curled up in my carpetbag under one of my scarves. He was ready to go home and see everyone. He missed them as much as I did when we were gone.

Death had to see how toxic this situation was. Yes, he'd let down his guard with me and shown me another side of him, but on the turn of a dime, he'd snap. Something about me called the darkness in him, and the anger always crept back. Even when he didn't outwardly show it, I felt it.

He had to see ending this was for the best.

The only times we were good together were when we were naked, and he'd taken that off the table in an attempt to control me—a seriously destructive move, especially if he was trying to build some kind of real relationship with me. But he wasn't. I got the feeling he was waiting for the inevitable—my demise, just like the rest of them.

There was so much I didn't understand about this place, about his motives. He said I needed to work it out for myself but then blocked me at every turn. I promised him I'd try, but I was getting nowhere. Jazzy's twenty-first birthday was fast approaching, and if I couldn't convince him to release me, I'd be trapped here, trapped in his anger and loathing until whatever killed his previous consorts killed me too.

I pulled the covers higher and stared at the ceiling, trying to calm my racing heart. I knew all these things, but goddess, I missed him. I missed those small calm moments when he looked at me in a way that curled my toes, and I missed his grin, and that laugh, and the way he touched me, kissed me. No one had ever made me feel as wonderful or as fucking awful as he could.

My eyes grew heavy, and I let them drift closed, allowing the darkness to pull me under for maybe the last time in this room.

The sky outside the castle window was dark and heavy. She pressed her hand to the glass, a sob falling from her lips. The weight of her pain was unbearable. She was scared and lonely, so incredibly lonely. Hand trembling, she picked up a knife and, holding it tight, brought it to her throat....

The room spun, and a female walked outside. She was running, running through the forest. Running with nowhere to go. She fell, but she didn't get up. She lay in the dirt and prayed her heart would stop, that it would just stop.

I woke with my heart pounding. Two different females this time, and their agony was like an ache in my bones, my soul. Their pain and loneliness were my own.

A dark, intoxicating scent reached me, and I knew I wasn't in my room alone anymore. Shoving myself up to my elbows, I blinked into the darkness. Death stood at the end of my bed in only a pair of dark trousers. His hairless, tattooed chest almost glowed under the muted light coming through the window.

His head was dipped like he was praying, his hands at his sides, fingers curled into fists. I sat up, but he said nothing, and neither did I for the longest time.

Finally, I wrapped my arms around my knees. "They killed themselves, didn't they? Your consorts ended their own lives?"

He lifted his head and sucked in a breath when his bright blue eyes locked on me. No shadows, no darkness, just clear, vibrant blue. "All but one, yes."

The one at the cliff. She hadn't jumped; she'd been pushed. "Why?"

"Because they were never meant to be here."

"I don't understand."

"You need to try."

I wanted to scream in frustration. "Will that happen to me? Eventually, will I...?"

"No," he said, voice breaking.

"Why not me? Why am I different?"

"Because it was always you... because it had to be you," he rasped.

I didn't understand. I didn't understand any of this. "Death—"

"I need you," he choked out. "I need my consort. I need you, Zinnia."

He'd said all he could. He could tell me no more. I had two choices: I could push for something he couldn't give me, or I could let it go, at least for tonight. I didn't know what the future held for me, for us, but however you looked at it, it wasn't good. In this moment, he needed me, and I could admit that right then, I needed him as well. What I'd seen had shaken me; those females, they'd pulled me down into the depths of their pain. I didn't know what it meant, and I couldn't think, not when Death was the only one who could drive the ache from my bones and the loneliness from my soul.

I tossed back the covers. "Then take me," I said softly into the heavy silence surrounding us.

His chest expanded sharply. "You still want me?"

Grabbing the bottom of the shirt I wore, I pulled it up and off, tossing it aside, leaving me in only my underwear. "Yes."

He took an abrupt step forward, and then he was striding around the bed. Leaning in, he hooked me around the waist and tugged me down on the mattress before covering me.

He stared at me, looking deeply into my eyes. "You have no idea just how precious you are to me, none," he rasped. "Trying to protect you, to force you to bend to my will by punishing you, was a greater punishment for me. I have not slept for days, my body aches constantly, my hands itch to touch you, and my heart feels as if it's being impaled by poisonous spikes whenever I see you. So much of the anger you feel when you're with me is directed at myself."

"But even more is directed at me," I whispered.

"Yes."

"And you won't tell me why?"

He shook his head. "I can't, but I need you to know that you're not to blame. That the anger I feel doesn't diminish how much I worship you, and that it is born from frustration over a situation that you have no control over. That's all I can tell you."

"What if I never work any of this out? What if I never learn the truth on my own?"

His Adam's apple slid up and down his throat. "I have to believe you will."

For the sake of his own sanity, he was deep in denial, and I felt the pressure of that, of saving him, of saving us both, immensely. I cupped the side of his face. "If you truly love me, Mors, then you need to let me go. Release me... it's the only way to save me from the same fate as the females that came before me."

751

His breathing was erratic, heavy. "Saving you, protecting you, is my greatest desire, but what you ask... I can't. I can't do it, love."

If we kept talking, we'd end up arguing. I didn't understand any of this, and he couldn't tell me. So instead of begging him to make me understand —something I knew he couldn't do—I brushed my thumb along his lower lip. "Then kiss me."

He slid the tips of his fingers down the side of my face, the roughened skin bringing every one of my nerve endings alive. "I am yours to command, my queen," he said, and then he covered my mouth with his and kissed me achingly slow and with a reverence that made my heart ache and my head spin.

He slid his hands along my side, over my waist, his fingers digging into flesh and muscle, massaging, worshipping. I wrapped my arms around him, running my hands over the smooth, muscled skin of his back, and tangled my legs with his, holding him close. The kiss deepened, and my world narrowed to him, to this. Fire built inside me, so hot that I was afraid I'd burn to ash and float away if Death didn't hold me down.

When I couldn't take it any longer, I wrapped my legs around his hips, desperate to feel him against me. Desperate for the sweet relief only he could give me. "Mors, I need you," I pleaded against his lips as my hands slid around his waist.

He lifted his hips away from me, giving me room, and I quickly undid his pants, shoving them down. His kiss became more urgent, a fierceness of need that more than matched my own. He wore nothing underneath, and his cock, hot and heavy and impossibly hard, fell into my hand. I squeezed him, stroked him, and he growled against my lips.

Gripping my underwear, he tore them from my body, his hand sliding up until his fingers were gliding through my slick folds, pressing against my opening. "Are you ready for me, love? Because I can't wait."

"So ready." I took his length in my hand and led him to me, pressing the head of his cock to my opening; then I lifted my hips, taking the tip inside me.

He groaned. "You so easily erase all traces of my control," he said roughly and grabbed my wrists, lifting them over my head. "Infuriating, irresistible, brave little witch." He pressed sucking kisses along my throat. "You terrify me. You beguile me." He kissed along my jaw and looked down at me. "You fucking own me."

Then he slid inside me, a slow, steady glide that had my mouth falling open as a needy, raw sound left me. He kept that pace, sliding out just as slow, then filling me, stretching me to my limits, and the whole time, he watched me, watched the play of my features as he made me feel things I didn't know I was capable of feeling.

752

His expression was set, determined, while his big body trembled above me, his muscles jumping, his veins and tendons standing out. I clung to him when he thrust inside me and stayed there, rocking against me, hitting me deep. I whimpered when the first orgasm rushed forward, crying out when I started coming around him so hard, all I could do was hold on.

"I'm going to fuck you all night, so when you leave me tomorrow, you'll feel me with you. I need you to feel me with you," he rasped.

He thrust faster, deeper. "Mors—"

"Will you think of me, my love? Will you think of me while you're gone?"

There was no missing the desperation in his voice. "Yes," I said, telling him the truth.

He thrust faster still. "I'll be counting down the minutes until you return," he said, his eyes flashing, the shadows swirling. "Without you, I am only darkness. Without you, I am a starless sky. I am nothing."

Tears burned my eyes. The things he said... I could love this male, this version of Death, and I could believe that he loved me—but it never lasted.

Sliding his hand between us, he rubbed my clit as he fucked me harder, kissing me, breathing my air and sharing his. Our hearts slammed together as if they were one, our bodies caught in a violent rhythm, an animalistic dance that came so naturally, as if we'd been doing this dance our entire lives, an eternity, not just weeks.

Arching against him, I cried out as I came again. Death hissed, grabbing my thigh and holding it high, the other hand cupping my face. "You are my beginning and my end, my everything, my sweet Stella," he groaned and came, pulsing fiercely inside me, grinding against me, filling me over and over until we were both spent.

And this time when he called me Stella, it didn't feel wrong—it felt so right.

Wrapping his arms around me, he rolled to his side. We stayed like that, me locked in Death's arms while we caught our breath. He pressed his lips to my forehead. "Rest while you can. The night has only just begun."

›)➤●《‹‹

Death was gone when I woke, and I wouldn't lie, I was disappointed.

My feelings for him were complex, but there was no denying that I did have feelings for him, strong ones. But we'd said all that needed to be said last night, all that could be said. He'd taken me all night, only letting me take short naps before he reached for me again, and I gave myself over to him willingly.

My body still ached, and my skin felt branded by his hands, his mouth, and he was right, I felt him. With every step I took, I felt him inside me. I quickly showered and dressed, then braided my hair. I was about to leave, but something stopped me. There was something I felt compelled to do first. Rummaging around in my pack, I found the small wooden box that I'd made when I was a kid. I used to keep my earrings in. I took them out, zipping them in the side pocket of my pack, then grabbing a piece of paper from the small desk in the corner, I quickly wrote a note, folded it, put it inside the box, and placed it beside the bed. Then I slid on my pack, and Hemlock scurried up my arm and climbed inside; he'd be asleep before we made it out of the castle. I looked around my room a final time and took in all the other little things that sat on shelves and on the dresser, the pictures and the keepsakes, and then my own now here for eternity with the rest. I didn't know what was going to happen, what the future held, but this place, this room—the females that came before me—were now part of my story, and I wanted to be remembered along with them.

I picked up the rest of my things and headed downstairs. I said my goodbyes to Egon and Lyle, then walked out the wide front doors—and pulled up short.

Death stood outside, waiting.

He said nothing, just held out his hand. I took it, and we headed down the stairs and started down the skull path that led to the gateway. He'd never walked me to the gate. He always left the castle before I did, moody and quiet. I glanced up at him now. He kept his eyes trained forward, a look on his face I couldn't read, but his hand gripped mine tighter.

"Will you be seeing the hounds while you're away?" he asked, still not looking down at me.

"Probably. Why?"

His jaw tightened. "Hounds are unpredictable. But then so are wolf shifters... and crows. Just make sure you're careful."

"None of them would ever hurt me," I said. "You have nothing to worry about."

He didn't reply. Was he jealous?

"Death?"

"Mors," he said.

That was the first time he'd ever asked me to call him that. "Mors?"

"Yes."

"I'm not going to sleep with anyone while I'm gone. You have no reason to be jealous."

He stopped, forcing me to do the same. "While you're away, I am sick with jealousy, not just of other males, but of everyone who gets to be in your presence, Zinnia, when I can't be."

He was trapped here, unable to move through the mortal world, at least not in his corporal form. He could use Somnus to visit dreams, and his soul could leave here when he recruited a reaper, like he had with Magnolia, but otherwise, he was stuck. "I'm sorry," I said lamely; there was nothing else I could say or do to make that easier on him.

He started walking again.

The gateway loomed ahead, and I had a rush of adrenaline. I was going to see my sister again. My heart filled with happiness, and there was no hiding it, but there was no denying how much I would miss Death while I was gone or how much I'd grown to care for him—more than I'd allowed myself to admit. But that still didn't mean we were right for each other.

His hand still gripped mine as the gateway opened, holding me close to him, not wanting to let me go.

Jasmine was on the other side, Ren with her. I could see them, but they couldn't see me yet; we weren't close enough.

"Zinnia," Death said, bringing my attention back to him. "You've seen a side of me that I'm not proud of, but know that I want you here with me more than anything—I need you to know that." He smiled, and there was pain in his eyes. "And when the lunar month is over, I want you to return to me. Promise you'll do that, love. Will you promise me that?"

I searched his eyes, the darkness swirling in the blue, as if he was barely holding the shadows at bay. "You know I will. We have a bargain."

"You said if I truly loved you, I should let you go, that releasing you was the only way to save you," he said, his thumb sliding over my cheek as he looked at me. "If that's what I must do to prove it to you, then... Zinnia Thornheart, I release you from your bargain."

My legs went weak. "You're releasing me?" It was what I'd wanted for so long, what I'd asked for, but still, his words were like a dagger to my heart.

"After your month away, whether you return to me or not, the choice is yours, little witch." The shadows swallowed more of his bright blue eyes. "But I'm begging you... choose me over everything and everyone, over a life with them, over the possibility of death here with me." He pressed a soft kiss to my lips. "Choose me," he said roughly, then released my hand and strode away.

I watched him go, unable to look away.

His cloak swirled around him, covering him as he walked, as his staff appeared in his hand, thumping on the ground with each step he took away from me, as he disappeared around the bend in the path.

It was harder than it should be to turn away. I looked at my sister, and goddess, my heart felt as if it were being torn in two.

Go. Leave. I snatched up my bags before I did something stupid, like go after him, and stepped through the gate and into Jazzy's arms.

My sister squeezed me tight. "I'm so glad you're home."

I watched the gate close behind her, locking me out of Limbo, and the ache in my chest returned more painful than ever before.

What the hell was I going to do?

CHAPTER 22

Zinnia

As soon as I walked into the clubhouse, I was handed a drink. A moment later, the music was turned up, and my cousins swooped in, pulling me in for a round of tight hugs while Hemy got pats and treats and kisses.

My cousins had made sure I was walking into a party when I stepped into the room with Jazzy and Ren, and I needed that—anything to help me stop thinking about Death and what he'd said to me.

To stop me from focusing on the awful feeling of dread inside me that I couldn't shake.

Everyone was here—all my cousins and their mates, Asher and a few more wolves from Draven's pack, and all Bram's brothers—and just for tonight, I was choosing oblivion with people I cared about. I'd think about the choice I had to make tomorrow or the next day. I had four weeks to think about it, four weeks away from Death and the choice he'd thrown at me before I left.

A full lunar month without his mood swings and demands, his unpredictable rages and unexplainable, hurtful anger.

Twenty-eight days without his growls or his kisses, without the feel of his arms around me or the devastating, swoony, and heart-stopping things he said to me, taking me by surprise.

I was jostled from the thoughts flying about my head by a pair of massive arms coming around me and lifting me off my feet before I was engulfed in the kind of hug that had the power to take all your worries away, at least for a little while. "Fucking good to see you, Zinny," Relic said against my ear, holding me tight.

His heat seeped through me, and I hugged him back just as fiercely. "You too, my friend."

He finally put me down, and I looked up into his handsome face. "You wanna get shit-faced?"

He grinned, flashing those white teeth and fangs. "I don't get shit-faced, babe. Male as big as me, packing this much muscle, impossible." He flexed and winked, and I burst out laughing. "But more than happy to drink you under the table, lightweight."

"We'll see who the lightweight is." I gave him a shove toward one of the standing tables where Magnolia and Bram had wandered over to.

I curled my arm around Mags's neck when I reached her and planted a kiss on her cheek. "You wanna try my new potion?" she said, sliding over a shot glass full of something purple.

"How fast will it get me wasted?"

She winked. "Let's start with this one and see how we go."

I downed the sweet-tasting potion, and a moment later, I was hit with a wave of euphoria. Whatever was in Mags's potion had my serotonin levels shooting through the roof. "Another!" I cried.

Then Jazzy was there, and Rose and Willow and Iris, and we were dancing—well, Iris was more swaying with how heavily pregnant she was. Relic took my hand, spinning me around, and we were all laughing and singing. I sank into it, letting Mags's potion do its thing—letting it take me out of my own head, just for a little while.

◦)⟩ ❂ ⟨(◦

I let my head slide across the back of the couch and land on Relic's shoulder. "I think I'm all partied out."

"Like I said, lightweight," he muttered and wrapped his arm around me. "You have a good night, babe?"

The party was still going, but it'd thinned out. Wills had gone downstairs to be with Warrick and Vi. Rose and Ronan and Iris and Draven had left a little while ago, and Mags and Bram were sitting on the opposite couch talking in that way couples obsessed with each other did, as if there were no one else in the room, while Jazzy was on Ren's knee on a chair beside us, making out.

"I had a great night. Being with all my favorite people, it's hard not to." I rested my hand on his stomach and tilted my head back to look at him. "Thanks for hanging with me tonight," I said and yawned. I was still feeling the effects of the potion and the beers, and my eyelids drooped.

Blue eyes filled my mind, wild and glowing, and I jolted awake.

Relic frowned. "Okay?"

I blinked up at him. "I think I drifted off for a second."

He grinned, flashing his killer dimples. "I'll be your pillow anytime."

"You're too charming for your own good, and the biggest flirt I've ever met." I huffed out a laugh.

"It's a skill I've perfected over the multiple centuries of my existence. It's a gift," he said, dropping his voice so it was low and growly.

"Relic, you seriously are a handsome devil, but that growly, dirty thing you're doing, as hot as it is, won't work on me," I said with a smirk. He wasn't being serious; he just was the flirtiest bastard I'd ever met.

"Baby, I gotta try. I've been angling for a feisty little witch of my own for a few years now, but I'm starting to think I've lost my touch 'cause every one of your cousins, your sister, and now you have flat-out rejected me," he said, that handsome-as-sin grin still on his face.

"You have no trouble picking up females."

"This is true, but I did think, just for a moment there, when we hung out in my room that time, that you might have actually considered taking me up on my offer of a night you'd never forget," he said, looking cocky as hell.

He was right. Who wouldn't consider it? A sound like a roar filled my head, and I jolted, sucking in a sharp breath. What the hell was that?

I shook it off and gave Relic a little shove. "Possibly," I said and rolled my eyes. "Just for a moment."

It was after my first month with Death; he'd ignored me, except for when he watched me, freaking me the hell out.

Before Death's bargain, I'd been working, using my powers to help people by speaking with their loved ones who'd crossed over, helping lost souls move on, or vanquishing evil ones. I'd felt lost while I was away that first month, disconnected from who I was, confused. Relic had been there, just doing what he did, being the truly awesome male that he was.

"I knew it." He winked. "If you ever change your mind, baby, you know where to find me."

I chuckled and shook my head. He'd offered me an escape from the pain I was feeling. No bullshit or pretense that it would be more than a good time.

He'd offered me a night of orgasms and, because it was Relic, no doubt some laughter as well. I'd wanted to go to his room with him when he'd asked, and I had, but we'd ended up talking, and I'd fallen asleep on his bed. I'd woken in the night, Relic beside me. He'd been awake, chest bare and hard as hell behind his worn jeans. I'd been about to roll toward him, but a voice in my head, Death's voice calling me his, roaring it in my mind, had stopped me.

It was like Death had been there.

And a moment ago, he'd been here as well, hadn't he? He'd been in my head, looking through my eyes right at Relic. He had to be with Somnus, and as soon as I'd drifted off, even though it was just for a split second, he'd had an opening.

"You okay, Zinny?" Relic asked, tucking my hair behind my ear.

I sat up straighter, shaking off the tiredness. "Ah... yeah. All good." Relic didn't want me, and I didn't want him, not now. That night in his room, I thought he must have been feeling as lost as me. "She's out there, you know? I know she is. She's waiting, Relic. You just have to find her."

His cocky grin slipped, the look in his eyes flattening. I had no idea how much he felt. Lucifer created the hounds and gave them the ability to feel lust, anger, and loyalty, but the rest didn't come easy. Relic was second-gen, though, still hundreds of years old, but not as old as Warrick and not directly created by Lucifer. I'd never asked, and he'd never said what his emotional range was. Some of the others faked it, but I didn't think that's what Relic was doing. He felt more than them; I was sure of it. Maybe not as much as us mortals, but definitely more.

"You know I love making a female feel good, babe, but sometimes, all I'm fucking after is a simple touch, a hug, you know? That's all. As for a mate, I'm good. I have brothers who've been waiting a fuck of a lot longer than me. They should be first," he said, and it was as serious as I'd ever heard him. "It wouldn't be right."

Hounds were extremely tactile, craved touch, and loved hugs, and what he'd just said broke my heart a little. "That's not how this works, and if you need a hug, I'm here... well, when I am here. But if she's out there, you'll find each other. Whose turn it is or if we're ready has nothing to do with it. The fates do whatever the hell they like." I knew that better than most. I gave his big, rough-skinned hand a squeeze and stood.

"The fates are evil bitches," he said and took a sip of his beer.

Or maybe they were the only ones who actually knew what was good for us, and we needed to just stop fighting it and give in.

·)·)·●·(·(·

It was late when we got back to Jazzy and Ren's place. They'd gone straight to bed, and I'd popped earplugs in when sounds started drifting down the hall that I sure as hell did not want to hear.

I'd also had plenty of opportunities to tell Jazzy or one of my cousins what Death had said to me before I'd left Limbo, but I hadn't.

"But I'm begging you... choose me over everything and everyone, over a life with them, over the possibility of death here with me."

"Choose me."

I squeezed my eyes closed and curled my fingers into fists. Why the hell had he said that? We could have carried on as we were for just a little longer. Now he was going to force my hand. He was going to make me choose. I wasn't in love with him—but I felt something. There was this pull inside me, distant but strong. Incredibly strong. Not love—it couldn't be—but something... something else. And even if what I felt for him did run deeper, even if I was falling for him, how could I choose him? How could I leave behind my sister? My family? I couldn't. Goddess, this hurt. I hated him for doing this to me, and I hated myself for even feeling the slightest bit conflicted about this. The answer should be easy. He forced me into a bargain I didn't want. He'd taken me away from everyone I loved.

This should be easy.

Then why the hell wasn't it?

CHAPTER 23

Zinnia

THE WIND BLEW *outside the castle. As she numbly sat on the couch in front of the fire, she stared down at the small vial gripped in her shaky, paint-stained fingers. It was full of something dark and noxious smelling. She was so cold, empty, broken. A tear slid down her cheek as she pulled out the cork and poured it into her mouth. Pain burned her throat and gut, scorched through her veins. Blood coming from her nose and eyes dripped from her chin onto her hands. She screamed, but not from the pain—from the relief.*

The room spun away to another place, looking through another female's eyes —no, this time, I was looking through my eyes.

Death stood among the trees, his cloak covering him. Snarls and growls came from beneath his hood.

Rage.

He slammed his staff down on the ground, and the earth shook beneath my feet.

"Mors," I called, running toward him, but he was moving farther and farther away from me. I called his name again, trying to reach him.

The world around me froze, and so did I.

Death tilted his head back and roared.

I gasped, shoving back the covers as I sat bolt upright. Then I was frozen, trying to find purchase. I was caught between the horror of the first vision and the desperate fear of the second.

Gods, I didn't know if my brain had conjured the vision of me and Death, or... or if that really had been him and something was terribly wrong.

Rubbing my face, I tried to wake myself up as I slid my feet into the slippers Jazzy had waiting for me and dragged on my favorite oversized cardigan that Else had knitted me years ago, which reached my knees. Hemy scurried across the mattress, and I held out my hand so he could run up and perch on my shoulder. He burrowed under my hair. "Morning, my sweet boy."

I walked out and found Jaz was at the kitchen counter. She was smearing butter on toast and had a butterfly of some variety on top of her head. "You have a good sleep?" she asked, lighting up when she saw me.

I pulled my earplugs out and held them up. "Thanks to these, yes." I popped them in my pocket. "Listening to my sister enthusiastically bone her mate isn't something I ever want to hear again."

She flushed. "Oh shit, sorry."

I shrugged. "It was gross, but it also made me happy that you're so happy and apparently getting laid really well."

She snorted and shook her head. "Yes, I most definitely am, but let's never mention that again." She held up her toast. "Want some?"

"Deal." I rounded the counter and popped two pieces in the toaster. "Ren home?"

"Nope, he had to go to work." She poured me a coffee and slid it over. "How's the head?"

"I mainly stuck to Mags's potion, so not bad at all. Our cousin has a gift," I said and took a sip.

"She really does." Her gaze held mine for a moment, and I saw the questions there, so many, but she took a bite out of her toast instead.

Now would be the perfect time to tell Jazzy everything that had happened. She was dying to ask me how my time in Limbo had been, but everyone tiptoed around the subject now, though. They waited for me to bring it up first, because I'd made it clear that's what I wanted. I opened my mouth to tell her what was happening, but the words wouldn't come out. I didn't know where to start or how to make her understand the way I was feeling. Everything was so messy and confusing, I just wanted to keep it to myself for a while longer.

You're keeping it to yourself because you haven't decided what you're going to do, and that would hurt your baby sister.

"So Else and Aunt Daisy are having a dinner tonight, just the family. You'll be there, right?" Jazzy said and sipped her coffee.

"Absolutely. I have a few things I need to do today, but I'll meet you there later. Can I borrow your car?" I said as nerves filled me.

"Or course. Anything I can help you with?"

My nerves shot higher. "No, not this time. Thanks, though."

››)·◕·(‹‹

"Do you have any white snakeroot?" I asked Wills, who was working at her store, The Cauldron, today, and pressed a kiss to Violet's peachy-colored hair. She was strapped to her mother's front, fast asleep. Hemy poked his head out of my bag, saw that Vi was asleep, and, disappointed, disappeared again.

Wills chuckled and broke off a piece of bread from her sandwich sitting on the counter. "We're all out, and our next delivery's not for a couple weeks. The council are being hard-asses on certain ingredients, and snake-root's on the restricted list." She rested her hip on the counter. "What are you using it for?" She held the bread, and Hemy's nose appeared, twitching; then he took it and vanished again. "Something important? Anything to do with your bargain?"

I shook my head. "I have a job," I said, lying through my teeth. "An old soul, like really old. I'm thinking I'll need a little more juice to make contact."

"I hope…" Her green eyes held mine. "I hope you haven't given up, Zin, because we haven't. Jazzy hasn't stopped trying to find a way to free you from Death—none of us have."

Guilt filled me. I should have told my sister this morning what was going on, but I didn't know how. Everything was so complicated. "I appreciate it, I do, but whatever happens, I'll be okay," I said and gripped the edge of the counter when another wave of guilt washed through me.

She nodded, not looking convinced. "As for the snakeroot, I know of a place that has a steady supply, but it's in the demon part of town. Yeah, they mostly follow the rules there—Rune runs a pretty tight ship—but still, going alone, no matter who you are or how capable you are, wouldn't be a good idea," she said, changing the subject back. She knew when not to push, and I loved that about her.

"Cool, where do I need to go?"

"There's a store—Malicious Brew. Give me a few hours, and then War can take Vi, and I'll come with."

If I hung out with Willow all day, there would eventually be questions, questions I wasn't ready to answer, that I didn't know how to answer. "Thanks, Wills, but I told my clients I'd get back to them this morning. I'll call Relic to keep me company."

My cousin looked disappointed, which just made me feel even more guilty. "I'll see you tonight, though? At your mom's for dinner."

"I guess I can let you off the hook this time then, but I want some one-on-one hang time and soon, okay?" she said, studying me way too closely. Out of all my cousins, Wills and I were the most alike, in appearance and personality, and she always seemed to know when I was hiding something.

"Absolutely."

I texted Relic as I headed out and asked if he could meet me. Relic being Relic, he immediately agreed. Traffic was heavy, and by the time I could park and let him know where I was, he was already close.

I found him a street over, standing by his bike, tall, in worn jeans and his leather vest, tapping away at his phone. The hound grinned when he saw me. "Just couldn't stay away from me?"

Hemlock poked his head out of my bag to see where we were and who we were with, and Relic gave his head a scratch. I snorted. "You wish."

"You have no idea. But since sex is off the cards, I'm happy to display my superior fighting abilities and protect a damsel in distress."

"I'm not a damsel."

He planted one of his massive hands on top of my head and mussed my hair. "Whatever you say, princess."

"You've been going to Willow's movie nights, huh?"

He chuckled, low and rough. "Of course, can't you see how evolved I've become? My emotional education is coming along nicely. I'm almost like a *real boy*."

"Jesus."

He winked. "So what are we doing here?"

This street was kind of a no-man's-land. Humans avoided it because, even though they didn't know demons existed, their flight instincts kept them away; they sensed there were predators nearby and avoided this part of the city all on their own, but as soon as we rounded the corner, we were in demon central. These demons could pass as human, though— that was one of the main prerequisites to live here. You also needed to know how to follow rules and not hurt humans. The forest-dwelling demons had none of those things. "I need some ingredients for a job I'm doing today."

The demons looked our way as we passed, but as soon as they saw Relic, they averted their eyes. Demons were naturally afraid of hellhounds. Lucifer used them to control the demons in Hell, and the fear was built into their DNA.

"Yeah? You found that job quick," he said, his gaze sliding to me. "Must be some kind of a record."

He knew I was up to something, or he at least suspected it. That's what you get for hanging out with a hound. "My client made the booking before I went to Limbo," I said, adding another lie to the list that day.

"Right," he said, making it obvious he didn't believe a word.

"Just up here," I said, relieved when I saw a sign with *Malicious Brew* scrawled on it swinging above the door.

I pushed open the door and walked in. I'd never smelled anything like it —not bad, just... busy. So many scents of herbs, plants, elixirs that I wasn't used to.

Relic looked around, tilted back his head, and sniffed the air. "This shit is burning my fucking nostrils." He scowled. "I don't like this, Zinny. It's too much. I can't smell anything else. No nose, no idea what the fuck's coming..."

The beads hanging in front of a door at the back of the room made a musical sound as they were drawn back, and a small female walked out. The demon was short and curvy and had bloodred hair that hung down her back in waves. Her face was humanoid and utterly stunning. She had a slightly upturned nose and full pink lips. She took several steps out, then slammed on the brakes, her unusual peridot eyes widening when she saw Relic. Her gaze sliced to the patch on his leather vest and the Devil Dogs MC emblem.

"I didn't do anything," she said. "Whatever they told you, I'm inno-cent." She lifted her hands and backed up a step like she was going to bolt. "I didn't do anything. Don't take me back... please... don't..."

"Not here to take you back to Hell, demon," Relic said. "So slow your roll and take a fucking breath."

She blinked up at him several times. "You're not?"

"Nope."

"He's just keeping me company," I said quickly because she still looked ready to turn and run. "I'm here for a couple of ingredients, that's all."

She kind of slumped in relief, then scowled. "What the fuck is wrong with you, witch? You brought a freaking hellhound into my shop? I almost pissed myself." She turned her scowl on Relic. "And you should know better." She shook her head. "Hounds, man. Meatheads, the lot of you."

Relic's head jerked back. "What did you call me, demon?"

"You heard me." She straightened her spine. "Lucifer didn't send you for me. You can't do shit, so save the intimidation bullshit for the next demon you drag back to Hell."

"Well, this has gotten off to a great start," I said as Relic strode past me and up to the little female.

She tried to step back, but he grabbed her arm and held her still while she squirmed to get away. He dipped lower, sniffing her head.

"What the hell do you think you're doing, mutt?" she yelled, and I saw she had fangs, short but sharp. "Let me the hell go."

"You're not just demon."

Her fight stopped instantly, and she blinked up at him. "How do you know that?"

"I can smell it." He smirked down at her. "Can't quite make out what else you are, but looking at you, I'd say a gremlin or maybe a troll."

She shrieked and slammed her knee up, aiming for Relic's nuts but only managing to get him midthigh. She was far too short to reach, but I doubted many beings could reach a hound's nuts that way, honestly. I respected her for trying, though. He deserved it.

"Okay, back up," I said to Relic.

He ignored me, wholly focused on the little demon in his grip.

"Meathead," she muttered again and started tapping her fingers against the side of her thigh, one after the other, over and over again.

"You couldn't handle my meathead, gremlin," he said and flashed her his fangs.

Okay, we were straying into some other weird freaking territory here that I did not want to be a part of. "So do you have any white snakeroot?" I asked.

"You do realize that gremlins don't actually exist? They're a myth." She pressed her hand to his chest and shoved, but he didn't move. "It's pretty cringe that you don't know that."

She shoved a second time, and again, Relic didn't budge; he did release her this time, though. He tilted his head to the side. "You have a very smart mouth for someone so small and annoying."

"And you have a giant head and ridiculous... muscles." She flushed. "You look like a deformed Sasquatch."

"Now I'm embarrassed for you, Gremmy, if we're talking about things that don't exist."

"Don't call me Gremmy," she gritted out, her fingers tapping against her thigh again.

"But it suits you"—Relic flashed her that thousand-watt grin— "Gremmy."

He was enjoying himself.

She crossed her arms tight over her chest. She was pissed, but I also saw the way she trembled. She was scared and doing her best to hide it. She was still a demon, and he was a huge hellhound invading her space. It was like a giant cat toying with an injured mouse. I wasn't sure Relic noticed.

"Leave," she said.

"I don't think so," he said back, definitely enjoying himself.

She looked down, her lids blinking rapidly, and then she sucked in a breath, teeth clenched, and looked back up. "I want you to leave, you giant pain in the ass. I want you to leave my shop now." Her voice was raised, pitched high. No, not scared—terrified. She was still desperately trying to be brave in the face of the huge male towering over her, and Relic missed it completely. Honestly, I was surprised.

"If I were in your ass, Gremmy, I promise it would only hurt for a minute, and then I'd make it feel real good."

She hissed.

"Okay," I said, stepping forward. "If you could just get the ingredients I need, we'll leave. Right, Relic?"

He winked down at her. "Sure."

She spun away, strode down one of the aisles crowded with ingredients, snatched something off the end, then stomped up to me and shoved it in my hands. "Now leave."

I slid my hand in my pocket for money. "I need to pay you."

"I don't care. Just leave."

I quickly pulled out some cash, more than what it was worth, but after what I'd just witnessed, she deserved a tip. I dropped the money on the counter, then grabbed Relic's arm and shoved him from the store.

He let me, but not without a little resistance.

The sound of the bolt being thrown behind us came as soon as we walked out. I spun around as the demon flipped the Open sign to Closed, then disappeared out of view, but not before I got a glimpse of exactly how rattled she looked.

"What the hell *was that*?" I asked Relic when we started walking.

"What?" He was still grinning.

"You terrified that female, then sexually harassed her," I said, because looking at him right now, the hound was clueless.

He stopped in his tracks. "No, I didn't... That's not what happened."

"I've never heard you speak to a female that way." Hounds were protective of females, worshipped them in a lot of ways—they did not harass or scare them.

Relic frowned down at me, glanced back at the shop, then back at me. "No... she wasn't afraid. She was—"

"She was shaking. You're a hellhound, and she's a demon. She was trying to hide it, but she was terrified. I thought she was actually going to cry for a moment." I wasn't trying to make him feel like shit, but he needed to be aware of what just happened back there.

"Cry?" he said, his voice so rough, it lifted goose bumps all over me. "No..." He looked back at the shop again. "No," he repeated.

"Yes."

"Fuck." He started back toward the shop, and I grabbed his arm.

"What are you doing?"

"I don't make females cry. I don't scare them, and I don't... sexually harass them." He actually looked nauseous.

"Going back there now will only make it worse. She wants you gone, and you need to respect that."

He stopped, looking confused and shaken. "Fuck," he said again and let me tug him back the way we were going.

He didn't say much after that, and he was distracted when he gave me a hug before he left for his shift at the Hell Fire, the hellhounds' bar. I watched him leave and then headed for home and our cemetery.

It was early afternoon by the time I got there. Sometimes I found it easier to call on spirits at our cemetery. It was a place of great power, and without any real information to go on, I needed all the help I could get.

The cemetery was quiet when I arrived, no Aunt Daisy or Arthur here today, thankfully. Daisy was probably in the kitchen getting ready for tonight. She went all out when she had us all under one roof. Closing the wide iron gates behind me, I ran my fingers over headstones, saying their names as I walked by, telling my loved ones, my ancestors, how much I missed and loved them, finally stopping beside my grandmother's grave.

"Hey, Gran," I said and sat on the ground. Daisy and Art had planted chamomile all over the grounds. It had spread everywhere, which was what they'd wanted. When Art cut the grass now, it smelled amazing.

"I need your help to find some people," I whispered as I slipped my bag over my head and set it beside me. Hemy scurried out and trotted to the herb garden to nibble on the basil. "I know you're resting, and I hate to disturb you, but I'm not sure I can do this alone. You see, Gran, I need to make a decision, one that should be simple, but now... now it's not." Death said he loved me, and I wasn't sure what I felt, but I felt... something. Something unexplainable. It was wide and deep and so incredibly strong, but also it felt... distant. I didn't understand it, and I needed to understand it.

Opening my bag, I pulled out the thimble, the book, and the small pot of dried paint I'd taken from my bedroom back in Limbo and placed them in front of me. I'd never met any of these females, besides Aster. I didn't know their names. I didn't know anything about them. All I had that told me anything of who they were, were my visions and these items. Worn and well-used items they'd taken the time to bring with them when they'd made their own journey to Limbo, however that came about. Items that had been left behind, survived when they hadn't.

Females Death had cared for, possibly loved.

And as much as I didn't want to consider it, there was this unsettling feeling inside me. Death was prone to bouts of rage and jealousy, of unreasonable and controlling behavior. The cloak was darkness, and sometimes, it pulled him into the shadows.

He said if I left him, he'd let the cloak take him, that he'd let the shadows and the darkness take hold. Death had remained covered, preferring the shadows, when I first went to Limbo, and I'd believed him capable of anything. I didn't know how easy it was for him to slip back into that place, but if he had when he was with his consorts, if he'd let his anger take hold, perhaps he'd done something, something terrible, when he was lost to the shadows. Something that had pushed them to do what they had, to hurt themselves.

Even thinking it made me feel sick with guilt, but I had to be sure.

Taking a tiny piece of snakeroot from my bag, I placed it in a small square of soft leather. Then I added one verbena leaf, three drops of agarwood oil, and two of juniper oil and placed it on the ground. Then I took a ball of string from my bag and cut a length off. Making a slice in my palm, I let my blood pool, then smeared it on the string before gathering up the leather square into a small pouch and tying it closed with the blood-soaked string.

Rubbing the pouch between my hands, I mixed everything together, warming it until its fragrance reached me and the oil soaked the leather through. I swiped the oily pouch over the items I'd taken from my room in Limbo, and then I squeezed my sliced palm and dripped some blood on Gran's grave as an offering before dropping more blood in a circle around everything.

Slipping off my shoes, I pressed my feet into the soft chamomile lawn that had grown over Gran's grave, digging my toes in, pulling power straight from the source. I let the magic that still flowed through Gran's bones reach out to me and latched on to it.

I gasped as it filled me, twisting around my own magic and lifting it higher and higher. Closing my eyes, I let the spell wrap around me, let the words come, let them form and build to call on Death's consorts, to ask them to show me the way, until they finally spilled from my lips. "Thank you, Mother, for the gifts you have given me, for the love you have bestowed upon me. I call on you, my sisters, sisters who came before, who loved and laughed and hoped for a life of peace and warmth, my sisters who were taken too soon. I call on you to come forward, to show me who you were and how you were taken. I ask for your help, dear sisters, to guide me, to lead me to the right path." I squeezed my hand tighter, and warm blood trickled over my hand and into the small circle. "Show me, sisters."

The world spun around me—but there were no souls to be found, only a suffocating darkness, a void, and it was cold and incredibly lonely.

Tears slid down my face. I felt so much, so much pain and fear as if it were my own.

A sob burst from me as I searched, but they weren't there. It was as if they were nothing.

As if they had ceased to exist.

CHAPTER 24

Zinnia

THE TABLE WAS laden with food; Daisy and Else had outdone themselves. Everyone I loved was in the same place, sitting around the table laughing and talking, and I tried to let it fill me so I could shake the awful empty feeling inside me, but what happened at the cemetery lingered, clinging to me like a cold hand around the back of my neck, not letting go.

I rubbed my arms and smiled when Vi gave Hemy another wide grin. He was besotted with her, performing for my tiny cousin, running down my arm and up Willow's, then peeking at Violet through Willow's hair. He did it again, and Violet giggled uncontrollably. Hemy spun around, triumphant.

"You little show-off," I said and scratched his head when he ran back to me.

"I need a Hemy," Wills said. "Imagine everything I'd get done with him keeping my little drama queen busy when I'm trying to make dinner or pee or just take a shower." She turned to Ren, who was sitting beside War. "I have asked my loyal familiar to go fox and entertain his niece, but he won't do it."

"Because I want her to love me for me, and not because I'm a fuzzy, cute woodland animal," he said with a smirk. "And thanks to Jaz's mural, she's now obsessed with them."

Jazzy chuckled. "I can't help it if I'm just that talented."

"Would you go crow and flap around to entertain babies and small children?" Ren asked Bram.

He shrugged. "Depends. If they were my own kids, then yeah, but then they'll probably have their own wings, so I'm not sure I'll need to."

Mags spun to face him. "And then I'll be left standing there while you all fly off and leave me behind." Her lips turned down. "I'm jealous already, and we don't even have kids yet."

"I'll carry you, babe," Bram said and kissed the top of her head.

"There's always the broom," Else said at her spot beside Daisy.

"What broom?" Iris asked, her hand dropping from her massive belly and grabbing the edge of the table. She was due in a few months, but with twins, she looked ready to have them now.

"Don't even think about it," Draven said to his mate, who still thought she could do everything she used to.

"What broom?" Mags asked, impatient.

Daisy frowned at Else. "Hey, we made a pact never to bring that up."

"Oopsie," Else said. Stan, Else's devoted and deceased familiar, stood behind her, chuckling, amused by her as always. Only Jaz and I could see him and knew he was there. He'd asked us not to tell her.

"When I asked if we had a family broom, you said we didn't," Rose said from her spot on Ronan's lap.

"We lied," Else said. "None of you could be trusted not to do something crazy with it." She shrugged. "But your daughter's mated to a crow, Daisy, so I think she should have it." She sipped her wine. "There's a hat as well."

"Else!" Aunt Daisy said. "What has gotten into you?"

"A hat like *a hat*, the pointy kind that most families have, but you said we didn't," Wills said.

"It doesn't do anything," Daisy said. "And if you knew about the hat, then you'd know there was a broom."

"Because it hasn't found its new owner. Jaz and Zinny haven't tried it on for size yet. Maybe it belongs to one of them," Else said.

Brooms, pointed hats, cauldrons—they were the things that humans associated with witches, but there was a reason for that. All covens supposedly had those things, items of power. They were tangible, things you could see and touch, unlike actual magic, and during the witch trials, the connection between the witches tried and those particular items had been noted, hence the association to this day.

Else stood slowly, then shuffled from the room. Stan followed her. He was always with her; the only time he left her side was when she was asleep, but he never went far.

"I can't believe you never told us we had them," Mags said.

"We tried the hat on each of you when you were babies. It didn't claim any of you, so we put it away," Daisy said, looking guilty. "Honestly, I was kind of scared of it. It's old and powerful. Who knows what it can do when it finds its owner?"

Else shuffled back in carrying both. Mags jumped up, and Else handed her the broom. "Fly, my pretty," she said and cackled.

Bram frowned, looking it over. "If you use that thing, you have to wear a helmet."

Mags looked disgusted. "A *helmet*. No way. None of my ancestors would have worn one."

"And I bet there were a whole lot of witches walking around with concussions." He gave it another once-over. "I don't know about this. You could break your damn neck."

"No, I won't," Mags said, running her hand over it.

Else placed the hat on Jazzy's head. "It won't toss her off, and she won't fall. Once you're in the air, you're stuck on it until you land." The hat was worn rich brown leather. Soft, the point at the top not super tall, not like in fairy stories. It was too big for Jazzy, though, and covered her eyes.

"See, nothing to worry about," Mags said to her mate, eyes shining with glee.

Else plucked the hat off Jasmine's head. "Nope, not yours. It might be destined for one of the babies," she said. "Could be Vi's or one of the twins." She moved behind me and put it on my head.

The moment she did, something happened. The room spun, the world shifting around me, followed by a massive surge of power flowing through my body. It was meant for me. I felt it. The hat had been waiting for me, and I knew instantly that if I was wearing it, any spell I used would be boosted.

"Whoa," Rose said. "It shrunk down to fit."

"How does it feel, Zinny?" Wills asked.

I had to take several breaths while the power surge settled. "Yeah, it feels... right. Good." That was the only way I knew how to describe it.

Else took it off my head and set it on the kitchen counter. "Then it's yours, my girl. It belongs to you now."

"Looks good too," Mags said.

"Thanks, Else." I took her hand.

She smiled, so much love in her eyes and warmth on her weathered face. "I had a feeling that the time was right," she said, then grabbed for the chair, stumbling.

"Else!" Daisy shot to her feet, but Warrick was there first, scooping her up.

Else went limp in his arms.

774

›)›‐●‐((‹

Else looked so small in her bed, covers pulled up to her chin, her long silver hair, wavy and soft, spread out on her pillow. Stan lay on the bed behind her, his arm around her.

They were the loves of each other's lives, but then they'd been torn from each other when Stan was murdered. He'd only been twenty-one years old.

He looked up at me now and shook his head.

Else wasn't coming back from whatever this was. Jasmine was standing behind me, and she rushed from the room, trying not to let anyone else see that she was about to cry. Stan had made us keep our promise, and we had; we never told our aunt or anyone else that he was with her. He'd wanted her to move on, to at least try and have a full life without him, and he knew she wouldn't be able to if she knew he was there.

She never really had, though. There was Connor, the sweet old guy she was kind of dating, but they'd never really been more than good friends. She'd never gotten over Stan, and she hadn't really tried because she didn't want to get over him. He was it for her.

Mags was kneeling on the floor beside her. "Else?"

She opened her eyes slowly. "Don't you yell at me," she said to Magnolia. "I didn't tell you because worrying gives a body ulcers. I've seen other healers, the best, and there's nothing anyone can do. My time's up, pumpkin," she said, her usually strong voice sounding weak.

Daisy brushed her hair back. "I won't give up, Else. There has to be something—"

"It's my heart, Daisy... and nothing can be done." She wrapped her fingers around Daisy's hand. "I'm ready to go. I'm... I'm so goddamn ready to see my Stan."

CHAPTER 25

Zinnia

Home: Week Two

DEATH CALLED MY NAME, *his voice echoing through the trees. His roars and unhinged growls should terrify me, but they didn't. I needed to find him.* "Mors!"

But the faster I ran toward him, the farther he got from me. I sobbed, tripping over tree roots and sliding in the mud. Blood dripped from my grazed palms, and each step grew more difficult than the last.

"Zinnia!" *he roared.*

I sat up with a gasp, my heart thundering in my chest. Hemlock was curled in close, sensing my distress even in sleep. "I'm okay, my sweet boy." It was a lie, and I wasn't fooling him or myself.

The dreams had been constant. Every night the last two weeks since I'd been home. I'd dreamed of Death calling for me, and every night I tried to find him in that forest, and I couldn't. It felt so real, but he was always out of reach. He needed me, but I couldn't get close to him. If Somnus was helping him, he'd be able to come to me, though. He'd be able to talk to me, like he had when I was fifteen.

But he hadn't done that. Maybe it was just a dream? It had to be because he'd talk to me if he was really there. He would.

There was a tap at my bedroom door before it opened. Jasmine walked in carrying a mug of coffee. "You sleep okay?"

"Yeah," I lied and took the mug, sitting up. "Any news?"

"She's still the same."

Else had deteriorated, but she was hanging on. I shoved back the covers. "Let me quickly get dressed, and we can head back."

We walked into Aunt Daisy's house a short time later. Wills was at the kitchen table, Rose beside her. They both looked exhausted.

"How is she?" Jaz asked.

"She's comfortable, but she's getting weaker," Rose said, her eyes filled with pain.

>)⧽●⧼((

Home: Week Three

I was surrounded by stars. I was alone and so scared. The stars spun past, faster and faster, darkness flashing to light—

I hit the ground so hard, I cried out.

I blinked up at the sky, then looked down at myself. I was naked, lying on the grass.

A giggle fell from my lips as I wiggled my toes.

"Stella?" a rough voice called.

I woke with a jolt, my gaze slicing to Else. She was still asleep.

"You okay?" Jaz asked from her seat beside me.

Another week had passed of nightly dreams or visions—I still didn't know what. Every night, I felt Death close and was never able to reach him, and I saw those females, their lives and their deaths, feeling their fear and not understanding any of it... All while sitting with my cousins at Else's bedside watching her get weaker and frailer by the day.

Right now, though, it was just me and Jazzy in here with Else.

"Nightmare?" Jaz asked.

"I'm... I'm not sure."

She studied me. "You look exhausted."

I was. Every time I fell asleep, another vision or dream came to me, and now this, this weird vision of the night sky, of Death, but in the past, of him calling out her name, calling Stella. I felt as if I were losing my damn mind.

"I'll go get us a coffee," she said.

"Thanks."

She walked out, and I looked back at Else. She was watching me. "Hey," I said and took her hand.

"Spill," she rasped. "I've been watching you the last few weeks. I may be on my death bed, but I'm not blind."

My mouth went dry. "There's nothing to tell."

"Now you're gonna lie? Right to your dying aunt's face?"

Her body may be weak, but her mind was still just as sharp. "So much has happened, Else. I'm not sure where to start—"

"Then give me the highlights." And for a moment there, she sounded like her old bossy self.

"Right, the highlights." I leaned forward, resting my elbows on my knees, and gave her hand a light squeeze before I let it all go, everything I'd been holding inside. "I'm not the only consort Death's had. He's had... well, I'm not sure of the actual number, but all have died horribly. I've tried to contact them, but I can't, and he won't tell me anything. Apparently, I have to work it all out myself. His brother, Somnus, lives in the Dream Realm protecting their younger sister from their mother, Nox. Her name's Marigold, and she's in a temple Death created as a child in the Night Realm. She's been locked in stasis for some reason since she was three, but I have no idea how old she truly is. Up until last month, Death never touched me. Now... things have, ah... well, progressed. He says he loves me, Else, that he'll release me from our bargain, but he wants me to choose him, even if that means death... for me. Even if that means leaving everyone I love and only being with him for as long as I survive. And those females, the one's that came before me, I... I feel them, but I can't reach them. There's nothing, just... goddess, there's just an empty void. And I have these visions, or maybe they're just dreams, I don't know, but in them, Death comes to me, but I can't reach him. I also have visions of the past, of those females, of their lives, their deaths, but that's all they can give me, and I have no idea what any of it means."

Else blinked up at me. "Boy, you weren't kidding. And that was just the highlights?"

I chuckled and wiped away the stray tear that had fallen without me realizing it. "I had a full-on month in Limbo."

"You can say that again, Zinny girl." She squeezed my hand back. "Did you know the mother and Nox hate each other?"

"They do? Why?"

"Not sure, but they fell out over something a very long time ago. It's mentioned in a few history books."

"I had no idea."

She shrugged a narrow shoulder. "Gods are touchy, and they get bent out of shape easily." Her eyes cleared and locked on me. "As for Death... well, nothing is ever as it seems. Do you love him?"

"Things have been far from smooth sailing. I... I care about him, deeply.

There's this connection, a magnetism pulling me toward him that's so strong, sometimes I feel like I'm being torn in two, but love...."

"Okay, let me put it this way, pumpkin. If you dropped that brick wall you've built around yourself, if you forget the other consorts and the visions and the brother and Nox and the kid in stasis and all the other things, if you shove that all aside, and it's just you and him, do you think you could love him?"

My heart thumped in my chest, and my palms grew sweaty. I was on the verge of hyperventilating. "I... I..."

She gave my hand another squeeze. "I'll take that as a yes."

Fuck.

"I just, I don't know what any of it means, what the visions are trying to tell me."

She studied my face, her eyes bright with life even though her body was failing her. "What if they're not just visions? What if they're something else?"

I stilled. "Like what? An alternate realm? Another timeline? Nox beaming a lie into my brain? I'm due to go back in less than a week, and I still have no idea what I'm going to do."

She shrugged a frail shoulder. "I wish I had the answers for you, but what I do know is it never hurts to look at something from a different angle. To wipe the slate clean when you're having no luck and try again."

>>◦●◦<<

Home: Week Four

Death stood behind me, his hands on my rounded belly. "Are you afraid?" he asked.

I shook my head. "How can I be afraid when I have you by my side? How can I be afraid when we're about to meet our child?"

"Aster," he rasped against my ear. "My star, my love, my light."

I woke with my hands on my flat stomach. I was in my room at Jasmine's house. No round belly. No baby. No Death. Loss washed through me with such force, I had to bite back a sob. I wanted the vision back; I wanted it all back.

Aster, the first of Death's consorts. She'd given him a child.

The visions were becoming more intense, more real. More brutal on my frail emotions. I was raw from my days with Else and my nights in the past —Death's past.

I shoved back the covers and quickly got dressed. My time was up. I was supposed to go back tomorrow, or not, a decision that, on paper, should be easy. Life or death? Who wouldn't choose life?

But either way, I wasn't going to leave my family, not yet, not while they still needed me.

Snatching my phone off the bedside table, I checked for missed calls or texts. Nothing, thank the goddess. Else was still here, still with us.

Shoving on my boots, I scooped up Hemlock, put him on my shoulder, and walked out. Jazzy and Ren were already gone. I didn't bother with breakfast; my stomach was too knotted and filled with nerves, and the sadness from that dream still hovered around me like a dark cloud. My hands fell to my stomach. For a moment, I'd felt what it would be like to be pregnant, something I would never experience for myself, and I wanted it back; I wanted to be back in that dream with Death.

Stop.

You're losing your damn mind.

Shoving my hands in my pockets, I walked through the field where Ren had built my sister her dream house and headed down the road to Daisy's house. Mags and Bram had been staying in Bram's tree house in the back-yard every night instead of heading to the crow village like they did a few nights a week. Good thing since I needed to talk to her, like now.

It was still pretty early, so instead of heading inside the house, I walked around the side to the backyard. The light was on in the kitchen; Daisy and Art were in there with Rose. I needed to speak with Mags before anyone saw me. They'd known what date it was, even if no one had said anything to me, because this situation was already hard enough. Jazzy had been avoiding me the last few days, and I got it. She was already hurting enough. Knowing her sister was about to leave while Else was like this, it was too much for her, for everyone.

I climbed the ladder to the tree house and knocked on the door.

Bram opened it a few seconds later. "Zinny, hey." He frowned. "Every-thing okay?"

His black hair was tied back, the sides freshly shaven. He had a few new markers tattooed on the right side of his head since my last visit, and going by the massive knife strapped to his thigh and the frustration in his eyes, he was about to leave on a job. My cousin's mate was an assassin, and he and his brothers frequently had to vanish for days on end to do what needed to be done. "How long will you be gone?" I asked him.

"I'll be back by morning, all going to plan." He pushed the door wide, letting me in.

Mags was standing at the kitchen counter, sipping a coffee. "Hey, Zinny. Hey, Hemy."

Bram strode over to her, pulled her into his arms, and kissed her. When the kiss ended, he rested his forehead against hers and said something low for her ears only. Then he kissed her again, gave me a chin lift, and walked out. A moment later, he dove off the small balcony, his wings exploding from his back and catching the air, and then he was gone.

I turned back to Mags. "Okay?"

She leaned on the counter. "Yeah, I mean, I hate it when he goes, but I'm usually fine. It's just now, with Else..." She shook her head. "I just want everyone close, you know?" Her eyes lifted to me, and she bit her lip. "Sorry."

Yeah, no one had forgotten that I was supposed to leave tomorrow. "That's kind of why I'm here. I need your help, Mags."

She straightened. "What do you need?"

I wanted to hug her right then. She'd do anything for me; they all would.

"Do you think you could get a message to Death?" My baby cousin was one of Death's reapers due to a whole shitty situation that happened when she and Bram got together. I knew she went to Limbo frequently, but I never saw her, and she couldn't reach me. When she delivered a soul, she went straight to that soul's "individual Limbo," and she hadn't found a way to veer off the path and find me, but surely there was a way for her to reach Death. There had to be.

She studied me closely. "What kind of message?"

"I'm not leaving, not yet, not while I can still be with Else, and not when my family needs me. I don't know if it's possible, but do you think you can find a way to get a message to him for me and tell him that?"

She put down her mug and rounded the counter. "I have no direct line to Death. He doesn't communicate with me at all. I feel the call to collect a soul, and I deliver it—that's it."

"Can you try anyway?"

"I'm... I'm not sure how." She looked as frustrated as I felt.

My only other option was to go to the gateway and wait, hope he came, and try to explain, but that would take most of the day, and I didn't want to be away from Else that long. "Sorry to ask. I just... I didn't know what else to do."

She chewed her lip again. "Let me try, okay? I'll see what I can do." She walked to her shelf and pulled down an old book of spells and a wooden bowl. "I think I have an idea, but I'll need to really focus."

I needed this to work.

"Call me if there's any change with Else," she said and took a small vial from the shelf as well. "If this is going to work, I'll know pretty quickly. I'll come find you when it's done."

›)) ● ((‹

Else was sleeping more than she was awake now. This was agony.

Connor, her friend, sat beside her. He was holding her hand, talking to her softly, telling her how much he cared about her, how much he was going to miss her. Rose and Iris sat beside me, and we were all struggling to hold back our tears. One slipped down my cheek, and I quickly dashed it away.

Stan, as always, was her constant, even if she didn't know it, though I wondered if she felt him now. There was a peace in her eyes when she was awake that was impossible to miss, as if she knew he was waiting for her.

Mags opened the door and walked in. I'd left her place two hours ago. Her gaze went from Else to me before she made her way to my side and took the seat beside me. She looked exhausted, dark rings under her eyes and fresh bandages on one of her arms. Whatever she'd done had taken a lot of blood, and she'd drained her power.

"I found my way there," she said quietly. "Not to Death, but there was a demon, Lyle. He said he'd pass on your message."

I sagged in relief and grabbed her hand. "Thank you."

She gave it a squeeze. "Anytime."

A weird pressure built in my chest as I sat there, as if I felt the hours, the minutes and seconds ticking down.

I wasn't leaving in the morning, and I honestly didn't know if I'd ever walk through that gateway ever again.

CHAPTER 26

Zinnia

THE LAST TWO days had been brutal.

I shoved my hand under my pillow and stared out the window. Clouds had gathered throughout the day, and the darkness of the night sky was almost oppressive.

Else wasn't eating, was barely drinking; she'd given up. She was ready to go, but Mags especially was having trouble accepting it. She'd been poring over the healing volumes in the library. Aunt Daisy was constantly baking and cooking, deep in denial, and the rest of us were just trying to squeeze in whatever time we had left with Else, one of the most amazing, stubborn, brilliant, loving females we'd ever met.

I was feeling so many things—guilt, sadness, and, yeah, confusion. I missed Death. Admitting that to myself hadn't been easy. Allowing myself to admit that I had feelings for a god who had a room full of things, treasured possessions from his previous, deceased consorts, felt like a kind of self-harm. What kind of idiot falls for a male who couldn't promise them anything at all, not even life?

What kind of idiot contemplated going back to that?

How could I do it knowing my family was already suffering, knowing they were about to lose Else? Considering leaving, with the possibly of never making it back, was selfish.

Letting myself fall in love with Death was so goddamn selfish.

I clung to my pillow tighter and let my eyes drift closed. I needed him, was desperate to see him, and sleep was the only way, even if it was painful. My lids grew heavy almost immediately; it'd been a long day. I sank into it and invited the darkness in.

The ground was cold, damp against my bare feet, and I shivered. The skull path stretched ahead of me, leading to the castle. Whispers, cries, and screams echoed through the forest. It was dark, and the feeling of dread that surrounded me had me gasping for breath.

I looked down at myself. I was wearing the dress, the black dress Nox had made me wear, the one Death had torn off me. Lifting the skirts, I ran as fast as I could. I rounded the bend, and the castle loomed ahead. A single candle was glowing in a window on the upper level. Death's room.

I ran up the castle stairs and pushed open the entrance doors. Silence greeted me. A stillness filled the massive stone building as if it had been submerged, as if it now sat at the bottom of the Night Sea.

"Mors!" I called his name as I stepped inside.

The floor was cracked by big, jagged fissures that went from one side to the other. Shards of shattered glass and broken furniture littered the ground. No one walked out—no Egon, no Lyle. They were gone; everyone was gone.

Gathering up my dress again, I rushed up the stairs and down the hall to Death's bedroom door. It was closed. I didn't know if the heavy wood was keeping everyone out or keeping him in because I felt a dark energy through it. Dark and filled with fury. I pressed my hand to it. "Mors?"

Nothing, not a sound came from inside.

Hand shaking, I turned the handle and pushed open the door.

I searched the dark room, but I couldn't see him—until my gaze slid to the bed. A shadowy figure lay there, unmoving. "Mors?" Nothing. I stepped closer. "It's me." I reached down and touched his shoulder. "Mors?"

He spun to face me with a feral snarl.

"I'm here," I whispered.

One moment, he was on the bed; the next, he was in front of me, looming over me, backing me up. Light flared, the fire on the other side of the room igniting. He was in his cloak, the hood obscuring half of his face. "You didn't come," he growled. "I waited and you didn't come."

I opened my mouth, but it slammed shut. I tried, but I couldn't open it; I couldn't speak.

Death shook his head. "No more lies from those lips, consort. No more."

My gaze slid over him. His shoulders heaved with his fury. His cloak hung open, revealing a strip of his naked body beneath. His chest and stomach were tight, his cock impossibly hard. I pressed my hand to his chest, over the intricate stars tattooed there, and pleaded with my eyes for him to understand.

He gathered up the front of my dress. "If you won't stay with me, I'll have you here in your dreams. I'll own you here, little witch," he snarled.

I wanted to tell him he could have me. That no matter where I was, I was his and he was mine, but he wouldn't let me speak, too lost in his rage to see, to see me. I let him hook his arm around my waist and pin me to the wall. I wrapped my arms around his neck and hung on tight when he tore my underwear from my body.

"I hate you," he said roughly, "for doing this to me." He nipped my earlobe. "Why did you do this to me?" His voice was a desperate plea. He swung my leg around his hip, and I lifted the other one, hanging on. "Why?" he growled and slammed inside me.

I tried to cry out, but no sound came; all I could do was hold on as he took me, pouring all his pain and rage into me.

"You break me and break me, and I let you." He made a sobbing, gasping sound. "I let you destroy me." He fucked me harder, fisting my hair and tilting my head back. "I won't do this again." He shook his head. "I won't do it."

He thrust into me over and over, nipping, sucking on my skin, my mouth, while he made sounds like a wounded animal, while he fed me his hate and anger and lust and gave me no choice but to take it, not letting me give him anything at all.

I wrapped my arms around him tighter, hanging on, clawing at his back. The darkness surrounded us, and his face shifted, transforming as the shadows gathered, turning him into the God of Death, my god. He slammed into me until there was no holding it back, and I tried, I tried so hard, because I had an awful feeling that when this ended, nothing would be the same again.

He sank his teeth into the side of my throat, and I screamed silently, still unable to make a sound, coming hard around him. My body jarred against the wall, and he thrust into me two more times and came as well, grinding into me until we were both spent.

Finally, he lifted his head, looking down at me, his face nothing but a skull, the blue of his eyes gone, obscured by shadow. "No more," he rasped, and then he stepped back.

My body stayed suspended against the wall, and Death lifted his hands.

"No more," he roared like a wounded beast, then jerked his hands to the side.

My world spun—

I slammed against the mattress, waking with a cry.

I gripped my stomach, my chest, my head. I felt as if I were being torn apart. Tears soaked my cheeks, and I realized my pain wasn't physical. No, what I was feeling was my heart breaking. Everything was a mess; something was happening to Death. That wasn't a dream; it was real, what had happened between us. He was in pain, and I'd caused it.

Someone knocked on my door. "Zinny, it's Else. Quickly, get dressed."

785

-))⟩-●-(((-

We were all in Else's small room. Not everyone that loved her was here—it would be impossible to fit them all in this house—but the people who knew her best, who had been lucky enough to know what it was to be loved, really loved, by her, cared for by her, and fiercely protected by her, were gathered in this room.

The small space was overflowing with so many emotions; there was sadness, of course, but mostly there was love.

Magnolia held one of Else's hands, and Daisy, the other. Stan looked at me, his gaze sliding between me and Jasmine, and he smiled. *"Thank you,"* he said.

We'd been the only people he'd been able to communicate with for so very long, and now he and Else would finally be together again.

I took Jasmine's hand, and we walked forward. I crouched beside the bed, and Jazzy kept hold of my hand. "You know we love you, Else. So much. You were there for us when our own mother couldn't be, so when I tell you this, you have to promise not to be mad at us... or Stanley."

Else took a ragged breath. "Spill."

I brushed my hand over the back of hers, so frail now when she'd always been such strength for us, for all of us. "He made us promise not to tell you, but he's been here, right here, by your side since he died. He's been a friend to me and to Jazzy, a confidant, and an example of what true love looks like, because, goddess... he loves you, so very much. It's so big, Else, so beautiful. He's standing right there"—I motioned to where he stood just in front of us—"and he's been standing there, at your side, for over fifty years. Laughing at your jokes, making eyes at you as if the sun and the moon rose and fell with you, and waiting. Waiting until you could finally be together again."

Jaz came down beside me and gently touched her soft hair. "You have nothing to fear, Else. Not one thing. Stanley will be there to greet you with open arms. You'll be together forever."

A tear slid down her wrinkled cheek. "He's... there?" She looked to the spot beside her.

I nodded.

Another tear slid down her face. "I thought... I-I t-thought he'd gone... but then I felt him. I-I've been..."

Her breathing became more labored, and Jaz and I stepped back to make room for our cousins. Mags climbed onto the bed beside her. Everyone surrounded her. Daisy started the chant, and then, one by one, we all joined in. We were saying words of love, of faith, calling on the mother to usher her safely into the arms of her loved ones. As the words overlapped, they became more a melody than a chant—a song so sweet and so filled with warmth, Else smiled, her gaze moving around the room to everyone here.

Stan stepped forward. "See you on the flip side," he said to me and Jazzy, and then he held out his hand to Else.

CHAPTER 27

Zinnia

Elswyth Beatrix Thornheart died at 2:48 a.m., surrounded by her loved ones on a crisp and cloudy winter's night.

Jasmine and I watched her soul rise from her body, and when Stanley greeted her, pulling her into his arms and holding her tight, she transformed, becoming the bold, stunningly beautiful young witch she had once been. Her hair, long and black, hung down her back as she smiled at him.

"She's with Stanley," I said to my aunt and cousins. "She's young again and so incredibly beautiful."

"They're walking away holding hands," Jasmine added with a shaky smile.

We'd spent the rest of the night preparing her body for the burial. We didn't like to wait to return our dead to the earth, to the mother. Everyone that could, made it to the funeral the following day. Nearly all our coven was there, and Connor arrived with a van full of witches from the Coven Elders' Assembly. Numerous council members and nearly everyone from Draven's pack as well as Bram's brothers and their aunt attended. The hounds arrived on their bikes, all dressed in black, and Ren's parents came too. Our cemetery was usually warded, but for today, we'd dropped it to allow everyone in to pay their respects. It was crowded, and the hounds and wolves had offered to make sure no one who shouldn't be there got in or took anything that they shouldn't.

People were still assholes, and the Thornheart cemetery was still one of the most coveted cemeteries in the city and farther afield.

Now, it was late evening, and everyone was gathered in the backyard at Daisy's house. There was a fire, and we were all eating, drinking, and sharing our memories of Else. It was hard to believe she was actually gone. It still didn't feel real.

And I felt so incredibly guilty because I couldn't stop thinking about Death and what happened in my dream just before Else died. Something was terribly wrong. That was no dream. It was him; he'd been with me.

But when I'd finally fallen back into bed in the early hours of the morning, he hadn't come back. I'd wanted to see him again, to talk to him, if he'd let me, but I hadn't dreamed at all. I had this sick, awful feeling inside me that I might never see him again—and I realized that wasn't something I could abide.

I didn't want to give him up, to never see him again, but I didn't want to leave my family either, especially now—and yeah, I sure as hell didn't want to die.

I glanced around the yard, and suddenly I found it hard to breathe. I needed to be alone, to think. I should say goodbye, but instead, I slipped away, down the side of the house, and broke into a run as soon as I reached the street, desperate to release the pressure building inside me, to burn off the awful feeling that wouldn't go away, screaming at me that something was wrong, that Death needed me, that I was making a mistake.

I made it back to Jasmine and Ren's place, but I couldn't bring myself to go inside. The house was empty, but I thought I'd lose my mind if I walked in there, if I went to my room and pretended that this was my life now, that I was fine and that never returning to Limbo was what I wanted. Instead, I sat beneath Jasmine's favorite tree. She loved this spot and sat here all the time. I rested my head against the rough trunk, listening to the insects and the rustle of the spruce trees.

My chest was hollow, so incredibly empty, as if some fundamental part of me had been scooped out, and the only way to feel whole again was to go back—to him. How could that be? How could I actually be considering giving it all up, every part of me, possibly my life, just to be with him again? I shoved my fingers in my hair.

"*Do you love him?*" Else's words filtered through my mind. "*Okay, let me put it this way, pumpkin, if you dropped that brick wall you've built around yourself, if you forget the other consorts and the visions and the brother and Nox and the kid in stasis and all the other things, if you shove that all aside, and it's just you and him, do you think you could love him?*"

I hadn't been able to answer her then, but it was obvious, wasn't it? Why else would I be torn over this? Why else would the pull to return to him be so strong?

Because I loved him.

So much that I was considering giving up everything—my life—to be with him again.

All of a sudden, holding myself up was too much. My body ached from crying the last two days, and emotionally I was drained. I lay on my side, my hand to the soft grass, and let the vibrations from the earth, from the mother, fill me, trying to let them restore me. Hemlock crawled out of his bag and curled up under my chin, and I closed my eyes, willing the darkness to come, to take me under as I let the exhaustion weigh down my limbs, my head, my stomach and chest, until I felt as if I were becoming one with the earth. I let it surround me in its familiar embrace and soothe the pain.

My eyes drifted closed.

I screamed as pain tore through me.

"That's it, love, push," Death said against my damp hair. "She's nearly here."

I bared down, squeezing his hand, and pushed again as another contraction gripped my rounded belly.

Death grinned, his eyes glistening as he reached between my legs. "One more, Aster."

I pushed hard, delivering our tiny daughter into the protection of her father's hands.

"She's here," he said, wrapping her in the blanket I'd made for her.

He lifted her, placing her on my chest, and I held her carefully as tears of happiness, of contentment and love, filled me. "You're finally here." I kissed her. "Hello, Marigold."

I jolted awake, blinking into the darkness. I didn't move, barely breathed.

"What if they're not visions? What if they're something else?"

Again, Else's words filled my head, and the truth filled my heart.

They weren't visions—they were memories. When I dreamed of them, of the others, I was watching, but now when I dreamed of Aster, I wasn't just looking through her eyes; I *was* her.

As soon as the realization hit me, waves of energy crashed through my body. I cried out as my back arched, bowing against the strength of it.

"Zinnia!"

Jasmine's voice was muffled, drowned out as it all came back. Right from the beginning. In the night sky beside Death, Nox taking him away from me, turning him into flesh and blood. Missing him so much, my light began to dim. Finally being plucked from the sky, Nox standing over me, blood rushing through newly created veins.

Being reunited with Death. I'd been wearing the black gown, the fabric like fine cobwebs and made from night and shadows—the one Death ripped from me when he saw it. Nox had used it to hurt him, to taunt him. And it had, because my soul was connected to his, was created to be at his side.

I saw it all. Me, Death, and Marigold, how happy the three of us were together—but then something happened to me after her birth. I'd been afraid all the time, so very fragile. Nox reached out to me; she was in my ear, in my head, twisting my fragile mind, making me believe Death would hurt our daughter, hurt me.

I'd taken Marigold, and I'd run. Nox's demons had promised to take me to her, but it was only Marigold that Nox wanted. She'd been there the day at the cliffs. She ordered her demons to snatch Marigold from my back. She ordered them to push me over.

Oh goddess, I'd left him. Nox had somehow poisoned my mind, and I'd run from him.

I'd left Death.

I'd taken his daughter, and we'd left him all alone.

Death had raged at me, had been so full of anger toward me, because I'd left him in my first life, and he'd been protective to the point of controlling because he was terrified Nox and her demons would get to me again.

And he was furious because I didn't remember any of it—because I didn't remember him.

My soul had come back, over and over and over—but Death had never opened himself up again. My mind continued to feed me visions, so many all at once. I was staring through their eyes, the females that came after, the females I'd seen in my visions, their lives—their deaths.

In all of them, Death was in his cloak, drowning in darkness and rage, and in all the visions, the females housing my soul cringed away from him.

He never let me back into his heart or his bed—not until now.

Not until he found me.

Because Death was mine.

This time, it wasn't just reincarnation; this was rebirth. I'd been given another chance to get it all back, to get the love of my life back, to get my daughter back. Oh goddess, I wanted them back.

Death had been mine almost since the beginning of time. He looked at me, touched me, spoke to me like he knew me, because he did. He'd shown me the cave, the tree house, places we'd spent time loving each other, because he wanted me to remember. He raged at me, sometimes hated me, because I looked at him like a monster, like a stranger, the way I had after

I'd given birth to Marigold, after Nox had poisoned my mind, when we'd been everything to each other. Everything.

The world around me rushed back into focus. I was in my room, and Ren was laying me on my bed. Jasmine was leaning over me, eyes wide with fear.

"I'm not hurt," I said and pushed myself up. My heart ached, the feeling of loss unbearable. I missed my consort; I ached for him, and I ached for my child, locked in Death's temple, frozen in time. No, I hadn't birthed her— Aster had—*but I was Aster*. I was his Stella. We were one and the same. I flew out of bed.

"Zinnia? What's going on?"

I loved my sister, and she loved me, but she didn't need me, not anymore. She had Ren now, and as much as leaving her killed me, Death needed me; our daughter needed me. I forced myself to slow down, and I took her face in my hands. "There is so much I want to tell you, but it's... so big, too big. I don't know how. All I can say is, Death loves me so much, Jazzy, and I love him. We belong together. I have to go, and I don't know what happens next, but I might not be able to—"

"Don't say it." She gripped me tight. "I don't want you to leave." Tears welled in her eyes.

I swiped them away. "You're so strong, Jaz. You don't need me anymore." I glanced up at Ren. "You have your own family now."

"I'll always need you," she choked.

"And I'll always need you, and I promise, I'll find a way to reach you. I promise, but my family is waiting for me, and I have to go."

She wrapped her arms around me tight, and I clung to her, pouring a lifetime of love into my baby sister—a lifetime that I might have to miss. "Love you, Jazzy."

"Love you too, Zinny."

I looked at Ren again over her shoulder, and he nodded. He had this. He had her. I didn't need to worry; he would always have her back.

I pressed a kiss to the top of her head. "I need to pack."

"Okay." She smiled shakily. "But before you leave, I have something for you. Something you need to take home with you."

Half an hour later, I was watching Jasmine's car drive away and walking into Oldwood Forest. "Stay hidden," I said to Hemy.

I wasn't sure if Death's protection would still work, so I gripped my knife tight. I heard demons, saw several, but they didn't see me. Either he was expecting me, or he was hoping I'd come. I let that fill me with hope; I needed it, especially after our last encounter in my dreams.

When I walked into the clearing, a demon was sitting there, leaning against a tree near the pile of rocks and boulders that would form the gateway to Limbo. He was playing with his phone, snickering at whatever he was doing.

He didn't look up, didn't see me. With Death's protection surrounding me still, I should be able to walk right up, open it, and walk through, and he wouldn't be any the wiser. I'd seen demons here before—this wasn't unusual—but still I approached cautiously, watching him closely.

The demon, apart from the greenish tinge to his skin, looked fairly humanoid. He tapped something out on his phone with a grin. Still, he gave no sign that he saw me at all. He couldn't; Death had made sure of it. I don't know why I was feeling so anxious. Maybe because I was so close to being back with Death and Marigold that I was terrified something would go wrong.

I made a slice in my palm and lifted my hand to drip my blood onto the rocks and boulders that would form the gateway.

One moment, the demon was by the tree; the next, he'd grabbed my wrist and shoved something cold and hard onto one of my fingers. My blood hit the boulders a moment later, and I yelled the words to open the gate as I swiped my blade at him.

He released my wrist and shoved my hand away, backing up with a smirk. "A gift from Nox."

The gateway opened behind me as I looked down at the tarnished gold band now on my hand and watched in horror as it turned liquid and swirled around my finger, sinking into my flesh, into bone. I screamed as pain shot up my arm.

"Have fun," the demon said before he slammed his foot into my stomach, pushing me through the gateway.

I fell through, hitting the path hard. Cold immediately seeped into me, through me. I lay there, looking around. Something wasn't right. The forest smelled dank, like decay; the air was heavy with it. Mossy strands hung from the trees, and the feeling of dread and sorrow was so thick, it took everything in me not to curl in a ball and give in to it, to sob from the hopelessness that sank deeper inside me. This was what I felt when I first met Death; this was what radiated from him and twisted inside me when I'd first come here. For months, I'd felt this—but somehow, it was worse now, so much worse.

Get up. He needs you.

It physically hurt to move, but somehow, I pulled myself off the ground and got to my feet. Scanning the area, I realized this wasn't the path I usually walked along. This wasn't the way back to Death. I was somewhere else. In Limbo, but somewhere I'd never been before.

My finger throbbed, blood oozing from around the dull gold embedded in my flesh. Shaking out my hand, I grabbed my hunting knife from the ground beside me. Nox, the evil bitch, was the reason I died the first time. She'd stolen our daughter, and then her demons had killed me on her order. I forced myself to walk. Whatever she had in store for me, I would not let her win, not this time. The path ahead seemed endless, and I walked faster, faster, then broke into a run.

I ran and ran for so long, my legs were close to giving out, but I never got anywhere. The same trees, the same path—it all remained the same. I was getting nowhere. Panting, I stopped, looking around me.

Death always warned me to stay on the skull path. Nox wanted me to stray from it. She wasn't giving me any other choice. The goddess was dangerous, especially when she felt threatened, which meant I was close. I was close to breaking whatever curse she had on Death, and she wanted me gone for good.

Well, she wasn't going to win. I would not die, not this time, and I wouldn't abandon Death, not ever again.

Gripping my knife tight, I did the only thing I could. I stepped off the path—

And into a cottage.

The forest was gone, and I was in a room... filled with dolls.

Stumbling back, I knocked one off the shelf. What the actual fuck was this? Everything was pink and frilly, and there were dolls, weird leather-looking dolls, in different colored, lacy dresses covering every surface. Hemy wriggled against me through the bag. "Don't move. Stay where you are until I tell you to come out," I whispered.

He stilled immediately, doing as I said.

The door opened, and a man walked in. He was huge, dressed in dirty jeans and a grungy navy-and-black flannel shirt like a lumberjack. His gaze sliced to me, eyes widening.

I held up my hands. "I'm sorry. I'm not sure how I got here—"

"Who are you? Why are you with my babies?" he said, eyeing me suspiciously. "You can't have them," he yelled. "You can't have them!"

CHAPTER 28

Death

I'D WAITED at the gateway for fucking hours, feet rooted to the ground, willing it to open, for Zinnia to walk through.

But she hadn't come.

Gripping the edge of the window, I took in the forest below the castle. The decay was setting in, my despair turning Limbo back into the desolate, cold, and joyless nothing it had been before I finally found her and brought her home.

As I'd stood at the gateway, I'd told myself that maybe she got the days mixed up or the date, maybe she was hurt and couldn't make it. Night had turned to day, then back to night as the shadows swirled thicker around me, calling me back to darkness.

I'd finally forced myself to walk away, to come back to the castle, and I'd done the only thing I could, something I'd done more than once since she left this time, something I hated doing—I'd used Somnus to find her.

Zinnia hadn't been hurt—she just hadn't chosen me.

In my despair, I'd lain there, willing her to come, to me, to join me in the Dream Realm, and she had. She'd come to the castle, come to my room, and I'd taken her like a fucking monster, taking everything I could from her one last time. I hadn't let her talk, and I'd fed off her warmth, the feel of her skin, the smell of her hair, like a fucking leech. I'd absorbed it all—and then I'd released her.

I didn't want to hear her apologies or her regrets. I didn't want to hear the reasons she wouldn't be returning, so I hadn't given her the option.

Never again.

I couldn't do this again.

My Stella's soul was always meant to be with me, but only someone powerful and loyal and prepared to sacrifice it all to be with me could draw me from the cloak. Someone without fear. I thought Zinnia was that female; I believed it with everything in me. I still did, but that didn't matter if she didn't want me. I knew what would happen next if I'd kept her here. I knew what happened next because I'd seen it. I'd held the limp, bleeding, poisoned bodies in my hands. I'd buried them.

Still, before the darkness took me completely, before I let her go forever and my world went back to the cold and empty void it was before I brought Zinnia here, I had to be close to her just one more time. Just once more.

Striding down the hall, I walked into Somnus's room. My brother lay there peacefully. He let me use his power to reach her; he had for centuries. I was the only being he allowed near him while he slumbered after all he'd been through. I didn't want to use him again this way, but this would be the last time. The very last.

Lying on the bed beside my brother, I wrapped my hand around his, closed my eyes, and let the dreaming in.

Darkness swam around me, a whirlpool of images and sounds flashing past. I knew where to find Zinnia. As soon as Somnus told me she existed, finding her here had been as easy as breathing.

But this time, I was met with an empty void. Nothingness. As if she didn't exist anymore.

I knew this feeling from when she'd concealed herself from me the first time.

She'd done it again. She'd locked me out.

I roared into the void, the last tendrils of hope sinking to the bottom of the ocean of dreams around me, into the darkest depths, and vanishing without a trace. I sank with them, swallowed by the dark, unforgiving waves, letting the cold soak into my bones.

Mors sucked in his last gasping breath, filling his lungs with putrid water, until only Death remained.

›)› ◉ ‹(‹

Zinnia

796

"I don't want your, ah... babies," I said as the shock and alarm in his eyes turned to something else, something that made me try to step back once more, only to hit the shelf of dolls behind me again.

"Who sent you? You can't have them. They're mine. *They're mine!*" He swung wildly, taking me by surprise. His fist connected with the side of my head, and my legs gave out.

Everything went dark.

I woke tied to a chair in only my underwear, with odd shapes drawn all over me in permanent marker. I pulled at the ropes biting into my wrists and ankles, but they were too tight. This was his Limbo. This room or house of dolls and horror was the lumberjack's Limbo, and somehow, I'd just walked into it.

The chair scraped as I tried to fight my way out of my ropes while I frantically searched the room for Hemy. I couldn't get free. Panting, I looked down at one of the shapes, this one drawn on my thigh, the rest all butting up against one another as if he was trying to fit in as many of them on my available skin as possible. It kind of reminded me of when Daisy would sew. She'd lay out her piece of fabric and pin the pattern onto it, moving the thin tissue around to fit each piece as best as she could, so as not to waste any of her fabric. My gaze sliced around the room, and I took a better look at the dolls.

Oh fuck. They weren't made of leather—they were made of skin.

They were all made of *skin*.

This was some fucked-up *Silence of the Lambs* shit, and Nox had offered me up to the lumberjack so he could add to his doll collection. *Fucking bitch.* Hemy tore out from under my clothes in a pile on the floor, running to me. Thank the goddess he was okay.

Humming came from the next room, and so did footsteps moving around on a hardwood floor. He was about to come back in here and carve me up. I fought harder, trying to wriggle my hands out of the rope strapping them to the arms of the chair. I couldn't get free. "Fuck this. Stay back," I said to Hemy. My feet were on the floor, and I rocked forward, standing at a weird bent-over angle then, and ran back, crashing hard against the wall. One of the legs snapped. I slammed into the wall a second time as the door opened. More of the chair broke away. The lumberjack stormed in, carrying a massive knife.

"No!" he yelled, running at me.

I spun around as he reached me, slamming the broken chair into him with all my strength. He fell, and I crashed down on top of him. The chair collapsed completely, what was left of it breaking apart. I quickly rolled away and jumped to my feet, shaking off the now-loose ropes and broken wood.

The big male rolled to his hands and knees to get up.

"Hemy!" I called, spun, and ran from the room. Hemy darted ahead, leading me through the house, where more skin dolls filled every available space, to the dining room and down a long hall.

The lumberjack pounded after me, the knife still in his hand. "Come back," he yelled. "Come back."

Like fuck. Hemy led me into a kitchen.

A door.

The lumberjack exploded into the room behind me, and I dove for the door, twisting the handle, and threw myself out—

And hit a stone floor.

I was dressed again, and Hemlock was back in his bag. I tugged up my sleeve. The patterns on my skin were gone. I turned slowly, taking in the room. A TV was going on the opposite side, big couches were scattered around, and there was a pool table.

I was in the hellhounds' den, belowground in the common room. It looked a little different, but that's exactly where I was.

Scrambling off the floor, I gripped my knife. This was supposed to throw me off, make me drop my guard, but that wasn't happening.

"Who the fuck are you?" a deep, rough voice growled.

I spun around. A huge male with long hair and a scruffy beard stood there. Most definitely a hellhound.

His head tilted to the side, eyes narrowing. "Willow?"

I shook my head. "Her cousin. Zinnia." I gripped my knife tighter. "And who the fuck are you?"

He grinned, flashing white teeth and fangs. "Axton, a good friend of your cousin, and the alpha's right hand."

CHAPTER 29

Zinnia

THE MASSIVE HOUND was watching me closely.

I had no idea how long he'd been in Limbo, but I'd never heard anyone talk about him. The hounds spoke of the brothers they'd lost, but no one had ever mentioned a male named Axton. Because they were created by Lucifer; once their bodies were burned, their life forces should automatically go back to Hell. At least, that was the way it was supposed to work.

"Why are you here?" I asked him.

Nox had sent me here, to this hound, for a reason. Most likely to disarm me, maybe get me to drop my guard. Hellhounds were protective of females; they always said themselves that they worshipped them, which was why I'd been so surprised by the way Relic had treated that demon. It was so far out of character for him, for any hellhound.

His jaw worked. "I lost my head, sweetheart," he said, voice deep. "But none of my brothers were around to burn my body, so my life force was trapped here instead of going home." His shoulders kind of slumped. "Now I'm stuck here, walking around this fucking replica of our den alone."

Not only was that awful, it made logical sense as to why he was here. "I'm sorry," I said and meant it. Maybe Nox thought I'd feel so sorry for the hellhound, it would stop me in my tracks, or the comfort of the familiar would slow me down. She was wrong. Nothing would stop me. "I'm so sorry that happened to you, and if you tell me where your body is, maybe I'll be able to get a message back to War when I get out of here. They can find it, burn it. Free you from this place."

A smile transformed his handsome face. "You'd do that for me?" Like all the hounds, there was something compelling about him. They were all handsome in their own way.

"Of course. War's family, and that makes you family."

A roar came from behind him, followed by cheers and howls.

I lifted my knife. "What the hell is that? I thought you were here alone?"

His fingers curled into fists. "I am. But I can still hear them. Death taunts me. He lets me hear my brothers, but I can never find them."

That was torture. "I'll talk to Death. I'll ask him to make this more bearable for you until I can get my message to War."

"You have Death's ear?"

"I did... hopefully, I still do." Hopefully, he hadn't given up on me completely. I just needed to get to him. "I'm sorry you're stuck here like this, but I have to leave."

He shoved his fingers through his hair. "I get it... can you just... will you stay for a little while? I'm... I'm so lonely, Zinnia. So fucking lonely."

This male was War and Relic's brother; they loved him, no doubt missed him terribly. Maybe they didn't know he was dead? Maybe they just thought he'd left or was in Hell, serving Lucifer. The hounds all took turns controlling the demons there, spending time between Hell and Roxburgh. Whatever had happened, my heart ached for him. "Maybe... just for a little while."

His expression lightened, his smile returning.

"I can't stay long, though."

He nodded. "Of course." His gaze slid to the couch. "Can we just sit on the couch? I'm not trying to be a creep. I just want to feel someone close. I haven't been touched by another being in... in so long. Not trying to cop a feel, Zinnia. I just want a hug, yeah?"

Everything he'd told me was plausible, and with what I knew of the hounds, their feelings about females and their unwavering loyalty, I truly didn't think he wanted to hurt me. Hounds were devoid of certain emotions, but they were extremely tactile; they liked touch, needed it. It would've been torture for Axton without it and without his brothers. Yes, Nox was trying to slow me down, and staying here with Axton was playing right into her hands, but I could spare him ten minutes before I left. "Okay then."

He took a shuddery breath. "Thank you," he said, the sincerity in his voice clear. He walked to the couch, looking awkward, and it pulled at my heart strings.

So I sat and waved him forward. He closed the space between us and sat beside me; then he slid down, resting his head on my lap, and wrapped his arms around my middle with a sigh.

"Better?" I rubbed his back, and light glinted off the gold wrapped around my finger. It'd stopped bleeding, but it hurt like hell. It wasn't hard to work out that whatever it was had me trapped in this limbo loop. I just needed some time—time not being chased by insane lumberjacks or emotionally propping up lonely hellhounds—to figure out how to get it off.

"Fuck, this is... I needed this, thank you," he rasped.

"No problem." I gasped a little when he tightened his arms around me.

"Sorry," he muttered. "So have you spent much time at the clubhouse?"

"Yeah, when I'm in Roxburgh. Willow and War have a daughter now, and Wills has these movie nights for the hounds and anyone who wants to come along."

"Yeah?"

"Yeah, and Relic is a really good friend."

He snorted.

"What?"

"Relic's a piece of shit."

I blinked down at him, confused. The hounds didn't do that; they didn't talk shit about one another. They had disagreements, sure, but I'd never heard them say shit about each other, not like that. "You didn't get along?"

"Relic, like the others, thinks the sun shines out of the alpha's ass."

"You and War didn't get on? I thought you were his right hand?"

He shrugged. "Maybe I exaggerated. I should've been alpha."

Unease slid through me.

Axton's eyes drifted shut, and he breathed deep. He made a low groan, then breathed in again.

He was scenting me.

I glanced down, and my unease increased. His dick was straining against the zipper of his jeans. *Fuck.* Something was seriously wrong here. He was lying to me. If the hounds lost one of their own, if he was damaged beyond the possibility of healing, they'd find him and burn him and send him home. They were the best trackers around. I was an idiot. Why didn't I think of that? I'd looked at him, and I'd seen Relic and War and the other males I cared about; I imagined what it would have been like for one of them. If the hounds wanted to send him back to Hell, they wouldn't have stopped looking for him until they found him.

"Haven't been with a female in a long time, Zinnia. You know we need it. Making a hound go without fucking for as long as I have is the worst kind of torture. You'll let me fuck you, won't you? You'll be my bitch and get on all fours, won't you, witch?"

Fear sliced through me, but I made myself breathe easy. I had to play this carefully. "I'm Death's consort. He wouldn't like it if I was with anyone else."

He chuckled. "If you're his, then why are you here? Why hasn't he come for you? Nah, that's not it. You afraid of how big I am? A lot of females are. You'll only cry for a little while, but then I'll stretch you out, and you'll be fine."

I wanted to vomit. Now I knew why he was here. War had sent him here. "I have to admit, I've always wanted to sleep with a hound. Do you promise to be careful? At least to start with?"

He reached down and squeezed his hard-on. "Sure. I'll go easy if you let me call you Willow. You look like her with all that red hair. Been wanting to fist that hair for a long fucking time."

Fuck. Warrick most definitely sent him here on purpose.

"A bit weird for me, but sure, whatever floats your boat," I said. "Do you mind if I take a shower first? I've been traveling, so I feel pretty gross."

"I like you all dirty," he said roughly.

"I'll be quick."

He sat up, his fingers wrapping around my throat. "You try anything, and you'll pay, understand, Willow?"

"I understand, Ax—"

"War. You call me War or Warrick from now on."

Fuck. Fuck. Fuck. "Okay, War."

He smiled. "You know where my quarters are?"

I nodded.

"Shower, then get in bed on all fours and wait for me."

I nodded again.

He released me, and I got off the couch and forced myself not to run for the door.

"In case you were wondering, the stairs that lead out of the den aren't there," he said and grinned before I could walk through it. "Just in case you were wondering."

I shrugged. "Nope." What the fuck was I going to do? As I rushed down the hall, howls and cheers echoed around me, as if more hounds were here. It sounded so real. I broke into a run. Hemy poked his head out of the bag, a little hiss leaving him, sensing the danger.

"I'll get us out of here. I will," I said to him.

There had to be another way out. I didn't know why, but I ran toward those howls, the familiar sounds of the hounds I knew and loved. They led me to a pit. Willow had told me about it—a place where they trained, blew off steam, or settled any disagreements.

My feet paused at the door as a scene played out before me. Warrick and Axton were in the pit, and it was surrounded by hounds. Ren was there, and Willow as well. They looked so real, but when I tried to touch one of them, my hand went right through.

Warrick advanced, fisted Axton's hair, and dragged him to the edge of the pit, smashing his face into the charred packed-earth wall. Axton dropped to his hands, and War yanked his head back again.

The bravado had dropped from Axton's face, and he shook his head. "No... please, Alpha..."

"Fucking coward," Lothar said to Willow.

"I'll leave... I'll never come back," Axton said.

Warrick stared down at him. "You attacked my female, you made her bleed, and then you dared to challenge me. The former alone is enough for me to put you to death, and the latter you walked into willingly, knowing exactly what the consequences of defeat were."

"No... please..."

War snapped the other male's neck, then pulled a knife from his boot and hacked off his head.

"Jesus," Willow said.

"If he doesn't take his head, he could survive. We heal from most injuries," Jagger said to her.

The hounds gathered around the pit and lifted their hands palms up. Flames danced across their skin, licking over their thick fingers.

Warrick shook his head, and silence filled the room.

The hounds lowered their gazes as they curled their fingers into fists, extinguishing their fires. "What's going on?" Willow asked Jagger.

"Burning him would send him back to Hell. Leaving his body to rot means he will be in eternal limbo."

"I didn't think you had souls?"

"We don't, it's more our... life force, our essence, for want of a better term."

War met his brothers' eyes, one by one, rage rolling off him. "You lay your hands on my female, you dare touch what's mine, and I will fucking end you. You challenge me for head of this pack, you enter the pit prepared to fight to the death. You'll get no mercy here."

Growls and grunts of approval echoed around them.

Axton had attacked Willow and challenged War. If it were the challenge alone, he wouldn't be here, but attacking Willow had been his fatal mistake.

The scene flickered, and it started all over again, the cheers and howls filling the room.

I ran back the way I came, searching my mind, trying to remember everything Willow had said about the den. There would be another way out of here; there had to be.

Then I remembered something. When Wills was telling me about how she and War first got together, she told me about a door in Warrick's room that led up to the clubhouse that females would knock on, trying to get him to let them in. It had to be the way out.

Axton would be coming for me soon, so I had to be quick. I sprinted to War's quarters and shut myself in, throwing the bolt after me. It was heavy, strong, made to give a hellhound pause, but it wouldn't hold for long. Spinning back, I took in the room. This was how it was before War renovated, before he opened it up, combining several rooms for him, Wills, and Violet. Which meant less for me to search, thank fuck. I scanned every inch of exposed wall, but there was no door. Had all the doors been taken? Was that the real reason Nox had sent me here, because there was no way out?

There was a tall dresser against the wall; it looked built-in, but it was definitely big enough to cover a door. I rushed over, running my hands around the edge. Not built-in. I tried to shift it.

The door handle rattled. "Let me in, Willow," Axton said.

"Just a minute... War. I want everything perfect for you," I called back and threw my back into it. The dresser scraped against the floor. Hemlock hissed again, scurrying out of my bag and onto my shoulder.

"What are you doing in there?" he called.

Yes! A door. Thank fuck. "I'm making it nice. Now be patient," I called back, doing my best impersonation of Willow.

I shoved again, and it scraped forward some more.

"Open the fucking door. Now, Willow!" he roared and smashed against the heavy wood.

I dragged the dresser forward a bit more, enough for me to squeeze in behind. He crashed against the charred wood again, trying to break in. I tried the handle, but the door was locked. Cursing, I pulled out my knife and worked on the hinges while Axton roared and continued to slam against the door. Thank fuck it was made by hounds; any other door would have buckled instantly.

I got the first hinge out, and then the second came easily, but the last was wedged tight. I dug my blade in and smacked my palm against the handle of my knife over and over.

The door crashed open behind me as the last hinge gave. Hemy shrieked and hissed, and I slammed my shoulder into the door, and it dropped as the dresser went flying.

Axton roared and reached for me as I fell through—

My hands landed on damp grass. It was night, a false moon lighting the area enough that I could still see everything clearly. I was in a small clearing, surrounded by trees. Hemlock was on the grass beside me, and I scooped him up. "It's okay," I said and stood—bumping against something behind me. An iron gate. One that I'd seen before.

A shriek echoed through the trees, and then another one. The same sounds I'd heard when I'd seen Death with the undead.

Only this time, I was on the wrong side of the gate.

I slid my knife free, gripping it tight as more shrieks filled the night. There was movement in the shadows, slow, awkward movement. They were coming. Then, one by one, they shuffled forward. There were three of them, and as they got closer and I got a better look at them, flashes of memory assaulted me.

I knew them from my visions. They'd each housed my soul at some point—the females who had cringed away from Death when he'd brought them to the castle. He'd sensed my soul, but it hadn't been enough. For some reason, they hadn't been enough to draw him from the cloak.

They'd all suffered, never content, never complete, sad, alone, confused, always pining for something, for someone, and not knowing what it was. It was Death. He was the missing piece, but they never saw him, they never got to see beneath the cloak, and without him, they'd ended their own lives full of despair, and Death's hope had been shattered over and over again. He blamed himself, his guilt unbearable.

"Whether you return to me or not, the choice is yours, little witch. But I'm begging you... choose me over everything and everyone, over a life with them, over the possibility of death here with me."

"Choose me."

Death didn't see the shell, not really; he saw my soul, the only thing that could make him whole again, make us both whole again. I'd been with him since almost the dawn of time, taken from him over and over again. Then when he'd finally found me and I'd drawn him from the cloak, from the shadows, and he'd allowed himself to hope—I hadn't recognized him. I hadn't remembered the love we shared.

He'd been waiting, hoping I'd remember, but I hadn't.

Until now.

I looked up at the females around me. Empty shells somehow still here, trapped, probably until I broke Nox's curse.

This was torture.

I remembered every tragic life these females had led—that *I* had led.

There was only one way to end this, for them and me. I had to get to Death.

"It's time to set you free," I choked, pressing my hand into the grass and placing the tip of my blade to the base of my gold-wrapped finger. Gritting my teeth, I thrust the knife down on it with force—slicing my finger off with a cry.

Everything paused; the females blinked at me, not moving. Hemy squeaked, and then the world around me shifted—

I was back on the skull path, just inside the gateway.

Quickly grabbing a shirt from my pack, I tore it into strips and wrapped the bleeding stump where my finger had been; then I started down the path. This was the way home, finally. I recognized the forest, but it looked as dark and desolate as it had when I first arrived, and it felt the same as well. The horror and pain, the despair, it was all I could do to keep walking.

Hemy emerged from my pack, then scurried back in, feeling what I did.

We rounded the bend, and the castle came into view. It was like I was living out the dream I'd had. I walked quicker, breaking into a run, taking the steps to the main doors two at a time, shoving them open.

The air was punched from my lungs. It was dark and cold, a mess of broken furniture—and the floor was cracked from one side to the other.

Movement caught my eye. Egon. He lifted his head from where he sat in the shadows. He stared at me as if I were a hallucination.

"Egon?"

He jolted and shot to his feet. "My lady?"

"Where is he?"

"You've been gone... so very long." He shook his head. "It's too late. He's... my lord is not the male you left."

An awful feeling crawled through me. "How long? How long have I been gone?"

"In human time?"

I stilled. "Yes."

Sympathy filled his eyes. "Twelve months."

I rocked back, grabbing onto the broken table so I didn't fall down. "Twelve months? I've been gone a full year?" I choked, shaking my head. "I was here."

Egon twisted his fingers in front of himself. "He couldn't feel you... you were gone. He thought..." His gaze dropped to my forearm, where my scar was, where the tattoo the demon had given me to hide from Death had once been.

He thought I'd hidden from him? *Oh goddess, no.* "Is he in his room?" I choked.

The demon glanced up to the second floor. "It's too dangerous."

I took off, running up the stairs, ignoring Egon calling after me, and moved along the shadowed hall to his door. A year? How could that be? Flinging the door open, I rushed inside. It was dark, the air stale. It smelled like actual death. Like a corpse had been left to rot away to nothing, and now only bones and dust remained.

"Mors?" I rasped, walking deeper into the room, using his name that he'd forbidden me to use for so long because it hurt, it hurt to hear it from me when I didn't remember who he was.

Nothing.

I didn't need to search the room; I knew exactly where he was. He was on the bed, draped in his cloak, unmoving.

Biting my lip, I moved to his side. "I'm here. I've come back to you," I choked out.

Nothing.

"Mors."

His cloak swirled.

"Please, look at me."

Slowly, he lifted his head, then turned to me.

His hood slipped back, and I swallowed down a cry of agony. His face was skin stretched over bone. There was barely anything left of him.

Then he opened his mouth and roared.

CHAPTER 30

Zinnia

THE FORCE of his rage had me cowering, his roar so loud, the windows rattled. The sounds of the forest went silent.

He stared blindly ahead, not seeing me, so lost in his despair and rage, he saw nothing else.

"It's me, Zinnia... your Stella," I choked out. "Mors, it's me."

He blinked, his gaze clearing just for a moment.

I cupped his skeletal face. "I came back."

One of his hands snapped out, and he caught me by the throat, his face contorting. "You left," he said, his voice rolling through the room like thunder, lifting the hair on the back of my neck.

I shook my head. "I'm right here. Your beloved. Look at me, please. I'm right here."

He snarled, his head moving in an odd way before he lurched forward, yanked me onto the bed, and shoved me down. I lay still while he loomed over me, searching my face, his features contorted in rage. "Stupid little witch," he said in a voice that sent ice down my spine. "You should never have come back here, because I will never let you leave. Whatever deal we had is void." There was nothing but rage in his voice.

He had completely reverted to the male he was when I first came here—

I felt it—but worse. He was so hollow, like a husk of himself. Mors was buried deep beneath the surface, and Death was fully in the driver seat.

I reached up to touch his face again. "Mors—"

"Do not call me that," he snarled. "I am the God of Death."

"And I am your consort," I said softy. "Yours."

He shook his head. "You never came back."

"I did. I'm right here. You have to believe me. I came back, but—"

One moment, he was looming over me; the next, he was up, hauling me off the bed. He slammed open the door, dragged me down the hall and into my old room. "Stay out of my way." He shoved me inside and walked away, leaving me to be forgotten like the others, so deep in the cloak, so deep in denial.

I wasn't giving up; I would bring him back. He said he'd let the cloak take him if I left, but the darkness and shadows couldn't have him. He was mine.

I grabbed the dresser to hold myself up, a rush of dizziness making my limbs weak.

"My lady?"

Egon stood at the door, his face etched in concern. I held up my hand. "I've lost some blood. How good are you with a needle and thread?"

Color drained from his face. "You're injured. Sit. I'll return momentarily."

Sitting heavily on the bed, I rubbed my hand over my face. I needed rest for the fight ahead. I would bring him back one battle at a time until I won the war. I had to; anything else was unacceptable.

Egon rushed back in with his basket of healing supplies, and I carefully unwrapped my hand.

The demon gasped. "What happened?"

"I cut it off. It was the only way to get back to him," I said, pain radiating up my entire arm. "There's some balm in my pack. Use it after you sew it up."

Egon nodded, mixing a tincture with a sedative and antibiotic herbs to prevent infection. He handed it to me, and I gulped it back, then lay down and gave in to the tiredness. I was back. I'd made it back to him.

I woke in the early hours of the morning drenched in sweat and shivering. The tincture hadn't worked. Egon had sewn me up and used the balm, but my hand was tight, obviously swollen. Infection had set in, and I had a fever. I struggled to regain consciousness, but it was impossible.

"My lady?" Egon was sitting beside the bed. He quickly got up and lifted my head, spooning a tonic into my mouth. I felt him unwrap my hand, checking it; then the scent of Else's healing balm reached me, and I instantly missed her again. Tears welled in my eyes before the tiredness took over again.

Death

Noises were coming from downstairs. Banging and crashing and talking. Shoving myself up off the bed, I strode to the door and flung it open. Whoever the fuck was disturbing my peace would pay with their head.

I reached the bottom of the stairs and stopped, surprised at what I saw.

Egon had ignored my order to leave the castle as it was and to remove himself and leave me here alone to rot.

Instead, he'd allowed more people into my home, and they were cleaning the destruction I'd caused in the main room and, by the sounds of it, in several other parts of the castle as well. "Egon," I roared.

Egon rushed by, ignoring me, carrying a bowl full of something strong smelling.

I grabbed his shoulder, stopping him, fighting back the savage rage that lived inside me now, that had returned stronger than ever before. "What the fuck are you still doing here? And why are all these people in my home? I want everyone gone." I wanted to be left alone.

He looked up at me stubbornly. The demon had been with me for centuries, and never once in all that time had he given me so much as a look of defiance, but that was what I was looking at now. "Do not test me, demon. You will do as you are told."

Egon squared his shoulders. "I will not. Her ladyship is unwell. I won't leave her in that state, and I will not allow her to live in squalor."

Every muscle in my body seized, razor blades eviscerating my insides. *Her ladyship?* A snarl was torn from me. "Do not mention her in my presence again. She made her choice. You are delusional. That female is never returning, now leave."

Egon blinked up at me several times. "Are you so deep in darkness that you do not know a dream from reality? She has returned. She returned last night." He rushed past. "Come and see for yourself if you don't believe me."

He was wrong. It was only a dream. She came home in my dreams, in my fucking nightmares. I had them every night. I shook my head, trying to clear it. Was I still asleep? Was this some sick trick of my warped mind? I shook my head again, forcefully, but I didn't wake, because I already was. And even though I tried to resist because what he said wasn't true, it couldn't be true, I stormed after Egon, up the stairs and to her old room— where I'd thrown her last night, *in a fucking dream.*

The door was open, and Egon was murmuring softly. "Please swallow, my lady. You need to drink this."

I rounded the door—and an invisible fist slammed into my chest. "No... it was a dream," I choked. "I'm still dreaming."

"It is not," Egon said. "Now help me. She's fighting an infection, and she's far too hot. I need you to hold her up so I can feed her some of my tonic."

I grabbed for the door as my legs buckled beneath me. She was here. She was in her bed, in my castle.

I didn't trust this. How could I trust this? "What the fuck is this? Why is she here now?"

"You will have to ask her that yourself, but if you don't help me now, she may die. She's strong, but we could still lose her. So either stand there and stare and let her die, or get over here and help me."

I lurched forward, and my throat grew so fucking tight, I was struggling to breathe. "Where is she hurt?"

Egon motioned her bandaged hand. "She lost a finger," he said as I carefully lifted her head for Egon to spoon some of his tonic into her mouth.

"How?"

"She cut it off herself with an unwashed blade. She said she did it to get back to you."

I stared down at her, desperately trying to swallow. A snarl curled my lip in disbelief even as my heart thumped hard in my chest. "This is a lie."

Egon growled, surprising me again. "She is right there, my lord. In your arms. You have lost her so many times—I was here with you, and I know what that did to you—but, my lord, this time, she has returned. She came back..." He swallowed audibly. "She chose you."

)))·◉·(((

Zinnia

I blinked up into Death's emaciated face. My sight swam, and my body ached. He stared at me, gaze hard. He took my wounded hand in his and lifted it. I tried to speak, to say something, but I was too damn weak. Then my eyelids were too heavy, and I let them slide shut.

When I woke again, a scream pierced the room. It went on and on. I wanted it to stop, but then I realized the scream was coming from me. Stabbing pain radiated through my body, and my limbs were so heavy, and I was so hot, so incredibly hot. I kicked at the covers. The T-shirt I was wearing was soaked, plastered to my skin. Egon was there; he held a straw to my lips, and I drank the cool water before my vision went dark and I was submerged again.

The next time I woke, I was so cold, my teeth chattered. I was in water. There was something hot against my back, surrounding me. The cold water stung so badly, I sobbed and begged for it to stop. A deep voice rolled over me. It was comforting, insistent, but the cold remained. They held me in the water until I thought I might die.

My eyes blinked open again. It was dark, the fire crackling and flickering across the room, bathing it in a muted orange glow. I was in my room at the castle. Lifting my hand, I looked at the bandages and wriggled the fingers I still had. The swelling had gone down. I'd beaten the infection.

"How do you feel?"

My head twisted to the chair beside me. I couldn't see him, but Death sat there, watching me from the shadows. "A lot better."

"Any pain?"

"Nothing I can't handle." The stabbing pain through my body was still there—no, not as sharp as before, but still very much there. I wasn't going to tell Death that, though, not yet. To him, I'd been gone a year. He felt betrayed, abandoned. I didn't want him to hold back or hide what he was feeling because he was concerned for me or thought me still in the throes of a fever and confused.

"Why are you here?" he asked coldly.

I pushed myself up. It was hard, but again, I refused to show him any weakness in this moment. "I'm here because this is where I belong, with my consort."

He went utterly still. "You expect me to believe you suddenly woke up one morning and decided you wanted to be with me?"

His voice was deep and broken and chilled me to the bone. I shifted under the covers so I was facing him, even though I still couldn't see his face. "To you, I've been gone a year. For me, only a month and eight days have passed since I left here."

"Is that right?"

He didn't believe me. "Yes." I slid my legs out from under the covers and pressed my feet to the cool stone floor. "I sent you a message that I'd be late. Magnolia said she got through to Lyle."

"I received no message, witch."

"Else was dying. I couldn't leave her or my family, so I stayed until she passed." I slid to the edge of the bed. "The night of her funeral... I finally learned the truth."

"What truth?" he said harshly.

"I lay in a field after her burial, and I slept." I eased off the bed. "I had visions of you... of us..." I swallowed, emotion clogging my throat. "All the things you wanted to tell me but couldn't. That you desperately wanted me to remember—"

"Lies," he snarled.

I ignored him and kept talking. "I was in the night sky... but then you left me all alone, and I missed you so much. Nox created me. She gifted me to you. We were so happy. I saw my belly swollen with our daughter, saw you take her in your arms when I gave birth to her." I stepped closer. "I remember, Mors. I remember everything. Every single life I had without you after that because I didn't know, because I didn't remember that you and Marigold are *everything* to me." I closed the space between us and reached into the shadows of his cloak, cupping his hollow face. "Every time I didn't choose you." I moved in between his legs. "But I know now, I remember, and I choose you, my love—"

He snarled and snatched my hand away from his face. Gripping my wrist, he stood. He backed me up until we stood in front of the fire. I didn't fight as he gripped my jaw and stared deep into my eyes. No, I wanted him to see the truth, to see me. His hand curled around the back of my head and his face went to my throat. I held still as he pressed his nose to my skin and dragged it up, breathing deep.

My pulse raced wildly. "Death..."

He pulled away suddenly, flinching, and a look transformed his face, like he'd been sucker-punched—pain, sharp and fierce filled his eyes, followed by brutal disappointment—then rage. "You are a liar, an imposter." He bared his teeth. "When I look into your hollow eyes, now that I finally can, I see nothing. I feel nothing. You don't even smell like Zinnia." His mouth twisted. "It's a good likeness, I'll give you that. You almost had me fooled there for a moment. Nox outdid herself this time, but you have no soul, creature. You're an imposter—"

"I'm not an imposter. I have a soul... It's me—"

"Zinnia has been gone an entire year. She left, she concealed herself from me, and she ran."

"I was trapped going from one damned soul to the next, trapped in the worlds you created for them. I couldn't get out—"

"Lies," he roared again. "You are one of Nox's creatures sent to torment me."

He searched my eyes again, and hatred flashed down at me. He truly didn't see me; something was stopping him from *seeing me*.

"Egon," Death yelled.

The demon open the door. "My lord?"

"Choose four demons to escort Nox's creature back to her. I won't have her here."

"But, my lord—"

"Do as I say."

"I won't do it," he said.

Death snarled and flung his hand out, slamming the door and shutting Egon out. I stared up at Death, begging him to see me. "How do I know everything I just told you? How can I know those things if I'm something Nox created?"

"Nox knows exactly what happened, and she has spies everywhere, as you well know," he bit out.

"You're wrong," I said, trying to pull from his hold. "Look at me."

He shook me brutally. "All I see when I look at you is a lie. Be thankful I don't just end you here and now. The only reason I'm letting you live is so you can deliver a message."

"What message?"

"She will never win." Then he dragged me to the door, flung it open, towed me along the hall and down the stairs. There was a group of demons sweeping the floor, and Death ordered them to come to him.

Four of them rushed over, and Death shoved me at them. "Take her to the Night Realm and deliver her to Nox. I want her gone tonight."

They instantly obeyed, towing me from the main room in only a T-shirt and underwear, my feet bare and fresh blood oozing from my bandage.

I called for Mors, but he did nothing, he said nothing.

He let them take me.

The demons dragged me from the castle and into the night.

CHAPTER 31

Death

I STOOD OUTSIDE, listening to the sounds of the night. There had been no light here for a year, only darkness. My realm was part of me, and I felt as black and cold inside as it was out here.

Nox lived to cause me pain. How could you despise your children so much? I would give anything to have Marigold with me, to end the curse my twisted bitch of a mother put on me and have her back. Sometimes, just the thought of my daughter shattered me into a million pieces. If it weren't for Somnus taking care of her, I would have lost my mind long ago.

But that wasn't enough for Nox; no, she wanted to destroy me in every way possible. Her curse had blocked Zinnia's soul from remembering me, from remembering us and our life together, and had bound Magnolia to her realm.

Surrounded by her demons, Nox sat in her temple plotting ways to fuck with me. She'd even gone as far as creating a soulless creature to impersonate the only female I had ever wanted—the mother of my child—and make me think the end of the curse was near, that I could have my family back with me like we'd once been.

Another god more malicious and evil didn't exist.

I strode back inside, and even though I told myself not to, I stopped at Zinnia's bedroom door. My Zinnia. When I first saw her when she was only fifteen years old, something had reached through the shadows and tugged sharply. Her soul had been back many times before. Somnus would find her, would take me to her, and I'd bring them back to the castle. But none of them had been able to reach me; they'd cringed away in fear, in horror. And I'd stayed in the shadows, trapped in darkness.

Zinnia wasn't just a vessel for her soul; she and Aster were one and the same. Zinnia hadn't been second best or a replacement for the female I'd lost; she *was* my beloved. And somehow, I loved her more now than I ever had. My soul had ached for hers. We were meant to walk side by side, but again, she'd run from me. Nox had cursed me to be alone, which meant she would always run from me. I would always lose her.

On our journey to the Outer Realm, I'd taken her to the cave we'd lived in together so very long ago, then to the tree house where we'd spent countless hours in each other's arms, but nothing had worked, not the castle, or the bedroom she'd slept in when she first came here, not Egon, and not me, nothing had made her remember.

All she had to do was *fucking remember*, and the curse would be broken. Just remember she loved me, choose to be with me of her own free will, and we'd be together again and our daughter would finally be released from Nox's grip.

My hand lifted, curling around the door handle to her room. The demons had dragged that creature from my castle the day before, and I was still shaken. For a moment, I'd truly believed she was back, that she wanted me. I realized now that was an impossibility.

Walk away.

My feet wouldn't move, wouldn't carry me away to my own room, where I would lie back down and let myself waste away for eternity. I stared at the door. I shouldn't go in there; it would do no good to surround myself with her things, with the shadows of her existence here with me. But I couldn't stop myself. I turned the handle and shoved the door open.

Something darted across the room—something white. It flew toward me, trying to escape. I scooped it up, lifting it higher to get a good look at the rodent.

Nox had actually gone as far as creating a familiar for her creature? It squeaked and wriggled in my hand frantically, trying to get away.

I gritted my teeth, and tightened my grip, about to squeeze, about to tear it to pieces and have this be over with, but it stilled suddenly, staring at me, its little nose twitching. Bringing it closer, I stared into its tiny black eyes, reaching inside the soulless creature—

I froze. "How do you have a soul?"

He squeaked again.

"Hemlock?" I choked.

He squeaked again and started wriggling frantically. I loosened my grip, and he scurried up my arm and down my side, then ran to the pack sitting on the ground. He scrambled inside... and then something was tossed out. I picked it up. A finger—Zinnia's finger—and it was wrapped in enchanted gold. Fuck, embedded in the flesh. Only the gods had access to this; it would poison whoever it touched, conceal them—shroud their soul.

No.

I spun around, and my gaze landed on a small pot sitting on the dresser. A plant of some kind. I strode over to it. No, an herb covered with tiny purple flowers. *Vervain.* I remembered the way Zinnia had described it when I was with her in her garden. She'd brought it with her. She'd brought it here because she wanted to make this her home—because she'd chosen me.

A tiny wooden box sat beside the bed, I'd seen it before, after she'd left, but thought nothing of it. She'd touched it; I felt her. Picking it up now, I opened it. There was a piece of paper inside. I unfolded it.

If you're reading this, you're one of the lucky ones. Fate chose you to be his. I know it doesn't feel that way now, and I know you're scared, but take my advice— don't waste time being afraid. Instead, make the most of whatever time you have with him. Love him.

Zinnia, consort to Mors, the God of Death.

"Zinnia," I choked out. She'd come back for me, and I'd sent her away.

Scooping up Hemlock and Zinnia's things, I ran from the room and pounded down the stairs.

"My lord?" Egon said.

"I'm going after Zinnia."

"Thank the gods."

I rushed out of the castle and whistled loudly. A moment later, Raze and Zuri ran from the trees. Egon was already at my side with the girth straps and bridles we'd need, and Lyle rushed out with provisions and strapped them to Zuri while I swung up onto Raze. Lyle was shaking, and there were tears in his eyes.

Then I remembered what Zinnia said. "Look at me, Lyle."

He trembled harder but did as he was told. "You were approached by one of my reapers, given a message, weren't you?"

He nodded, and tears spilled down his cheeks.

Fuck. "Why didn't you tell me? Why would you keep it from me?"

"Nox," he choked out. "One of her demons threatened to hurt my mate and my son. He said he was always watching. He saw the reaper, he knew what the message was, and he said I wasn't to tell you, or he'd kill them."

Egon growled. "You betrayed his lordship? What were you thinking?"

"Where is the demon now?" I asked.

"H-he lives in the forest."

"I'll take care of the demon," Egon said, fury in his eyes.

"And you," I said to Lyle, "you will not leave the castle until I return, and you better pray that her ladyship is alive." Because if she wasn't, I would tear Limbo apart. I would destroy it, balance be damned. I would throw the universe into chaos until I found her again.

He spun and ran inside.

"I'll make sure he doesn't leave," Egon said and straightened his shoulders, fighting back his own emotions.

I gave the older demon a nod and nudged Raze. He took off, Zuri right behind him.

They had a day's head start. I wasn't stopping until I reached my consort.

›)›·●·(‹‹

Zinnia

We'd spent the night out in the forest. The demons had placed some kind of icons around our camp to prevent anything from attacking us. It'd worked, but the farther away from the castle we got, the creepier they seemed to get, and I realized it wasn't what skulked in the forest that I really needed to be worried about.

The four of them watched me now, and one of them actually wiped drool from the corner of his mouth while he did it.

"Why does Death send you to his mother?" he asked. "Why does his lordship want you banished from his realm?"

"We should get going," I said and winced as I stood. My feet were all cut up, and I was frozen to the bone. Moving meant they were distracted. Moving meant they had other things to focus on than me. I needed them to get me through this forest, and then I could figure out what to do next. I was a sitting duck on my own, and the pain from the fever still had me weakened and struggling. Add in the cold, and my magic was seriously weakened as well. I wasn't going to fight these assholes until we were close to the tree house Death had taken me to, if it was still there. I was counting on it still being there. I was pretty sure I knew where it was. I'd be able to rest up there, get warm, then work out my next step before I made my way back to the castle.

I would make Death listen to me.

The pain in my limbs intensified, and my core temperature changed so suddenly, my heart jumped in my chest. I wasn't shivering anymore; I was sweating. When the demons around me spoke, I could see their breath on the cold air. The last thing I should be was hot.

My fever was coming back. "We need to move," I said, because it was only a matter of time before my magic was completely gone and I was delirious, possibly unconscious, and utterly at the mercy of these demons, who didn't know the meaning of the word.

"We'll move when we're good and ready, female," another demon said.

"Your master told you to deliver me to Nox. Perhaps you should do as you're told," I said, trying to insert authority into my voice—not easy when I was standing in only a T-shirt with sweat dripping down my face.

"He's not here, though, is he? He won't give you a second thought now that he knows you're an imposter. He and his mother don't exactly talk, so how will he know if you make it to the Night Realm or not?"

"Death knows everything, and you'd be fools to cross him." I tried to keep the fear from my voice while I called on my weakened magic, letting it build and swirl inside me. They weren't going to leave me any other choice but to fight them here. *Shit.*

"Death has forgotten you exist. There's only one female he wants, and you're not her. The moment we left with you, he forgot all about you." The demon stood and cracked his neck. "I'm not really in the mood to journey all the way to the Night Realm. What about you?" he asked his friend.

The drooling one stood, swiping his nose with the back of his hand. "Nah, I'd rather stay here."

Grunting their agreement, the others stood as well.

I lifted my hands and called on the anger burning in my gut. "You want to know what I am?" I said as flames appeared, dancing above my palms. "A witch. A witch who has killed more than her fair share of demons. Come any closer, and I will incinerate you." Maybe I could brazen this out, make them believe I was at full power and send them running.

A wave of pain washed through me, and I stumbled to the right. The drooler lunged, and I sent a bolt of fire at him, setting his feet on fire. *Shit.*

He stomped and cursed while his buddies laughed it up.

I was trying to set the asshole on fire, not just singe his shoe leather. I was screwed.

"Is that all you got, witch?" one of the demons said, chuckling.

"No, that was just a warning. Now back the fuck up, or I'll burn you to a crisp," I said through clenched teeth, fighting to stay conscious.

He grabbed the demon closest to him by the back of the shirt and threw him toward me.

With a cry, I fired my power at him. His shirt ignited, and he yanked it off and stomped it out. They all laughed again and rushed me. Screaming, I called on every bit of magic I had left and let it rush from me with force. The demons were knocked back, but they jumped back up. If I'd been at full power, I would have blown them yards way. If I'd been at full power, I would have set them all on fire and removed their heads one at a time.

As it was, I could barely stand.

They came running back, and I tried to fight. I swung and kicked and bit and scratched, but there were four of them. They overpowered me, slamming me into the ground. The air was knocked from my lungs, and I fought for breath as they pinned me down.

One minute, one of the demons was looming over me, trying to shove his disgusting body between my legs; the next, the ground was shaking and the demon was flying through the air. The earth cracked and branches snapped. I rolled, pushing myself up so I was sitting. The demons were screaming, suspended five feet in the air, backs bowed, heads tilted up, arms and legs thrust back. Death sat on the back of Raze, his hand lifted and aimed at them, rage contorting his emaciated face.

He climbed off Raze and walked over to them. His hand was black and he reached up and grabbed the first demon by the throat. The demon screamed as blood poured from his mouth, brain matter slid from his ears, and then he disintegrated, turning to ash. The others screamed in terror as he gave them all the same treatment one by one.

Then, finally, when nothing but ash remained, his gaze slid to me.

I couldn't read his expression. I didn't know what he was thinking or feeling.

Unsteadily, I climbed to my feet.

Death started walking, his cloak opening, flowing behind him, and in only a pair of trousers, I saw just how much damage he'd done to himself. He was skin and bone. He didn't stop until he was standing in front of me. So incredibly tall, he towered over me. I tilted my head back. "Mors...."

He lifted his blackened hand and held it in front of my face. I tried to jerk back, but he grabbed me with the other one, holding me in place. Power flowed into me from his palm, and I felt it tug on something, something foreign, something that shouldn't be there. My mouth opened on a cry as it was drawn out, as Death manipulated it in midair, then flung it on the ground. A golden liquid. I watched as it ran together, forming a mass that hardened into solid gold.

"What was that?" I gasped, looking up at Death.

"Enchanted gold. It's poisonous unless you're a god," he said, staring into my eyes, searching.

"Mors?"

He flinched, then dropped to his knees. Trembling, he wrapped his thin body around me. "Forgive me," he choked out. "Forgive me, my love."

My heart pounded in my chest as I slid my hands under his hood and slipped it off. It dropped, and I tilted his head back, exposing his drawn face and the agony shining from his blue eyes. "You see me?" I asked.

"I see the past and the future. I see my heart in your eyes and my soul sitting in the palm of your hand." He stared deeper into my eyes. "I see you, my perfect, feisty, incredibly powerful witch, and I see your soul, a soul that is more familiar to me than the stars in the sky. I see the life we shared together, the loss, the heartache, and the joy. You have been mine since the dawn of creation. I see you, my love, and finally..." His throat worked, and a tear slid down his sunken-in cheek. "You see me too."

Tears welled in my eyes, and I leaned down, pressing my lips to his. They were cool, not hot like they usually were. "How can I help you?" I rasped.

"Kiss me again," he choked out. "The more I'm in your presence—the more you look at me like that, talk to me, touch me—the more I will be pulled from the shadows."

When I first came to Limbo, he'd stayed concealed because, under his cloak, he'd wasted away. That was why he'd finally been able to go without it, because I'd been with him long enough that he'd been restored. I lowered myself to the ground in front of him and pressed my body to his.

"Are you hurt, love? Did they hurt you?" he said in a pained voice.

I shook my head. "I'm not hurt."

His mouth slid down the side of my cheek, seeking my mouth, and I turned toward him, offering it to him. He kissed me again, deeper, more urgently. I shivered, and he surrounded us with his cloak, in his dark, rich, smooth scent. Warmth washed over me, the world around us disappearing. We were no longer in the forest; we were in the night sky, stars blinking above. Death lowered me to the ground, and it was like I was lying on the softest mattress.

"I need you," I whispered against his lips.

"You have me, my beautiful consort, for an eternity."

"Eternity?"

"Not even death can reach you now. You will forever be by my side."

Finally, I got my forever with the love of my life. "When they tore our daughter from my back and I fell to my death, I vowed to return to you." My hands trembled as I touched his face. "I'm sorry it's taken me so long."

He made an agonized sound. "No one will ever take you from me again."

I ran my hands up his back, my fingers sliding over his cool skin, feeling every rib, every bone on his skeletal form. I held him closer, running my hands over him, touching him, whispering to him, doing whatever I needed to heal him, to bring every part of him back to me.

I kissed him more fiercely. "I love you," I said as tears slid down my cheeks. "I've missed you." A sob left me. "I didn't know how much, but now I do, and it hurts so much that I've been parted from you for so long."

He groaned. "Time was stolen from us, but our love transcends all. What we share will survive even the end of times."

He slid my shirt up and off, his cold, trembling hands moving over my breasts. I reached between us and shoved down my underwear, kicking them aside, then quickly undid his pants and took him in my hand. His narrow hips moved between mine as I led him to me, wrapping my legs around his waist.

"My love," he groaned as he slid inside me, filling me.

We moved together under the shadows and stars of his cloak, and with every glide of my hand down his back, I felt him transform. My beautiful Death. He was perfect to me no matter how he looked. When he stared into my eyes, he saw the soul beneath, and I did as well. But when he thrust into me next, the sharpness of his bones under skin had been replaced by flesh and muscle. He wasn't cold anymore; he was so incredibly warm.

He moved faster, and I rocked with him, lifting my hips, crying out when he hit me so deep. He moaned my name against my ear, and I clung to him as he claimed me, as we were reunited again, just two more stars in the sky.

I came with a sob, shaking and clinging to him as he groaned, coming with me.

Panting, we lay in each other's arms.

He rose up, staring down at me, sliding the tip of his finger along my hairline and down the side of my face. "This was destined. You made it so," he said roughly, and then his hand went to his chest, right over the three stars tattooed there. "I've been waiting so long to have you back, my little witch, my Zinnia... and our Marigold."

He'd carried us on his chest, me and Marigold, a part of him, surrounded by him, and now I knew what the constant ache in mine was. It was them. "Let's go and get our daughter."

CHAPTER 32

Zinnia

THE PASS over the Night Sea had been rough as hell. Thankfully, things had calmed, and I breathed in the ocean air as Mors gently held my wrist while he carefully worked the glove he'd made me over my hand. I'd slathered the wound with numbing balm and padded it. It was still raw and hurt like hell more often than not, but the balm was helping. I'd work on healing it properly when we got back to the castle. For now, I needed to be ready for whatever waited for us. I needed to be able to hold my knife and use my magic. I had to be ready to fight.

"How does that feel?" he asked.

I wriggled my remaining fingers and thumb, then pulled out my knife, gripping it. "Feels good."

"Your goal when we hit land is to stay alive at all costs, understand?" he said roughly. "You get yourself killed again, and I'll be seriously pissed off."

He said it lightly, but the depth of fear in his eyes told the truth. "I'm not going to die." I didn't want to hurt him, but I had to ask, "What will happen to the others, the undead?"

"They rose when you came to Limbo. They felt it, your soul, and were drawn to it. It was part of Nox's twisted curse. They will finally be at peace now that it's broken." He shook his head, pain in his eyes. "I failed them," he choked out. "They suffered, and I didn't know how to help them."

823

Which was why Alga had screamed "give it back" at me. She'd wanted her soul back, her life back. "None of this is your fault. Nox is responsible for all of it."

"I was so desperate to have you back that when Somnus found your soul, I couldn't resist it. I was deep in the cloak, lost in the dark, and three times, I took innocent females from their worlds and brought them to the castle, only thinking of my own pain, desperate to get you and Marigold back... but it was never right, and because of that, none of them were able to draw me from the cloak. So I stayed in darkness. I ignored them, neglected them. I didn't protect them like I should have. None of those females were strong enough to house such a powerful soul—a soul they never should have been given—and they were driven to madness by it. They ended their own lives."

"So you stopped looking."

He nodded. "Somnus found your soul again and again, and I refused to bring them to the castle only to watch them suffer the same." Pain filled his eyes. "Feeling you so close but not being able to reach you, hurting innocent females over and over again... I couldn't do it anymore. Then Som found you, and something was... different. For the first time in centuries, I let him take me to you, and as soon as I felt your presence, as soon as I saw you, I knew you were the one, that this time was different. But you vanished completely, and I didn't know what the fuck to do. Then I sensed some kind of connection to you in your cousin and I thought you had somehow disguised yourself... or fuck, I don't know, but I was drawn to her soul because of you, desperate for you, and when you finally revealed yourself to me, it was the happiest and most terrifying day of my long existence." His gaze stayed steady on me. "So I need you to promise me that you won't leave me again."

"I promise. You have nothing to worry about. My magic is at full power. I feel strong, strong enough to keep both myself and our daughter alive if it comes to that."

Those magnetic blue eyes met mine, and there was no missing the concern. "It can't be easy navigating the female you once were with the one you are now. If this starts to feel like too much, if you're struggling to cope with all that's changed or you get scared and feel the urge to run from me—"

I pressed my hand to his chest. "I'm not going anywhere. Yes, I'm Aster, the female you loved, the female who gave birth to our daughter, and everything she was—her thoughts and feelings—they're mine now. But I'm also Zinnia, a powerful witch, a Thornheart, and Jasmine's big sister. I don't know how to explain it other than for the first time in my entire life, and that includes my very first life, I feel whole, as if a missing piece of me has been returned. Like this was how it was always meant to be." I slid my hand up to the side of his throat. "I'm stronger now in every way. Stronger than I've ever been. This life has made me stronger. Before, I was born fully grown. I was naïve, I trusted too easily, and didn't understand the world I'd been thrust into. Nox could never get in my head now like she did back then, and I will never, ever willingly leave you, understand?"

His fingers delved into my hair, and he pressed a kiss to my forehead. "Okay."

"Okay," I said.

He released a rough breath. "As strong as you are, you leave Nox to me. Don't engage with her. Don't let her goad you into an attack. She lost. The curse was broken when you came back to me of your own free will. She has to let us get Marigold and leave." He tucked my hair behind my ear and slid his thumb along my jaw.

"But she won't," I said. "That's what's supposed to happen when the curse is broken, but it won't be that easy."

"No, it won't. My mother hates to lose. She has nothing left, nothing to amuse herself but hurting others. She lost her humanity a long time ago, and to her, this is a game. Entertainment." He shook his head. "Until she realizes she's lost, and then things will get really dangerous."

I squared my shoulders. "I won't let her tear us apart again. I won't let her do it."

Shadows swirled around him. "Neither will I."

I turned, looking toward land. Nox's temple stood in the distance, glinting under the moon. "Do you think she knows we're coming?"

He wrapped his arms around me. "Count on it."

When we were close enough, we dropped anchor and climbed into the dinghy. Fog had moved in, making it impossible to see anything, and the oars creaked as we made our way to shore as silently as we could. Hemlock was in a hard case strapped around my waist that Death had made for him. It was like an iron bum bag with little bars on either end. He hadn't protested when I put him inside. It was a trade-off—the cage or he had to go back to the castle. My familiar knew my moods and understood that shit was about to go down. He hadn't made a peep since we left the ship.

I scanned the shore. "I can't see anything moving out there."

"Me either," he said, "but they're there."

Ice slid down my spine.

"Okay?" he asked, not missing a thing.

"I'm fine. A little fear's healthy."

"If we get separated—"

"If we get separated, we carry on with the plan. You distract Nox, and I'll get Marigold, and then we'll meet you back here," I said and closed my eyes for a moment, visualizing it, manifesting the moment we got on the boat and sailed away. All of us safe, together. Then I whispered a spell, calling on the mother for her help. It wasn't the first time I'd tried to call on her, to reach her, but I wasn't sure she heard me or that it was even possible here. Still, I tried because we needed all the help we could get.

The dinghy scraped against the beach, and I opened my eyes. Quickly and quietly, I stepped out, slipping on my pack and sliding my knife from its sheath.

Mors grabbed my other hand and draped us in his cloak so we blended with the shadows. We headed away from the path that led to Nox's temple. No point taking the most obvious route and making it easy for them.

We headed up the side of the cliff; it was steep and slippery, dangerous, but it not only avoided Nox, it was a more direct route. I looked up the cliff face to the sharp edge high above and shuddered.

"What is it?"

My mouth had gone dry, my palms sweaty. "Marigold was taken from me... just up there." My gaze locked on the edge. "That's where they pushed me over." I turned to him. "The vow I made that day, to come back, to get my revenge, to make them pay... that's why I kept coming back, no matter how hopeless it felt, because I wanted my family back, and to make Nox pay for what she did to us." A vow made in death is one of the strongest there was.

"I want her to pay as well. I've wanted to make her suffer, to torture her until she ended the curse, to watch her blood drain from her evil body until she was gray and lifeless, but the night needs its goddess despite how heartless and insane she is. Like Hell needs Lucifer, the Dream Realm needs Somnus, and Limbo needs Death." He stopped me, turning me to face him. He looked stricken. "I felt them take you from me that day. I felt it, and I heard your vow. That's why I searched, why Somnus searched. I knew you were coming back to me." His hand was trembling when he cupped the side of my face. "I knew balance between the realms had to be maintained, but still I fought Nox. We battled for so very long. Blood was spilled, but no one won—no one could win. There was only one way to win, and that was to break her curse. I had to walk away from our baby girl because Nox bound her to her realm. I was forced to take her to my temple and put her in stasis to keep her safe. There was no way I'd let Nox have our child. I refused to let her near Mari. It nearly fucking killed me, losing you both."

His thumb swiped my cheek. "But that incredible—fuck, *magnificent* rage you unleashed is what brought you back to me. Nox never counted on that. You're right. Without that vow, you wouldn't be standing in front of me now. I would have lost you and Marigold both forever. There would have been no hope." He shook his head. "But that rage, it's what could get you killed now. I can feel it, Zinnia. It's stronger now than it ever was before. I can't die. My soul can't be taken from me. But I won't risk you. You are immortal now, yes, but not if she takes your head. So until we get Marigold, until we're back at the castle, you are still vulnerable. Only then will you be able to walk by my side for eternity, finally safe. I can't lose you again. I can't wait century after century and hope you come back or that you'll remember us. I can't fucking do it, Zinnia. You are strong and powerful—that's why I know you can bring our daughter home—but where Nox is concerned, let it be my rage that fights for us, let it be me."

As much as I wanted to destroy Nox, he was right. I wasn't strong enough. My rage alone wasn't enough to defeat her. But taking the power back from her would cut her at the knees. "I won't do anything stupid. I won't risk our happily ever after."

He smiled, and my knees went weak; then he kissed me.

A branch snapped, and we froze. I smelled them before I saw them. Demons, all three of them in Nox's colors. "They can't be far ahead," one of them said, tilting his head back and scenting the air.

They couldn't see us under his cloak.

But then he stilled and sniffed again.

Death nodded. We needed to make a move, use our element of surprise. I nodded back. Ready. Death thrust his hand out through the cloak, grabbed a demon by the throat, then tore off his head, turning him to ash. I exploded from our cover, slashing the throat of one with my knife, then threw another back with a burst of magic. The demon grabbed his throat with a gurgled cry, and I dug my blade into his chest and dragged it down, spilling his innards, before wrenching his head back and hacking his head off while Death dispatched the other one.

My consort tilted his head to the side, listening, his blue eyes glowing. "There are more, but they're farther away. Let's go."

We scrambled up the steep track. Once we got to the top, we'd be more exposed, and we'd have to make a run for it. My thigh muscles burned, and my chest ached with a rage so intense, I had to grit my teeth. The darkness was oppressive when we reached the top; Nox was trying to make it as hard as possible for us, but it only helped our cover. If she thought the dark would stop us from finding our way back to Death and Somnus's temple, she was so wrong.

My child was close. I felt her. I felt that little girl's beating heart right beside mine. Nothing would stop me from getting to her.

As we neared the top, voices drifted down. Death dropped his cloak around us once more. There were at least four demons up there, waiting. They were scanning the cliff's edge. Death grabbed up a rock and tossed it halfway across the clearing. It cracked against a tree at the edge, and the demons spun that way, running toward the forest.

We quickly scrambled over the edge and ran toward the tree line on the opposite side of the wide clearing.

We burst into the trees, and Death wrapped an arm around me, holding us still so he could listen again.

"Let's go," he said when he heard nothing.

We walked for a while without any sign of demons, but they'd be at the temple waiting. If they didn't manage to stop us on the way, they'd be waiting for us there. The whole time we walked, I inwardly focused on building my power, on harnessing my magic. I slipped my finger through Hemy's cage, checking on him, and he gave my finger a little nibble to tell me he was okay.

The distant *hoot* of Nox's owl came from somewhere above us.

Death stilled, tilting his head to the side as the sound of movement filled the forest around us. He cursed. "Demons."

"We can fight."

"There's too many." He held my gaze. "When I throw off the cloak, I want you to make yourself as small as possible and stay under it, understand?"

"No, we can—"

"They'll want to take me to Nox. I'm going to let them. When it's clear, go and get Marigold."

"Mors, hang on—"

"We knew this might happen. I won't risk you getting hurt." The look in his eyes said it wasn't up for debate. "I know you can fight," he said, knowing I'd try to anyway, "but I'm counting on you to get to Mari, to get our daughter. Just do what I said, and the temple will let you in."

I nodded. I hated it, but he was right. "You can trust me," I said. "I won't leave without her."

"I know you won't," he said. "Just stay under the cloak and stick to the shadows."

"But the cloak, it doesn't know me."

"It knows you." He brushed the backs of his fingers down the side of my cheek. "It's made of the night sky, love. It remembers you, missed you, and it wants to protect you."

We'd talked about this happening. We had a plan. I knew what to do. "I'll meet you at the beach."

"I'll see you there," he said before he shoved off the cloak.

I dropped to the dark, overgrown forest floor, and the cloak settled over me like a dark shadow.

"Where is she?" one of the demons demanded.

Death roared like a wounded lion. "You killed her. You took her from me."

Good plan. They'd think I was dead. I wasn't sure how long they'd buy it, but it'd give me a head start.

The sound of a fist hitting flesh came next, of demons screaming and snarling. The sound of their fighting grew more distant as he led them away from me. Silence slowly surrounded me until all I could hear were my own shallow breaths, and still, I didn't move, not yet.

Finally, when I was sure I was alone, I slowly, so slowly, pushed back the hood and looked around.

Standing, I turned, taking in my surroundings—

A male leaned against a tree.

I snatched up my knife and lifted my hand, my magic swirling.

He held up his hands. "Don't shoot. I'm not one of them. Well, they think I am, but my loyalties lie elsewhere."

He had humanoid features and the pointed ears of the fae. "Who are you loyal to?"

"Somnus," he said, holding my gaze.

"I don't believe you, and I don't have time for you." My magic grew higher.

"He was right—you are powerful." He stepped away from the tree, his hands still up. "I'm not going to hurt you, Zinnia. I want to help you get Marigold back. That's the plan, right? Death distracts the demons while you go for your daughter. I can help you."

My alarm bells weren't ringing, but I wasn't going to just lower my hand and believe him. "Who are you to Somnus?"

"The love of his life. He and I met in my dreams a very long time ago." He took a step forward. "I'll help you, and you'll take me to him."

There was genuine pain in his eyes, but my daughter's life was at stake. "Prove it."

"He said you'd be a tough nut to crack." The male smiled. "He said you have an herb garden outside the kitchen, and he enjoyed your dinner together, that you're strong and threw him off-balance. You reprimanded him when he not so subtly tried to convince you that your place was with his brother. You asked him when he'd last done something for himself and told him that he wasn't practicing what he preached."

No one else could know that. How could they?

I took him in. He was a lithe male, with larger blades strapped to his thighs and smaller ones strapped to his chest. You didn't arm yourself like that unless you knew how to use them.

"Grab her," a demon yelled, charging through the forest toward us with three others right behind him.

I backed up, gripping my knife tighter.

The male claiming to be Somnus's lover moved so fast, he was nothing but a blur. Steel flashed as knives flew, taking all four demons down. The male strode forward, and pulling one of his larger knives free, he relieved them of their heads. He slid his knife back in its sheath, brushed the ash from his sleeves, and glanced back at me. "Believe me now?" he said with a cocky grin.

I wasn't sure I could trust him, but he could have let those demons take me. He was also obviously skilled with a blade and could have incapacitated me easily by now, but he hadn't. The sound of more demons coming echoed through the trees.

"If anything happens to me or our daughter, Death will hunt you down and torture you until you pray for death, understand?"

He inclined his head. "As he should." He glanced over his shoulder as the demons grew closer.

"What's your name?" I asked.

"Pascal. Shall we get the fuck out of here, then?"

I nodded, spun, and sprinted toward the temple.

CHAPTER 33

Zinnia

It was quiet, way too freaking quiet.

"How are you getting in there?" Pascal asked.

There were several yards between us and the temple. So far, we hadn't seen any demons scouting the place, but they had to be there. I slid the vial from my pack. "Death's blood."

"Are you sure it'll work?"

"No, but Death said it would. It's our only hope right now." I still wasn't sure if this male could be trusted, though every instinct I had said he could be. I tucked the blood safely back in my pocket and slid out my small knife. I made a slice in my palm and then whispered a magic-boosting spell.

"What the hell are you doing?" Pascal asked, sounding horrified.

My power instantly shot higher. "I'm a witch. My coven uses blood to spell and for a power boost. If we get attacked, I'm going to need my magic at full strength."

His head jerked back. "You're a witch?"

"Yes, why?" I said, narrowing my eyes at him.

He shook his head, but a small smile teased his lips. "No reason."

I didn't have time for whatever that was. "You ready?"

He nodded. "If the demons come, leave them to me. Your priority is to get the door open. They can't follow us in, so you get the door open, and we're safe."

Pascal had a nice face. The guy was handsome, charming, and Somnus had mentioned him by name at our dinner. He'd said he'd trust him with his life, with Marigold's life. "If you are who you say you are, Somnus will be pretty pissed if I let you get hacked into tiny pieces by a bunch of demons."

He chuckled. "You think they'll get the chance? You've seen what I can do."

This was true; the male was skilled.

I turned back to the temple. Marigold was just inside. I almost had her in my arms. I just had to get through that door, and I'd have had my baby back. I'd have my daughter.

Lightning flashed in the distance, cracking through the sky right over Nox's tower.

"They're fighting," Pascal said. "Last time they fought like this, it felt as if the world were ending."

The first time Nox killed me, they'd battled. I hadn't asked Death how. "Death's powers are weakened here."

Pascal shrugged. "They don't seem weakened anymore."

He'd better be okay. "We need to make a move."

He nodded, jaw tightening with determination. "Just get to Marigold, and leave the rest to me."

"If you betray me, if you turn on me—"

"I won't."

"If you do, if my daughter gets hurt because of you, I will hex you. I'll make you wish you were dead," I said, meaning every word of it, the words coming from my gut, an oath wrapped in power.

He dipped his chin. "And I'd deserve it." He slipped one of his blades from his chest holder, sliced his palm with a wince, and grabbed mine. "I will never betray you, Zinnia, or anyone you love." Our blood mingled, binding his words in a blood oath.

Okay, I was definitely starting to like this guy. "Glad we're on the same page."

He grinned. "Me too. I sure as hell wouldn't want to be your enemy."

"Wise." Death's cloak was like a stormy sky gathering around me. It sensed the temple as well.

I dug one of Mags's potions from my pack and handed it to him. "Wait until the demons are close, then throw it. The glass needs to smash, but get the hell out of the way fast."

His brow lifted as he slid it in his pocket. "What does it do?"

"Melts faces off."

832

His eyes widened, and then he grinned again. "Excellent."

Taking the vial of Death's blood from my pocket, I poured some on my palm, and the shadows slid along my arm, around my hand. I turned to Pascal. He stood beside me, a wicked curved knife in each hand, twirling them slowly as he scanned the area around us. "Ready?"

He flashed another grin. "Let's do it."

"In three, we run."

He dipped his chin.

I held up three fingers. *Three. Two. One.*

We both exploded out of the trees and made a run for the temple door. The demons hiding, guarding the place, hadn't been expecting us. They'd obviously bought Death's lie. We made it to the door, and I copied the symbol Death had done when we first came here, drawing it in his blood while Pascal guarded my back.

Demons swarmed us, closing in.

The shadows gathered thicker around my hand, and the door rumbled; then slowly, shuddering, it finally swung open. "Come on!" I called to Pascal.

"I'm right behind you," he said, fending off the demons, using those knives, moving with a kind of grace, a dance, like nothing I'd ever seen before.

I ran in, my heart slamming against the back of my ribs. Every muscle in my body trembled, adrenaline pounding through me as I slowed and walked weak-kneed down the hall toward my daughter. She'd been in stasis so long, so very long. There was no way she could know who I was. When she went to sleep, I was someone else. My heart knew her, though, and my memories were so vivid. Her birth, the weight of her in my arms, the way she smelled, the sound of her voice—it was all there, so real, as if it were this body, this life, that had experienced all of it.

Taking a deep breath, I pressed my hand, still stained with Death's blood, to the door in front of me and whispered the words he'd given me to gain access.

The last barrier between me and my daughter. The door swung open and I walked into the room.

She lay there, so small, her eyes closed, her little cheeks pink, her hair spread out on the pillow. I'd chosen Death, and the curse was broken, but I had no idea how to wake her up.

Goddess, my heart ached looking at her. Her father was a god, and I really didn't know what made up the other half of Marigold. I'd been a star made mortal—but if this was what the fates had planned, then the female I was now was what she needed, and I was where I was supposed to be. I had to go with my gut. I was a witch, and that meant using magic, the blood of my coven, and my gifts from the mother.

It was all I had, and I prayed it was all I'd need.

Dropping my pack on the ground, I slid my spelling knife from my pocket and pricked the tip of my finger. There was blood still on her forehead, Death's, and I let instinct guide me, pressing mine to it. "Wake up, Marigold," I whispered. Power slid down my arm, but it was wrong, not strong enough. I needed something, something more. Panic filled me, my heart pounding faster. What the hell was I supposed to do? Death was counting on me; Marigold was counting on me.

I tried it again, but again nothing.

I sucked in a breath.

Magic.

I felt magic around me—not mine, but magic I recognized. So familiar it was as if I were home with my family, but no, it wasn't mine—it was Marigold's.

She was a witch, and somehow, her ancient bloodline was connected to mine.

I shook as I held Marigold's tiny hand. "Wake up, baby girl."

She didn't move.

Something caught the corner of my eye. My pack. Something had slipped out made of worn brown leather. The hat that Else had given me. Picking it up, I moved it around, studying it. My hands tingled. It was vibrating, a low hum of power running through it like it did when I was in Aunt Daisy's kitchen. Lifting it higher, I placed it on my head.

It was hard to describe, but there was this... this knowing as soon as I put it on. The hat was guiding me, so I closed my eyes and followed. The world seemed to expand, open up. The magic pulsing through it transcended space, reaching out. I felt home, I felt Roxburgh, and I felt my sister and cousins, my aunt.

I needed them. I needed their help.

I reached out.

·)) ◗ ● ◖ ((·

Rose

My hairbrush slipped from my fingers, clattering to the counter. A vision filled my mind, fuzzy but growing clearer—no, it was more than that.

"Rose?"

Ronan walked in behind me, and I felt him move in close, his front to my back, his arms sliding around my waist when he realized what was happening, supporting me as I let whatever this was reach me.

The picture finally cleared.

Zinnia.

My legs went weak, and if it weren't for Ronan, I would have hit the floor. *Oh, thank you, goddess.* She'd been gone for a year, no word, no idea if she was okay—if she was even alive.

Zinny was in a room, a small child beside her. I gasped in a breath, because in that moment, I knew the things my cousin did, I knew everything, and I gasped from the enormity of it. The child was hers, and she needed us to help wake her up.

Zinnia was reaching for me, for us. She needed us.

I gasped out another breath, the vision dissipating until I was back in my bathroom with my mate. "I need to gather everyone at the cemetery."

Twenty minutes later, I stood in a circle in the middle of the cemetery with Mom, Jazzy, Mags, Iris, and Willow. We clasped hands, power flowing through us, building, twisting.

I closed my eyes and invited Zinnia back in.

"I can feel her," I called over the wind now whipping around us. "On the count of three, send her everything you've got."

"We got you, Zinny," Jazzy said, tears sliding down her face, her eyes bright with joy, with relief that her big sister was alive. "Let's give her all the power she needs."

"One, two... three." Power surged through me, and I cried out, holding on, holding it inside me. I wouldn't let go until the right moment.

I closed my eyes, and a vision of Zinnia standing over the child filled my mind once more. Her red hair flew around her face. "Now," she yelled, calling out to us.

"Now," I called back and released it, sending every bit of magic we had through the connection between us.

›)⟩ ⦿ ⟨((‹

Zinnia

I pressed my finger to the blood on Marigold's forehead, mixing my blood with Death's as power surged through me and into my daughter's tiny body. She jolted, her mouth opening on a small cry.

I yanked my hand away, and the connection between Rose and me fell away. *Oh goddess.*

"Marigold?" I brushed her hair back from her face. She had to be okay. "Wake up for Mommy."

Her eyelids quivered.

"Marigold?"

She blinked once, twice—then stared up at me with wide blue eyes.

My heart felt as if it exploded in my chest, and my hand shook as I brushed her hair back again. "Hello, baby," I whispered.

She sat up, and her hair, long and soft and as black as night, fell around her shoulders.

We stared at each other, those wide blue eyes identical to Death's searching mine.

Then finally, she reached up, her hand touching my jaw, still blinking as if she was trying to clear her vision, and then she tilted her head to the side like Death often did and smiled. "Mommy."

She felt it. Oh goddess, she felt the connection between us the same way I did. A tear streaked down my cheek as I scooped her up and held her to me.

She wrapped her little arms around me tight. "I've been waiting for you," she said in her sweet little voice.

"I'm so sorry. I'm so sorry I took so long, baby." I stood, carrying her from the room as Pascal burst through the doors, covered in blood and ash. He was scratched and bruised, but thankfully, nothing life-threatening.

"Pascal!" Marigold cried, her eyes lighting up.

He dipped into a bow and grinned at her. "Lady Marigold, princess of Limbo, queen of all witches, as always, I am at your service."

She giggled.

"We spent a lot of time together in the Dream Realm, didn't we, Mari, with Uncle Somnus."

She nodded, then rested her head on my shoulder.

"Queen of witches?" I'd definitely felt her magic. I'd been right; the other half of Marigold's DNA was witch, and somehow, her bloodline was connected to my coven.

"You know your soul was once a star, yes?" Pascal said.

It seemed impossible, but it was true. "Yes."

"Well, you had sisters, and when you were pulled from the sky, they fell with you, but they were scattered to different realms. You and your sisters were the very first witches. No, they didn't practice magic like you do, but the magic was there."

"How do you know this?"

"I've been around a very long time, Zinnia, in the Night Realm and a part of Nox's court." His mouth twisted, hatred filling his eyes. "She truly is an evil bit—" His gaze slid to Marigold.

836

"But that doesn't explain how my and Mari's bloodlines are connected now."

"One of your sisters fell to earth, and your family descends from her. That's why it worked this time, why the fates chose you to break the curse and wake Marigold..." He smiled gently. "It was always going to be you. It had to be you."

My heart pounded in my chest. I'd been a witch in my first life as well. That's why my dying vow wasn't in vain—it was wrapped in magic.

"Love the hat, by the way," Pascal said, looking me over.

"So do I, you have no idea how much," I said and pressed my nose to Marigold's head, breathing her in.

"Can we go home now?" she said sleepily.

Pascal read my instant concern. "She'll be sleepy for a little while, until she gets used to being awake."

I tilted my head to the doors and raised a brow in question.

Pascal nodded. "I made good use of your potion."

I tucked Mari in close. "Yeah, baby, we can go home now."

The forest was quiet when we left. We had to hide a few times from demon scouts, but we made it back to the beach without too much trouble. When we reached the dinghy, three demons were waiting for us. Pascal's hands were a blur as he took them out easily with his knives.

Now we just had to wait for Death.

But the lightning and thunder hadn't slowed; it intensified, and I was getting seriously worried.

Death was a part of me now, and his rage was bigger than I'd ever felt it, and the more time that passed, the more lost to it he became. He was buried so deep in his hatred, in his need to hurt Nox for all she'd done to him and his brother and to me and Marigold, he couldn't get back out.

I knew if I didn't do something, he'd lose all sense of time and place; he'd be trapped in that rage and struggle to find a way back out.

I had to do something, and I had to do it now.

"You need to go with Uncle Pascal, okay, Marigold? Mommy will be back soon."

Pascal turned to me, alarm on his face. "What are you doing?"

I looked up at the sky as lightning forked through it, and a moment later, a boom rumbled so loud, the ground shook. "I need to go and get him."

"It's too dangerous," he said, shaking his head.

"I don't have a choice." I handed my daughter to Pascal, and he took her, holding her in a way that let me know he'd done it before in her dreams. "Take her to the ship and wait there. If I'm not back by morning, go without us."

Pascal jerked back. "What? No."

"The only thing that matters is keeping Marigold safe. If we're not back by morning, get her to the castle, to Somnus."

"Zinnia—"

"Promise me," I said.

"Hang on a minute—"

"*Promise me.*"

His jaw tightened. "I promise."

"Thank you. Now get in the boat." I kissed Marigold's soft cheek. "I'll see you soon."

"No," she whimpered. "No, Mommy."

"It's going to be okay." I opened the cage strapped to my waist, and Hemy scurried out. "This is Hemlock, my familiar. He's going to be sad without me. Can you look after him for me until I come back?"

Her eyes lit up as she gently stroked his back, nodding.

"Good girl. He likes lots of cuddles and treats. Do you think you can do that?"

She nodded again as I handed him to her. I kissed his furry little head. "Look after her," I said to him.

He squeaked that he would, a fierce look on his sweet face.

I gave Marigold one more kiss, then started back the way we'd come.

The kind of power Death and Nox had wasn't something I understood, but that went both ways. They didn't understand magic. We worked on different frequencies; we drew our powers from different places, in different ways. That was my advantage, my only advantage. Still, I needed more than magic; I needed the power of a goddess.

This time, when I called for the mother, I did it with the magic of my family behind it, amplifying it. This time, I had the hat. The mother was volatile, and she hated being disturbed. But our coven had worshipped her faithfully for generations. We gave and we gave, and it was time she gave back.

Breathing deep, I let my soul call out her name, her true name.

Terra.

CHAPTER 34

Death

"You took everything from me," Nox screamed. "I created you and your brother. He was *mine*, and you snatched him away." Lightning danced across her fingers before she fired it at me.

I fired back, knocking it away easily. She screamed again, her fury cracking thunder above us. Nox was far older, and because of that, she had always been stronger than me, but she'd only stayed that way from the gifts she'd received from other gods—gifts she'd received from selling Somnus to whoever wanted to use him and his powers.

She didn't have Somnus now, though, and she hadn't for a very long time, and the gifts she'd been given had all been used up. She was weaker than me now. Fury burned in her eyes but also fear, because she knew it as well. Her skin and hair were singed from my lightning, and she was panting hard from the exertion.

The last time I'd been able to break through the block she had on my power was after she'd murdered my consort and stolen my child. Sheer rage had done it. She'd been stronger than she was now, and the curse had prevented me from taking Marigold from the Night Realm. I'd only been able to take her to my temple, so at least Nox couldn't get near her.

Breaking the curse had been a massive drain on my mother, and once I got to her temple, I'd easily shattered the bind she had on me. My powers throbbed through me now, wild and unstoppable.

She swiped away the sweat that poured down her face with shaking hands and held them out in front of her.

I almost had her, and I would not leave until her body lay charred and broken on the ground, until I'd heard her scream in agony and not just fury. I couldn't kill her, but I could break her. I could break her so badly that she would take centuries to recover.

My vision burned red as I slammed my staff on the ground and another bolt of lightning shot from the top of it. Dark laughter fell from me when it hit its mark, knocking her back. "You can't win. You can barely stand," I snarled and hit her with another bolt.

She flew back, slamming into a marble column, then hit the ground. I stalked toward her, towering over her, holding up my staff, that glowed bright with power.

A smirk curled her lips. "I murdered your consort once, and I will do it again. No matter how long it takes, I will take her from you."

"You won't get near her."

"You know I can." Triumph lit her eyes. "I already got to her once. I gave Fluke my blood to mark her so you couldn't find her." Her eyes flashed. "You love to punish me, you took you and your brother from me. So if I can't be with my children, then neither can you. Marigold is mine, and you will never have another." She smiled, and it was pure evil. "Fluke took her womb so if you ever did find her, she would never be able to give you another child. Now what do you say?"

"I say you are poison, and I will not stop until you are broken and alone," I snarled with all the hatred in my heart.

She actually frowned in confusion. "Did you not hear me? She is barren."

Nox truly thought I would reject Zinnia over her inability to bare children. "I already know the evil you did."

"Then why are we fighting? What use is she to you now?"

Unconditional love wasn't something she had ever understood. Loving someone with your whole heart and not asking for or wanting anything in return was foreign to her. "Use? I love her. She is all I need. All I will ever need."

"I don't believe you." Nox shook her head, eyes wild. "Give me Somnus, and you can have Marigold."

She didn't get it. She was also in no position to make any deals, and she knew it as well. She knew she was losing.

"I already have Marigold."

I spun around at the sound of Zinnia's voice. She strode toward us, dressed in all leather, my cloak flowing around her, her wild red hair spilling out from under a pointed leather hat. She was beautiful and fearless, and she shouldn't fucking be here. "Stay back," I growled.

She shook her head. "This needs to end, now." Her gaze sliced to my mother. "Sorry the whole 'I took your consort's womb' thing wasn't the gotcha moment you were hoping for. You thought it was the ace up your sleeve, that you'd tell him, and he'd leave me?" She shook her head. "You really don't understand how love works, huh?"

"You will not win," Nox shrieked, getting to her feet.

Zinnia's lips moved, but she wasn't talking; she was spelling under her breath, chanting as she strode closer. Ignoring Nox, her green eyes came to me. "It's time to go now, Mors," she said gently. "You need to stop fighting. Marigold's waiting for us."

I looked between her and Nox. "Not yet. Not until she's bleeding and broken." I tried to pull her behind me, but power sparked off her, throwing my hand away.

Nox straightened, triumph on her face. "I created him, and now you can watch as I destroy him."

I stepped in front of Zinnia and lifted my staff—

She touched my arm and shook her head as she moved back around me. "No, my child," she said in a voice that wasn't her own, not anymore. Her eyes, now black, glowed with otherworldly power—with godly power. "Your mother and I have a few things to discuss."

Nox flinched, stumbling back in shock. "Terra?"

Terra? Mother Nature, the Great Goddess, the creatress of all life, or the mother, as the witches who worshipped her called her. I felt her now, dark and light magic, her incredible power flowing through Zinnia's body.

"You created him, did you?" Terra said.

Nox flinched.

"Who is the creatress of all life, Nox?" She shook her head. "You played but a small part in the creation of your sons, and you know it. Without me helping you, they would not exist, and neither would Aster and her sisters. You begged me for help, and what did you do after I gave you what you wanted? You abused them. You used and bartered with my creations to increase your own power, and then you hid here from me in the Night Realm." She laughed. "You cannot hide anymore. Zinnia Thornheart has made it possible for me to reach you anytime I like. Make no mistake, you may not harm my creations, and now Zinnia has been possessed by a goddess, you cannot harm her either."

Nox shrieked. "You do not come to my realm and tell me what I can and cannot do—"

Zinnia's hands flew up, the power of a goddess flowing from her, and

841

she slammed Nox back down before she lifted her off the ground and held her against the column behind her. "I can and I have. I am older than you, stronger than you, and you will do as I say, or I will tear you apart piece by piece." Terra strode up to her. "Do we understand each other?"

She shook, fighting it, but Terra was right—her power was far stronger. "Fine," Nox bit out. "Now release me and leave my realm. Leave!" she shrieked.

Zinnia's head tilted back, her body jolting, and I felt the goddess leave her. Zinnia stepped back as Nox hit the ground. I grabbed my consort around the waist and pulled her back. Zinnia shook in my arms but not from fear, from fury.

"You fuck with me or my consort, you come near Marigold or Somnus or Pascal..." Her hands curled into fists. "If you try and hurt any of my family again, I will call Terra back. I will let her have me, and she will tear you apart, because she wants to. I felt it, her hatred of you. All she needs is a reason, and if I give her one, she will destroy you. She's already proven she can create gods. She can replace you."

Nox stared at her, full of fury that she couldn't unleash.

Zinnia dismissed her, then turned to me, taking my hand. "Our daughter is waiting for us."

I didn't dare fight her on it; I didn't want to. No, I let my exquisite, strong, beautiful, fierce consort lead me from Nox's temple.

)) ● ((

"Thank you for what you did for Zinnia and for protecting my daughter," I said to Pascal. "Anything you need or want, please ask. I owe you a debt, and I won't ever forget it."

The male turned from the ocean to me. "You owe me nothing. It was my honor, my lord. I've spent a lot of time with Marigold in the Dream Realm." He smiled. "I'm extremely fond of her and your brother."

"He'll be awake when we return," I said.

Pascal's chest expanded on a sharp indrawn breath. "I know."

"Will this be the first time you've seen each other out of the dreaming?" "Yes."

I could feel how much he cared for Som, and I could feel the goodness inside him. "All will be well," I said, not sure how to reassure him. But I knew my brother. If he'd allowed Pascal around Marigold, he trusted and cared for him.

Leaving Pascal to contemplate his reunion with Somnus, I headed below to the cabin. When I opened the door and slipped inside, I stilled. Zinnia lay on her side, Marigold tucked in close. Her little arm was wrapped around her mother's neck, her fingers in Zinnia's hair. Hemy was curled up behind Mari, tucked in close. Pulling off my shirt, I climbed on the bed behind my consort and wrapped my arms around all of them.

"Hey," Zinnia said softly.

"Did I wake you?"

"No, I couldn't sleep." I heard her swallow. "All my life, I've had this feeling that something was missing, that there was this hole in my chest, that I'd been born with a fundamental part of me missing. I don't feel that way anymore."

I lifted up and looked down at her. "You don't?"

A tear slid down her cheek, and she shook her head. "How could I when I have everything I've ever wanted right here in this bed? The male I love more than life itself, who owns my soul, and a daughter who is my entire heart."

"And you own me, heart and soul, my precious consort." I leaned in and pressed a soft kiss to her lips. "Thank you, Zinnia, for choosing me, for pulling me from the shadows and loving me. Now, we have an eternity to look forward to, and I promise you that nothing will ever part us again." I wrapped them both tighter in my arms, holding them safe.

"Nothing," she said softly.

EPILOGUE

Zinnia

Four years later

MARIGOLD SKIPPED AROUND THE HEADSTONES, Hemlock on her shoulder, Violet's hand gripped in hers, while the rest of her cousins followed in a disorderly line. "Keep up, Kai," she called.

Rose and Ronan's baby, Kai, had his father's dark hair and his mother's blue eyes. He was holding Torin's hand, and they were babbling away to each other like they were speaking their own language. Torin was big for his age, but according to Warrick, all hellhounds were. They were both fourteen months old, and Rose and Willow had given birth only two weeks apart.

Mari loved spending time with her cousins; she also loved that she was the oldest and could be in charge. Her black hair was in a long braid down her back, swishing from side to side as she glanced back and rolled her eyes at Tate and Raff, Iris and Draven's twins. Tate had gone wolf, and Raff was hanging on to his tail, cracking up every time he tugged on it and made his brother yelp, while Iris's familiar, Nia, bounded along beside them, barking with excitement.

"Not long now, and there'll be two more mini monsters in the coven," I said to Jaz and Mags, who were gathering rosemary beside me, Iris, Rose, and Wills, who were currently filling our jars with cemetery dirt.

Jazzy chuckled, butterflies dancing around her head as she snipped off another sprig of rosemary. "Thank the goddess we have Mari. We won't have to lift a finger."

Mags straightened with a groan. "I'm thinking sooner rather than later for me. This little girl wants to come early. I'm sure of it."

They were due three months apart, both having girls, but Mags was positive her baby was going to make an appearance earlier than she should.

"It'll be fine," Wills said. "Mom's brewing you an elixir that'll keep that little girl where she needs to be for a little while longer."

"It works," Rose said, sitting on the picnic blanket under the oak tree. "I used it for Kai."

Iris poured a glass of lemonade. "Anyone want one?"

"None for me. We need to get going," I said and shielded my eyes, looking over at my daughter. "Time to go, Mari."

She hugged her cousins and ran over to the picnic blanket. There wasn't much left over from lunch, but Marigold had put a cupcake aside for her father. She carefully wrapped it in a napkin and cradled it gently in her hands, then turned to me. "All ready."

"Hang on a minute. I think you're forgetting something," Mags said.

Marigold giggled, then made the rounds, hugging everyone else and laughing harder when they gave her big smacking kisses on her cheeks.

Jazzy gave me a hug. "You'll be here for the ceremony next week?"

"I wouldn't miss it." It was something we did every year to honor the loved ones we'd lost. All our coven would gather here.

After another round of goodbyes, Mari and I headed off.

Twenty minutes later, we were pulling up at the entrance to Oldwood Forest. I parked the car and Mari watched me closely as I did the spell to conceal it until we needed it again. She was already doing simple spells at seven. She was a natural. My baby would be a powerful witch one day. I felt the magic inside her growing every day.

I took her hand, and we walked into the forest. Night was falling, and moonlight filtered through the trees. Like her father, Marigold loved the dark.

"When do you think my familiar will come, Mommy?" she asked as we walked.

"I wish I could give you an answer, baby, but a familiar finds you when the time is right and not before."

Her eyes lit up. "What do you think they'll be?"

"I don't know, but whatever they are, they'll be perfect for you." Hemy squeaked his agreement from my shoulder.

We were free to move between Limbo and Roxburgh now. Though Death still worried while we were gone, he didn't try to stop us. We had an eternity ahead of us, the three of us, and he'd finally allowed himself to believe it.

Marigold ran across the clearing when we reached it, and I laughed and ran after her. She jumped up and down with excitement while I made a small slice in my hand to open the gateway.

The stones rumbled, rolling and reshaping, and a moment later, it was open.

We stepped through onto the skull path, and the gate closed behind us.

"Daddy!" Mari cried and took off.

I looked up as Mors rounded the corner, tall and broad and utterly gorgeous. He grinned wide when he saw us, scooping his daughter up as soon as she reached him.

"Did you have fun with your cousins?" he asked.

"We played in the cemetery, and had a picnic, and I brought you a cupcake." She thrust it out, and he took it.

He leaned in and pressed a kiss to my lips. "I'm glad you're back."

I grinned up at him. "Me too."

"Tell me, Daddy!" Marigold said.

He looked down at her. "Again?"

"Yes, again," she said excitedly.

"Your wish is my command, princess," he said in his beautiful voice.

She tilted her head back in anticipation, looking at the night sky, a sky Death had created, replicated, when he built this realm from the ground up. "Which one was Mommy?"

"See the small cluster of stars above us? They were your mommy and her sisters."

"And they landed in different realms when Mommy came to Earth," Mari said, jumping ahead because she'd heard this more times than I could count.

"That's right," he said. "See the two bright stars to the left—"

"That was you and Uncle Somnus."

"Right, again, and the cute little star twinkling closest to me, the brightest one in the cluster, that's your mommy."

She blinked up at the sky. "And you loved her even then."

"I did," he said in a low, rough voice.

She sighed. "I love that story."

Yes, she did. She had her father point out those stars almost every night. He curled his arm around my shoulders and pulled me in close. "I missed you both."

We'd only been gone half the day, but we didn't like being away from each other for very long. I wrapped my arm around his waist. "We missed you too."

We rounded the bend, and the castle came into view. Lyle's son, Ryker, stood on the steps waiting, a son I had no idea existed until we brought Mari home. Death's castle hadn't exactly been a very welcoming place, and neither had Death before Marigold and I moved in and changed things. Now, Lyle's mate helped around the castle as well, and Ryker was there all the time. He and Mari had fast become best friends. As soon as Mari saw him, she called his name. Death put her down, and she took off to play, Hemlock bounding after her.

"Follow me," my consort said and led us away from the castle. "Somnus and Pascal are watching Mari tonight."

I looked at him. "Oh?"

He waved his hand, and a path appeared in front of us. "Did you think I'd forget our anniversary?"

The anniversary of the curse being broken, of us finally being together the way we were always meant to be. As we walked, Death's cloak swirled around him, and my clothes evaporated, replaced by a black dress made of night that looked like fine cobwebs. It was no longer torn and old, like it had been in Nox's temple. It had been restored to how it once was when the mother created it and me, like Death's cloak had been for him. A clearing opened up ahead of us. It glowed with soft lighting from the stars, from the moon. A table was to one side, and when he waved his hand, food, candles, and wine appeared. Then he clicked his fingers, and the sound of his piano playing echoed around us.

I gazed up at him. "This is... it's beautiful."

He smiled, his cloak swirling, his eyes glowing blue and utterly gorgeous. "Anything for my perfect consort, my wife, my precious guiding star."

Then we swayed to the music, dressed in nothing but the night sky and wrapped in each other's arms.

Also by Sherilee Gray

Rocktown Ink:

Beg For You

Sin For You

Meant For you

Bad For You

All For You

Just for You

The Smith Brothers:

Mountain Man

Wild Man

Solitary Man

Boosted Hearts:

Swerve

Spin

Slide

Spark

Axle Alley Vipers:

Crashed

Revved

Wrecked

Stand Alone Novels:

Breaking Him

While You Sleep

Romantic suspense

Lawless Kings:

Shattered King

Broken Rebel

Beautiful Killer

Ruthless Protector

Glorious Sinner

Merciless King

About the Author

Sherilee Gray is a kiwi girl and lives in beautiful New Zealand with her husband and their two children. When she isn't writing sexy contemporary or paranormal romance, searching for her next alpha hero on Pinterest, or fueling her voracious book addiction, she can be found dreaming of far off places with a mug of tea in one hand and a bar of chocolate in the other.

To find out about new releases, giveaways, events and other cool stuff, sign up for my <u>newsletter</u>!

www.sherileegray.com

www.ingramcontent.com/pod-product-compliance
Lightning Source LLC
Chambersburg PA
CBHW071955110726
47910CB00005B/1545